# CHILDREN OF THE SOIL

# CHILDREN OF THE SOIL.

BY

HENRYK SIENKIEWICZ,

AUTHOR OF

"WITH FIRE AND SWORD," "THE DELUGE," "PAN MICHAEL,"
"WITHOUT DOGMA," "YANKO THE MUSICIAN,"
"LILLIAN MORRIS," ETC.

*AUTHORIZED AND UNABRIDGED TRANSLATION FROM THE POLISH BY*

JEREMIAH CURTIN.

**Fredonia Books**
**Amsterdam, The Netherlands**

Children of the Soil

by
Henryk Sienkiewicz

ISBN: 1-58963-555-8



Reprinted from the 1898 edition

Fredonia Books
Amsterdam, The Netherlands
http://www.fredoniabooks.com



In order to make original editions of historical works available to scholars at an economical price, this facsimile of the original edition of 1898 is reproduced from the best available copy and has been digitally enhanced to improve legibility, but the text remains unaltered to retain historical authenticity.

# INTRODUCTORY STATEMENT.

THE title of this book in the original is Rodzina Polanieckich (The Family of the Polanyetskis); "Children of the Soil" has been substituted, because of the difficulty of the Polish title for American and English readers, because the Polanyetskis are called children of the soil in the text of the volume, and because all the other characters are children of the soil in the same sense.

For most readers this book will have a double interest, — the interest attaching to a picture of Polish life, and the general human interest inseparable from characters like those presented in the narrative of Pan Stanislav's fortunes.

The Poles form a part of the great Slav race, which has played so important a rôle in the world's history already, and which is destined to play a far more important one yet in the future.

The argument involved in the career and meditations of Pan Stanislav is of interest to every person in civilized society; it is an argument presented so clearly, and reinforced with such pointed examples, that neither comment nor explanation is needed.

Were it not for the change of title, I might escape even this brief statement; but now I may add that the following translation was made in many places, in different countries, at various intervals, and at moments snatched from other work. I began "Children of the Soil" in Cahirciveen, Ireland, and continued it in London, Edinburgh, Fort William near the foot of Ben Nevis, Rome, Naples, and Florence, Tsarskoe Selo, Russia, and South Uist, an island of the Outer Hebrides. From the Outer Hebrides I was called home before I wished to come, and left that little granite kingdom in the Atlantic with sincere regret.

The translation was finished in Warren, Vermont, and revised carefully. To new readers of Sienkiewicz I may state that Pan, Pani, and Panna, when prefixed to names, mean Mr., Mrs., and Miss respectively

JEREMIAH CURTIN.

# CHILDREN OF THE SOIL.

## CHAPTER I.

It was the first hour after midnight when Pan Stanislav Polanyetski was approaching the residence in Kremen. During years of childhood he had been twice in that village, when his mother, a distant relative of the present owner of Kremen, was taking him home for vacation. Pan Stanislav tried to remember the place, but to do so was difficult. At night, by the light of the moon, everything took on an uncertain form. Over the bushes, fields, and meadows, a white mist was lying low, changing the whole region about into a shoreless lake, as it were, — an illusion increased by choruses of frogs in the mist.

It was a July night, very calm and perfectly bright. At moments, when the frogs became silent, landrails were heard playing in the dew; and at times, from afar, from muddy ponds, hidden behind reeds, the call of the bittern sounded as if coming from under the earth.

Pan Stanislav could not resist the charm of that night. It seemed to him familiar in some way; and that familiarity he felt all the more, since he had returned only the previous year from abroad, where he had spent his first youth and had become engaged afterward in mercantile matters. Now, while entering that sleeping village, he recalled his childhood, memorable through his mother, now five years dead, and because the bitterness and cares of that childhood, compared with the present, seemed perfect bliss to him.

At last the brichka rolled up toward the village, which began with a cross standing on a sand mound. The cross, inclining greatly, seemed ready to fall. Pan Stanislav remembered it because in his time under that mound had been buried a man found hanging from a limb in the neighboring forest, and afterward people were afraid to pass by that spot in the night-time.

Beyond the cross were the first cottages, but the people were sleeping; there was no light in any window. As far as the eye could reach, only roofs of cottages were gleaming on the night background of the sky, lighted up by the moon, and the roofs appeared silvery and blue. Some cottages were washed with lime and seemed bright green; others, hidden in plum orchards, in thickets of sunflowers or pole beans, barely came out of the shadow. In the yards, dogs barked, but in their sleep, as it were, accompanying the croaking of frogs, the calling of landrails and bitterns, and all those sounds with which a summer night speaks, and which strengthen the impression of silence still more.

The brichka, moving slowly along the soft sandy road, entered at last a dark alley, spotted only here and there by the moonlight, which pushed in between the leaves. Beyond the alley, night watches whistled; and in the open was seen a white dwelling, in which some windows were lighted. When the brichka rattled up to the entrance, a serving-man hurried out of the house and began to assist Pan Stanislav to alight; but in addition the night watch appeared and two white dogs, evidently very young and friendly, for, instead of barking, they began to fawn and to spring on the guest, showing such delight at his coming that the watch had to moderate their effusiveness with a stick.

The man took Pan Stanislav's things from the brichka, and after a moment the guest found himself in a dining-room where tea was waiting. Nothing had changed from the time of his childhood. At one wall was a sideboard in walnut; at one end of this a clock with heavy weights and a cuckoo; at the other were two badly painted portraits of women in robes of the eighteenth century; in the centre of the room stood a table with a white cloth, and surrounded by chairs with high arms. That room, lighted brightly, full of steam rising from a samovar, seemed rather hospitable and gladsome.

Pan Stanislav began to walk along the side of the table; but the squeaking of his boots struck him in that silence, therefore he went to the window and looked through the panes at the yard filled with moonlight. Over this yard the two white dogs, which had greeted him so effusively, were chasing each other.

After a time the door of the next room opened, and a young lady entered in whom Pan Stanislav divined the daughter of the master of Kremen by his second wife; at sight of her he stepped from the window curtains, and, approaching the table in his squeaking boots, bowed, and announced his name. The young lady extended her hand, and said, —

"We learned of your arrival from the despatch. Father is a trifle ill, and was obliged to lie down; but he will be glad to see you in the morning."

"I am not to blame for coming so late," answered Pan Stanislav; "the train reaches Chernyov only at eleven."

"And from Chernyov it is ten miles to Kremen. Father tells me that this is not your first visit."

"I came here with my mother when you were not in the world yet."

"I know. You are a relative of my father."

"I am a relative of Pan Plavitski's first wife."

"Father esteems family connections very highly, even the most distant," said the young lady; and she began to pour out tea, pushing aside from time to time the steam, which, rising from the samovar, veiled her eyes. When conversation halted, only the tick of the clock was heard. Pan Stanislav, who was interested by young ladies, looked at Panna Plavitski carefully. She was a person of medium height, rather slender; she had dark hair, a face calm, but subdued, as it were, a complexion sunburnt somewhat, blue eyes, and a most shapely mouth. Altogether it was the face of a self-possessed and delicate woman. Pan Stanislav, to whom she seemed not ill-looking, but also not beautiful, thought that she was rather attractive; that she might be good; and that under that exterior, not too brilliant, she might have many of those various qualities which young ladies in the country have usually. Though he was young, life had taught him one truth, — that in general women gain on near acquaintance, while in general men lose. He had heard also touching Panna Plavitski, that the whole management in Kremen — a place, by the way, almost ruined — lay on her mind, and that she was one of the most overworked persons on earth. With reference to those cares, which must weigh on her, she seemed calm and unmoved; still he thought that surely she must wish to sleep. This was evident, indeed, by her eyes, which blinked in spite of her, under the light of the hanging lamp.

The examination would have come out on the whole in her favor, were it not that conversation dragged somewhat. This was explained by the fact that they saw each other for the first time in life ; besides, she received him alone, which might be awkward for a young lady. Finally, she knew that Pan Stanislav had not come to make a visit, but to ask for money. Such was the case in reality. His mother had given, a very long time before, twelve thousand and some rubles for a mortgage on Kremen, which Pan Stanislav wished to have redeemed, — first, because there were enormous arrears of interest, and second, since he was a partner in a mercantile house in Warsaw, he had entered into various transactions and needed capital. He had promised himself beforehand to make no compromise, and to exact his own absolutely. In affairs of that sort, it was a point with him always to appear unyielding. He was not such by nature, perhaps ; but he had made inflexibility a principle, and therewith a question of self-love. In consequence of this, he overshot the mark frequently, as people do who argue something into themselves. Hence, while looking at that agreeable, but evidently drowsy young lady, he repeated to himself, in spite of the sympathy which was roused in him, —

"That is all well, but you must pay."

After a while he said, "I have heard that you busy yourself with everything ; do you like land management ?"

"I love Kremen greatly," answered she.

"I too loved Kremen when I was a boy ; but I should not like to manage the place, — the conditions are so difficult."

"Difficult, difficult. We do what we can."

"That is it, — you do what you can."

"I assist father, who is often in poor health."

"I am not skilled in those matters, but, from what I see and hear, I infer that the greater number of agriculturists cannot count on a future."

"We count on Providence."

"Of course, but people cannot send creditors to Providence."

Panna Plavitski's face was covered with a blush; a moment of awkward silence followed; and Pan Stanislav said to himself, —

"Since thou hast begun, proceed farther ;" and he said. —

TO HIS EXCELLENCY,

HON. FREDERIC T. GREENHALGE,

Governor of Massachusetts.

---

SIR,—You are at the head of a Commonwealth renowned for mental culture; you esteem the Slav Race and delight in good literature;—to you I beg to dedicate this volume, in the hope that it will give pleasure to you and to others in that State which you govern so acceptably.

JEREMIAH CURTIN

WARREN, VERMONT,
April 19, 1895.

"You will permit me to explain the object of my coming."

The young lady looked at him with a glance in which he might read, "Thou hast come just now; the hour is late. I am barely alive from fatigue: even the slightest delicacy might have restrained thee from beginning such a conversation." She answered aloud, —

"I know why you have come; but it may be better if you will speak about that with my father."

"I beg your pardon."

"But I beg pardon of you. People have a right to mention what belongs to them, and I am accustomed to that; but to-day is Saturday, and on Saturday there is so much work. Moreover, in affairs of this sort, you will understand — sometimes, when Jews come, I bargain with them; but this time I should prefer if you would speak with my father. It would be easier for both."

"Then till to-morrow," said Pan Stanislav, who lacked the boldness to say that in questions of money he preferred to be treated like a Jew.

"Perhaps you would permit me to pour you more tea?"

"No, I thank you. Good-night." And, rising, he extended his hand; but the young lady gave hers far less cordially than at the greeting, so that he touched barely the ends of her fingers. In going, she said, —

"The servant will show you the chamber."

And Pan Stanislav was left alone. He felt a certain discontent, and was dissatisfied with himself, though he did not wish to acknowledge that fact in his heart. He began even to persuade himself that he had done well, since he had come hither, not to talk politely, but to get money. What was Panna Plavitski to him? She neither warmed nor chilled him. If she considered him a churl, so much the better; for it happens generally that the more disagreeable a creditor, the more people hasten to pay him.

But his discontent was increased by that reasoning; for a certain voice whispered to him that this time it was not merely a question of good-breeding, but also in some degree of compassion for a wearied woman. He felt, besides, that by acting so urgently he was satisfying his pose, not his heart, all the more because she pleased him. As in that sleeping village and in that moonlight night he had found something special, so in that young lady he found something which he had looked for in vain in foreign women, and which moved him more than he expected. But people are often ashamed of feelings which are very good. Pan Stanislav was ashamed of emotions, especially; hence he determined to be inexorable, and on the morrow to squeeze old Plavitski without mercy.

Meanwhile the servant conducted him to the bed-chamber. Pan Stanislav dismissed him at once, and was alone. That was the same chamber which they gave him, when, during the life of Plavitski's first wife, he came to Kremen with his mother; and remembrances beset him again. The windows looked out on a garden, beyond which lay a pond; the moon was looking into the water, and the pond could be seen more easily than in former times, for it was hidden then by a great aged ash-tree, which must have been broken down by a storm, since on that spot there was sticking up merely a stump with a freshly broken piece at the top. The light of the moon seemed to centre on that fragment, which was gleaming very brightly. All this produced an impression of great calm. Pan Stanislav, who lived in the city amid mercantile labors, therefore in continual tension of his physical and mental powers, and at the same time in continual unquiet, felt that condition of the country around him as he would a warm bath after great toil. He was penetrated by relief. He tried to reflect on business transactions, how were they turning, would they give loss or profit, finally on Bigiel, his partner, and how Bigiel would manage various interests in his absence, — but he could not continue.

Then he began to think of Panna Plavitski. Her person, though it had made a good impression, was indifferent to him, even for this reason, that he saw her for the first time; but she interested him as a type. He was thirty years old and something more, therefore of the age in which instinct, with a force almost invincible, urges a man to establish a domestic hearth, take a wife, and have a family. The greatest pessimism is powerless against this instinct; neither art nor any calling in life protects a man against it. In consequence of this, misanthropes marry in spite of their philosophy, artists in spite of their art, as do all those men who declare that they give to their objects not a half, but a whole soul. Exceptions confirm the principle that, in general, men cannot live a conventional lie and swim against the currents of nature. For the great part, only those do not marry for whom the same power that creates marriage stands in the way of it; that is, those whom love has deceived. Hence, celibacy in advanced life, if not always, is most frequently a hidden tragedy.

Stanislav Polanyetski was neither a misanthrope nor an artist; neither was he a man proclaiming theories against marriage. On the contrary, he wanted to marry, and he was convinced that he ought to marry. He felt that for him the time had arrived; hence he looked around for the woman. From that came the immense interest which women roused in him, especially unmarried ones. Though he had spent some years in France and Belgium, he had not sought love among married women, even among those who were over giddy. He was an active and occupied person, who contended that only idle men can romance with married women, and in general that besieging other men's wives is possible only where men have very much money, little honor, and nothing to do, consequently in a society where there is a whole class long since enriched, sunk in elegant idleness, and of dishonest life. He was himself, in truth, greatly occupied, hence he wished to love in order to marry; therefore only unmarried women roused in him curiosity of soul and body. When he met a young lady, the first question he asked himself was, "Is she not the woman?" or at least, "Is she not the kind of woman?" At present his thoughts were circling around Panna Plavitski in this manner. To begin with, he had heard much of her from her relative living in Warsaw; and he had heard things that were good and even touching. Her calm, mild face was before his eyes now. He recalled her hands, very shapely, with long fingers, though somewhat sunburnt, her dark blue eyes, then the slight shadow over her mouth. Her voice too pleased him. Notwithstanding all this, he repeated his promise that he would make no compromise and must have his own; still he was angry at the fate which had brought him to Kremen as a creditor. Speaking to himself in mercantile language, he repeated in spirit, "The quality is good, but I will not 'reflect,' as I did not come for it."

Still he "reflected," and that to such a degree that after he had undressed and lain down, he could not sleep for a long time. The cocks began to crow, the window panes were growing pale and green; but under his closed eyelids he saw yet the calm forehead of Panna Plavitski, the shadow over her mouth, and her hands pouring out the tea. Then, when sleep became overpowering, it seemed to him as though he were holding those hands in his own and drawing her toward him, and she was pulling back and turning her head aside, as if to escape a kiss. In the morning he woke late, and remembering Panna Plavitski, thought, "Ah, she will look like that!"

## CHAPTER II.

HE was roused by the servant, who brought coffee and took his clothes to be brushed. When the servant brought them back, Pan Stanislav asked if it were not the custom of the house to meet in the dining-room for coffee.

"No," answered the servant; "because the young lady rises early, and the old gentleman sleeps late."

"And has the young lady risen?"

"The young lady is at church."

"True, to-day is Sunday. But does not the young lady go to church with the old gentleman?"

"No; the old gentleman goes to high Mass, and then goes to visit the canon, so the young lady prefers early Mass."

"What do they do here on Sunday?"

"They sit at home; Pan Gantovski comes to dinner."

Pan Stanislav knew this Gantovski as a small boy. In those times they nicknamed him "Little Bear," for he was a thick little fellow, awkward and surly. The servant explained that Pan Gantovski's father had died about five years before, and that the young man was managing his estate in the neighboring Yalbrykov.

"And does he come here every Sunday?"

"Sometimes he comes on a week day in the evening."

"A rival!" thought Pan Stanislav. After a while he inquired, —

"Has the old gentleman risen?"

"It must be that he has rung the bell, for Yozef has gone to him."

"Who is Yozef?"

"The valet."

"And who art thou?"

"I am his assistant."

"Go and inquire when it will be possible to see the old gentleman."

The servant went out and returned soon.

"The old gentleman sends to say that when he dresses he will beg you to come."

"Very well."

The servant went out; Pan Stanislav remained alone and waited, or rather was bored, a good while. Patience began to fail him at last; and he was about to stroll to the garden, when Yozef came with the announcement that the old gentleman begged him to come.

Yozef conducted him then to a chamber at the other end of the house. Pan Stanislav entered, and at the first moment did not recognize Pan Plavitski. He remembered him as a person in the bloom of life and very good-looking; now an old man stood before him, with a face as wrinkled as a baked apple, — a face to which small blackened mustaches strove in vain to lend the appearance of youth. Hair as black as the mustaches, and parted low at the side of the head, indicated also pretensions as yet unextinguished.

But Plavitski opened his arms: "Stas! how art thou, dear boy? Come hither!" And, pointing to his white shirt, he embraced the head of Pan Stanislav, and pressed it to his bosom, which moved with quick breathing.

The embrace continued a long time, and for Pan Stanislav, much too long. Plavitski said at last, —

"Let me look at thee, Anna, drop for drop! My poor beloved Anna!" and Plavitski sobbed; then he wiped with his heart finger[1] his right eyelid, on which, however, there was not a tear, and repeated,—

"As like Anna as one drop is like another! Thy mother was always for me the best and the most loving relative."

Pan Stanislav stood before him confused, also somewhat stunned by a reception such as he had not expected, and by the odor of wax, powder, and various perfumes, which came from the face, mustaches, and shirt of the old man.

"How is my dear uncle?" asked he at last, judging that this title, which moreover he had given in years of childhood to Plavitski, would answer best to the solemn manner of his reception.

"How am I?" repeated Plavitski. "Not long for me now, not long! But just for this reason I greet thee in my house with the greater affection, — I greet thee as a father. And if the blessing of a man standing over the grave, and who at the same time is the eldest member of the family, has in thy eyes any value, I give it thee."

And seizing Pan Stanislav's head a second time, he kissed it and blessed him. The young man changed still more, and constraint was expressed on his face. His mother was

[1] Third, or ring finger

a relative and friend of Plavitski's first wife: to Plavitski himself no affectionate feelings had ever attracted her, so far as he could remember; hence the solemnity of the reception, to which he was forced to yield, was immensely disagreeable to him. Pan Stanislav had not the least family feeling for Plavitski. "This monkey," thought he, "is blessing me instead of talking money;" and he was seized by a certain indignation, which might help him to explain matters clearly.

"Now sit down, dear boy," said Plavitski, "and be as if in thy own house."

Pan Stanislav took a seat, and began, "Dear uncle, for me it is very pleasant to visit uncle. I should have done so surely, even without business; but uncle knows that I have come also on that affair which my mother —"

Here the old man laid his hand on Pan Stanislav's knee suddenly. "But hast thou drunk coffee?" asked he.

"I have," answered Pan Stanislav, driven from his track.

"Marynia goes to church early. I beg pardon, too, that I have not given thee my room; but I am old, I am accustomed to sleep here. This is my nest" Then, with a circular sweep of the hand, he directed attention to the chamber.

Unconsciously Pan Stanislav let his eyes follow the motion of the hand. On a time this chamber had been to him a ceaseless temptation, for in it had hung the arms of Plavitski. The only change in it was the wall, which in the old time was rose-colored, and represented, on an endless number of squares, young shepherdesses, dressed *à la Watteau*, and catching fish with hooks. At the window stood a toilet-table with a white cover, and a mirror in a silver frame. On the table was a multitude of little pots, vials, boxes, brushes, combs, nail files, etc. At one side, in the corner, was a table with pipes and pipe-stems with amber mouth-pieces; on the wall, above the sofa, was the head of a wild boar, and under it two double-barrelled guns, a hunting-bag, horns, and, in general, the weapons of hunting; in the depth was a table with papers, open shelves with a certain number of books. Everywhere the place was full of old furniture more or less needed and ornamental, but indicating that the occupant of the chamber was the centre around which everything turned in that house, and that he cared greatly for himself. In one word, it was the chamber of an old single man, — an egotist full of petty anxiety for his personal comfort, and full of pretensions. Pan Stanislav did not need long reflection to divine that Plavitski would not give up his chamber for anything, nor to any man.

But the hospitable host inquired further, "Was it comfortable enough for thee? How didst thou spend the night?"

"Perfectly; I rose late."

"But thou wilt stay a week or so with me?"

Pan Stanislav, who was very impulsive, sprang up from his chair.

"Does n't uncle know that I have business in Warsaw, and a partner, who at present is doing all our work alone? I must go at the earliest; and to-day I should like to finish the business on which I have come."

To this Plavitski answered with a certain cordial dignity, "No, my boy. To-day is Sunday; and besides, family feeling should go before business. To-day I greet thee, and receive thee as a blood relative; to-morrow, if thou wish, appear as a creditor. That is it. To-day my Stas has come to me, the son of my Anna. Thus will it be till to-morrow; thus should it be, Stas. This is said to thee by thy eldest relative, who loves thee, and for whom thou shouldst do this."

Pan Stanislav frowned a little, but after a while he answered, "Let it be so till to-morrow."

"Anna spoke through thee then. Dost smoke a pipe?"

"No, only cigarettes."

"Believe me, thou doest ill. But I have cigarettes for guests."

Further conversation was interrupted by the rattle of an equipage at the entrance.

"That is Marynia, who has come from early Mass," said Plavitski.

Pan Stanislav looked out through the window, and saw a young lady in a straw hat stepping out of the equipage.

"Hast made the acquaintance of Marynia?" asked Plavitski.

"I had the pleasure yesterday."

"She is a dear child. I need not tell thee that I live only for her —"

At that moment the door opened, and a youthful voice asked, "May I come in?"

"Come in, come in; Stas is here!" answered Plavitski.

Marynia entered the chamber quickly, with her hat hanging by ribbons over her shoulder; and when she had embraced her father, she gave her hand to Pan Stanislav. In her rose-colored muslin, she looked exceedingly graceful and pretty. There was about her something of the character of Sunday, and with it the freshness of that morning, which was bright and calm. Her hair had been ruffled a little by her hat; her cheeks were blooming; and youth was breathing from her person. To Pan Stanislav, she seemed more joyous and more shapely than the previous evening.

"High Mass will be a little later to-day," said she to her father; "for immediately after Mass the canon went to the mill to prepare Pani Siatkovski; she is very ill. Papa will have half an hour yet."

"That is well," said Plavitski; "during that time thou wilt become more nearly acquainted with Stas. I tell thee, drop for drop like Anna! But thou hast never seen her. Remember, too, Marynia, that he will be our creditor to-morrow, if he wishes; but to-day he is only our relative and guest."

"Very well," answered the young lady; "we shall have a pleasant Sunday."

"You went to sleep so late yesterday," said Pan Stanislav, "and to-day you were at early Mass."

She answered merrily, "The cook and I go to early Mass that we may have time afterward to think of dinner."

"I forgot to mention," said Pan Stanislav, "that I bring you salutations from Pani Emilia Hvastovski."

"I have not seen Emilia for a year and a half, but we write to each other often. She is about to visit Reichenhall, for the sake of her little daughter."

"She was ready to start when I saw her."

"But how is the little girl?"

"She is in her twelfth year; she has grown beyond measure, and is pale. It does not seem that she is very healthy."

"Do you visit Emilia often?"

"Rather often. She is almost my only acquaintance in Warsaw. Besides, I like Pani Emilia very much."

"Tell me, my boy," inquired Plavitski, taking a pair of fresh gloves from the table, and putting them into a breast-pocket, "what is thy particular occupation in Warsaw?"

"I am what is called an 'affairist:' I have a commission house in company with a certain Bigiel. I speculate in wheat and sugar, sometimes in timber; in anything that gives profit."

"I have heard that thou art an engineer?"

"I have my specialty. But on my return I could not find occupation at any factory, and I began at mercantile transactions, all the more readily that I had some idea of them. But my specialty is dyeing."

"How dost thou say?" inquired Plavitski.

"Dyeing."

"The times are such now that one must take up anything," said Plavitski, with dignity. "I am not the man to take that ill of thee. If thou wilt only retain the honorable old traditions of the family, no occupation brings shame to a man."

Pan Stanislav, to whom the appearance of the young lady had brought back his good nature, and who was amused by the sudden "grandezza" of the old man, showed his sound teeth in a smile, and answered, —

"Praise God for that!"

Panna Plavitski smiled in like manner, and said, "Emilia, who likes you very much, wrote to me once that you conduct your business perfectly."

"The only difficulty in this country is with Jews; still competition is easy. And with Jews it is possible to get on by abstaining from anti-Semitic manifestoes. As to Pani Emilia, however, she knows as much about business as does her little Litka."

"Yes; she has never been practical. Had it not been for her husband's brother, Pan Teofil Hvastovski, she would have lost all she has. But Pan Teofil loves Litka greatly."

"Who does n't love Litka? I, to begin with, am dying about her. She is such a marvellous child, and such a favorite; I tell you that I have a real weakness for her."

Panna Marynia looked attentively at his honest, vivacious face, and thought, "He must be a little whimsical, but he has a good heart."

Plavitski remarked, meanwhile, that it was time for Mass, and he began to take farewell of Marynia in such fashion as if he were going on a journey of some months; then he made the sign of the cross on her head, and took his hat. The young lady pressed Pan Stanislav's hand with more life than at the morning greeting; he, when sitting in the little equipage, repeated in his mind, "Oh, she is very nice, very sympathetic."

Beyond the alley, by which Pan Stanislav had come the night before, the equipage rolled over a road which was beset here and there with old and decayed birches standing at unequal distances from one another. On one side stretched a potato-field, on the other an enormous plain of wheat, with heavy bent heads, which seemed to sleep in the still air and in the full light of the sun. Before the carriage, magpies and hoopoes flew among the birches. Moving along paths through the yellow sea of wheat, and hidden in it to their shoulders, went village maidens with red kerchiefs on their heads, which resembled blooming poppies.

"Good wheat," said Pan Stanislav.

"Not bad. What is in man's power is done, and what God gives He gives. Thou art young, my dear, so I give thee a precept, which in future will be of service to thee more than once, 'Do always that which pertains to thee, and leave the rest to the Lord God.' He knows best what we need. The harvest will be good this year; I know that beforehand, for when God is going to touch me with anything, He sends a sign."

"What is it?" asked Pan Stanislav, with astonishment.

"Behind my pipe-table — I do not know whether thou hast noted where it stands — a mouse shows himself to me a number of days in succession when any evil is coming."

"There must be a hole in the floor."

"There is no hole," said Plavitski, closing his eyes, and shaking his head mysteriously.

"One might bring in a cat."

"I will not bring in a cat, for if it is the will of God that that mouse should be a sign to me, or forewarning, I shall not go against that will. Nothing has appeared to me this year. I mentioned this to Marynia; maybe God desires in some way to show that He is watching over our family. Listen, my dear; people will say, I know, that we are ruined, or at least in a very bad state. Here it is; judge for thyself: Kremen and Skoki, Magyerovka and Suhotsin, contain about two hundred and fifty vlokas of land; on that there is a debt of thirty thousand rubles to the society, not more, and about a hundred thousand mortgage, including thy sum. Therefore we have about a hundred and thirty thousand. Let us estimate only three thousand rubles a vloka; that will make seven hundred and fifty thousand, —altogether eight hundred and eighty thousand —"

"How is that?" asked Pan Stanislav, with astonishment; "uncle is including the debt with the property."

"If the property were worth nothing, no one would give me a copper for it, so I add the debt to the value of the property."

Pan Stanislav thought, "He is a lunatic, with whom it is useless to talk ;" and he listened further in silence.

"I intend to parcel out Magyerovka. The mill I will sell; but in Skoki and Suhotsin I have marl, and knowest thou at how much I have estimated it? At two million rubles."

"Has uncle a purchaser?"

"Two years ago a certain Shaum came and looked at the fields. He went away, it is true, without speaking of the business; but I am sure that he will come again, otherwise the mouse would have appeared behind the pipe-table."

"Ha! let him come again."

"Knowest thou another thing that comes to my head? Since thou art an 'affairist,' take up this business. Find thyself partners, that is all."

"The business is too large for me."

"Then find me a purchaser; I will give ten per cent of the proceeds."

"What does Panna Marynia think of this marl?"

"Marynia, how Marynia? She is a golden child, but still a child! She believes that Providence watches over our family."

"I heard that from her yesterday."

Meanwhile they had drawn near Vantory and the church, on a hill among linden-trees. Under the hill stood a number of peasant-wagons with ladder-like boxes, and some brichkas and carriages. Pan Plavitski made the sign of the cross, and said, "This is our little church, which thou must remember. All the Plavitskis lie here, and I, too, shall be lying here soon. I never pray better than in this place."

"There will be many people, I see," said Pan Stanislav.

"Gantovski's brichka, Zazimski's coach, Yamish's carriage, and a number of others are there. Thou must remember the Yamishes. She is an uncommon woman; he pretends to be a great agriculturist and a councillor, but he is an old dotard, who never did understand her."

At that moment the bell began to sound in the church tower.

"They have seen us, and are ringing the bell," said Plavitski; "Mass will begin this moment. I will take thee, after Mass, to the grave of my first wife; pray for her, since she was thy aunt. She was an honest woman; the Lord light her."

Here Plavitski raised his finger again to rub his right eye. Pan Stanislav therefore asked, wishing to change the conversation, —

"But was not Pani Yamish once very beautiful? or is this the same one?"

Plavitski's face gleamed suddenly. He thrust out for one moment the end of his tongue from his blackened little mustaches, and patting Pan Stanislav on the thigh, said, —

"She is worth a sin yet, — she is, she is."

Meanwhile they drove in, and after walking around the church, entered the sacristy at the side; not wishing to push through the crowd, they sat on side seats near the altar. Plavitski occupied the collator's place, in which were also the Yamishes. Yamish was a man very old in appearance, with an intelligent face, but weighed down; she was a woman well toward sixty, dressed almost like Panna Marynia, — that is, in a muslin robe and a straw hat. The bows, full of politeness, which Pan Plavitski made to her, and the kind smiles with which she returned them, showed that between those two reigned intimate relations founded on mutual adoration. After a while the lady, raising her glasses to her eyes, began to observe Pan Stanislav, not understanding apparently who could have come with Pan Plavitski. In the seat behind them one of the neighbors, taking advantage of the fact that Mass had not begun yet, was finishing some narrative about hunting, and repeated a number of times to another neighbor, "My dogs, well — " then both stopped their conversation, and began to speak to Plavitski and Pani Yamish so audibly that every word reached the ears of Pan Stanislav. The priest came out to the altar then.

At sight of the Mass and that little church, Pan Stanislav's memory went back to the years of his childhood, when he was there with his mother. Wonder rose in him involuntarily when he thought how little anything changes in the country, except people. Some are placed away in consecrated earth; others are born. But the new life puts itself into the old forms; and to him who comes from afar, after a long absence, all that he saw long ago seems of yesterday. The church was the same; the nave was filled, as of old, with flaxen-colored heads of peasants, gray coats, red and yellow kerchiefs with flowers on the heads of the maidens; it had precisely the same kind of odor of incense, of sweet flag, and the exhalations of people. Outside one of the windows grew the same birch-tree, whose slender branches, thrown against the panes by the wind as it rose, cast shade which gave a green tinge to light in the church. But the people were not the same: some of the former ones were crumbling quietly into dust, or had made their way from beneath the earth in the form of grass; those who were left yet were somehow bent, as if going under ground gradually. Pan Stanislav, who plumed himself on avoiding all generalizing theories, but who in reality had a Slav head, which, as it were, had not emerged yet from universal existence, occupied himself with them involuntarily; and all the time he was thinking that there is still a terrible precipice between that passion for life innate in people and the absoluteness of death. He thought, also, that perhaps for this reason all systems of philosophy vanish, like shadows; but Mass is celebrated, as of old, because it alone promises further and unbroken continuity.

Reared abroad, he did not believe in it greatly; at least, he was not certain of it. He felt in himself, as do all people of to-day, the very newest people, an irrestrainable repugnance to materialism; but from it he had not found an escape yet, and, what is more, it seemed to him that he was not seeking it. He was an unconscious pessimist, like those who are looking for something which they cannot find. He stunned himself with occupations to which he was habituated; and only in moments of great excess in that pessimism did he ask himself, What is this all for? Of what use is it to gain property, labor, marry, beget children, if everything ends in an abyss? But that was at times, and did not become a fixed principle. Youth saved him from this, not the first youth, but also not a youth nearing its end, a certain mental and physical strength, the instinct of self-preservation, the habit of work, vivacity of character, and finally that elemental force, which pushes a man into the arms of a woman. And now from the recollections of childhood, from thoughts of death, from doubts as to the fitness of marriage, he came to this special thought, that he had no one to whom he could give what was best in him; and then he came to Panna Marynia Plavitski, whose muslin robe, covering a young and shapely body, did not leave his eyes. He remembered that when he was leaving Warsaw, Pani Emilia, a great friend of his and of Panna Marynia's, had said laughingly, —

"If you, after being in Kremen, do not fall in love with Marynia, I shall close my doors against you." He answered her with great courage that he was going only to squeeze out money, not to fall in love, but that was not true. If Panna Plavitski had not been in Kremen, he would surely have throttled Plavitski by letter, or by legal methods. On the way he had been thinking of Panna Marynia and of how she would look, and he was angry because he was going for money, too. Having talked into himself great decision in such matters, he determined above all to obtain what belonged to him, and was ready rather to go beyond the mark than not to reach it. He promised this to himself, especially the first evening, when Marynia, though she had pleased him well enough, had not produced such a great impression as he had expected, or rather had produced a different one; but that morning she had taken his eye greatly. "She is like the morning herself," thought he; "she is nice and knows that she is nice, — women always know that."

This last discovery made him somewhat impatient, for he wished to return as soon as possible to Kremen, to observe the young woman further. In fact, Mass was over soon. Plavitski went out immediately after the blessing, for he had two duties before him, — the first, to pray on the graves of his two wives who were lying under the church; the second, to conduct Pani Yamish to her carriage. Since he wished to neglect neither of these, he had to count with time. Pan Stanislav went with him; and soon they found themselves before the stone slabs, erected side by side in the church wall. Plavitski kneeled and prayed awhile with attention; then he rose, and wiping away a tear, which was hanging really on his lids, took Pan Stanislav by the arm, and said, "Yes, I lost both; still I must live."

Meanwhile Pani Yamish appeared before the church door in the company of her husband, of those two neighbors who had spoken to her before Mass, and of young Gantovski. At sight of her Pan Plavitski bent to Pan Stanislav's ear and said, —

"When she enters the carriage, take notice what a foot she has yet."

After a while both joined the company; bows and greetings began. Pan Plavitski presented Pan Polanyetski; then, turning to Pani Yamish, he added, with the smile of a man convinced that he says something which no common person could have hit upon, —

"My relative, who has come to embrace his uncle, and squeeze him."

"We will permit only the first; otherwise he will have an affair with us," said the lady.

"But Kremen[1] is hard," continued Plavitski; "he will break his teeth on it, though he is young."

Pani Yamish half closed her eyes. "That ease," said she, "with which you scatter sparks, *c'est inoui!* How is your health to-day?"

"At this moment I feel healthy and young."

"And Marynia?"

"She was at early Mass. We wait for you both at five. My little housekeeper is breaking her head over supper. A beautiful day."

"We shall come if neuralgia lets me, and my lord husband is willing."

"How is it, neighbor?" asked Plavitski.

"I am always glad to go," answered the neighbor, with the voice of a crushed man.

"Then, *au revoir.*"

"*Au revoir,*" answered the lady; and turning to Pan Stanislav, she reached her hand to him. "It was a pleasure for me to make your acquaintance."

Plavitski gave his arm to the lady, and conducted her to the carriage. The two neighbors went away also. Pan Stanislav remained a while with Gantovski, who looked at him without much good-will. Pan Stanislav remembered him as an awkward boy; from the "Little Bear," he had grown to be a stalwart man, somewhat heavy perhaps in his movements, but rather presentable, with a very shapely,

[1] Kremen means flint in Polish.

light-colored mustache. Pan Stanislav did not begin conversation, waiting till the other should speak first; but he thrust his hands into his pockets, and maintained a stubborn silence.

"His former manners have remained with him," thought Pan Stanislav, who felt now an aversion to that surly fellow.

Meanwhile Plavitski returned from Yamish's carriage.

"Hast taken notice?" asked he of Pan Stanislav, first of all. "Well, Gantos," said he then, "thou wilt go in thy brichka, for in the carriage there are only two places."

"I will go in the brichka, for I am taking a dog to Panna Marynia," answered the young man, who bowed and walked off.

After a while Pan Plavitski and Pan Stanislav found themselves on the road to Kremen.

"This Gantovski is uncle's relative, I suppose?" asked Pan Stanislav.

"The tenth water after a jelly. They are very much fallen. This Adolph has one little farm and emptiness in his pocket."

"But in his heart there is surely no emptiness?"

Pan Plavitski pouted. "So much the worse for him, if he imagines anything. He may be good, but he is simple. No breeding, no education, no property. Marynia likes him, or rather she endures him."

"Ah, does she endure him?"

"See thou how it is: I sacrifice myself for her and stay in the country; she sacrifices herself for me and stays in the country. There is no one here; Pani Yamish is considerably older than Marynia; in general, there are no young people; life here is tedious: but what 's to be done? Remember, my boy, that life is a series of sacrifices. There is need for thee to carry that principle in thy heart and thy head. Those especially who belong to honorable and more prominent families should not forget this. But Gantovski is with us always on Sunday for dinner; and to-day, as thou hast heard, he is bringing a dog."

They dropped into silence, and drove along the sand slowly. The magpies flew before them from birch to birch, this time in the direction of Kremen. Behind Plavitski's little carriage rode in his brichka Pan Gantovski, who, thinking of Pan Stanislav, said to himself, —

"If he comes as a creditor to squeeze them, I 'll break his neck: if he comes as a rival, I 'll break it too."

From childhood, he had cherished hostile feelings toward Polanyetski. In those days they met once in a while. Polanyetski used to laugh at him; and, being a couple of years older, he even beat him.

Plavitski and his guest arrived at last, and, half an hour later, all found themselves at table in the dining-room, with Panna Marynia. The young dog, brought by Gantovski, taking advantage of his privilege of guest, moved about under the table, and sometimes got on the knees of those present with great confidence and with delight, expressed by wagging his tail.

"That is a Gordon setter," said Gantovski. "He is simple yet; but those dogs are clever, and become wonderfully attached."

"He is beautiful, and I am very grateful to you," answered Marynia, looking at the shining black hair and the yellow spots over the eyes of the dog.

"Too friendly," added Plavitski, covering his knees with a napkin.

"In the field, too, they are better than common setters."

"Do you hunt?" asked Pan Stanislav of the young lady.

"No; I have never had any desire to do so. And you?"

"Sometimes. But I live in the city."

"Art thou much in society?" inquired Plavitski.

"Almost never. My visits are to Pani Emilia, my partner Bigiel, and Vaskovski, my former professor, an oddity now, — those are all. Of course I go sometimes to people with whom I have business."

"That is not well, my boy. A young man should have and preserve good social relations, especially when he has a right to them. If a man has to force his way, the question is different; but as Polanyetski, thou hast the right to go anywhere. I have the same story, too, with Marynia. The winter before last, when she had finished her eighteenth year, I took her to Warsaw. Thou 'lt understand that the trip was not without cost, and that for me it required certain sacrifices. Well, and what came of it? She sat for whole days with Pani Emilia, and they read books. She is born a recluse, and will remain one. Thou and she might join hands."

"Let us join hands!" cried Pan Stanislav, joyously.

"I cannot, with a clear conscience," answered Marynia;

"for it was not altogether as papa describes. I read books with Emilia, it is true; but I was much in society with papa, and I danced enough for a lifetime."

"You have no fault to find?"

"No; but I am not yearning."

"Then you did not bring away memories, it seems?"

"Evidently there remained with me only recollections, which are something different."

"I do not understand the difference."

"Memory is a magazine, in which the past lies stored away, and recollection appears when we go to the magazine to take something."

Here Panna Marynia was alarmed somewhat at that special daring with which she had allowed herself this philosophical deduction as to the difference between memory and recollection; therefore she blushed rather deeply.

"Not stupid, and pretty," thought Pan Stanislav; aloud he said, "That would not have come to my head, and it is so appropriate."

He surveyed her with eyes full of sympathy. She was in fact very pretty; for she was laughing, somewhat confused by the praise, and also delighted sincerely with it. She blushed still more when the daring young man said, —

"To-morrow, before parting, I shall beg for a place, — even in the magazine."

But he said this with such joyousness that it was impossible to be angry with him; and Marynia answered, not without a certain coquetry, —

"Very well; and I ask reciprocity"

"In such case, I should have to go so often to the magazine that I might prefer straightway to live in it."

This seemed to Marynia somewhat too bold on such short acquaintance; but Plavitski broke in now and said, —

"This Stanislav pleases me. I prefer him to Gantos, who sits like a misanthrope."

"Because I can talk only of what may be taken in hand," answered the young man, with a certain sadness.

"Then take your fork, and eat."

Pan Stanislav laughed. Marynia did not laugh: she was sorry for Gantovski; therefore she turned the conversation to things which were tangible.

"She is either a coquette, or has a good heart," thought Pan Stanislav again.

But Pan Plavitski, who recalled evidently his last winter visit in Warsaw, continued, "Tell me, Stas, dost thou know Bukatski?"

"Of course. By the way, he is a nearer relative to me than to uncle."

"We are related to the whole world, — to the whole world literally. Bukatski was Marynia's most devoted dancer. He danced with her at all the parties."

Pan Stanislav began to laugh again: "And for all his reward he went to the magazine, to the dust-bin. But at least it is not necessary to dust him, for he is as careful of his person as uncle, for instance. He is the greatest dandy in Warsaw. What does he do? He is manager of fresh air, which means that when there is fair weather he walks out or rides. Besides, he is an original, who has peculiar little closets in his brain. He observes various things of such kind as no other would notice. Once, after his return from Venice, I met him and asked what he had seen there. 'I saw,' said he, 'while on the Riva dei Schiavoni, half an egg-shell and half a lemon-rind floating: they met, they struck, they were driven apart, they came together; at last, paf! the half lemon fell into the half egg-shell, and away they went sailing together. In this see the meaning of harmony.' Such is Bukatski's occupation, though he knows much, and in art, for instance, he is an authority."

"But they say that he is very capable."

"Perhaps he is, but capable of nothing. He eats bread, and that is the end of his service. If at least he were joyous, but at bottom he is melancholy. I forgot to say that besides he is in love with Pani Emilia."

"Does Emilia receive many people?" inquired Marynia.

"No. Vaskovski, Bukatski, and Mashko, an advocate, the man who buys and sells estates, are her only visitors.

"Of course she cannot receive many people; she has to give much time to Litka."

"Dear little girl," said Pan Stanislav, "may God grant at least that Reichenhall may help her."

And his joyous countenance was covered in one moment with genuine sadness. Marynia looked at him with eyes full of sympathy, and in her turn thought a second time, "Still he must be kind really."

But Plavitski began to talk as if to himself. "Mashko, Mashko — he too was circling about Marynia. But she did not like him. As to estates, the price now is such that God pity us."

"Mashko is the man who declares that under such conditions it is well to buy them."

Dinner came to an end, and they passed into the drawing-room for coffee; while at coffee Pan Plavitski, as his wont was in moments of good-humor, began to make a butt of Gantovski. The young man endured patiently, out of regard for Marynia, but with a mien that seemed to say, "Ei! but for her, I would shake all the bones out of thee." After coffee Marynia sat down at the piano, while her father was occupied with patience. She played not particularly well, but her clear and calm face was outlined pleasantly over the music-board. About five Pan Plavitski looked at the clock and said, —

"The Yamishes are not coming."

"They will come yet," answered Marynia.

But from that moment on he looked continually at the clock, and announced every moment that the Yamishes would not come. At last, about six, he said with a sepulchral voice, —

"Some misfortune must have happened."

Pan Stanislav at that moment was near Marynia, who in an undertone said, —

"Here is a trouble! Nothing has happened, of course; but papa will be in bad humor till supper."

At first Pan Stanislav wished to answer that to make up he would be in good-humor to-morrow after sleeping; but, seeing genuine anxiety on the young lady's face, he answered, —

"As I remember, it is not very far; send some one to inquire what has happened."

"Why not send some one over there, papa?"

But he answered with vexation, "Too much kindness; I will go myself;" and ringing for a servant, he ordered the horses, then stopping for a moment he said, —

"*Enfin*, anything may happen in the country; some person might come and find my daughter alone. This is not a city. Besides, you are relatives. Thou, Gantovski, may be necessary for me, so have the kindness to come with me."

An expression of the greatest unwillingness and dissatisfaction was evident on the young man's face. He stretched his hand to his yellow hair and said, —

"Drawn up at the pond is a boat, which the gardener could not launch. I promised Panna Marynia to launch it; but last Sunday she would not let me, for rain was pouring, as if from a bucket."

"Then run and try. It is thirty yards to the pond; thou wilt be back in two minutes."

Gantovski went to the garden in spite of himself. Plavitski, without noticing his daughter or Pan Stanislav, repeated as he walked through the room, —

"Neuralgia in the head; I would bet that it is neuralgia in the head; Gantovski in case of need could gallop for the doctor. That old mope, that councillor without a council, would not send for him surely." And needing evidently to pour out his ill humor on some one, he added, turning to Pan Stanislav, "Thou 'lt not believe what a booby that man is."

"Who?"

"Yamish."

"But, papa!" interrupted Marynia.

Plavitski did not let her finish, however, and said with increasing ill humor, "It does not please thee, I know, that she shows me a little friendship and attention. Read Pan Yamish's articles on agriculture, do him homage, raise statues to him; but let me have my sympathies."

Here Pan Stanislav might admire the real sweetness of Marynia, who, instead of being impatient, ran to her father, and putting her forehead under his blackened mustaches, said, —

"They will bring the horses right away, right away, right away! Maybe I ought to go; but let ugly father not be angry, for he will hurt himself."

Plavitski, who was really much attached to his daughter, kissed her on the forehead and said, "I know thou hast a good heart. But what is Gantovski doing?"

And he called through the open gate of the garden to the young man, who returned soon, wearied out, and said, —

"There is water in the boat, and it is drawn up too far; I have tried, and I cannot —"

"Then take thy cap and let 's be off, for I hear the horses have come."

A moment later the young people were alone.

"Papa is accustomed to society a little more elegant than that in the country," said Marynia; "therefore he likes

Pani Yamish, but Pan Yamish is a very honorable and sensible man."

"I saw him in the church; to me he seemed as if crushed."

"Yes; for he is sickly, and besides has much care."

"Like you."

"No, Pan Yamish manages his work perfectly; besides, he writes much on agriculture. He is really the light of these parts. Such a worthy man! She too is a good woman, only to me she seems rather pretentious."

"An ex-beauty."

"Yes. And this unbroken country life, through which she has become rather rusty, increases her oddness. I think that in cities oddities of character and their ridiculous sides efface one another; but in the country, people turn into originals more easily, they grow disused to society gradually, a certain old-fashioned way is preserved in intercourse, and it goes to excess. We must all seem rusty to people from great cities, and somewhat ridiculous."

"Not all," answered Pan Stanislav; "you, for example."

"It will come to me in time," answered Marynia, with a smile.

"Time may bring changes too."

"With us there is so little change, and that most frequently for the worse."

"But in the lives of young ladies in general changes are expected."

"I should wish first that papa and I might come to an agreement about Kremen."

"Then your father and Kremen are the main, the only objects in life for you?"

"True. But I can help little, since I know little of anything."

"Your father, Kremen, and nothing more," repeated Pan Stanislav.

A moment of silence came, after which Marynia asked Pan Stanislav if he would go to the garden. They went, and soon found themselves at the edge of the pond. Pan Stanislav, who, while abroad, had been a member of various sporting clubs, pushed to the water's edge the boat, which Gantovski could not manage; but it turned out that the boat was leaky, and that they could not row in it.

"This is a case of my management," said Marynia, laughing; "there is a leak everywhere. And I know not how to find an excuse, since the pond and the garden belong to me only. But before it is launched I will have the boat mended."

"As I live, it is the same boat in which I was forbidden to sail when a boy."

"Quite possibly. Have you not noticed that things change less by far, and last longer than people? At times it is sad to think of this."

"Let us hope to last longer than this moss-covered boat, which is as water-soaked as a sponge. If this is the boat of my childhood, I have no luck with it. In old times I was not permitted to sail in it, and now I have hurt my hand with some rusty nail."

Saying this, he drew out his handkerchief and began to wind it around a finger of his right hand, with his left hand, but so awkwardly that Marynia said, —

"You cannot manage it; you need help;" and she began to bind up his hand, which he twisted a little so as to increase the difficulty of her task, since it was pleasant for him to feel her delicate fingers touching his. She saw that he was hindering her, and glanced at him; but the moment their eyes met, she understood the reason, and, blushing, bent down as if tying more carefully. Pan Stanislav felt her near him, he felt the warmth coming from her, and his heart beat more quickly.

"I have wonderfully pleasant memories," said he, "of my former vacations here; but this time I shall take away still pleasanter ones. You are very kind, and besides exactly like some flower in this Kremen. On my word, I do not exaggerate."

Marynia understood that the young man said that sincerely, a little too daringly perhaps, but more through innate vivacity than because they were alone; she was not offended, therefore, but she began to make playful threats with her pleasant low voice, —

"I beg you not to say pretty things to me; if you do, I shall bind your hand badly, and then run away."

"You may bind the hand badly, but stay. The evening is so beautiful."

Marynia finished her work with the handkerchief, and they walked farther. The evening was really beautiful. The sun was setting; the pond, not wrinkled with a breath of wind, shone like fire and gold. In the distance, beyond the water, the alders were dozing quietly; the nearer trees were outlined with wonderful distinctness in the ruddy air. In the yard beyond the house, storks were chattering.

"Kremen is charming, very charming!" said Pan Stanislav.

"Very," answered Marynia.

"I understand your attachment to this place. Besides, when one puts labor into anything, one is attached to it still more. I understand too that in the country it is possible to have pleasant moments like this; but, besides, it is agreeable here. In the city weariness seizes men sometimes, especially those who, like me, are plunged to their ears in accounts, and who, besides, are alone. Pan Bigiel, my partner, has a wife, he has children, — that is pleasant. But how is it with me? I say to myself often: I am at work, but what do I get for it? Grant that I shall have a little money, but what then? — nothing To-morrow ever the same as to-day: Work and work. You know, Panna Plavitski, when a man devotes himself to something, when he moves with the impetus of making money, for example, money seems to him an object. But moments come in which I think that Vaskovski, my original, is right, and that no one whose name ends in *ski* or *vich* can ever put his whole soul into such an object and rest in it exclusively. He declares that there is in us yet the fresh memory of a previous existence, and that in general the Slavs have a separate mission. He is a great original, a philosopher, and a mystic. I argue with him, and make money as I can; but now, for example, when I am walking with you in this garden, it seems to me in truth that he is right."

For a time they walked on without speaking. The light became ruddier every instant, and their faces were sunk, as it were, in that gleam. Friendly, reciprocal feelings rose in them each moment. They felt pleasant and calm in each other's society. Of this Pan Stanislav was sensible seemingly, for, after a while, he remarked, —

"That is true, too, which Pani Emilia told me. She said that one has more confidence, and feels nearer to you in an hour than to another in a month. I have verified this. It seems to me that I have known you for a long time. I think that only persons unusually kind can produce this impression."

"Emilia loves me much," answered Marynia, with simplicity; "that is why she praises me. Even if what she says were true, I will add that I have not the power to be such with all persons."

"You made on me, yesterday, another impression, indeed; but you were tired then and drowsy."

"I was, in some degree."

"And why did you not go to bed? The servants might have made tea for me, or I might have done without it."

"No; we are not so inhospitable as that. Papa said that one of us should receive you. I was afraid that he would wait himself for you, and that would have injured him; so I preferred to take his place."

"In that regard thou mightst have been at ease," thought Pan Stanislav; "but thou art an honest maiden to defend the old egotist." Then he said, "I beg your pardon for having begun to speak of business at once. That is a mercantile habit. But I reproached myself afterward. 'Thou art this and that kind of man,' thought I; and with shame do I beg your pardon."

"There is no cause for pardon, since there is no fault. They told you that I occupy myself with everything; hence you turned to me."

Twilight spread more deeply by degrees. After a certain time they returned to the house, and, as the evening was beautiful, they sat down on the garden veranda. Pan Stanislav entered the drawing-room for a moment, returned with a footstool, and, bending down, pushed it under Marynia's feet.

"I thank you, I thank you much," said she, inclining, and taking her skirt with her hand; "how kind of you! I thank you much."

"I am inattentive by nature," said he; "but do you know who taught me a little carefulness? Litka. There is need of care with her; and Pani Emilia has to remember this."

"She remembers it," answered Marynia, "and we will all help her. If she had not gone to Reichenhall, I should have invited her here."

"And I should have followed Litka without invitation."

"Then I beg you in papa's name, once and for all."

"Do not say that lightly, for I am ready to abuse your kindness. For me it is very pleasant here; and as often as I feel out of sorts in Warsaw, I'll take refuge in Kremen."

Pan Stanislav knew this time that his words were intended to bring them nearer, to establish sympathy between them; and he spoke with design, and sincerely. While speaking, he looked on that mild young face, which, in the light of the setting sun, seemed calmer than usual. Marynia raised to him her blue eyes, in which was the question, "Art speaking by chance, or of purpose?" and she answered in a somewhat lower voice, —

"Do so."

And both were silent, feeling that really a connection between them was beginning.

"I am astonished that papa is not returning," said she, at last.

The sun had gone down; in the ruddy gloaming, an owl had begun to circle about in slow flight, and frogs were croaking in the pond.

Pan Stanislav made no answer to the young lady's remark, but said, as if sunk in his own thoughts: "I do not analyze life; I have no time. When I enjoy myself, — as at this moment, for instance,—I feel that I enjoy myself; when I suffer, I suffer, — that is all. But five or six years ago it was different. A whole party of us used to meet for discussions on the meaning of life, — a number of scholars, and one writer, rather well known in Belgium at present. We put to ourselves these questions: Whither are we going? What sense has everything, what value, what end? We read the pessimists, and lost ourselves in various baseless inquiries, like one of my acquaintances, an assistant in the chair of astronomy, who, when he began to lose himself in interplanetary spaces, lost his reason; and, after that, it seemed to him that his head was moving in a parabola through infinity. Afterward he recovered, and became a priest. We, in like manner, could come to nothing, rest on nothing, — just like birds flying over the sea without a place to light on. But at last I saw two things: first, that my Belgians were taking all this to heart less than I,—we are more naive; second, that my desire for labor would be injured, and that I should become an incompetent. I seized myself, then, by the ears, and began to color cottons with all my might. After that, I said in my mind: Life is among the rights of nature; whether wise or foolish, never mind, it is a right. We must live, then; hence it is necessary to get from life what is possible. And I wish to get something. Vaskovski says, it is true, that we Slavs are not able to stop there; but that is mere talk. That we cannot be satisfied with money alone, we will admit. But

I said to myself, besides money there are two things: peace and — do you know what, Panna Plavitski? — woman. For a man should have some one with whom to share what he has. Later, there must be death. Granted. But where death begins, man's wit ends. 'That is not my business,' as the English say. Meanwhile, it is needful to have some one to whom a man can give that which he has or acquires, whether money or service or fame. If they are diamonds on the moon, it is all the same, for there is no one to learn what their value is. So a man must have some one to know him. And I think to myself, who will know me, if not a woman, if she is only wonderfully good and wonderfully reliable, greatly mine and greatly beloved? This is all that it is possible to desire; for from this comes repose, and repose is the one thing that has sense. I say this, not as a poet, but as a practical man and a merchant. To have near me a dear one, that is an object. And let come then what may. Here you have my philosophy."

Pan Stanislav insisted that he was speaking like a merchant; but he spoke like a dreamer, for that summer evening had acted on him, as had also the presence of that youthful woman, who in so many regards answered to the views announced a moment earlier. This must have come to Pan Stanislav's head, for, turning directly to her, he said, —

"This is my thought, but I do not talk of it before people usually. I was brought to this somehow to-day; for I repeat that Pani Emilia is right. She says that one becomes more intimate with you in a day than with others in a year. You must be fabulously kind. I should have committed a folly if I had not come to Kremen; and I shall come as often as you permit me."

"Come, — often."

"I thank you." He extended his hand, and Marynia gave him hers, as if in sign of agreement.

Oh, how he pleased her with his sincere, manly face, with his dark hair, and a certain vigor in his whole bearing and in his animated eyes! He brought, besides, so many of those inspirations which were lacking in Kremen, — certain new horizons, running out far beyond the pond and the alders which hemmed in the horizon at Kremen. They had opened in one day as many roads as it was possible to open. They sat again a certain time in silence, and their minds wandered on farther in silence as hastily as they had during speech. Marynia pointed at last to the light, which was increasing behind the alders, and said, "The moon."

"Aha! the moon," repeated Pan Stanislav.

The moon was, in fact, rising slowly from behind the alders, ruddy, and as large as a wheel. Now the dogs began to bark; a carriage rattled on the other side of the house; and, after a while, Plavitski appeared in the drawing-room, into which lamps had been brought. Marynia went in, Pan Stanislav following.

"Nothing was the matter," said Plavitski. "Pani Hrometski called. Thinking that she would go soon, they did not let us know. Yamish is a trifle ill, but is going to Warsaw in the morning. She promised to come to-morrow."

"Then is all well?" asked Marynia.

"Well; but what have you been doing here?"

"Listening to the frogs," answered Pan Stanislav; "and it was pleasant."

"The Lord God knows why He made frogs. Though they don't let me sleep at night, I make no complaint. But, Marynia, let the tea be brought."

Tea was waiting already in another room. While they were drinking it, Plavitski described his visit at the Yamishes. The young people were silent; but from time to time they looked at each other with eyes full of light, and at parting they pressed each other's hands very warmly. Marynia felt a certain heaviness seizing her, as if that day had wearied her; but it was a wonderful and pleasant kind of weariness. Afterward, when her head was resting on the pillow, she did not think that the day following would be Monday, that a new week of common toil would begin; she thought only of Pan Stanislav, and his words were sounding in her ears: "Who will know me, if not a woman, if she is only wonderfully good and wonderfully reliable, greatly mine and greatly beloved?"

Pan Stanislav, on his part, was saying to himself, while lighting a cigarette in bed, "She is kind and shapely, charming; where is there such another?"

## CHAPTER III.

But the following day was a gray one, and Panna Plavitski woke with reproaches. It seemed to her that, the day before, she had let herself be borne away on some current farther than was proper, and that she had been simply coquetting with Pan Stanislav. She was penetrated with special dissatisfaction, for this reason principally: that Pan Stanislav had only come as a creditor. She had forgotten that yesterday; but to-day she said to herself, "Undoubtedly it will come to his head that I wanted to win him, or to soften him;" and at this thought the blood flowed to her cheeks and her forehead. She had an honest nature and much ambition, which revolted at every idea that she might be suspected of calculation. Believing now in the possibility of such a suspicion, she felt in advance as if offended by Pan Stanislav. Withal, there was one thought which was bitter beyond every expression: she knew that, as a rule, a copper could not overtake a copper in the treasury of Kremen; that there was no money; and that if, in view of the proposed parcelling of Magyerovka, there were hopes of having some in future, her father would make evasions, for he considered other debts more urgent than Pan Stanislav's. She promised herself, it is true, to do all in her power to see him paid absolutely, and before others; but she knew that she was not able to effect much. Her father assisted her willingly in management; but in money matters he had his own way; and it was rarely that he regarded her opinion. His rôle consisted really in evading everything by all means, — by promises never kept, by delays, by presenting imaginary calculations and hopes, instead of reality. As the collection of debts secured by mortgage on land is difficult and tedious, and defence may be kept up almost as long as one wishes, Plavitski held on to Kremen, thanks to his system. In the end, all this threatened ruin inexorable, as well as complete; but, meanwhile, the old man considered himself "the head of affairs," and listened the more unwillingly to the opinions and counsels of his daughter, since he suspected at once that she doubted his "head." This offended his self-esteem to the utmost. Marynia had passed, because of this "head" and its methods, through more than one humiliation. Her country life was only an apparent ideal of work and household occupations. There was wanting to it neither bitterness nor pain; and her calm countenance indicated, not only the sweetness of her character, but its strength, and a great education of spirit. The humiliation which threatened her this time, however, seemed harder to bear than the others.

"At least, let him not suspect me," said she to herself. But how could she prevent his suspicion? Her first thought was to see Pan Stanislav before he met her father, and describe the whole state of affairs to him; treat him as a man in whom she had confidence. It occurred to her then that such a description would be merely a prayer for forbearance, for compassion; and hence a humiliation. Were it not for this thought, Marynia would have sent for him. She, as a woman noting keenly every quiver of her own heart and the hearts of others, felt half consciously, half instinctively, that between her and that young man something was foreshadowed; that something had begun, as it were; and, above all, that something might and must be inevitable in the future, if she chose that it should be; but, as affairs stood, it did not seem to her that she could choose. Only one thing remained, — to see Pan Stanislav, and efface by her demeanor yesterday's impressions; to break the threads which had been fastened between them, and to give him full freedom of action. Such a method seemed best to her.

Learning from the servants that Pan Stanislav not only had risen, but had drunk tea and gone out to the road, she decided to find him. This was not difficult, since he had returned from his morning walk, and, standing at the side wall of the entrance, which was grown over with wild grapevines, was talking with those two dogs which had fawned on him so effusively at his arrival. He did not see her at once; and Marynia, standing on the steps, heard him saying to the dogs, —

"These big dogs take pay for watching the house? They eat? They don't bark at strangers, but fawn on them. Ei! stupid dogs, lazy fellows!"

And he patted their white heads. Then, seeing her through the openings of the grape-vines, he sprang up as quickly as if thrown from a sling, and stood before her, glad and bright-faced.

"Good-morning. I have been talking with the dogs. How did you rest?"

"Thank you." And she extended her hand to him coldly; but he was looking at her with eyes in which was to be seen most clearly how great and deep a pleasure the sight of her caused him. And he pleased poor Marynia not less; he simply pleased her whole soul. Her heart was oppressed with regret that she had to answer his cordial good-morning so ceremoniously and coldly.

"Perhaps you were going out to look after affairs? In that case, if you permit, I will go with you. I must return to the city to-day; hence one moment more in your company will be agreeable. God knows if I could I would remain longer. But now I know the road to Kremen."

"We beg you to come, whenever time may permit."

Pan Stanislav noticed now the coolness of her words, of her face; and began to look at her with astonishment. But if Marynia thought that he would do as people do usually, — accommodate himself to her tone readily and in silence, — she was mistaken. Pan Stanislav was too vivacious and daring not to seek at once for the cause; so, looking her steadfastly in the eye, he said, —

"Something is troubling you."

Marynia was confused.

"You are mistaken," replied she.

"I see well; and you know that I am not mistaken. You act toward me as you did the first evening. But then I made a blunder: I began to speak of money at a wrong time. Yesterday I begged your pardon, and it was pleasant, — how pleasant! To-day, again, it is different. Tell me why!"

Not the most adroit diplomacy could have beaten Marynia from her path. It seemed to her that she could chill him and keep him at a distance by this demeanor; but he, by inquiring so directly, rather brought himself nearer, and he continued to speak in the tone of a man on whom an injustice had been wrought: —

"Tell me what is the matter; tell me! Your father said I was to be a guest yesterday, and a creditor to-day. But that is fol— that is nothing! I do not understand such distinctions; and I shall never be your creditor, rather your debtor. For I am already indebted to you, and grateful for yesterday's kindness; and God knows how much I wish to be indebted to you always."

He looked into her eyes again, observing carefully whether there would not appear in them yesterday's smile; but Marynia, whose heart was oppressed more and more, went on by the way which she had chosen: first, because she had chosen it; and second, lest by acknowledging that to-day she was different, she might be forced to explain why she was so.

"I assure you," said she, at last, with a certain effort, "that either you were mistaken yesterday, or you are mistaken to-day. I am always the same, and it will always be agreeable to me if you bear away pleasant memories."

The words were polite, but uttered by a young woman so unlike her of yesterday that on Pan Stanislav's face impatience and anger began to appear.

"If it is important for you that I should feign to believe this, let it be as you wish. I shall go away, however, with the conviction that in the country Monday is very different from Sunday."

These words touched Marynia; for from them it seemed as if Pan Stanislav had assumed certain rights by reason of her conduct with him yesterday. But she answered rather with sadness than with anger, —

"How can I help that?"

And after a while she went away, saying that she had to go and wish good-day to her father. Pan Stanislav remained alone. He drove away the dogs, which had tried to fawn on him anew, and began to be angry.

"What does this mean?" asked he in his mind. "Yesterday, kind; to-day, surly, — altogether a different woman. How stupid all this is, and useless! Yesterday, a relative; to-day, a creditor! What is that to her? Why does she treat me like a dog? Have I robbed any one? She knew yesterday, too, why I came. Very well! If you want to have me as a creditor — not Polanyetski — all right. May thunderbolts crush the whole business!"

Meanwhile Marynia ran into her father's chamber. Plavitski had risen, and was sitting, attired in his dressing-gown, before a desk covered with papers. For a while he turned to answer the good-day of his daughter, then occupied himself again with reading the papers.

"Papa," said Marynia, "I have come to speak of Pan Stanislav. Does papa —"

But he interrupted her without ceasing to look at the papers, —

"I will bend thy Pan Stanislav in my hand like wax."

"I doubt if that will be easy. Finally, I should wish that he were paid before others, even with the greatest loss to us."

Plavitski, turning from the desk, gazed at her, and asked coolly, —

"Is this, I pray, a guardianship over him, or over me?"

"It is a question of our honor."

"In which, as thou thinkest, I need thy assistance?"

"No, papa; but —"

"What pathetic day has come on us? What is the matter with thee?"

"I merely beg, papa, by all —"

"And I beg thee also to leave me. Thou hast set me aside from the land management. I yielded; for, during the couple of years that remain to me in life, I have no wish to be quarrelling with my own child. But leave me even this corner in the house, — even this one room, — and permit me to transact such affairs as it is possible to transact here."

"Dear papa, I only beg —"

"That I should move out into a cottage, which, for the fourth time, thou art choosing for me?"

Evidently the old man, in speaking of the "pathetic day," wished merely that no one should divide this monopoly with him. He rose now, in his Persian dressing-gown, like King Lear, and grasped at the arm of his chair; thus giving his heartless daughter to understand that, if he had not done this, he should have fallen his whole length on the floor, stricken down by her cruelty. But tears came to her eyes, and a bitter feeling of her own helplessness flowed to her heart. For a while she stood in silence, struggling with sorrow and a wish to cry; then she said quietly, "I beg pardon of papa," and went out of the room.

A quarter of an hour later, Pan Stanislav entered, at the request of Plavitski, but ill-humored, irritated through striving to master himself.

Plavitski, after he had greeted his visitor, seated him at his side in an armchair prepared previously, and, putting his palm on the young man's knee, said, —

"Stas, but thou wilt not burn this house? Thou wilt not

kill me, who opened my arms to thee as a relative; thou wilt not make my child an orphan?"

"No," answered Pan Stanislav; "I will not burn the house, I will not cut uncle's throat, and I will not make any child an orphan. I beg uncle not to talk in this manner, for it leads to nothing, and to me it is unendurable."

"Very well," said Plavitski, somewhat offended, however, that his style and manner of expression had found such slight recognition; "but remember that thou didst come to me and to this house when thou wert still a child."

"I came because my mother came; and my mother, after the death of Aunt Helen, came because uncle did not pay interest. All this is neither here nor there. The money rests on a mortgage of twenty-one years. With the unpaid interest, it amounts to about twenty-four thousand rubles. For the sake of round numbers, let it be twenty thousand; but I must have those twenty, since I came for them."

Plavitski inclined his head with resignation. "Thou didst come for that. True. But why wert thou so different yesterday, Stas?"

Pan Stanislav, who half an hour earlier had put that same question to Marynia, just sprang up in his chair, but restrained himself and said, —

"I beg you to come to business."

"I do not draw back before business; only permit me to say a couple of words first, and do not interrupt me. Thou hast said that I have not paid the interest. True. But knowest thou why? Thy mother did not give me all her property, and could not without permission of a family council. Perhaps it was worse for you that the permission was not given, but never mind. When I took those few thousand rubles, I said to myself: The woman is alone in the world with one child; it is unknown how she will manage, unknown what may happen. Let the money which she has with me be her iron foundation; let it increase, so that at a given moment she may have something for her hands to seize hold on. And since then I have been in some fashion thy savings bank. Thy mother gave me twelve thousand rubles; to-day thou hast in my hands almost twenty-four thousand. That is the result. And wilt thou repay me now with ingratitude?"

"Beloved uncle," answered Pan Stanislav, "do not take me, I pray, for a greater dunce than I am, nor for a madman. I say simply that I am not caught with such chaff; it is too coarse. Uncle says that I have twenty-four thousand rubles; where are they? I am asking for them, without talk, and moreover such talk."

"But be patient, I pray thee, and restrain thyself, even for this reason, that I am older," answered Plavitski, offended and with dignity.

"I have a partner, who in a month will contribute twelve thousand rubles to a certain business. I must pay the same amount. I say clearly and declare that, after two years of annoyance with letters, I cannot and will not endure any longer."

Plavitski rested his arm on the desk, his forehead on his palm, and was silent. Pan Stanislav looked at him, waiting for an answer; he gazed with increasing displeasure, and in his mind gave himself this question: "Is he a trickster or a lunatic; is he an egotist, so blinded to himself that he measures good and evil by his own comfort merely; or is he all these together?"

Meanwhile Plavitski held his face hidden on his palm, and was silent.

"I should like to say something," began Pan Stanislav, at last.

But the old man waved his hand, indicating that he wished to be alone with his thoughts for a time yet. On a sudden he raised his face, which had grown radiant, —

"Stas," said he, "why are we disputing, when there is such a simple way out of it?"

"How?"

"Take the marl."

"What?"

"Bring thy partner, bring some specialist; we will set a price on my marl, and form a company of three. Thy — what 's his name? Bigiel, is n't it? will pay me so much, whatever falls to him; thou wilt either add something or not; and we 'll all go on together. The profits may be colossal."

Pan Stanislav rose. "I assure you," said he, "that there is one thing to which I am not accustomed, that is to be made sport of. I do not want your marl; I want only my money; and what you tell me I regard simply as an unworthy or stupid evasion."

A moment of oppressive silence followed. Jove's anger began to gather on the brows and forehead of Plavitski. For a while he threatened boldly with his eyes, then, moving quickly to the hooks on which his weapons were hanging, he took down a hunter's knife, and, offering it to Pan Stanislav, said, —

"But there is another way, strike!" and he opened his dressing-gown widely; but Pan Stanislav, mastering himself no longer, pushed away the hand with the knife, and began to speak in a loud voice, —

"This is a paltry comedy, nothing more! It is a pity to lose words and time with you. I am going away, for I have had enough of you and your Kremen; but I say that I will sell my debt, even for half its value, to the first Jew I meet. He will be able to settle with you."

Then the right hand of Plavitski was stretched forth in solemnity.

"Go," said he, "sell. Let the Jew into the family nest; but know this, that the curse, both of me and of those who have lived here, will find thee wherever thou art."

Pan Stanislav rushed out of the room, white with rage. In the drawing-room he cursed as much as he could, looking for his hat; finding it at last, he was going out to see if the brichka had come, when Marynia appeared. At sight of her he restrained himself somewhat; but, remembering that she it was, precisely, who was occupied with everything in Kremen, he said, —

"I bid farewell to you. I have finished with your father. I came for what belonged to me; but he gave me first a blessing, then marl, and finally a curse. A nice way to pay debts!"

There was a moment in which Marynia wished to extend her hand to him and say, —

"I understand your anger. A while ago I was with father also, and begged him to pay you before all others. Deal with us and with Kremen as may please you; but do not accuse me, do not think that I belong to a conspiracy against you, and retain even a little esteem for me."

Her hand was already extending, the words were on her lips, when Pan Stanislav, rousing himself internally, and losing his balance still more, added, —

"I say this because, when I spoke to you the first evening, you were offended, and sent me to your father. I give thanks for the effective advice; but, as it was better for you than for me, I will follow my own judgment hereafter."

Marynia's lips grew pale; in her eyes were tears of

indignation, and, at the same time, of deep offence. She raised her head, and said, —

"You may utter what injuries you like, since there is no one to take my part;" then she turned to the door, with her soul full of humiliation and almost despair, because those were the only returns she had received for that labor in which she had put her whole strength and all the zeal of her honest young soul. Pan Stanislav saw, too, that he had exceeded the measure. Having very lively feelings, he passed in one instant to compassion, and wished to hurry after her to beg her pardon; but it was late: she had vanished.

This roused a new attack of rage. This time, however, the rage included himself. Without taking farewell of any one, he sat in the brichka, which came up just then, and drove out of Kremen. In his soul such anger was seething that for a time he could think of nothing but vengeance. "I will sell it, even for a third of the value," said he to himself, "and let others distrain you. I give my word of an honest man that I will sell. Even without need, I will sell out of spite!"

In this way his intention was changed into a stubborn and sworn resolve. Pan Stanislav was not of those who break promises given to others or themselves. It was now a mere question of finding a man to buy a claim so difficult of collection; for to receive the amount of it was, without exaggeration, to crack a flint with one's teeth.

Meanwhile the brichka rolled out of the alley to the road in the open field. Pan Stanislav, recovering somewhat, began to think of Marynia in a form of mind which was a mosaic composed of the impressions which her face and form had made on him, — of recollections of the Sunday conversation; of repulsion, of pity, of offence, animosity; and, finally, dissatisfaction with himself, which strengthened his animosity against her. Each of these feelings in turn conquered the others, and cast on them its color. At times he recalled the stately figure of Marynia, her eyes, her dark hair, her mouth, pleasing, though too large, perhaps; finally, her expression; and an outburst of sympathy for her mastered him. He thought that she was very girlish; but in her mouth, in her arms, in the lines of her whole figure, there was something womanly, something that attracted with irresistible force. He recalled her mild voice, her calm expression, and her very evident goodness. Then, at thought of how harsh he had been to her before going, — at thought of the tone with which he had spoken to her, — he began to curse himself. "If the father is an old comedian, a trickster, and a fool," said he to himself; "and if she feels all this, she is the unhappier. But what then? Every man with a bit of heart would have understood the position, taken compassion on her, instead of attacking the poor overworked child. I attacked her. I!" Then he wanted to slap his own face; for at once he imagined what might have been, what an immeasurable approach, what an exceptional tenderness would have arisen, if, after all the quarrels with her father, he had treated her as was proper, — that is, with the utmost delicacy. She would have given him both hands when he was leaving; he would have kissed them; and he and she would have parted like two persons near to each other. "May the devils take the money!" repeated he to himself; "and may they take me!" And he felt that he had done things which could not be corrected. This feeling took away the remnant of his equilibrium, and pushed him all the more along that road, the error of which he recognized. And he began a monologue again, more or less like the following, —

"Since all is lost, let all burn. I will sell the claim to any Jew; let him collect. Let them fly out on to the pavement; let the old man find some office; let her go as a governess, or marry Gantovski." Then he felt that he would agree to anything rather than the last thought. He would twist Gantovski's neck. Let any one take her, only not such a wooden head, such a bear, such a dolt. Beautiful epithets began to fall on the hapless Gantovski; and all the venom passed over on to him, as if he had been really the cause of whatever had happened.

Arriving in such a man-eating temper at Chernyov, Pan Stanislav might, perhaps, like another Ugolino, have gnawed at once into Gantovski with his teeth, "where the skull meets the neck," if he had seen him at the station. Fortunately, instead of Gantovski's "skull," he saw only some officials, some peasants, a number of Jews, and the sad, but intelligent face of Councillor Yamish, who recognized him, and who, when the train arrived soon, invited him — thanks to good relations with the station-master — to a separate compartment.

"I knew your father," said he; "and I knew him in his brilliant days. I found a wife in that neighborhood. I remember he had then Zvihov, Brenchantsa, Motsare, Rozvady in Lubelsk, — a fine fortune. Your grandfather was one of the largest landowners in that region; but now the estate must have passed into other hands."

"Not now, but long since. My father lost all his property during his life. He was sickly; he lived at Nice, did not take care of what he had, and it went. Had it not been for the inheritance which, after his death, fell to my mother, it would have been difficult."

"But you are well able to help yourself. I know your house; I have had business in hops with you through Abdulski."

"Then Abdulski did business with you?"

"Yes; and I must confess that I was perfectly satisfied with our relations. You have treated me well, and I see that you manage affairs properly."

"No man can succeed otherwise. My partner, Bigiel, is an honest man, and I am not Plavitski."

"How is that?" asked Yamish, with roused curiosity.

Pan Stanislav, with the remnant of his anger unquenched, told the whole story.

"H'm!" said Yamish; "since you speak of him without circumlocution, permit me to speak in like manner, though he is your relative."

"He is no relative of mine: his first wife was a relative and friend of my mother, — that is all; he himself is no relative."

"I know him from childhood. He is rather a spoiled than a bad man. He was an only son, hence, to begin with, his parents petted him; later on his two wives did the same. Both were quiet, mild women; for both he was an idol. During whole years matters so arranged themselves that he was the sun around which other planets circled; and at last he came to the conviction that everything from others was due to him, and nothing to others from him. When conditions are such that evil and good are measured by one's own comfort solely, nothing is easier than to lose moral sense. Plavitski is a mixture of pompousness and indulgence: of pompousness, for he himself is ever celebrating his own glory; and indulgence, for he permits himself everything. This has become almost his nature. Difficult circumstances came on him. These only a man of character can meet; character he never had. He began to evade, and in the end grew accustomed to evasion. Land ennobles, but land also spoils us. An acquaintance of mine, a bankrupt, said once to me, 'It is not I who evade, but my property, and I am only talking for it.' And this is somewhat true, — truer in our position than in any other."

"Imagine to yourself," answered Pan Stanislav, "that I, who am a descendant of the country, have no inclination for agriculture. I know that agriculture will exist always, for it must; but in the form in which it exists to-day I see no future for it. You must perish, all of you."

"I do not look at it in rose-colors either. I do not mention that the general condition of agriculture throughout Europe is bad, for that is known. Just consider. A noble has four sons; hence each of these will inherit only one-fourth of his father's land. Meanwhile, what happens? Each, accustomed to his father's mode of living, wishes to live like the father; the end is foreseen easily. Another case: A noble has four sons; the more capable choose various careers; you may wager that the least capable remains on the land. A third case: what a whole series of generations have acquired, have toiled for, one light head ruins. Fourth, we are not bad agriculturists, but bad administrators. Good administration means more than good cultivation of land; what is the inference, then? The land will remain; but we, who represent it at present under the form of large ownership, must leave it most likely. Then, do you see, when we have gone, we may return in time."

"How is that?"

"To begin with, you say that nothing attracts you to land; that is a deception. Land attracts, and attracts with such force that each man, after he has come to certain years, to a certain well-being, is unable to resist the desire of possessing even a small piece of land. That will come to you too, and it is natural. Finally, every kind of wealth may be considered as fictitious, except land. Everything comes out of land; everything exists for it. As a banknote is a receipt for metallic money in the State Bank, so industry and commerce and whatever else you please is land turned into another form; and as to you personally, who have come from it, you must return to it."

"I at least do not think so."

"How do you know? To-day you are making property; but how will you succeed? And that, too, is a question of the future. The Polanyetskis were agriculturists; now one of them has chosen another career. The majority of sons of agriculturists must choose other careers also, even because they cannot do otherwise. Some of them will fail; some will succeed and return — but return, not only with capital, but with new energy, and with that knowledge of exact administration which is developed by special careers. They will return because of the attraction which land exercises, and finally through a feeling of duty, which I need not explain to you."

"What you say has this good side, that then my such-an-uncle-not-an-uncle Plavitski will belong to a type that has perished."

Pan Yamish thought a while and said, —

"A thread stretches and stretches till it breaks, but at last it must break. To my thinking, they cannot hold out in Kremen, even though they parcel Magyerovka. But do you see whom I pity? — Marynia. She is an uncommonly honest girl. For you do not know that the old man wanted to sell Kremen two years ago; and that that did not take place partly through the prayers of Marynia. Whether this was done out of regard to the memory of her mother, who lies buried there, or because so much is said and written about the duty of holding to the soil, it is sufficient that the girl did what she could to prevent the sale. She imagined, poor thing, that if she would betake herself with all power to work, she could do everything. She abandoned the whole world for Kremen. For her it will be a blow when the thread breaks at last, and break it must. A pity for the years of the girl!"

"You are a kind person, councillor!" cried Pan Stanislav, with his accustomed vivacity.

The old man smiled. "I love that girl: besides, she is my pupil in agriculture; of a truth it will be sad when she is gone from us."

Pan Stanislav fell to biting his mustaches, and said at last, "Let her marry some man in the neighborhood, and remain."

"Marry, marry! As if that were easy for a girl without property. Who is there among us? Gantovski. He would take her. He is a good man, and not at all so limited as they say. But she has no feeling for him, and she will not marry without feeling. Yalbrykov is a small estate. Besides, it seems to the old man that the Gantovskis are something inferior to the Plavitskis, and Gantovski too believes this. With us, as you know, that man passes for a person of great family who is pleased to boast himself such. Though people laugh at Plavitski, they have grown used to his claim. Moreover, one man raises his nose because he is making property, another because he is losing it, and nothing else remains to him. But let that pass. I know one thing, whoever gets Marynia will get a pearl."

Pan Stanislav had in his mind at that moment the same conviction and feeling. Sinking, therefore, into meditation, he began again to muse about Marynia, or, rather, to call her to mind and depict her to himself. All at once it even seemed to him that he would be sad without her; but he remembered that similar things had seemed so to him more than once, and that time had swept away the illusion. Still he thought of her, even when they were approaching the city; and when he got out at Warsaw, he muttered through his teeth,—

"How stupidly it happened! how stupidly!"

## CHAPTER IV.

On his return to Warsaw, Pan Stanislav passed the first evening at the house of his partner, Bigiel, with whom, as a former schoolmate, he was connected by personal intimacy.

Bigiel, a Cheh by descent, but of a family settled in the country for a number of generations, had managed a small commercial bank before his partnership with Pan Stanislav, and had won the reputation of a man not over-enterprising, it is true, but honorable and uncommonly reliable in business. When Pan Stanislav entered into company with him, the house extended its activity, and became an important firm. The partners complemented each other perfectly. Pan Stanislav was incomparably more clever and enterprising; he had more ideas and took in a whole affair with greater ease; but Bigiel watched its execution more carefully. When there was need of energy, or of pushing any one to the wall, Pan Stanislav was the man; but when it was a question of careful thought, of examining interests from ten sides, and of patience, Bigiel's rôle began. Their temperaments were directly opposite; and for that reason, perhaps, they had sincere friendship for each other. Preponderance was relatively on the side of Pan Stanislav. Bigiel believed in his partner's uncommon capacity; and a number of ideas really happy for the house, which Pan Stanislav had given, confirmed this belief. The dream of both was to acquire in time capital sufficient to build cotton-mills, which Bigiel would manage, and Pan Stanislav direct. But, though both might count themselves among men almost wealthy, the mills were in a remote future. Less patient, and having many relatives, Pan Stanislav tried, it is true, immediately after his return from abroad, to direct to this object local, so-called "our own," capital; he was met, however, with a general want of confidence. He noticed at the same time a wonderful thing: his name opened all doors to him, but rather injured than helped him in business. It might be that those people who invited him to their houses could not get it into their heads that one of themselves, hence a man of good family and with a name ending in *ski*, could conduct any business successfully. This angered Polanyetski to such a degree that the clever Bigiel had to quench his outburst by stating that such want of confidence was in fact caused by years of experience. Knowing well the history of different industrial undertakings, he cited to Pan Stanislav a whole series of cases, beginning with Tyzenhaus, the treasurer, and ending with various provincial and land banks, which had nothing of the country about them except their names, — in other words, they were devoid of every home basis.

"The time has not come yet," said Bigiel; "but it will come, or, rather, it is in sight. Hitherto there have been only amateurs and dilettanti; now for the first time are appearing here and there trained specialists."

Pan Stanislav who, in spite of his temperament, had powers of observation rather well developed, began to make strange discoveries in those spheres to which his relatives gave him access. He was met by a general recognition for having done something. This recognition was offered with emphasis even; but in it there was something like condescension. Each man let it be known too readily that he approved Polanyetski's activity, that he considered it necessary; but no one bore himself as if he considered the fact that Polanyetski was working at some occupation as a thing perfectly common and natural. "They all *protect* me," said he; and that was true. He came also to the conclusion that if, for example, he aspired to the hand of any of the young ladies of so-called "society," his commercial house and his title of "affairist" would, notwithstanding the above recognition, have injured more than helped him. They would rather give him any of those maidens if, instead of a lucrative business, he had some encumbered estate, or if, while living as a great lord, he was merely spending the interest of his capital, or even the capital itself.

When he had made dozens of observations of this kind, Pan Stanislav began to neglect his relatives, and at last abandoned them altogether. He restricted himself to the houses of Bigiel and Pani Emilia Hvastovski, and to those male acquaintances who were a necessity of his single life. He took his meals at François's with Bukatski, old Vaskovski, and the advocate Mashko, with whom he discussed and argued various questions; he was often at the theatre and at public amusements of all kinds. For the rest, he led rather a secluded life; hence he was unmarried yet, though he had great and fixed willingness to marry, and, besides, sufficient property.

Having gone after his return from Kremen almost directly to Bigiel's, he poured out all his gall on "uncle" Plavitski, thinking that he would find a ready and sympathetic listener; but Bigiel was moved little by his narrative, and said, —

"I know such types. But, in truth, where is Plavitski to find money, since he has none? If a man holds mortgages, he should have a saint's patience. Landed property swallows money easily, but returns it with the greatest difficulty."

"Listen, to me, Bigiel," said Pan Stanislav; "since thou hast begun to grow fat and sleep after dinner, one must have a saint's patience with thee."

"But is it true," asked the unmoved Bigiel, "that thou art in absolute need of this money? Hast thou not at thy disposal the money that each of us is bound to furnish?"

"I am curious to know what that is to thee, or Plavitski. I have money with him; I must get it, and that is the end of the matter."

The entrance of Pani Bigiel, with a whole flock of children, put a curb on the quarrel. She was young yet, dark-haired, blue-eyed, very kind, and greatly taken up with her children, six in number, — children liked by Pan Stanislav uncommonly; she was for this reason his sincere friend, and also Pani Emilia's. Both these ladies, knowing and loving Marynia Plavitski, had made up their minds to marry her to Pan Stanislav; both had urged him very earnestly to go to Kremen for the money. Hence Pani Bigiel was burning with curiosity to know what impression the visit had made on him. But as the children were present, it was impossible to speak. Yas, the youngest, who was walking on his own feet already, embraced Pan Stanislav's leg and began to pull it, calling "Pan, Pan!" which in his speech sounded, "Pam, Pam!" two little girls, Evka and Yoasia, climbed up without ceremony on the knees of the young man; but Edzio and Yozio explained to him their business. They were reading the "Conquest of Mexico," and were playing at this "Conquest." Edzio, raising his brows and stretching his hands upwards, spoke excitedly, —

"I will be Cortez, and Yozio a knight on horseback; but as neither Evka nor Yoasia wants to be Montezuma, what can we do? We can't play that way, can we? Somebody must be Montezuma; if not, who will lead the Mexicans?"

"But where are the Mexicans?" asked Pan Stanislav.

"Oh," said Yozio, "the chairs are the Mexicans, and the Spaniards too."

"Then wait, I'll be Montezuma; now take Mexico!"

An indescribable uproar began. Pan Stanislav's vivacity permitted him to become a child sometimes. He offered such a stubborn resistance to Cortez that Cortez fell to denying him the right to such resistance, exclaiming, not without historic justice, that since Montezuma was beaten, he must let himself be beaten. To which Montezuma answered that he cared little for that; and he fought on. In this way the amusement continued a good while. And Pani Bigiel, unable to wait for the end, asked her husband at last, —

"How was the visit to Kremen?"

"He did what he is doing now," answered Bigiel, phlegmatically: "he overturned all the chairs, and went away."

"Did he tell thee that?"

"I had no time to ask him about the young lady; but he parted with Plavitski in a way that could not be worse. He wants to sell his claim; this will cause evidently a complete severance of relations."

"That is a pity," answered Pani Bigiel.

At tea, when the children had gone to bed, she questioned Pan Stanislav plainly concerning Marynia.

"I do not know," said he; "perhaps she is pretty, perhaps she is not. I did not linger long over the question."

"That is not true," said Pani Bigiel.

"Then it is not true; and she is lovable and pretty, and whatever you like. It is possible to fall in love with her, and to marry her; but a foot of mine will never be in their house again. I know perfectly why you sent me there; but it would have been better to tell me what sort of a man her father is, for she must be like him in character, and if that be true, then thanks for the humiliation."

"But think over what you say: 'She is pretty, she is lovable, it is possible to marry her,' and then again: 'She must be like her father.' These statements do not hold together."

"Maybe not; it is all one to me! I have no luck, and that is enough."

"But I will tell you two things: first, you have come

back deeply impressed by Marynia; second, that she is one of the best young ladies whom I have seen in life, and he will be happy who gets her."

"Why has not some one taken her before now?"

"She is twenty-one years old, and entered society not long since. Besides, don't think that she has no suitors."

"Let some other man take her."

But Pan Stanislav said this insincerely, for the thought that some other man might take her was tremendously bitter for him. In his soul, too, he felt grateful to Pani Bigiel for her praises of Marynia.

"Let that rest," said he; "but you are a good friend."

"Not only to Marynia, but to you. I only ask for a sincere, a really sincere, answer. Are you impressed or not?"

"I impressed? to tell the truth, — immensely."

"Well, do you see?" said Pani Bigiel, whose face was radiant with pleasure.

"See what? I see nothing. She pleased me immensely, — true! You have no idea what a sympathetic and attractive person she is; and she must be good. But what of that? I cannot go a second time to Kremen, I came away in such anger. I said such bitter things, not only to Plavitski, but to her, that it is impossible."

"Have you complicated matters much?"

"Rather too much than too little."

"Then a letter might soften them."

"I write a letter to Plavitski, and beg his pardon! For nothing on earth! Moreover, he has cursed me."

"How, cursed?"

"As patriarch of the family; in his own name and the names of all ancestors. I feel toward him such a repulsion that I could not write down two words. He is an old pathetic comedian. I would sooner beg her pardon; but what would that effect? She must take her father's part; even I understand that. In the most favorable event, she would answer that my letter is very agreeable to her; and with that relations would cease."

"When Emilia returns from Reichenhall we will bring Marynia here under the first plausible pretext, and then it will be your work to let misunderstandings vanish."

"Too late, too late!" repeated Pan Stanislav; "I have promised myself to sell the claim, and I will sell it."

"That is just what may be for the best."

"No, that would be for the worst," put in Bigiel; "but I will persuade him not to sell. I hope, too, that a purchaser will not be found."

"Meanwhile Emilia will finish Litka's cure." Here Pani Bigiel turned to Pan Stanislav: "You will learn now how other young ladies will seem to you after Marynia. I am not so intimate with her as Emilia is, but I will try to find the first convenient pretext to write to her and find out what she thinks of you."

The conversation ended here. On the way home, Pan Stanislav saw that Marynia had taken by no means the last place in his soul. To tell the truth, he could hardly think of aught else. But he had at the same time the feeling that this acquaintance had begun under unfavorable conditions, and that it would be better to drive the maiden from his mind while there was time yet. As a man rather strong than weak mentally, and not accustomed to yield himself to dreams simply because they were pleasant, he resolved to estimate the position soberly, and weigh it on all sides. The young lady possessed, it is true, almost every quality which he demanded in his future wife, and also she was near his heart personally. But at the same time she had a father whom he could not endure; and, besides the father, a real burden in the form of Kremen and its connections.

"With that pompous old monkey I should never live in peace; I could not," thought Pan Stanislav. "For relations with him are possible only in two ways: it is necessary either to yield to him (to do this I am absolutely unable), or to shake him up every day, as I did in Kremen. In the first case, I, an independent man, would enter into unendurable slavery to an old egotist; in the second, the position of my wife would be difficult, and our peace might be ruined.

"I hope that this is sober, logical reasoning. It would be faulty only if I were in love with the maiden already. But I judge that this is not the case. I am occupied with her, not in love with her. These two are different. *Ergo*, it is necessary to stop thinking of Marynia, and let some other man take her."

At this last idea, a feeling of bitterness burned him vividly, but he thought, "I am so occupied with her that this is natural. Finally, I have chewed more than one bitter thing in life; I will chew this one as well. I suppose also that it will be less bitter each day."

But soon he discovered that besides bitterness there remained in him also a feeling of sorrow because the prospects had vanished which had been opening before him. It seemed to him that a curtain of the future had been raised, and something had shown him what might be; then the curtain had fallen on a sudden, and his life had returned to its former career, which led finally to nothing, or rather led to a desert. Pan Stanislav felt in every case that the old philosopher Vaskovski was right, and that the making of money is only a means. Beyond that, we must solve life's riddle in some fashion. There must be an object, an important task, which, accomplished in a manner straightforward and honorable, leads to mental peace. That peace is the soul of life; without it life has, speaking briefly, no meaning.

Pan Stanislav was in some sense a child of the age; that is, he bore in himself a part of that immense unrest which in the present declining epoch is the nightmare of mankind. In him, too, the bases on which life had rested hitherto were crumbling. He too doubted whether rationalism, stumbling against every stone at the wayside, could take the place of faith; and faith he had not found yet. He differed, however, from contemporary "decadents" in this, — that he had not become disenchanted with himself, his nerves, his doubts, his mental drama, and had not given himself a dispensation to be an imbecile and an idler. On the contrary, he had the feeling, more or less conscious, that life as it is, mysterious or not mysterious, must be accomplished through a series of toils and exploits. He judged that if it is impossible to answer the various "whys," still it behooves a man to do something because action itself may, to a certain degree, be an answer. It may be inconclusive, it is true; but the man who answers in that way casts from himself at least responsibility. What remains then? The founding of a family and social ties. These must, to a certain degree, be a right of human nature and its predestination, for otherwise people would neither marry nor associate in societies. A philosophy of this kind, resting on Pan Stanislav's logical male instinct, indicated marriage to him as one of the main objects of life. His will had for a long time been turned and directed to this object. A while before, Panna Marynia seemed to him the pier "for which his ship was making in that gloomy night." But when he understood that the lamp on that pier had not been lighted for him, that he must sail farther, begin a new voyage over unknown seas, a feeling of weariness and regret seized him. But his reasoning seemed to him logical, and he went home with an almost settled conviction that "it was not yet that one," and "not yet this time."

Next day, when he went to dine, he found Vaskovski and Bukatski at the restaurant. After a while Mashko also came in, with his arrogant, freckled face and long side whiskers, a monocle on his eye, and wearing a white waistcoat. After the greeting, all began to inquire of Pan Stanislav touching his journey, for they knew partly why the ladies had insisted on his personal visit, and, besides, they knew Marynia through Pani Emilia.

After they had heard the narrative, Bukatski, transparent as Sevres porcelain, said with that phlegm special to him, —

"It is war, then? That is a young lady who acts on the nerves, and now would be the time to strike for her. A woman will accept more readily the arm offered on a stony path than on a smooth road."

"Then offer an arm to her," said Pan Stanislav, with a certain impatience.

"See thou, my beloved, there are three hindrances. First, Pani Emilia acts on my nerves still more; second, I have a pain in my neck every morning, and in the back of my head, which indicates brain disease; third, I am naked."

"Thou naked?"

"At least now. I have bought a number of Falks, all *avant la lettre*. I have plucked myself for a month, and if I receive from Italy a certain Massaccio, for which I have been bargaining, I shall ruin myself for a year."

Vaskovski, who from his features, or rather from the freckles on his face, was somewhat like Mashko, though much older, and with a face full of sweetness, fixed his blue eyes on Bukatski, and said, —

"And that too is a disease of the age, — collecting and collecting on all sides!"

"Oh, ho! there will be a dispute," remarked Mashko.

"We have nothing better to do," said Pan Stanislav.

And Bukatski took up the gauntlet.

"What have you against collecting?"

"Nothing," answered Vaskovski. "It is a kind of old-womanish method of loving art, worthy of our age. Do you not think there is something decrepit about it? To my thinking, it is very characteristic. Once people bore within them enthusiasm for high art: they loved it where it was, in museums, in churches; to-day they take it to their own private cabinets. Long ago people ended with collecting; to-day they begin with it, and begin at oddities. I am not talking at Bukatski; but to-day the youngest boy, if he has a little money, will begin to collect — and what? Not objects of art, but its oddities, or in every case its trifles. You see, my dear friend, it has seemed to me always that love and amateurism are two different things; and I insist that a great amateur of women, for example, is not a man capable of lofty feeling."

"Perhaps so. There is something in that," said Pan Stanislav.

"How can this concern me?" inquired Mashko, passing his fingers through his English side whiskers. "It contains, to begin with, the decree of an ancient pedagogue about modern times."

"Of a pedagogue?" repeated Vaskovski. "Why, since a morsel of bread fell to me, as from heaven,[1] I renounced the slaughter of innocents and the rôle of Herod; secondly, you are mistaken in saying that I utter a decree. Almost with joy I see and note new proofs every hour that we are at the end of an epoch, and that a new one will begin shortly."

"We are in the open sea, and will not turn to shore soon," muttered Mashko.

"Give us peace," said Pan Stanislav.

But the unconquered Vaskovski continued, —

"Amateurism leads to refinement; in refinement great ideals perish, and yield to desire for enjoyment. All this is nothing but paganism. No one can realize to what a degree we are paganized. But is there something? There is the Aryan spirit, which does not ossify, which never grows cold, — a spirit which has within it the divine afflatus, hence creative power; and this spirit feels hampered in pagan fetters. The reaction has set in already, and a rebirth in Christ will begin in this field, as in others. That is undoubted."

Vaskovski, who had eyes like a child, — that is, reflecting only external objects and ever fixed, as it were, on infinity,

[1] He had received an inheritance some time before.

— fixed them on the window, through which were visible gray clouds pierced here and there by sun-rays.

"It is a pity that my head aches, for that will be a curious epoch," said Bukatski.

But Mashko, who called Vaskovski "a saw," and was annoyed by his discussions, begun from any cause or without cause, took from the side-pocket of his coat a cigar, bit off the end, and, turning to Pan Stanislav, said, —

"Here, Stas, wouldst thou really sell that claim on Kremen?"

"Decidedly. Why dost thou ask?"

"Because I might consider it."

"Thou?"

"Yes. Thou knowest that I consider this kind of business frequently. We can talk about it. I cannot say anything certain to-day; but to-morrow I will ask thee to send me the mortgage on Kremen, and I will tell thee whether the thing is possible. Perhaps after dinner to-morrow thou wilt come to me to drink coffee; we may settle something then."

"Well. If anything is to be done, I should prefer it done quickly; for the moment I finish with Bigiel, I wish to go abroad."

"Whither art thou going?" asked Bukatski.

"I do not know. It is too hot in the city. Somewhere to trees and water."

"Another old prejudice," said Bukatski. "In the city there is always shade on one side of the street, which there is not in the country. I walk on the shady side quietly and feel well; therefore I never go out of the city in summer."

"But Professor, art thou not going somewhere?" asked Pan Stanislav.

"Of course. Pani Emilia has been urging me to go to Reichenhall. Perhaps I shall go."

"Then let us go together. It is all one to me where I go. I like Salzburg, and, besides, it will be pleasant to see Pani Emilia and Litka."

Bukatski stretched forth his transparent hand, took a tooth-pick from a glass, and, picking his teeth, began to speak in his cool and careless voice, —

"There is such a mad storm of jealousy raging within me that I am ready to go with you. Have a care, Polanyetski, lest I explode, like dynamite."

There was something so amusingly contradictory between the words and the tone of Bukatski that Pan Stanislav laughed, but after a while he answered, —

"It had not occurred to me that it is possible to fall in love with Pani Emilia. Thank thee for the idea."

"Woe to you both!" said Bukatski.

## CHAPTER V.

NEXT day, after an early dinner at Bigiel's, Pan Stanislav betook himself to Mashko's at the appointed hour. The host was waiting for him evidently; for in the study he found an exquisite coffee service ready, and glasses for liqueurs. Mashko himself did not appear at once, however; for, as the servant said, he was receiving some lady. In fact, his voice and the words of a woman came through the door from the drawing-room.

Meanwhile, Pan Stanislav fell to examining Mashko's ancestors, a number of whose portraits were hanging on the walls. The authenticity of these the friends of the young advocate doubted. A certain cross-eyed prelate afforded Bukatski a special subject for witticisms; but Mashko was not offended. He had determined, cost what it might, to force on the world himself, his ancestors, his genius for business, knowing that, in the society in which he moved, people would ridicule him, but no one would have energy to attack his pretensions. Possessing energy, limitless insolence, and a real turn for business besides, he determined to force himself upward by those qualities. People who did not like him called him shameless; and he was, but with calculation. Coming from a family uncertain even as to its nobility, he treated people of undoubted ancient families as if he were of incomparably better birth than they, people who were of undoubted wealth, as if he were wealthier than they. And this succeeded: those tactics of his were effective. He was careful not to fall into complete ridicule; but he had marked out for himself in this procedure uncommonly wide margins. At last he reached the point which he sought: he was received everywhere, and had established his credit firmly. Certain transactions brought him really generous profits; but he did not hoard money. He judged that the time for that had not come yet, and that he must invest more in the future, with the intent that it would repay him in the way which he wanted. He did not squander money, and was not over liberal, for he looked on those as marks of a parvenu; but, when the need came, he showed himself, to use his own phrase, "solidly munificent." He passed for a very smooth man in business, and, above all, a man of his word. His word rested on credit, it is true; but it kept him in a high position, which in turn permitted him to make really important transactions. He did not draw back before trifles. He possessed daring, and a certain energy which excluded long hesitation; he had faith, too, in his own fortune. Success strengthened that faith. He did not know, in fact, how much property he had; but he handled large sums of money, and people considered him wealthy.

Finally, Mashko's life motive was vanity, rather than greed. He wanted to be rich, it is true; but, beyond all, he wanted to pass for a great lord in English fashion. He went so far as to adapt his exterior thereto, and was almost proud of his personal ugliness: it seemed to him even aristocratic. There was, indeed, a certain something, which, if not uncommon, was at least peculiar, in his pouting mouth, in his broad nostrils, and the red freckles on his face. There was a certain power and brutality, such as the English have sometimes, and that expression was increased by his monocle. To wear this, he had to rear his head somewhat; and when he passed his fingers through his light side whiskers, he reared it still more.

Pan Stanislav could not endure the man at first, and concealed his dislike even too slightly. Later on he became accustomed to him, especially since Mashko treated him differently from others,—perhaps through secret regard; perhaps because, wishing to gain in advance a man so demanding, to act otherwise would be to expose himself to an immediate account, disagreeable in the best case. At last, the young men, by meeting often, grew used to each other's weaknesses, and endured each other perfectly. On this occasion, for example, when Mashko had conducted the lady to the door, he showed himself in the study, set aside for the moment his greatness, and, greeting Pan Stanislav, began to speak like an ordinary mortal, not like a great lord or an Englishman.

"With women! with women! *c'est toujours une mer à boire* (there is always a sea to drink). I have invested their little capital, and I pay them the interest most regularly. Not enough! They come at least once a week to inquire if there has not been some earthquake."

"What wilt thou say to me?" asked Pan Stanislav.

"First of all, drink some coffee."

And, igniting the alcohol under the lamp, he added, —

"With thee there will be no delay. I have seen the mortgage. The money is not easy of recovery; but we need not look on it as lost. Evidently the collection will involve costs, journeys, etc. Hence I cannot give thee what the face of the mortgage indicates; but I will give two-thirds, and pay in three instalments in the course of a year."

"Since I have said to myself that I would sell the claim, even for less than the face of it, I agree. When will the first instalment be paid?"

"In three months."

"Then I will leave my power of attorney with Bigiel in case I must go on a journey."

"But art thou going to Reichenhall?"

"Possibly."

"Ai! Who knows but Bukatski has given thee an idea?"

"Every one has his own thoughts. Thou, for example. Why art thou buying this claim on Kremen? The business is too small for thee, is it not?"

"Among great affairs small ones too are transacted. But I will be outspoken. Thou knowest that neither my position nor my credit belongs to the lowest; both one and the other will increase when I have behind me a piece of land, and that such a large one. I have heard myself from Plavitski that he would sell Kremen. I will suppose that he is still more inclined now, and that it will be possible to acquire all that property cheaply, even very cheaply, for some payments, for some unimportant ready money, with a life annuity in addition; I shall see! Afterward, when it is put in order a little, like a horse for the market, it may be sold; meanwhile I shall have the position of a landholder, which, *entre nous*, concerns me very greatly."

Pan Stanislav listened to Mashko's words with a certain constraint, and said, —

"I must tell thee plainly that the purchase will not be easy. Panna Plavitski is very much opposed to selling. She, in woman fashion, is in love with her Kremen, and will do all she can to retain it in the hands of herself and her father."

"Then in the worst case I shall be Plavitski's creditor, and I do not think that the money will be lost to me. First, I may sell it, as thou hast; second, as an advocate, I can dispose of it with far greater ease. I may myself find means of paying, and indicate them to Plavitski."

"Thou canst foreclose too, and buy it at auction."

"I might if I were some one else, but to foreclose would be devilishly unbecoming in Mashko. No; other means will be found, to which ready consent may be given by Panna Plavitski herself, for whom, by the way, I have great esteem and regard."

Pan Stanislav, who at that moment was finishing his coffee, put his cup suddenly on the table. "Ah," said he, "and it is possible in that way to get at the property." Again a feeling of great anger and bitterness seized him. At the first moment he wished to rise, say to Mashko, "I will not sell the claim!" and go out. He restrained himself, however, and Mashko, passing his fingers through his side whiskers, answered,—

"But if?—I can assure thee, on my word, that at this moment I have no such plan; at least I have not placed it before myself definitely. But if?—I made the acquaintance of Panna Plavitski once in Warsaw, in the winter, and she pleased me much. The family is good, the property ruined, but large, and can be saved. Who knows? Well, that is an idea like any other. I am perfectly loyal with thee, as, for that matter, I have been always. Thou didst go there as if for money, but I knew why those ladies sent thee. Thou hast returned, however, as angry as the devil; therefore I take it that thou hast no intentions. Say that I am mistaken, and I will withdraw at once, not from the plan, for, as I have assured thee, I have no plan yet, but even from thinking over it as something possible. I give thee my word on that. In the opposite case, however, do not hold to the position, 'Not for me, not for any one,' and do not bar the lady's way. But now I listen to thee."

Pan Stanislav, recalling his reasonings of yesterday, thought also that Mashko was right when he said that in such a case he ought not to bar any one's road to the lady, and after a certain time he said,—

"No, Mashko, I have no intentions touching Panna Plavitski. Thou art free to marry her or not. I will say, nevertheless, openly, there is one thing which does not please me, though for me it is profitable; namely, that thou art buying this claim. I believe that thou hast no plan yet; but in case thou shouldst have one, it will seem somewhat strange— But any pressure, any trap—this, however, is thy affair."

"It is so much my affair that if some one else, and not

thou, had said this, I should have been quick to remind him. I may tell thee, however, that should I form such a plan, which I doubt, I shall not ask the hand of Panna Plavitski as interest for my money. Since I can say to myself conscientiously that I would buy the debt in any case, I have the right to buy it. Above all, as matters stand to-day, I wish to buy Kremen, for I need it; hence I am free to use all honorable means which may lead to that end."

"Very well; I will sell. Give directions to write the contract, and send it, or bring it thyself to me."

"I have directed my assistant. It is ready, and needs only the signatures."

In fact, the contract was signed a quarter of an hour later. Pan Stanislav, who spent the evening of that day at Bigiel's, was in such anger as he had never been before; Pani Bigiel could not hide her vexation; and Bigiel, thinking the whole over carefully said, toward the end of the evening, with his usual balance and deliberation, —

"That Mashko has a plan is beyond doubt. The question is merely whether he is deceiving thee by saying that he has no plan, or is deceiving himself!"

"God preserve her from Mashko!" answered Pani Bigiel. "We all saw that she pleased him greatly."

"I supposed," said Bigiel, "that a man like Mashko would look for property, but I may be mistaken. It may be also that he wants to find a wife of good stock, strengthen thereby his social position, become related to numerous families, and at last take into his hands the business of a certain whole sphere of society. That also is not badly calculated, especially since, if he uses his credit, which will be increased by Kremen, it may with his cleverness clear him in time."

"And as you say," remarked Pan Stanislav, "Panna Plavitski pleases him really. I remember now that Plavitski said something too on this subject."

"What then?" asked Pani Bigiel; "what will happen then?"

"Panna Plavitski will marry Pan Mashko if she wishes," said Pan Stanislav.

"But you?"

"Oh I am going to Reichenhall straightway."

## CHAPTER VI.

In fact, Pan Stanislav went a week later to Reichenhall; but before that he received a letter from Pani Emilia inquiring about his journey to Kremen. He did not write in return, for he intended to answer the letter orally. He heard too, but only on the eve of his departure, that Mashko had gone to Kremen the day before; and that news touched him more than he thought it would. He said to himself, it is true, that he would forget the affair when no farther away than Vienna; but he could not forget it, and he had his head so occupied with thinking whether Panna Plavitski would marry Mashko or not, that he wrote to Bigiel from Salzburg, as it were on business, but really asking him to send news of Mashko. He listened without attention to the discussions of his travelling companion, Vaskovski, about the mutual relations of nationalities in Austria, and the mission of modern nations in general. More than once he was so occupied with thinking about Marynia that he simply did not answer questions. It astonished him, too, that at times he saw her as clearly as if she had been standing before him, not only as an exact image, but as a living person. He saw her pleasant, mild face, with shapely mouth, and the little ensign on the upper lip; the calm gaze of her eyes, in which were visible the attention and concentration with which she listened to his words; he saw her whole posture, lithe, supple, from which came the warmth of great and genuine maiden youthfulness. He remembered her bright robe, the tips of her feet, peeping from under it, her hands, delicate, though slightly sunburnt, and her dark hair, moved by the breeze in the garden. He had never thought that there could be a memory almost palpable, and that the memory of a person seen during such a brief time. But he understood this to be a proof of how deep an impression she had, in truth, made on him; and when at moments it passed through his head that all this, which had fixed itself thus in his memory, might be possessed by Mashko, he could hardly believe it. In those moments his first feeling, which was, moreover, in accord with his active nature, was an irresistible impulse to hinder it. He had to remember then that the affair was decided already, and that he had resolved to drop Panna Plavitski.

He and Vaskovski reached Reichenhall early in the morning; and that very day, before they had learned the address of Pani Emilia, they met her and Litka in the park. She had not expected to see either, especially Pan Stanislav, and was sincerely delighted when she met them; her delight was darkened only by this, that Litka, a child exceptionally sensitive, and ailing with asthma and heart-disease, was still more delighted, so much delighted, indeed, that she had a violent palpitation of the heart, with stifling and almost a swoon.

Such attacks were frequent with her; and, when this one passed, calmness came back to all faces. On the way to the house, the child held "Pan Stas" by the hand, and in her eyes, usually pensive, there shone deep delight. From time to time she pressed his hand, as if to convince herself that he had come really to Reichenhall and was near her. Pan Stanislav had simply no time to speak to Pani Emilia, or to make an inquiry, for Litka was showing him Reichenhall, and chattering unceasingly; she wanted to show him all the nice places at once. Every moment she said, —

"This is nothing yet. Thumsee is prettier; but we will go there to-morrow."

Then turning to her mother, "Mamma will let me go, is n't it true? I can walk much now. It is not far. Mamma will let me go, will she not?"

At moments again she pushed away from Pan Stanislav, and, without dropping his hand, looked at him with her great eyes, repeating, —

"Pan Stas, Pan Stas!"

Pan Stanislav showed her the greatest tenderness, or tenderness as great as an elder brother might show; time after time he chided her good-naturedly, —

"Let the kitten not run so; she will choke."

And she nestled up to him, pouted, and answered, as if in anger, —

"Hush, Pan Stas!"

Pan Stanislav glanced, however, frequently at the serene face of Pani Emilia, as if desiring to let her know that he wished to converse with her. But there was no opportunity, since she did not like to destroy Litka's joyousness, and preferred to leave their mutual friend in her possession exclusively. Only after dinner, which they ate in the garden together, amid foliage and the twittering of sparrows, when Vaskovski had begun to tell Litka about birds, and the love which Saint Francis Assisi had felt for them, and the child, with her head on her hand, was lost completely in listening, did Pan Stanislav turn to Pani Emilia and ask, —

"Do you not wish to walk to the end of the garden?"

"I do," answered she. "Litka, stay here a minute with Pan Vaskovski; we will come back in that time."

They walked along, and Pani Emilia asked immediately,—

"Well, what?"

Pan Stanislav began to tell; but whether it was that he wished to appear better before Pani Emilia, or that he determined to reckon with that delicate nature, or, finally, that the last thoughts concerning Marynia had attuned him to a note more sensitive than usual, it is sufficient that he changed the affair altogether. He confessed, it is true, to a quarrel with Plavitski, but he was silent touching this, that before his departure from Kremen he had answered Marynia almost with harshness; besides, he did not spare praises on her in his story, and finally he finished, —

"Since that debt became a cause of misunderstanding at once between me and Plavitski, — a thing which must be reflected on Panna Marynia, — I chose to sell it; and just before I left Warsaw, I sold it to Mashko."

Pani Emilia, who had not the slightest conception of business, and, besides, was of a simplicity truly angelic, remarked, —

"You did well. There should be no such thing as money between you."

Ashamed to deceive such a simple soul, he answered, —

"True! Or rather the contrary, I think I did badly. Bigiel, too, is of the opinion that it was not well. Mashko may press them; he may put various demands before them; he may offer Kremen for sale. No, that was not a delicate act, nor one to bring us nearer; and I should not have committed it, were it not that I came to the conviction that it was necessary to drive all that out of my head."

"But no; do not say so. I believe that there is predestination in everything; and I believe, too, that Providence designed you for each other."

"I do not understand that. If that be true, then I need

not do anything, for in every case I must marry Panna Plavitski."

"I have a woman's head, and say stupid things, perhaps; but it seems to me that Providence wills and arranges everything for the best, but leaves people freedom. Frequently they do not wish to follow that which is predestined, and this is why so many are unhappy."

"Maybe. It is difficult, however, to follow anything but one's own convictions. Reason is like a lantern, which God puts in our hands. Who will assure me meanwhile that Panna Marynia will marry me?"

"I ought to have news from her of your visit to Kremen, and I wonder that so far I have none. I think that a letter will come to-morrow at latest, for we write every week to each other. Does she know of your departure for Reichenhall?"

"She does not. I did not know myself when in Kremen where I should go."

"That is well; for she will be outspoken, though she would be so in any case."

The first day's conversation ended here. In the evening it was decided at Litka's request to walk to Thumsee, and go in the morning so as to dine at the lake, return in a carriage, or on foot, if Litka was not tired and they could return before sunset. The two men presented themselves at the lady's villa before nine in the morning. Pani Emilia and Litka were dressed and waiting on the veranda; both were so like visions that Vaskovski, the old pedagogue, was astonished at sight of them.

"The Lord God makes perfect flowers of people sometimes," said he, pointing at mother and daughter from a distance.

Indeed, Pani Emilia and Litka were admired by all Reichenhall. The first, with her spiritualized, angelic face, appeared the incarnation of love, motherly tenderness, and exaltation; the other, with her great pensive eyes, yellow hair, and features that were almost too delicate, seemed rather the idea of an artist than a living little girl. Bukatski, the decadent, said that she was formed of mist made just a trifle rosy by light. Indeed, there was something in the little maiden, as it were, not of earth, which impression was heightened by her illness and exceeding sensitiveness. Her mother loved her blindly; those who surrounded her loved her also; but attention did not spoil this child, exceptionally sweet by nature.

Pan Stanislav, who visited Pani Emilia in Warsaw a number of times every week, was sincerely attached to both mother and daughter. In a city where woman's reputation is less respected than anywhere else in the world, scandal was created by this, without the least cause, of course; for Pani Emilia was as pure as an infant, and simply carried her exalted head in the sky as if she knew not that evil existed. She was even so pure that she did not understand the necessity of paying attention to appearances. She received gladly those whom Litka loved; but she refused a number of good offers of marriage, declaring that she needed nothing on earth except Litka. Bukatski alone insisted that Pani Emilia acted on his nerves. Pan Stanislav adapted himself to those azure heights surrounding that crystal woman, so that he never approached her with a thought dimmed by temptation.

Now he answered with simplicity Vaskovski's remark, —

"In truth, they both seem marvellous."

And, greeting them, he repeated more or less the same thing to Pani Emilia, as something that in the given case had attracted his attention. She smiled with pleasure, — likely because the praise included Litka, — and, gathering up her skirt for the road, she said, —

"I received a letter to-day, and have brought it to you."

"May I read it right away?"

"You may; I beg you to do so."

They set out by the forest road for Thumsee, — Pani Emilia, Vaskovski, and Litka in advance, Pan Stanislav a little behind them, his head bent over the letter, which was as follows: —

My dear Emilka, — To-day I have received thy litany of questions, and will answer at once, for I am in haste to share my thoughts with thee. Pan Stanislav Polanyetski went from here on Monday; hence, two days ago. The first evening I received him as I receive every one, and nothing whatever came to my head; but the next day was Sunday. I had time to spare; and almost the entire afternoon we were not only together, but alone, for papa went to the Yamishes. What shall I say? Such a sympathetic, sincere, and, at the same time, honest man! From what he said of Litka and of thee, I saw at once that he has a good heart. We walked a long time by the pond in the garden. I bound up his hand, for he cut himself with the boat. He spoke so wisely that I forgot myself in listening to his words. Ah, my Emilka, I am ashamed to confess it, but my poor head was turned a little by that evening. Thou knowest, moreover, how alone I am and overworked, and how rarely I see men like him. It seemed to me that a guest had come from another world, and a better one. He not only pleased, but captivated me with his heartiness, so that I could not sleep, and was thinking all the time of him. It is true that in the morning he quarrelled with papa, and even I received a little; though God sees how much I would give that there might be no question of that kind between us. At the first moment it touched me greatly; and if that ugly man had known how much I cried in my chamber, he would have pitied me. But, afterward, I thought that he must be very sensitive; that papa was not right; and I am not angry now I will say, also, in thy ear, that a certain voice whispers to me continually that he will not sell to any one the claim which he has on Kremen, if only to be able to come here again. That he parted in such anger with papa is nothing. Papa himself does not take it to heart; for those are his ways, not his convictions or feelings. Pan Stanislav has in me a true friend, who, after the sale of Magyerovka, will do everything to end all causes of misunderstanding, and in general all those nasty money questions. He will have to come then, even to take what belongs to him, — is it not true? It may be also that I please him a little That a man as quick as he is should say something bitter gives no cause for wonder. Speak not of this when thou seest him, and do not scold him; God keep thee from that. I know not why I feel a certain confidence that he will do no injustice to me, or papa, or my beloved Kremen; and I think it would be well in the world if all were like him.

My dear, I embrace thee and Litka most heartily. Write to me of her health minutely, and love me as I do thee.

When he had finished reading, Pan Stanislav put the letter in the side-pocket of his coat, which he buttoned. Then he pushed his hat down to the back of his head, and felt a certain intense desire to break his cane into small bits and throw them into the river: he did not do this, however; he only began to mutter, while gritting his teeth, —

"Yes; very well. Thou knowest Polanyetski! Be confident that he will not injure thee! Thou wilt come out in safety."

Then he addressed himself as follows, —

"Thou hast thy deserts; for she is an angel, and thou art not worthy of her." And again a desire seized him to break his cane into bits. Now he saw clearly that the soul of that maiden had been ready to give itself with all faith and trust to him; and he prepared for her one of those painful and wounding disillusions, the memory of which, fixed once and forever, pains eternally. To sell the claim was nothing; but to sell it to a man wishing to buy it with the intention which Mashko had, was to say to the woman, "I do not want thee; marry him, if it please thee." What a bitter disillusion for her, after all that he had said to her on that Sunday, — after those words friendly, open, and at the same time intended to enter her heart! They were chosen for that purpose, and he felt that she had taken them in that sense. He might repeat as often as he pleased that they bound him to nothing; that in the first meeting and in the first conversation which a man has with a woman, he merely pushes out horns, like a snail, and tries the ground to which he has come. That would be no consolation to him now. Besides, he was not merely not in humor for self-justification, but wished rather to give himself a slap on the face. He saw for the first time so definitely that he might have received Marynia's heart and hand; and the more real that possibility was to him, the more the loss seemed irreparable. Moreover, from the moment of reading that letter, a new change appeared in him. His own reasoning that now he ought to let Marynia go, seemed pitiful and paltry. With all his faults, Pan Stanislav had a grateful heart; and that letter moved him to a high degree, by the kindness and understanding, by the readiness to love, which were revealed in it. Hence the remembrance of Marynia became rosy in his heart and mind all at once, — became rosy even with such power that he thought, —

"As God is in heaven, I shall fall in love with her now!" And such a tenderness seized him that in presence of it even anger at himself had to yield. He joined the company after a while, and, pushing forward a little with Pani Emilia, said, —

"Give me this letter."

"With the greatest pleasure. Such an honest letter, is it not? And you did not confess to me that she suffered somewhat at parting; but I will not reprove, since she herself takes you under her protection."

"If it would help, I would beg you to beat me; but there is nothing to be said, for those are things incurable."

Pani Emilia did not share this opinion; on the contrary, seeing Pan Stanislav's emotion, she felt sure that an affair in which both sides had such vivid feelings was in the best state and must end satisfactorily. At that very thought her sweet face became radiant.

"We shall see after some months." said she.

"You do not even divine what we may see," said Pan Stanislav, thinking of Mashko.

"Remember," continued Pani Emilia, "that he who once wins Marynia's heart will never be disappointed."

"I am certain of that," answered he, gloomily; "but also such hearts, when once wounded, do not return again."

They could not speak further, for Litka and Pan Vaskovski caught up with them. After a while the little girl took Pan Stanislav, as usual, for her own exclusive property. The forest, sunk in the mild morning light of a fair day, occupied her uncommonly; she began to inquire about various trees; every little while she cried out with pleasure, —

"Mushrooms!"

But he answered mechanically, thinking of something else, —

"Mushrooms, kitten, mushrooms."

At last the road descended, and they beheld Thumsee under their feet. In the course of half an hour they came down to a beaten path, stretching along the shore, on which were visible here and there wooden foot-piers, extending a few yards into the lake. Litka wished to look from near by at big fish which were visible in the clear water. Pan Stanislav, taking her by the hand, led her out on to one of the piers.

The fish, accustomed to crumbs thrown by visitors, instead of fleeing, approached still nearer, and soon a whole circle surrounded Litka's feet. In the blue water were visible the golden-brown backs of the carp, and the gray spotted scales of the salmon trout, while the round eyes of these creatures were fixed on the little girl as if with an expression of entreaty.

"Coming back, we will bring lots of bread," said Litka. "How strangely they look at us! What are they thinking of?"

"They are thinking very slowly," said Pan Stanislav; "and only after an hour or two will they say: 'Ah! here is some little girl with yellow hair and rosy dress and black stockings.'"

"And what will they think of Pan Stas?"

"They will think that I am some gypsy, for I have not yellow hair."

"No. Gypsies have no houses."

"And I have no house, Litka. I had the chance of one, but I sold it."

He uttered this last phrase in a certain unusual manner, and in general there was sadness in his voice. The little girl looked at him carefully; and all at once her sensitive face reflected his sadness, just as that water reflected her form. When they joined the rest of the company, from time to time she raised her sad eyes with an inquiring and disturbed expression. At last, pressing more firmly his hand, which she held, she asked, —

"What troubles Pan Stas?"

"Nothing, little child; I am looking around at the lake, and that is why I do not talk."

"I was pleasing myself yesterday, thinking to show Pan Stas Thumsee."

"Though there are no rocks here, it is very beautiful. But what house is that on the other side?"

"We will take dinner there."

Pani Emilia was talking merrily with Vaskovski, who, carrying his hat in his hand, and seeking in his pockets for a handkerchief to wipe his bald head, gave his opinions about Bukatski, —

"He is an Aryan," concluded he; "and therefore in continual unrest, he is seeking peace. He is buying pictures and engravings at present, thinking that thus he will fill a void. But what do I see? This, those children of the century bear in their souls an abyss like this lake, for example; besides, the abyss in them is bottomless, and they think to fill it with pictures, strong waters, amateurship, dilettantism, Baudelaire, Ibsen, Maeterlinck, finally dilettante science. Poor birds, they are beating their heads against the sides of their cages! It is just as if I tried to fill this lake by throwing in a pebble."

"And what can fill life?"

"Every sincere idea, all great feelings, but only on condition that they begin in Christ. Had Bukatski loved art in the Christian way, it would have given him the peace which he is forced to seek."

"Have you told him that?"

"Yes, that and many other things. I urge him and Pan Stanislav always to read the Life of Saint Francis of Assisi. They are not willing to do so, and laugh at me. Yet he was the greatest man and the greatest saint of the Middle Ages, — a saint who renewed the world. If such a man were to come now, a renewal in Christ would follow, still more sincerely and with greater completeness."

Midday approached, and with it heat. The forest began to have the odor of resin; the lake became perfectly smooth in the calm air full of glitter, and, while reflecting the spotless blue of the sky, seemed to slumber.

At last they reached the house and the garden, in which there was a restaurant, and sat under a beech-tree at a table already laid. Pan Stanislav called a waiter in a soiled coat, ordered dinner, then looked about silently at the lake and the mountains around it. A couple of yards from the table grew a whole bunch of iris, moistened by a fountain fixed among stones. Pani Emilia, looking at the flowers, said, —

"When I am at a lake and see irises, I think that I am in Italy."

"For nowhere else are there so many lakes or so many irises," answered Pan Stanislav.

"Or so much delight for every man," added Vaskovski. "For many years I go there in the autumn to find a refuge for the last days. I hesitated long between Perugia and Assisi, but last year Rome gained the day. Rome seems the anteroom to another life, in which anteroom light from the next world is visible already. I will go there in October."

"I envy you sincerely," said Pani Emilia.

"Litka is twelve years old," began Vaskovski.

"And three months," interrupted Litka.

"And three months: therefore for her age she is very small and a great little giddy-head; it is time to show her various things in Rome," continued Vaskovski. "Nothing is so remembered as that which is seen in childhood. And though childhood does not feel many things completely, nor understand them, that comes later, and comes very agreeably, for it is as if some one were to illuminate on a sudden impressions sunk in shadow. Come with me to Italy in October."

"In October I cannot; I have my woman's reasons, which detain me in Warsaw."

"What are they?"

Pani Emilia began to laugh.

"The first and most important, but purely womanly, reason, is to marry that gentleman sitting there so gloomy," said she, pointing to Pan Stanislav, "but really so much in love."

He woke from thoughtfulness, and waved his hand. But Vaskovski inquired with his usual naıveté of a child, —

"Always with Marynia Plavitski?"

"Yes," replied Pani Emilia. "He has been in Kremen, and it would be vain for him to deny that she took his heart greatly."

"I cannot deny," answered Pan Stanislav.

But further conversation was interrupted in an unpleasant manner, for Litka grew weak on a sudden. In a moment she was choking, and had one of her attacks of palpitation of the heart, which alarmed even doctors. The mother seized her at once in her arms; Pan Stanislav ran to the restaurant for ice; Vaskovski began to draw the garden bench with effort toward the table, so that she might stretch on it and breathe with more freedom.

"Thou art wearied, my child, art thou not?" asked Pani Emilia, with pale lips. "See, my love, it was too far — Still the doctor permitted. So anxious! But this is nothing; it will pass, it will pass! My treasure, my love!" And she began to kiss the damp face of the little girl.

Meanwhile Pan Stanislav came with ice, and after him the mistress of the place hurried out with a pillow in her hand. They laid the little girl on the bench, and while Pani Emilia was wrapping the ice in a napkin, Pan Stanislav bent over the child and asked, —

".How art thou, kitten?"

"I was only choking a little; but I am better," answered she, opening her mouth, like a fish to catch breath.

She was not much better, however, for even through her dress one could see how violently the little sick heart was beating in her breast. But under the influence of ice, the attack decreased gradually, and at last ceased altogether, leaving behind only weariness. Litka began again to smile at her mother, who also recovered from her alarm somewhat. It was needful to strengthen the child before they returned home. Pan Stanislav ordered dinner, which was scarcely touched by any one except Litka, for all looked at her from moment to moment with secret fear lest the choking might seize her a second time. An hour passed in this way. Guests began now to enter the restaurant. Pani Emilia wished to go home, but she had to wait for the carriage, which Pan Stanislav had sent for to Reichenhall.

The carriage came at last, but new alarm was in wait for them. On the road, though they moved at a walk and the road was very smooth, even light jolting troubled Litka, so that when they were just near Reichenhall, a choking attacked her again. She begged permission to get out of the carriage; but it appeared that walking wearied her. Then Pani Emilia decided to carry the child. But Pan Stanislav, anticipating that motherly devotion, which moreover was not at all in proportion to the woman's strength, said, —

"Come, Litus, I will carry thee. If not, mamma will weary herself and be sick."

And without asking further, he lifted her lightly from the ground, and carried her with perfect ease on one arm only; to assure both her and Pani Emilia that it did not trouble him in the least, he said playfully, —

"When such a kitten is walking on the ground, she seems not at all heavy; but now, see where those great feet are hanging. Hold on by my neck; thou wilt be steadier."

And he went on, as firmly as he could, and quickly, for he wished the doctor to attend her as soon as possible; as he went, he felt her heart beating against his shoulder, and she, while grasping him with her thin, meagre arms, repeated, —

"Let me down; I cannot — Let me down!"

But he said, —

"I will not. Thou seest how bad it is to be tired out from walking. In future we will take a big easy armchair on wheels; and when the child is wearied, we will seat her in it, and I will push her."

"No, no!" said Litka, with tears in her voice.

He carried her with the tenderness of an elder brother or a father; and his heart was overflowing: first, because really he loved that little maid; and second, because this came to his head of which he had never thought before, — or, at least, had never felt clearly, — that marriage opens the way to fatherhood and to all its treasures of happiness. While carrying that little girl, who was dear to him, though a stranger, he understood that God had created him for a family; not only to be a husband, but a father; also that the main object and meaning of life were found specially in the family. And all his thoughts flew to Marynia. He felt now with redoubled force that of women whom he had met so far he would have chosen her for a wife before all. and would wish her to be the mother of his children.

## CHAPTER VII.

During some days that succeeded the choking, Litka was not ill, but she felt weak; she went out, however, to walk, because the doctor not only ordered her to go, but recommended very urgently moderate exercise up hill. Vaskovski went to the doctor to learn the condition of her health. Pan Stanislav awaited the old man's return in the reading-room, and knew at once from his face that he was not a bearer of good tidings.

"The doctor sees no immediate danger," said Vaskovski; "but he condemns the child to an early death, and in general gives directions to watch over her, for it is impossible, he says, to foresee the day or the hour."

"What a misfortune, what a blow!" said Pan Stanislav, covering his eyes with his hand. "Her mother will not be able to survive her. One is unwilling to believe in the death of such a child."

Vaskovski had tears in his eyes. "I asked whether she must suffer greatly. 'Not necessarily,' said the doctor; 'she may die as easily as if falling asleep.'"

"Did he tell the mother anything about her condition?"

"He did not. He said, it is true, that there was a defect of the heart; but he added that with children such things often disappear without a trace. He has no hope himself."

Pan Stanislav did not yield to misfortune easily.

"What is one doctor!" said he. "We must struggle to save the child while there is a spark of hope. The doctor may be mistaken. We must take her to a specialist at Monachium, or bring him here. That will alarm Pani Emilia, but it is difficult to avoid it. Wait; we can avoid it. I will bring him, and that immediately. We will tell Pani Emilia that such and such a celebrated doctor has come here to see some one, and that there is a chance of taking counsel concerning Litka. We must not leave the child without aid. We need merely to write to him, so that he may know how to talk to the mother."

"But to whom will you write?"

"To whom? Do I know? The local doctor here will indicate a specialist. Let us go to him at once, and lose no time."

The matter was arranged that very day. In the evening the two men went to Pani Emilia. Litka was well, but silent and gloomy. She smiled, it is true, at her mother and her friend; she showed gratitude for the tenderness with which they surrounded her; but Pan Stanislav had not power to amuse her. Having his head filled with thoughts of the danger which threatened the child, he considered her gloom a sign of increasing sickness and an early premonition of near death, and with terror he said in his soul that she was not such as she had been; it seemed as if certain threads binding her to life had been broken. His fear increased still more when Pani Emilia said, —

"Litka feels well, but do you know what she begged of me to-day? To go back to Warsaw."

Pan Stanislav with an effort of will put down his alarm, and, turning to the little one, said while feigning joyfulness, —

"Ah, thou good-for-nothing! Art thou not sorry for Thumsee?"

The little maid shook her yellow hair.

"No!" answered she, after a time, and in her eyes tears appeared; but she covered these quickly with her lids, lest some one might see them.

"What is the matter with her?" thought Pan Stanislav.

A very simple thing was the matter. In Thumsee she had learned that her friend, her "Pan Stas," her dearest comrade, was to be taken from her. She had heard that he loved Marynia Plavitski; until then she had felt sure that he loved only her and mamma. She had heard that mamma wanted him to marry Marynia; but up to that time she, Litka, had looked on him as her own exclusive property. Without knowing clearly what threatened her, she felt that this "Pan Stas" would go, and that a wrong would be done her, the first which she had experienced in life. She would have suffered less if some one else had inflicted the wrong; but, just think, her mamma and "Pan Stas" were wronging her! That seemed a vicious circle out of which the child knew not how to escape and could not. How could she complain to them of what they were doing! Evidently they wanted this, wished it; it was necessary for them, and they would be happy if it happened. Mamma said that "Pan Stas" loved Panna Marynia, and he did not deny; therefore Litka must yield, must swallow her tears, and be silent in presence of her mamma even.

And she hid in herself her first disappointment in life. Yes, she had to yield; but because grief is a bad medicine for a heart sick already, this yielding might be more thoroughly and terribly tragic than any one around her could imagine.

The specialist came two days later from Monachium, and remaining two days, confirmed fully the opinion of the doctor in Thumsee. He set Pani Emilia at rest, though he told Pan Stanislav that the life of the child might continue months and years, but would be always as if hanging on a thread which might break from any cause. He gave directions to spare the little girl every emotion, as well joyous as sad, and to watch over her with the greatest alertness.

They surrounded her therefore with care and attention. They spared her even the slightest emotion, but they did not spare her the greatest, which was caused by Marynia's letters. The echo of the one which came a week later struck her ears, which were listening then diligently. True, it might dispel her fears touching "Pan Stas," but it was a great shock to her. Pani Emilia had hesitated all day about showing Pan Stanislav that letter. He had been asking daily for news from Kremen; she had to lie simply to conceal the arrival of the letter. Finally, she felt bound to tell the truth, so that he might know the difficulties which he had to encounter.

The next evening after receiving the letter, when she had put Litka to sleep, she began conversation herself on this subject.

"Marynia has taken it greatly to heart that you sold the claim on Kremen."

"Then you have received a letter?"

"I have."

"Can you show it to me?"

"No; I can only read you extracts from it. Marynia is crushed."

"Does she know that I am here?"

"It must be that she has not received my letter yet; but it astonishes me that Pan Mashko, who is in Kremen, has not mentioned it to her."

"Mashko went to Kremen before I left Warsaw; and he was not sure that I would come here, especially as I told him that doubtless I should change my plan."

Pani Emilia went to her bureau for the package of letters. Returning to the table, she trimmed the lamp, and, sitting opposite Pan Stanislav, took the letter from the envelope.

"You see," said she, "that for Marynia it is not a question of the sale alone. You know that her head was a little imaginative, therefore this sale had for her another meaning. A great disenchantment has met her indeed!"

"I should not confess to any other person," said Pan Stanislav, "but I will to you. I have committed one of the greatest follies of my life, but I have never been so punished."

Pani Emilia raised her pale blue eyes to him with sympathy.

"Poor man, are you so captivated, then, by Marynia? I do not ask through curiosity, but friendship, for I should like to mend everything, but wish to be certain."

"Do you know what conquered me?" broke in Pan Stanislav, excitedly, — "that first letter. In Kremen she pleased me; I began to think about her. I said to myself that she would be more agreeable and better than others. She is such precisely as I have been seeking. But what next? Long before, I had said to myself that I would not be a soft man, and yield what belongs to me. You understand that when a man makes a principle of anything, he holds to it even for pride's sake. Besides, in each one of us there are, as it were, two distinct persons; the second of these criticises whatever is done by the first one. This second man began to say to me: 'Drop this affair; you cannot live with the father.' In truth, he is unendurable. I resolved to drop the affair. I got rid of the claim. That is how it happened. Only later did I find that I could not dismiss the thought of Panna Plavitski; I had always this same impression: 'She is such as thou art seeking.' I saw that I had committed a folly, and was sorry. When that letter came, and I convinced myself that on her side there was a feeling that she could love me and be mine, I loved her. And I give you my word that either I am losing my head, or this is true. It is nothing while a man is fancying something; but when he sees that there were open arms before him, what a difference! That letter conquered me; I cannot help myself."

"I prefer not to read you all this letter," said Pani Emilia, after a while. "Naturally she writes that the brief dream ended by an awakening more sudden than she had looked for. She writes that Pan Mashko is very considerate in money questions, though he wishes them to turn to his profit."

"She will marry him, as God is in heaven!"

"You do not know her. But of Kremen she writes: 'Papa has a wish to dispose of his property, and settle in Warsaw. Thou knowest how I love Kremen, how I grew up with it; but in view of what has happened, I doubt whether my work can be of service. I shall make one more struggle to defend the dear bit of land. Still papa says that his conscience will not let him imprison me in the country, and this is all the more bitter, since it is as if I were the question. Indeed, life seems at times to be touching on irony. Pan Mashko offers papa three thousand life annuity, and the whole amount for the parcelling of Magyerovka. I do not wonder that he seeks his own profit, but through such a bargain he would get the property for almost nothing. Papa himself said to him, "In this way, if I live one year I shall get from Kremen three thousand, for Magyerovka is mine anyhow." Pan Mashko answered that in the present state of affairs the creditors would take the money for Magyerovka; but if papa agrees to the conditions proposed he will receive ready money and may live thirty years, perhaps longer. Which is true also. I know that this project pleases papa in principle; the only question with him is to get as much as he can. In all this there is one consolation,—that if we live in Warsaw, I shall see thee, dear Emilia, and Litka oftener. Sincerely and from my whole soul do I love you both, and know that on your hearts at least I can count always.'"

"So then I deprived her of Kremen, but sent her a suitor," said Pan Stanislav, after a moment of silence.

While saying this, he did not know that Marynia had put almost the same words into the letter. Pani Emilia had omitted them purposely, not wishing to wound him.

During the last visit of the Plavitskis in Warsaw, Mashko had made some advances for the hand of Marynia; she had no need, therefore, of great keenness to divine his reason for buying the claim and coming to Kremen. Just in this was the bitterness that filled her heart, and the deep offence which she felt that Polanyetski had inflicted on her.

"It is absolutely needful to explain all this," said Pani Emilia.

"I have sent her a suitor!" repeated Pan Stanislav. "I cannot even make the excuse that I did not know of Mashko's designs."

Pani Emilia turned Marynia's letter in her delicate fingers some time, and then said suddenly,—

"It cannot rest this way. I wanted to unite you with her because of my friendship for both of you, but now there is a motive the more; to wit, your suffering. It would be a reproach for me to leave you as you are, and I cannot. Do not lose hope. There is a pretty French proverb, and a very ugly Polish one, about woman's strength and will. In truth, I wish greatly to help you."

Pan Stanislav seized her hand and raised it to his lips.

"You are the best and most honorable person that I have met in the world."

"I have been very happy," answered Pani Emilia; "and since I think that there is only one road to happiness, I wish those who are near me to go by it."

"You are right. That road, or none! Since I have life, I wish that life to be of use to some one else and to me."

"As to me," said Pani Emilia, laughing, "since I have undertaken the rôle of matchmaker for the first time in life, I wish to be of service. But it is necessary to think what must be done now."

Saying this, she raised her eyes. The light of the lamp fell directly on her delicate face, which was still very youthful; on her light hair, which was somewhat disarranged above her forehead. There was something in her so bewitching and at the same time so virginal that Pan Stanislav, though he had a head occupied with other things, recalled the name, "maiden widow," which Bukatski had given her.

"Marynia is very candid," said she, after a moment's thought, "and will understand better if I write the pure truth to her. I will tell her what you told me: that you went away much pleased with her; that what you have done was done without reckoning with yourself, purely under the influence of the thought that you could not come to an agreement with her father; but at present you regret this most sincerely, you beg her not to take it ill, and not to take away the hope that she will yield to entreaty."

"And I will write to Mashko that I will purchase the debt of him at whatever profit he likes."

"See," said Pani Emilia, smiling, "that sober, calculating Pan Stanislav, who boasts that he has freed himself from the Polish character and from Polish fickleness."

"Yes, yes!" cried Pan Stanislav, with a more joyous tone. "Calculation consists in this, to spare nothing on an object that is worth it." At that moment, however, he grew gloomy and said, "But if she answers that she is Mashko's betrothed?"

"I will not admit that. Pan Mashko may be the most honorable of men, but he is not for her. She will not marry without affection. I know that Mashko did not please her at all. That will never take place; you do not know Marynia. Only do, on your part, what you can, and be at rest as to Mashko.'

"Then, instead of writing, I will telegraph to him to-day. He cannot stop in Kremen long at one time, and must receive my despatch in Warsaw."

## CHAPTER VIII.

MASHKO's answer, which Pan Stanislav received two days later, was, "I bought Kremen yesterday."

Though it might have been foreseen from Marynia's letter that affairs would take this and no other turn, and the young man was bound to be prepared for it, the news produced the impression of a thunder-clap. It seemed to him that a misfortune had happened, as sudden as it was incurable, — a misfortune for which the whole responsibility fell on him. Pani Emilia, knowing better than any one else Marynia's attachment to Kremen, had also a presentiment which she could not conceal, that by this sale the difficulty of bringing these two young people nearer each other would be increased greatly.

"If Mashko does not marry Marynia," said Pan Stanislav, "he will strip old Plavitski in such fashion as to save himself and leave the old man without a copper. If I had sold my claim to the first usurer I met, Plavitski would have wriggled out, paid something, promised more; and the ruin of Kremen would have been deferred for whole years, in the course of which something favorable might have happened; in every case there would have been time to sell Kremen on satisfactory conditions. Now, if they are left without a copper, the fault will be mine."

But Pani Emilia looked on the affair from another side: "The evil is not in this alone," said she, "that Kremen is sold. You have caused this sale, and that immediately after seeing Marynia. If some one else had done so, the affair would not have such a significance; but the worst is just this, that Marynia was greatly confident that you would not act thus."

Pan Stanislav felt this as vividly as she; and since he was accustomed to give himself a clear account of every position, he understood also that Marynia was the same as lost to him. In view of this, one thing remained, — to acknowledge the fact and seek another wife. But Pan Stanislav's whole soul revolted against this. First, his feeling for Marynia, though sudden, strengthened neither by time nor nearer acquaintance, though resting mainly on the charm.

almost exclusively physical, which her form had wrought on him, had grown considerably in recent days. Her letter effected this, and the conviction that he had inflicted a wrong on her. Compassion for her seized him now, and he could not think of her without emotion; in consequence of this, the feeling itself increased through two causes, which play a very important rôle in each masculine heart. First, that energetic, muscular man could never yield passively to the course of events. His nature simply could not endure this. The sight of difficulty roused him to action particularly. Finally, his self-love also was opposed to letting Marynia go. The thought which he must acknowledge to himself sometimes, — that he was only a springe in the hand of that Mashko and one of the means to his objects; that he had let himself be abused, or at least used by the advocate, — filled him with rage. Though Mashko should not receive Marynia's hand, though the affair should end with Kremen, even that was more than Pan Stanislav could suffer. Now an irrestrainable desire seized him to go and take the field against Mashko, to throw a stone under his feet, to cross his further plans, at least, and show him that his keenness of an advocate was not enough in a meeting with real manly energy. All these, as well as the more noble motives, urged Pan Stanislav with irresistible force to undertake something, to do something. Meanwhile the position was such that there remained well-nigh nothing to do. Precisely in this contradiction was hidden the tragedy. To remain in Reichenhall, let Mashko carry out his plans, extend his nets, work for the hand of Panna Plavitski — no! not for anything! But what was he to do? To this last question there was no answer. For the first time in life Pan Stanislav felt as if he were chained; and the less he was accustomed to such a position, the more did he bear it with difficulty. He learned too, for the first time, what sleeplessness means, what excited nerves are. Since Litka, during the days just preceding, felt worse again, there hung over the whole society a leaden atmosphere in which life was becoming unendurable.

After a week another letter came from Marynia. This time there was no mention either of Pan Stanislav or Mashko. Marynia wrote only about the sale of Kremen, without complaint, and without explanation of how the affair had taken place. But from this alone he might infer how deeply the sale had wounded her.

It would have pleased Pan Stanislav more had she complained. He understood clearly, too, that silence in the letter touching him showed how far he had been excluded from the heart of that lady, while silence touching Mashko might show directly the opposite. Finally, if she valued that Kremen so much, she might return to it by giving her hand to its present owner; perhaps she had become reconciled by that thought. Old Plavitski had his prejudices of a noble, it is true, and Pan Stanislav counted on them; but, considering the man as an egotist above all, he admitted that in the present case he would sacrifice his daughter and his prejudices.

In the end of ends, to remain with folded arms at Reichenhall, and wait for news as to whether Pan Mashko would be pleased to offer his hand to Panna Plavitski, became for Pan Stanislav simply impossible. Litka, too, from time to time begged her mother to return to Warsaw. Pan Stanislav determined, therefore, to return, all the more as the time was approaching when he and Bigiel had to begin a new affair.

This decision brought him great solace at once. He would return; he would examine the position with his own eyes, and perhaps undertake something. In every case it would be better than sitting at Reichenhall. Both Pani Emilia and Litka heard the news of his departure without surprise. They knew that he had come only for a few weeks, and they hoped to see him soon in Warsaw. Pani Emilia was to go in the middle of August. For the rest of the month she decided to remain with Vaskovski in Salzburg, and return then to Warsaw. Meanwhile she promised to inform Pan Stanislav of Litka's health frequently, and besides correspond with Marynia and learn what her thoughts really were touching Mashko.

On the day of his departure, Pani Emilia and Litka, with Vaskovski, took farewell of him at the station. When in the compartment, he was rather sorry to go. Happen what might, he knew not how things would turn out at Warsaw; here he was surrounded by persons who were the sincerest well-wishers that he had in the world. Looking out through the window, he beheld the sad eyes of Litka raised toward him, and the friendly face of Pani Emilia, with the same feeling as if they had been his own family. And again that uncommon beauty of the young widow struck him,—her features, delicate to the verge of excess, her angelic expression of face, and her form perfectly maidenlike, dressed in black.

"Farewell," said Pani Emilia, "and write to us from Warsaw; we shall see each other in three weeks or sooner."

"In three weeks," repeated Pan Stanislav. "I will write certainly. Till we meet again, Litus!"

"Till we meet again! Bow from me to Evka and Yoasia."

"I will do so."

And he stretched out his hand through the window again: "Till our next meeting! Remember your friend."

"We will not forget; we will not forget. Do you wish me to repeat a novena for your intention?" asked Pani Emilia, smiling.

"Thank you for that too. Do so. Till we meet again, Professor."

The train moved that moment. Pani Emilia and Litka waved their parasols till the more frequent puffing of the engine hid, with rolls of steam and smoke, the window through which Pan Stanislav was looking.

"Mamma," asked Litka, "is it really necessary to say a novena for Pan Stas?"

"Yes, Litus. He is so kind to us, we must pray to God to make him happy."

"But is he unhappy?"

"No — that is — seest thou, every one has trouble, and he has his."

"I know; I heard in Thumsee," said the little girl. And after a while she added in a low voice, —

"I will say a novena."

But Professor Vaskovski, who was so honest that he could not hold his tongue, said after a time to Pani Emilia, when Litka had gone forward, —

"That is a golden heart, and he loves you both as a brother. Now that the specialist has assured us that there is not the least fear, I can tell everything. Pan Stanislav brought him here purposely, for he was alarmed about the little girl in Thumsee."

"Did he bring him?" asked Pani Emilia. "What a man!" And tears of gratitude came to her eyes. After a while she said, "But I will reward him, for I will give him Marynia."

Pan Stanislav went away with a heart full of good wishes and gratitude to Pani Emilia, for the man who has failed and for that reason falls into trouble, feels the friendship of people more keenly than others. Sitting in the corner of the compartment, with the image of Pani Emilia fresh in his mind, he said to himself, —

"If I had fallen in love with her! What rest, what certainty of happiness! An object in life would have been found; I should know for whom I am working, I should know whose I am, I should know that my existence has some meaning. She says, it is true, that she will not marry, but me! — she might, who knows? That other is perfection, perhaps, but she may have a very dry heart."

Here he feels suddenly: "Still I can think calmly about Pani Emilia; while at every recollection of that other a certain unquiet seizes me, which is at once both bitter and agreeable. I am drawn by something toward that other. I have just pressed Pani Emilia's hand, and that pressure has left no sensation; while even now I remember the warm palm of Marynia, and feel a certain species of quiver at the very thought of it."

As far as Salzburg, Pan Stanislav thought only of "that other." This time his thoughts began to take the form. if not of resolves, at least of questions, — how is he to act toward her, and what in this state of affairs is his duty?

"It is not to be denied that I caused the sale of Kremen," said he to himself. "Kremen had for her not only the money value, which might perhaps have been drawn from it had the sale not been hastened, but also the value with which her heart was bound to the place. I have deprived her of both. Briefly speaking, I have wronged her. I have acted legally; but for a conscience made up of something more than paragraphs, that is not sufficient. I have offended her, I confess, and I must correct my fault in some way. But how? Buy Kremen from Mashko? I am not rich enough. I might perhaps do so by dissolving partnership with Bigiel and withdrawing all my capital; but that is materially impossible. Bigiel might fail, should I do that; hence I will not do it. There is one other way, — to keep up relations as best I can with Plavitski, and propose later on for the hand of his daughter. If rejected, I shall have done at least what behooves me."

But here that second internal man, of whom Pan Stanislav made mention, raised his voice and began, —

"Do not shield thyself with a question of conscience. If Panna Plavitski were ten years older and ugly, thou mightst have caused in the same way the sale of Kremen, and taken from her everything which thou hast taken, and still it would not have come to thy head to ask for her hand. Tell thyself straightway that Panna Plavitski draws thee, as with nippers, by her face, her eyes, her lips, her arms, her whole person, and do not tempt thyself."

But, in general, Pan Stanislav held that second internal man firmly, and treated him sometimes with very slight ceremony. Following this method, he said to him, —

"First, thou knowest not, fool, that even in that case I should not try to make good the injury. That at present I wish to make it good by proposing for the lady is natural. Men always ask to marry women who please them, not those for whom they feel repulsion. If thou hast nothing better to say, then be silent."

The internal man ventured a few more timid remarks, as, for instance, that Plavitski might give command to throw Pan Stanislav downstairs; that in the best case he might not permit him to cross the threshold. But somehow Pan Stanislav was not afraid of this. "People," thought he, "do not use such means now; and if the Plavitskis do not receive me, so much the worse for them."

He admitted, however, that if they had even a little tact they would receive him. He knew that he would see Marynia at Pani Emilia's.

Meditating in this way, he arrived at Salzburg. There was one hour till the arrival of the train from Monachium, by which he was to go to Vienna; hence he decided to walk about the town. That moment he saw in the restaurant the bright-colored pea-jacket of Bukatski, his monocle, and his small head, covered with a still smaller soft cap.

"Bukatski or his spirit!" cried he.

"Calm thyself, Pan Stanislav," answered Bukatski, phlegmatically, greeting him as if they had parted an hour before. "How art thou?"

"What art thou doing here?"

"Eating a cutlet."

"To Reichenhall?"

"Yes. But thou art homeward?"

"Yes."

"Thou hast proposed to Pani Emilia?"

"No."

"Then I forgive thee. Thou mayst go."

"Keep thy conceits for a fitter season. Litka is in very great danger."

Bukatski grew serious, and said, raising his brows, —

"Ai, ai! Is that perfectly certain?"

Pan Stanislav told briefly the opinion of the doctor. Bukatski listened for a while; then he said, —

"And is a man not to be a pessimist in this case? Poor child and poor mother! In the event of misfortune, I cannot imagine in any way how she will endure it."

"She is very religious; but it is terrible to think of this."

"Let us walk through the town a little," said Bukatski; "one might stifle here."

They went out.

"And a man in such straits is not to be a pessimist!" exclaimed Bukatski. "What is Litka? Simply a dove! Every one would spare her; but death will not spare her."

Pan Stanislav was silent.

"I know not myself now," continued Bukatski, "whether to go to Reichenhall or not. In Warsaw, when Pani Emilia is there, even I can hold out. Once a month I propose to her, once a month I receive a refusal; and thus I live from the first of one month to the first of the next. The first of the month has just passed, and I am anxious for my pension. Is the mother aware of the little girl's condition?"

"No. The child is in danger; but perhaps a couple of years remain yet to her."

"Ah! perhaps no more remain to any of us. Tell me, dost thou think of death often?"

"No. How would that help me? I know that I must lose the case; therefore I do not break my head over it, especially before the time."

"In this is the point, — we must lose, but still we keep up the trial to the end. This is the whole sense of life, which otherwise would be simply a dreary farce, but now it is a dull tragedy as well. As to me, I have three things at present to choose from: to hang myself, go to Reichenhall, or go to Monachium to see Boecklin's pictures once more. If I were logical, I should choose the first; since I am not, I'll choose Reichenhall. Pani Emilia is worth the Boecklins, both as to outline and color."

"What is to be heard in Warsaw?" asked on a sudden Pan Stanislav, who had had that question on his lips from the first of the conversation. "Hast thou seen Mashko?"

"I have. He has bought Kremen, he is a great landholder, and, since he has wit, he is using all his power not to seem too great. He is polite, sensible, flattering, accessible; he is changed, not to my advantage, it is true, for what do I care? but surely to his own."

"Is n't he going to marry Panna Plavitski?"

"I hear that he wants to. Thy partner, Bigiel, said something of this, also that Mashko bought Kremen on conditions more than favorable. Thou wilt find clearer news in the city."

"Where are the Plavitskis at present?"

"In Warsaw. They are living in the Hotel Rome. The young woman is not at all ugly. I called on them as a cousin, and talked about thee."

"Thou mightst have chosen a more agreeable subject for them."

"Plavitski, who is glad of what has happened, told me that thou hadst done them a service, without wishing it certainly, but thou hadst done it. I asked the young lady how it was that she saw thee in Kremen for the first time. She answered that during her visit in Warsaw thou must have been in foreign countries."

"In fact, I was gone then on business of the firm to Berlin, and I remained there some time."

"Indeed, I did not observe that they were offended at thee. I heard so much, however, of the young lady's love of country life, that she must, I admit, be a little angry at thee for having taken Kremen from her. In every case, she does not show any anger."

"Perhaps she will show it only to me; and the opportunity will not be lacking, for I shall visit them immediately after my return."

"In that case do me one little service: marry the lady, for of two evils I prefer to be thy cousin rather than Mashko's."

"Very well," replied Pan Stanislav, curtly.

## CHAPTER IX.

AFTER his return to Warsaw, Pan Stanislav went first of all to Bigiel, who told him minutely the conditions on which Kremen was sold. Those conditions were very profitable for Mashko. He bound himself to pay at the end of a year thirty-five thousand rubles, which were to come from the parcelling of Magyerovka, and besides to pay three thousand yearly till the death of Pan Plavitski. To Pan Stanislav the bargain did not seem at first too unfavorable for Plavitski; but Bigiel was of another opinion.

"I do not judge people too hastily," said he; "but Plavitski is an incurable old egotist who has sacrificed the future of his child to his own comfort, and, besides, he is frivolous. In this case the annuity is placed as it were on Kremen; but Kremen, as a ruined estate, on which there is need to spend money, has a fictitious value. If Mashko puts it in order, very well; if not, in the most favorable event he will fall behind in payment, and Plavitski may not see a copper for years. What will he do then? He will take Kremen back. But before that time Mashko will contract new debts, even to pay the old ones; and, in case of his bankruptcy, God knows how many creditors will stretch their hands after Kremen. Finally, all depends on the honesty of Mashko, who may be a correct man, but he is carrying on business riskily; if he takes one false step, it may ruin him. Who knows if this very purchase of Kremen be not such a step? — for, wishing to bring the estate into order, he must draw on his credit to the utmost. I have seen men who succeeded a long time until they turned to buying great estates."

"The ready money for Magyerovka will remain with the Plavitskis always," said Pan Stanislav, as if wishing to quiet his own fears for their future.

"If old Plavitski does not eat it up, or play it away, or waste it."

"I must think of something. I caused the sale; I must help."

"Thou?" asked Bigiel, with astonishment. "I thought that thy relations were broken forever."

"I shall try to renew them. I will visit the Plavitskis to-morrow."

"I do not know that they will be glad to see thee."

"And I myself do not know."

"Dost wish I will go with thee? For it is a question of breaking the ice. They may not receive thee alone. It is a pity that my wife is not here. I sit by myself whole evenings and play on the violoncello. During the day I have time enough too; I can go with thee."

Pan Stanislav, however, refused, and next day he dressed himself with great care and went alone. He knew that he was a presentable man; and though usually he did not think much of this, he resolved now to omit nothing which might speak in his favor. On the way he had his head full of thoughts as to what he should say, what he should do in this case or that one, and he tried to foresee how they would receive him.

"I will be as simple and outspoken as possible," said he to himself; "that is the best method absolutely."

And, before he noted it, he found himself at the Hotel Rome. His heart began to beat then more quickly.

"It would not be bad," thought he, "if I should not find them at home. I could leave a card and see later on if Plavitski would acknowledge my visit."

But straightway he said to himself, "Don't be a coward," and went forward. Learning from the servant that Plavitski was at home, he sent in his card, and after a while was invited to enter.

Plavitski was sitting at a table writing letters, drawing at intervals smoke from a pipe with a great amber mouthpiece. At sight of Pan Stanislav he raised his head, and, looking at him through gold-rimmed glasses, said,—

"I beg, I beg!"

"I learned from Bigiel that you and Panna Plavitski were in Warsaw," said Pan Stanislav, "and I came to pay my respects."

"That was very pretty on thy part," answered Plavitski, "and, to tell the truth, I did not expect it. We parted in a bitter manner and through thy fault. But since thou hast felt it thy duty to visit me, I, as the older, open my arms to thee a second time."

The opening of the arms, however, was confined to reaching across the table a hand, which Pan Stanislav pressed, saying in his own mind,—

"May the Evil One take me, if I come here to thee, and if I feel toward thee any obligation!" After a while he asked, "You and your daughter are coming to live in Warsaw?"

"Yes. I am an old man of the country, accustomed to rise with the sun and to work in the fields; it will be grievous for me in your Warsaw. But it was not right to imprison my child; hence I made one sacrifice more for her."

Pan Stanislav, who had spent two nights in Kremen, remembered that Plavitski rose about eleven in the forenoon, and that he labored specially about the business of Kremen, not its fields; he passed this, however, in silence, for he had a head occupied with something else at that moment. From the chamber which Plavitski occupied, an open door led to another, which must be Marynia's. It occurred to Pan Stanislav, who was looking in the direction of that door from the time of his entrance, that perhaps she did not wish to come out; therefore he inquired, —

"But shall I not have the pleasure of seeing Panna Marynia?"

"Marynia has gone to look at lodgings which I found this morning. She will come directly, for they are only a couple of steps distant. Imagine to thyself a plaything, not lodgings. I shall have a cabinet and a sleeping-room; Marynia also a very nice little chamber, — the dining-room is a trifle dark, it is true; but the drawing-room is a candy-box."

Here Plavitski passed into a narrative concerning his lodgings, with the volubility of a child amused by something, or of an old lover of comfort, who smiles at every improvement. At last he said, —

"I had barely looked around when I found myself at home. Dear Warsaw is my old friend; I know her well."

But at that moment some one entered the adjoining room.

"That is Marynia, surely," said Plavitski. "Marynia, art thou there?" called he.

"I am," answered a youthful voice.

"Come here; we have a guest."

Marynia appeared in the door. At sight of Pan Stanislav, astonishment shone on her face. He, rising, bowed; and when she approached the table, he stretched out his hand in greeting. She gave him her own with as much coldness as politeness. Then she turned to her father, as if no one else were present in the room, —

"I have seen the lodgings; they are neat and comfortable, but I am not sure that the street is not too noisy."

"All streets are noisy," answered Plavitski. "Warsaw is not a village."

"Pardon me; I will go to remove my hat," said Marynia. And, returning to her room, she did not appear for some time.

"She will not show herself again," thought Pan Stanislav.

But evidently she was only arranging her hair before the mirror, after removing her hat; she entered a second time, and asked, —

"Am I interrupting?"

"No," said Plavitski, "we have no business now, for which, speaking in parenthesis, I am very glad. Pan Polanyetski has come only through politeness."

Pan Stanislav blushed a little, and, wishing to change the subject, said, —

"I am returning from Reichenhall; I bring you greetings from Pani Emilia and Litka, and that is one reason why I made bold to come."

For a moment the cool self-possession on Marynia's face vanished.

"Emilia wrote to me of Litka's heart attack," said she. "How is she now?"

"There has not been a second attack."

"I expect another letter, and it may have come; but I have not received it, for Emilia addressed it very likely to Kremen."

"They will send it," said Plavitski; "I gave directions to send all the mail here."

"You will not go back to the country, then?" asked Pan Stanislav.

"No; we will not," answered Marynia, whose eyes recovered their expression of cool self-possession.

A moment of silence followed. Pan Stanislav looked at the young lady, and seemed to be struggling with himself. Her face attracted him with new power. He felt now more clearly that in such a person precisely he would find most to please him, that he could love such a one, that she is the type of his chosen woman, and all the more her coldness became unendurable. He would give now, God knows what, to find again in those features the expression which he saw in Kremen, the interest in his words, and the attention, the transparency in those eyes full of smiles and roused curiosity. He would give, God knows what, to have all this return, and he knew not by what method to make it return, by a slow or a quick one; for this cause he hesitated. He chose at last that which agreed best with his nature.

"I knew," said he, suddenly, "how you loved Kremen, and in spite of that, perhaps, it is I who caused its sale. If that be the case, I tell you openly that I regret the act acutely, and shall never cease to regret it. In my defence I cannot even say that I did it while excited, and without intent. Nay, I had an intent; only it was malicious and irrational. All the greater is my fault, and all the more do I entreat your forgiveness."

When he had said this, he rose. His cheeks were flushed, and from his eyes shone truth and sincerity; but his words remained without effect. Pan Stanislav went by a false road. He knew women in general too slightly to render account to himself of how far their judgments, especially their judgments touching men, are dependent on their feelings, both transient and permanent. In virtue of these feelings, anything may be taken as good or bad money; anything interpreted for evil or good, recognized as true or false; stupidity may be counted reason, reason stupidity, egotism devotion, devotion egotism, rudeness sincerity, sincerity lack of delicacy. The man who in a given moment rouses dislike, cannot be right with a woman, cannot be sincere, cannot be just, cannot be well-bred. So Marynia, feeling deep aversion and resentment toward Pan Stanislav from the time of Mashko's coming to Kremen, took sincerity simply ill of him. Her first thought was: "What kind of man is this who recognizes as unreasonable and bad that which a few days ago he did with calculation?" Then Kremen, the sale of the place, Mashko's visit and the meaning of that visit, which she divined, were for her like a wound festering more and more. And now it seemed to her that Pan Stanislav was opening that wound with all the unsparingness of a man of rough nature and rude nerves.

He rose, and with eyes fixed on her face, waited to see if a friendly and forgiving hand would not be extended to him, with a clear feeling that one such stretching forth of a hand might decide his fate; but her eyes grew dark for a moment, as if from pain and anger, and her face became still colder.

"Let not that annoy you," said she, with icy politeness.

"On the contrary, papa is very much satisfied with the bargain and with the whole arrangement with Pan Mashko."

She rose then, as if understanding that Pan Stanislav wished to take leave. He stood a moment stricken, disappointed, full of resentment and suppressed anger, full of that feeling of mortification which a man has when he is rejected.

"If that is true, I desire nothing more."

"It is, it is! I did a good business," concluded Plavitski.

Pan Stanislav went out, and, descending a number of steps at a time with hat pressed down on his head, he repeated mentally, —

"A foot of mine will not be in your house again."

He felt, however, that, if he were to go home, anger would stifle him; he walked on, therefore, not thinking whither his feet were bearing him. It seemed to him at that moment that he did not love Marynia, that he even hated her; but still he thought about her, and if he had thought more calmly he would have told himself that the mere sight of her had affected him deeply. He had seen her now a second time, had looked on her, had compared that image of her which he had borne in his memory with the reality; the image became thereby still more definite, more really attractive, and acted the more powerfully on him. And, in spite of the anger, in the depth of his soul an immense liking for her raised its head, and a delight in the woman. There existed, as it were, for him two Marynias, — one the mild, friendly Marynia of Kremen, listening and ready to love; the other that icy young lady of Warsaw, who had rejected him. A woman often becomes dual in this way in the heart of a man, which is then most frequently ready to forgive this unfriendly one for the sake of that loved one. Pan Stanislav did not even admit that Marynia could be such as she had shown herself that day; hence there was in his anger a certain surprise. Knowing his own undeniable worth, and being conceited enough, he carried within him a conviction, which he would not acknowledge to himself, that it was enough for him to extend his hand to have it seized. This time it turned out differently. That mild Marynia appeared suddenly, not only in the rôle of a judge, who utters sentences and condemns, but also in the rôle, as it were, of a queen, with whom it is possible to be in favor or disfavor. Pan Stanislav could not accustom himself to this thought, and he struggled with it; but such is human nature that, when he learned that for that lady he was not so much desired as he had thought, that she not only did not over-value him, but esteemed him lower than herself, in spite of his displeasure, offence, and anger, her value increased in his eyes. His self-love was wounded; but, on the other hand, his will, in reality strong, was ready to rush to the struggle with difficulties, and crush them. All these thoughts were circling chaotically in his head, or, instead of thoughts, they were rather feelings torn and tearing themselves. He repeated a hundred times to himself that he would drop the whole matter, that he must and wished to do so; and at the same time he was so weak and small that somewhere in the most secret corner of his soul he was counting that very moment on the arrival of Pani Emilia, and on the aid which her arrival would bring him. Sunk in this mental struggle, he did not recollect himself till he was halfway on the Zyazd, when he asked, "Why the misery have I gone to Praga?" He halted. The day was fine and was inclining toward evening. Lower down, the Vistula was flowing in the gleam of the sun; and beyond it, and beyond the nearer clumps of green, a broad country was visible, covered on the horizon with a rosy and blue haze. Far away, beyond that haze, was Kremen, which Marynia had loved and which she had lost. Pan Stanislav, fixing his eyes on the haze, said to himself, —

"I am curious to know what she would have done had I given Kremen to her."

He could not imagine that to himself definitely; but he thought that the loss of that land was for her a great bitterness really, and he regretted it. In this sorrow his anger began to scatter and vanish as mist. His conscience whispered that he had received what he earned. Returning, he said to himself, "But I am thinking of all this continually."

And really he was. Never had he experienced, in the most important money questions, even half the disquiet, never had he been absorbed so deeply. And again he remembered what Vaskovski had said of himself, that his nature, like Pan Stanislav's, could not fix its whole power on the acquisition of money. Never had he felt with such clearness that there might be questions more important than those of wealth, and simply more positive. For the second time a certain astonishment seized him.

It was nearly nine when he went to Bigiel's. Bigiel was sitting in a spacious, empty house with doors opening on the garden veranda; he was playing on a violoncello in such fashion that everything through the house was quivering. When he saw Pan Stanislav he broke off a certain tremolo and inquired, —

"Hast thou been at the Plavitskis' to-day?"

"Yes."

"How was the young lady?"

"Like a decanter of chilled water. On such a hot day that is agreeable. They are polite people, however."

"I foresaw this."

"Play on."

Bigiel began to play "Traumerei," and while playing closed his eyes, or turned them to the moon. In the stillness the music seemed to fill with sweetness the house, the garden, and the night itself. When he had finished, he was silent for a time, and then said, —

"Knowest what? When Pani Emilia comes, my wife will ask her to the country, and with her Marynia. Maybe those ices will thaw then between you."

"Play the 'Traumerei' once more."

The sounds were given out a second time, with calmness and imagination. Pan Stanislav was too young not to be somewhat of a dreamer; hence he imagined that Marynia was listening with him to the "Träumerei," with her hand in his hands, with her head on his bosom, loving much, and beloved above all in the world.

## CHAPTER X.

Pan Plavitski was what is called a well-bred man, for he returned Pan Stanislav's visit on the third day. He did not return it on the second, for such haste would have indicated a wish to maintain intimate relations; and not on the fourth nor the fifth, for that would have shown a want of acquaintance with the habits of society, — but only within the period most specially and exclusively indicated by command of *savoir vivre.* Plavitski prided himself all his life on a knowledge of those commands, and esteemed them as his own; the observances of them he considered as the highest human wisdom. It is true that, as a man of sense, he permitted other branches of knowledge to exist, on condition, however, that they should not be overestimated; and especially, that they should not have the claim to force themselves on to people who were truly well-bred.

Pan Stanislav — for whom everything was desirable that would strengthen in any way the thread of further relations with Marynia — was hardly able to conceal his delight at the arrival of Plavitski. That delight was evident in his agreeable reception, full of good-humor. He must have been astonished, besides, at Plavitski, and the influence which the city had exercised on him. His hair shone like the wing of a raven; his little mustaches were sticking up, vying with the color of his hair; his white shirt covered a slender form; his scarf-pin and black vest gave a certain holiday brilliancy to his whole figure.

"On my word, I did not recognize my uncle at the first moment!" cried Pan Stanislav. "I thought that some youngster was coming."

"*Bon jour, bon jour!*" answered Plavitski. "The day is cloudy; a little dark here. It must be for that reason that thou didst mistake me for a stripling."

"Cloudy or clear, what a figure!" answered Pan Stanislav.

And seizing Plavitski by the side, without ceremony, he began to turn him around and say, —

"A waist just like a young lady's! Would that I might have such a one!"

Plavitski, offended greatly by such an unceremonious greeting, but still more delighted at the admiration roused by his person, said, defending himself, —

"*Voyons!* Thou art a lunatic. I might be angry. Thou art a lunatic!"

"But uncle will turn as many heads as he pleases."

"What dost thou say?" asked Plavitski, sitting down in an armchair.

"I say that uncle has come here for conquest."

"I have no thought whatever of that. Thou art a lunatic!"

"But Pani Yamish? or have n't I seen with my own eyes —"

"What?"

Here Plavitski shut one eye and thrust out the point of his tongue; but that lasted only an instant, then he raised his brows, and said, —

"Well, as to Pani Yamish? She is well enough in Kremen. Between thee and me, I cannot endure affectation, —it savors of the country. May the Lord God not remember, for Pani Yamish, how much she has tortured me with her affectation: a woman should have courage to grow old, then a relation would end in friendship; otherwise it becomes slavery."

"And my dear uncle felt like a butterfly in bonds?"

"But don't talk in that way," answered Plavitski, with dignity, "and do not imagine that there was anything between us. Even if there had been, thou wouldst not have heard a word about it from me. Believe me, there is a great difference between you of this and us of the preceding generation. We were not saints, perhaps; but we knew how to be silent, and that is a great virtue, without which what is called true nobility cannot exist."

"From this I infer that uncle will not confess to me where he is going, with this carnation in his buttonhole?"

"Oh, yes, yes! Mashko invited me to-day to dine with a number of other persons. At first I refused, not wishing to leave Marynia alone. But I have sat so many years in the country for her sake that in truth a little recreation is due to me. But art thou not invited?"

"No."

"That astonishes me: thou art, as thou sayest, an 'affairist'; but thou bearest a good family name. For that matter, Mashko is an advocate himself. But, in general, I confess that I did not suspect in Mashko the power to place himself as he has."

"Mashko could place himself even on his head —"

"He goes everywhere; all receive him. Once I had a prejudice against him."

"And has uncle none now?"

"I must acknowledge that he has acted with me in all that business of Kremen like a gentleman."

"Is Panna Marynia of the same opinion?"

"Certainly; though I think that Kremen lies on her heart. I got rid of it for her sake, but youth cannot understand everything. I knew about her views, however, and am ready to endure every bitterness with calm. As to Mashko, in truth, she cannot cast reproach at him for anything. He bought Kremen, it is true, but —"

"But he is ready to give it back?"

"Thou art of the family, so, speaking between us, I think that that is true. Marynia occupied him greatly, even during our former visit to Warsaw; but somehow the affair did not move. The maiden was too young; he did not please her sufficiently; I was a little opposed myself, for I was prejudiced as to his family. Bukatski sharpened his teeth at him, so it ended in nothing."

"It did not end, since it is beginning again."

"It is, for I am convinced that he comes of a very good family, once Italian and formerly called Masco. They came here with Queen Bona, and settled in White Russia at that time. He, if thou hast noticed it, has a face somewhat Italian."

"No; he has a Portuguese face."

"That is all one, however. But the plan to sell Kremen and still to keep it — no common head could have worked that out. As to Mashko — yes I think that such is his plan. Marynia is a strange girl, though. It is bitter to say this, that a man understands a stranger sooner than his own child. But if she will only say as Talleyrand did, '*Paris vaut la messe.*'"

"Ah, I thought that it was Henry IV. who said that."

"Thou didst, for thou art an 'affairist,' a man of recent times. History and ancient deeds are not to the taste of you young men, ye prefer to make money. Everything depends, then, on Marynia; but I will not hurry her. I will not, for, finally, with our connections, a better match may be found. It is necessary to go out a little among people and find old acquaintances. That is only toil and torment; but what is necessary, is necessary. Thou thinkest that I go to this dinner with pleasure. No! but I must receive young people sometimes. I hope too that thou wilt not forget us."

"No, no; I will not."

"Dost know what they say of thee?—that thou art making money infernally. Well, well, I don't know whom thou art like—not like thy father! In every case, I am not the man to blame thee, no, no! Thou didst throttle me without mercy, didst treat me as the wolf did the lamb; but there is in thee something which pleases me,—I have for thee a kind of weakness."

"The feeling is mutual," said Pan Stanislav.

In fact, Plavitski did not lie. He had an instinctive respect for property, and that young man, who was gaining it, roused in him a certain admiration, bordering on sympathy. He was not some poor relative who might ask for assistance; and therefore Plavitski, though for the moment he had no calculations in regard to Pan Stanislav, resolved to keep up relations with him. At the end of the visit he began to look around on the apartments.

"Thou hast fine lodgings!" said he.

That, too, was true. Pan Stanislav had a dwelling furnished as if he were about to marry. The furnishing itself caused him pleasure, for it gave a certain show of reality to his wishes.

Plavitski, looking around at the drawing-room, beyond which was another smaller apartment furnished very elegantly, inquired,—

"Why not marry?"

"I will when I can."

Plavitski smiled cunningly, and, patting Pan Stanislav on the knee, began to repeat,—

"I know whom; I know whom."

"Wit is needed in this case!" cried Pan Stanislav; "try to keep a secret from such a diplomat."

"Ah ha! whom? The widow, the widow—whom?"

"Dear uncle!"

"Well? May God bless thee, as I bless thee! But now I am going, for it is time to dine, and in the evening there will be a concert in Dolina."

"In company with Mashko?"

"No, with Marynia; but Mashko too will be there."

"I will go also, with Bigiel."

"Then we shall see each other. A mountain cannot meet a mountain, but a man may meet a man any time."

"As Talleyrand said."

"Till our next meeting, then!"

Pan Stanislav liked music at times; he had had no thought, though, of going to this concert; but when Plavitski mentioned it, a desire of seeing Mashko seized him. After Plavitski had gone, he thought some time yet whether to go or not; but it might be said that he did this for form's sake, since he knew in advance that he would not hold out and would go. Bigiel, who came to him for a business consultation in the afternoon, let himself be persuaded easily, and about four o'clock they were in Dolina.

The day, though in September, was so warm and pleasant that people had assembled numerously; the whole audience had a summer look. On all sides were bright-colored dresses, parasols, and youthful women, who had swarmed forth like many-colored butterflies, warmed by the sun. In this swarm, predestined for love, or already the object of that feeling and entertaining it, and assembled there for the pursuit of love and for music, Marynia also was to appear. Pan Stanislav remembered his student years, when he was enamoured of unknown maidens whom he sought in throngs of people, and made mistakes every moment, through similarity of hat, hair, and general appearance. And it happened now to him, to mistake at a distance a number of persons for Marynia, — persons more or less like her; and now, as before, whenever he said to himself, "This is she!" he felt those quivers at the heart, that disquiet which he had felt formerly. To-day, however, anger came on him, for this seemed to him ridiculous; and, besides, he felt that such eagerness for meetings and interviews, by occupying a man, and fixing his attention on one woman, increases the interest which she excites, and binds him all the more to her.

Meanwhile the orchestra began to play before he could find her for whom he was looking. It was necessary to sit down and listen, which he did unwillingly, secretly impatient with Bigiel, who listened with closed eyes. After the piece was ended, he saw at last Plavitski's shining cylinder, and his black mustaches; beyond him the profile of Marynia. Mashko sat third, calm, full of distinction, with the mien of an English lord. At times he talked to Marynia, and she turned to him, nodding slightly.

"The Plavitskis are there," said Pan Stanislav. "We must greet them."

"Where dost thou see them?"

"Over there, with Mashko."

"True. Let us go."

And they went.

Marynia, who liked Pani Bigiel, greeted Bigiel very cordially. She bowed to Pan Stanislav not with such coolness as to arrest attention; but she talked with Bigiel, inquiring for the health of his wife and children. In answer, he invited her and her father very earnestly to visit them on the following week, at his place in the country.

"My wife will be happy, very happy!" repeated he. "Pani Emilia too will come."

Marynia tried to refuse; but Plavitski, who sought entertainment, and who knew from his former stay in Warsaw that Bigiel lived well, accepted. It was settled that they would dine, and return in the evening. The trip was an easy one, for Bigiel's villa was only one station distant from Warsaw.

"Meanwhile sit near us," said Plavitski; "right here a number of seats are unoccupied."

Pan Stanislav had turned already to Marynia, —

"Have you news from Pani Emilia?"

"I wished to ask if you had," answered she.

"I have not; but to-morrow I shall inquire about Litka by telegram."

Here the conversation stopped. Bigiel took the seat next to Plavitski, Pan Stanislav on the outside. Marynia turned to Mashko again, so that Pan Stanislav could see only her profile, and that not completely. It seemed to him that she had grown somewhat thin, or at least her complexion had become paler and more delicate during her stay of a few weeks in Warsaw; hence her long eyelashes were more sharply defined and seemed to cast more shade. Her whole form had become more exquisite, as it were. The effect was heightened by a careful toilet and equally careful arrangement of hair, the style of which was different from what it had been. Formerly she wore her hair bound lower down, now it was dressed more in fashion; that is, high under her hat. Pan Stanislav noted her elegant form at a glance, and admired with his whole soul the charm of it, which was evident in everything, even in the way in which she held her hands on her knees. She seemed very beautiful to him. He felt again with great force that if every man bears within him his own type of female charm, which is the measure of the impression that a given woman makes on him, Marynia is for him so near his type that she and it are almost identical, and, looking at her, he said to himself, —

"Oh to have such a wife, to have such a wife!"

But she turned to Mashko. Perhaps she turned even too often; and if Pan Stanislav had preserved all his coolness of blood, he might have thought that she did so to annoy him, and that was the case, perhaps. Their conversation must have been animated, however, for, from time to time, a bright blush flashed over her face.

"But she is simply playing the coquette with him," thought Pan Stanislav, gritting his teeth. And he wanted absolutely to hear what they were saying; that was difficult, however. The audience, during the long intervals, was noisy enough. Separated by two persons from Marynia, Pan Stanislav could not hear what she said; but after a new piece of music had been finished, he heard single words and opinions from Mashko, who had the habit of speaking with emphasis, so as to give greater weight to each word.

"I like him," said Mashko. "Every man has a weakness; his weakness is money — I am grateful to him, for he persuaded me — to Kremen — I think, besides, that he is a sincere well-wisher of yours, for he has not spared — I confess, too, that he roused my curiosity."

Marynia answered something with great vivacity; then Pan Stanislav heard again the end of Mashko's answer, —

"A character not formed yet, and intelligence perhaps less than energy, but a nature rather good."

Pan Stanislav understood perfectly that they were talking of him, and recognized Mashko's tactics equally well. To judge, as it were, with reason and impartially, rather, to praise, or at least to recognize various qualities, and at the same time to strip them of every charm, was a method well known to the young advocate. Through this he raised himself to the exceptional, and, as it were, higher position of a judge. Pan Stanislav knew, too, that Mashko spoke not so much with intent to lower him, as to exalt himself, and that likely he would have said the same thing of every other young man in whom he might suspect a possible rival.

They were finally the tactics which Pan Stanislav himself might have used in a similar case; this did not hinder him, however, from considering them in Mashko as the acme of perversity, and he determined to pay him if the opportunity offered.

Toward the end of the concert he was able to see how far Mashko was assuming the rôle of suitor. When Marynia, wishing to tie her veil, had removed her gloves and they had fallen from her knees, Mashko raised them and held them, together with her parasol; at the same time he took her wrap from the side of the chair and placed it across his arm, so as to give it to her when they were leaving the garden, — in a word, he was entirely occupied with the lady, though he preserved the coolness and tact of a genuine man of society. He seemed also sure of himself and happy. In fact, Marynia, beyond the brief conversation with Bigiel, talked only with Mashko during the time when she was not listening to the music. When they moved toward the gate, she went with him and before her father. Again Pan Stanislav saw her smiling profile turning to Mashko. While talking, they looked into each other's eyes. Her face was vivacious, and her attention directed exclusively to what he was saying. She was, in fact, coquetting with Mashko, who saw it himself, without admitting, however, for a moment, in spite of his cleverness, that she could do so merely to worry Pan Stanislav.

Before the gate a carriage was waiting in which Mashko seated her and her father. He began then to take leave of them; but Marynia, inclining toward him, said, —

"How is this? Papa has invited you; is it not true, papa?"

"He was to come with us," said Plavitski.

Mashko took his seat in the carriage, and they drove away, exchanging bows with Bigiel and Pan Stanislav. The two friends walked on a good while in silence; at last Pan Stanislav said, feigning calmness in his voice, —

"I am curious to know if they are betrothed."

"I do not think they are," said Bigiel; "but it is tending that way."

"I too see that."

"I thought that Mashko would seek property. But he is in love, and that may happen even to a man who is thinking only of a career. Mashko is in love. Besides, by taking her he will free himself from paying for Kremen. No, the business is not so bad as it seems, and the lady is very pretty; what is true, is true."

And they were silent again. But Pan Stanislav felt so oppressed that he could not control himself.

"This thought that she will marry him is simply a torment to me. And this helplessness! I should prefer anything to such helplessness. I speak to thee openly. What a stupid and ridiculous rôle I have played in the whole affair!"

"Thou hast gone too far, — that may happen to any one; that thou wert her father's creditor is the fault of remarkable circumstances. Thy understanding of such matters differs utterly from his: thou and he are men from two different planets, hence the misunderstanding. Perhaps the affair was too sharply put by thee; but when I think it all over, too great mildness was not proper, even out of regard to Panna Marynia. By making too great abatements thou wouldst have made them for her, — is it not true? What would have resulted? This, that she helped her father in exploiting thee. No; it was for thee to finish the matter."

Here the prudent Bigiel checked himself, thought a moment, and said, —

"And as to thy rôle, there is one escape: to withdraw completely, leave events to their course, and tell thyself that all is going according to thy idea."

"How will it help me," cried Pan Stanislav, violently, "to say that, when all is going against my idea? — and since I feel foolish, there is no help for it. How could there be? To begin with, I did all this myself, and now I want to undo it. All my life I have known what I wanted, but this time I have acted as if I did n't know."

"There are passages in life to be forgotten."

"That may be, my dear man, but meanwhile interest in life falls away. Is the question whether I am well or ill, rich or naked, the same to me now as it once was? I feel sick at the very thought of the future. Thou art established and connected with life; but what am I? There was a prospect; now there is none. That gives a great distaste for things."

"But surely Panna Marynia is not the only woman on earth."

"Why say that? She is the only one now; were there another, I should think of that other. What is the use of such talk? In this lies the question, in this the whole evil, — that she is the only one. A year from now a tile may fall on my head, or I may find another woman: what will happen to-morrow I know not; but that the deuce is taking me to-day, I do know. This is connected in me with other things too, of which to-day I do not care to speak. In external life it is necessary to eat bread in peace, — is not that true? In internal life it is the same. And this is an urgent affair; but I defer internal life till after marriage, for I understand that new conditions work out a new way of thinking, and moreover, I wish to finish one thing before beginning another. But everything grows involved, — not only involved, but vanishes. Barely has something appeared when it is gone. This is the case now. I live in uncertainty. I would prefer if they were already betrothed, for then all would end of itself."

"I tell thee only this," said Bigiel: "when I was a boy, I got a thorn in me sometimes; it pained much less to draw the thorn out myself than to let some one else draw it."

"In that thou art right," said Pan Stanislav, who added after a while, "The thorn may be drawn if it has not gone in too deeply, and one can seize it. But what are comparisons! When a thorn is drawn out, nothing is lost; but my hope of the future is ruined."

"That may be true; but if there is no help for it?"

"To accept that view is just what grieves the man who is not an imbecile."

The conversation stopped here. At the moment of parting Pan Stanislav said, —

"By the way, I should prefer not to be with you on Sunday."

"Maybe thou wilt do well to stay away."

## CHAPTER XI.

A SURPRISE was waiting at home for Pan Stanislav; he found the following despatch from Pani Emilia, "I leave here for home to-morrow evening; Litka is well." This return was unexpected, or at least uncommonly hurried; but since the despatch contained an assurance as to Litka's health, Pan Stanislav understood that Pani Emilia was returning for the sole purpose of occupying herself with his affair, and his heart rose in gratitude. "There is an honest nature," said he to himself; "that is a friend." And with thankfulness there rose in his heart such hope, as if Pani Emilia had the ring of an enchantress, or a magic rod, with which she could change the heart of Panna Marynia in an instant. Pan Stanislav did not know clearly how this could be done; but he knew that one person at least wished him well with deep sincerity, would speak for him, would justify him, would exalt his heart and character and diminish prejudices, which the course of events had accumulated against him. He calculated that Pani Emilia would be very persevering, and that for her this would be a question of duty. A man who is troubled by something is glad to find a person on whom to put responsibility. So in moments of rising bitterness, especially, it seemed to Pan Stanislav that Pani Emilia was responsible for his relations with Marynia; for if she had not shown that letter from which Marynia's readiness to love him was evident, he would have been able to take his mind and heart from her. Perhaps this was true, since in the history of his feelings this letter did in fact play a leading part. It showed him how near happiness had been, almost secured; to what extent in her own mind Marynia had given him heart and soul. It is more difficult to throw away happiness which is not only desired, but begun; and, had it not been for that letter, Pan Stanislav might have regretted the past less, forgotten it more easily, and reconciled himself to the position more readily. At present he thought it even her duty to help him with all her power. Finally, he understood that the affair would move, as it were, of itself; he hoped to see Marynia often, and in conditions most favorable, since he would see her in a house where he was loved and esteemed, and where like feelings must be communicated to each guest. All this strengthened Pan Stanislav's hope; but it added new links to those which bound his thoughts to Marynia. Previously he had promised himself not to go to Bigiel's (on Sunday); now he changed his decision, thinking that, if only health permitted, Pani Emilia too would take part in the trip. Aside from reasons connected with Marynia, he rejoiced from his whole soul to see the beloved faces of Pani Emilia and Litka, who were his greatest attachments in life so far.

That same evening he wrote a few words to Plavitski touching the arrival, supposing that Marynia would be thankful for that information; he gave notice at Pani Emilia's, so that servants would be waiting in the morning with tea; and he hired a commodious carriage to take her and Litka to their home.

Next morning at five he was at the station; while waiting for the train, he began to run briskly along the platform to warm himself somewhat, since the morning was cool. Remote objects, the station buildings, and the cars standing on the near rails, were sunk in fog, which, very dense near the ground, became rose-colored and shining higher up, announcing that the day would be pleasant. Except officials and servants, there was no one on the platform yet, because of the early hour; gradually, however, people began to arrive. All at once two forms came out of the fog; in one of these Pan Stanislav, with beating heart, recognized Marynia, who was hastening, with her maid, to greet Pani Emilia. As he had not expected the meeting, he was greatly confused at the first moment. She stopped short, as if astonished or troubled. After a while, however, he approached and extended his hand to her, —

"Good-day!" said he. "And truly it will be a good day for us both if our travellers arrive."

"Then is it not certain?" asked Marynia.

"Of course it is certain, unless something unlooked for prevents. I received a despatch yesterday, and sent the news to Pan Plavitski, thinking that you would be glad to hear it."

"Thank you. The surprise was so pleasant!"

"The best proof of that is that you have risen so early."

"I have not lost the habit of early rising yet."

"We came too soon. The train will arrive only in half an hour. Meanwhile I advise you to walk, for the morning is cool, though the day promises to be fine."

"The fog is clearing," said Marynia, raising her blue eyes, which to Pan Stanislav seemed violet in the light of the morning.

"Do you wish to walk along the platform?"

"Thank you; I prefer to sit in the waiting-room."

And, nodding, she went away. Pan Stanislav began to fly with hurried steps along the platform. It was somewhat bitter to think that she would not remain; but he explained to himself that perhaps this was not proper, and, besides, the bitterness was overcome by the pleasant thought of how the coming of Pani Emilia would bring them nearer, and how many meetings it would cause. A certain wonderful solace and good-humor continued to rise in him. He thought of the violet eyes of Marynia, and her face made rosy by the coolness of the morning; he rushed past the windows of the hall in which she was sitting, and said to himself almost joyfully, —

"Ah, ha! sit there, hide thyself! I will find thee." And he felt with greater force than ever how dear she might become to him, if she would be kind even in a small degree.

Meanwhile bells sounded; and a few minutes later, in the fog, still dense at the earth, though the sky above was blue, appeared the dim outlines of the train, which, as it approached, became more clearly defined. The engine, puffing interrupted clumps of smoke, rolled in with decreasing movement, and, stopping, began with noise and hissing to belch forth under its front wheels the useless remnant of steam.

Pan Stanislav sprang to the sleeping-car; the first face at the window was Litka's, which at sight of him grew as radiant as if a sudden sunbeam had fallen on it. The little girl's hands began to move joyously, beckoning to Pan Stanislav, who was in the car in one moment.

"My dearest little kitten!" cried he, seizing Litka's hand, "and hast thou slept; art thou well?"

"I am well; and we have come home. And we'll be together — and good-day, Pan Stas!"

Right behind the little girl stood Pani Emilia, whose hand "Pan Stas" kissed very cordially; and he began to speak quickly, as people do at time of greeting, —

"Good day to the dear lady. I have a carriage. You

can go at once. My servant will take your baggage; I ask only for the check. They are waiting for you at home with tea. Pray give the check. Panna Plavitski is here too."

Panna Plavitski was waiting, in fact, outside the car; and she and Pani Emilia shook hands, with faces full of smiles. Litka looked for a moment at Marynia, as if hesitating; after a while, however, she threw herself on her neck with her usual cordiality.

"Marynia, thou wilt go with us to tea," said Pani Emilia. "It is ready, and thou art fasting, of course."

"Thou art tired, travelling all night."

"From the boundary we slept as if killed; and when we woke, we had time to wash and dress. In every case we must drink tea. Thou wilt go with us?"

"I will, with the greatest pleasure."

But Litka began to pull at her mother's dress.

"Mamma, and Pan Stas."

"But, naturally, Pan Stas too, — he thought of everything. Thanks to him, everything is ready. He must go with us, of course."

"He must; he must!" cried Litka, turning to Pan Stanislav, who answered, smiling, —

"Not he must; but he wants to."

And after a moment all four took their places in the carriage. Pan Stanislav was in excellent humor. Marynia was before him, and at his side little Litka. It seemed to him that the morning brightness was entering him, and that better days were beginning. He felt that henceforth he would belong to an intimate circle of beings bound together by comradeship and friendship, and in that circle would be Marynia. Now she was sitting there before him, near his eye, and near the friendship which both felt for Pani Emilia and Litka. Meanwhile all four were talking joyously.

"What has happened, Emilka," asked Marynia, "that thou hast come so soon?"

"Litka begged so every day to come home."

"Dost not like to live abroad?" asked Pan Stanislav.

"No."

"Homesick for Warsaw?"

"Yes."

"And for me? Now tell quickly, or it will be bad."

Litka looked at her mother, at Marynia, and then at Pan Stanislav: and at last she said, —

"And for Pan Stas too."

"Take this for that!" said Pan Stanislav, and he seized her little hand to kiss it; but she defended herself as she could. At last she hid her hand. He, turning to Marynia, and showing his sound white teeth, said, —

"As you see, we are always quarrelling; but we love each other."

"That is the way generally," answered Marynia.

And he, looking her straight and honestly in the eyes, said, —

"Oh that it were the way generally!"

Marynia blushed slightly and grew more serious, but said nothing, and began to converse with Pani Emilia.

Pan Stanislav turned to Litka.

"But where is Professor Vaskovski? Has he gone to Italy?"

"No. He stopped at Chenstohova, and will come the day after to-morrow."

"Is he well?"

"He is."

Here the little girl looked at her friend, and said, —

"But Pan Stas has grown thin; has n't he, mamma?"

"Indeed he has," answered Pani Emilia.

Pan Stanislav was changed somewhat, for he had been sleeping badly, and the cause of that sleeplessness was sitting before him in the carriage. But he laid the blame on cares and labor in his business. Meanwhile they arrived at Pani Emilia's.

When the lady went to greet her servants, Litka ran after her. Pan Stanislav and Marynia remained alone in the dining-room.

"You have no nearer acquaintance here, I suppose, than Pani Emilia?" said Pan Stanislav.

"None nearer; none so beloved."

"In life kindness is needed, and she is very kind and well-wishing. I, for example, who have no family, can look on this as the house of a relative. Warsaw seems different to me when they are here." Then he added, with a voice less firm, "This time I comfort myself also with their arrival, because there will be at last something mutual and harmonious between us."

Here he looked at her, with a prayer in his eyes, as if he wished to say, "Give me a hand in conciliation; be kind to me, too, since a pleasant day has come to us."

But she, just because she could not be for him altogether indifferent, went always farther in the direction of dislike. The more he showed cordial kindness, the more sympathetic he was, the more his action seemed to her unheard of, and the more offended she felt at heart.

Having a delicate nature, and being, besides, rather timid, and feeling really that a reply, if too ill-natured, might spoil the day's harmony, she preferred to be silent; but he did not need an answer in words, for he read in her eyes as follows: The less you try to improve our relations, the better they will be; and they will be best if most distant. His joy was quenched in one moment; anger took its place, and regret, still stronger than anger, — for it rose from that charm which nothing could conquer, and to which Pan Stanislav yielded himself with the conviction, too, that the gulf between him and Marynia was in reality growing deeper each day. And now, looking on her sweet and kind face, he felt that she was as dear as she was lost irrecoverably.

The arrival of Litka put an end to that interval, grievous to him beyond description. The little girl ran in with great delight, her hair in disorder, a smile on her lips; but seeing them, she stopped suddenly, and looked now at one, now at the other, with her dark eyes. At last she sat down quietly at a table with tea. Her joyousness had vanished too, though Pan Stanislav, confining the pain in his heart, strove to talk and be gladsome.

But he turned scarcely any attention to Marynia; he occupied himself only with Pani Emilia and Litka; and, wonderful thing! Marynia felt that as an additional bitterness. To the series of offences still another was added.

On the following day Pani Emilia and Litka were invited to tea in the evening at the Plavitskis'. Plavitski invited Pan Stanislav too, but he did not go. And such is human nature that this again touched Marynia. Dislike, as well as love, demands an object. Involuntarily Marynia looked toward the door all the evening, till the hour struck in which it was certain that Pan Stanislav would not come; then she began to coquet so with Mashko that she transfixed Pani Emilia with amazement.

## CHAPTER XII.

MASHKO was a very clever man, but full of self-love; he had no reason, however, not to take the kindness which Marynia showed him in good earnest. The unequal degree of it he attributed a little to coquetting, a little to the changing disposition of the young lady; and though the latter filled him with a certain alarm, this alarm was not great enough to restrain him from taking a decisive step.

Bigiel divined the true state of affairs when he declared that Mashko was in love. Such was the case really. At first Panna Plavitski pleased him in a high degree; afterward, when he had thought the pros and cons over, he came to the conviction that the pros had prevailed. The young advocate valued property, it is true; but, gifted with great sobriety of mind, and understanding perfectly the conditions in which he found himself, he concluded that a very wealthy lady he could not find and would not get. Richly dowered young ladies were found either among the aristocracy of descent, — and for him their thresholds were too lofty, — or among the world of financiers, who sought connections with families bearing names more or less famous. Mashko knew perfectly that his painted bishops and armored men, whom Bukatski ridiculed, would not open bankers' safes to him. He understood that even if they had been less fantastic, his profession of advocate would itself be a certain *diminutio capitis* in the eyes of great financial whales. On the other hand, he had, in truth, a certain racial repugnance to that kind of connection; while maidens of good descent had the uncommon attraction which they have for parvenus generally.

Panna Plavitski had no dower, or at least a very insignificant one. In taking her, however, he would free himself from all obligations to the Plavitskis created by the purchase of Kremen. Secondly, by connecting himself with a good family, he would endeavor to bring in a whole group of noble clients, and this might be a very real profit; finally, through the family relations of Marynia, he might in time manage the business of a number, or a number of tens, of really wealthy families, — a thing which had long been the object of his efforts.

The Plavitskis, like all who are a little above middling country families, had indeed relatives whom they did not greatly recognize; they had also others who did not greatly recognize them. This, however, was done not so much from reasons of pride as involuntarily, by virtue of a certain social selection, through which people seek in society persons who are more or less in the same conditions of life as they themselves are. Great family festivals united such separated relatives temporarily; and Mashko not only found it agreeable to think that at his wedding there would be perfectly well-sounding names, but he foresaw various possible profits. The question would be merely one of cleverness to give people of this kind an idea that it would be well on their part, good and safe, to intrust their business to a man noted for energy, and, more than all, one of their own class, since he is a relative. That would be something like a dower given to a poor cousin. Mashko, taking note of his own qualities, hoped to force himself on them, and in time tower above them. He knew that this man or that would come at first to him for such counsel as he might find in conversation with an acquaintance, or a distant relative, who happened to understand various questions; later on, as the counsels proved good, he would come oftener, and at last put everything into the hands of the counsellor. Helping others in this fashion, he could himself sail out into broad waters, clear Kremen in time, advance to considerable property, throw aside at last legal pursuits, which he did not like, and which he considered only as a means of reaching his object, and fix himself finally in lofty spheres of society as an independent man, and at the same time a representative of superior landed property resting on a firm basis. He had foreseen all this, calculated and counted, before he determined to try for the hand of Panna Plavitski.

He had not foreseen, however, one thing; to wit, that he would fall in love to such a degree as he had. For the time this made him angry, for he judged that too strong a feeling was something opposed to the balance which a man of high society should preserve at all times. That balance was one of his illusions. If he had had no need of forcing himself into that society, or had been born in it, he might have permitted himself to love to his heart's satisfaction.

In spite of all his keenness, he had not understood that one of the chief privileges of this society, which considers itself privileged, is freedom. For this reason he was not altogether content when his heart melted too much in presence of Marynia. But, on the other hand, the object toward which he strove grew identified the more in him with that personal happiness which was verging almost on intoxication.

These were new things for him, so new that the brightness of those unknown horizons blinded him. Mashko had arrived at thirty and some years of his life without knowing what rapture is. Now he understood what happiness and charms were described by that word, for he was enraptured with Marynia to the depth of his soul. Whenever Plavitski received him in his room, and she was in the adjoining one, Mashko was with her in thought to such a degree that hardly could he understand what the old man was saying.

When she entered, there rose in his heart feelings utterly unknown to him hitherto, — feelings tender and delicate, which made him a better man than he was usually. His blue eyes changed their ordinary steel and cold gleam to an expression of sweetness and delight; the freckles on his face, by which he called to mind Professor Vaskovski, became still more distinct; his whole form lost its marks of formality, and he passed his fingers through his light side whiskers, not like an English lord, but an ordinary love-stricken mortal. He rose at last so high that he wished not only his own good, but her good, evidently not understanding it otherwise than through him and in him.

He was so much in love that, if rejected, he might become dangerous, especially in view of his want of moral development, his great real energy, and lack of scruples. Till then he had not loved, and Marynia roused first in him all that was capable of loving. She was not a brilliant beauty; but she possessed in the highest degree the charm of womanliness, and that womanliness was the reason that she attracted energetic natures specially. In her delicate form there was something in common with a climbing plant; she had a calm face, clear eyes, and a mouth somewhat thoughtful, — all this, taken together, did not produce a mighty impression at the first glance, but after a time every man, even the most indifferent, saw that there was in her something peculiar, which made him remember that he had in his presence a woman who might be loved.

In so far as Mashko felt himself better than usual. and

in reality was so during that epoch of his life, in that far had the spiritual level of Marynia sunk since the Plavitskis came to Warsaw. The sale of Kremen had deprived her of occupation and a moral basis of life. She lacked a lofty object. Besides, the course of events had accumulated in her bitterness and dissatisfaction, which turn always to the injury of the heart. Marynia felt this herself distinctly; and a few days after that evening when Pan Stanislav did not come to them, she began first to speak of this to Pani Emilia, when at twilight they were left by themselves in the drawing-room adjoining Litka's chamber.

"I see," said she, "that we are not so outspoken with each other as we used to be. I have wished to speak with thee openly, and I cannot bring myself to do so, for it has seemed to me that I am not worthy of thy friendship."

Pani Emilia brought her sweet face up to Marynia's head, and began to kiss her on the temples.

"Ai, thou Marynia, Marynia! What art thou saying, thou, always calm and thoughtful?"

"I say so, for in Kremen I was more worthy than I am now. Thou wilt not believe how attached I was to that corner. I had all my days occupied, and had some sort of wonderful hope that in time something very happy would come to me. To-day all that has passed; and I cannot find myself in this Warsaw, and, what is worse, I cannot find my former honesty. I saw how astonished thou wert because I was coquetting with Pan Mashko. Do not tell me that thou didst not see it. And dost thou think that I myself know why I acted so? It must be because I am worse, or from some anger at myself, at Pan Stanislav, at the whole world. I do not love Mashko; I will not marry him. Therefore I act dishonestly, and with shame I confess it; but moments come in which I should like to do an intended injustice to some one. Thou shouldst break thy old friendship with me, for in truth I am other than I have been."

Here tears began to roll down Marynia's face, and Pani Emilia fell to quieting her and fondling her all the more; at last she said,—

"Pan Mashko is striving for thee most evidently; and I thought, I confess, that thou hadst the intention of accepting him. I tell thee now sincerely that that pained me, for he is not the man for thee; but, knowing thy love for

Kremen, I admitted thy wish to return to it in this way."

"At first I had such thoughts, it is true. I wished to persuade myself that Pan Mashko pleased me; I did not like to repulse him. It was a question with me of something else too, but it was a question also of Kremen. But I could not convince myself. I do not want even Kremen at such a price; but precisely in this lies the evil. For, in such a case, why am I leading Pan Mashko into error, why am I deluding him? Through simple dishonesty."

"It is not well that thou art deluding him; but it seems to me that I understand whence that flows. From repugnance to some one else, and from the offence given by him. Is it not true? Console thyself, however, with this, that the evil is not beyond remedy; for thou mayst change thy action with Pan Mashko to-morrow. And, Marynia, it is needful to change it while there is time yet, while nothing is promised."

"I know, Emilia; I understand that. But see, when I am with thee I feel as formerly, like an upright and honest woman; I understand, that not only a word binds, but conduct. And he may say that to me."

"Then tell him that thou hast tried to convince thyself that thou wert in love with him, but could not. In every case, that is the only way."

Silence followed; but both Marynia and Pani Emilia felt that they had not begun yet to talk of that which, if it did not concern both, concerned Pani Emilia most seriously. So, taking Marynia's hands, she said, —

"Now confess, Marynia, thou art coquetting with Mashko because thou art offended by Pan Stanislav?"

"That is true," answered Marynia, in a low voice.

"But does not this mean that the impression of his visit to Kremen, and of thy first conversations with him, are not effaced yet?"

"Better if it were."

Pani Emilia began to stroke her dark hair. "Thou wilt not believe how good, clever, and noble a man he is. For us he has some friendship. He has liked Litka always; this makes me grateful from my whole soul to him. But thou knowest what an unardent and lukewarm feeling friendship is usually. He in this regard even is exceptional. When Litka was sick in Reichenhall, wilt thou believe it, he brought a celebrated doctor from Monachium; but, not wishing to alarm us, he said that the doctor had come to another patient, and that we should take advantage of his presence. Think what care and kindness! He is extremely reliable, a man to be trusted; and he is energetic and just. There are intelligent men, but without energy; others have energy, but lack delicacy of heart. He unites one to the other. I forgot to tell thee that when Litka's property was in danger, and when my husband's brother set about saving it, he found the greatest aid in Pan Stanislav. If Litka were grown up, I would give her to no one in the world with such confidence as to him. I could not even recount to you how much kindness we have experienced from him."

"If as much as I have of evil, then very much."

"Marynia, he did not intend that. If thou couldst but know how he suffers for his rashness, and how sincerely he acknowledges his fault touching thee."

"He told me that himself," answered Marynia. "I, my Emilka, have pondered much over this, — to tell the truth, I have not thought of another thing; and I cannot find that he is to blame. In Kremen he was so pleasant that it seemed to me — to thee alone will I say this; for to thee I have written it already — that on the Sunday evening which he passed in our house I went to sleep with my head and heart so filled with him that I am ashamed to speak of it now. And I felt that one day longer, one friendly word more on his part, and I should love him for my lifetime. It seemed to me that he also — The next day he went away in anger. The fault was my father's; it was mine also. I was able to understand that; and dost remember the letter I wrote thee at Reichenhall? Precisely the same trust which thou hast in him, I too had. He went away; I myself do not know why I thought, that he would return, or would write to me. He did not return; he did not write. Something told me that he would not take away Kremen; he took it. And afterward — I know that Pan Mashko talked with him openly, and he urged Pan Mashko, and assured him that he was thinking of nothing himself. Oh, my Emilia! If it please thee, he is not to blame; but how much harm has he done to me! Through him I have lost not only a beloved corner in which I was working; but more, I have lost faith in life, in people, in this, — that better and nobler things in this world conquer the low and the evil. I have become worse. I tell thee sincerely that I cannot find myself. He had the right to act as he has acted.

I admit that; I say so, and do not say that he is guilty. But he has broken some vital spring in me. There is no cure for that; it cannot be mended. How can it? What is it to me that a change rose in him afterward; that he regrets what he did; that he would be ready even to marry me? What is that to me, if I, who almost loved him, not only do not love him now, but must guard against repugnance? That is worse than if I did not care for him. I know what thy wish is; but life must be built on love, not on repugnance. How can I give my hand to him with that feeling of offence in my soul and with that regret, that through him, guilty or not guilty, so much has been lost to me? Thou thinkest that I do not see his charm; but what can I do, when the more I see him, the more I am repulsed, and if I had to choose I should choose Pan Mashko, though he is less worthy? To everything good which thou canst say of him I agree; but to everything I answer: I do not love him; I never will love him."

Pani Emilia's eyes were filled with tears. "Poor Pan Stas," said she, as if to herself. And after a moment of silence she asked, "And art thou not sorry for him?"

"I am sorry for him when I think of him as he was in Kremen; I am sorry for him when I do not see him. But from the moment that I see him, I feel nothing but—repulsion."

"Yes; because thou knowest not how unhappy he was in Reichenhall, and now he is still more unhappy. He has no one in the world."

"He has thy friendship, and he loves Litka."

"My Marynia, that is something different. I am thankful to him from my whole soul for his attachment to Litka; but that is something different altogether, and thou knowest thyself that he loves thee a hundred times more than Litka."

In the chamber it had grown dark already; but soon the servant brought in a lamp, and, placing it on the table, went out. By the lamplight Pani Emilia beheld a whitish form crouched on the sofa near the door which led to Litka's room.

"Who is there? Is that Litka?"

"I, mamma."

In her voice there was something; Pani Emilia rose and went hurriedly toward her.

"When didst thou come out? What is the matter?"

"I feel so ill in some way."

Pani Emilia sat down on the sofa, and, drawing the little girl up to her, saw tears in her eyes.

"Art thou crying, Litus? What is the matter?"

"Oh, so sad, so sad!"

And, inclining her head to her mother's shoulder, she began to cry. She was in reality sad, for she had learned that "Pan Stas" was more unhappy than in Reichenhall, and that he loves Marynia a hundred times more than her. That evening, when going to sleep and in her nightdress, she nestled up to her mother's ear and whispered, —

"Mamma, mamma, I have one very great sin on my conscience."

"My poor little girl, what is troubling thee?"

She whispered in a still lower voice, "I do not like Panna Marynia."

## CHAPTER XIII.

Pani Emilia, with Litka and Marynia, and with them Plavitski, were going to the Bigiels to dine at their country house, which stood in a forest at the distance of one hour and a half from the city. It was a fine day in September; there were myriads of glittering spider-webs in the air and on the stubbles. Leaves still fresh and green adhered to the trees yet; here and there, through leafy openings, were visible as it were fountains and bouquets of red and yellow. That pale and faded autumn brought to Marynia's mind her occupations in the country, the odor of grain in the barns, the fields with stacks, and the clear extent of the meadows, bounded way off somewhere on the horizon by stretches of alder. She felt a yearning for that life and that composure, in comparison with which the city, notwithstanding the labor which seethed in its every-day existence, but which Marynia was unable to appreciate, seemed to her idle and empty. She felt now that that life in which she had found her own worth and merit was lost beyond return to her, and on the other hand there was not outlined before her anything that could take its place and redeem it. She might, it is true, return by becoming Pani Mashko; but her heart was filled with bitterness at that thought alone, and Mashko, with his Warsaw self-confidence, with his freckles and his side whiskers, with his aping an English lord, seemed to her simply repulsive. Never had she felt withal a deeper feeling against Pan Stanislav, who had taken Kremen from her, and put Mashko in place of it. She was disgusted with Mashko at that moment, and it seemed to her that she hated Pan Stanislav. She saw before her life with her father on the pavement of Warsaw, without an object, without occupation, without an ideal, with regret for the past and in view of the past, and with emptiness in the future. For this reason that calm autumn day, instead of quieting her, filled her with bitterness and sorrow. On the whole, the journey was not joyous. Litka sat in gloom because "Pan Stas" was not with them. Pani Emilia gave all attention to her, fearing lest that gloomy feeling might be connected with her health. Plavitski alone was in genuine good-humor, especially at the beginning of the journey. In his buttoned frock-coat, with a red flower in the buttonhole, with a light-colored overcoat, and with mustaches as pointed as needles, he thought himself beautiful, and was sprightly, since rheumatism, which he felt at times, was not troubling him, by reason of the good weather; secondly, before him sat one of the most presentable women in Warsaw, who, as he supposed, would not remain indifferent to so many charms, or in any case would esteem them in so far as she would be able to note them. Let her say at least to herself, "Oh, what a charming man that must have been!" In the worst event, Plavitski would have been satisfied with such a retrospective recognition. In this hope he was really enchanting; for at one time he was lofty and fatherly, at another sportive, setting out with the theory that young men of the present do not know how to act politely with ladies. In politeness, as he told Pani Emilia, he went as far as mythology, which was true under a certain aspect, for he looked at her as would a satyr.

But all this was received with a faint smile and with too little attention, hence he grew offended at last and began to speak of something else; namely, that, thanks to the relations of his daughter, he would become acquainted with the bourgeoisie, of which he was glad, however, for hitherto he had seen that society only on the stage, but it is necessary in life to meet the most varied kinds of people, for it is possible to learn something from each of them. He added finally, that it is the duty of certain circles not to estrange the commonalty, but on the contrary to gather them in, and thus plant in them sound principles; therefore he who had striven always to fulfil his social duties did not halt before that mission. Here the noble expression of his face took on a certain style of pensiveness, and in that state of feeling they drove up to the villa of the Bigiels.

It stood in a forest of unmixed pines, in the neighborhood of other villas, among old trees, which in places were felled, in places standing in groups of a few, or of a few tens. They seemed to wonder a little what such a new house was doing among them in the old forest stillness; but they hospitably shielded it from the wind; on fine days they surrounded it with balsamic air, permeated with the odor of gum and resin.

The Bigiels, with a row of children, came out to meet the guests. Pani Bigiel, who liked Marynia much, greeted her very cordially, desiring, besides, to prepossess her thereby for Pan Stanislav; she considered that the better Marynia understood how pleasant it might be for her among them, the less difficulty would she make.

Plavitski, who, during his previous stay with Marynia in Warsaw, had made the acquaintance of the Bigiels at Pani Emilia's, but had limited himself to leaving cards with them simply, showed himself now such a gracious prince as was possible only to the most refined man, who at the same time was fulfilling his mission of gathering in the "bourgeoisie."

"At the present day it is agreeable for any man to find himself under the roof of a person like you; but all the more for me, since my cousin, Polanyetski, has entered the career of commerce and is your partner."

"Polanyetski is a strong man," answered Bigiel, with directness, pressing the gloved hand of Plavitski.

The ladies retired for a moment to remove their hats; then, the air being quite warm, they returned to the veranda.

"Is Pan Stanislav not here yet?" inquired Pani Emilia.

"He has been here since morning," answered Bigiel; "but now he is visiting Pani Kraslavski. The place is near by," added he, turning to Marynia; "not even half a verst distant. There are summer residences everywhere about, and those ladies are our nearest neighbors."

"I remember Panna Terka Kraslavski since the time of the carnival," said Marynia. "She was always very pale."

"Oh, she is very pale yet. The past winter she spent in Pau."

Meanwhile the little Bigiels, who loved Litka wonderfully, drew her out to play in front of the house. The little girls showed her their gardens, made in the sand among the pines, in which gardens, to tell the truth, nothing would grow. These surveys were interrupted every little while by the girls, who stood on their toes and kissed Litka's cheeks; she, bending her beautiful flaxen head, returned these kisses with tenderness.

But the boys wanted their share as well. First, they stripped to the stalk the georgina at the house, gathering for Litka the most beautiful blossoms; then they disputed about this, — what play does Litka like; and they went to Pani Emilia for information. Edzio, who had the habit of speaking in a very loud voice, and closing his eyes at the same time, called out, —

"Please, Pani, I say that she likes ball better, only I don't know that you will let her play ball."

"Yes; if she will not run, for that hurts her."

"Oh, she will not, Pani; we will throw the ball so that it will go straight to her every time, then she will not run any. And if Yozio does n't know how to throw that way, let her throw the ball."

"I want to play with her," said Yozio, pitifully. And at the very thought that he might be deprived of that pleasure, his mouth took the form of a horseshoe and began to quiver; but Litka anticipated his outburst of sorrow, saying, —

"I will throw to thee, Yozio; I 'll throw to thee very often."

Yozio's eyes, already moist, began to smile at once.

"They will not hurt her," said Bigiel to Pani Emilia. "This is remarkable: the boys are what is called regular tearers; but with her they are wonderfully careful. It is Pan Stanislav who has trained them in this devotion to her."

"Such lovely children! there are few in the world like them," remarked Pani Emilia.

In a moment the children gathered in a group to arrange the play. In the middle of the group stood Litka, the oldest and the tallest; and though the little Bigiels were well-behaved children, she, with her sweet, poetic face and features, almost over-refined, seemed, among those ruddy, round faces, like a being from another planet. Pani Bigiel turned attention to that first of all.

"Is she not a real queen?" asked she. "I say truly that never can I look at her sufficiently."

"She is so noble in appearance," added Bigiel.

And Pani Emilia looked at her only one with a glance in which there was a sea of love. The children ran apart now, and stood in a great circle forming, on the gray background of fallen pine needles, parti-colored spots, which seemed as small under the immense pines as colored mushrooms.

Marynia went from the veranda and stood near Litka, to assist her in catching the ball, for which it was necessary to run, and in that way save her from exertion.

On the broad forest road leading to the villa, Pan Stanislav appeared at that moment. The children did not notice him at once; but he took in with a glance the veranda, as well as the space in front; and, seeing the bright robe of Marynia under a pine, he hastened his steps. Litka, knowing her mamma's alarm at every more animated movement which she made, and, not wishing to disquiet her for anything, stood almost without stirring from her place, and caught on her club only those balls which came directly toward her. Marynia ran after all that went farther. By reason of that running, her hair was loosened so that she had to arrange it; and, at the moment when Pan Stanislav was coming in at the gate, she stood bent backward somewhat and with arms raised to her head.

He did not take his eyes from her, and saw no one save her. She seemed to him on that broad space younger and smaller than usual, and therewith so maidenlike, so unapproachably attractive, so created for this, that a man should put his arms around her and press her to his bosom; she was so feminine, so much the dearest creature on earth, — that never till that moment had he felt with such force how he loved her.

At sight of him, the children threw down their balls and clubs, and ran with a cry to meet him. The amusement was stopped. Litka at the first instant sprang also toward Pan Stas, but restrained herself on a sudden, and looked with her great eyes, now toward him, now toward Marynia.

"But thou art not rushing to meet Pan Polanyetski," said Marynia.

"No."

"Why, Litus?"

"Because —"

And her cheeks flushed somewhat, though the child did not know and did not dare to express her thought, which might be expressed in the words: "Because he does not love me any more; he loves only thee, and looks only at thee."

But he approached, freeing himself from the children, and repeating, —

"Do not hang on, little rogues, or I 'll throw you."

And he extended his hand to Marynia, looking at her in the eyes, with an entreaty for a pleasant smile and a greeting even a whit less indifferent than usual; then he turned to Litka, —

"But is the dearest kitten well?"

At sight of him, and under the influence of his voice, she, forgetting all the suffering of her little heart, gave him both hands, saying, —

"Oh, yes, well; but yesterday Pan Stas did not come to us, and it was sad. To-day I 'll take Pan Stas to mamma to give account."

After a while all were on the veranda.

"How are Pani Kraslavski and her daughter?" asked Pani Emilia.

"They are well, and are coming here after dinner," answered Pan Stanislav.

Just before dinner Professor Vaskovski came, bringing Bukatski, who had returned to Warsaw the evening before. His intimacy with the Bigiels permitted him to come without being invited; and the presence of Pani Emilia was too great a temptation to be resisted. He met her, however, without a trace of sentiment, in his usual jesting fashion; she was glad to see him, for he amused her with his strange and original way of uttering ideas.

"Were you not going to Monachium and Italy?" asked she, when they had sat down to dinner.

"Yes; but I forgot a card-knife in Warsaw, and came back to get it."

"Oh, that was a weighty reason."

"It always makes me impatient that people do everything from weighty reasons. What privilege have weighty reasons, that every man must accommodate himself to them? Besides, I gave, without wishing it, the last services to a friend, for yesterday I was at the funeral of Lisovich."

"What! that thin little sportsman?" inquired Bigiel.

"The same. And imagine that to this moment I cannot escape astonishment that a man who played the jester all his life could bring himself to such a serious thing as death. Simply I cannot recognize my Lisovich. At every step a man meets disappointment."

"But," said Pan Stanislav, "Pani Kraslavski told me that Ploshovski, he with whom all the women of Warsaw were in love, shot himself in Rome."

"He was a relative of mine," said Plavitski.

This news affected Pani Emilia mainly. She scarcely knew Ploshovski himself, but she had often seen his aunt, for whom her husband's elder brother was agent. She knew also how blindly this aunt loved her sister's son.

"My God, what a misfortune!" said she. "But is it true? A young man so capable, so wealthy — poor Panna Ploshovski!"

"And such a great estate will be without an heir," added Bigiel. "I know their property, for it is near Warsaw. Old Panna Ploshovski had two relatives: Pani Krovitski, though she was distant, and Leo Ploshovski, who was nearer. Neither are living now."

These words moved Plavitski again. He was indeed some sort of a distant relative of Panna Ploshovski, and even had seen her two or three times in his life; but there remained to him merely the remembrance of fear, for she had told him the bitter truth each time without circumlocution, or rather, speaking simply, had scolded him as much as he could hold. For this reason, in the further course of his life he avoided her most carefully, and all communication between them was stopped, though on occasions he liked to say a word in society of his relationship with a family so well known and important. He belonged to that category of people, numerous in our country, who are convinced that the Lord God created for their special use an easy road to fortune through inheritance, and who consider every hope of that kind as certain. He cast a solemn glance, therefore, on the assembly, and said, —

"Perhaps, too, Providence decided that those properties should pass to other hands, which are able to make better use of them."

"I met Ploshovski abroad once," said Pan Stanislav; "and on me he made the impression of a man altogether uncommon. I remember him perfectly."

"He was so brilliant and sympathetic," added Pani Bigiel.

"May God show him mercy!" said Professor Vaskovski. "I too knew him; he was a genuine Aryan."

"Azoryan," said Plavitski.

"Aryan," repeated the professor.

"Azoryan," corrected Plavitski, with emphasis and dignity.

And the two old men looked at each other with astonishment, neither knowing what the other wanted, and this to the great delight of Bukatski, who, raising his monocle, said, —

"How is that, Aryan or Azoryan?"

Pan Stanislav put an end to the misunderstanding by explaining that Azorya was the name of the family escutcheon of the Ploshovskis, that therefore it was possible to be at once an Aryan and an Azoryan; to which Plavitski agreed unwillingly, making the parenthetical remark that whoso bears a decent name, need not be ashamed of it, nor modify it.

Bukatski, turning to Pani Emilia, began to converse in his usual frigid tone, —

"One kind of suicide alone do I consider justifiable, suicide for love; therefore I am persuading myself for a number of years to it, but always in vain."

"They say that suicide is cowardice," put in Marynia.

"This is a reason too why I do not take my life: I am excessively brave."

"Let us not speak of death, but of life," said Bigiel, "and of that which is best in it, health. To the health of Pani Emilia!"

"And Litka," added Pan Stanislav.

Then he turned to Marynia and said, "To the health of our mutual friends!"

"Most willingly," answered Marynia.

Then he lowered his voice and continued, "For see, I consider them not only as friends of mine, but also — how is it to be expressed?— as advocates. Litka is a child yet, but Pani Emilia knows to whom friendship may be offered. Therefore if a certain person had a prejudice against me, even justly; if I had acted with that person not precisely as I should, or simply ill, and if that person knew me to be suffering from my act, — that person ought to think that I am not the worst of men, since Pani Emilia has sincere good-will for me."

Marynia was confused at once; she was sorry for him. He finished in a still lower voice, —

"But in truth I am suffering. This is a great question for me."

Before she had answered, Plavitski raised a health to Pani Bigiel, and made a whole speech, the substance of which was that the Queen of Creation is no other than woman; therefore all heads should incline before woman, as the queen, and, for this reason, he had bowed down all his life before woman in general, and at present he bowed before Pani Bigiel in particular.

Pan Stanislav from his soul wished him to choke, for he felt that he might have received some kind word from Marynia, and he felt that the moment had passed. In fact, Marynia went to embrace Pani Bigiel; on her return she did not resume the interrupted conversation, and he dared not ask her directly for an answer.

Immediately after dinner came Pani and Panna Kraslavski: the mother, a woman about fifty years old, animated, self-confident, talkative; the daughter, the complete opposite of her mother, formal, dry, cold, pronouncing "tek," instead of "tak," but for the rest with a full, though pale face, reminding one somewhat of the faces of Holbein's Madonnas.

Pan Stanislav began out of malice to entertain her; but, looking from time to time at the fresh face and blue eyes of Marynia, he said to himself, "If thou hadst given even one kind word! thou,—thou, the pitiless." And he grew more and more angry, so that when Panna Kraslavski said "memme" instead of "mamma," he inquired harshly,—

"Who is that?"

"Memme," however, displayed her whole supply of facts, or rather suppositions, concerning the suicide of Ploshovski.

"Imagine," said she, with warmth, "it came to my head at once that he shot himself because of the death of Pani Krovitski. Lord light her soul! she was a coquette, and I never liked her. She coquetted with him so that I was afraid to take Terka to any place where they were together, because her conduct was simply a bad example for such a young girl. What is true, is true! Lord light her soul! Terka, too, had no sympathy for her."

"Ah, Pani," said Pani Emilia, "I have always heard that she was an angel."

And Bukatski, who had never seen Pani Krovitski in his life, turned to Pani Kraslavski and said phlegmatically,—

"Madame, *je vous donne ma parole d'honneur* that she was an archangel."

Pani Kraslavski was silent a moment, not knowing what to answer; then, flushing up, she would have answered something sharp, were it not that Bukatski, as a man of wealth, might in a given event be a good match for Terka. Pan Stanislav enjoyed the same consideration in her eyes; and for these two exclusively she kept up summer relations with the Bigiels, whom she did not recognize when they met her by chance on the street.

"With gentlemen," said she, "every presentable woman is an angel or an archangel. I do not like this, even when they say it to me about Terka. Pani Krovitski might be a good person, but she had no tact; that is the whole question."

In this way conversation about Ploshovski dropped, the

more since the attention of Pani Kraslavski was turned exclusively to Pan Stanislav, who was entertaining Panna Terka. He was entertaining her a little out of anger at himself, a little out of anger at Marynia, and he tried to convince himself that it was pleasant for him near her; he tried even to find in her a charm, and discovered that her neck was too slender and her eyes as it were quenched eyes, which grew lively and turned inquiringly at him when there was no place for a question. He observed, too, that she might be a quiet despot, for when the mother began to talk too loudly, Panna Terka put her glasses to her eyes and looked at her attentively; and under the influence of that look the mother lowered her voice, or grew silent altogether. In general, Panna Terka annoyed him immensely; and if he occupied himself more with her than he ever had before, he did so from sheer desperation, to rouse at least a shade of jealousy in Marynia. Even people of sound sense grasp at such vain methods when the misery of their feelings presses them too keenly. These methods produce usually results opposite to those intended, for they increase the difficulty of subsequent approach and explanations; besides, they merely strengthen the feeling cherished in the heart of the person using them. Toward the end Pan Stanislav longed so much for Marynia that he would have agreed to listen even to an unpleasant word from her, if he could only approach her and speak; and still it seemed to him more difficult now than an hour before. He drew a deep breath when the visit was over, and the guests were preparing to go. Before that, however, Litka approached her mother, and, putting her arms around her neck, whispered. Pani Emilia nodded, and then approached Pan Stanislav, —

"Pan Stanislav," said she, "if you do not think of spending the night here, ride with us. Marynia and I will take Litka between us, and there will be room enough."

"Very well. I cannot pass the night here; and I am very thankful," answered he; and, divining easily who the author of this plan was, he turned to Litka and said, —

"Thou, my best little kitten, thou."

She, holding to her mother's dress, raised to him her eyes, half sad, half delighted, asking quietly, —

"Is that good, Pan Stas?"

A few minutes later they started. After a fine day there came a night still finer, a little cool, but all bright and silvery from the moon. Pan Stanislav, for whom the day had passed grievously and in vain, breathed now with full breast, and felt almost happy, having before him two beings whom he loved very deeply, and one whom he loved beyond everything on earth. By the light of the moon he saw her face, and it seemed to him mild and peaceful. He thought that Marynia's feelings must be like her face in that moment; that perhaps her dislike of him was softening amid that general quiet.

Litka dropped into the depth of the seat, and appeared to be sleeping. Pan Stanislav threw a shawl, taken from Pani Emilia, over her feet, and they rode on a while in silence.

Pani Emilia began to speak of Ploshovski, the news of whose death had impressed her deeply.

"There is hidden in all that some unusually sad drama," said Pan Stanislav; "and Pani Kraslavski may be right in some small degree when she insists that these two deaths are connected."

"There is in suicide," said Marynia, "this ghastly thing, that one feels bound to condemn it; and while condemning there is an impression that there should be no sympathy for the misfortune."

"Sympathy," answered Pan Stanislav, "should be had for those who have feeling yet, — hence for the living."

The conversation ceased, and they went on again for some time in silence. After a while Pan Stanislav pointed to the lights in the windows of a house standing in the depth of a forest park, and said, —

"That is Pani Kraslavski's villa."

"I cannot forgive her for what she said of that unfortunate Pani Krovitski," said Pani Emilia.

"That is simply a cruel woman," added Pan Stanislav; "but do you know why? It is because of her daughter. She looks on the whole world as a background which she would like to make as black as possible, so that Panna Terka might be reflected on it the more brightly. Perhaps the mother had designs sometime on Ploshovski; perhaps she considered Pani Krovitski a hindrance, — hence her hatred."

"That is a nice young lady," said Marynia.

"There are persons for whom behind the world of social forms begins another and far wider world; for her nothing begins there, or rather everything ends. She is simply an automaton, in whom the heart beats only when her mother winds it with a key. For that matter, there are in society very many such young ladies; and even those who give themselves out for something different are in reality just like her. It is the eternal history of Galatea. Would you believe, ladies, that a couple of years since an acquaintance of mine, a young doctor, fell in love to distraction with that puppet, that quenched candle. Twice he proposed, and twice he was rejected; for those ladies looked higher. He joined the Holland service afterwards, and died there somewhere, with the fever doubtless; for at first he wrote to me inquiring about his automaton, and later on those letters ceased to come."

"Does she know of this?"

"She does; for as often as I see her, I speak of him. And what is characteristic is this, — that the memory of him does not ruffle her composure for an instant. She speaks of him as of any one else. If he expected from her even a posthumous sorrow, he was deceived in that also. I must show you, ladies, sometime, one of his letters. I strove to explain to him her feeling; he answered me, 'I estimate her coolly, but I cannot tear my soul from her.' He was a sceptic, a positive man, a child of the age; but it seems that feeling makes sport of all philosophies and tendencies. Everything passes; but feeling was, is, and will be. Besides, he said to me once, 'I would rather be unhappy with her than happy with another.' What is to be said in this case? The man looked at things soundly, but could not tear his soul away, — and that was the end of it."

This conversation ended also. They came out now on to a road planted with chestnut-trees, the trunks of which seemed rosy in the light of the carriage lamps.

"But if any one has misfortune, he must endure it," said Pan Stanislav, following evidently the course of his own thoughts.

Meanwhile Pani Emilia bent over Litka, —

"Art sleeping, child?" inquired she.

"No, mamma," answered Litka.

## CHAPTER XIV.

"I HAVE never run after wealth," said Plavitski; "but if Providence in its inscrutable decrees has directed that even a part of that great fortune should come to our hands, I shall not cross its path. Of this not much will come to me. Soon I shall need four planks and the silent tear of my child, for whom I have lived; but here it is a question of Marynia."

"I would turn your attention to this," said Mashko, coldly, — "that, first of all, those expectations are very uncertain."

"But is it right not to take them into consideration?"

"Secondly, that Panna Ploshovski is living yet."

"But sawdust is dropping out of the old woman. She is as shrivelled as a mushroom!"

"Thirdly, she may leave her property for public purposes."

"But is it not possible to dispute such a will?"

"Fourthly, your relationship is immensely distant. In the same way all people in Poland are related to one another."

"She has no nearer relatives."

"But Polanyetski is your relative."

"No. God knows he is not! He is a relative of my first wife, not mine."

"And Bukatski?"

"Give me peace! Bukatski is a cousin of my brother-in-law's wife."

"Have you no other relatives?"

"The Gantovskis claim us, as you know. People say that which flatters them. But there is no need of reckoning with the Gantovskis."

Mashko presented difficulties purposely, so as to show afterward a small margin of hope, therefore he said, —

"With us people are very greedy for inheritances; and let any inheritance be in sight, they fly together from all sides, as sparrows fly to wheat. Everything in such cases depends on this: who claims first, what he claims, and finally through whom he claims. Remember that an energetic man, acquainted with affairs, may make something out of nothing; while, on the other hand, a man without energy or acquaintance with business, even if he has a good basis of action, may effect nothing."

"I know this from experience. All my life I have had business up to this." Here Plavitski drew his hand across his throat.

"Besides, you may become the plaything of advocates," added Mashko, "and be exploited without limit."

"In such a case I could count on your personal friendship for us."

"And you would not be deceived," answered Mashko, with importance. "Both for you and Panna Marynia I have friendship as profound as if you belonged to my family."

"I thank you in the name of the orphan," answered Plavitski; and emotion did not let him speak further.

Mashko put on dignity, and said, "But if you wish me to defend your rights, both in this matter, which, as I said, may prove illusive, and in other matters, then give me those rights." Here the young advocate seized Plavitski's hand, —

"Respected sir," continued he, "you will divine that of which I wish to speak; therefore hear me to the end patiently."

He lowered his voice; and although there was no one in the room, he began to speak almost in a whisper. He spoke with force, with dignity, and at the same time with great self-command, as befitted a man who never forgot who he was nor what he offered. Plavitski closed his eyes at moments; at moments he pressed Mashko's hand; finally, at the end of the conference, he said, —

"Come to the drawing-room; I will send in Marynia. I know not what she will say to you; in every case, let that come which God wills. I have at all times known your value; now I esteem you still more — and here!"

The arms of Plavitski opened wide, and Mashko bent toward them, repeating, not without emotion, but always with lofty dignity, —

"I thank, I thank —"

After a while he found himself in the drawing-room.

Marynia appeared with a face which had grown very pale; but she was calm. Mashko pushed a chair toward her, seated himself in another, and began, —

"I am here by the approval of your father. My words can tell you nothing beyond what my silence has told already, and which you have divined. But since the moment has come in which I should mention my feelings explicitly, I do this then with all confidence in your heart and character. I am a man who loves you, on whom you may lean; therefore I put in your hands my life, and I beg you from the bottom of my heart to consent to go with me."

Marynia was silent for a moment, as if seeking words, then she said, —

"I ought to answer you clearly and sincerely. This confession is for me very difficult; but I do not wish such a man as you to deceive himself. I have not loved you; I do not love you, and I will not be your wife, even should it come to me never to be any one's."

Then a still more prolonged silence followed. The spots on Mashko's face assumed a deeper hue, and his eyes cast cold steel gleams.

"This answer," said he, "is as decided as it is painful to me and unexpected. But will you not give yourself a few days to consider, instead of rejecting me decisively at this moment?"

"You have said that I divined your feelings; I had time then to make my decision, and the answer which I gave you, I give after thorough reflection."

Mashko's voice became dry and sharp now, —

"Do you think that by virtue of your bearing with me, I had not the right to make such a proposal?"

And he was sure in that moment that Marynia would answer that he understood her bearing incorrectly, that there was nothing in it authorizing him to entertain any hope, — in one word, that she would seek the crooked road taken usually by coquettes who are forced to redeem their coquetry by lying; but she raised her eyes to him and said, —

"My conduct with you has not been at times what it should have been; I confess my fault, and with my whole soul I beg pardon for it."

Mashko was silent. A woman who evades rouses contempt; a woman who recognizes her fault dashes the weapon from the hand of every opponent in whose nature, or even in whose education, there lies the least spark of knightly feeling. Besides this, there is one final method of moving the heart of a woman in such a case, and that is to overlook her fault magnanimously. Mashko, though he saw before him a precipice, understood this, and determined to lay everything on this last card. Every nerve in him quivered from anger and offended self-love; but he mastered himself, took his hat, and, approaching Marynia, raised her hand to his lips.

"I knew that you loved Kremen," said he; "and I bought it for one purpose only, to lay it at your feet. I see that I went by a mistaken road, and I withdraw, though I do so with endless sorrow; I beg you to remember that. Fault on your part there has not been, and is not. Your peace is dearer to me than my own happiness; I beg you, therefore, as an only favor, not to reproach yourself. And now farewell."

And he went out.

She sat there motionless a long time, with a pale face and a feeling of oppression in her soul. She had not expected to find in him so many noble feelings. Besides, the following thought came to her head, "That one took Kremen from me to save his own; this one bought it to return it to me." And never before had Pan Stanislav been so ruined in her thoughts. At that moment she did not remember that Mashko had bought Kremen, not from Pan Stanislav, but from her father; second, that he had bought it profitably; third, that though he wished to return it, he intended to take it again with her hand, thus freeing himself from the payments which weighed on him; and finally, to take the matter as it was in reality, neither Pan Stanislav nor any one else had taken Kremen from her, — Plavitski had sold it because he was willing and found a purchaser. But at that moment she looked on the matter in woman fashion, and compared Mashko with Pan Stanislav, exalting the former beyond measure, and condemning the latter beyond his deserts. Mashko's action touched her so much that if she had not felt for him simply a repulsion, she would have called him back. For a while it seemed to her even that she ought to do so, but strength failed her.

She did not know either that Mashko went down the stairs with rage and despair in his soul; in fact, a precipice had opened before him. All his calculations had deceived him: the woman whom he loved really did not want him, and rejected him; and though she had striven to spare him in words, he felt humbled as never before. Whatever he had undertaken in life hitherto, he had carried through always with a feeling of his own power and reason, with an unshaken certainty of success. Marynia's refusal had taken that certainty from him. For the first time he doubted himself; for the first time he had a feeling that his star was beginning to pale, and that perhaps an epoch of defeats was beginning for him on all fields on which he had acted hitherto. That epoch had begun even. Mashko had bought Kremen on conditions exceptionally profitable, but it was too large an estate for his means. If Marynia had not rejected him, he would have been able to manage; he would not have needed to think of the life annuity for Plavitski, or the sum which, according to agreement, came to Marynia for Magyerovka. At present he had to pay Marynia, Pan Stanislav, and the debts on Kremen, which must be paid as soon as possible, for, by reason of usurious interest, they were increasing day by day, and threatening utter ruin. For all this he had only credit, hitherto unshaken, it is true, but strained like a chord; Mashko felt that, if that chord should ever snap, he would be ruined beyond remedy.

Hence at moments, besides sorrow for Marynia, besides the pain which a man feels after the loss of happiness, anger measureless, almost mad, bore him away, and also an unbridled desire for revenge. Therefore, when he was entering his residence, he muttered through his set teeth, —

"If thou do not become my wife, I 'll not forgive thee for what thou hast done to me; if thou become my wife, I 'll not forgive thee either."

Meanwhile Plavitski entered the room in which Marynia was sitting, and said, —

"Thou hast refused him, or he would have come to me before going."

"I have, papa."

"Without hope for the future?"

"Without hope. I respect him as no one in the world, but I gave him no hope."

"What did he answer?"

"Everything that such a high-minded person could answer."

"A new misfortune. Who knows if thou hast not deprived me of a morsel of bread in my old age? But I knew that no thought of this would come to thee."

"I could not act otherwise; I could not."

"I have no wish to force thee; and I go to offer my sufferings there where every tear of an old man is counted."

And he went to Lour's to look at men playing billiards. He would have consented to Mashko; but at the root of the matter he did not count him a very brilliant match, and, thinking that Marynia might do better, he did not trouble himself too much over what had happened.

Half an hour later Marynia ran in to Pani Emilia's.

"One weight at least has fallen from my heart," began she. "I refused Pan Mashko to-day decisively. I am sorry for him; he acted with me as nobly and delicately as only such a man could act; and if I had for him even a small spark of feeling, I would return to him to-day."

Here she repeated the whole conversation with Mashko. Even Pani Emilia could not reproach him with anything; she could not refuse a certain admiration, though she had blamed Mashko for a violent character, and had not expected that, in such a grievous moment for himself, he would be able to show such moderation and nobleness. But Marynia said, —

"My Emilka, I know thy friendship for Pan Stanislav, but judge these two men by their acts, not their words, and compare them."

"Never shall I compare them," answered Pani Emilia "comparison is impossible in this case. For me, Pan Stanislav is a nature a hundred times loftier than Mashko, but thou judgest him unjustly. Thou, Marynia, hast no right to say, 'One took Kremen from me; the other wished to give it back.' Such was not the case. Pan Stanislav did not take it from thee at any time; but to-day, if he could, he would return it with all his heart. Prepossession is talking through thee."

"Not prepossession, but reality, which nothing can change."

Pani Emilia seated Marynia before her, and said, "By all means, Marynia, prepossession, and I will tell thee why. Thou art not indifferent to Pan Stanislav now."

Marynia quivered as if some one had touched a wound which was paining her; and after a while she replied, with changed voice, —

"Pan Stanislav is not indifferent to me; thou art right. Everything which in me could be sympathy for him has turned to dislike; and hear, Emilka, what I will tell thee. If I had to choose between those two men, I should choose Mashko without hesitation."

Pani Emilia dropped her head; after a while Marynia's arms were around her neck.

"What suffering for me, that I cause thee such pain! but I must tell truth. I know that in the end thou, too, wilt cease to love me, and I shall be all alone in the world."

And really something like that had begun. The young women parted with embraces and kisses; but still, when they found themselves far from each other, both felt that something between them had snapped, and that their mutual relations would not be so cordial as hitherto.

Pani Emilia hesitated for a number of days whether to repeat Marynia's words to Pan Stanislav; but he begged her so urgently for the whole truth that at last she thought it necessary, and that she would better tell it. When all had been told, he said, —

"I thank you. If Panna Plavitski feels contempt for me, I must endure it; I cannot, however, endure this, — that I should begin to despise myself. As it is, I have gone too far. My dear lady, you know that if I have done her a wrong, I have tried to correct it, and gain her forgiveness. I do not feel bound to further duties. I shall have grievous moments; I do not hide that from you. But I have not been an imbecile, and am not; I shall be able to bring myself to this, — I shall throw all my feelings for Panna Plavitski through the window, as I would something not needed in my chamber, I promise that sacredly."

He went home filled with will and energy. It seemed to him that he could take that feeling and break it as he might break a cane across his knee. This impulse lasted a number of days. During that time he did not show himself anywhere, except at his office, where he talked with Bigiel of business exclusively. He worked from morning till evening and did not permit himself even to think about Marynia in the daytime.

But he could not guard himself from sleepless nights. Then came to him the clear feeling that Marynia might love him, that she would be the best wife for him, that he would be happy with her as never with any one else, and that he would love her as his highest good. The regret born of these thoughts filled his whole existence, and did not leave him any more, so that sorrow was consuming his life and his health, as rust consumes iron. Pan Stanislav began to grow thin; he saw that the destruction of a feeling gives one sure result, — the destruction of happiness. Never had he seen such a void before him, and never had he felt, with equal force, that nothing would fill it. He saw, too, that it was possible to love a woman not as she is, but as she might be; therefore his heart-sickness was beyond measure. But, having great power over himself, he avoided Marynia. He knew always when she was to be at Pani Emilia's, and then he confined himself at home.

It was only when Litka fell ill again that he began to visit Pani Emilia daily, passing hours with the sick child, whom Marynia attended also.

## CHAPTER XV.

But poor Litka, after a new attack, which was more terrible than any preceding it, could not recover. She spent days now lying on a long chair in the drawing-room; for at her request the doctor and Pani Emilia had agreed not to keep her in bed the whole time. She liked also to have Pan Stanislav sitting near her; and she spoke to him and her mother about everything that passed through her mind. With Marynia she was silent usually; but at times she looked at her long, and then raised her eyes to the ceiling, as if wishing to think out a thought, and give herself an account of something. More than once these meditations took place when she was left alone with her mother. On a certain afternoon she woke as if from a dream, and turning to her mother, said, —

"Mamma, sit near me here on the sofa."

Pani Emilia sat down; the child put her arms around her neck, and, resting her head on her shoulder, began to speak in a caressing voice, which was somewhat enfeebled.

"I wanted to ask mamma one thing, but I do not know how to ask it."

"What is thy wish, my dear child?"

Litka was silent a moment, collecting her thoughts; then she said, —

"If we love some one, mamma, what is it?"

"If we love some one, Litus?"

Pani Emilia repeated the question, not understanding well at first what the little girl was asking, but she did not know how to inquire more precisely.

"Then what is it, mamma?"

"It is this, — we wish that one to be well, just as I wish thee to be well."

"And what more?"

"And we want that person to be happy, want it to be pleasant in the world for that person, and are glad to suffer for that person when in trouble."

"And what more?"

"To have that one always with us, as thou art with me; and we want that one to love us, as thou lovest me."

"I understand now," said Litka, after a moment's thought; "and I think myself that that is true,—that it is that way."

"How, kitten?"

"See, mamma, when I was in Reichenhall, mamma remembers? at Thumsee I heard that Pan Stas loves Panna Marynia; and now I know that he must be unhappy, though he never says so."

Pani Emilia, fearing emotion for Litka, said,—

"Does not this talk make thee tired, kitten?"

"Oh, no, not a bit, not a bit! I understand now: he wants her to love him, and she does not love him; and he wants her to be near him always, but she lives with her father, and she will not marry him."

"Marry him?"

"Marry him. And he is suffering from that, mamma; is n't it true?"

"True, my child."

"Yes, I know all that; and she would marry him if she loved him?"

"Certainly, kitten; he is such a kind man."

"Now I know."

The little girl closed her eyes, and Pani Emilia thought for a while that she was sleeping; but after a time she began to inquire again,—

"And if he married Marynia, would he cease to love us?"

"No, Litus; he would love us always just the same."

"But would he love Marynia?"

"Marynia would be nearer to him than we. Why dost thou ask about this so, thou kitten?"

"Is it wrong?"

"No, there is nothing wrong in it, nothing at all; only I am afraid that thou wilt weary thyself."

"Oh, no! I am always thinking of Pan Stas anyhow. But mamma must n't tell Marynia about this."

With these words ended the conversation, after which Litka held silence for a number of days, only she looked more persistently than before at Marynia. Sometimes she took her hand and turned her eyes to the young woman, as if wishing to ask something. Sometimes when Marynia and Pan Stanislav were near by, she gazed now on her, now on him, and then closed her lids. Often they came daily, sometimes a number of times in the day, wishing to relieve

Pani Emilia, who permitted no one to take her place in the night at Litka's bedside; for a week she had been without rest at night, sleeping only a little in the day, when Litka herself begged her to do so. Still Pani Emilia was not conscious of the whole danger which threatened the little girl; for the doctor, not knowing what that crisis of the disease would be, whether a step in advance merely, or the end, pacified the mother the more decisively because Pan Stanislav begged him most urgently to do so.

She had a feeling, however, that Litka's condition was not favorable, and, in spite of assurances from the doctor, her heart sank more than once from alarm. But to Litka she showed always a smiling and joyous face, just as did Pan Stanislav and Marynia; but the little girl had learned already to observe everything, and Pani Emilia's most carefully concealed alarm did not escape her.

Therefore on a certain morning, when there was no one in her room but Pan Stanislav, who was occupied with inflating for her a great globe of silk, which he had brought as a present, the little girl said, —

"Pan Stas, I see sometimes that mamma is very anxious because I am sick."

He stopped inflating the globe, and answered, —

"Ai! she does n't dream of it. What is working under thy hair? But it is natural for her to be anxious; she would rather have thee well."

"Why are all other children well, and I alone always sick?"

"Nicely well! Were n't the Bigiel children sick, one after another, with whooping-cough? For whole months the house was like a sheepfold. And did n't Yozio have the measles? All children are eternally sick, and that is the one pleasure with them."

"Pan Stas only talks that way, for children are sick and get well again." Here she began to shake her head. "No; that is something different. And now I must lie this way all the time, for if I get up my heart beats right away; and the day before yesterday, when they began to sing on the street, and mamma was n't in the room, I went to the window a little while, and saw a funeral. I thought, 'I, too, shall die surely.'"

"Nonsense, Litus!" cried Pan Stanislav; and he began to inflate the globe quickly to hide his emotion, and to show the child how little her words meant. But she went on with her thought, —

"It is so stifling for me sometimes, and my heart beats so — mamma told me to say then 'Under Thy protection,' and I say it always, for I am terribly afraid to die! I know that it is nice in heaven, but I should n't be with mamma, only alone in the graveyard; yes, in the night."

Pan Stanislav laid down the globe suddenly, sat near the long chair, and. taking Litka's hand, said,—

"My Litus, if thou love mamma, if thou love me, do not think of such things. Nothing will happen to thee; but thy mother would suffer if she knew what her little girl's head is filled with. Remember that thou art hurting thyself in this way."

Litka joined her hands: "My Pan Stas, I ask only one thing, not more."

He bent his head down to her: "Well, ask, kitten, only something sensible."

"Would Pan Stas be very sorry for me?"

"Ah! but see what a bad girl!"

"My Pan Stas, tell me."

"I? what an evil child, Litus! Know that I love thee, love thee immensely. God preserve us! there is no one in the world that I should be so sorry for. But be quiet at least for me, thou suffering fly! thou dearest creature!"

"I will be quiet, kind Pan Stas."

And in the moment when Pani Emilia came, and he was preparing to go, she asked, —

"And Pan Stas is not angry with me?"

"No, Litus," answered Pan Stanislav.

When he had gone to the antechamber he heard a light knocking at the door; Pani Emilia had given orders to remove the bell. He opened it and saw Marynia, who came ordinarily in the evening. When she had greeted him, she asked, —

"How is Litka to-day?"

"As usual."

"Has the doctor been here?"

"Yes. He found nothing new. Let me help you!"

Saying this, he wished to take her cloak, but she was unwilling to accept his services, and refused. Having his heart full of the previous talk with Litka, he attacked her most unexpectedly, —

"What I offer you is simple politeness, nothing more;

and even if it were something more, you might leave your repugnance to me outside this threshold, for inside is a sick child, whom not only I, but you, profess to love. Your response lacks not merely kindness, but even courtesy. I would take in the same way the cloak of any other woman, and know that at present I am thinking of Litka, and of nothing else."

He spoke with great passionateness, so that, attacked suddenly, Marynia was a little frightened; indeed, she lost her head somewhat, so that obediently she let her cloak be taken from her, and not only did not find in herself the force to be offended, but she felt that a man sincerely and deeply affected by alarm and suffering might talk so, therefore a man who was really full of feeling and was good at heart. Perhaps, too, that unexpected energy of his spoke to her feminine nature; it is enough that Pan Stanislav gained on her more in that moment than at any time since their meeting at Kremen, and never till then was she so strongly reminded of that active young man whom she had conducted once through the garden. The impression, it is true, was a mere passing one, which could not decide their mutual relations; but she raised at once on him her eyes, somewhat astonished, but not angry, and said, —

"I beg your pardon."

He had calmed himself, and was abashed now.

"No; I beg pardon of you. Just now Litka spoke of her death to me, and I am so excited that I cannot control myself; pray understand this, and forgive me."

Then he pressed her hand firmly, and went home.

## CHAPTER XVI.

On the following day Marynia offered to stay at Pani Emilia's till Litka should recover perfectly. Litka supported this offer, which Pani Emilia, after a short opposition, was forced to accept. In fact, she was dropping down from weariness; the health of the sick girl demanded unceasing and exceptional watchfulness, for a new attack might come at any instant. It was difficult to calculate or be sure that a servant, even the most faithful, would not doze at the very moment in which speedy assistance might save the child's life; hence the presence of Marynia was a real aid to the anxious mother, and calmed her.

As to Plavitski, he preferred to eat at the restaurant, and made no trouble. Marynia, moreover, went in every day to inquire about his health and bring domestic accounts into order; then she returned to Pani Emilia to sit half the night by the little girl.

In this way Pan Stanislav, who passed at Pani Emilia's all the time free from occupation, and received, or rather dismissed with thanks, those who came to inquire for Litka's health, saw Marynia daily. And she in truth amazed him; Pani Emilia herself did not show more anxiety for the child, and could not nurse her more carefully. In a week Marynia's face had grown pale from watching and alarm; there were dark lines beneath her eyes; but her strength and energy seemed to grow hourly. There was in her also so much sweetness and kindness, something so calm and delicate in the services which she rendered Litka, that the child, despite the resentment which she cherished in her little soul, began to be kind to her; and when she went for some hours to her father, Litka looked for her with yearning.

Finally the little girl's health seemed to improve in the last hours. The doctor permitted her to walk in the chamber and sit in an armchair, which on sunny days was pushed to the door opening on the balcony, so that she might look at the street and amuse herself with the movement of people and carriages.

At such times Pan Stanislav, Pani Emilia, and Marynia stood near her frequently; their conversation related to what was passing on the street. Sometimes Litka was wearied, and, as it were, thoughtful; at other times, however, her child nature got the upper hand, and everything amused her, — hence the October sun, which covered the roofs, the walls, and the panes of the shop windows with a pale gold; the dresses of the passers-by; the calling of the hucksters. It seemed that those strong elements of life, pulsating in the whirl of the city, entered the child and enlivened her. At times wonderful thoughts came to her head; and once, when before the balcony a heavy wagon was pushing past which carried lemon-trees in tubs, and these, though tied with chains, moved with the motion of the wagon, she said, —

"Their hearts do not palpitate." And then, raising her eyes to Pan Stanislav, she asked, —

"Pan Stas, do trees live long?"

"Very long; some of them live a thousand years."

"Oh, I would like to be a tree. And which does mamma like best?"

"The birch."

"Then I would like to be a little birch; and mamma would be a big birch, and we should grow together. And would Pan Stas like to be a birch?"

"If I could grow somewhere not far from the little birch."

Litka looked at him shaking her head somewhat sadly, said, —

"Oh, no! I know all now; I know near what birch Pan Stas would like to grow."

Marynia was confused, and dropped her eyes on her work; Pan Stanislav began to stroke lightly with his palm the little blond head, and said, —

"My dear little kitten, my dear, my — my — "

Litka was silent; from under her long eyelids flowed two tears, and rolled down her cheeks. After a while, however, she raised her sweet face, radiant with a smile, —

"I love mamma very much," said she, "and I love Pan Stas, and I love Marynia."

## CHAPTER XVII.

Professor Vaskovski inquired every day about the health of the little one; and though most frequently they did not receive him, he sent her flowers. Pan Stanislav, meeting him somewhere at dinner, began thanking him in Pani Emilia's name.

"Asters, only asters!" said Vaskovski. "How is she to-day?"

"To-day not ill, but, in general, not well; worse than in Reichenhall. Fear for each coming day seizes one; and at the thought that the child may be missing —"

Here Pan Stanislav stopped, for further words failed him; at last he burst out, —

"What is the use in looking for mercy? There is nothing but logic, which says that whoso has a sick heart must die. And may thunderbolts split such existence!"

Now came Bukatski, who, when he had learned what the conversation was, attacked the professor; even he, as he loved Litka, rebelled in his soul at thought of that death which was threatening her.

"How is it possible to deceive oneself so many years, and proclaim principles which turn into nothing in view of blind predestination?"

But the old man answered mildly: "How, beloved friends, estimate with your own measure the wisdom of God and His mercy? A man under ground is surrounded by darkness, but he has no right to deny that above him are sky, sun, heat, and light."

"Here is consolation," interrupted Pan Stanislav; "a fly could n't live on such doctrines. And what is a mother to do, whose only and beloved child is dying?"

But the blue eyes of the professor seemed to look beyond the world. For a time he gazed straightforward persistently; then he said, like a man who sees something, but is not sure that he sees it distinctly, "It appears to me that this child has fixed herself too deeply in people's hearts to pass away simply, and disappear without a trace. There is something in this, — something was predestined to her;

she must accomplish something, and before that she will not die."

"Mysticism," said Bukatski.

But Pan Stanislav interrupted: "Oh, that it were so, mysticism or no mysticism! Oh, that it were so! A man in misfortune grasps even at a shadow of hope. It never found place in my head that she had to die."

But the professor added, "Who knows? she may survive all of us."

Polanyetski was in that phase of scepticism in which a man recognizes certainty in nothing, but considers everything possible, especially that everything which at the given time his heart yearns for; he breathed therefore more easily, and received certain consolation.

"May God have mercy on her and Pani Emilia!" said he. "I would give money for a hundred Masses if I knew they would help her."

"Give for one, if the intention be sincere."

"I will, I will! As to the sincerity of intention, I could not be more sincere if the question involved my own life."

Vaskovski smiled and said, "Thou art on the good road, for thou knowest how to love."

And all felt relieved in some way. Bukatski, if he was thinking of something opposed to what Vaskovski had said, did not dare mention it; for when people in presence of real misfortune seek salvation in faith, scepticism, even when thoroughly rooted, pulls its cap over its ears, and is not only cowardly, but seems weak and small.

Bigiel, who came in at that moment, saw more cheerful faces, and said, —

"I see by you that the little one is not worse."

"No, no," said Pan Stanislav; "and the professor told us such wholesome things that he might be applied to a wound."

"Praise be to God! My wife gave money for a Mass to-day, and went then to Pani Emilia's. I will dine with you, for I have leave; and, since Litka is better, I will tell you another glad news."

"What is it?"

"Awhile ago I met Mashko, who, by the way, will be here soon; and when he comes, congratulate him, for he is going to marry."

"Whom?" asked Pan Stanislav.

"My neighbor's daughter."

"Panna Kraslavski?"

"Yes."

"I understand," said Bukatski; "he crushed those ladies into dust with his grandeur, his birth, his property, and out of that dust he formed a wife and a mother-in-law for himself."

"Tell me one thing," said the professor; "Mashko is a religious man —"

"As a conservative," interrupted Bukatski, "for appearance' sake."

"And those ladies, too," continued Vaskovski.

"From habit —"

"Why do they never think of a future life?"

"Mashko, why dost thou never think of a future life?" cried Bukatski, turning to the advocate, who was coming in at that moment.

Mashko approached them and asked, "What dost thou say?"

"I will say Tu felix, Mashko, nube!" (Thou, Mashko, art fortunate in marriage!)

Then all began to offer congratulations, which he received with full weight of dignity; at the end he said, —

"My dear friends, I thank you from my whole heart; and, since ye all know my betrothed, I have no doubt of the sincerity of your wishes."

"Do not permit thyself one," said Bukatski.

"But Kremen came to thee in season," interjected Pan Stanislav.

Indeed, Kremen had come to Mashko in season, for without it he might not have been accepted. But for that very cause the remark was not agreeable; hence he made a wry face, and answered, —

"Thou didst make that purchase easy; sometimes I am thankful to thee, and sometimes I curse thee."

"Why so?"

"For thy dear Uncle Plavitski is the most annoying, the most unendurable figure on earth, omitting thy cousin, who is a charming young lady; but from morning till evening she rings changes on her never to be sufficiently regretted Kremen, through all the seven notes, adding at each one a tear. Thou art seldom at their house; but, believe me, to be there is uncommonly wearisome."

Pan Stanislav looked into his eyes and answered, "Listen, Mashko: against my uncle I have said everything that could hit him; but it does not follow, therefore, that I am to listen patiently if another attacks Plavitski, especially a man who has made profit by him. As to Panna Marynia, she is sorry, I know, for Kremen; but this proves that she is not an empty puppet, or a manikin, but a woman with a heart; dost understand me?"

A moment of silence followed. Mashko understood perfectly whom Pan Stanislav had in mind when he mentioned the empty doll and manikin; hence the freckles on his face became brick-colored, and his lips began to quiver. But he restrained himself. He was in no sense a coward; but even the man who is most daring has usually some one with whom he has no wish to quarrel, and for Mashko Polanyetski was such a one. Therefore, shrugging his shoulders, he said,—

"Why art thou angry? If that is unpleasing to thee —"

But Pan Stanislav interrupted, "I am not angry; but I advise thee to remember my words." And he looked him in the eyes again.

Mashko thought, "If thou wilt have an adventure anyhow, thou canst have it."

"Thy words," said he, "I can remember; only do thou take counsel also from me. Permit not thyself to speak in that tone to me, else I might forget myself also, and call thee to reckoning."

"What the deuce —" began Bukatski. "What is the matter with thee?"

But Pan Stanislav, in whom irritation against Mashko has been gathering for a long time, would beyond doubt have pushed matters to extremes had not Pani Emilia's servant rushed into the room at that moment.

"I beg," said he, with a panting voice; "the little lady is dying!"

Pan Stanislav grew pale, and, seizing his hat, sprang to the door. A long, dull silence followed, which Mashko interrupted at last.

"I forgot," said he, "that everything should be forgiven him at present."

Vaskovski, covering his eyes with his hands, began to pray. At length he raised his head and said, —

"God alone has bridled death, and has power to restrain it."

A quarter of an hour later, Bigiel received a note from his wife with the words, "The attack has passed."

## CHAPTER XVIII.

Pan Stanislav hurried to Pani Emilia's, fearing that he would not find Litka living; for the servant told him on the way that the little lady was in convulsions, and dying. But when he arrived, Pani Emilia ran to meet him, and from the depth of her breast threw out in one breath the words, "Better! better!"

"Is the doctor here?"

"He is."

"But the little one?"

"Is sleeping."

On the face of Pani Emilia the remnants of fear were struggling with hope and joy. Pan Stanislav noticed that her lips were almost white, her eyes dry and red, her face in blotches; she was mortally wearied, for she had not slept for twenty-four hours. But the doctor, a young man, and energetic, looked on the danger as passed for the time. Pani Emilia was strengthened by what he told her in presence of Pan Stanislav, especially this: "We should not let it come to a second attack, and we will not."

There was real consolation in these words, for evidently the doctor considered that they were able to ward off another attack; still there was a warning that another attack might be fatal. But Pani Emilia grasped at every hope, as a man falling over a precipice grasps at the branches of trees growing out on the edge of it.

"We will not; we will not!" repeated she, pressing the doctor's hand feverishly.

Pan Stanislav looked into his eyes unobserved, wishing to read in them whether he said this to pacify the mother, or on the basis of medical conviction, and asked as a test, —

"You will not leave her to-day?"

"I do not see the least need of staying," answered he. "The child is exhausted, and is like to sleep long and soundly. I will come to-morrow, but to-day I can go with perfect safety." Then he turned to Pani Emilia, —

"You must rest, too. All danger has passed; the patient

should not see on your face any suffering or alarm, for she might be disturbed, and she is too weak to endure that."

"I could not fall asleep," said Pani Emilia.

The doctor turned his pale blue eyes to her, and, gazing into her face with a certain intensity, said slowly, —

"In an hour you will lie down, and will fall asleep directly; you will sleep unbrokenly for six or eight hours, — let us say eight. To-morrow you will be strong and refreshed. And now good-night."

"But drops to the little one, if she wakes?" asked Pani Emilia.

"Another will give the drops; you will sleep. Good-night." And he took farewell.

Pan Stanislav wished to follow him to inquire alone about Litka, but he thought that a longer talk of that kind might alarm Pani Emilia; hence he preferred to omit it, promising himself that in the morning he would go to the doctor's house and talk there with him. After a while, when he was alone with Pani Emilia, he said, —

"Do as the doctor directed; you need rest. I promise to go to Litka's room now, and I will not leave her the whole night."

But Pani Emilia's thoughts were all with the little girl; so, instead of an answer, she said to him directly, —

"Do you know, after the attack, she asked several times for you before she fell asleep. And for Marynia too. She fell asleep with the question, 'Where is Pan Stas?'"

"My poor beloved child, I should have come anyhow right after dinner. I flew here barely alive. When did the attack begin?"

"In the forenoon. From the morning she was gloomy, as if foreboding something. You know that in my presence she says always that she is well; but she must have felt ill, for before the attack she sat near me and begged me to hold her hand. Yesterday, I forgot to tell you that she put such strange questions to me: 'Is it true,' inquired she, 'that if a sick child asks for a thing it is never refused?' I answered that it is not refused unless the child asks for something impossible. Some idea was passing through her head evidently, for in the evening, when Marynia ran in for a moment, she put like questions to us. She went to sleep in good humor, but this morning early she complained of stifling. It is lucky that I sent for the doctor before the attack, and that he came promptly."

"It is the greatest luck that he went away with such certainty that the attack would not be repeated. I am perfectly sure that that is his conviction," answered Pan Stanislav.

Pani Emilia raised her eyes: "The Lord God is so merciful, so good, that —"

In spite of all her efforts, she began to sob, for repressed alarm and despair were changed to joy in her, and she found relief in tears. In that noble and spiritualized nature, innate exaltation disturbed calm thought; by reason of this, Pani Emilia never gave an account to herself of the real state of affairs; now, for example, she had not the least doubt that Litka's illness had ended once for all with this recent attack, and that thenceforth a time of perfect health would begin for the child.

Pan Stanislav had neither the wish nor the heart to show her a middle road between delight and despair; his heart rose with great pity for her, and there came to him one of those moments in which he felt more clearly than usually how deeply, though disinterestedly, he was attached to that enthusiastic and idealistic woman. If she had been his sister, he would have embraced her and pressed her to his bosom; as it was, he kissed her delicate, thin hands, and said, —

"Praise be to God; praise be to God! Let the dear lady think now of herself, and I will go to the little one and not stir till she wakes." And he went.

In Litka's chamber there was darkness, for the window-blinds were closed, and the sun was going down. Only through the slats did some reddish rays force their way; these lighted the chamber imperfectly and vanished soon, for the sky began to grow cloudy. Litka was sleeping soundly. Pan Stanislav, sitting near her, looked on her sleeping face, and at the first moment his heart was oppressed painfully. She was lying with her face toward the ceiling; her thin little hands were placed on the coverlid; her eyes were closed, and under them was a deep shadow from the lashes. Her pallor, which seemed waxen in that reddish half-gloom, and her open mouth, finally, the deep sleep, — gave her face the seeming of such rest as the faces of the dead have. But the movement of the ruffles on her nightdress showed that she was living and breathing. Her respiration was even calm and very regular. Pan Stanislav looked for a long time at that sick face, and felt again, with full force, what he had felt often, when he thought of himself, — namely, that nature had made him to be a father; that, besides the woman of his choice, children might be the immense love of his life, the chief object and reason of his existence. He understood this, through the pity and love which he felt at that moment for Litka, who, a stranger to him by birth, was as dear to him then as would have been his own child.

"If she had been given to me," thought he; "if she lacked a mother, — I would take her forever, and consider that I had something to live for."

And he felt also that were it possible to make a bargain with death, he would have given himself without hesitation to redeem that little "kitten," over whom death seemed then to be floating like a bird of prey over a dove. Such tenderness seized him as he had not felt till that hour; and that man, of a character rather quick and harsh, was ready to kiss the hands and head of that child, with a tenderness of which not even every woman's heart is capable.

Meanwhile it had grown dark. Soon Pani Emilia came in, shading with her hand a blue night-lamp.

"She is sleeping?" asked she, in a low voice, placing the lamp on the table beyond Litka's head.

"She is," answered Pan Stanislav, in an equally low voice.

Pani Emilia looked long at the sleeping child.

"See," whispered Pan Stanislav, "how regularly and calmly she breathes. To-morrow she will be healthier and stronger."

"Yes," answered the mother, with a smile.

"Now it is your turn. Sleep, sleep! otherwise I shall begin to command without pity."

Her eyes continued to smile at him thankfully. In the mild blue light of the night-lamp she seemed like an apparition. She had a perfectly angelic face; and Pan Stanislav thought in spite of himself that she and Litka looked really like forms from beyond the earth, which by pure chance had wandered into this world.

"Yes," answered she; "I will rest now. Marynia has come, and Professor Vaskovski. Marynia wishes absolutely to remain."

"So much the better. She manages so well near the little girl. Good-night."

"Good-night."

Pan Stanislav was alone again, and began to think of Marynia. At the very intelligence that he would see her soon he could not think of aught else; and now he put the question to himself: "In what lies this wonderful secret of nature in virtue of which I, for example, did not fall in love with Pani Emilia, decidedly more beautiful than Marynia, likely better, sweeter, more capable of loving, — but with that girl whom I know incomparably less, and, justly or unjustly, honor less?" Still with every approach of his to Marynia there rose in him immediately all those impulses which a man may feel at sight of a chosen woman, while a real womanly form, like that of Pani Emilia, made no other impression on him than if she had been a painting or a carving. Why is this, and why, the more culture a man has, the more his nerves become subtile, and his sensitiveness keener, the greater difference does he make between woman and woman? Pan Stanislav had no answer to this save the one which that doctor in love with Panna Kraslavski had given him: "I estimate her coolly, but I cannot tear my soul from her." That was rather the description of a phenomenon than an answer, for which, moreover, he had not the time, since Marynia came in at that moment.

They nodded in salutation; he raised a chair then, and put it down softly at Litka's bed, letting Marynia know by a sign that she was to sit there. She began to speak first, or rather, to whisper.

"Go to tea now. Professor Vaskovski is here."

"And Pani Emilia?"

"She could not sit up. She said that it was a wonder to her, but she must sleep."

"I know why: the doctor hypnotized her, and he did well. The little girl is indeed better."

Marynia gazed into his eyes; but he repeated, —

"She is really better — if the attack will not return, and there is hope that it will not."

"Ah! praise be to God! But go now and drink tea."

He preferred, however, to whisper to her near by and confidentially, so he said, —

"I will, I will; but later. Let us arrange meanwhile so that you may rest. I have heard that your father is ill. Of course you have been watching over him."

"Father is well now, and I wish to take Emilia's place absolutely. She told me that the servants had not slept either all last night, for the child's condition was alarming before the attack. It is needful now that some one be on the watch always. I should wish, therefore, so to arrange that we — that is, I, you, and Emilka — should follow in turn."

"Very well; but to-day I will remain. If not here, I shall be at call in the next chamber. When did you hear of the attack ?"

"I did not hear of it. I came as I do usually in the evening to learn what was to be heard."

"Pani Emilia's servant hurried to me while I was dining. You can imagine easily how I flew hither. I was not sure of finding her alive. What wonder, since during dinner I talked almost all the time of Litka with Bukatski and Vaskovski, till Mashko came with the announcement of his marriage."

"Is Mashko going to marry ?"

"Yes. The news has not gone around yet; but he announced it himself. He marries Panna Kraslavski; you remember her ?"

"She who was at the Bigiels that evening. She is a good match for Mashko, Panna Kraslavski."

There was silence for a moment. Marynia, who, not loving Mashko, had rejected his hand, but who more than once had reproached herself for her conduct with regard to him, thinking that she had exposed him to deception and suffering, could find only comfort in the news that the young advocate had borne the blow so easily. Still the news astonished her for the time, and also wounded her. Women, when they sympathize with some one, wish first that some one to be really unhappy, and, secondly, they wish to alleviate the misfortune themselves; when it turns out that another is able to do that, they undergo a certain disillusion. Marynia's self-love was wounded also doubly. She had not thought that it would be so easy to forget her; hence she had to confess that her idea of Mashko as an exceptional man had no basis. He had been for her hitherto a kind of ace in the game against Pan Stanislav; now he had ceased to be that. She felt, therefore, let matters be as they might, somewhat conquered. This did not prevent her, it is true, from informing Pan Stanislav, with a certain accent of truth, that his news caused her sincere and deep joy, but at bottom she felt in some sort offended by him because he had told her.

For a certain time Pan Stanislav had acted with her very reservedly, and in nothing had he betrayed what was happening within him. He did not feign to be too cool, for they had to meet; therefore, in meeting her he maintained even a certain kindly freedom, but for this very reason she judged that he had ceased to love her, and such is human nature, that though the old offence was existing yet, and had even increased in the soul of the young woman, though her first disillusion had changed as it were into a spring, giving forth new bitterness continually, still the thought that her repugnance was indifferent to him irritated Marynia. Now it seemed to her that Pan Stanislav must even triumph over her mistake as to Mashko; and at this, that in every case she, who shortly before had the choice between Mashko and him, has that choice no longer, and will fall, as it were, into a kind of neglect somewhat humiliating.

But he was far from such thoughts. He was glad, it is true, that Marynia should know that, by exalting Mashko above him, she had been mistaken fundamentally; but he had not dreamed even of taking pleasure in this or triumphing because of her isolation, for at every moment and at that time more than any other he was ready to open his arms to her, press her to his bosom, and love her. He was working, it is true, continually and even with stubbornness to break in himself those feelings; but he did this only because he saw no hope before him, and considered it an offence against his dignity as a man to put all the powers of his soul and heart into a feeling which was not returned. To use his own expression, he wished to avoid surrender, and he did avoid surrender, to the best of his power; but he understood perfectly that such a struggle exhausts, and that even if it ends with victory it brings a void, instead of happiness. Besides, he was far yet from victory. After all his efforts he had arrived at this only, — that his feeling was mingled with bitterness. Such a ferment dissolves love, it is true, for the simple reason that it poisons it; and in time this bitterness might have dissolved love in Pan Stanislav's heart. But what an empty result! Sitting then near Marynia and looking at her face and head, shone on by the light of the lamp, he said to himself, "If only she wished!" That thought made him angry; but since he wanted to be sincere with himself, he had to confess that if only she wished he would bend to her feet with the greatest readiness. What an empty result, then, and what a position without escape! For he felt that the misunderstanding between them had increased so much that even if Marynia desired a return of those moments passed in Kremen, self-love and fear of self-contradiction would close her lips. Their relations had become so entangled that they might fall in love more easily a second time than come to an understanding.

After a short conversation there was silence between them, interrupted only by the breathing of the sick child and the slight, but mournful, sounds of the window-panes, on which fine rain was striking. Outside, the night had grown wet; it was autumnal, bringing with it oppression, gloom, pessimism, and discontent. Equally gloomy seemed that chamber, in whose dark corners death appeared to be lurking. Hour followed hour more slowly. All at once forebodings seized Pan Stanislav. He looked at Litka on a sudden, and it seemed to him madness to suppose that she could recover. Vain was watching! vain were hopes and illusions! That child must die! she must all the more surely, the dearer she was. Pani Emilia will follow her; and then there will be a desert really hopeless. What a life! See, he, Polanyetski, has those two, the only beings in the world who love him, — beings for whom he is something; therefore it is clear that he must lose them. With them there would be something in life to which he could adhere; without them there will be only nothingness and a certain kind of future, blind, deaf, unreasoning, with the face of an idiot.

The most energetic man needs some one to love him. Otherwise he feels death within, and his energy turns against life. A moment like that had come now to Pan Stanislav. "I do not know absolutely why I should not fire into my forehead," thought he, "not from despair at losing them, but because of the nothing without them. If life must be senseless, there is no reason to permit this senselessness, unless through curiosity to learn how far it can go." But this thought did not appear in him as a plan; it was rather the effort of a man writhing at the chain of misfortune, a burst of anger in a man seeking some one against whom to turn. In Pan Stanislav this anger turned suddenly on Marynia. He did not know himself why; but it seemed to him at once that all the evil which had happened, had happened through her. She had brought into their circle a dislike not there before, suffering not there before, and had thrown, as it were, some stone into their smooth water; and now the wave, which was spreading more and more widely, covered not only him, but Pani Emilia and Litka. As a man governing himself by judgment, not by nerves, he understood how vain were reproaches of this sort; still he could not put down the remembrance that before Marynia came it was better in every way, and so much better even, that he might consider that as a happy period of his life. He loved then only Litka, with that untroubled, fatherly feeling, which did not and could not bring bitterness for a moment. Who knows, besides, if in time he might not have been able to love Pani Emilia? She, it is true, had not for him other feelings than those of friendship, but perhaps only because he did not desire other feelings. High-minded women frequently refuse themselves feelings which go beyond the boundary of friendship, so as not to render difficult and involved the life of some one who might, but does not wish to become dear. Meanwhile in the depth of the soul lies a calm secret melancholy; they find sweetness and consolation in the tenderness permitted by friendship.

Pan Stanislav, by becoming acquainted with Marynia, gave her at once the best part of his feelings. Why? for what purpose? Only to give himself suffering. Now, to complete the misfortune, that Litka, the one ray of his life, had died, or might die any moment. Pan Stanislav looked again at her, and said in his soul,—

"Remain even, thou dear child; thou knowst not how needful thou art to me and to thy mother. God guard thee; what a life there will be without thee!"

Suddenly he saw that the eyes of the child were looking at him. For a while he thought himself mistaken, and did not dare to stir; but the little maiden smiled, and finally she whispered,—

"Pan Stas."

"It is I, Litus. How dost thou feel?"

"Well; but where is mamma?"

"She will come right away. We had a great struggle to make her go to bed to sleep, and we hardly persuaded her."

Litka turned her head, and, seeing Marynia, said,—

"Ah! is that Aunt Marynia?"

For some time she had called her aunt.

Marynia rose, and, taking the vial which stood on the shelf, poured drop after drop into a spoon; then she gave them to Litka, who, when she had finished drinking, pressed her lips to Marynia's forehead.

A moment of silence followed; then the child said, as if to herself, —

"There is no need of waking mamma."

"No; no one will wake her," answered Pan Stanislav. "All will be as Litus wishes."

And he began to stroke her hand, which was lying on the coverlid. She looked at him, repeating, as was her wont, —

"Pan Stas, Pan Stas!"

For a while it seemed that she would fall asleep; but evidently the child was thinking of something with great effort, for her brows rose. At last, opening widely her eyes, she looked now at Pan Stanislav, and now at Marynia. In the room nothing was heard save the sound of rain on the windows.

"What is the matter with the child?" asked Marynia.

But she, clasping her hands, whispered in a voice barely audible, "I have a great, great prayer to Aunt Marynia, but — I am afraid to say it."

Marynia bent her mild face toward the little girl.

"Speak, my love; I will do everything for thee."

Then the little girl, seizing her hand, and pressing it to her lips, whispered, —

"I want Aunt Marynia to love Pan Stas."

In the silence which followed after these words was to be heard only the somewhat increased breathing of the little girl. At last the calm voice of Marynia was heard, —

"Very well, my love."

A spasm of weeping seized Pan Stanislav suddenly by the throat; everything, not excluding Marynia, vanished from his eyes before that child, who, at such a moment, sick, powerless, and in the face of death, thought only of him.

Litka asked further, —

"And will aunt marry Pan Stas?"

In the light of the blue lamp Marynia's face seemed very pale; her lips quivered, but she answered without hesitation, —

"I will, Litus."

The little girl raised Marynia's hand to her lips a second time; her head fell on the pillow, and she lay for a while with closed lids; after some time, however, two tears flowed down her cheeks. Then followed a longer silence; the rain was beating against the window-panes. Pan

Stanislav and Marynia were sitting motionless without looking at each other; both felt, however, that their fates had been decided that night, but they were as it dazed by what had happened. In the chaos of thought and feelings neither of them knew how to note or indicate what was passing within them. In that silence, which was kept instinctively, lest perchance they might look each other in the eyes, hour followed hour. The clock struck midnight, then one; about two Pani Emilia slipped in like a shadow.

"Is she sleeping?" inquired she.

"No, mamma," answered Litka.

"Art thou well?"

"Well, mamma."

And when Pani Emilia sat near her bed, the little one embraced her neck; and, nestling her yellow head at her breast, she said, —

"I know now, mamma, that when a sick child begs for anything, people never refuse."

And she nestled up to her mother some time yet; then, drawing out each word as sleepy children do, or very tired ones, she said, —

"Pan Stas will not be sad any more; and I will tell mamma why — "

But here her head became heavy on her mother's breast, and Pani Emilia felt the cold sweat coming on the hands of the child, as well as on her temples.

"Litus!" exclaimed she, with a suppressed, frightened voice.

And the child began, —

"I feel so strange, so weak — "

Her thoughts grew dim; and after a while she continued, —

"Oh, the sea is rolling — such a big sea! — and we are all sailing on it. Mamma! mamma!"

And a new attack came, dreadful, pitiless. The little girl's body was drawn in convulsions, and her eyesight turned toward the back of her head. There was no chance of illusion this time; death was at hand, and visible in the pale light of the lamp, in the dark corner of the room, in the sound of the window-panes, stricken by the rain, and in the noise of the wind, full of terrified voices and cries.

Pan Stanislav sprang up and ran for the doctor. In a quarter of an hour both appeared before the closed doors of the room, uncertain whether the child was living yet, and they disappeared through it immediately, — first Pan Stanislav, then the doctor, who, from the moment that they had pulled him out of bed, kept repeating one phrase, "Is it fear or emotion?"

Some of the servants, with sleepy and anxious faces, were gathered at the door, listening; and in the whole house followed a silence, long continued, which weighed down like lead.

It was broken at last by Marynia, who was the first to come out of the closed chamber, her face as pale as linen and she said hurriedly, —

"Water for the lady! the little lady is living no longer."

## CHAPTER XIX.

AUTUMN, in its last days, smiles on people at times with immense sadness, but mildly, like a woman dying of decline. It was on such a mild day that Litka's funeral took place. There is pain mingled with a certain consolation in this, — that those left behind think of their dead and feel the loss of them. Pan Stanislav, occupied with the funeral, was penetrated by that calm and pensive day with still greater sadness; but, transferring Litka's feelings to himself, he thought that the child would have wished just such a day for her burial, and he found in this thought a certain solace. Till that moment he had not been able simply to measure his sorrow; such knowledge comes later, and begins only when the loved one is left in the graveyard, and a man returns by himself to his empty house. Besides, preparations for the funeral had consumed Pan Stanislav's whole time. Life has surrounded with artificial forms, and has complicated, such a simple act as death. Pan Stanislav wished to show Litka that last service, which, moreover, there was no one else to perform. All those springs of life through which man thinks, resolves, and acts, were severed in Pani Emilia by the death of her child. This time the wind seemed too keen for the fleece of the lamb. Happily, however, excessive pain either destroys itself, or benumbs the human heart. This happened with Pani Emilia. Pan Stanislav noticed that the predominant expression of her face and eyes was a measureless, rigid amazement. As in her eyes there were no tears, so in her mouth there were no words, — merely a kind of whisper, at once tragic and childish, showing that her thought did not take in the misfortune, but hovered around the minutiæ accompanying it; she seized at these, and attended to them with as much carefulness as if her child were alive yet. In the room, now turned into a chamber of mourning, Litka, reposing on a satin cushion amid flowers, could want nothing; meanwhile the heart of the mother, grown childish from pain, turned continually to this: what could be lacking to Litka? When they tried to remove her from the body, she offered no resistance; she merely lost the remnant of her consciousness, and began to groan, as if pained beyond endurance.

Pan Stanislav and her husband's brother, Pan Hvastovski, who had come just before the funeral, strove to lead her away at the moment Litka was covered with the coffin-lid; but when Pani Emilia began to call the little one by name, courage failed the two men.

The procession moved at last with numerous torches, and drew after it a train of carriages, preceded by priests, chanting gloomily, and surrounded by a crowd of the curious, who in modern cities feed their eyes with the sorrow of others, as in ancient times they fed them in the circus with the blood of people.

Pani Emilia, attended by her husband's brother, and having Marynia at her side, walked also behind the caravan with dry and expressionless face. Her eyes saw only one detail, and her mind was occupied with that alone. It had happened that a lock of Litka's flaxen, immensely abundant hair was outside the coffin. Pani Emilia did not take her eyes from it the whole way, repeating again and again, "O God, O God! they have nailed down the child's hair!"

In Pan Stanislav's sorrow, weariness, nervous disturbance, resulting from sleeplessness, became a feeling of such unendurable oppression that at moments he was seized by an invincible desire to turn back when he had gone half-way, — return home, throw himself on a sofa, not think of anything, not wish anything, not love any one, not feel anything. At the same time this revulsion of self-love astounded him, made him indignant at himself: he knew that he would not return; that he would drain that cup to the bottom, that he would go to the end, not only because it would happen so, but because sorrow for Litka, and attachment to her, would be stronger than his selfishness. He felt, too, at that moment, that all his other feelings were contracted and withered, and that for the whole world he had in his heart merely nothing, at least, at that moment. For that matter his thoughts and feelings had fallen into perfect disorder, composed of external impressions received very hastily, observations made, it was unknown why, and mixed all together mechanically with a feeling of sorrow and pain. At times he looked at the houses past which the procession was moving, and he distinguished their colors. At times some shop sign caught his eye; this he read, not knowing why he did so. Then again he thought that the priests had ceased to sing, but would begin directly; and he was waiting for that renewed continuance of sad voices, as if in a kind of dread. At times he reasoned like a man who, waking from sleep, wishes to give himself an account of reality: "Those are houses," said he to himself; "those are signs; that is the odor of pitch from the torches; and there on the bier lies Litka; and we are going to the graveyard." And all at once there rose in him a wave of sorrow for that sweet, beloved child, for that dear face which had smiled so many times at him. He recalled her from remoter and from recent days, remembered her in Reichenhall, where he carried her when returning from Thumsee; and later at Bigiel's, in the country; and in Pani Emilia's house, when she said that she wanted to be a birch-tree; and finally, when, a few hours before her death, she entreated Marynia to marry him. Pan Stanislav did not say directly to himself that Litka loved him as a grown woman loves, and that, in betrothing him to Marynia, she had performed an act of sacrifice, for the feelings of the little girl were not known, and could not be defined with precision; he felt perfectly, however, that there was something like that love in her, and that the sacrifice took place, flowed, in fact, from that deep and exceptional attachment which Litka had felt for him. Since the loss of even those who are dearest is felt most of all through the personal loss which we suffer, Pan Stanislav began to repeat to himself: "That was the one soul that loved me truly; I have no one in the whole world now." And, raising his eyes to the coffin, to that tress of blond hair which was waving in the wind, he cried out in spirit to Litka with all those tender expressions with which he had spoken to her while in life. Finally, he felt that tears were choking him, because that was a call without echo. There is something heart-rending in the indifference of the dead. When the one who reflected every word and glance has become indifferent, when the loving one is icy, the one who was near in daily life, and next the heart, is full of solemnity, and far away, it avails not to repeat to one's self: "Death, death!" In addition to all pain connected with the loss, there is a harrowing deception, as if an injustice to the heart had been wrought by that lifeless body, which remains deaf to our pain and entreaty. Pan Stanislav had, in this manner, at the bottom of his soul, a feeling that Litka, by taking herself from him, and going to the region of death, had done an injustice; and from being one who is near, she had become one remote; from being a confidant, she had become formal, far away, lofty, sacred, and also perfectly indifferent to the despair of her mother and the deep loneliness of her nearest friend. There was much selfishness in those feelings of Pan Stanislav; but were it not for that selfishness, which, first of all, has its own loss and loneliness in mind, people, especially those who believe in life beyond the grave and its happiness, would feel no grief for the dead.

The procession passed out at last from the city to clearer and more open spaces, and beyond the barrier advanced along the cemetery wall, which was fronted with a garland of beggars, and with garlands of immortelles and evergreens intended for grave mounds. The line of priests in white surplices, the funeral procession with torches, the hearse with the coffin, and the people walking behind it, halted before the gate; there they removed Litka. Pan Stanislav, Bukatski, Hvastovski, and Bigiel bore her to the grave of her father.

That silence, and the void which, after each funeral, is waiting for people at home when they return from fresh graves, seemed this time to begin even at the cemetery. The day was calm, pale, with here and there the last yellowed leaves dropping from the trees without a rustle. The funeral procession was belittled amid these wide, pale spaces, which, studded with crosses, seemed endless, — as if, in truth, that cemetery opened into infinity. The black, leafless trees with tops formed of slender branches, as it were, vanishing in the light, gray and white tombstones resembling apparitions, the withered leaves on the ground, covering long and straight alleys, — all these produced at once a genuine impression of Elysian fields of some sort, fields full of deep rest, but full also of deep, dreamy melancholy, certain "cold and sad places" of which the gloomy head of Cæsar dreamed, and to which now was to come one more "animula vagula."

The coffin stopped at last above the open grave. The piercing "Requiem æternam" was heard, and then "Anima ejus." Pan Stanislav, through the chaos of his thoughts and impressions, and through the veil of his own sorrow, saw, as in a dream, the stony face and glassy eyes of Pani

Emilia, the tears of Marynia, which irritated him at that moment, the pale face of Bukatski, on whose features the expression was evident that his philosophy of life, having no work to do at that graveyard, had left him and Litka's coffin at the gate. When each threw a handful of sand on the coffin-lid, he followed the example of others; when they lowered the coffin on straps into the depth of the grave, and closed the stone doors, something seized him anew by the throat, so that all of which he had been thinking, and had learned hitherto, was changed into one nothingness. He repeated in his soul the simple words: "Till we meet, Litus!" — words which, when he recalled them afterwards, seemed to have no relation to the torturing mental storm within him. This was the end. The funeral procession began to decrease and melt away. After a time Pan Stanislav was roused by the wind, which came from afar from between the crosses. He saw now at the grave Pani Emilia with Marynia, Pani Bigiel, Vaskovski, and Litka's uncle; he said to himself that he would go out last, and waited, repeating in his soul, "Till we meet, Litus!" He was thinking of death, and of this, — that he, too, would come to this place of monuments, and that it is an ocean into which all thoughts, feelings, and efforts are flowing. It seemed to him then as if he and all who were there at the grave, or had returned home, were on a ship sailing straight to the precipice. Of life beyond the grave he had no thought at that moment.

Meanwhile the short autumn twilight came on; the crosses grew still less distinct. The old professor and Pan Hvastovski conducted Pani Emilia to the cemetery gate without resistance on her part. Pan Stanislav repeated once more, "Till we meet, dear child!" and passed out.

Beyond the gate he thought: "It is fortunate that the mother is unconscious, for what a terrible thought to leave a child there alone. The dead forsake us, but we too forsake them."

In fact, he saw from a distance the carriage in which Pani Emilia was riding away, and it seemed to him that such an order of things in the world has in it something revolting. Still when he had sat down alone in his droshky, he felt a moment of selfish relief, flowing from the feeling that a certain torturing and oppressive act had been ended, after which would come rest. On returning to his own dwelling, it appeared empty, without a ray of gladness, without consolation or hope; but when at tea, he stretched himself on the sofa, an animal delight in repose after labor took possession of him, with a feeling of solace, and even as it were of satisfaction, that the funeral was over and Litka was buried. He remembered then the opinion of a certain thinker: "I know no criminals; I know only honest people, and they are disgusting." Pan Stanislav seemed to himself repulsive at that moment.

In the evening he remembered that it was needful to inquire about Pani Emilia, whom Marynia was to take for some weeks to her own house. While going out, he saw a photograph of Litka on the table, and kissed it. A quarter of an hour later he rang the bell at the Plavitskis'.

The servant told him that Plavitski had gone out, but that Professor Vaskovski and Father Hylak were there beside Pani Emilia. Marynia received him in the drawing-room; her hair was badly dressed, her eyes red; she was almost ugly. But her former way of meeting him had changed entirely, as if she had forgotten all offences in view of more unhappy subjects.

"Emilia is with me," whispered she, "and is in a bad state; but it seems that at least she understands what is said. Professor Vaskovski is with her. He speaks with such feeling. Do you wish to see Emilia absolutely?"

"No. I have come merely to inquire how she feels, and shall go away directly."

"I do not know — she might like to see you. Wait a moment; I will go and say that you are here. Litka loved you so; for that reason alone perhaps it would be pleasant for Emilia to see you."

"Very well."

Marynia went to the next chamber; but evidently did not begin conversation at once, for to Pan Stanislav there came from the door, not her voice, but that of Vaskovski, full of accents of deep conviction, and also, as it were, of effort, striving to break through the armor of insensibility and suffering.

"It is as if your child had gone to another room after play," said the old professor; "and as if she were to return at once. She will not return, but you will go to her. My dear lady, look at death, not from the side of this world, but from the side of God. The child lives and is happy; for, being herself in eternity, she considers this separation from you as lasting one twinkle of an eye. Litka is living," continued he, with emphasis; "she is living and happy. She sees that you are coming to her, and she stretches forth her hands to you; she knows that in a moment you will come, for from God's point of view life and pain are less than the twinkle of an eye, — and then eternity with Litka. Think, dearest lady, with Litka in peace, in joy, — without disease, without death. Worlds will pass away, and you will be together."

"It would be well were that certain," thought Pan Stanislav, bitterly. But after a while he thought, "If I felt that way, I should have some cause to go in; otherwise not."

Still in spite of this thought he went in, not waiting even for Marynia's return; for it seemed to him that if he had no cause, he had a duty, and he was not free to be cowardly in presence of the suffering of others. Selfishness is "cotton in the ears against human groans," and excuses itself in its own eyes by saying that nothing can be said to great suffering to relieve it. Pan Stanislav understood that this was the case, and was ashamed to withdraw comfortably instead of going to meet the sorrow of a mother. When he entered, he saw Pani Emilia sitting on the sofa; above the sofa was a lamp, and lower than the lamp a palm, which cast a shadow on that unhappy head, as if gigantic fingers were opened above it. Near Pani Emilia sat Vaskovski, who was holding her hands and looking into her face. Pan Stanislav took those hands from him, and, bending down, began to press them to his lips in silence.

Pani Emilia blinked a while, like a person striving to rise out of sleep; then she cried suddenly, with an unexpected outburst, —

"Remember how she —"

And she was borne away by a measureless weeping, during which her hands were clasped, her lips could not catch breath, and her bosom was bursting from sobs. At last strength failed her, and she fainted. When she recovered, Marynia led her to her own chamber. Pan Stanislav and Vaskovski went to the adjoining reception-room, where they were detained by Plavitski, who had come in just that moment.

"Such a sad person in the house," said he, — "it spoils life terribly. A little peace and freedom should be due to me; but what is to be done, what is to be done? I must descend to the second place, and I am ready."

At the end of half an hour Marynia came with the announcement that at her request Pani Emilia had gone to bed, and was a little calmer. Pan Stanislav and Vaskovski took leave, and went out.

They walked along in a dense fog, which rose from the earth after a calm day, hiding the streets and forming particolored circles around the lamps. Both were thinking of Litka, who was passing her first night among the dead, and at a distance from her mother. To Pan Stanislav this seemed simply terrible, not for Litka, but for Pani Emilia, who had to think of it. He meditated also over the words spoken by Vaskovski, and said at last, —

"I heard thy words. If they gave her solace, it is well; but if that were true, we should make a feast now, and rejoice that Litka is dead."

"But whence dost thou know that we shall not be happy after death?"

"Wilt thou tell me whence thou hast the knowledge that we shall?"

"I do not know; I believe."

There was no answer to this; therefore Pan Stanislav said, as if to himself, "Mercy, empyrean light, eternity, meeting; but what is there in fact? The corpse of a child in the grave, and a mother who is wailing from pain. Grant that death has produced thy faith at least; yet it brings doubt, because thou art grieving for the child. I am grieving still more; and this grief casts on me directly the question, 'Why did she die? Why such cruelty?' I know that this question is a foolish one, and that milliards of people have put it to themselves; but, if this knowledge is to be my solace, may thunderbolts split it! I know, too, that I shall not find an answer, and for that very reason I want to gnash my teeth and curse. I do not understand, and I rebel; that is all. That is the whole result, which thou canst not recognize as the one sought for."

Vaskovski answered also, as if speaking to himself, "Christ rose from the dead, for He was God; but He rose as man, and He passed through death. How can I, poor worm, do otherwise than magnify the Divine Will and Wisdom in death?"

To this Pan Stanislav answered, —

"It is impossible to talk with thee!"

"It is slippery," answered Vaskovski; "give me thy arm." And, taking Pan Stanislav by the arm, he leaned on him, and said, "My dear friend, thou hast an honest and a loving heart; thou didst love that little girl greatly, thou wert ready to do much for her. Do this one thing now,— whether thou believest or not,—say for her, 'Eternal rest!' If thou think that that will be no good to her, say to thyself, 'I can do no more, but I will do that.'"

"Give me peace!" answered Pan Stanislav.

"That may not be needful to her, but thy remembrance of her will be dear; she will be grateful, and will obtain the grace of God for thee."

Pan Stanislav remembered how Vaskovski, at news of Litka's last attack, said that the life of the child could not be purposeless, and that if she had to die she was predestined to do something before death; and now he wished to attack Vaskovski on this point, when the thought flashed on him that, before her death, Litka had united him with Marynia; and it occurred to him that perhaps she had lived for this very purpose. But at that moment he rebelled against the thought. Anger at Marynia seized him; he was full of stubbornness, and almost contempt.

"I do not want Marynia at such a price!" thought he, gritting his teeth; "I do not! I have suffered enough through her. I would give ten such for one Litka."

Meanwhile Vaskovski, trotting near him, said,—

"Nothing is to be seen at a step's distance, and the stones are slippery from fog. Without thee I should have fallen long ago."

Pan Stanislav recovered himself, and answered,—

"Whoso walks on the earth, professor, must look down, not up."

"Thou hast good legs, my dear friend."

"And eyes which see clearly, even in a fog like this which surrounds us. And it is needful, for we all live in a fog, and deuce knows what is beyond it. All that thou sayest makes on me such an impression as the words of a man who would break dry twigs, throw them into a torrent, and say, Flowers will come from these. Rottenness will come, nothing more. From me, too, this torrent has torn away something from which I am to think that a flower will rise? Folly! But here is thy gate. Good-night!"

And they separated. Pan Stanislav returned to his own house barely alive, he was so weary; and, when he had lain down in bed, he began to torture himself with thoughts further continued, or rather with visions. To begin with, before his eyes appeared the figure of Pani Emilia, powerless from pain; she was sitting in Marynia's parlor, under the palm-leaf, which was hanging over her head like an immense ill-omened hand, with outspread, grasping fingers, and it cast a shadow on her face. "I might philosophize over that till morning," muttered he. "Everything out of which life is constructed is a hand like that, from which a shadow falls, — nothing more. But if there were a little mercy besides, the child would not have died; but with what Vaskovski says, you could n't keep life in a sparrow."

Here he remembered, however, that Vaskovski not only spoke of death, but begged him also to say "eternal rest" for Litka. Pan Stanislav began now to struggle with himself. His lips were closed through lack of a deep faith that Litka might hear his "eternal rest," and that it might be of good to her. He felt, besides, a kind of shame to speak words which did not flow from the depth of his conviction, and felt also the same kind of shame not to say the "eternal rest." "For, finally, what do I know?" thought he. "Nothing. Around is fog and fog. Likely nothing will come to her from that; but, let happen what may, that is in truth the only thing that I can do now for my kitten, — for that dear child, — who was mindful of me on the night that she died."

And he hesitated for a time yet; at last he knelt and said, "eternal rest." It did not bring him, however, any solace, for it roused only the more sorrow for Litka, and also anger at Vaskovski, because he had pushed him into a position in which he had either to fall into contradiction with himself or be, as it were, a traitor to Litka. He felt, finally, that he had had enough of that kind of torment, and he determined to go early in the morning to his office and occupy himself with Bigiel on the first commercial affair that presented itself, if it were only to tear away his thought from the painful, vicious circle in which for some days he had been turning.

But in the morning Bigiel anticipated him, and came to his house; maybe, too, with the intent to occupy him. Pan Stanislav threw himself with a certain interest into the examination of current business; but he and Bigiel were not long occupied, for an hour later Bukatski came to say farewell to them.

"I am going to Italy to-day," said he, "and God knows when I shall return. I wish to say to you both, Be in good health. The death of that child touched me more than I thought it would."

"Art thou going far?"

"Oh, there would be much talk in the answer. With us, this is how it happens: Be a Buddhist, or whatever may please thee, the kernel of the question is this: one believes a little, trusts a little in some sort of mercy, and thus lives. Meanwhile, what happens? Reality slaps us daily in the face, and brings us into mental agony and anguish, into moral straits. With us, one is always loving somebody, or is tormented with somebody's misfortune; but I do not want this. It tortures me."

"How will the Italians help thee?"

"How will they help me? They will, for in Italy I have the sun, which here I have not; I have art, which here I have not, and I feel for it a weakness; I have chianti,[1] which does good to the catarrh of my stomach; and finally, I have people for whom I care nothing and nothing, and who may die for themselves in hundreds without causing me any bitterness.

"I shall look at pictures, buy what I need, nurse my rheumatism, my headache; and I shall be for myself a more or less elegant, a more or less well nourished, a more or less healthy animal, — which, believe me, is still the kind and condition of life most desired. Here I cannot be that beast which, from my soul, I wish to be."

"Thou art right, Bukatski. We, as thou seest, are sitting with our accounts, also somewhat for this, — to become more idiotic, and not think of aught else. When we acquire such a fortune as thou hast, I don't know how it is with Bigiel, but I will follow in thy steps."

"Then till we see each other again in time and space!" said Bukatski.

A while after his departure, Pan Stanislav said, —

"He is right. How happy I should be, for example, if I had not become attached to that child and Pani Emilia! In this respect we are incurable, and we spoil our lives voluntarily. He is right. In this country one is always loving some person or something; it is an inherited disease. Eternal romanticism, eternal sentimentalism, — and eternally pins in the heart."

"Old Plavitski bows to thee," said Bigiel. "That man loves nobody but himself."

[1] An Italian wine.

"In reality, this is perhaps true; but he lacks the courage to tell himself that that is permissible and necessary. Nay, what is more, he is convinced that it is needful to act otherwise; and through this he is in continual slavery. Here, though a man have a nature like Plavitski's, he must feign even to himself that he loves some one or something."

"But will you visit Pani Emilia to-day?" asked Bigiel.

"Of course! If I were to say, for example, 'I have the malaria,' I should not cure myself by saying so."

And, in fact, not only was he at Pani Emilia's that day, but he was there twice; for at his first visit he did not find the ladies at home. To the question where his daughter was, Plavitski answered, with due pathos and resignation, "I have no daughter now." Pan Stanislav, not wishing to tell him fables, for which he felt a sudden desire, went away, and returned only in the evening.

This time Marynia herself received him, and informed him that Pani Emilia had slept for the first time since Litka's funeral. While saying this, she left her hand a certain time in his. Pan Stanislav, in spite of all the disorder in which his thoughts were, could not avoid noticing this; and, when he looked at last with an inquiring glance into her eyes, he discovered that the young lady's cheeks flushed deeply. They sat down, and began to converse.

"We were at Povanzki," said Marynia, "and I promised Emilia to go there with her every day."

"But is it well for her to remember the child so every day, and open her wounds?"

"But are they healed?" answered Marynia, "or is it possible to say to her, 'Do not go'? I thought myself that it would not be well, but grew convinced of the contrary. At the graveyard she wept much, but was the better for it. On the way home she remembered what Professor Vaskovski had told her, and the thought is for her the only consolation, — the only."

"Let her have even such a one," answered Pan Stanislav.

"You see, I did not dare to mention Litka at first, but she speaks of her all the time. Do not fear to speak to her of the child, for it gives her evident solace."

Here the young lady continued in a lower, and, as it were, an uncertain voice, "She reproaches herself continually for having listened to the assurances of the doctor the last night, and gone to sleep; she is sorry for those last moments, which she might have passed with Litka, and that thought tortures her. To-day, when we were returning from the graveyard, she asked about the smallest details. She asked how the child looked, how long she slept, whether she took medicine, what she said, whether she spoke to us; then she implored me to remember everything, and not omit a single word."

"And you did not omit anything?"

"No."

"How did she receive it?"

"She cried very, very much."

Both grew silent, and were silent rather long; then Marynia said,—

"I will go and see what is happening to her."

After a while she returned.

"She is sleeping," said the young lady. "Praise be to God!"

Indeed, Pan Stanislav did not see Pani Emilia that evening; she had fallen into a kind of lethargic slumber. At parting, Marynia pressed his hand again long and vigorously, and inquired almost with submission,—

"You do not take it ill of me that I repeated to Pani Emilia Litka's last wish?"

"At such moments," answered Pan Stanislav, "I cannot think of myself: for me it is a question only of Pani Emilia; and if your words caused her solace, I thank you for them."

"Till to-morrow, then?"

"Till to-morrow."

Pan Stanislav took farewell, and went out. While descending the steps, he thought,—

"She considers herself my betrothed."

And he was not mistaken; Marynia looked on him as her betrothed. She had never been indifferent to him; on the contrary, the greatness of his offence had been for her the measure of that uncommon interest which he had roused in her. And though, during Litka's illness and funeral, he could discover in himself unfathomable stores of selfishness, he seemed to her so good that she was simply unable to compare him with any one. Litka's words did the rest. In real truth, her heart desired love first of all; and now, since before Litka's death she had made her a promise, since she had bound herself to love and to marry, it seemed to her that even if she had not loved, it was her duty to command herself, and that she was not free at present not to love. Pan Stanislav had entered the sphere of her duty; she belonged to those straightforward, womanly natures, not at all rare even now, for whom life and duty mean one and the same thing, and who for this reason bring good-will to the fulfilment of duty, and not only good, but persistent will.

Such a will brings with it love, which lights like the sun, warms like its heat, and cherishes like the blue, mild sky. In this way life does not become a dry, thorny path, which pricks, but a flowery one, which blooms and delights. This country maiden, straightforward in thought, and at once simple and delicate in feelings, possessed that capacity for life and happiness in the highest degree. So, when Pan Stanislav had gone, she, in thinking about him, did not name him in her mind otherwise than "Pan Stas," for he had indeed become her "Pan Stas."

Pan Stanislav, on his part, when lying down to sleep, repeated to himself somewhat mechanically, "She considers herself my betrothed."

Litka's death, and the events of the last days, had pushed Marynia, not only in his thoughts, but in his heart, to more remote, and even very remote places. Now he began to think of her again, and at the same time of his future. All at once he beheld, as it were, a cloud of countless questions, to which, at that moment, at least, he had no answer. But he felt fear in presence of them; he felt that he lacked strength and willingness to undertake this labor. Again he began to live with the former life; again to fall into that sentimental, vicious circle; again to disquiet himself; again to make efforts, and struggle over things which bring only bitterness, — to struggle with himself over questions of feeling. Would it not be better to labor with Bigiel on accounts, — make money, — so as to go sometime, like Bukatski, to Italy, or some other place where there is sun, art, wine good for the stomach, and, above all, people to whom one is indifferent, whose happiness will not enliven the heart of a stranger, but in return whose death or misfortune will not press a single tear from him.

## CHAPTER XX.

During all the mental struggles through which Pan Stanislav had passed, the interests of his commercial house were developed favorably. Thanks to Bigiel's sound judgment, diligence, and care, current business was transacted with a uniform thoroughness which removed every chance of dissatisfaction or complaint from the patrons of the house. The house gained reputation every day, extended its activity slowly and regularly, and was growing rich. Pan Stanislav, on his part, labored, not indeed with such mental peace as hitherto, but no less than Bigiel. He passed the morning hours daily in the office; and the greater his mental vexation, the deeper his misunderstanding with Marynia since her coming to Warsaw, the more earnest was his labor. This labor, often difficult, and at times requiring even much intense thought, but unconnected with the question which pained him, and incapable of giving any internal solace, became, at last, a kind of haven, in which he hid from the storm. Pan Stanislav began to love it. "Here, at least, I know what I am doing, and whither I am tending; here everything is very clear. If I do not find happiness, I shall find at least that enlargement of life, that freedom, which money gives; and all the better for me if I succeed in stopping at that." Recent events had merely confirmed him in those thoughts; in fact, nothing but suffering had come to him from his feelings. That sowing had yielded a bitter harvest, while the only successes which he had known, and which in every case strengthen and defend one against misfortune, were given by that mercantile house. Pan Stanislav thought with a certain surprise that this was true; but it was not. He himself felt the narrowness of that satisfaction which the house could give; but he said to himself at the same time, "Since it cannot be otherwise, this must be accepted; and it is safer to stop here, for it is better to be only a merchant, who succeeds, than a dreamer, who fails in everything." Since Litka's death, then, he resolved all the more to stifle in himself those impulses to which reality did not answer, and which had brought him nothing but regrets. Evidently Bigiel was pleased with a state of mind in his partner which could bring only profit to the house.

Still Pan Stanislav could not grow wholly indifferent in a few weeks to all that with which, on a time, his heart had been connected. Hence he went sometimes to visit Litka, whose gravestone was covered in the morning with white winter frost. Twice he met Pani Emilia and Marynia in the cemetery. Once he attended them home to the city, and Pani Emilia thanked him for remembering the little girl. Pan Stanislav noticed that she did this with evident calmness; he understood the cause of this calmness when, at parting, she said to him, —

"I keep always in mind now that for her separation from me is as short as one twinkle of an eye; and you know not what comfort it is to me that at least she is not yearning."

"Well, what I know not, I know not," said Pan Stanislav, in his soul. Still the deep conviction of Pani Emilia's speech struck him. "If these are illusions," thought he, "they are really life-giving, since they are able to draw forth juices for life from the dungeon of the grave."

Marynia asserted, besides, in her first conversation with Pan Stanislav, that Pani Emilia lived only through that thought, which alone softened her grief. For whole days she mentioned nothing else, and said, with such persistence, that from God's point of view death is separation for one twinkle of an eye, that she began to alarm Marynia.

"She talks, too, of Litka," said Marynia, in conclusion, "as if the child had not died, and as if she should see her to-morrow."

"That is happy," answered Pan Stanislav. "Vaskovski rendered tangible service; such a nail in the head gives no pain."

"Still, she is right, for it is so."

"I will not contradict you."

Marynia was alarmed, it is true, by the persistence with which Pani Emilia returned to one thought; but on the other hand she herself did not look on death otherwise. Hence that tinge of scepticism, evident in Pan Stanislav's words, touched her a little, and pained her; but, not wishing to let this be evident, she changed the conversation.

"I gave directions to enlarge Litka's photograph," said she. "Yesterday they brought me three copies; one I will give Emilia. I feared at first that it would excite her too much, but now I see that I may give it; nay, more, it will be very dear to her."

She rose then, and went to a bookcase on which were some photographs in a wrapper; these she took, and, sitting at Pan Stanislav's side before a small table, opened them.

"Emilia told me of a certain talk which you had with Litka a short time before her death, when the child wished you three to be birches growing near one another. Do you remember that talk?"

"I do. Litka wondered that trees live so long; she thought awhile what kind of tree she would like to be, and the birch pleased her most."

"True; and you said that you would like to grow near by, therefore, around these photographs I wish to paint birches on a passe-partout. Here I have begun, you see, but I have no great success. I cannot paint from memory."

Then she took one of the photographs, and showed Pan Stanislav the birches painted in water-colors; but since she was a little near-sighted, she bent over her work, so that her temple for one moment was near Pan Stanislav's face. She was no longer that Marynia of whom he had dreamed when returning evenings from Pani Emilia's, and who at that time had filled his whole soul for him. That period had passed: his thoughts had gone in another direction; but Marynia had not ceased to be that type of woman which produced on his masculine nerves an impression exceptionally vivid; and now, when her temple almost touched his own, when, with one glance of the eye, he took in her face, her cheeks slightly colored, and her form bent over the picture, he felt the old attraction with its former intensity, and the quick blood sent equally quick thoughts to his brain. "Were I to kiss her eyes and mouth now," thought he, "I am curious to know what she would do;" and in a twinkle the desire seized him to do so, even were he to offend Marynia mortally. In return for long rejection, for so much fear and suffering, he would like such a moment of recompense, and of revenge, perhaps, with it. Meanwhile, Marynia, while examining the painting, continued, —

"This seems worse to-day than yesterday; unfortunately trees have no leaves now, and I cannot find a model."

"The group is not bad at all," said Pan Stanislav; "but

if these trees are to represent Pani Emilia, Litka, and me, why have you painted four birches?"

"The fourth represents me," said Marynia, with a certain timidity; "I, too, have a wish sometimes to grow with you."

Pan Stanislav looked at her quickly; and she, wrapping the photographs up again, said, as it were, hurriedly, —

"So many things are connected in my mind with the memory of that child. During her last days I was with her and Emilia almost continually. At present Emilia is one of the nearest persons on earth to me. I belong to them as well as you do; I know not clearly how to explain this. There were four of us, and now there are three, bound together by Litka, for she bound us. When I think of her now, I think also of Emilia and of you. This is why I decided to paint the four birches; and you see there are three photographs, — one for Emilia, one for me, and one for you."

"I thank you," said Pan Stanislav, extending his hand to her. Marynia returned the pressure very cordially, and said, —

"For the sake of her memory, too, we should forget all our former resentments."

"This has happened already," answered Pan Stanislav; "and as for me, I wish that it had happened long before Litka's death."

"My fault began then; for this I beg forgiveness," and she extended her hand to him.

Pan Stanislav hesitated awhile whether to raise it to his lips; but he did not raise it, he only said, —

"Now there is agreement."

"And friendship?" asked Marynia.

"And friendship."

In her eyes a deep, quiet joy was reflected, which enlivened her whole face with a mild radiance. There was in her at the moment so much kindness and trustfulness that she reminded Pan Stanislav of that first Marynia whom he had seen at Kremen when she was sitting on the garden veranda in the rays of the setting sun. But since Litka's death he had been in such a frame of mind that he considered remembrances like that as unworthy of him; hence he rose and began to take leave.

"Will you not remain the whole evening?" asked Marynia.

"No, I must return."

"I will tell Emilia that you are going," said she, approaching the door of the adjoining room.

"She is either thinking of Litka at present, or is praying; otherwise she would have come of herself. Better not interrupt her; I will come to-morrow in any case."

Marynia approached him, and, looking into his eyes, said with great cordiality, "To-morrow and every day. Is it not true? Remember that you are 'Pan Stas' for us now."

Since Litka's death Marynia had named him thus for the second time, so in going home he thought, "Her relations to me are changed thoroughly. She feels herself simply as belonging to me, for she bound herself to that by the promise given the dying child; she is ready even to fall in love with me, and will not permit herself not to love. With us there are such women by the dozen." And all at once he fell into anger.

"I know those fish natures with cold hearts, but sentimental heads filled with so-called principles, — everything for principle, everything for duty, nothing spontaneous in the heart. I might sigh out my last breath at her feet and gain nothing; but when *duty* commands her to love me, she will love even really."

Evidently Pan Stanislav in his wanderings abroad had grown used to another kind of women, or at least he had read of them in books. But since with all this he had a little sound judgment too, that judgment began to speak thus to him, —

"Listen, Polanyetski," it said. "These are exceptional natures because they are uncommonly reliable: on them one may build; on them a life may be founded. Art thou mad? With thee it was a question of finding a wife, not an ephemeral love affair."

But Pan Stanislav did not cease to resist, and he answered his judgment, "If I am to be loved, I want to be loved for my own sake."

Judgment tried once more to explain that it was all one how love began; since later on he could be loved only for his own sake, that in the present case, after his recent efforts and vexations, it was almost miraculous, almost providential, that something natural had intervened in a way to break resistance immediately; but Pan Stanislav did not cease from being furious. At last judgment was strengthened by that attraction and pleasure which he found in Marynia, by virtue of which he saw in her more charms than in any other woman; this attraction spoke in its turn, —

"I do not know if thou love her, and I care not; but to-day, when her arm and face approached thee, thou wert near jumping out of thy skin. Why is it that such a shiver does not pass through thee when thou art near another? Think what a difference in that."

But to everything Pan Stanislav answered: "A fish, a duty-bound fish." And again the thought came to him, "Catch her, if thou prefer that to any other kind. People marry; and for thee, it is time. What more dost thou want, is it a kind of love which thou wouldst be the first to laugh into ridicule? Thy love has died out. Suppose it has; but the attraction remains, and the conviction, too, that this woman is reliable and honest."

"True," thought he further, "but from love, whether stupid or wise, comes choice, and have I that at present? No, for I hesitate, while formerly I did not hesitate; second, I ought to decide which is better, — Panna Plavitski, or debit and credit in the house of Bigiel and Polanyetski. Money gives power and freedom; the best use is made of freedom when a man carries no one in his heart or on his shoulders." Thus meditating, he reached home, and lay down to sleep. During the night he dreamed of birches on sand hills, calm blue eyes, and a forehead shaded with dark hair, from which warmth was beating.

## CHAPTER XXI.

SOME mornings later, before Pan Stanislav had gone to his office, Mashko appeared.

"I come to thee on two affairs," said he, "but I will begin with money, so as to leave thee freedom of action; shall I, or not?"

"My dear friend, I attend to money questions in my office, so begin with the other."

"The money matter is not a question of thy house, but a private one; for this reason I prefer to speak of it privately. I am going to marry, as thou knowest; I need money. I have to make payments as numerous as the hairs on my head, and the wherewithal does not correspond. The term is near to pay the first instalment of my debt to thee for the claim on Kremen; canst thou extend the time another quarter?"

"I will be frank," replied Pan Stanislav; "I can, but I am unwilling to do so."

"Well, I will be equally sincere, and ask what thou wilt do in case I fail to pay."

"The like happens in the world," answered Pan Stanislav; "but this time thou art looking on me as simpler than I am, for I know that thou wilt pay."

"Whence is that certainty?"

"Thou art going to marry, and marry a fortune; how expose thyself to the evil fame of bankruptcy? Thou wilt squeeze money from under the earth, perhaps, but thou wilt pay."

"Even Solomon could not pour out of the empty."

"Because he did not take lessons from thee. My dear friend, no one is listening to us, so I may say that all thy life thou hast been doing nothing else."

"Then thou art sure that I will pay thee?"

"I am."

"Thou art right; I wanted of thee a favor to which I have no claim. But even I feel wearied at last of all this, — to take something here and thrust it in there; to live eternally in such a whirl passes human power in the long run. I am sailing, as it were, into the harbor. In two months I shall be on a new footing, but meanwhile I am using the last of my steam; 'tis not in thy way to oblige me; the position is difficult. There is a small forest in Kremen; I will cut that and pay, since there is no other way."

"What forests are there in Kremen? Old Plavitski shaved off everything that could be taken."

"There is a large oak grove behind the house, toward Nedzyalkov."

"True, there is."

"I know that thou and Bigiel take up such affairs. Buy that forest; it will spare me the search for a purchaser, and he and thou can come out of the business with profit."

"I will discuss it with Bigiel."

"Then thou wilt not refuse in advance?"

"No; if thou give it cheaply, I may even take the forest myself. But in such matters I need to calculate the possible profits or losses; I want also to know thy terms. Make thy own estimates. Send me thy list; how many trees there are, and what kinds."

"I will send it in an hour."

"In that case I will give thee an answer in the evening."

"I advise thee beforehand of one thing,—thou wilt not have the right to cut oak for two months."

"Why is that?"

"Because Kremen will lose greatly by losing that ornament; hence I propose that it be resold to me after the marriage, of course at a good profit to thee."

"We shall see."

"Besides, I have marl in Kremen; thou hast spoken to me of this. Plavitski reckoned it at millions,—that, of course, is nonsense; but in the hands of clever men it might be made a paying business. Think that over, too, with Bigiel; I would take thee into partnership."

"Should the business seem good, we may take it; our house exists to gain profit."

"Then we will talk of the marl later on; but now I return to the oak. Let the general outline of our bargain be this,—that I, instead of the first payment, give thee the oak grove, or a part of it, according to estimate. I give it in some sense in pledge, and thou art obliged not to cut trees before the close of the following quarter."

"I can do that; evidently there will be questions later on as to removal of the oak, which we shall mention when writing the contract, if, in general, we write one."

"Then there is at least one burden off my head," said Mashko, rubbing his forehead with his hand. "Imagine that I have ten or fifteen such every day, not counting conversations on business with Pani Kraslavski, which are more wearying than all else, and then waiting on my betrothed, who" — here Mashko interrupted himself for a moment, but suddenly waved his hand, and added — "which also is not easy."

Pan Stanislav looked at him with amazement. On the lips of Mashko, who, in every word, followed society observances so closely, this was something unheard of. Mashko, however, spoke on, —

"But let that pass; thou knowest how near we were to quarrelling before Litka's death. I had not in mind thy great love for that little maiden; I forgot that thou wert disturbed and annoyed. I acted rudely; the fault was on my side entirely, and I beg thy pardon."

"That is a forgotten affair," said Pan Stanislav.

"I revive it because I have a service to beg of thee. The affair is of this kind: I have not friends, blood relatives; I have n't them, or if I have, it is not worth while to exhibit them. Now, I must find groomsmen, and, in truth, I do not know well where to look for them. I have managed the business of various young lords, as thou knowest; but to ask the first young fellow whom I meet, because he has a title, does not beseem me, and I am unwilling to do so. With me it is a question of having groomsmen who are people of position, and, I tell thee openly, with prominent names. Those ladies, too, attach great importance to this matter. Wilt thou be a groomsman for me?"

"In other circumstances I would not refuse; but I will tell thee how it is. Look at me: I have no crape on my hat nor white tape on my coat, therefore I am not in mourning; but I give thee my word that I am in deeper mourning than if my own child were dead."

"That is true; I had not thought of that," said Mashko. "I beg thy pardon."

These words impressed Pan Stanislav.

"But if this is very important; if, in truth, thou art unable to find another, — let it be according to thy wish; but I say sincerely that for me, after such a funeral, it will be difficult to assist at a wedding."

Pan Stanislav did not say, it is true, at such a wedding,

but Mashko divined his thought. "There is another circumstance, too," continued he. "Thou must have heard of a certain poor little doctor, who fell in love to the death with thy betrothed. She was free not to return his love, no man will reproach her for that; but he, poor fellow, went his way somewhere to the land where pepper grows, and the deuce took him. Dost understand? I was in friendship with that doctor; he confided his misfortune to me, and wept out his secret. Dost understand? In these conditions to be groomsman for another — say thyself."

"And did that man really die of love for my betrothed?"

"But hast thou not heard of it?"

"Not only have I not heard, but I cannot believe my own ears."

"Knowest thou what, Mashko, marriage changes a man; but I see that betrothal does also, — I do not recognize thee simply."

"Because, as I have said, I am so weary that breath fails me, and at such times the mask falls."

"What dost thou mean by that?"

"I mean that there are two kinds of people, — one, of people who never limit themselves by anything, and arrange their modes of action according to every circumstance; the other, of people having a certain system which they hold to with more or less sequence. I belong to the second. I am accustomed to observe appearances, and, what is more, accustomed so long that at last it has become a second nature to me. But, for example, when travelling in time of great heat, a moment may come on the man who is most *comme il faut*, when he will unbutton not only his coat, but his shirt; such a moment has come on me, therefore I unbutton."

"This means? —"

"It means that I am transfixed with astonishment that any man could fall in love to the death with my betrothed, who is, as thou on a time didst give me to understand, cold, formal, and as mechanical in words, thoughts, and movements as if wound up with a key; that is perfectly true, and I confirm it. I do not wish thee to hold me for a greater wretch than I am; I do not love her, and my wife will be as formal as my betrothed. I loved Panna Plavitski, who rejected me. Panna Kraslavski I take for her property. Call this iniquity, if it suit thee to do so; I will answer that such iniquity has been committed, or will be committed, by thousands among those so-called honorable people, to whom thou art ready to give thy hand. Moreover, life does not flow on in delight for people thus married, but also not in tragedy; they limp, but go forward. Later on they are aided by years spent together, which bring a species of attachment, by children who are born to them; and they get on in some fashion. Such are most marriages, for the majority choose to walk on the earth, rather than scale summits. Sometimes there are even worse marriages: when a woman wishes to fly, and a man to creep, or *vice versa*, there is no chance for an understanding. As to me, I have worked like an ox. Coming from a reduced family, I wished to gain distinction, I confess. If I had consented to remain an obscure attorney, and acquire merely money, perhaps I should have unlocked and thrown open to my son the door to light; but I have no love for my children before they come into the world, hence I wished not only to have money myself, but to be somebody, to mean something, to occupy a position, to have such weight as with us it is possible to have, at least in society. From this it has happened that what the advocate gained, the great lord expended; position obliges. This is why I have not money. Struggling of this sort has wearied me. Opening holes in one place to fill them in another, — for this reason I marry Panna Kraslavski; who again marries me for the reason that, if I am not really a great lord, amusing himself in the legal career, I am so apparently. The match is even; there is no injustice to any one, and neither has tricked the other, or, if it please thee, we have tricked each other equally. Here is the whole truth for thee; now despise me if thou wish."

"As God lives, I have never respected thee more," answered Pan Stanislav; "for now I admire not thy sincerity merely, but also thy courage."

"I accept the compliment because thou art candid; but in what dost thou see courage?"

"In this, — that having so few illusions as to Panna Kraslavski, thou art going to marry her."

"I marry her because I am more wise than foolish. I looked for money, it is true; but thinkest thou that for money I would marry the first woman I met who possessed it? By no means, my dear friend. I take Panna Kraslavski, and I know what I am doing. She has her great qualities, indispensable under the circumstances in which

I take her, and in which she marries me. She will be a cold, unagreeable wife, sour, and even contemptuous, in so far as she does not fear me; but, on the other hand, Panna Kraslavski, as well as her mother, has a religious respect for appearances, — for what is fitting, or, speaking generally, for what is polite. This is one point. Further, there is not even one germ in her from which love intrigues could grow; and life with her, be it disagreeable as it may, will never end in scandal. This is the second. Third, she is pedantic in everything, as well in religion as in fulfilment of all the duties which she may take on herself. This is, indeed, a great quality. I shall not be happy with her, but I can be at peace; and who knows if this is not the maximum possible to ask of life, and I tell thee, my dear friend, that when a man takes a wife he should think before all of future peace. In a mistress seek what pleases thee, — wit, temperament, a poetical form of sensitiveness. But with a wife one must live years; seek in her that on which one can rely, — seek principles."

"I have never thought thee a fool," said Pan Stanislav; "but I see that thou hast more wit than I suspected."

"Our women — take those, for example, of the money world — are formed really on the French novel; and what comes of that is known to thee."

"More or less; but to-day thou art so eloquent that I listen to thy description with pleasure."

"Well, a woman becomes her own God and her own measure of right."

"And for her husband?"

"A chameleon and a tragedy."

"This happens a little in the world of much money and no traditions; there everything is appearance and toilet, beneath which sits not a soul, but a more or less exquisite wild beast. And this wealthy and elegant world, amusing itself, and permeated with artistic, literary, and even religious dilettantism, wields the baton and directs the orchestra."

"Not yet with us."

"Not yet altogether. For that matter, there are exceptions, even in the society mentioned; all the more must there be outside it. Yes, there are women of another kind among us, — for instance, Panna Plavitski. Oh, what security, and withal what a charm of life, with a woman like her! Unhappily, she is not for me."

"Mashko, I was ready to recognize in thee cleverness, but I did not know thee to have enthusiasm."

"What's to be done? I was in love with her, but now I am going to marry Panna Kraslavski."

Mashko pronounced the last words, as if in anger, then followed a moment of silence.

"Then thou wilt not be my groomsman?"

"Give me time to consider."

"In three days I am going away."

"To what place?"

"To St. Petersburg. I have business there; I will stay about two weeks."

"I will give my answer on thy return."

"Very well; to-day I will send thee the estimate of my oak in three sizes. To save the instalment!"

"And the conditions on which I will buy it."

Here Mashko took leave and went out. Pan Stanislav hastened to his office. After a conversation with Bigiel, he decided, if the affair should seem practicable and profitable, to buy the oak alone. He could not account to himself why he felt a certain wonderful desire to be connected with Kremen. After business hours he thought also of what Mashko had said of Panna Plavitski. He felt that the man had told the truth, and that, with a woman of this kind, life might be not only safe and peaceful, but full of charm; he noticed, however, that in those meditations he rendered justice rather to the type of which Marynia was a specimen, than to Marynia in person. He observed also in himself a thousand inconsistencies; he saw that he felt a certain repugnance, and even anger, at the thought of loving any one or anything, or letting his heart go into bonds and knots, usually fastened so firmly that they were painful. At the very thought of this he was enraged, and repeated in spirit, "I will not; I have had enough of this! It is an unwholesome exuberance, which leads people only to errors and suffering." At the same time he took it ill, — for example, that she did not love him with a certain exuberant and absolute love, and opened her heart to him only when duty commanded. Afterward, when he did not want love, he was astonished that it began to pall on him so easily, and that he desired Marynia far more when she was opposed, than now, when she was altogether inclined to him.

"All leads to this at last," thought he: "that man himself does not know what he wants, or what he must hold to; that is his position. May a thunderbolt split it! Panna Plavitski has more good qualities than she herself suspects. She is dutiful, just, calm, attractive; my thoughts draw me toward her; and still I feel that Panna Plavitski is not for me what she once was, and that the devils have taken something that was in me. But what is it? As to the capacity for loving," continued Pan Stanislav, in his monologue, "I have come to the conclusion that loving is most frequently folly, and loving too much folly at all times; hence I should now be content, but I am not."

After a while it came to his mind that this was merely a species of weakness, — such, for example, as follows an operation in surgery, or an illness that a man has passed through, — and that positive life will fill out in time that void which he feels. For him positive life was his mercantile house. When he went to dine, he found Vaskovski and two servants, who winked at each other when they saw how the old man at times held motionless an uplifted fork with a morsel of meat on it, and fell to thinking of death, or talking to himself. Professor Vaskovski had for some time been holding these monologues, and spoke to himself on the street so distinctly that people looked around at him. His blue eyes were turned on Pan Stanislav for a while vacantly; then he roused himself, as if from sleep, and finished the thought which had risen in his head. "She says that this will bring her near the child."

"Who says?" inquired Pan Stanislav.

"Pani Emilia."

"How will she be nearer?"

"She wants to become a Sister of Charity."

Pan Stanislav grew silent under the impression of that news. He was able to meditate over that which passed through his head, to expel feeling, to philosophize on the unwholesome excesses of the society in which he lived; but in his soul he had two sacred images, — Litka and Pani Emilia. Litka had become simply a cherished memory, but he loved Pani Emilia with a living, brotherly, and most tender affection, which he never touched in his meditations. So for a time he could not find speech; then he looked sternly at Vaskovski, and said, —

"Professor, thou art persuading her to this. I do not

enter into thy mysticism and ideas from beneath a dark star, but know this, — that thou wilt take her life on thy conscience; for she has not the strength to be a Sister of Charity, and will die in a year."

"My dear friend," answered Vaskovski, "thou hast condemned me unjustly without a hearing. Hast thou stopped to consider what the expression 'just man' means?"

"When it is a question of one dear to me, I jeer at expressions."

"She told me yesterday of this, most unexpectedly, and I asked, 'But, my child, will you have the strength? That is arduous labor.' She smiled at me, and said: 'Do not refuse me, for this is my refuge, my happiness. Should it seem that I have not strength enough, they will not receive me; but if they receive me, and my strength fails afterward, I shall go sooner to Litka, and I am yearning so much for her.' What had I to answer to such a choice, and such simplicity? What art thou able to say, even thou, who art without belief? Wouldst thou have courage to say: 'Perhaps Litka is not in existence; a life in labor, in charity, in sacrifice, and death in Christ, may not lead to Litka at all'? Invent another consolation; but what wilt thou invent? Give her another hope, heal her with something else; but with what wilt thou heal her? Besides, thou wilt see her thyself; speak to her sincerely. Wilt thou have courage to dissuade her?"

"No," answered Pan Stanislav, briefly; and after a while he added, "Only suffering on all sides."

"One thing might be possible," continued Vaskovski. "To choose instead of Sisters of Charity, whose work is beyond her strength, some contemplative order; there are those in whom the poor human atom is so dissolved in God that it ceases to lead an individual existence, and ceases to suffer."

Pan Stanislav waved his hand. "I do not understand these things," said he, dryly, "and I do not look into them."

"I have here somewhere a little Italian book on the Ladies of Nazareth," said Vaskovski, opening his coat. "Where did I put it? When going out, I stuck it somewhere."

"What can the Ladies of Nazareth be to me?"

But Vaskovski, after unbuttoning his coat, unbuttoned his shirt in searching; then he thought a while and said, "What am I looking for? I know that little Italian book. In a couple of days I am going to Rome for a long, very long time. Remember what I said, that Rome is the antechamber to another world. It is time for me to go to God's antechamber. I would persuade Emilia greatly to go to Rome, but she will not leave her child; she will remain here as a Sister of Charity. Maybe, however, the order of Nazareth would please her; it is as simple and mild as was primitive Christianity. Not with the head, my dear, for there they know better what to do, but with the heart, childlike but loving."

"Button thy shirt, professor," said Pan Stanislav.

"Very good; I will button it. I have something at my heart, and I would tell it thee; thou art as mobile as water, but thou hast a soul. Seest thou, Christianity not only is not coming to an end, as some philosophizing, giddy heads imagine, but it has only made half its way."

"Dear professor," said Pan Stanislav, mildly, "I will listen to what thou hast to tell me willingly and patiently, but not to-day; for to-day I am thinking only of Pani Emilia, and there is simply a squeezing at my throat. This is a catastrophe."

"Not for her, since her life will be a success, and her death also."

Pan Stanislav began to mutter, "As God lives, not only every mightier feeling, but simple friendship, ends in regret; never has any attachment brought me a thing except suffering. Bukatski is right: from general attachments there is nothing but suffering, from personal attachments nothing but suffering; and now live, man, in the world so surrounded."

The conversation broke off, or rather was turned into the monologue of Professor Vaskovski, who began a discourse with himself about Rome and Christianity. After dinner they went out on the street, which was full of the sound of sleighbells and the gladsome winter movement. Though in the morning of that day snow had fallen in sufficient abundance, toward evening the weather had become fair, calm, and frosty.

"But, professor, button thy shirt."

"Very well; I will button it," answered Vaskovski; and he began to draw the holes of his vest to the buttons of his frockcoat.

"Still I like that Vaskovski," said Pan Stanislav, to himself, when on the way home. "If I were to grow attached to him for good, the deuce would take him surely, for such is my fate. Fortunately I am insensible enough to him so far." And thus he persuaded himself untruly, for he had a sincere friendship for Vaskovski, and the man's fate was not indifferent in the least to him. When he reached home, Litka's face smiled at him from a large photograph as he entered; this had been sent by Marynia during his absence, and moved Pan Stanislav to the depth of his soul. He experienced, moreover, this species of emotion whenever he remembered Litka on a sudden, or saw unexpectedly one of her portraits. He thought then, that love for the child, hidden away somewhere in the depth of his heart, rose suddenly with its previous vividness and power, penetrating his whole being with indescribable tenderness and sorrow. This revival of sorrow was even so painful that he avoided it as a man avoids a real suffering usually. This time, however, there was something sweet in his emotion. Litka was smiling at him by the light of the lamp, as if she wished to say "Pan Stas;" around her head on the white margin of the picture were four green birches. Pan Stanislav stopped and looked for a long time; at last he thought, "I know in what may be the happiness of life, in children!" But he said to himself a few moments later, "I never shall love my own as I loved that poor child." The servant entered now and gave him a letter from Marynia, which came with the photograph. She wrote as follows: —

"My father asks me to pray you to spend the evening with us. Emilia has moved to her own house, and receives no visits to-day. I send you Litka's photograph, and beg you to come without fail. I wish to speak with you of Emilia. Papa has invited Pan Bigiel, who has promised to come; therefore you and I can talk quietly."

Pan Stanislav, after reading the letter, dressed, read a certain time, then went to the Plavitskis'. Bigiel had been there a quarter of an hour, and was playing piquet with Plavitski; Marynia was sitting at some distance, by a small table, occupied in work of some kind. After he had greeted all, Pan Stanislav sat near her, —

"I thank you most earnestly for the photograph," began he. "I saw it unexpectedly, and Litka stood before my eyes in such form that I could not control myself. Moments like that are the measure of sorrow, of which a man cannot even give account to himself. I thank you most earnestly, and for the four birches too. Touching Pani Emilia, I know everything from Vaskovski. Is this merely a project, or a fixed resolve?"

"Rather a fixed resolve," answered Marynia; "and what do you think?"

Marynia raised her eyes to him as if waiting for some counsel.

"She has not strength for it," said she, finally.

Pan Stanislav was silent a while; then he opened his arms helplessly, and said, —

"I have talked about this with Vaskovski. I attacked him, since I thought that the idea was his; but he swore to me that he had nothing to do with it. He asked then what other consolation I could think out for her, and I could give him no answer. What in life has remained to her really?"

"What?" returned Marynia, in a low voice.

"Do I not understand, think you, whence that resolve came? She does not wish to violate her religious principles in any way, but she wants to die as soon as possible; she knows that those duties are beyond her strength, and therefore she assumes them."

"True," answered Marynia; and she inclined her face so closely to her work that Pan Stanislav saw only the parting of the dark hair on her small head. Before her stood a box full of pearls, which she was sewing on to various articles to be used in a lottery for benevolent purposes; and tears, which were flowing from her eyes, began to drop on those pearls.

"I see that you are weeping," said Pan Stanislav.

She raised tearful eyes to him, as if to say, "Before thee I shall not hide tears," and answered, "I know that Emilia is doing well, but such a pity — "

Pan Stanislav, partly from emotion, and partly because he knew not himself what to answer, kissed her hand for the first time.

Pearls began then to drop more thickly from Marynia's eyes, so that she had to rise and go out. Pan Stanislav approached the players, as Plavitski was saying in a sour, outspoken tone, to his partner, —

"Rubicon after Rubicon. Ha! it is difficult. You represent new times, and I old traditions. I must be beaten."

"What has that to do with piquet?" asked Bigiel, calmly.

Marynia returned soon, with the announcement that tea was ready; her eyes were somewhat red, but her face was clear and calm. When, a little later, Bigiel and Plavitski sat down at cards again, she conversed with Pan Stanislav in that quiet, confiding tone which people use who are very near to each other, and who have many mutual relations. It is true that those mutual relations between them had been created by the death of Litka and the misfortune of Pani Emilia, — hence the conversation could not be gladsome; but in spite of that, Marynia's eyes, if not her lips, smiled at Pan Stanislav, and were at once thoughtful and clear.

Later in the evening, after his departure, Marynia did not name him in her mind, when she thought of him, otherwise, than "Pan Stas."

Pan Stanislav, on his part, returned home feeling calmer by far than he had since Litka's death. While pacing his chamber, he made frequent halts before the little girl's photograph, and looked, too, at the four birches painted by Marynia. He thought that the bond fastened between him and Marynia by Litka was becoming closer each day, as if without any one's will, and simply by some mysterious force of things. He thought, too, that if he lacked the former original desire to make that bond permanent, his courage would almost fail to cut it decisively, especially so soon after Litka's death. Late in the night he sat down to the lists sent by Mashko. At times, however, he made mistakes in the reckoning, for he saw before him Marynia's head inclining forward, and her tears falling on the box of pearls.

Next morning he bought the oak in Kremen, very profitably, for that matter.

## CHAPTER XXII.

MASHKO returned in two weeks from St. Petersburg, well pleased with his arrangements for credit, and bringing important news, which had come to him, as he stated, in a way purely confidential, — news not known yet to any man. The preceding harvest had been very poor throughout the whole empire; here and there hunger had begun to appear. It was easy to divine, therefore, that, before spring, supplies would be gone in whole neighborhoods, and that the catastrophe of hunger might become universal. In view of this, people of the inner circle began to whisper about the chance of stopping the grain export; and this kind of echo Mashko brought back, with the assurance that it came to his ears through people extremely well versed in affairs. This news struck Pan Stanislav so vividly that he shut himself in for some days, pencil in hand; then he hurried to Bigiel with the proposition that the ready money at command of the house, as well as its credit, should be turned to prompt purchases of grain. Bigiel was afraid, but he began by being afraid of every new enterprise. Pan Stanislav did not conceal from him that this would be a large operation, on the success or failure of which their fate might depend. Complete failure, however, was little likely, and success might make them really rich at one sweep. It was to be foreseen that, in view of the lack of grain, prices would rise in every event. It was also to be foreseen that the law would limit the possibility of making new contracts with foreign merchants, but would respect contracts made before its promulgation; but even if it failed in this regard, the rise of prices in the country itself was a thing almost certain. Pan Stanislav had foreseen and calculated everything, in so far as man could; and Bigiel, who, in spite of his caution, was a person of judgment, was forced to confess that the chances of success were really considerable, and that it would be a pity to miss the opportunity.

In fact, after a number of new consultations, during which Bigiel's opposition grew weaker and weaker, they decided on that which Pan Stanislav wished: and after a certain time their chief agent, Abdulski, went out with power to make contracts in the name of the house, as well for grain on hand as for grain not threshed yet.

After Abdulski's departure, Bigiel went to Prussia. Pan Stanislav remained alone at the head of the house, toiled from morning till evening, and made scarcely a visit. But time did not drag, for he was roused by hope of great profit and a future of fuller activity.

Pan Stanislav, in throwing himself into that speculation, and drawing in Bigiel, did so, first of all, because he thought it good; but he had another thought, too, — the mercantile house with all its affairs was too narrow a field for his special training, abilities, and energies, and Pan Stanislav felt this. Finally, what was the question in affairs handled by the house? To buy cheap, sell dear, and put the profit in a safe; that was its one object. Purchases direct, or through another, — nothing more. Pan Stanislav felt confined in those limits. "I should like to dig up something, or make something," said he to Bigiel, in moments of dissatisfaction and distaste; "at the root of the matter we are simply trying to direct to our own pockets some current from that stream of money which is flowing in the business of men, but we produce nothing."

And that was true. Pan Stanislav wished to advance to property, to acquire capital, and then undertake some very large work, giving a wider field for labor and creativeness.

The opportunity had come, as it seemed to him; hence he grasped with both hands at it. "I will think of other things afterward," thought he.

By "other things," he meant his affairs of mind and heart, — that is, his relations to religion, people, country, woman. He understood that to be at rest in life one must explain these relations, and stand on firm feet. There are men who all their lives do not know their position with reference to these principles, and whom every wind turns toward a new point. Pan Stanislav felt that a man should not live thus. In his state of mind, as it then was, he saw that these questions might be decided in a manner direct to dryness, as well as positive to materialism, and in general negatively; but he understood that they must be decided.

"I wish to know clearly whether I am bound to something or not," thought he.

Meanwhile he labored, and saw people little; he could

not withdraw from them altogether. He convinced himself, also, that questions most intimately personal cannot be decided otherwise than internally, otherwise than by one's own brain or heart, within the four walls of the body; but that most frequently certain external influences, certain people, near or distant, hasten the end of meditation, and the decisions flowing from it. This happened at his farewell with Pani Emilia, who was now shortening daily, and almost feverishly, the time before her entrance on her novitiate with the Sisters of Charity.

Amid all his occupations, Pan Stanislav did not cease to visit her; but a number of times he failed to find her at home. Once he met Pani Bigiel at her house, and also Pani and Panna Kraslavski, whose presence constrained him in a high degree. Afterward, when Marynia informed him that Pani Emilia would begin her novitiate in a few days, he went to take farewell of her.

He found her calm and almost joyous, but his heart was pained when he looked at her. Her face was transparent in places, as if formed of pearl; the blue veins appeared through the skin on her temples.

She was very beautiful, in a style almost unearthly, but Pan Stanislav thought: "I will take the last leave of her, for she will not hold out even a month; from one more attachment, one more grief and unhappiness."

She spoke to him of her decision as of a thing the most usual, to be understood of itself, — the natural outcome of what had happened, the natural refuge from a life deprived of every basis. Pan Stanislav understood that for him to dissuade her would be purely conscienceless, and an act devoid of sense.

"Will you remain in Warsaw?" asked he.

"I will, for I wish to be near Litka; and the mother superior promised that I should be in the house first, and afterward, when I learn something, in one of the hospitals. Unless unusual events come to pass, while I am in the house I shall be free to visit Litka every Sunday."

Pan Stanislav set his teeth, and was silent; he looked only at the delicate hands of Pani Emilia, thinking in his soul, —

"She wishes to nurse the sick with those hands."

But at the same time he divined that she wanted, beyond all, something else. He felt that under her calmness and resignation there was immense pain, strong as death, and calling for death with all the powers of her heart and soul; but she wished death to come without her fault, not through her sin, but her service, — her reward for that service was to be her union with Litka.

And now, for the first time, Pan Stanislav understood the difference between pain and pain, between sorrow and sorrow. He, too, loved Litka; but in him, besides sorrow for her, and remembrance of her, there was something else, — a certain interest in life, a certain curiosity touching the future, certain desires, thoughts, tendencies. To Pani Emilia there remained nothing, — it was as if she had died with Litka; and if anything in the world occupied her yet, if she loved those who were near her, it was only for Litka, through Litka, and in so far as they were connected with Litka.

These visits and that farewell were oppressive to Pan Stanislav. He had been deeply attached to Pani Emilia, but now he had the feeling that the cord binding them had snapped once and forever, that their roads parted at that moment, for he was going farther by the way of life; she, however, wished her life to burn out as quickly as possible, and had chosen labor, — blessed, it is true, — but beyond her strength, so as to make death come more quickly.

This thought closed his lips. In the last moments, however, the attachment which he had felt for her from of old overcame him; and he spoke with genuine emotion while kissing her hand.

"Dear, very dear lady, may God guard and comfort you!"

Here words failed him; but she said, without dropping his hand, —

"Till I die, I shall not forget you, since you loved Litka so much. I know, from Marynia, that Litka united you and her; and for that reason I know that you will be happy, otherwise God would not have inspired her. As often as I see you in life, I shall think that Litka made you happy. Let her wish be accomplished at the earliest, and God bless you both!"

Pan Stanislav said nothing; but, when returning home, he thought, —

"Litka's will! She does not even admit that Litka's will can remain unaccomplished; and how was I to tell her that the other is not for me now what she once was?"

Still Pan Stanislav felt with increasing distinctness that

it was not right to remain as he was any longer, and that those bonds connecting him with Marynia ought soon to be tightened, or broken, so as to end the strange condition, and the misunderstandings and sorrows which might rise from it. He felt the need of doing this quickly, so as to act with honor; and new alarm seized him, for it seemed that, no matter how he acted, his action would not bring him happiness.

When he reached home, he found a letter from Mashko, which read as follows,—

"I have called on thee twice to-day. Some lunatic has insulted me before my subordinates on account of the oak which I sold thee. His name is Gantovski. I need to speak with thee, and shall come again before evening."

In fact, he ran in before the expiration of an hour, and asked, without removing his overcoat, —

"Dost thou know that Gantovski?"

"I know him; he is a neighbor and relative of the Plavitskis. What has happened, and how has it happened?"

Mashko removed his overcoat, and said, —

"I do not understand how news of the sale could get out, for I have not spoken of it to any one; and it was important for me that it should not become known."

"Our agent, Abdulski, went to Kremen to look at the oak. Gantovski must have heard of the sale from him."

"Listen; this is the event. To-day Gantovski's card is brought into my office; not knowing who he is, I receive the man. A rough fellow enters, and asks if 't is true that I sold the oak, and if I wish to depopulate a part of Kremen. Evidently I reply by asking how that may concern him. He answers that I have bound myself to pay old Plavitski a yearly annuity from Kremen; and that, if I ruin the place by a plundering management, there will be nothing through which to compel me. In answer, as thou canst understand, I advise him to take his cap, button up closely, in view of the frost, and go to the place whence he came. Hereupon he falls to making an uproar, calling me a cheat and a swindler. At last he says that he lives in the Hotel Saxe, and goes out. Hast thou the key to this? Canst thou tell me its meaning?"

"Of course. First, this Gantovski is of limited mind, by nature he is rude; second, for whole years he has been in love with Panna Plavitski, and has wished to be her knight."

"Thou knowest that I have rather cool blood; but, in truth, it seems at times a dream. That a man should permit himself to insult me because I sell my own property, simply passes human understanding."

"What dost thou think of doing? Old Plavitski will be the first to warm Gantovski's ears, and force him to beg thy pardon."

Mashko's face took on such a cold and determined expression of wrath that Pan Stanislav thought, —

"Well, 'the bear' has brewed beer of a kind that he did not expect; now he must drink it."

"No one has ever offended me without being punished, and no one ever will. This man not only has insulted me, but has done me a wrong beyond estimation."

"He is a fool, simply irresponsible."

"A mad dog, too, is irresponsible, but people shoot him in the head. I talk, as thou seest, coolly; listen, then, to what I say: a catastrophe has come to me, from which I shall not rise."

"Thou art speaking coolly; but anger is stifling thee, and thou art ready to exaggerate."

"Not in the least; be patient, and hear me to the end. The position is this: If my marriage is stopped, or even put off, a few months, the devils will take me, with my position, my credit, my Kremen, and all that I have. I tell thee that I am travelling with the last of my steam, and I must stop. Panna Kraslavski does not marry me for love, but because she is twenty-nine years of age, and I seem to her, if not the match she dreamed of, at least a satisfactory one. If it shall seem that I am not what she thinks, she will break with me. If those ladies should discover to-day that I sold the oak in Kremen from necessity, I should receive a refusal to-morrow. Now think: the scandal was public, for it was in presence of my subordinates. The matter will not be kept secret. I might explain to those ladies the sale of the oak, but yet I shall be an insulted man. If I do not challenge Gantovski, they may break with me, as a fellow without honor; if I challenge him, — remember that they are devotees, and, besides, women who keep up appearances as no others that I know, — they will break with me then as a man of adventures. If I shoot Gantovski, they will break with me as a murderer; if he hits me, they will break with me as an imbecile, who lets himself be insulted and beaten.

In a hundred chances there are ninety that they will act in this way. Is it clear to thee now why I said that the devils will take me, my credit, my position, and Kremen in addition?"

Pan Stanislav waved his hand with all the easy egotism to which a man can bring himself in reference to another, who, at the bottom of things, is of little account to him.

"Bah!" said he; "maybe I will buy Kremen of thee. But the position is difficult. What dost thou think, then, of doing with Gantovski?"

To this Mashko answered: "So far I pay my debts. Thou dost not wish to be my groomsman; wilt thou be my second?"

"That is not refused," answered Pan Stanislav.

"I thank thee. Gantovksi lives in the Hotel Saxe."

"I will be with him to-morrow."

Immediately after Mashko's departure, Pan Stanislav went to spend the evening at Plavitski's; on the road he thought, —

"There are no jokes with Mashko, and the affair will not finish in common fashion; but what is that to me? What are they all to me, or I to them? Still, how devilishly alone a man is in the world!"

And all at once he felt that the only person on earth who cared for him, and who thought of him, not as a thing, was Marynia.

And, in fact, when he came, he knew from the very pressure of her hand that this was true. She said to him, in greeting, with her mild and calm voice, —

"I had a presentiment that you would come. See, here is a cup waiting for you."

## CHAPTER XXIII.

When Pan Stanislav came to the Plavitskis' he found there Gantovski. The young men greeted each other at once with evident coldness and aversion. There was not in the whole world that day an unhappier man than Gantovski. Old Plavitski bantered him as usual, and even more than usual, being in excellent humor because of his relative, the old lady from whom he expected a considerable inheritance. Gantovski's presence was awkward for Marynia; and she strove in vain to hide this annoyance by kindness and a cordial reception. At last Pan Stanislav almost feigned not to see him. It was evident, too, that Gantovski had not confessed anything before old Plavitski, and that he was trembling lest Pan Stanislav might refer to his adventure with Mashko, or tell it outright.

Pan Stanislav understood this at once, as well as the advantage over "the bear" which was given him by his silence; wishing to use it in the interest of Mashko, he was silent for a time, but could not forego the pleasure of punishing Gantovski in another way. He occupied himself the whole evening with Marynia, as he had not done since Litka's death. This filled Marynia with evident delight. Leaving Gantovski to her father, she walked with Pan Stanislav through the room and talked confidentially; then they sat under the palm, where Pan Stanislav had seen Pani Emilia after the funeral, and talked about her approaching admission to the order of Sisters of Charity. To Gantovski it seemed at times that only people who were betrothed could speak in that way; and he felt then what must be felt by a soul not in purgatory, for in purgatory a soul has hope yet before it, but what is felt by a soul when entering the gate with the inscription "*Lasciate ogni speranza*" (Leave every hope). Seeing them together in this way, he thought, too, that perhaps Polanyetski had bought the oak with the land so as to obtain for Marynia even a part of Kremen, and therefore with her will and knowledge. And this being the case, the hair rose on his head at the mere thought of how he had blundered in raising a scandal with Mashko. Plavitski, on his part, hearing his half conscious, but altogether inappropriate answers, amused himself still more at the expense of the "rustic," who on the city pavement had lost what remained of his wit. Plavitski considered himself now as the model of a man of the "capital."

The moment came, however, when the young men were left alone, for Marynia was occupied with tea in the next room, and Plavitski had gone for cigars to his study; Pan Stanislav turned then to Gantovski, —

"Let us go together after tea," said he; "I wish to speak with you touching your collision with Pan Mashko."

"Of course," answered Gantovski, gloomily, understanding that Polanyetski was Mashko's second.

Meanwhile they had to remain for tea, and sit long enough after that, for Plavitski did not like to go to bed early, and summoned Gantovski to a game of chess. During the play, Marynia and Pan Stanislav sat apart and conversed with animation, to the heartfelt torment of "the bear."

"The arrival of Gantovski must be pleasing to you," said Pan Stanislav, all at once, "for it brings Kremen to your mind."

Astonishment flashed over Marynia's face that he was the first to mention Kremen. She had supposed that, in virtue of a tacit agreement, he would cover that question with silence.

"I think no more now of Kremen," answered she, after a pause.

This statement was not true, for in her heart's depth she was sorry for the place in which she had been reared, — the place of her labor for years, and of her shattered hopes; but she thought herself forced to speak thus by duty, and by the feeling for Pan Stanislav, which was increasing continually.

"Kremen," added she, with a voice of some emotion, "was the cause of our earliest quarrel; and I wish now for concord, concord forever."

While saying this, she looked into Pan Stanislav's eyes with a coquetry full of sweetness, which a bad woman is able to put on at any time, but an honest woman only when she is beginning to love.

"She is wonderfully kind," thought he. Straightway he added aloud, "You might have a fabulous weapon against me, for you might lead me to perdition with kindness."

"I do not wish to lead you to that," replied she.

And in sign that she did not, she began to shake her dark, shapely head laughingly; and Pan Stanislav looked at her smiling face, and her mouth a trifle too large, and said mentally, —

"Whether I love her, or love her not, no one attracts me as she does."

In fact, she had never occupied him and never pleased him more, even when he felt no shade of doubt that he loved her, and when he was struggling with that feeling. But at last he took farewell of her, for it had grown late; and after a while he and Gantovski found themselves on the street.

Pan Stanislav who never had been able to guard himself from impulsiveness, stopped the unfortunate "bear," and asked almost angrily, —

"Did you know that it was I who bought the oak at Kremen?"

"I did," answered Gantovski; "for your agent, that man who says that he is descended from Tartars — I forget what his name is — was at my house in Yalbrykov, and told me that it was you."

"Why, then, did you make the scandal with Pan Mashko, not with me?"

"Do not push me to the wall so," answered Gantovski, "for I do not like it. I raised the scandal with him, not with you, because the Plavitskis have nothing to do with you; but that man is obliged to pay them yearly from Kremen the amount he has engaged to pay, and if he ruins Kremen, he will have nothing to pay from. If you wished to know why I attacked him, you know now."

Pan Stanislav had to confess in his soul that there was a certain justice in Gantovski's answer; hence he began the conversation at once from another side, —

"Pan Mashko has begged me to be his second, that's why I interfere in this question. I shall call on you to-morrow as a second; but as a private man, and a relative, though a distant one, of Pan Plavitski, I can tell you to-day only this, — that you have rendered the poorest service to Pan Plavitski, and if he and his daughter are left without a morsel of bread, they will have you to thank for it. This is the truth!"

Gantovski's eyes became perfectly round.

"Without a morsel of bread? They will thank me for it?"

"That is the position," repeated Pan Stanislav. "But listen carefully. Without reference to the result of the scandal, the circumstances are such that it may have the most fatal results. I say this to you, on my word: you have, perhaps, ruined Pan Plavitski, and taken from him and his daughter the way, or rather the means, of living."

If Gantovski really did not like to be pressed to the wall, it was time for him then to show his dislike; but Gantovski had lost his head utterly, and stood in amazement, with open mouth, unable to find an answer; and only after a time did he begin, —

"What? How? In what way? Be sure that it will not come to that, even if I have to give them Yalbrykov."

"Pan Gantovski," interrupted Pan Stanislav, "it is a pity to lose words. I have known your neighborhood from the time I was a little boy. What is Yalbrykov, and what have you in Yalbrykov?"

It was true, Yalbrykov was a poor little village, with nine vlokas of land; and, besides, Gantovski had, as is usual, inherited debts higher than his ears; so his hands dropped at his sides. It occurred to him, however, that perhaps matters did not stand as Pan Stanislav represented them; and he grasped at this thought as at a plank of salvation.

"I do not understand what you say," said he. "God is my witness that I would choose my own ruin rather than injure the Plavitskis; and know this, that I would be glad to twist the neck of Pan Mashko; but, if it is necessary, — if it is a question of the Plavitskis, — then let the devils take me first!

"Immediately after the scandal, I went to Pan Yamish, who is here at the session, and told him all. He said that I had committed a folly, and scolded me, it is true. If it were a question of my skin, it would be nothing, — I would not move a finger; but, since it touches something else, I will do what Pan Yamish tells me, even should a thunderbolt split me next moment. Pan Yamish lives at the Hotel Saxe, and so do I."

They parted on this; and Gantovski went to his hotel, cursing Mashko, himself, and Polanyetski. He felt that it must be as Polanyetski had said, — that some incurable misfortune had happened, — and that he had wrought grievous injustice against that same Panna Marynia for whom he would have given his last drop of blood; he felt that if there had been for him any hope, he had destroyed it completely. Plavitski would close his door on him. Panna Marynia would marry Polanyetski, unless he did n't want her. But who would not want her? And, at the same time, Pan Gantovski saw clearly that among those who might ask her hand, he was the last man she would marry. "What have I? Nothing," said he to himself; "that measly Yalbrykov, nothing more, — neither good name nor money. Every man knows something; I alone know nothing. Every one means something; I alone mean nothing. That Polanyetski has learning and money; but that I love her better, — the devils to me for that, and as much to her, if I am such an idiot that through loving I harm instead of helping her."

Pan Stanislav, on his way home, thought of Gantovski in the same way, and in general had not for him even one spark of sympathy. At home he found Mashko, who had been waiting an hour, and who said, as greeting, —

"Kresovski will be the other second."

Pan Stanislav made somewhat of a wry face, and answered, —

"I have seen Gantovski."

"And what?"

"He is a fool."

"He is that, first of all. Hast thou spoken to him in my name?"

"Not in thy name. As a relative of Pan Plavitski, I told him that he had given Pan Plavitski the worst service in the world."

"You gave no explanations?"

"None. Hear me, Mashko: it is a question for thee of complete satisfaction; it is no point for me that ye should shoot each other. In virtue of what I have told Gantovski, he is ready to agree to all thy conditions. Happily, he has committed himself to Yamish. Yamish is a mild, prudent man, who understands also that Gantovski has acted like an idiot, and will be glad to give him a lesson."

"Very well," said Mashko. "Give me a pen and piece of paper."

"Thou hast them at the desk."

Mashko sat down and wrote. When he had finished, he gave the written sheet to Pan Stanislav, who read as follows: —

"I testify this day that I attacked Pan Mashko while I was drunk, in a state of unconsciousness, and without giving myself account of what I was saying. To-day, having become sober, in presence of my seconds, the seconds of Pan Mashko, and the persons who were present at the scene, I acknowledge my act as rude and senseless, and turn with the greatest sorrow and contrition to the good sense and kindness of Pan Mashko, begging him for forgiveness, and acknowledging publicly that his conduct was and is in everything above the judgment of men like me."

"Gantovski is to declaim this, and then subscribe it," said Mashko.

"This is devilishly unmerciful; no one will agree to it," said Pan Stanislav.

"Dost thou acknowledge that this fool has permitted to himself something unheard of with reference to me?"

"I do."

"And remember what result this adventure may have for me?"

"It is impossible to know that."

"Well, I know; but I will tell thee only this much, — those ladies will regret from their souls that they are bound to me, and will use every pretext which will excuse them before society. That is certain; I am ruined almost beyond rescue."

"The devil!"

"Thou canst understand now that what is troubling me must be ground out on some one, and that Gantovski must pay me for the injustice in one form or another."

"Neither have I any tenderness for him. Let it be so," said Pan Stanislav, shrugging his shoulders.

"Kresovski will come for thee to-morrow morning at nine."

"Very well."

"Then, till we meet again. By the way, should you see Plavitski to-morrow, tell him that his relative, Panna Ploshovski, from whom he expected an inheritance, has died in Rome. Her will was here with her manager, Podvoyni, and is to be opened to-morrow."

"Plavitski knows of that already, for she died five days ago."

Pan Stanislav was left alone. For a certain time he thought of his money without being able to foresee a method by which he might receive it from the bankrupt Mashko, and the thought disturbed him. He remembered, however, that the debt could not be removed from the mortgage on Kremen until it was paid in full; that in this last case he would continue as he had been previously, — a creditor of Kremen. Kremen, it is true, was not a much better debtor than Mashko, hence this was no great consolation; but for the time he was forced to be satisfied with it. Later on, something else also came to his head. He remembered Litka, Pani Emilia, Marynia, and he was struck by this, — how the world of women, a world of feelings purely, a world whose great interest lies in living in the happiness of those near us, differs from the world of men, a world full of rivalry, struggles, duels, encounters, angers, torments, and efforts for acquiring property. He recognized at that moment what he had not felt before, — that if there be solace, repose, and happiness on earth, they are to be sought from a loving woman. This feeling was directly opposed to his philosophy of the last few days, hence it disturbed him. But, in comparing further those two worlds, he could not withhold the acknowledgment that that feminine and loving world has its foundation and reason of existence.

If Pan Stanislav had been more intimate with the Holy Scriptures, beyond doubt the words, "Mary has chosen the better part," would have occurred to him.

## CHAPTER XXIV.

KRESOVSKI was almost an hour late on the following morning. He was, according to a noted description among us, one of the administrators of fresh air in the city, — that is, one of the men who do nothing. He had a name sufficiently famous, and had squandered rather a large fortune. On these two foundations he lived, he went everywhere, and was recognized universally as a man of good breeding. How the above titles can provide a man everything is the secret of great cities; it is enough that not only Kresovski's position was recognized and certain, but he was considered a person to whom it was possible to apply with safety in delicate questions. In courts of honor he was employed as an arbiter; in duels, as a second. High financial circles were glad to invite him to dinners, weddings, christenings, and solemnities of that sort, since he had a patrician baldness, and a countenance extremely Polish; hence he ornamented a table perfectly.

He was a man in the essence of things greatly disenchanted with people, a little consumptive, and very satirical. He possessed, however, a certain share of humor, which permitted him to see the laughable side of things, especially of very small things; in this he resembled Bukatski somewhat, and made sport of his own fault-finding. He permitted others to make sport of it also, but within measure. When the measure was passed, he straightened himself suddenly, and squeezed people to excess; in view of this he was looked on as dangerous. It was said of him that in a number of cases he had found courage where many would have lacked it, and that, in general, he could "carry his nose high." He did not respect any one nor anything, except his own really very noble physiognomy; time, especially, he did not respect, for he was late always and everywhere. Coming in to Pan Stanislav's on this occasion, he began at once, after the greeting, to explain his tardiness, —

"Have you not noticed," asked he, "that if a man is in a real hurry, and very anxious to hasten, the things he needs most vanish purposely? The servant seeks his hat,

— it is gone; looks for his overshoes,— they are not there; hunts for his pocket-book, — it is not to be had. I will wager that this is so always."

"It happens thus," said Pan Stanislav.

"I have, in fact, invented a cure. When something has gone from me as if it had fallen into water, I sit down, smile, and say aloud: 'I love to lose a thing in this way, I do passionately;' my man looks for it, becomes lively, stirs about, passes the time, — that is very wholesome and agreeable. And what will you say? Right away the lost article is found."

"A patent might be taken for such an invention," answered Pan Stanislav; "but let us speak of Mashko's affair."

"We must go to Yamish. Mashko has sent me a paper which he has written for Gantovski. He is unwilling to change a word; but it is an impossible statement, too harsh, — it cannot be accepted. I understand that a duel is waiting for us, nothing else; I see no other outcome."

"Gantovski has intrusted himself to Pan Yamish in everything, and he will do all that Yamish commands. But Yamish, to begin with, is also indignant at Gantovski; secondly, he is a sick man, mild, calm, so that who knows that he may not accept such conditions."

"Pan Yamish is an old dotard," said Kresovski; "but let us go, for it is late."

They went out. After a while the sleigh halted before the hotel. Pan Yamish was waiting for them, but he received them in his dressing-gown, for he was really in poor health. Kresovski, looking at his intelligent, but careworn and swollen face, thought, —

"He is really ready to agree to everything."

"Sit down, gentlemen," said Pan Yamish; "I came only three days ago, and though I do not feel well, I am glad, for perhaps the affair may be settled. Believe me that I was the first to rub the ears of my water-burner."

Here he shrugged his shoulders, and, turning to Pan Stanislav, inquired, —

"What are the Plavitskis doing? I have not visited them yet, though I long to see my golden Marynia."

"Panna Marynia is well," answered Pan Stanislav.

"But the old man?"

"A few days ago a distant relative of his died, — a very wealthy woman; he is counting, therefore, on an inheritance. He told me so yesterday; but I hear that she has left all her property for benevolent purposes. The will is to be opened to-day or to-morrow."

"May God have inspired her to leave something to Marynia! But let us come to our affair. I need not tell you, gentlemen, that it is our duty to finish it amicably, if we can."

Kresovski bowed. Introductions like this, which he had heard in his life God knows how often, annoyed him.

"We are profoundly convinced of this duty."

"So I had hoped," answered Yamish, benevolently. "I confess myself that Pan Gantovski had not the least right to act as he did. I recognize even as just that he should be punished for it; hence I shall persuade him to all, even very considerable, concessions, fitted to assure proper satisfaction to Pan Mashko."

Kresovski took from his pocket the folded paper, and gave it, with a smile, to Pan Yamish, saying, —

"Pan Mashko demands nothing more than that Pan Gantovski should read this little document, to begin with, in presence of his own and Pan Mashko's seconds, as well as in presence of Pan Mashko's subordinates, who were present at the scene, and then write under it his own respected name."

Pan Yamish, finding his spectacles among his papers, put them on his nose, and began to read. But as he read, his face grew red, then pale; after that he began to pant. Pan Stanislav and Kresovski could scarcely believe their eyes that that was the same Pan Yamish who a moment before was ready for every concession.

"Gentlemen," said he, with a broken voice, "Pan Gantovski has acted like a water-burner, like a thoughtless man; but Pan Gantovski is a noble, and this is what I answer in his name to Pan Mashko."

When he said this, he tore the paper in four pieces, and threw them on the floor.

The thing had not been foreseen. Kresovski began to meditate whether Yamish had not offended his dignity of a second by this act, and in one moment his face began to grow icy, and contract like that of an angry dog; but Pan Stanislav, who loved Pan Yamish, was pleased at his indignation.

"Pan Mashko is injured in such an unusual degree that he cannot ask for less; but Pan Kresovski and I foresaw your answer, and it only increases the respect which we have for you."

Pan Yamish sat down, and, being somewhat asthmatic, breathed rather heavily for a time; then he grew quiet, and said, —

"I might offer you an apology on the part of Pan Gantovski, but in other expressions altogether; I see, however, that we should be losing time merely. Let us talk at once of satisfaction, weapon in hand. Pan Vilkovski, Pan Gantovski's other second, will be here soon; and if you can wait, we will fix the conditions immediately."

"That is called going straight to the object," said Kresovski, who quite agreed with Pan Yamish.

"But from necessity, — and sad necessity," replied Yamish.

"I must be in my office at eleven," said Pan Stanislav, looking at his watch; "but, if you permit, I will run in here about one o'clock, to look over the conditions and sign them."

"That will do. We cannot draw up conditions that will rouse people's laughter, that I understand and inform you; but I count on this, — that you, gentlemen, will not make them too stringent."

"I have no thought, I assure you, of quarrelling to risk another man's life." So saying, Pan Stanislav started for his office, where, in fact, a number of affairs of considerable importance were awaiting him, and which, in Bigiel's absence, he had to settle alone. In the afternoon he signed the conditions of the duel, which were serious, but not too stringent. He went then to dinner, for he hoped to find Mashko in the restaurant. Mashko had gone to Pani Kraslavski's; and the first person whom Pan Stanislav saw was Plavitski, dressed, as usual, with care, shaven, buttoned, fresh-looking, but gloomy as night.

"What is my respected uncle doing here?" asked Pan Stanislav.

"When I have trouble, I do not dine at home usually, and this to avoid afflicting Marynia," answered Plavitski. "I go somewhere; and as thou seest, the wing of a chicken, a spoonful of preserve, is all that I need. Take a seat with me, if thou hast no pleasanter company."

"What has happened?"

"Old traditions are perishing; that has happened."

"Bah! this is not a misfortune personal to uncle."

Plavitski glanced at him gloomily and solemnly. "To-day," said he, "a will has been opened."

"Well, and what?"

"And what? People are saying now throughout Warsaw: 'She remembered her most distant relatives!' Nicely did she remember them! Marynia has an inheritance, has she? Knowest thou how much? Four hundred rubles a year for life. And the woman was a millionnaire! An inheritance like that may be left to a servant, not to a relative."

"But to uncle?"

"Nothing to me. She left fifteen thousand rubles to her manager, but mentioned no syllable about me."

"What is to be done?"

"Old traditions are perishing. How many people gained estates formerly through wills, and why was it? Because love and solidarity existed in families."

"Even to-day I know people on whose heads thousands have fallen from wills."

"True, there are such, — there are many of them; but I am not of the number."

Plavitski rested his head on his hand, and from his mouth issued something in the style of a monologue.

"Yes, always somewhere somebody leaves something to somebody." Here he sighed, and after a while added, "But to me no one leaves anything, anywhere, at any time."

Suddenly an idea equally cruel and empty occurred to Pan Stanislav on a sudden to cheer up Plavitski; therefore he said, —

"Ai! she died in Rome; but the will here was written long ago, and before that one there was another altogether different, as people tell me. Who knows that in Rome a little codicil may not be found, and that my dear uncle will not wake up a millionnaire some day?"

"That day will not come," answered Plavitski. Still the words had moved him; he began to gaze at Polanyetski, to squirm as if the chair on which he was sitting were a bed of torture, and said, at last, "And you think that possible?"

"I see in it nothing impossible," answered Pan Stanislav, with real roguish seriousness.

"If the wish of Providence."

"And that may be."

Plavitski looked around the hall; they were alone. He pushed back his chair on a sudden, and, pointing to his shirt-bosom, said, —

"Come here, my boy!"

Pan Stanislav inclined his head, which Plavitski kissed twice, saying at the same time, with emotion,—

"Thou hast consoled me; thou hast strengthened me. Let it be as God wills, but thou hast strengthened me. I confess to thee now that I wrote to Panna Ploshovski only to remind her that we were living. I asked her when the rent term of one of her estates would end; I had not, as thou knowest, the intention to take that place, but the excuse was a good one. May God reward thee for strengthening me! The present will may have been made before my letter. She went to Rome later; on the way she must have thought of my letter, and therefore of us; and, to my thinking, that is possible. God reward thee!"

After a while his face cleared up completely; all at once he laid his hand on Pan Stanislav's knee, and, clicking with his tongue, cried,—

"Knowest what, my boy? Perhaps in a happy hour thou hast spoken; and might we not drink a small bottle of Mouton-Rothschild on account of this codicil?"

"God knows that I cannot," said Pan Stanislav, who had begun to be a little ashamed of what he had said to the old man. "I cannot, and I will not."

"Thou must."

"'Pon my word, I cannot. I have my hands full of work, and I will not befog my head for anything in the world."

"A stubborn goat,—a regular goat! Then I will drink half a bottle to the happy hour."

So he ordered it, and asked,—

"What hast thou to do?"

"Various things. Immediately after dinner I must be with Professor Vaskovski."

"What kind of a figure is that Vaskovski?"

"In fact," said Pan Stanislav, "an inheritance has fallen to him from his brother, who was a miner,—an inheritance, and a considerable one. But he gives all to the poor."

"He gives to the poor, but goes to a good restaurant. I like such philanthropists. If I had anything to give the poor, I would deny myself everything."

"He was ailing a long time, and the doctor ordered him to eat plentifully. But even in that case he eats only what is cheap. He lives in a poor chamber, and rears birds. Next door he has two large rooms; and knowest, uncle, who passes the night in them? Children whom he picks up on the street."

"It seemed to me right away that he had something here," said Plavitski, tapping his forehead with his finger.

Pan Stanislav did not find Vaskovski at home; hence after an interview with Mashko he dropped in to see Marynia about five in the afternoon. His conscience was gnawing him for the nonsense he had spoken to Plavitski. "The old man," said he to himself, "will drink costly wines on account of that codicil; while to my thinking they are living beyond their means already. The joke should not last too long."

He found Marynia with her hat on. She was going to the Bigiels', but received him, and since he had not come for a long time, he remained.

"I congratulate you on the inheritance," said he.

"I am glad myself," replied she; "it is something sure, and in our position that is important. For that matter, I should like to be as rich as possible."

"Why so?"

"You remember what you said once, that you would like to have enough to establish a manufactory, and not carry on a mercantile house. I remember that; and since every one has personal wishes, I should like to have much, much money."

Then, thinking that she might have said too much, and said it too definitely, she began to straighten the fold of her dress, so as to incline her head.

"I came, for another thing, to beg your pardon," said Pan Stanislav. "To-day at dinner I told a pack of nonsense to Pan Plavitski, saying that Panna Ploshovski had changed her will, perhaps, and left him a whole estate. Beyond my expectation he took it seriously. I should not wish to have him deceive himself; and if you will permit me, I will go at once to him and explain the matter somehow."

"I have explained it to him already," said Marynia, smiling; "he scolded me, and that greatly. You see how you have involved matters. You have cause indeed to beg pardon."

"Therefore I beg."

And, seizing her hand, he began to cover it with kisses; and she left it with him completely, repeating as if in sarcasm, but with emotion, —

"Ah, the wicked Pan Stas, the wicked Pan Stas!"

That day Pan Stanislav felt on his lips till he fell asleep the warmth of Marynia's hand; and he thought neither of Mashko nor Gantovski, but repeated to himself with great persistence, —

"It is time to decide this."

## CHAPTER XXV.

KRESOVSKI, with a doctor and a case containing pistols, entered one carriage, Pan Stanislav with Mashko another, and the two moved toward Bielany. The day was clear and frosty, full of rosy haze near the ground. The wheels turned with a whining on the frozen snow; the horses were steaming, and covered with frost; on the trees abundant snow was resting.

"Frost that is frost," said Mashko. "Our fingers will freeze to the triggers. And the delight of removing one's furs!"

"Then be reconciled; make no delay. My dear man, tell Kresovski to begin the work straightway."

Here Mashko wiped his damp eye-glass, and added, "Before we reach the place, the sun will be high, and there will be a great glitter from the snow."

"Finish quickly, then," answered Pan Stanislav. "Since Kresovski is in time, there will be no waiting for the others; they are used to early rising."

"Dost know what makes me anxious at this moment?" asked Mashko. "This, that there is in the world one factor with which no one reckons in his plans and actions, and through which everything may be shattered, involved, and ruined, — human stupidity. Imagine me with ten times the mind that I have, and unoccupied with the interests of Pan Mashko. Imagine me, for example, some great statesman, some Bismark or Cavour, who needs to gain property to carry out his plans, and who calculates every step, every word, — what then? A beast like this comes along, stupid beyond human reckoning, and carries all away on his horns. That is something fabulous! Whether this fellow will shoot me or not, is the least account now; but the brute has spoiled my life-work."

"Who can calculate such a thing?" said Pan Stanislav. "It is as if a roof were to fall on thy head."

"For that very reason rage seizes me."

"But as to his shooting thee, don't think of that."

Mashko recovered, wiped his glass again, and began, —

"My dear, I see that from the moment of our starting thou hast been observing me a little, and now 't is thy wish to add to my courage. That is natural. On my part, I must calm thee; and on my word I give assurance that I will not shame thee. I feel a little disquiet, — that is simple; but knowest why? That which constitutes danger of life, the firing at one, is nothing. Let weapons be given me and him; let us into the woods. God knows that I should fire away at that idiot half a day, and meet his shots half a day. I have had a duel already, and know what it is. It is the comedy that disconcerts one, the preparations, the seconds, the idea that men will look at thee, and the fear touching how thou wilt appear, how thou wilt acquit thyself. It is simply a public exhibition, and a question of self-love, — nothing more. For nervous natures a genuine trial. But I am not over nervous. I understand, also, that in this regard I am superior to my opponent, for I am more accustomed to men. 'T is true such an ass has less imagination, and is not able to think; for example, how he would look as a corpse; how he would begin to decay, and so on. Still I shall be able to command myself better. Besides, I will tell thee another thing: Philosophy is philosophy; but in matters like this the decisive elements are temperament and passion. This duel will not bring me to anything, will not save me in any regard; on the contrary, it may bring me to trouble. But still I cannot deny it to myself, so much indignation has collected in my soul, I so hate that idiot, and would like so to crush and trample him, — that I cease to reason. Thou mayest be certain of one thing, — that as soon as I see the face of the blockhead I shall forget disquiet, forget the comedy, and see only him."

"I understand that well enough," said Pan Stanislav.

And the spots on Mashko's face increased and became blue from the frost, wherewith he had a look as stubborn as it was ugly.

Meanwhile they arrived. Almost simultaneously squeaked the carriage bringing Gantovski, with Yamish and Vilkovski. When they alighted, these gentlemen saluted their opponents; then the seven, counting the doctor, withdrew to the depth of the forest to a place selected on the preceding day by Kresovski.

The drivers, looking at the seven overcoats outlined strangely on the snow, began to mutter to themselves.

"Do you know what is going to happen?" asked one.

"Is it my first time?" answered the other.

"Let the world grow polite; let fools go to fight!"

Meanwhile the seven, clattering on in their heavy overshoes, and blowing lines of white steam from their nostrils, went toward the other end of the forest. On the way, Yamish, somewhat against the rules binding in such cases, approached Pan Stanislav, and began, —

"I wished sincerely that my man should beg pardon of Pan Mashko, but under the conditions it is not possible."

"I proposed to Mashko, too, to tone down that note, but he would not."

"Then there is no escape. All this is immensely foolish, but there is no escape!"

Pan Stanislav did not answer, and they walked on in silence. Pan Yamish began to speak again, —

"But I hear that Marynia Plavitski has received some inheritance?"

"She has, but a small one."

"And the old man?"

"He is angry that the whole property is not left to him."

Yamish tapped his forehead with his glove. "He has a little something here, that Plavitski;" then, looking around, he said, "Somehow we are going far."

"We shall be on the ground in a moment."

And they went on. The sun had risen above the undergrowth; from the trees there fell bluish shadows on the snow; but more and more light was coming into the forest every instant. The crows and daws, hidden somewhere among the tree-tops, shook the snow, dry as down, and it fell without noise to the ground, forming under the trees little pointed piles. Everywhere there was immense silence and rest. Men alone were disturbing it to shoot at each other.

They halted at last on the edge of the forest where it was clean. Then Yamish's short discourse concerning the superiority of peace over war was listened to by Mashko and Gantovski with ears hidden by fur collars. When Kresovski loaded the pistols, each made his choice; and the two, throwing their furs aside, stood opposite each other with the barrels of their weapons turned upward.

Gantovski breathed hurriedly; his face was red, and his mustaches were in icicles. From his whole posture and face it was clear that the affair disconcerted him greatly; that through shame and force of will he controlled himself; and that, had he followed the natural bent of his feelings, he would have sprung at his opponent and smashed him with the butt of his pistol, or even with his fist. Mashko, who previously had feigned not to see his opponent, looked at him now with a face full of hatred, stubbornness, and contempt. His cheeks were all in spots. He mastered himself more, however, than Gantovski; and, dressed in a long frock-coat, with a high hat on his head, with his long side-whiskers, he seemed too stiff, too much like an actor playing the rôle of a duelling gentleman.

"He will shoot 'the bear' like a dog," thought Pan Stanislav.

The words of command were heard, and two shots shook the forest stillness. Mashko turned then to Kresovski, and said coolly, —

"I beg to load the pistols."

But at the same moment at his feet appeared a spot of blood on the snow.

"You are wounded," said the doctor, approaching quickly.

"Perhaps; load the pistols, I beg."

At that moment he staggered, for he was wounded really. The ball had carried away the very point of his kneepan. The duel was interrupted; but Gantovski remained some time yet on the spot with staring eyes, astonished at what had happened.

After the first examination of the wound he approached, however, pushed forward by Yamish, and said as awkwardly as sincerely, —

"Now I confess that I was not right in attacking you. I recall everything that I said, and I beg your pardon. You are wounded, but I did not wish to wound you." After a moment, when he was going away with Yamish and Vilkovski, he was heard to say, "As I love God most sincerely, it was a pure accident; I intended to fire over his head."

Mashko did not open his mouth that day. To the question of the doctor if the wound caused much pain, he merely shook his head in sign that it did not.

Bigiel, who had just returned from Prussia with his pockets full of contracts, when he heard all that had happened, said to Pan Stanislav, —

"Mashko seems an intelligent man, but, as God lives, every one of us has some whim in his head. He, for example, has credit; he has many splendid business cases; he might have a considerable income, and make a fortune. But no, he wants to force matters, strain his credit to the utmost, buy estates, give himself out as a great proprietor, a lord,—be God knows what, only not what he is. All this is wonderful, and the more so that it is so common. More than once I think that life in itself is not bad, but that all ruin it through want of mental balance, and certain devilish whims,—through a kind of wasp, which every one has behind his collar. I understand that a man wants to have more than he has, and to mean more than he means; but why strive for it in fantastic fashion? I am first to recognize energy and cleverness in Mashko; but, taking everything into consideration, he has something here, as God is true, he has."

Bigiel now tapped his forehead with his finger a number of times.

Meanwhile Mashko, with set teeth, was suffering, since his wound, though not threatening life, was uncommonly painful. In the evening he fainted twice in presence of Pan Stanislav. Afterward, weakness supervened, during which that boldness of spirit which had upheld the young advocate through the day gave way completely. When the doctor departed, after dressing the wound, Mashko lay quietly for a time, and then began,—

"But I am in luck!"

"Do not think of that," answered Pan Stanislav; "thou wilt get more fever."

But Mashko continued, however, "Insulted, ruined, wounded,—all at one blow."

"I repeat to thee that this is no time to think of that."

Mashko rested his elbow on the pillow, hissed from pain, and said,—

"Never mind; this is the last time that I shall converse with a decent man. One week or two from now I shall be of those whom people avoid. What do I care for this fever? There is something so unendurable in ruin so complete, in a wreck of fate so utter, that the first idiot, the first goose that comes along will say: 'I knew that long ago; I foresaw that.' So it is: all of them foresee everything after the event; and of him whom the thunderbolt has struck, they make in addition a fool, or a madman."

Pan Stanislav recalled Bigiel's words at that moment. But Mashko, by a marvellous coincidence, spoke on in such fashion as if wishing to answer those words.

"And dost think that I did not give account to myself that I was going too sharply; that I was hurrying with too much force; that I wanted to be something greater than I was; that I carried my nose too high? No one will render me that justice; but knowest thou that I said it to myself? But I said to myself, too: 'It is needful to do this; this is the one way to rise to distinction. Maybe things are wrong, maybe life, in general, goes backward; but had it not been for that adventure unforeseen, and of unfathomable stupidity, I should have succeeded just because I was such as I was. If I had been a modest man, I should not have got Panna Kraslavski. With us it is necessary always to pretend something; and if the devils take me, it is not through my pride, but that blockhead."

"But how the deuce art thou to know surely that thy marriage will fail?"

"My dear man, thou hast no knowledge of those women. They agreed on Pan Mashko through lack of something better, for Pan Mashko had good success. But if any shadow falls on my property, my position, my station, they will throw me aside without mercy, and then roll mountains on to me to shield themselves before the world of society. What knowledge hast thou of them? Panna Kraslavski is not Panna Plavitski."

A moment of silence followed, then Mashko spoke further, with a weakening voice: "She could have rescued me. For her I should have gone on another road,—a far quieter one. In such conditions Kremen would have been saved; the debt on it would have fallen away, as well as Plavitski's annuity. I should have waded out. Dost thou know that, besides, I fell in love with her in student fashion? It came so, unknown whence. But she chose rather to be angry with thee than love me. Now I understand; there is no help for it."

Pan Stanislav, who did not relish this conversation, interrupted it, and spoke with a shadow of impatience,—

"It astonishes me that a man of thy energy thinks everything lost, while it is not. Panna Plavitski is a past on which thou hast made a cross, by proposing to Panna Kraslavski. As to the present, thou wert attacked, it is true; but thou hast fought, thou wert wounded, but in such a way that in a week thou wilt be well; and finally, those ladies have not announced that they break with thee. Till thou hast that, black on white, thou hast no right to talk thus Thou art sick, and that is why thou art reading funeral services over thyself prematurely. But I will tell thee another thing. It is for thee to let those ladies know what has happened. Dost wish, I will go to them to-morrow, then they will act as they please; but let them be informed by thy second, not by city gossips."

Mashko thought a while, and said: "I wished to write in every case to my betrothed; but if thou go, it will be better. I have no hope that she will hold to me, but it is needful to do what is proper. I thank thee. Thou wilt be able to present the affair from the best side,—only not a word touching troubles of any kind. Thou must lessen the sale of the oak to zero, to a politeness which I wished to show thee. I thank thee sincerely. Say that Gantovski apologized."

"Hast thou some one to sit with thee?"

"My servant and his wife. The doctor will come again, and bring a surgeon. This pains me devilishly, but I am not ill."

"Then, till we meet again."

"Be well. I thank thee—thou art—"

"Sleep soundly."

Pan Stanislav went out. Along the way he meditated on Mashko's course, and meditated with a species of anger:

"He is not of the romantic school; still he is inclined to pretend something of that sort. Panna Plavitski! he loved her—he would have gone by another road—she might have saved him!—this is merely a tribute to sentimentality, and, besides, in false coin, since a month later he proposed to that puppet—for money's sake! Maybe I am duller-witted; I do not understand this, and do not believe in disappointments cured so easily. Had I loved one woman, and been disappointed, I do not think that I should marry another in a month. Devil take me if I should! He is right, however, that Marynia is of a different kind from Kraslavski. There is no need whatever to discuss that; she is different altogether! different altogether!"

And that thought was immensely agreeable to Pan Stanislav. When he reached home, he found a letter from Bukatski, who was in Italy, and a card from Marynia, full of anxiety and questions concerning the duel. There was a request to send news early in the morning of what had happened, especially to inform her if everything was really over, and if no new encounter was threatened. Pan Stanislav, under the influence of the idea that she was different from Panna Kraslavski, answered cordially, more cordially even than he wished, and commanded his servant to deliver the note at nine the next morning. Then he set about reading Bukatski's letter, shrugging his shoulders from the very beginning. Bukatski wrote as follows:—

May Sakya Muni obtain for thee blessed Nirvana! Besides this, tell Kaplaner not to forward my three thousand rubles to Florence, but to keep them at my order. These days I have resolved to entertain the design of forming the plan of becoming a vegetarian. Dost note how decisive this is? If the thought does not annoy me, if this plan becomes a determination, and the determination is not beyond my power, I shall cease to be a flesh-eating animal; and life will cost me less money. That is the whole question. As to thee, I beg thee to be satisfied with everything, for life is not worth fatigue.

I have discovered why the Slavs prefer synthesis to analysis. It is because they are idlers, and analysis is laborious. A man can synthesize while smoking a cigar after dinner. For that matter, they are right in being idlers. It is comfortably warm in Florence, especially on Lung-Arno. I walk along for myself and make a synthesis of the Florentine school. I have made the acquaintance here of an able artist in water-colors,—a Slav, too, who lives by art; but he proves that art is swinishness, which has grown up from a mercantile need of luxury, and from over-much money, which some pile up at the expense of others. In one word, art is, to his thinking, meanness and injustice. He fell upon me as upon a dog, and asserted that to be a Buddhist and to be occupied with art is the summit of inconsistency; but I attacked him still more savagely, and answered, that to consider consistency as something better than inconsistency was the height of miserable obscurantism, prejudices, and meanness. The man was astonished, and lost speech. I am persuading him to hang himself, but he does n't want to. Tell me, art thou sure that the earth turns around the sun, or is n't this all a joke? For that matter, it is all one to me! In Warsaw I was sorry for that child who died, and here too I think of her frequently. How stupid that was! What is Pani Emilia doing? People have their rôle in the world fixed beforehand, and her rôle came to her with wings and suffering. Why was she good? She would have been happier otherwise. As to thee, O man, show me one kindness. I beg thee, by all things, marry not. Remember that if thou marry, if thou have a son, if thou toil to leave him property, thou wilt do so only for this: that that son may be what I am, irreparably so. Farewell burning energy, farewell mercantile house, commission firm, O transitory form, vicious toil, effort for money, future father of a family, rearer of children and trouble. Embrace for me Vaskovski. He, too, is a man of synthesis May Sakya Muni open thy eyes to know that it is warm in the sun and cool in the shade, and to lie down is better than to stand! Thy

BUKATSKI.

"Hash!" thought Pan Stanislav. "All this is artificial, all self-deception through a kind of exaggeration. But if a man accustoms himself to this, it will become in time a second nature to him, and, meanwhile, the devils take his reason; his energy and soul decay like a corpse. A man may throw himself headlong into such a hole as Mashko has, or into such a one as Bukatski. In both cases he will go under the ice. What the devil does it mean? Still there must be some healthy and normal life; only it is needful to have a little common sense in the head. But for a man like Bigiel, it is not bad in the world. He has a wife whom he loves, children whom he loves; he works like an ox. At the same time he has a great attachment for people, loves music and his violoncello, on which he plays in the moonlight, with his face raised toward the ceiling. It cannot be said that he is a materialist. No; in him one thing agrees with another somehow, and he is happy."

Pan Stanislav began to walk through the room, and look from time to time at Litka's face, smiling from between the birches. The need of balancing accounts with his own self seized hold of him with increasing force. Like a merchant, he set about examining his debit and credit, which, for that matter, was not difficult. On the credit side of his life, his feeling for Litka once occupied the chief place; she was so dear to him in her time that if a year before it had been said, "Take her as your own child," he would have taken her, and considered that he had something to live for. But now this relation was only a remembrance, and from the rubric of happiness it had passed over to the rubric of misfortune. What was left? First of all, life itself; second, that mental dilettantism, which in every case is a luxury; further, the future, which rouses curiosity; further, the use of material things; and finally, his commercial house. All this had its value; but Pan Stanislav saw that there was a lack of object in it. As to the commercial house, he was pleased with the successes which he experienced, but not with the kind of work which the house demanded; on the contrary, that kind of work was not enough for him, — it was too narrow, too poor, and angered him. On the other hand, dilettantism, books, the world of mind, — all had significance as an ornament of life, but could not become its basis. "Bukatski," said Pan Stanislav to himself, "has sunk in this up to his ears: he wished to live with it, and has become weak, incompetent, barren. Flowers are good; but whoso wishes to breathe the odor of them exclusively will poison himself." In truth, Pan Stanislav did not need to be a great sage to see around him a multitude of people who were out of joint, whose health of soul mental dilettantism had undermined, — just as morphine undermines one's health of body.

This dilettantism had wrought much harm to him, too, if only in this, — that it had made him a skeptic. He had been saved from grievous disease only by a sound organism, which felt the absolute need of expending its superfluous energy. But what will come later? Can he continue in that way? To this Pan Stanislav answered now with a decisive No! Since the business of his house could not fill out his life, and since it was simply perilous to fill it out with dilettantism, it was necessary to fill it out with something else, — to create new worlds, new duties, to open up new horizons; and to do this, he had to do one thing, — to marry.

On a time when he said this to himself, he saw before him a certain undefined form, uniting all the moral and physical requisites, but without a body and without a name. Now it was a real figure; it had calm blue eyes, dark hair, a mouth a trifle too large, and was called Marynia Plavitski. Of any one else there could not be even mention; and Pan Stanislav placed her before himself with such vividness that the veins throbbed in his temples with more life. He was perfectly conscious, however, that something was lacking then in his feeling for Marynia, — namely, that around which the imagination lingers, which dares not ask anything, but hopes everything; which fears, trembles, kneels; which says to the loved woman, "At thy feet;" the love in which desire is at the same time worship, homage, — a feeling which adds a kind of mystic coloring to the relations of a man to a woman; which makes of the man, not merely a lover, but a follower. That had gone. Pan Stanislav, in thinking now of Marynia, thought soberly, almost insolently. He felt that he could go and take her, and have her; and if he did so, it would be for two reasons: first, because Marynia was for him a woman more attractive than all others; and second, reason commanded him to marry, and to marry her.

"She is wonderfully reliable," thought he; "there is nothing in her fruitless or dried up. Egotism has not destroyed the heart in her; and it is undoubted that such a one will not think merely of what belongs to her. She is honesty incarnate, duty incarnate; and in life the only need will be to prevent her from thinking too little of herself. If reason commands me to marry, I should commit a folly, were I to look for another."

Then he asked whether, if he abandoned Marynia, he would not act dishonorably. Litka had united them. Something in his heart revolted at the very thought of opposing the will and sacrifice of that child. If he wished, however, to act against that will, should he have borne himself as he had? No. In such an event he ought not to have shown himself at the Plavitskis' since Litka's death, nor have seen Marynia, nor kissed her hand, nor let himself be borne away by the current which had borne him, — by the power of events, perhaps, — but borne him so far that to-day he would disappoint Marynia, and fall in her eyes to the wretched position of a man who knows not himself what he wishes. For he would have to be blind not to see that Marynia considers herself his betrothed; and that, if she were not disquieted by his silence so far, it was simply because she ascribed it to the mourning which both had in their hearts for Litka.

"Looking, then," said Pan Stanislav, "from the side of reason and conservative instinct, from the side of sense and honor, I ought to marry her. Therefore what? Therefore I should be an imbecile if I hesitated, and did not consider the question as settled. It is settled."

Then he drew breath, and began to walk through the room. Under the lamp lay Bukatski's letter. Pan Stanislav took it, and read from the place where his eyes fell by chance.

"I beg thee, by all things, marry not. Remember that if thou marry, if thou have a son, if thou toil to leave him property, thou wilt do so only for this: that that son may be what I am."

"Here is a nice quandary for thee," said Pan Stanislav, with a certain stubbornness. "I will marry. I will marry Marynia Plavitski; dost hear? I will gain property; and if I have a son, I will not make of him a decadent; dost understand?"

And he was pleased with himself. A little later he looked at Litka, and felt that a sudden emotion seized him.

A current of sorrow for her, and of feeling, rose with a new power in his heart. He began to converse with the child, as in important moments of life people speak usually with beloved dead, —

"Thou art pleased, kitten? Is it not true?" asked he. And she smiled at him from among the birches painted by Marynia; she seemed to blink at him, and to answer, —

"True, Pan Stas; true."

That evening, before going to bed, he took back from the servant the note which was to be given to Marynia in the morning, and wrote another still more affectionate, and in the following words, —

Dear Lady, — Gantovski made a scene with Mashko — rather an awkward one — from which a duel came. Mashko is slightly wounded. His opponent begged his pardon on the spot. There will be no further results, save this: that I am still more convinced of how kind you are, and thoughtful and excellent; and to-morrow, if you permit, I will come with thanks to kiss your beloved and dear hands. I will come in the afternoon; for, in the morning, after visiting my office, I must go to Pani Kraslavski's, and then say farewell to Professor Vaskovski, though, were it possible, I should prefer to begin the day not with them. Polanyetski.

After writing these words, he looked at the clock, and, though it was eleven already, he gave command to deliver the letter, not in the morning, but straightway.

"Thou wilt go in through the kitchen," said he to the servant; "and, if the young lady is asleep, thou wilt leave it."

When alone, he said the following words to the lady, —

"Thou art a very poor diviner, unless thou divine why I am coming to-morrow!"

## CHAPTER XXVI.

PANI KRASLAVSKI received Pan Stanislav with great astonishment, because of the early hour; but still she received him, thinking that he had come for some uncommon reason. He, on his part, without long introductions, told her what had happened, disguising at the same time only what was necessary for shielding Mashko from suspicion of bankruptcy or unfavorable business.

He noticed that the old lady, while he was talking, kept her green eyes — made, as it were, of stone, and devoid of glitter — fixed on him, and that no muscle of her face moved. Only when he had ended did she say, —

"There is one thing in all this which I do not understand. Why did Pan Mashko sell the oak? That is no small ornament to any residence."

"Those oaks stand far from the house," answered Pan Stanislav, "and injure the land, — for nothing will grow in the shade of them; and Pan Mashko is a practical man Besides, to tell the truth, we are old friends, and he did that through friendship for me. I am a merchant; I needed the oak, and Pan Mashko let me have all he could spare."

"In such an event, I do not understand why that young man —"

"If you are acquainted with Pan Yamish," interrupted Pan Stanislav, "he, because he lives near both Kremen and Yalbrykov, will explain to you that that young man is not of perfect mind, and is known as such in the whole neighborhood."

"In that case Pan Mashko was not obliged to fight a duel with him."

"In such matters," answered Pan Stanislav, with a shade of impatience, "we have different ideas from ladies."

"You will permit me to say a couple of words to my daughter."

Pan Stanislav thought it time to rise and take farewell; but since he had come, as it were, on a reconnaissance, and wished to take some information to Mashko, he said, —

"If the ladies have any message to Pan Mashko, I am going to him directly."

"In a moment," answered Pani Kraslavski.

Pan Stanislav remained alone and waited rather long, so long indeed that he began to be impatient. At last both ladies appeared. Though her hair had not been dressed with sufficient care, the young lady, in a white chemisette and a sailor's tie, seemed to Pan Stanislav quite beautiful, in spite of a slight inflammation of the eyes, and a few pimples on her forehead, which were powdered. There was about her a certain attractive languor, from which, having risen very late apparently, she had not been able yet to rouse herself, and a certain equally charming morning carelessness. For the rest, there was no emotion on her bloodless face.

After salutations were exchanged with Pan Stanislav, she said, with a cool, calm voice, —

"Be so kind as to tell Pan Mashko that I was greatly pained and alarmed. Is the wound really slight?"

"Beyond a doubt."

"I have begged mamma to visit Pan Mashko; I will take her, and wait in the carriage for news. Then I will go again for mamma, and so every day till Pan Mashko has recovered. Mamma is so kind that she consents to this."

Here a slight, barely evident blush passed over her pale face. To Pan Stanislav, for whom her words were an utter surprise, and whom they pierced with astonishment, she seemed then perfectly comely; and a moment later, when going to Mashko, he said to himself, —

"Well, the women are better than they seem. But they are two decanters of chilled water; still the daughter has some heart. Mashko did not know her, and he will have an agreeable surprise. The old woman will go to him, will see all those bishops and castellans with crooked noses over which Bukatski amused himself so much; but she will believe in Mashko's greatness."

Meditating in this way, he found himself in Mashko's house, and had to wait, for he came at the moment of dressing the wound. But barely had the doctor gone, when Mashko gave command to ask him to enter, and, without even a greeting, inquired, —

"Well, hast thou been there?"

"How art thou; how hast thou slept?"

"Well. But never mind — hast thou been there?"

"I have. I will tell thee briefly. In a quarter of an hour Pani Kraslavski will be here. The young lady told me to say that she would bring her mother, and would wait to hear how thou art; and to tell thee that she is greatly alarmed, that she is very unhappy, but thanks God that there is nothing worse. Thou seest, Mashko! I add, besides, that she is good-looking, and has attracted me. Now I am going, for I have no time to wait."

"Have mercy; wait a moment. Wait, my dear; I have not a fever, and if thou speak through fear —"

"Thou art annoying," said Pan Stanislav; "I give thee my word that I tell the truth, and that thou hast spoken ill of thy betrothed prematurely."

Mashko dropped his head on the pillow, and was silent for a time; then he said, as if to himself, —

"I shall be ready to fall in love with her really."

"That is well. Be in health; I am going to take farewell of Vaskovski."

But instead of going to Vaskovski, he went to the Plavitskis', whom he did not find at home, however. Plavitski was never at home, and of Marynia they said that she had gone out an hour before. Usually when a man is going to a woman who rouses vivid interest in him, and makes up his mind on the way what to say to her, he has rather a stupid face if he finds that she is not at home. Pan Stanislav felt this, and was vexed. He went to a greenhouse, however, bought a multitude of flowers, and had them sent to Marynia. When he thought of the delight with which she would receive them, and with what a beating heart she would wait for evening, he was so pleased that after dinner he dropped into Vaskovski's in the very best humor.

"I have come to take farewell, Professor; when dost thou start on the journey?"

"How art thou, my dear?" answered Vaskovski. "I had to delay for a couple of days; for, as thou seest, I am wintering various small boys here."

"Young Aryans, I suppose, who in hours of freedom draw purses out of pockets?"

"No, they are good souls; but I cannot leave them without care. I must seek out a successor who will live in my place."

"But who would roast himself here? How dost thou live in such heat?"

"Because I sit without a coat; and wilt thou permit me

not to put it on? It is a little warm here; but perspiration is wholesome, and these little feathered creatures crave heat."

Pan Stanislav looked around. In the room there were at least a dozen and a half of buntings, titmice, finches. Sparrows, accustomed evidently to be fed, looked in in flocks through the window. The professor kept in his room only birds purchased of dealers; sparrows he did not admit, saying that if he did there would be no end to their numbers, and that it would be unjust to receive some and reject others. The chamber birds had cages fastened to the walls and the inner sash of the window, but went into them only at night; during daylight they flew through the chamber freely, filling it with twitter, and leaving traces on books and manuscripts, with which all the corners and the tables were filled.

Some of the birds which had become very tame sat on Vaskovski's head even. On the floor husks of hemp-seed cracked under one's feet. Pan Stanislav, who knew that chamber thoroughly, still shrugged his shoulders, and said,—

"All this is very good, but that the professor lets them light and sing on his head; that, God knows, is too much! Besides, it is stifling here."

"That is the fault of Saint Francis of Assisi," answered Vaskovski, "for I learned from him to love these little birds. I have even a pair of doves, but they are home-stayers."

"Thou wilt see Bukatski, of course; I received a letter from him, — here it is."

"May I read it?"

"I give it to thee for that very purpose."

Vaskovski read the letter, and said when he had finished, "I have always liked this Bukatski; he is a good soul, but — he has a little something here!" Vaskovski began, to tap his forehead with his fingers.

"This is beginning to amuse me," exclaimed Pan Stanislav. "Imagine to thyself, Professor, for a certain number of days some one taps himself on the forehead and says of some one of our acquaintance, 'He has something here!' A charming society!"

"If it is a little so, it is a little so!" answered Vaskovski, with a smile. "And knowest thou what this is? It is the usual Aryan trouble of soul; and in us, as Slavs, there is more of that than in the west, for we are the youngest

Aryans, and therefore neither reason nor heart have settled yet into a balance. We are the youngest Aryans: we feel with more vividness; we take everything to heart more feverishly; and we arrange ourselves to the practice of life with more passion. I have seen much; I have noticed this for a long time. What wonderful natures! Just look, for example, the German students can carouse, — that does n't hinder them from either working or fashioning themselves into practical people; but let a Slav take this habit, and he is lost, he will do himself to death! And so with everything. A German will become a pessimist and write volumes on this, — that life is despair; but he will drink beer meanwhile, rear children, make money, cultivate his garden, and sleep under a feather tick. A Slav will hang himself, or ruin himself with mad life, with excess, smother himself in a swamp into which he will wade purposely. My dear, I remember men who Byronized themselves to death. I have seen much; I have seen men who, for example, took a fancy to peasants, and ended with drinking vodka in peasant dramshops. There is no measure with us, and there cannot be, for in us, to the excessive acceptance of every idea, are joined frivolousness and knowest what vanity. O my God, how vain we are! how we wish to push ourselves forward always, so that we may be admired and gazed at! Take this Bukatski: he has sunk in scepticism up to his ears in fact; in pessimism, Buddhism, decadency, and in what else besides — do I know? — and in these too there is a chaos at present. He has sunk so deeply that those miasmas are really poisoning him; but dost thou think that with this he is not posing? What wonderful natures! those who are most sincere, who have the most vivid feelings, taking all things to heart most powerfully, — are at the same time comedians. When a man thinks of this, he loves them, but he wants to laugh and to weep."

Pan Stanislav recalled how during his first visit to Kremen he had told Marynia of his Belgian times, when, living with some young Belgians, occupying himself with pessimism, he noticed finally that he took all these theories far more to heart than the Belgians, and that, through this, these theories spoiled his life more. Hence he said now, —

"Professor, thy speech is truthful. I have seen such things too, and the devils will take us all."

Vaskovski fixed his mystic eyes on the frosty window-panes, and said, —

"No; some one else will take us all. That hotness of blood, that capacity for accepting an idea, are the great basis of the mission which Christ has designed for the Slavs." Here Vaskovski pointed to a manuscript stained by the birds, and said mysteriously, —

"I am going with that; that is the labor of my life. Dost wish I will read from it?"

"As God lives, I have n't time; it is late already."

"True. It is growing dark. Then I will tell thee in brief words. Not only do I think, but I believe most profoundly, that the Slavs have a great mission."

Here Vaskovski halted, began to rub his forehead, and said, —

"What a wonderful number, — 'three.' There is some mystery in it."

"Thou wert going to speak of a mission," said Pan Stanislav, disquieted.

"Never fear; the one has connection with the other. There are three worlds in Europe: the Roman, the German, and the Slav. The first and second accomplished what they had to do. The future is for that third."

"And what has that third to do?"

"Social conditions, justice, the relations of man to man, the life of individuals, and that which is called private life, are founded on Christian science, no matter what comes. The incoherence of men has deformed this science, but still everything stands on it. Only the first half of the problem is solved, — the first epoch. There are people who think that Christianity is nearing its end. No; the second epoch is about to begin. Christ is in the life of individuals, but not in history. Dost understand? To bring Him into history, to found on Him the relations of peoples, to create the love of our neighbor in the historical sense, — that is the mission which the Slav world has to accomplish. But the Slavs are deficient in knowledge yet; and the need is to open their eyes to this mission."

Pan Stanislav was silent, for he had nothing to answer.

Vaskovski continued: "This is what I have been pondering over a lifetime, and have explained in this work." Here he pointed to a manuscript. "This is the labor of my life. Here *this* mission is outlined."

"On which meanwhile the buntings are — " thought Pan Stanislav. "And surely it will be that way a long time." But aloud he said, "And it is thy hope, Professor, that when such a work is printed — "

"No; I hope nothing. I have a little love, but I am a man too insignificant, too weak in mind. This will vanish, as if some one had thrown a stone into water; but there will be a circle. Let some chosen one come later on; for I know that what is predestined will not fail. He will not refuse the mission even if he wishes. There is no use in bending men from their predestination, nor in changing them by force. What is good in a different place may be bad in this, for God made us for another use. The labor is vain. Vainly too wilt thou persuade thyself that thy only wish is to gain money; thou, like others, must follow the voice of predestination and nature."

"I am following it indeed, for I am going to marry; that is, if I be accepted."

Vaskovski embraced him.

"I wish thee happiness! This is perfect! May God bless thee! I know that the little maid indicated it to thee. But remember how I told thee that she had something to do, and that she would not die till she had done it. May God give her light, and a blessing to both of you! Besides, Marynia is golden."

"And to thee, beloved Professor, a happy journey and a successful mission!"

"And to thee, thy wish for thyself."

"What do I wish?" asked Pan Stanislav, joyfully. "Well, so, half a dozen little missionaries."

"Ah rogue! thou wert always a rogue!" answered Vaskovski. "But fly off, fly off; I will visit thee once more."

Pan Stanislav flew out, sat on a droshky, and gave command to take him to the Plavitskis'. On the road he was arranging what to say to Marynia; and he prepared a little speech, partly sentimental, and partly sober, as befits a positive man who has found really that which he was seeking, but who also is marrying through reason. Evidently Marynia looked for him much later; for there was no light in the chamber, though the last gleam of twilight was quenched. Pan Stanislav, for a greeting, began to kiss both her hands, and, forgetting completely his wise introduction, asked in a voice somewhat uncertain and excited, —

"Have you received the flowers and the letter?"

"I have."

"And did you guess why I sent them?"

Marynia's heart beat with such force that she could not answer.

Pan Stanislav inquired further, with a still more broken voice, —

"Do you agree to Litka's wish, — do you want me?"

"I do," answered Marynia.

Then he, in the feeling that it was proper to thank her, sought words in vain; but he pressed her hands more firmly to his lips, and, holding them both, drew her gently nearer and nearer. Suddenly a flame seized him; he put his arms around her, and began to seek her lips with his own. But Marynia turned away her head so that he could kiss only the hair on her temples. For a while only their hurried breathing was heard in the darkness; at last Marynia wrested herself from his arms.

A few moments later the servant brought a light. Pan Stanislav, recovering himself, was alarmed at his own boldness, and looked into Marynia's eyes with disquiet. He was sure that he had offended her, and was ready to beg her forgiveness. But he saw with wonder that there were no traces of anger in her face. Her eyes were downcast, her cheeks flushed, her hair disarranged somewhat; it was evident that she was disturbed and, as it were, dazed, but withal only penetrated with the perfect sweetness of that fear which comes to a woman who is loved, and who, in passing over the new threshold, feels that she must yield something there, but who passes over and yields because she wishes. She loves, and she is obliged to yield in view of the rights which she accords to the man.

But a vivid feeling of gratitude passed through Pan Stanislav at sight of her. It seemed to him then that he loved her as he had loved of old, before Litka's death. He felt also that in that moment he could not be too delicate nor too magnanimous; hence, taking her hand again, he raised it to his lips with great respect, and said, —

"I know that I am not worthy of you; there is no discussion on that point. God knows that I shall always do for you what is in my power."

Marynia looked at him with moist eyes and said, "If only you are happy."

"Is it possible not to be happy with you? I saw that from the first moment at Kremen. But afterward, you know, everything was spoiled. I thought you would marry Mashko, and how I worried —"

"I was angry, and I beg forgiveness — my dear — Pan Stas."

"This very day the professor said, 'Marynia is gold,'" exclaimed Pan Stanislav, with great ardor. "This is true! all say the same — not only gold, but a treasure — a very precious one."

Her kindly eyes began to smile at him: "Maybe a heavy one."

"Let not your head ache over that. I have strength enough; I shall be able to bear it. Now at least I have something to live for."

"And I," answered Marynia.

"Do you know that I have been here already to-day? I sent chrysanthemums later. After yesterday's letter to you, I said to myself, 'That is simply an angel, and I should lack, not only heart, but common-sense to delay any longer.'"

"I was so alarmed about that duel, and so unhappy. But is it all over now?"

"I give you my word, most thoroughly."

Marynia wanted to make further inquiries, but at that moment Plavitski came. They heard him cough a little, put away his cane, and remove his overcoat; he opened the door then, and, seeing them alone, said, —

"So you are sitting all by yourselves?"

But Marynia ran up to him, and placing her hands on his shoulders, and putting forth her forehead for a kiss, said, —

"As betrothed, papa."

Plavitski stepped back a little and inquired, "What dost thou say?"

"I say," answered she, looking quietly into his eyes, "that Pan Stanislav wishes to take me, and that I am very happy."

Pan Stanislav approached, embraced Plavitski heartily, and said, "I do with uncle's consent and permission."

But Plavitski exclaimed, "Oh, my child!" and, advancing with tottering step to a sofa, he sat on it heavily. "Wait a moment," said he, with emotion. "It will pass — do not mind me — my children! If that is needed, I bless you with my whole heart."

And he blessed them; wherewith still greater emotion mastered him, for, after all, he loved Marynia really. The voice stuck in his throat repeatedly; and the two young people heard only such broken expressions as, for example, "Some corner near you — for the old man, who worked all his life — an only child — an orphan."

They pacified him together, and pacified him so well that half an hour later Plavitski struck Pan Stanislav on the shoulder suddenly, and said, —

"Oh robber! Thou wert thinking of Marynia, and I was thinking thee a little — " He finished the rest in Pan Stanislav's ear, who grew red with indignation, and answered, —

"How could uncle suppose such a thing? If any one else had dared to say that — "

"Well, well, well!" answered Plavitski, smiling; "there is no smoke without fire."

That evening Marynia, taking farewell of Pan Stanislav, asked, —

"You will not refuse me one thing?"

"Nothing that you command."

"I have said long to myself that if a moment like the present should come, we would go to Litka together."

"Ah, my dear lady," answered Pan Stanislav; and she continued, —

"I know not what people will say; but what do we care for the world — what indeed?"

"Nothing. I am thankful to you from my heart and soul for the thought — My dear lady —my Marynia!"

"I believe that she looks at us and prays for us."

"Then she is our little patroness."

"Good-night."

"Good-night."

"Till to-morrow."

"Till to-morrow," said he, kissing her hands, — "till after to-morrow, daily;" and here he added in a low voice, "Until our marriage."

"Yes," answered Marynia.

Pan Stanislav went out. In his head and in his heart he felt a great whirl of feelings, thoughts, impressions, above which towered one great feeling, — that something unheard of in its decisiveness had happened; that his fate had been settled; that the time of reckoning, of wavering and changing, had passed; that he must begin a new life. And that feeling was not unpleasant to him, — nay, it verged on a kind of delight, especially when he remembered how he had kissed Marynia's hair and temples. That which was lacking in his feelings shrank and vanished almost utterly in this remembrance; and it seemed to Pan Stanislav that he had found everything requisite to perfect happiness. "I shall never grow sated with this," thought he; and it seemed to him simply impossible that he should. He remembered then the goodness of Marynia, and how reliable she was; how on such a heart and character he might build; how in living with her nothing could ever threaten him; how she would not trample on any quality of his, nor make it of no avail; how she would receive as gold that which in him was gold; how she would live for him, not for herself. And, meditating in this way, he asked what better could he find? and he wondered indeed at his recent hesitation. Still he felt that what was coming was a change so gigantic, so immensely decisive, that somewhere at the bottom, in the deepest corner of his soul, there was roused a kind of alarm before this unknown happiness. But he did not hesitate. "I am neither a coward nor an imbecile," thought he. "It is necessary to go ahead, and I will go."

Returning home, he looked at Litka; and immediately there opened before him, as it were, a new, clear horizon. He thought that he might have children, have such a bright dear head as this — and with Marynia. At the very thought his heart began to beat with greater life, and to the impulse of thoughts was joined such a solace of life as he had not known previously. He felt almost perfectly happy. Looking by chance at Bukatski's letter, which he took from his pocket before undressing, he laughed so heartily that the servant looked in with astonishment. Pan Stanislav wished to tell him that he was going to marry. He fell asleep only toward morning, but rose sprightly and fresh; after dressing, he flew to his office to announce the news to Bigiel at the earliest.

Bigiel embraced him, then, with his usual deliberation, proceeded to consider the affair, and said finally, —

"Reasoning the matter over, this is the wisest thing that thou hast done in life;" then, pointing to a box of papers, he added, "Those contracts ought to be profitable, but thine is still better."

"Is n't it?" exclaimed Pan Stanislav, boastfully.

"I will fly to tell my wife," said Bigiel, "for I cannot contain myself; but go thou home, and go for good. I will take thy place till the wedding, and during the honeymoon."

"Very well; I will hurry to see Mashko, and then Marynia and I will go to Litka."

"That is due from you both to her."

Pan Stanislav bought more flowers on the way, added a note to them that he would come soon, and dropped in to see Mashko. Mashko was notably better, under the care of Pani Kraslavski, and was looking for her arrival every moment. When he had heard the news, he pressed Pan Stanislav's hand with emotion, and said, —

"I will tell thee only one thing, — I do not know whether she will be happy with thee, but certainly thou wilt be happy with her."

"Because women are better than men," answered Pan Stanislav. "After what has happened to thee, I hope that thou art of this opinion."

"I confess that to this moment I cannot recover from astonishment. They are both better, and more mysterious. Imagine to thyself —" Here Mashko halted, as if hesitating whether to continue.

"What?" inquired Pan Stanislav.

"Well, thou art a discreet man, and hast given me, besides, such proofs of friendship that there may not be secrets between us. Imagine, then, that yesterday, after thy departure, I received an anonymous letter. Here, as thou art aware, the noble custom of writing such letters prevails. In the letter were tidings that Papa Kraslavski exists, is alive, and in good health."

"Which, again, may be gossip."

"But also may not be. He lives, probably, in America. I received the letter while Pani Kraslavski was here. I said nothing; but after a time, when she had examined those portraits, and began to inquire of my more distant family relations, I asked her, in turn, how long she had been a widow. She answered, —

"'My daughter and I have been alone in the world nine years; and those are sad events, of which I do not wish to speak to-day.'

"Observe that she did not say directly when her husband died."

"And what dost thou think?"

"I think that if papa is alive, he must be that kind of figure of which people do not speak, and that in truth those may be 'sad events.'"

"The secret would have come out long ago."

"Those ladies lived abroad some years. Who knows? That, however, will not change my plans in any way. If Pan Kraslavski is living in America, and does not return, he must have reasons; it is as if he were not in the world, then. In fact, I am gaining the hope now that my marriage will come to pass, for I understand that when people have something to hide, they exact less."

"Pardon my curiosity," said Pan Stanislav, taking his hat; "but with me it is a question of my money, and now touching the Kraslavskis. Dost thou know surely that these ladies have money?"

"It seems that they have much; still, I am playing against a card somewhat hidden. It is likely that they have much ready money. The mother told me repeatedly that her daughter would not need to look to her husband's property. I saw their safe; they keep a big house. I know nearly all the money-lenders — Jews and non-Jews — in Warsaw, and I know surely that these ladies are not in debt a copper to any one; as thou knowest thyself, they have a nice villa not far from the Bigiels. They do not live on their capital, for they are too prudent."

"Thou hast no positive figures, however?"

"I tried to get them, but in roundabout fashion. Not being too certain of my connection with the ladies, I could not insist overmuch. It was given me to understand that there would be two hundred thousand rubles, and perhaps more."

Pan Stanislav took leave, and on the way to the Plavitskis' thought, "All this is a kind of mystery, a kind of darkness, a kind of risk. I prefer Marynia."

Half an hour later he was driving with Marynia to the cemetery, to Litka. The day was warm, as in spring, but gray; the city seemed sullen and dirty. In the cemetery the melting snow had slipped in patches to the ground from the graves, and covered the yellow, half-decayed grass. From the arms of crosses and leafless tree-branches large drops were falling, which, borne from time to time by gusts of warm wind, struck the faces of Pan Stanislav and Marynia. These gusts pulled Marynia's dress, so that she had to hold it. They stopped at last before Litka's grave.

And here all was wet, sloppy, gloomy, half-stripped of the melting snow. The thought that that child, once so cared for, so loved, and so petted, was lying in that damp dungeon darkness, could hardly find a place in Pan Stanislav's head.

"All this may be natural," thought he; "but it is not

possible to be reconciled with death." And, in truth, whenever he visited Litka, he returned from the cemetery in a kind of irrepressible rebellion, with a species of passionate protest in his soul. These thoughts began to rend him in that moment also. It seemed to him simply terrible to love Litka, and to reconcile his love with the knowledge that a few steps lower down she is lying there, black and decaying. "I ought not to come," said he to himself, "for I grow mad, lose my head here, and lose every basis of life." But, above all, he suffered, for, if it is impossible not to think of death, it is equally impossible to explain it; hence everything touching it, which comes to the head, is, in so far as a man does not stretch forth his hand toward simple faith, at once despairing and shallow, trivial and common. "For me there is a greater question here than that of existence itself, but I am only able to answer with a commonplace. A perfectly vicious circle!"

And it was true; for if he considered, for example, that at the first thought of death everything becomes smoke, and he felt that unfortunately it does, he felt at the same time that thousands of people had come to that thought before he had, and that no one had found in it either solace or even such satisfaction as the discovery of a truth gives. Everything that he could say to himself was at once terrifying and petty. It was easy for him to understand that the whole life of man, general history, all philosophies, are at bottom merely a struggle with incessant death, — a struggle despairing, a struggle utterly senseless, and at the same time infinitely foolish and devoid of object, for it is lost in advance. But such reasoning could not bring him any comfort, since it was merely the confirmation of a new vicious circle.

For if the one object of all human efforts is life, and the only result death, the nonsense passes measure, and simply could not be accepted, were it not for that loathsome and pitiless reality, which turns beings beloved and living into rotten matter.

Pan Stanislav, during every visit to the cemetery, poisoned himself with such thoughts. To-day, while going, he thought that the presence of Marynia would liberate him from them; meanwhile, rather the opposite happened. Litka's death, which had broken in him trust in the sense and moral object of life, undermined in him also that first, former love for Marynia, which was so naive and free of doubt; now, when with Marynia, he was standing at Litka's grave, when that death, which had begun to be only a memory, had become again a thing almost tangible, its poisoning effect was increasing anew. Again it seemed to him that all life, consequently love, too, is merely an error, and the processes of life utterly useless and vain. If above life there is neither reason nor mercy, why toil, why love and marry? Is it to have children, become attached to them with every drop of one's blood, and then look on helplessly, while that blind, stupid, insulting, brutal force chokes them, as a wolf chokes a lamb, and come to their graves, and think that they are mouldering in damp and darkness? See, Litka is down there.

A day wonderfully gloomy only strengthened the bitterness of these feelings. At times, during his previous visits, the cemetery had seemed to Pan Stanislav a kind of great void in which life was dissolving, but in which every misfortune, too, was dissolving, — something enormously dreamy, soothing. To-day there was no rest in it. Pieces of snow fell from the trees and gravestones; ravens pushed about among the wet trees with their croaking. Sudden and strong blasts of wind hurled drops of moisture from the branches, and, driving them about, produced a certain desperate struggle around the stone crosses, which stood firm and indifferent.

Just then Marynia ceased praying, and said, with that slightly suppressed voice with which people speak in cemeteries, —

"Now her soul must be near us."

Pan Stanislav made no answer; but he thought first that he and Marynia were beings as if from two distinct worlds, and then that if there were even a particle of truth in what she said, all his mental struggles would be less important than that melting snow. "In such case," said he to himself, "there is dying and there are cemeteries, but there is simply no death."

Marynia began to place on the grave immortelles, which she had bought at the gate, and he to think hurriedly, rather by the aid of his impressions than his ideas, "In my world there is no answer to anything; there are only vicious circles, which lead to the precipice."

And this struck him, — that if such ideas of death as

Marynia had, did not come from faith, or if they had been unknown altogether, and if all at once some philosopher had formulated them as a hypothesis, the hypothesis would be recognized as the most genial of the genial, because it explains everything, gives an answer to questions, gives light, not only to life, but to death, which is darkness. Mankind would kneel with admiration before such a philosopher and such a scientific theory.

On the other hand, he felt that still something of Litka was there with them. She herself was falling into dust, but something had survived her; there remained, as it were, currents of her thought, of her will, of her feeling. This, — that she had brought him to Marynia; that they were betrothed; that they were then standing at her grave; that they were to be united; that their lives would go on together; that they would have children, who in their turn would live and love and increase, — what was that, if not such a current, which, coming forth from that child, might go on and on through eternity, renewing itself in an endless chain of phenomena? How then understand that from a mortal being should issue an immortal and ceaseless energy? Marynia, in the simplicity of her faith, had found an answer; Pan Stanislav had not.

And still Marynia was right. Litka was with them. Through Pan Stanislav's head there flew at that moment a certain hypothesis, dim, and not fixed in close thought yet, — a hypothesis, that, perhaps, all which man thinks during life, all that he wishes, all that he loves, is a hundred times more intangible, a hundred times more subtile, than ether, from which rises an astral existence, conscious of itself, either eternal or successively born into beings more and more perfect, more subtile, on to infinity. And it seemed to him that atoms of thought and feeling might collect into a separate individuality, specially because they came forth from one brain or one heart; that they are related, — hence tend to one another with the same mysterious principle by which physical elements combine to form physical individualities.

At present he had not time to meditate over this, but it seemed to him that he had caught something, that in the veil before his eyes, he saw, as it were, an opening that might turn out to be a deception; but at the moment, when he felt that still Litka was with them, he thought that her presence could be understood only in that manner.

Just then some funeral came, for, in the tower, which stood in the middle of the cemetery, the bell began to sound. Pan Stanislav gave Marynia his arm, and they went towards the gate. On the way Marynia, thinking evidently more about Litka, said, —

"Now I am certain that we shall be happy."

And she leaned more on Pan Stanislav's arm, for the gusts of wind had become so violent that it was difficult for her to resist them. One of these carried her veil around his neck. Reality began to call to him. He pressed the arm of the living woman to his side, and felt that loving, if it cannot ward away death, can at least harmonize life.

When they were seated in the carriage, he took Marynia's hand, and did not let it go during the whole way. At moments solace returned to him almost perfectly, for he thought that that maiden, true and kind to the core of her nature, would be able to make good what was lacking in his feeling, and revivify in him that which was palsied. "My wife! my wife!" repeated he, in mind, looking at her; and her honest, clear eyes answered, "Thine."

When they arrived at the house, Plavitski had not returned from his walk before dinner; they were all by themselves then. Pan Stanislav sat down by her side, and under the influence of those thoughts which had passed through his head on the way, he said, —

"You declared that Litka was with us; that is true. I have always returned from the cemetery as if cut down; but it is well that we were there."

"It is; for we went as if for a blessing," said Marynia.

"I have that same impression; and, besides, it seems to me as if we were united already, or, at least, were nearer than before."

"True; and this will be both a sad and a pleasant remembrance."

He took her hand again, and said, —

"If you believe that we shall be happy, why defer happiness? My kind, my best, I, too, trust that it will be well with us; let us not defer the day. We have to begin a new life; let us begin it promptly."

"Make the decision. I am yours with all my soul."

Then he drew her toward him, as he had the day before, and began to seek her lips with his lips; and she, whether under the influence of the thought that his rights were greater on that day, or under the influence of awakening thoughts, did not turn her head away any more, but, half closing her eyes, she herself gave him her lips, as if they had been thirsty a long time.

## CHAPTER XXVII.

For Pan Stanislav began now the period of ante-nuptial cares and preparations. He had, it is true, a dwelling furnished for more than a year, — that is, from a period before he knew Marynia. At that time he made no denial when Bukatski laughed at the lodgings, seeing in them a proof of how anxious his friend was to marry. "Yes," said he; "I have property enough to permit this. I think, too, that I am doing something toward it, and that my plans are growing real."

Bukatski said this was prevision worthy of praise, and wondered that a man of such foresight did not engage also a nurse and a midwife. At times conversation of this kind ended in a quarrel, for Pan Stanislav could not let any one deny him sound judgment in worldly matters. Bukatski affirmed that it was bird romance, worthy of a bunting, to start with building a poetic nest. One friend contended that there could be no wiser method than to build a cage, if you want a bird; the other retorted that if the bird were not found yet, and the chase was uncertain, the cage was a joke on one's appetite. It ended with allusions to the slim legs of Bukatski, which, for him, made the chase after birds of all kinds impossible, even though they were wingless. Bukatski, on such occasions, fell into excellent humor.

Now, however, when the cage was ready, and the bird not only caught, but willing, there remained so much to be done that Pan Stanislav was seized more than once by surprise that an act so simple by nature as marriage, should be so complex in civilized societies. It seemed to him that if no one has the right to look into the moral side of the connection, since it is the outcome of genuine free-will, the formal side should be looked at still less.

But he thought so because he was not a law-giver, and was an impulsive man made impatient by the need of getting "papers." Once he had resolved on marriage, he ceased to think or to analyze, and hastened, as a man of action, to execute.

He was even filled more than once with pride, on comparing himself with such a man, for instance, as Ploshovski, whose history had been circling from mouth to mouth in society, before people had begun to learn it from his diary. "But I am of different metal," thought Pan Stanislav, with a certain satisfaction. At moments, again, when he recalled Ploshovski's figure, his noble, delicate, and also firmly defined profile, his refinement, subtlety, and mental suppleness, his rare gift of winning people, especially women, it occurred to him that he, Polanyetski, is a less refined type, less noble, and, in general, a man cut from ruder materials. But to this he answered that evidently, in the face of conditions in life and the resistance required by it, too much refinement is simply fatal to mind as well as body. In himself he saw also far more ability for living. "Finally," said he, "I can be of some service, while he would have been good only on social shelves with curiosities. I am able to win bread; he was able only to make pellets out of bread when baked. I know how, and I know well how, to color cotton; he only knew how to color women's cheeks. But what a difference between us with reference to women! That man over-analyzed his life and the life of the woman whom he loved; he destroyed her and himself by not being able to escape from the doubt whether he loved her sufficiently. I, too, have doubts whether my love is perfect; but I take my little woman, and should be an imbecile, not a man, to fear the future, and fail to squeeze from it in simple fashion what good and happiness it will let me squeeze."

Here Pan Stanislav, though he had forsworn analysis, began to analyze, not himself, it is true, but Marynia. He permitted this, however, only because he foresaw certainly favorable conclusions; he understood that, in calculating the future of two people, good-will on one side is not sufficient, and becomes nothing, if good will fails on the other. But he was convinced that in taking Marynia he was not taking a dead heart. Marynia had brought to the world not only an honest nature, but from years of childhood she had been in contact with work and with conditions in which she was forced to forget herself, so as to think of others. Besides, there was above her the memory of a mother, a kind of endless blessing from beyond the grave, — a mother whose calmness, candor, and uprightness, whose life, full of trials, were remembered to the present with the utmost respect, throughout the whole region of Kremen. Pan Stanislav knew this, and was persuaded that, building on the heart and character of Marynia, he was building on a foundation well-nigh immovable. More than once he recalled the words of a woman, an acquaintance and friend of his mother's, who, when some one asked her whether she was more anxious about the future of her sons than her daughters, answered, "I think only of my sons; for my daughters, in the worst case, can be only unhappy."

So it is! School and the world rear sons, and both may make them scoundrels; daughters, in whom the home ingrafts honorableness, can, in the worst case, be only unhappy. Pan Stanislav understood that this was true with regard to Marynia. So that if he analyzed her, his analysis was rather the examination of a jeweller and his admiration for his gems, than a scientific method intended to reach results unknown and unexpected.

Still he quarrelled once with Marynia very seriously, because of a letter from Vaskovski, which Pan Stanislav received from Rome a few weeks after the professor's departure, and which he read in its integrity to Marynia. This letter was as follows: —

My Dear, — I am lodging at Via Tritone, Pension Française. Visit my Warsaw lodgings; see if Snopchinski looks after my little boys properly, and if the birds of Saint Francis have seeds and water in plenty When spring comes, it will be needful to open the windows and cages; whichever bird wishes to stay, let it stay, and whichever one wishes to go, let it fly. The boys of the genus *homo sapiens* should have good food, since I left money therefor, and besides little moralizing, but much love. Snopchinski is a worthy man, but a hypochondriac. He says this comes from snows. When he is attacked by what he calls "chandra," he looks for whole weeks on his boots, and is silent; but one must talk with little boys, to give them confidence. This is all that touches Warsaw.

I am printing here in French, in the typography of the journal "L'Italie," that work of mine which I discussed with thee. They laugh at my French a little, and at me, but I am used to that. Bukatski came here. He is a good, beloved fellow! he has grown strange to the last degree, and says that he drags his feet after him, though I have not noticed it. He loves both Marynia and thee, and indeed every one, though he denies it. But when he begins to talk, one's ears wither. May the Lord God bless thee, dear boy, and thy honest Marynia! I should like to be at thy wedding, but I know not whether I shall finish my work before Easter; listen, therefore, now to what I tell thee, and know that I write this letter to that end. Do not think that the old man is talking just to talk. Thou knowest, besides, that I have been a teacher; that the inheritance from my brother freed me from that occupation, that I have had experience and have seen things. If ye have children, do not torture them with knowledge; let them grow up as God wills. I might stop here; but thou art fond of figures, hence I will give thee figures. A little child has as many hours of labor as a grown man in office, with this difference, that the man talks during office hours with his colleagues, or smokes cigarettes; the child must strain its attention continually, or lose the clew of lessons, and cease to understand what is said to it. The man goes home when his work is done; the child must prepare for the following day, which takes four hours from a capable child, from one less capable six. Add to this, that poorer pupils give lessons frequently, the rich take them, which, added, gives twelve hours. Twelve hours' labor for a child! Dost understand that, my dear? Canst thou realize what sickly natures must grow up in such conditions, — natures out of joint, inclined to the wildest manias, crooked, wilful? Dost thou understand how we are filling cemeteries with our children, and why the most monstrous ideas find supporters? Ah, at present they are limiting the hours of labor in factories even for grown people, but touching children at school philanthropy is silent. Oh, but that is a field! that is a service to be rendered; that is a coming glory and sainthood. Do not torture thy children with learning, I beg thee — and I beg Marynia; promise me both of you. I do not speak just to speak, as Bukatski says sometimes, but I speak from the heart; and this is the greatest reform for which future ages are waiting, the greatest after the introduction of Christ into history. Something wonderful happened to me in Perugia a few days since, but of that I will tell thee sometime, and now I embrace both of you.

Marynia listened to this letter, looking at the tips of her shoes, like that Snopchinski of whom the Professor wrote. But Pan Stanislav laughed, and said, —

"Have you ever heard anything like this? It is long before our marriage; but he is lamenting over our children, and takes the field on their behalf. This is somewhat the history of my nest."

After a while he added, "To tell the truth, the fault is mine; for I made him various promises." And, inclining so that he could see Marynia's eyes, he asked, "But what do you say to this letter?"

Pan Stanislav, inquiring thus, had chanced on that unhappy moment when a man is not himself, and acts not in accordance with his own nature. He was rather a harsh person generally, but not brutal, and at times was even capable of delicate acts, really womanlike. But now, in his look and in the question directed to a young lady so mimosa-like as Marynia, there was something simply brutal. She knew as well as others that after marriage come children; but this seemed to her something indefinite, not to be mentioned, or if mentioned, mentioned in allusions as delicate as lace, or in a moment of emotion, with beating heart, with loving lips at the ear, with solemnity, — as touching what is most sacred in a mutual future. Hence Pan Stanislav's careless tone outraged and pained her. She thought, "Why does he not understand this?" and she in turn acted not in accordance with her nature; for, as happens frequently with timid persons in moments of bitterness and confusion, they exhibit greater anger than they feel.

"You should not treat me in this way!" cried she, indignantly. "You should not speak to me in this way!"

Pan Stanislav laughed again with feigned gayety.

"Why are you angry?" inquired he.

"You do not act with me as is proper."

"I do not understand the question."

"So much the worse."

The smile vanished from his lips; his face grew dark, and he spoke quickly, like a man who has ceased to reckon with his words.

"Perhaps I am stupid; but I know what is right and what is not. In this way life becomes impossible. Whoever makes great things out of nothing must not blame others. But, since my presence is disagreeable, I go!"

And, seizing his hat, he bowed, and went out. Marynia did not try to detain him. For a while offence and anger stifled in her all other sensations; then there remained to her only an impression, as if from the blow of a club. Her thoughts scattered like a flock of birds. Above them towered only one dim idea: "All is over! he will not return!" Thus fell the structure which had begun to unite in such beautiful lines. Emptiness, nothingness, a torturing, because objectless life, and a chilled heart, — that is what remained to her. And happiness had been so near! But that which had taken place so suddenly was something so strange that she could not explain immediately. She went to the writing-desk, and began mechanically to arrange papers in it, with a certain objectless haste, as if there could be any reason at that moment for arranging them. Then she looked at Litka's photograph, and sat down quickly with her hands on her eyes and temples. After a time it occurred to her that Litka's will must be stronger than the will of them both, and a ray of hope shone in on her suddenly. She began to walk in the room, and to think on what had passed; she recalled Pan Stanislav, not only as he had been just then, but earlier, — two, three days, a week before. Her regret became greater than her feeling of offence, and it increased with her affection for Pan Stanislav. After a time she said in her soul that she was not free to forget herself; that it was her duty to accept and love Pan Stanislav as he was, and not strive to fix him to her ideas. "That is, he is a living man, not a puppet," repeated she, a number of times. And a growing feeling of fault seized her, and after that compunction. A heart submissive by nature, and greatly capable of loving, struggled against sound sense, which she possessed undoubtedly, and which now told her in vain that reason was not on Pan Stanislav's side, and that, moreover, she had said nothing which needed pardon. She said to herself, "If he has a good heart, even to a small extent, he will return;" but she was seized also with fear in view of the self-love of men in general, and of Pan Stanislav in particular, — she was too intelligent not to note that he cared greatly to pass for an unbending person. But considerations of that kind, which an unfriendly heart would have turned to his disadvantage, had made her tender only on his behalf.

Half an hour later she was convinced to the depth of her soul that the fault lay only on her side; that "she had tormented him so much already" that she ought to yield now, — that is, to be the first to extend a hand in conciliation. That meant in her mind to write a few peace-making words. He had suffered so much from that affair of Kremen that this was due to him. And she was ready even to weep over his fate. She hoped, withal, that he, the bad, ugly man, would estimate what it cost her to write to him, and would come that same evening.

It had seemed to her that nothing was easier than to write a few cordial phrases, which go directly from one heart to another. But how difficult! A letter has no eyes, which fill with tears; no face, which smiles both sadly and sweetly; no voice, which trembles; no hands to stretch forth. You may read and understand a letter as you like; it is merely black letters on paper as impassive as death.

Marynia had just torn the third sheet, when the face of Pan Plavitski, as wrinkled as a roast apple, and with mustaches freshly dyed, showed itself at the door partly open.

"Is Polanyetski not here?" inquired he.

"He is not, papa."

"But will he come this evening?"

"I do not know," answered she, with a sigh.

"If he comes, my child, tell him that I will return not later than an hour from now; and that I wish to speak with him."

"And I too wish to speak with him," thought Marynia.

And when she had torn the third sheet she took the fourth and was thinking whether to turn the whole quarrel into a jest, or simply to beg his pardon. The jest might not please him; in the pardon there was something warmer, but how difficult it was! If he had not fled, it would have sufficed to extend her hand; but he flew out as if shot from a sling, the irritable man, though so much loved.

And, raising her eyes, she began to work intently with her dark head, when on a sudden the bell sounded in the entrance. Marynia's heart was beating like a hammer; and through her head flew these questions, like lightning, —

"Is it he? Is it not he?"

The door opened; it was he.

He came in with the look of a wolf, his head down, his face gloomy. Evidently he was very uncertain how she would receive him; but she sprang up, her heart beating like a bird's heart; her eyes radiant, happy, touched greatly by his return; and, running to him, she laid her hands on his shoulders.

"But how good! how nice! And do you know, I wanted to write to you."

Pan Stanislav, pressing her hands to his lips, was silent for some time; at last he said, —

"You ought to give the order to throw me downstairs." In a rapture of thankfulness he drew her up to him, kissed her lips, eyes, temples, and hair, which became unbound in the pressure. In such moments it seemed to him always that he would find everything that goes to make great and perfect love. At last he released her and continued, —

"You are too good. Though that is better, it subdues me. I came to beg your forgiveness, nothing more. I regained my senses at once. I reproached myself for my last words, and I cannot tell you how sorry I was. I walked along the street, thinking to see you in the window, perhaps, and note from your face whether I might come in. After that I could not restrain myself, and returned."

"I beg pardon; it was my fault. You see the torn paper; I wrote and wrote."

He devoured with his eyes her hair, which she had arranged hastily. With blushing face, from which joy was beaming, with eyes laughing from happiness, she seemed to him more beautiful than ever, and desired as never before.

Marynia noticed, too, that he was looking at her hair; and confusion struggled with pure womanly coquetry. She had fastened it awkwardly by design, so that the tresses were falling more and more on her shoulders; while she said, —

"Do not look, or I 'll go to my room."

"But that is my wealth," said Pan Stanislav; "and in my life I have never seen anything like it."

He stretched his hands to her again, but she evaded.

"Not permitted, not permitted," said she; "as it is, I am ashamed. I ought to have left you."

Her hair, however, came gradually to order; then both sat down and conversed quietly, though looking into each other's eyes.

"And you wished really to write?" asked Pan Stanislav.

"You see the torn paper."

"I say that, in truth, you are too good."

She raised her eyes, and, looking at the shelf above the bureau, said, —

"Because the fault was mine. Yes; only mine."

And, judging that she could not be too magnanimous, she added after a moment, blushing to her ears and dropping her eyes, —

"For, after all, the professor is correct in what he writes about learning."

Pan Stanislav wanted to kneel down and kiss her feet Her charm and goodness not only disarmed him, but conquered him thoroughly.

"That I am annihilated is true," cried he, as if finishing some unexpressed thought with words. "You conquer me utterly."

She began to shake her head joyously. "Ei! I don't know; I am such a coward."

"You a coward? I will tell you an anecdote: In Belgium I knew two young ladies named Wauters, who had a pet cat, a mild creature, mild enough, it would seem, to be put to a wound. Afterward one of the young ladies received a tame hare as a gift. What do you think? The cat was so afraid that from terror he jumped on to every shelf and stove. One day the ladies went to walk; all at once they remembered that the cat was alone with the hare. 'But will not Matou hurt the hare?' 'Matou? Matou is so terrified that he is ready to go out of his skin!' And they walked on quietly. They came home an hour later. And guess what had happened? They found only the ears of the hare. That is precisely the relation of young ladies to us. They are afraid seemingly; but afterward nothing is left of us but ears."

And Pan Stanislav began to laugh, and Marynia with him; after a while he added, —

"I know that of me only ears will be left."

He did not tell the truth, however; for he felt that it would be otherwise. Marynia too, after thinking a while, said, —

"No; I have not such a character."

"That is better too; for I will tell you sincerely what conclusions I have drawn from my life observations: the greater egotism always conquers the less."

"Or the greater love yields to the less," answered Marynia.

"That comes out the same. As to me, I confess that I should like to hold some Herod, see, this way, in my hand" (here Pan Stanislav opened his fingers and then closed them into a fist); "but with such a dove as you, it is quite different. With you I think we shall have to fight to restrain you from too much self-abnegation, too much personal sacrifice. Such is your nature, and I know whom I take. For that matter all say so, and even Mashko, who is no Solomon, said: 'She may be unhappy with thee; thou with her, never.' And he is right. But I am curious to know how Mashko will be for his wife. He has a firm hand."

"But is he loved much?"

"Not so much as awhile ago, when a certain young lady coquetted with him."

"Yes; for he was n't so wicked as a certain 'Pan Stas.'"

"That will be a wonderful marriage. She is not ill-looking, though she is pale, and has red eyes. But Mashko marries for property. He admits that she does n't love him; and when that adventure with Gantovski took place (he is brave, too), he was certain that those ladies would choose the opportunity to break with him. Meanwhile it turned out just the opposite; and imagine, Mashko is now alarmed again, because everything moves as if on oil. It seems to him suspicious. There are certain strange things there; there exists also, as it seems, a Pan Kraslavski — God knows what there is not. The whole affair is stupid. There will be no happiness in it, — at least, not such as I picture to myself."

"And what do you picture to yourself?"

"Happiness in this, — to marry a reliable woman, like you, and see the future clearly."

"But I think it is in this, — to be loved; but that is not enough yet."

"What more?"

"To be worthy of that love, and to — "

Here Marynia was unable for a time to find words, but at last she said, —

"And to believe in a husband. and work with him."

## CHAPTER XXVIII.

Pan Stanislav was not mistaken. Everything went so favorably for Mashko, Pani and Panna Kraslavski acted so admirably, that he was more and more alarmed. At moments he laughed at this; and since he had had no secret from Pan Stanislav for some time, he said one day, with complete cynicism, —

"My dear, those are simply angels; but my hair stands on end, for something is hidden in this."

"Better thank the Lord God."

"They are too ideal; they are faultless; they are even without vanity. Yesterday, for example, I gave them to understand that I am an advocate only because to my thinking sons of the best families should undertake something in these times, be something. Guess what they answered? That that is as good a position as any other; that every employment is worthy in their eyes, provided it is work; and that only poor and empty natures could be ashamed of work. They shot out so many packages of commonplace that I wanted to answer with a sentence from copy-books, such as 'Honor is a steep cliff,' or something of that sort. Polanyetski, I tell thee there is something concealed there. I thought that it was papa, but it is not papa. I have news of him: he lives in Bordeaux; he calls himself De Langlais; and he has his own domestic hearth, not so much legally, as numerously, surrounded, which he maintains with a pension received from Pani Kraslavski."

"What harm is that to thee?"

"None whatever."

"If it is that way, they are unhappy women, — that is all."

"True; but if their income answers to the misfortune? Remember that I have burdens. Besides, seest thou, if they are such women as they pretend, and if, also, they are rich, I am ready to fall in love really, and that would be stupid; if it appears that they have nothing, or little, I am ready, also, to fall in love, and that would be still more stupid. She has charms for me."

"No; that would be the one wise thing in every case. But think of thyself, Mashko, a little of me and the Plavitskis. It is known to thee that I have not the habit of being mild in those matters, and the dates of payment are approaching."

"I'll fire up the boiler once more with credit. For that matter, thou and they have a mortgage on Kremen. In a couple of days there will be a betrothal party at Pani Kraslavski's, after which I hope to learn something reliable."

Here Mashko began a monologue, —

"But that a positive man, such as I am, should go into a forest in this way, passes belief. On the other hand, there is not a man, even among those who know best how every one stands, who would let himself doubt of Pani Kraslavski's property. And they are so noble!"

"Thy fears are probably baseless," interrupted Pan Stanislav, with certain impatience. "But thou, my dear fellow, art not positive in any sense, for thou hast been always pretending, and art pretending still, instead of looking to that which gives thee bread."

A few days later the betrothal party took place in fact. Marynia was there; for Pani Kraslavski, who liked Plavitski, whose relatives were known to her, did not avoid association with him as she did with the Bigiels. Mashko brought such of his acquaintances as had well-known names. They had monocles on their eyes, and their hair parted in the middle; for the greater part very young, and mainly not very quick-witted. Among them were the five brothers Vyj, who were called Mizio, Kizio, Bizio, Brelochek, and Tatus. They were nicknamed the five sleeping brothers, since they felt the impulses of life in their legs exclusively, and were active only in the carnival, but became perfectly torpid, at least in a mental sense, during Lent. Bukatski loved them, and amused himself with them. Baron Kot was there, who, because he had heard something from some one of a certain ancient Kot of Dembna, added always, when he was presented, "of Dembna," and who always answered everything that was said to him with: "*Quelle drôle d'histoire!*" Mashko was on the footing of *thou* with all these, though he treated them with a certain species of disregard, as well as Kopovski, — a young man with a splendid ideal head, and also splendid eyes without thought. Pan Stanislav and

Kresovski represented the category of Mashko's more clever friends. Pani Kraslavski had invited a number of ladies with daughters, among whom the five brothers circled carelessly and coolly, and whose maiden hearts fluttered at the approach of Kopovski, caring less for his mental resemblance to Hamlet, resting on this, — that if not he, his brain might be put into "a nutshell." A number of dignified bald heads completed the company.

Panna Kraslavski was dressed in white; in spite of her red eyes, she looked alluring. There was in her, indeed, a certain womanly charm, resting on a wonderful, almost dreamy repose. She recalled somewhat the figures of Perugini. At times she grew bright, like an alabaster lamp, in which a flame flashes up on a sudden; after a while she paled again, but paled not without charm. Dressed in a thin white robe, she seemed more shapely than usual. Pan Stanislav, looking at her, thought that she might have a heart which was dry enough, and a dry enough head, but she could be a genteel wife, especially for Mashko, who valued social gentility above everything else. Their manner toward each other seemed like a cool and pale day, in which the sun does not burn, but in which also a storm is not threatening. They were sitting at the end of the drawing-room, not too near, but also not too far, from the rest of the company; they occupied themselves with each other no more and no less than was proper. In his conversation with her as much feeling was evident as was required, but, above all, the wish to appear a "correct" betrothed; she paid him on her part in the same coin. They smiled at each other in a friendly way. He, as the future leader and head of the house, spoke more than she; sometimes they looked into each other's eyes, — in a word, they formed the most correct and exemplary couple of betrothed people that could be imagined, in the society sense of the term. "I should not have held out," said Pan Stanislav to himself. Suddenly he remembered that while she was sitting there in conventional repose, white, smiling, the poor little doctor, who could not "tear his soul from her," was in equal repose somewhere between the tropics turning to dust, under the ground, forgotten, as if he had never existed; and anger bore him away. Not only did he feel contempt for the heart of Mashko's betrothed, but that repose of hers seemed now bad taste to him, — a species of spiritual deadness, which once had been fashionable, and which, since they saw in it something demonic, the poets had struck with their thunderbolts, and which, in time, had grown vulgar, and dropped to be moral nonentity and folly. "First of all, she is a goose, and, moreover, a goose with no heart," thought Pan Stanislav. At that moment Mashko's alarm at the noble conduct of those ladies grew clear to him to such a degree that Mashko rose in his esteem as a man of acuteness.

Then he fell to comparing his own betrothed with Panna Kraslavski, and said to himself with great satisfaction, "Marynia is a different species altogether." He felt that he was resting mentally while looking at her. In so much as the other seemed, as it were, an artificial plant, reared, not in broad fresh currents of air, but under glass, in that much did there issue from this one life and warmth, and still the comparison came out to the advantage of Marynia, even in respect to society. Pan Stanislav did not overlook altogether "distinction," so-called, understanding that, if not always, it frequently answers to a certain mental finish, especially in women. Looking now at one, now at the other, he came to the conviction that that finish which Panna Kraslavski had was something acquired and enslaving, with Marynia it was innate. In the one it was a garment thrown on outside; in the other, the soul, — a kind of natural trait in a species ennobled through long ages of culture. Taking from Bukatski's views as many as he needed, — that is, as many as were to the point, — Pan Stanislav remembered that he had said frequently that women, without reference to their origin, are divided into patricians, who have culture, principles, and spiritual needs, which have entered the blood, and parvenues, who dress in them, as in mantillas, to go visiting. At present, while looking at the noble profile of Marynia, Pan Stanislav thought, with the vanity of a little townsman who is marrying a princess, that he was taking a patrician in the high sense of the word; and, besides, a very beautiful patrician.

Frequently women need only some field, and a little luck, to bloom forth. Marynia, who seemed almost ugly to Pan Stanislav when he was returning from the burial of Litka, astonished him now, at times, with her beauty. Near her Panna Kraslavski seemed like a faded robe near a new one; and if the fortune of Panna Plavitski had been on a level with her looks, she would have passed, beyond doubt, for a beauty. As it was, the five brothers, putting their glasses on their equine noses, looked at her with a certain admiration; and Baron Kot, of Dembna, declared confidentially that her betrothal was real luck, for had it not taken place, who knows but he might have rushed in.

Pan Stanislav could note also that evening one trait of his own character which he had not suspected, — jealousy. Since he was convinced that Marynia was a perfectly reliable woman, who might be trusted blindly, that jealousy was simply illogical. In his time he had been jealous of Mashko, and that could be understood; but now he could not explain why Kopovski, for example, with his head of an archangel and his brains of a bird, could annoy him, just because he sat next to Marynia, and doubtless was asking her more or less pertinent questions, to which she was answering more or less agreeably. At first he reproached himself. "Still, it would be difficult to ask her not to speak to him!" Afterward he found that Marynia turned to Kopovski too frequently, and answered too agreeably. At supper, while sitting next her, he was silent and irritated; and when she asked the reason, he answered most inappropriately, —

"I have no wish to spoil the impression which Pan Kopovski produced on you."

But she was pleased that he was jealous; contracting the corners of her mouth to suppress laughter, and looking at him sedately, she answered, —

"Do you find, too, that there is something uncommon in Pan Kopovski?"

"Of course, of course! When he walks the streets even, it seems that he is carrying his head into fresh air, lest the moths might devour it."

The corners of Marynia's mouth bore the test, but her eyes laughed evidently; at last, unable to endure, she said, in a low voice, —

"Outrageously jealous!"

"I? Not the least!"

"Well, I will give you an extract from our conversation. You know that yesterday there was a case of catalepsy during the concert; to-day they were talking of that near us; then, among other things, I asked Pan Kopovski if he had seen the cataleptic person. Do you know what he answered? 'Each of us may have different convictions.' Well, now, isn't he uncommon?"

Pan Stanislav was pacified, and began to laugh.

"But I tell you that he simply does n't understand what is said to him, and answers anything."

They passed the rest of the evening with each other in good agreement. At the time of parting, when the Plavitskis, having a carriage with seats for only two persons, were unable to take Pan Stanislav, Marynia turned to him and inquired, —

"Will the cross, whimsical man come to-morrow to dine with us?"

"He will, for he loves," answered Pan Stanislav, covering her feet with the robe.

She whispered into his ear, as it were great news, "And I too."

And although he at the moment of speaking was perfectly sincere, she spoke more truth. Mashko conducted Pan Stanislav home. On the road they talked of the reception. Mashko said that before the arrival of guests he had tried to speak to Pani Kraslavski of business, but had not succeeded.

"There was a moment," said he, "when I thought to put the question plainly, dressing it of course in the most delicate form. But I was afraid. Finally, why have I doubts of the dower of my betrothed? Only because those ladies treat me with more consideration than I expected. As a humor, that is very good; but I fear to push matters too far, for suppose that my fears turn out vain, suppose they have money really, and are incensed because my curiosity is too selfish. It is necessary to count with this also, for I may be wrecked at the harbor."

"Well, then," answered Pan Stanislav, "admit this, and for that matter it is likely that they have; but if it should turn out that they have not, what then? Hast a plan ready? Wilt thou break with Panna Kraslavski, or wilt thou marry her?"

"I will not break with her in any case, for I should not gain by it. If my marriage does not take place, I shall be a bankrupt. But if it does, I will state my financial position precisely, and suppose that Panna Kraslavski will break with me."

"But if she does not, and has no money?"

"I shall love her, and come to terms with my creditors. I shall cease to 'pretend,' as thy phrase is, and try to win bread for us both; I am not a bad advocate, as thou knowest."

"That is fairly good," answered Pan Stanislav, "but that does not pacify me touching the Plavitskis and myself."

"Thou and they are in a better position than others, for ye have a lien on Kremen. In a given case thou wilt take everything in thy firm grasp, and squeeze out something. It is worse for those who have trusted my word; and I tell thee to thy eyes that I am concerned more for them. I had, and I have great credit even now. That is my tender point. But if they give me time, I will come out somehow. If I had a little happiness at home, and a motive there for labor —"

They came now to Pan Stanislav's house, so Mashko did not finish his thought. At the moment of parting, however, he said suddenly, —

"Listen to me. In thy eyes I am somewhat crooked; I am much less so than seems to thee. I have *pretended*, as thou sayst, it is true! I had to wriggle out, like an eel, and in those wrigglings I slipped sometimes from the beaten road. But I am tired, and tell thee plainly that I wish a little happiness, for I have not had it. Therefore I wanted to marry thy betrothed, though she is without property. As to Panna Kraslavski, dost thou know that there are moments when I should prefer that she had nothing, but, to make up, that she would not drop me when she knows that I too have nothing. I say this sincerely — and now good-night."

"Well," said Pan Stanislav to himself, "this is something new in Mashko." And he entered the gate. Standing at the door, he was astonished to hear the piano in his apartments. The servant said that Bigiel had been waiting two hours for him.

Pan Stanislav was alarmed, but thought that if something unfavorable had caused his presence, he would not play on the piano. In fact, it turned out that Bigiel was in haste merely to get Pan Stanislav's signature for an affair which had to be finished early next morning.

"Thou mightest have left the paper, and gone to bed," said Pan Stanislav.

"I slept awhile on thy sofa, then sat at the piano. Once I played on the piano as well as on the violin, but now my fingers are clumsy. Thy Marynia plays probably; such music in the house is a nice thing."

Pan Stanislav laughed with a sincere, well-wishing laugh.

"My Marynia? My Marynia possesses the evangelical talent: her left hand does not know what her right hand is doing. Poor dear woman! She has no pretensions; and she plays only when I beg her to do so."

"Thou art as it were laughing at her," said Bigiel; "but only those who are in love laugh in that way."

"Because I am in love most completely. At least it seems so now to me; and in general I must say that it seems so to me oftener and oftener. Wilt thou have tea?"

"Yes. Thou hast come from Pani Kraslavski's?"

"I have."

"How is Mashko? Will he struggle to shore?"

"I parted with him a moment ago. He came with me to the gate. He says things at times that I should not expect from him."

Pan Stanislav, glad to have some one to talk with, and feeling the need of intimate converse, began to tell what he had heard from Mashko; and how much he was astonished at finding a man of romantic nature under the skin of a person of his kind.

"Mashko is not a bad man," said Bigiel. "He is only on the road to various evasions; and the cause of that is his vanity and respect for appearances. But, on the other hand, that respect for appearances saves him from final fall. As to the man of romance, which thou hast found in him —"

Here Bigiel cut off the end of a cigar, lighted it with great deliberation, wrinkling his brows at the same time, and, sitting down comfortably, continued, —

"Bukatski would have given on that subject ten ironical paradoxes about our society. Now something stuck in my head that he told me, when he attacked us because always we love some one or something. It seems to him that this is foolish and purposeless; but I see in this a great trait. It is necessary to become something in the world; and what have we? Money we have not; intellect, so-so; the gift of making our way in a position, not greatly; management, little. We have in truth this yet, — that almost involuntarily, through some general disposition, we love something or somebody; and if we do not love, we feel the need of love. Thou knowest that I am a man of deliberation and a merchant, hence I speak soberly. I call attention to this because of Bukatski. Mashko, for instance, in some other country, would be a rogue from under a dark star; and I know many such. But here even beneath the trickster thou canst scratch to the man; and that is simple, for, in the last instance, while a man has some spark in his breast yet, he is not a beast utterly; and with us he has the spark, precisely for this reason, that he loves something."

"Thou bringest Vaskovski to my mind. What thou art saying is not far from his views concerning the mission of the youngest of the Aryans."

"What is Vaskovski to me? I say what I think. I know one thing: take that from us, and we should fly apart, like a barrel without hoops."

"Well, listen to what I will tell thee. This is a thing decided in my mind rather long since. To love, or not to love some one, is a personal question; but I understand that it is needful to love something in life. I too have meditated over this. After the death of that child, I felt that the devil had taken certain sides of me; sometimes I feel that yet. Not to-day; but there are times — how can I tell thee? — times of ebb, exhaustion, doubts. And if, in spite of this, I marry, it is because I understand that it is necessary to have a living and strong foundation under a more general love."

"For that, and not for that," answered Bigiel the inexorable in judgment, "for thou are marrying not at all from purely mental reasons. Thou art taking a comely and honest young woman, to whom thou art attracted; and do not persuade thyself that it is otherwise, or thou wilt begin to pretend. My dear friend, every man has these doubts before marrying. I, as thou seest, am no philosopher; but ten times a day I asked myself before marriage, if I loved my future wife well enough, if I loved her as was necessary, had I not too little soul in the matter, and too many doubts? God knows what! Afterward I married a good woman, and it was well for us. It will be well for you too, if ye take things simply; but that endless searching in the mind and looking for certain secrets of the heart is folly, God knows."

"Maybe it is folly. I too have no great love for lying on my back and analyzing from morn in till night; but I cannot help seeing facts."

"What facts?"

"Such facts, for example, as this, that my feeling is not what it was at first. I think that it will be; I acknowledge that it is going to that. I marry in spite of these observations, as if they did not exist; but I make them."

"Thou art free to do so."

"And see what I think besides: still it is necessary that the windows of a house should look out on the sun; otherwise it will be cold in the dwelling."

"Thou hast said well," answered Bigiel.

## CHAPTER XXIX.

MEANWHILE winter began to break; the end of Lent was approaching, and with it the time of marriage for Pan Stanislav, as well as Mashko. Bukatski, invited as a groomsman to the former, wrote to him among other things as follows, —

"To thrust forth the all-creative energy from its universal condition, — that is, from a condition of perfect repose, — and force it by means of marriages concluded on earth to incarnate itself in more or less squalling particulars which require cradles and which amuse themselves by holding the great toe in the mouth, is a crime. Still I will come, because stoves are better with you than in this place."

In fact, he came a week before the holidays, and brought as a gift to Pan Stanislav a sheet of parchment ornamented splendidly with something in the style of a grave hour-glass, on which was the inscription, "Stanislav Polanyetski, after a long and grievous bachelorhood."

Pan Stanislav, whom the parchment pleased, took it next day about noon to Marynia. He forgot, however, that it was Sunday, and felt, as it were, disappointed, at finding Marynia with her hat on.

"Are you going out?" inquired he.

"Yes. To church. To-day is Sunday."

"Ah, Sunday! True. But I thought that we should sit here together. It would be so agreeable."

She raised her calm blue eyes to him, and said with simplicity, "But the service of God?"

Pan Stanislav received these words at once as he would have received any other, not foreseeing that, in the spiritual process which he was to pass through later on, they would play a certain rôle by reason of their directness, and said as if repeating mechanically, —

"You say the service of God. Very well! I have time; let us go together."

Marynia received this offer with great satisfaction.

"I am the happier," said she, on the way, "the more I love God."

"That, too, is the mark of a good nature; some persons think of God only as a terror."

And in the church that came again to his mind of which he had thought during his first visit to Kremen, when he was at the church in Vantory, with old Plavitski: "Destruction takes all philosophies and systems, one after another; but Mass is celebrated as of old." It seemed to him that in that there was something which passed comprehension. He who, because of Litka, had come in contact with death in a manner most painful, returned to those dark problems whenever he happened to be in a cemetery, or a church at Mass, or in any circumstances whatever in which something took place which had no connection with the current business of life, but was shrouded in that future beyond the grave. He was struck by this thought, — how much is done in this life for that future; and how, in spite of all philosophizing and doubt, people live as if that future were entirely beyond question; how much of petty personal egotisms are sacrificed for it; how many philanthropic deeds are performed; how asylums, hospitals, retreats, churches are built, and all on an account payable beyond the grave only.

He was struck still more by another thought, — that to be reconciled with life really, it is necessary to be reconciled with death first; and that without faith in something beyond the grave this reconciliation is simply impossible. But if you have faith the question drops away, as if it had never existed. "Let the devils take mourning; let us rejoice;" for if this is true, what more can be desired? Is there before one merely the view of some new existence, in the poorest case, wonderfully curious, — even that certainty amounts to peace and quiet. Pan Stanislav had an example of that, then, in Marynia. Because she was somewhat short-sighted, she held her head bent over the book; but when at moments she raised it, he saw a face so calm, so full of something like that repose which a flower has, and so serene, that it was simply angelic. "That is a happy woman, and she will be happy always," said he to himself. "And, besides, she has sense, for if, on the opposite side, there were at least certainty, there would be also that satisfaction which truth gives; but to torture one's self for the sake of various marks of interrogation is pure folly."

On the way home, Pan Stanislav, thinking continually of this expression of Marynia's, said, —

"In the church you looked like some profile of Fra Angelico; you had a face which was indeed happy."

"For I am happy at present. And do you know why? Because I am better than I was. I felt at one time offended in heart, and I was dissatisfied; I had no hope before me, and all these put together formed such suffering that it was terrible. It is said that misfortune ennobles chosen souls, but I am not a chosen soul. For that matter, misfortune may ennoble, but suffering, offence, ill-will, destroy. They are like poison."

"Did you hate me much then?"

Marynia looked at him and answered, "I hated you so much that for whole days I thought of you only."

"Mashko has wit; he described this once thus to me· 'She would rather hate you than love me.'"

"Oi! that I would rather, is true."

Thus conversing, they reached the house. Pan Stanislav had time then to unroll his parchment hour-glass and show it to Marynia; but the idea did not please her. She looked on marriage not only from the point of view of the heart, but of religion. "With such things there is no jesting," said she; and after a while she confessed to Pan Stanislav that she was offended with Bukatski.

After dinner Bukatski came. During those few months of his stay in Italy he had become still thinner, which was a proof against the efficacy of "chianti" for catarrh of the stomach. His nose, with its thinness, reminded one of a knife-edge; his humorous face, smiling with irony, had become, as it were, porcelain, and was no larger than the fist of a grown man. He was related both to Pan Stanislav and Marynia; hence he said what he pleased in their presence. From the threshold almost, he declared to them that, in view of the increasing number of mental deviations in the world at present, he could only regret, but did not wonder, that they were affianced. He had come, it is true, in the hope that he would be able to save them, but he saw now that he was late, and that nothing was left but resignation. Marynia was indignant on hearing this; but Pan Stanislav, who loved him, said, —

"Preserve thy conceit for the wedding speech, for thou must make one; and now tell us how our professor is."

"He has grown disturbed in mind seriously," replied Bukatski.

"Do not jest in that way," said Marynia.

"And so much without cause," added Pan Stanislav.

But Bukatski continued, with equal seriousness: "Professor Vaskovski is disturbed in mind, and here are my proofs for you: First, he walks through Rome without a cap, or rather, he walked, for he is in Perugia at present; second, he attacked a refined young English lady, and proved to her that the English are Christians in private life only, — that the relations of England to Ireland are not Christian; third, he is printing a pamphlet, in which he shows that the mission of reviving and renewing history with the spirit of Christ is committed to the youngest of the Aryans. Confess that these are proofs."

"We knew these ways before his departure; if nothing more threatens the professor, we hope to see him in good health."

"He does not think of returning."

Pan Stanislav took out his note-book, wrote some words with a pencil, and, giving them to Marynia, said, —

"Read, and tell me if that is good."

"If thou write in my presence, I withdraw," said Bukatski.

"No, no! this is no secret."

Marynia became as red as a cherry from delight, and, as if not wishing to believe her eyes, asked, —

"Is that true? It is not."

"That depends on you," answered Pan Stanislav.

"Ah, Pan Stas! I did not even dream of that. I must tell papa. I must."

And she ran out of the room.

"If I were a poet, I would hang myself," said Bukatski.

"Why?"

"For if a couple of words, jotted down by the hand of a partner in the house of Bigiel and Company, can produce more impression than the most beautiful sonnet, it is better to be a miller boy than a poet."

But Marynia, in the rapture of her joy, forgot the note-book, so Pan Stanislav showed it to Bukatski, saying, "Read."

Bukatski read: —

"After the wedding Venice, Florence, Rome, Naples. Is that well?"

"Then it's a journey to Italy?"

"Yes. Imagine, she has not been abroad in her life; and Italy has always seemed to her an enchanted land, which she has not even dreamed of seeing. That is an immense delight for her; and what the deuce wonder is there, if I think out a little pleasure for her?"

"Love and Italy! O God, how many times Thou hast looked on that! All that love is as old as the world."

"Not true! Fall in love, and see if thou 'lt find something new in it."

"My beloved friend, the question is not in this, that I do not love yet, but in this, — that I love no longer. Years ago I dug that sphinx out of the sand, and it is no longer a riddle to me."

"Bukatski, get married."

"I cannot. My sight is too faint, and my stomach too weak."

"What hindrance in that?"

"Oh, seest thou, a woman is like a sheet of paper. An angel writes on one side, a devil on the other; the paper is cut through, the words blend, and such a hash is made that I can neither read nor digest it."

"To live all thy life on conceits!"

"I shall die, as well as thou, who art marrying. It seems to us that we think of death, but it thinks more of us."

At that moment Marynia came in with her father, who embraced Pan Stanislav, and said, —

"Marynia tells me that 't is thy wish to go to Italy after the wedding."

"If my future lady will consent."

"Thy future lady will not only consent," answered Marynia, "but she has lost her head from delight, and wants to jump through the room, as if she were ten years of age."

To which Plavitski answered, "If the cross of a solitary old man can be of use in your distant journey, I will bless you."

And he raised his eyes and his hand toward heaven, to the unspeakable delight of Bukatski; but Marynia drew down the raised hand, and, kissing it, said with laughter, —

"There will be time for that, papa ; we are going away only after the wedding."

"And, speaking plainly," added Bukatski, "then there will be a buying of tickets, and giving baggage to be weighed, and starting, — nothing more."

To this Plavitski turned to the cynic, and said, with a certain unction. —

"Have you come to this, — that you look on the blessing of a lonely old man and a father as superfluous?"

Bukatski, instead of an answer, embraced Plavitski, kissed him near the waistcoat, and said, —

"But would the 'lonely old man' not play piquet, so as to let those two mad heads talk themselves out?"

"But with a rubicon?" asked Plavitski.

"With anything you like." Then he turned to the young couple: "Hire me as a guide to Italy."

"I do not think of it," answered Pan Stanislav. "I have been in Belgium and France, no farther. Italy I know not; but I want to see what will interest us, not what may interest thee. I have seen men such as thou art, and I know that through over-refinement they go so far that they love not art, but their own knowledge of it."

Here Pan Stanislav continued the talk with Marynia.

"Yes, they go so far that they lose the feeling of great, simple art, and seek something to occupy their sated taste, and exhibit their critical knowledge. They do not see trees; they search simply for knots. The greatest things which we are going to admire do not concern them, but some of the smallest things, of which no one has heard; they dig names out of obscurity, occupy themselves in one way or another, persuade themselves and others that things inferior and of less use surpass in interest the better and more perfect. Under his guidance we might not see whole churches, but we might see various things which would have to be looked at through cracks. I call all this surfeit, abuse, over-refinement, and we are simply people."

Marynia looked at him with pride, as if she would say, "Oh, that is what is called speaking!" Her pride increased when Bukatski said, —

"Thou art quite right."

But she was indignant when he added, —

"And if thou wert not right, I could not win before the tribunal."

"I beg pardon," said Marynia; "I am not blinded in any way."

"But I am not an art critic at all."

"On the contrary, you are."

"If I am, then, I declare that knowledge embraces a greater number of details, but does not prevent a love of great art; and believe not Pan Stanislav, but me."

"No; I prefer to believe him."

"That was to be foreseen."

Marynia looked now at one, now at the other, with a somewhat anxious face. Meanwhile Plavitski came with cards. The betrothed walked through the rooms hand in hand; Bukatski began to be wearied, and grew more and more so. Toward the end of the evening the humor which animated him died out; his small face became still smaller, his nose sharper, and he looked like a dried leaf. When he went out with Pan Stanislav, the latter inquired, —

"Somehow thou wert not so vivacious?"

"I am like a machine: while I have fuel within, I move; but in the evening, when the morning supply is exhausted, I stop."

Pan Stanislav looked at him carefully. "What is thy fuel?"

"There are various kinds of coal. Come to me: I will give thee a cup of good coffee; that will enliven us."

"Listen! this is a delicate question, but some one told me that thou hast been taking morphine this long time."

"For a very short time," answered Bukatski; "if thou could only know what horizons it opens."

"And it kills — Fear God!"

"And kills! Tell me sincerely, has this ever occurred to thee, that it is possible to have a yearning for death?"

"No; I understand just the opposite."

"But I will give thee neither morphine nor opium," said Bukatski, at length; "only good coffee and a bottle of honest Bordeaux. That will be an innocent orgy."

After some time they arrived at Bukatski's. It was the dwelling of a man of real wealth, seemingly, somewhat uninhabited, but full of small things connected with art and pictures and drawings. Lamps were burning in a number of rooms, for Bukatski could not endure darkness, even in time of sleep.

The "Bordeaux" was found promptly, and under the machine for coffee a blue flame was soon burning. Bukatski stretched himself on the sofa, and said, all at once, —

"Perhaps thou wilt not admit, since thou seest me such a filigree, that I have no fear of death."

"This one thing I have at times admitted, that thou art jesting and jesting, deceiving thyself and others, while really the joke is not in thee, and this is all artificial."

"The folly of people amuses me somewhat."

"But if thou think thyself wise, why arrange life so vainly?" Here Pan Stanislav looked around on bric-à-brac, on pictures, and added, "In all this surrounding thou art still living vainly."

"Vainly enough."

"Thou art of those who *pretend.* What a disease in this society! Thou art posing, and that is the whole question."

"Sometimes. But, for that matter, it becomes natural."

Under the influence of "Bordeaux" Bukatski grew animated gradually, and became more talkative, though cheerfulness did not return to him.

"Seest thou," said he, "one thing, — I do not pretend. All which I myself could tell, or which another could tell me, I have thought out, and said long since to my soul. I lead the most stupid and the vainest life possible. Around me is immense nothingness, which I fear, and which I fence out with this lumber which thou seest in this room; I do this so as to fear less. Not to fear death is another thing, for after death there are neither feelings nor thoughts. I shall become, then, a part also of nothingness; but to feel it, while one is alive, to know of it, to give account to one's self of it, as God lives, there can be nothing more abject. Moreover, the condition of my health is really bad, and takes from me every energy. I have no fuel in myself, therefore I add it. There is less in this of posing and pretending than thou wilt admit. When I have given myself fuel, I take life in its humorous aspect; I follow the example of the sick man, who lies on the side on which he lies with most comfort. For me there is most comfort thus. That the position is artificial, I admit; every other, however, would be more painful. And see, the subject is exhausted."

"If thou would undertake some work."

"Give me peace. To begin with, I know a multitude of things, but I don't understand anything; second, I am sick; third, tell a paralytic to walk a good deal when he cannot use his legs. The subject is exhausted! Drink that wine there, and let us talk about thee. That is a good lady, Panna Plavitski; and thou art doing well to marry her. What I said to thee there in the daytime does not count. She is a good lady, and loves thee."

Here Bukatski, enlivened and roused evidently by the wine, began to speak hurriedly.

"What I say in the daytime does not count. Now it is night; let us drink wine, and a moment of more sincerity comes. Dost wish more wine, or coffee? I like this odor; one should mix Mocha and Ceylon in equal parts. Now comes a time of more sincerity! Knowest thou what I think at bottom? I have no clear idea of what happiness fame may give, for I do not possess it; and since the Ephesian temple is fired, there is no opening to fame before me. I admit, however, so, to myself, that the amount of it might be eaten by a mouse, not merely on an empty stomach, but after a good meal in a pantry. But I know what property is, for I have a little of it; I know what travelling is, for I have wandered; I know what freedom is, for I am free; I know what women are — oi, devil take it! — too well, and I know what books are. Besides, in this chamber, I have a few pictures, a few drawings, a little porcelain. Now listen to what I will say to thee: All this is nothing; all is vanity, folly, dust, in comparison with one heart which loves. This is the result of my observations; only I have come to it at the end, while normal men reach it at the beginning."

Here he began to stir the coffee feverishly with a spoon; and Pan Stanislav, who was very lively, sprang up and said, —

"And thou, O beast! what didst thou say some months since, — that thou wert going to Italy because there no one loved thee, and thou didst love no one? Dost remember? Thou 'lt deny, perhaps."

"But what did I say this afternoon to thy betrothed? That thou and she had gone mad; and now I say that thou art doing well. Dost wish logic of me? To talk and to say something are two different things. But now I am more sincere, for I have drunk half a bottle of wine."

Pan Stanislav began to walk through the room and repeat: "But, as God lives, it is fabulous! See what the root of the matter is, and what they all say when cornered."

"To love is good, but there is something still better, — that is, to be loved. There is nothing above that! As to me, I would give for it all these; but it is not worth while to talk of me. Life is a comedy badly written, and without talent: even that which pains terribly is sometimes like a poor melodrama; but in life, if there be anything good, it is to be loved. Imagine to thyself, I have not known that, and thou hast found it without seeking."

"Do not say so, for thou knowest not how it came to me."

"I know; Vaskovski told me. That, however, is all one. The question is this, — thou hast known how to value it."

"Well, what dost thou wish? I understand that I am loved a little; hence I marry, and that is the end of the matter."

Thereupon Bukatski put his hand on Pan Stanislav's shoulder.

"No, Polanyetski; I am a fool in respect to myself, but not a bad observer of what is passing around me. That is not the end, but the beginning. Most men say, as thou hast, 'I marry, — that is the end;' and most men deceive themselves."

"That philosophy I do not understand."

"But thou seest what the question is? It is not enough to take a woman; a man should give himself to her also, and should feel that he does so. Dost understand?"

"Not greatly."

"Well, thou art feigning simplicity. She should not only feel herself owned, but an owner. A soul for a soul! otherwise a life may be lost. Marriages are good or bad. Mashko's will be bad for twenty reasons, and among others for this, of which I wish to speak."

"He is of another opinion. But, as God lives, it is a pity that thou art not married, since thou hast such a sound understanding of how married life should be."

"If to understand and to act according to that understanding were the same, there would not be the various, very various events, from which the bones ache in all of us. For that matter, imagine me marrying."

Here Bukatski began to laugh with his thin little voice. Joyfulness returned to him on a sudden, and with it the vision of things on the comic side.

"Thou wilt be ridiculous; but what should I be? Something to split one's sides at. What a moment that is! Thou wilt see in two weeks. For instance, how thou wilt dress for church. Here, love, beating of the heart, solemn thoughts, a new epoch in life; there, the gardener, with flowers, a dress-coat, lost studs, the tying of a cravat, the drawing on of patent-leather boots, — all at one time, one chaos, one confusion. Deliver me, angels of paradise! I have compassion on thee, my dear friend; and do thou, I beg, not take seriously what I say. There is a new moon now, and I have a mania for uttering commonplace sentiment at the new moon. All folly! — the new moon, nothing more! I have grown as soft-hearted as a ewe who has lost her first lamb; and may the cough split me, if I have n't uttered commonplace!"

But Pan Stanislav attacked him: "I have seen many vain things; but knowest thou what seems to me vainest in thee and those like thee? Thou and they, who absolve yourselves from everything, recognize nothing above you, and fear like fire every honest truth, for the one reason that some one might sometime declare it. How bad this is words cannot tell. As to thee, my dear friend, thou wert sincerer a while since than now. Again, thou 'rt a poodle, dancing on two legs; but I tell thee that ten like thee could not show me that I have not won a great prize in the lottery."

He took farewell of Bukatski with a certain anger; on the road home, however, he grew pacified and repeated continually: "See where the truth is; see what Mashko, and even Bukatski, says, when ready to be sincere; but I have won simply a great prize, and I will not waste what I have won."

When he entered his lodgings and saw Litka's photograph, he exclaimed, "My dearest kitten!" Up to the moment of sleeping he thought of Marynia with pleasure, and with the calmness of a man who feels that some great problem of life has been settled decisively, and settled well. For, in spite of Bukatski's words, he was convinced that, since he was going to marry, all would be decided and ended by that one act.

## CHAPTER XXX.

The "catastrophe," as Bukatski called it, came at last. Pan Stanislav learned by experience that if in life there are many days in which a man cannot seize his own thoughts, to such belong above all the day of his marriage. At times a number of these thoughts circled in his brain at one moment, and were so indefinite, that, speaking accurately, they were rather unconscious impressions than thoughts. He felt that a new epoch in life was beginning, that he was assuming great obligations which he ought to fulfil conscientiously and seriously; and at the same time, but exactly at the same time, he wondered that the carriage was n't coming yet, and expressed his astonishment in the form of a threat: "If those scoundrels are late, I'll break their necks for them." At moments a solemn, and, as it were, noble fear of that future for which he had assumed responsibility was mastering him; he felt within him a certain elevation, and in this feeling of elevation he began to lather his beard, and he thought whether on such an exceptional day it would not be exceptionally worth while to bring in a barber to his somewhat dishevelled hair. Marynia at the same time was at the basis of all his impressions. He saw her, as if present. He thought: "At this moment, she too is dressing, she is standing in her chamber in front of the mirror, she is talking to her maid, her soul is flying toward me, and her heart beats unquietly." That instant tenderness seized him and he said to himself, "But have no fear, honest soul, for, as God lives, I will not wrong thee;" and he saw himself in the future, kind, considerate, so that he began to look with a certain emotion at the patent-leather boots standing near the armchair, on which his wedding-suit was lying. He repeated from time to time too, "If to marry, then marry!" He said to himself that he was stupid to hesitate, for another such Marynia there was not on earth; he felt that he loved her, and thought at the same time that the weather was not bad, but that perhaps rain might fall; that it might be cold in the Church of the Visitation; that in an hour he would be kneeling by Marynia, that a white necktie is safer knotted than pinned; that marriage is indeed the most important ceremony in life; that there is in it something sacred, and that one must not lose one's head anyhow, for in an hour it will be over; to-morrow they will depart, and then the normal quiet life of husband and wife will begin.

These thoughts, however, flew away at moments like a flock of sparrows, into which some one has fired from behind a hedge suddenly, and it grew empty in Pan Stanislav's head. Then phrases of this kind came to his lips mechanically: "The eighth of April — to-morrow will be Wednesday! to-morrow will be Wednesday! my watch! to-morrow will be Wednesday!" Later he roused himself, repeated, "One must be an idiot!" and the scattered birds flew back again in a whole flock to his head, and began to whirl around in it.

Meanwhile Abdulski, the agent of the house of Polanyetski, Bigiel, and Company came in. He was to be the second groomsman, with Bukatski as first. Being a Tartar by origin and a man of dark complexion, though good-looking, he seemed so handsome in the dress-coat and white cravat that Pan Stanislav expressed the hope that surely he would marry soon. Abdulski answered, —

"The soul would to paradise;" then he commenced a pantomime, intended to represent the counting of money, and began to speak of the Bigiels. All their children wanted to be at the marriage. The Bigiels decided to take only the two elder ones; from this arose disagreements and difference of opinion, expressed on Pani Bigiel's side by means of slaps. Pan Stanislav, who was a great children's man, was exceedingly indignant at this, and said, —

"I'll play a trick on the Bigiels. Have they gone already?"

"They were just going."

"That is well; I will run in there on the way to Plavitski's, take all the children, and pour them out before Pani Bigiel and my affianced."

Abdulski expressed the conviction that Pan Stanislav would not do so; but he merely confirmed him thereby in his plan all the more. In fact, when he entered the carriage, they drove for the children directly. The governess, knowing Pan Stanislav's relations with the family, dared not oppose him; and half an hour later, Pan Stanislav, to the great consternation of Pani Bigiel, entered Plavitski's lodgings at the head of a whole flock of little Bigiels, in their every-day clothing, with collars awry, hair disarranged for the greater part, and faces half happy, half frightened, and, hurrying up to Marynia, he said, kissing her hands already enclosed in white gloves,—

"They wanted to wrong the children. Say that I did well."

This proof of his kind heart entertained and pleased Marynia; hence she was glad from her whole soul to see the children, and even glad of this,—that the assembled guests considered her future husband an original,—and glad because Pani Bigiel, straightening the crooked collars hurriedly, said in her worry,—

"What's to be done with such a madman?"

Somewhat of this opinion too was old Plavitski. But Pan Stanislav and Marynia were occupied for the moment with each other so exclusively that everything else vanished from their eyes. The hearts of both beat a little unquietly. He looked at her with a certain admiration. All in white, from her slippers to her gloves, with a green wreath on her head, and a long veil, she seemed to him other than usual. There was in her something uncommonly solemn, as in the dead Litka. Pan Stanislav did not make, it is true, that comparison; but he felt that this white Marynia, if not more remote from him, made him hesitate more than she of yesterday, arrayed in her ordinary costume. Withal she seemed less comely than usual, for the wedding wreath is becoming to women only exceptionally, and, besides, disquiet and emotion reddened her face; which, with the white robe, seemed still redder than it was in reality. But a wonderful thing! Just this circumstance moved Pan Stanislav. In his heart, rather kind by its nature, there rose a certain feeling resembling compassion or tenderness. He understood that Marynia's heart must be panting then like a captive bird, and he began to calm her; to speak to her with such good and kind words that he was astonished himself where he could find them in such numbers, and how they came to him so easily. But they came to him easily just because of Marynia. It was to be seen that she gave herself to him with a panting of the heart, but also with confidence; that she gave him her heart, her soul, and her whole being, her whole life, and that not only for good, but for every moment of her life—and to the end of it. In this regard no shadow rose in Pan Stanislav's mind, and that certainty made him better at that moment, more sensitive and eloquent, than he was ordinarily. At last they held each the other's hand and looked into each other's eyes, not only with love, but with the greatest friendship and confidence. Both felt the double reality. Yet a few moments, and that future will begin. But now the thoughts of both began to grow clear; and that internal disquiet, from which they had not been free, yielded more and more and turned into a solemn concentration of thought, as the religious ceremony drew near. Pan Stanislav's thoughts did not fly apart like sparrows; there remained to him only a certain astonishment, as it were, that he with all his scepticism had such a feeling even of the religious significance of the act which was about to be accomplished. At heart he was not a sceptic. In his soul there was hidden even a certain yearning for religious sensations; and if he had not returned to them it was only through a loss of habit and through spiritual negligence. Scepticism, at most, had shaken the surface of his thoughts, just as wind roughens the surface of water; the depths of which are still calm. He had lost, too, familiarity with forms; but to regain it was a work for the future and Marynia. Meanwhile this ceremony to which he must yield seemed to him so important, so full of solemnity and sacredness, that he was ready to proceed to it with bowed head.

But first he had another ceremony, which, equally solemn in itself, was disagreeable enough to Pan Stanislav; namely, to kneel before Pan Plavitski, whom he considered a fool, receive his blessing and hear an exhortation, which, as was known, Plavitski would not omit. Pan Stanislav had said in his mind, however, "Since I am to marry, I must pass through all which precedes it, and with a good face; little do I care what expression that monkey, Bukatski, will have at such moments." Therefore he knelt with all readiness at Marynia's side before her father, and listened to his blessing with an exhortation, which, by the way, was not long. Plavitski himself was moved really; his voice and his hands trembled; he was barely able to pronounce something in the nature of an adjuration to Pan Stanislav, not to prevent Marynia from coming even occasionally to pray at his grave before it was grown over completely with grass.

Finally, the solemnity of the moment affected Yozio Bigiel. Seeing Pan Plavitski's tears, seeing Marynia and Pan Stanislav on their knees (kneeling at Bigiel's house was not only a punishment, but frequently the beginning of more vigorous instruction), Yozio gave expression to his sympathy and fear by closing his eyes, opening his mouth, and breaking into as piercing a wail as he could utter. When the rest of the little Bigiels followed his example in great part, and all began to move, for the time to pass to the church had arrived, the grave of Pan Plavitski grown over with grass could not call forth an impression sufficiently elegiac.

Sitting in the carriage between Abdulski and Bukatski, Pan Stanislav hardly answered their questions in half words; he took no part in the conversation, but kept up a monologue with himself. He thought that in a couple of minutes that would come to pass of which he had been dreaming whole months; and which till the death of Litka he had desired with the greatest earnestness of his life. Here for the last time he was roused by a feeling of the difference between that past which not long since had vanished, and the present moment; but there was a difference. Formerly he strove and desired; to-day he only wished and consented. That thought pierced him like a shudder, for it shot through his head that perhaps there was lacking in his own personality that basis on which one may build. But he was a man able to keep his alarms in close bonds, and to scatter them to the four winds at a given moment. He said to himself, therefore: "First, there is no time to think of this; and second, reality does not answer always to imaginings; this is a simple thing." Then what Bukatski had said pushed again into his memory: "It is not enough to take, a man must give;" but he thought this a fabric of such fine threads that it had no existence whatever, and that life should be taken more simply, that there is no obligation to come to terms with preconceived theories. Here he repeated what he had said to himself frequently, "I marry, and that is the end." Then reality embraced him, or rather the present moment; he had nothing in his head but Marynia, the church, and the ceremony.

She on the way meanwhile implored God in silence to help her to make her husband happy; for herself she begged also a little happiness, being certain, moreover, that her dead mother would obtain that for her.

Then they went arm in arm between the lines of invited and curious people, seeing somewhat as through a mist lights gleaming in the distance on the altar, and at the sides faces known and unknown. Both saw more distinctly the face of Pani Emilia, who wore the white veil of a Sister of Charity, her eyes at once smiling and filled with tears. Litka came to the minds of both; and it occurred to them that it was precisely she who was conducting them to the altar. After a while they knelt down; before them was the priest, higher up the gleaming of the candles, the glitter of gold, and the holy face of the principal image. The ceremony commenced. They repeated after the priest the usual phrases of the marriage vow; and Pan Stanislav, holding Marynia's hand, was seized suddenly by emotion such as he had not expected, and such as he had not felt since his mother had brought him to first communion. He felt that that was not a mere every-day legal act, in virtue of which a man receives the right to a woman; but in that binding of hands, in that vow, there is present a certain mysterious power from beyond this world, — that it is simply God before whom the soul inclines and the heart trembles. The ears of both were struck then in the midst of silence by the solemn words, "*Quod Deus junxit, homo non disjungat;*" but Pan Stanislav felt that that Marynia whom he had taken becomes his body and blood, and a part of his soul, and that for her too he must be the same. That moment a chorus of voices in the choir burst out with "*Veni Creator,*" and a few moments after the Polanyetskis went forth from the church. On the way out, the arms of Pani Emilia embraced Marynia once again: "May God bless you!" and when they drove to the wedding reception, she went to the cemetery to tell Litka the news, that Pan Stas was married that day to Marynia.

## CHAPTER XXXI.

Two weeks later, in Venice, the doorkeeper of the Hotel Bauer gave Pan Stanislav a letter with the postmark of Warsaw. It was at the moment when he and his wife were entering a gondola to go to the church of Santa Maria della Salute, where on that day, the anniversary of her death, a Mass was to be offered for the soul of Marynia's mother. Pan Stanislav, who expected nothing important from Warsaw, put the letter in his pocket, and asked his wife, —

"But is it not a little too early for Mass?"

"It is; a whole half hour."

"Then perhaps it would please thee to go first to the Rialto?"

Marynia was always ready to go. Never having been abroad before, she simply lived in continual rapture, and it seemed to her that all which surrounded her was a dream. More than once, in the excess of her delight, she threw herself on her husband's neck, as if he had built Venice, as if she ought to thank him alone for its beauty. More than once she repeated, —

"I look and I see, but cannot believe that this is real."

So they went to the Rialto. There was little movement yet, because of the early hour; the water was as if sleeping, the day calm, clear, but not very bright, — one of those days in which the Grand Canal with all its beauty has the repose of a cemetery, the palaces seem deserted and forgotten, and in their motionless reflection in the water is that peculiar deep sadness of dead things. One looks at them then in silence, and as if in fear, lest by words the general repose may be broken.

Thus did Marynia look. But Pan Stanislav, less sensitive, remembered that he had a letter in his pocket, hence he drew it forth, and began to read. After a time he exclaimed, —

"Ah! Mashko is married; their wedding was three days after ours."

But Marynia, as if roused from a dream, inquired, while blinking, "What dost thou say?"

"I say, dreaming head, that Mashko's wedding is over."

She rested her head on his shoulder, and, looking into his eyes, inquired, —

"What is Mashko to me? I have my Stas."

Pan Stanislav smiled like a man who kindly permits himself to be loved, but does not wonder that he is loved; then he kissed his wife on the forehead, with a certain distraction, for the letter had begun to occupy him, and read on. All at once he sprang up, as if something had pricked him, and cried, —

"Oh, that is a real catastrophe!"

"What has happened?"

"Panna Kraslavski has a life annuity of nine thousand rubles, which her uncle left her; beyond that, not a copper."

"But that is a good deal."

"A good deal? Hear what Mashko writes: —

"'In view of this, my bankruptcy is an accomplished fact, and the declaration of my insolvency a question of time.'

"They deceived each other; dost understand? He counted on her property, and she on his."

"At least they have something to live on."

"They have something to live on; but Mashko has nothing with which to pay his debts, and that concerns us a little, — me, thee, and thy father. All may be lost."

Here Marynia was alarmed in earnest. "My Stas," said she, "perhaps thy presence is needed there; let us return, then. What a blow this will be to papa!"

"I will write Bigiel immediately to take my place, and save what is possible. Do not take this business to heart too much, my child. I have enough to buy a bit of bread for us both, and for thy father."

Marynia put her arms around his neck. "Thou, my good — With such a man one may be at rest."

"Besides, something will be saved. If Mashko finds credit, he will pay us; he may find a purchaser, too, for Kremen. He writes me to ask Bukatski to buy Kremen, and to persuade him to do so. Bukatski is going to Rome this evening, and I have invited him to lunch. I will ask him. He has a considerable fortune, and would have something to do. I am curious to know how Mashko's life will develop. He writes at the end of the letter:

"'I discovered the condition of affairs to my wife; she bore herself passively, but her mother is wild with indignation.'

"Finally he adds that at last he has fallen in love with his wife, and that if they should separate, it would be the greatest unhappiness in life for him. That lyric tale gives me little concern; but I am curious as to how all this will end."

"She will not desert him," said Marynia.

"I do not know; I thought myself once that she would not, but I like to contradict. Wilt thou bet?"

"No; for I do not wish to win. Thou ugly man, thou hast no knowledge of women."

"On the contrary, I know them; and I know them because all are not like this little one who is sailing now in a gondola."

"In a gondola in Venice, with her Stas," answered Marynia.

They were now at the church. When they went from Mass to the hotel, they found Bukatski, dressed for the road, in a cross-barred gray suit,—which, on his frail body, seemed too large, — in yellow shoes and a fantastic cravat, tied as fancifully as carelessly.

"I am going to-day," said he, after he had greeted Marynia. "Do you command me to prepare a dwelling in Florence for you? I can engage some palace."

"Then you will halt on the road to Rome?"

"Yes. First, to give notice in the gallery of your coming, and to put a sofa on the stairs for you; second, I halt for black coffee, which is bad throughout Italy in general, but in Florence, at Giacosa's, Via Tornabuoni, it is exceptionally excellent. That, however, is the one thing of value in Florence."

"What pleasure is there for you in always saying something different from what you think?"

"But I am thinking seriously of engaging nice lodgings on Lung-Arno for you."

"We shall stop at Verona."

"For Romeo and Juliet? Of course; of course! Go now; later you would shrug your shoulders if you thought of them. In a month it would be too late for you to go, perhaps."

Marynia started up at him like a cat; then, turning to her husband, said, —

"Stas, don't let this gentleman annoy me so!"

"Well," answered Pan Stanislav, "I will cut his head off, but after lunch."

Bukatski began to declaim:—

> "It is not yet near day:
> It was the nightingale, and not the lark,
> That pierc'd the fearful hollow of thine ear."

Then, turning to Marynia, he inquired, "Has Pan Stanislav written a sonnet for you?"

"No."

"Oh, that is a bad sign. You have a balcony on the street; has it never come once to his head to stand under your balcony with a guitar?"

"No."

"Oh, very bad!"

"But there is no place to stand here, for there is water."

"He might go in a gondola. With us it is different, you see; but here in Italy the air is such that if a man is in love really, he either writes sonnets, or stands under a balcony with a guitar. It is a thing perfectly certain, resulting from the geographical position, the currents of the sea, the chemical make-up of the air and the water: if a man does not write sonnets, or stand out of doors with a guitar, surely he is not in love. I can bring you very famous books on this subject."

"It seems that I shall be driven to cut his head off before lunch," said Pan Stanislav.

The execution, however, did not come, for the reason that it was just time for lunch. They sat down at a separate table, but in the same hall was a general one, which for Marynia, whom everything interested, was a source of pleasure, too, for she saw *real* English people. This made on her such an impression as if she had gone to some land of exotics; for since Kremen is Kremen, not one of its inhabitants had undertaken a similar journey. For Bukatski, and even Pan Stanislav, her delight was a source of endless jokes, but also of genuine pleasure. The first said that she reminded him of his youth; the second called his wife a "field daisy," and said that one was not sorry to show the world to a woman like her. Bukatski noticed, however, that the "field daisy" had much feeling for art and much honesty. Many things were known to her from books or pictures; not knowing others, she acknowledged this openly, but in her expressions there was nothing artificial or affected. When a thing touched her heart, her delight had no bounds, so that her eyes became moist. At one time Bukatski jested with her unmercifully; at another he persuaded her that all the connoisseurs, so called, have a nail in the head, and that she, as a sensitive and refined nature, and so far unspoiled, was for him of the greatest importance in questions of art; she would be still more important if she were ten years of age.

At lunch they did not talk of art, because Pan Stanislav remembered his news from Warsaw, and said, —

"I had a letter from Mashko."

"And I, too," answered Bukatski.

"And thou? They must be hurried there; Mashko must be pressed in real earnest. Is the question known to thee?"

"He persuades me, or rather, he implores me, to buy — dost thou know what?"

Bukatski avoided Kremen, knowing well what trouble it had caused, and was silent through delicacy toward Marynia.

But Pan Stanislav, understanding his intention, said, —

"Oh, my God! Once we avoided that name as a sore spot, but now, before my wife, it is something different. It is hard to be tied up a whole lifetime."

Bukatski looked at him quickly; Marynia blushed a little, and said, —

"Stas is perfectly right. Besides, I know that it is a question of Kremen."

"Yes, it is of Kremen."

"Well, and what?" asked Pan Stanislav.

"I should not buy it even because of this, — that the lady might have the impression that people are tossing it about like a ball."

"If I do not think at all of Kremen?" said Marynia, blushing still more. She looked at her husband; and he nodded in sign of praise and satisfaction.

"That is a proof," answered he, "that thou art a child of good judgment."

"At the same time," continued Marynia, "if Pan Mashko does not hold out, Kremen will either be divided, or go into usurers' hands, and that to me would be disagreeable."

"Ah, ha!" said Bukatski, "but if you do not think at all of Kremen?"

Marynia looked again at her husband, and this time with alarm; he began to laugh, however.

"Marynia is caught," said he.

Then he turned to Bukatski. "Evidently Mashko looks on thee as the one plank of salvation."

"But I am not a plank; look at me! I am a straw, rather. The man who wishes to save himself by such a straw will drown. Mashko has said himself more than once to me, 'Thou hast blunted nerves.' Perhaps I have; but I need strong impressions for that very reason. If I were to help Mashko, he would work himself free, stand on his feet, give himself out as a lord still further; his wife would personate a great lady, they would be terribly *comme il faut*, and I should have the stupid comedy, which I have seen already, and which I have yawned at. If, on the other hand, I do not help him, he will be ruined, he will perish, something interesting will happen, unexpected events will come to pass, something tragic may result, which will occupy me more. Now, think, both of you, I must pay for a wretched comedy, and dearly; the tragedy I can have for nothing. How is a man to hesitate in this case?"

"Fi! how can you say such things?" exclaimed Marynia.

"Not only can I say them, but I shall write them to Mashko; besides, he has deceived me in the most unworthy manner."

"In what?"

"In what? In this, that I thought: 'Oh, that is a regular snob! that is material for a dark personage; that is a man really without heart or scruples!' Meanwhile, what comes out? That at bottom of his soul he has a certain honesty; that he wants to pay his creditors; that he is sorry for that puppet with red eyes; that he loves her; that for him separation from her would be a terrible catastrophe. He writes this to me himself most shamelessly. I give my word that in our society one can count on nothing. I will settle abroad, for I cannot endure this."

Now Marynia was angry in earnest.

"If you say such things, I shall beg to break relations with you."

But Pan Stanislav shrugged his shoulders, and added: "In fact, thy talk is ever on some conceit to amuse thyself and others, and never wilt thou think with judgment and in human fashion. Dost understand, I do not persuade thee to buy Kremen, and all the more because I might have a certain interest to do so; but there would be some occupation for thee there, something to do."

Here Bukatski began to laugh, and said after a while,—

"I told thee once that I like, above all, to do what pleases me, and that it pleases me most to do nothing; hence it is that doing nothing I do what pleases me most. If thou art wise, prove that I have uttered nonsense. Take the second case: Suppose me a buckwheat sower; that, however, simply passes imagination. I, for whom rain or fine weather is merely the question of choosing a cane or an umbrella, would have, in my old age, to stand on one leg, like a stork, and look to see whether it pleases the sun to shine, or the clouds to drop rain. I should have to tremble as to whether my wheat is likely to grow, or my rape-seed shed, or rot fall on the potatoes; whether I shall be able to stake my peas, or furnish his Worship of Dogweevil as many bushels as I have promised; whether my plough-horses have the glanders, and my sheep the foot-rot. I should, in my old age, come to this,—that from blunting of faculties I would interject after every three words: 'Pan Benefactor,' or 'What is it that I wanted to say?' *Voyons! pas si bête!* I, a free man, should become a *glebæ adscriptus*, a 'Neighbor,' a 'Brother Lata,' a 'Pan Matsyei,' a 'Lechit.'"[1]

Here, roused a little by the wine, he began to quote in an undertone the words of Slaz in "Lilla Weneda":—

> "Am I a Lechit? What does this mean? Are boorishness,
> Drunkenness, gluttony, gazing from my eyes
> With the seven deadly sins, a passion for uproar,
> Pickled cucumbers, and escutcheons?"

"Argue with him," said Pan Stanislav, "especially when at the root of the matter he is partly right."

But Marynia, who as soon as Bukatski had begun to speak of work in the country, grew somewhat thoughtful, shook thoughtfulness now from her forehead, and said,—

"When papa was not well,—and never in Kremen has he been so well as recently,—I saved him a little in management, and later that work became for me a habit. Though God knows there was no lack of troubles, it gave me a pleasure that I cannot describe. But I did not understand the cause of this till Pan Yamish explained it. 'That,' said he, 'is the real work on which the world stands, and every other is either the continuation of it, or something artificial.' Later I understood even things

[1] Polish noble.

which he did not explain. More than once, when I went out to the fields in spring, and saw that all things were growing, I felt that my heart, too, was growing with them. And now I know why that is: In all other relations that a man holds there may be deceit, but the land is truth. It is impossible to deceive the land; it either gives, or gives not, but it does not deceive. Therefore land is loved, as truth; and because one loves it, it teaches one to love. And the dew falls not only on grain, and on meadows, but on the soul, as it were; and a man becomes better, for he has to deal with truth, and he loves, — that is, he is nearer God. Therefore I loved my Kremen so much."

Here Marynia became frightened at her own speech, and at this, what would "Stas" think; at the same time reminiscences had roused her. All this was reflected in her eyes as the dawn, and on her young face; and she was herself like the dawn.

Bukatski looked at her as he would at some unknown newly discovered master-piece of the Venetian school; then he closed his eyes, and hid half of his small face in his enormous fantastic cravat, and whispered, —

"*Délicieuse!*"

Then, thrusting forth his chin from his cravat, he said, —

"You are perfectly right."

But the logical woman would not let herself be set aside by a compliment.

"If I am right, you are not."

"That is another matter. You are right because it becomes you; a woman in that case is always right."

"Stas!" said Marynia, turning to her husband. But there was so much charm in the woman at that moment, that he also looked on her with delight, his eyes smiled, his nostrils moved with a quick motion; for a moment he covered her hand with his, and said, —

"Oh, child, child!"

Then he inclined to her, and whispered, —

"If we were not in this hall, I would kiss those dear eyes and that mouth."

And, speaking thus, Pan Stanislav made a great mistake, for at that moment it was not enough to feel the physical charm of Marynia, to be roused at the color of her face, her eyes, or her mouth, but it was necessary to feel the soul in her; to what an extent he did not feel it was shown by his fondling words, "O child, child!" She was for him at that moment only a charming child-woman, and he thought of nothing else.

Just then coffee was brought. To end the conversation, Pan Stanislav said,—

"So Mashko has come out a lover, and that after marriage."

Bukatski swallowed a cup of boiling coffee, and answered, "In this is the stupidity, that Mashko is the man, not in this,—that the love was after marriage. I have not said anything sensible. If I have, I beg pardon most earnestly, and promise not to do so a second time. I have burned my tongue evidently with the hot coffee! I drink it so hot because they tell me that it is good for headache; and my head aches, aches."

Here Bukatski placed his palm on his neck and the back of his head, and blinked, remaining motionless for a few seconds.

"I am talking and talking," said he, then, "but my head aches. I should have gone to my lodgings, but Svirski, the artist, is to come to me here. We are going to Florence together; he is a famous painter in water-colors, really famous. No one has brought greater force out of water-colors. But see, he is just coming!"

In fact, Svirski, as if summoned by a spell, appeared in the hall, and began to look around for Bukatski. Espying him at last, he approached the table.

He was a robust, short man, with hair as black as if he were an Italian. He had an ordinary face, but a wise, deep glance, and also mild. While walking, he swayed a little because of his wide hips.

Bukatski presented him to Marynia in the following words,—

"I present to you Pan Svirski, a painter, of the *genus* genius, who not only received his talent, but had the most happy idea of not burying it, which he might have done as well, and with equal benefit to mankind, as any other man. But he preferred to fill the world with water-colors and with fame."

Svirski smiled, showing two rows of teeth, wonderfully small, but white as ivory, and said,—

"I wish that were true."

"And I will tell you why he did not bury his talent," continued Bukatski; "his reasons were so parochial that it would be a shame for any decent artist to avow them. He loves Pognembin, which is somewhere in Poznan, or thereabouts, and he loves it because he was born there. If he had been born in Guadeloupe he would have loved Guadeloupe, and love for Guadeloupe would have saved him in life also. This man makes me indignant; and will the lady tell me if I am not right?"

To this Marynia answered, raising her blue eyes to Svirski, "Pan Bukatski is not so bad as he seems, for he has said everything that is good of you."

"I shall die with my qualities known," whispered Bukatski.

Svirski was looking meanwhile at Marynia, as only an artist can permit himself to look at a woman, and not offend. Interest was evident in his eyes, and at last he muttered, —

"To see such a head all at once, here in Venice, is a genuine surprise."

"What?" asked Bukatski.

"I say, that the lady is of a wonderfully well-defined type. Oh, this, for example" (here he drew a line with his thumb along his nose, mouth, and chin). "And also what purity of outline!"

"Well, is n't it true?" asked Pan Stanislav, with excitement. "I have always thought the same."

"I will lay a wager that thou hast never thought of it," retorted Bukatski.

But Pan Stanislav was glad and proud of that interest which Marynia roused in the famous artist; hence he said, —

"If it would give you any pleasure to paint her portrait, it would give me much more to have it."

"From the soul of my heart," answered Svirski, with simplicity; "but I am going to Rome to-day. There I have begun the portrait of Pani Osnovski."

"And we shall be in Rome no later than ten days from now."

"Then we are agreed."

Marynia returned thanks, blushing to her ears. But Bukatski began to take farewell, and drew Svirski after him. When they had gone out, he said, —

"We have time yet. Come to Floriani's for a glass of cognac."

Bukatski did not know how to drink, and did n't like

spirits; but since he had begun to take morphine, he drank more than he could endure, because some one had told him that one neutralized the other.

"What a delightful couple those Polanyetskis are!" said Svirski.

"They are not long married."

"It is evident that he loves her immensely. When I praised her, his eyes were smiling, and he rose as if on yeast."

"She loves him a hundred times more."

"What knowledge hast thou in such matters?"

Bukatski did not answer; he only raised his pointed nose, and said, as if to himself, —

"Oh, marriage and love have disgusted me; for it is always profit on one side, and sacrifice on the other. Polanyetski is a good man, but what of that? She has just as much sense, just as much character, but she loves more; therefore life will fix itself for them in this way, — he will be the sun, he will be gracious enough to shine, to warm, will consider her as his property, as a planet made to circle around him. All this is indicated to-day. She has entered his sphere. There is in him a certain self-confidence which angers me. He will have her with an income, but she will have him alone without an income. He will permit himself to love, considering his love as virtue, kindness, and favor; she will love, considering her love as a happiness and a duty. Look, if you please, at him, the divine, the resplendent! I want to go back and tell them this, in the hope that they will be less happy."

Meanwhile the two men had taken seats in front of Floriani's, and soon cognac was brought to them. Svirski thought some time over the Polanyetskis, and then inquired, —

"But if the position is pleasant for her?"

"I know that she has short sight; she might be pleased quite as well to wear glasses."

"Go to the deuce! glasses on a face like hers — "

"This makes thee indignant; but the other makes me — "

"Yes, for thou hast a kind of coffee-mill in thy head, which grinds, and grinds everything till it grinds it into fine dust. What dost thou want of love in general?"

"I, of love? I want nothing of love! Let the devil take him who wants anything of love! I have sharp pains in my shoulder-blades from it. But if I were other than

I am, if I had to describe what love ought to be, if I wanted anything of it, then I should wish — "

"What? hop! jump over!"

"That it were composed in equal parts of desire and reverence."

Then he drank a glass of cognac, and added after a while, —

"It seems to me that I have said something which may be wise, if it is not foolish. But it is all one to me."

"No! it is not foolish."

"As God lives, it is all one to me."

## CHAPTER XXXII.

After a stay of one week in Florence, Pan Stanislav received his first letter from Bigiel concerning the business of the house, and news so favorable that it almost surpassed his expectations. The law prohibiting export of grain because of the famine was proclaimed. But the firm had enormous supplies bought and exported previously; and because prices, especially at the first moment, had risen excessively abroad, Bigiel and Polanyetski began to do perfect business. Speculation, planned and carried through on a great scale, turned out so profitable that from well-to-do people, which they were before, they had become almost rich. For that matter Pan Stanislav had been sure of his business from the beginning, and entertained no fears; the news, however, pleased him both with reference to profit and his own self-love. Success intoxicates a man and strengthens his self-confidence. So, in talking with Marynia, he was not able to refrain from giving her to understand that he had an uncommon head, unquestionably higher than all those around him, like a tree the loftiest in the forest; that he is a man who always reaches the place at which he has aimed, — in a word, a kind of phœnix in that society, abounding in men who know not how to help themselves. In the whole world he could not have found a listener more willing and ready to accept everything with the deepest faith.

"Thou art a woman," said he, not without a shade of loftiness; "therefore why tell thee the affair from the beginning, and enter into details. To thee, as a woman, I can explain all best if I say thus: I was not in a condition yesterday to buy the medallion with a black pearl which I showed thee at Godoni's; to-day I am, and will buy it."

Marynia thanked him, and begged that he would not do so; but he insisted, and said that nothing would restrain him, that that was resolved on, and Marynia must consider herself the owner of the great black pearl, which, on such a white neck as hers, would be beautiful. Then he fell to kissing that neck; and when finally he had satisfied himself, but still felt the need of a listener of some sort, he began to walk in the room, smiling at his wife and at his own thoughts, saying, —

"I do not mention those who do nothing: Bukatski, for instance, who is known to be good for nothing, nor asses like Kopovski, who is known to have a cat's head; but take even men who do something, — men of mind seemingly. Never would Bigiel seize a chance on the wing: he would set to thinking over it, and to putting it off; to-day he would decide, and to-morrow be afraid, and the time would be gone. What is the point in question? First, to have a head, and second, to sit down and calculate. And if one decides to act, then act. It is needful, too, to be cool, and not pose. Mashko is no fool, one might think; but see what he has worked out! I have not gone his way, and shall not follow him."

Thus speaking, he continued to walk and to shake his thick, dark hair; and Marynia, who, in every case, would have listened to his words with faith, received them now as an infallible principle, all the more that they rested on tangible success.

He stopped before her at last, and said, —

"Knowest what I think? that coolness is judgment. It is possible to have an intelligent head, to take in knowledge as a sponge absorbs liquid, and still not to have sound, sober judgment. Bukatski is for me a proof of this. Do not think me vain; but if I, for instance, knew as much about art as he does, I should have a sounder judgment concerning it. He has read so much, and caught up so many opinions, that at last he has none of his own. Surely, from the materials which he has collected, I should have squeezed out something of my own."

"Oh, that is sure," said Marynia, with perfect confidence.

Pan Stanislav might have been right in a certain view. He was not a dull man by any means, and it may be that his intelligence was firmer and more compact than Bukatski's; but it was less flexible and less comprehensive. This did not occur to him. He did not think, also, that in that moment, under the influence of boastfulness, he was saying things before Marynia which the fear of ridicule and criticism would have restrained him from saying before strangers, sceptical persons. But he did not restrain himself before Marynia; he judged that if he could permit himself such little boastfulness before any one, it was before his wife. Besides, as he himself said, "He had taken her, and all was over." Moreover, she was his own.

In general, he had not felt so happy and satisfied at any time in life as then. He had experienced material success, and considered the future as guaranteed; he had married a woman, young, charming, and clever, for whom he had become a dogma, — and the position could not be otherwise, since her lips were not dry for whole days from his kisses, — and whose healthy and honest heart was filled with gratitude for his love. What could be lacking to him? What more could he wish? He was satisfied with himself, for he ascribed in great part to his own cleverness and merit, his success in so arranging life that everything promised peace and prosperity. He saw that life was bitter for other men, but pleasant for him, and he interpreted the difference to his own advantage. He had thought once that a man wishing peace had to regulate his connection with himself, with mankind, with God. The first two he looked on as regulated. He had a wife, a calling, and a future; hence he had given and secured to himself all that he could give and secure. As to society, he permitted himself sometimes to criticise it, but he felt that in the bottom of his soul he loved it really; that even if he wished, he could not do otherwise; that if in a given case it were necessary to go into water or fire for society, he would go, — hence he considered everything settled on that side too. His relation with God remained. He felt that should that become clear and certain, he might consider all life's problems settled, and say to himself definitely, "I know why I have lived, what I wanted, and why I must die." While not a man of science, he had touched enough on science to know the vanity of seeking in philosophy so-called explanations or answers which are to be sought rather in intuition, and, above all, in feeling, in so far as the one and the other of these are simple, — otherwise they lead to extravagance. At the same time, since he was not devoid of imagination, he saw before him, as it were, the image of an honest, well-balanced man, a good husband, a good father, who labors and prays, who on Sunday takes his children to church, and lives a life wonderfully wholesome from a moral point of view. That picture smiled at him; and in life so much is done for pictures. He thought that a society which had a great number of such citizens would be stronger and healthier than a society which below was composed of boors, and above of sages, dilettanti, decadents, and all those forbidden figures with sprained intellects. One time, soon after his acquaintance with Marynia, he had promised himself and Bigiel that on finishing with his own person, and with people, he would set about this third relation seriously. Now the time had come, or at least was approaching. Pan Stanislav understood that this work needed more repose than is found on a bridal trip, and among the impressions of a new life and a new country, and that hurry of hotels and galleries in which he lived with Marynia. But, in spite of these conditions, in the rare moments when he was with his own thoughts, he turned at once to that problem, which for him was at that time the main one. He was subject meanwhile to various influences, which, small in themselves, exercised a certain action, even because he refrained purposely from opposing them. Of these was the influence of Marynia. Pan Stanislav was not conscious of it, and would not have owned to its existence; still the continual presence of that calm soul, sincerely and simply pious, extremely conscientious in relation to God, gave him an idea of the rest and peace to be found in religion. When he attended his wife to church, he remembered the words which she said to him in Warsaw, "Of course; it is the service of God." And he was drawn into it, for at first he went to church with her always not to let her go alone, and later because it gave him also a certain internal pleasure, — such, for example, as the examination of phenomena gives a scientist specially interested in them. In this way, in spite of unfavorable conditions, in spite of journeys, and a line of thought interrupted by impressions of every sort, he advanced on the new road continually. His thoughts had at times great energy and decisiveness in this direction. "I feel God," said he to himself. "I felt Him at Litka's grave; I felt Him, though I did not acknowledge it, in the words of Vaskovski about death; I felt Him at marriage; I felt Him at home, in the plains, and in this country, in the mountains above the snow; and I only ask yet how I am to glorify Him, to honor and love Him? Is it as pleases me personally, or as my wife does, and as my mother taught me?"

In Rome, however, he ceased at first to think of these

things; so many external impressions were gathered at once in his mind that there was no room for reflection. Moreover, he and Marynia came home in the evening so tired that he remembered almost with terror the words of Bukatski, who, at times, when serving them as cicerone for his own satisfaction, said, "Ye have not seen the thousandth part of what is worth seeing; but that is all one, for in general it is not worth while to come here, just as it is not worth while to stay at home."

Bukatksi was then in a fit of contradiction, overturning in one statement what he had seemed to affirm in the preceding one.

Professor Vaskovski came, too, from Perugia to greet them, which pleased Marynia so much that she met him as she would her nearest relative. But, after satisfying her first outbursts of delight, she observed in the professor's eyes, as it were, a kind of melancholy.

"What is the matter?" inquired she. "Do you not feel well in Italy?"

"My child," answered he, "it is pleasant in Perugia, and pleasant in Rome — oh, how pleasant! Know this, that here, while walking on the streets, one is treading on the dust of the world. This, as I repeat always, is the antechamber to another life — but — "

"But what?"

"But people — you see, that is, not from a bad heart, for here, as well as everywhere, there are more good than bad people; but sometimes I am sad, for here, as well as at home, they look on me as a little mad."

Bukatski, who was listening to the conversation, said, —

"Then the professor has more cause for sadness here than at home."

"Yes," answered Vaskovski; "I have so many friends there, like you, who love me — but here, no — and therefore I am homesick."

Then he turned to Pan Stanislav: "The journals here have printed an account of my essay. Some scoff altogether. God be with them! Some agree that a new epoch would begin through the introduction of Christ and His spirit into history. One writer confessed that individuals treat one another in a Christian spirit, but that nations lead a pagan life yet. He even called the thought a great one; but he and all others, when I affirm this to be a mission which God has predestined to us, and other youngest of the Aryans, seize their sides from laughter. And this pains me. They give it to be understood also that I have a little here —"

And poor Vaskovski tapped his forehead with his finger. After a while, however, he raised his head and said, —

"A man sows the seed in sadness and often in doubt; but the seed falls on the field, and God grant that it spring up!"

Then he began to inquire about Pani Emilia; at last he turned to them his eyes, which were as if wakened from sleep, and asked naively, —

"But it is pleasant for you to be with each other?"

Marynia, instead of answering, sprang to her husband, and, nestling her head up to his shoulder, said, —

"Oh, see, Professor, this is how we are together, — so!"

And Pan Stanislav stroked her dark head with his hand

## CHAPTER XXXIII.

A WEEK later Pan Stanislav took his wife to Svirski's on Via Margutta. Svirski they saw almost daily. They had grown accustomed to the artist and liked him; now he was to paint Marynia's portrait. At the studio they found the Osnovskis, with whom acquaintance was made the more easily since the ladies had met some years before at a party, and Pan Stanislav had been presented on a time to Pani Osnovski, at Ostend; he needed merely to remember her now. Pan Stanislav, it is true, did not recollect whether at that epoch, when, after looking at every young and presentable woman, he asked himself, "Is it this one?" he had asked this touching the present Pani Osnovski; he might have done so, however, for she had the reputation then of being a comely, though rather flighty young person. Now she was a woman of six or seven and twenty, very tall, a fresh, though dark brunette, with cherry lips, dishevelled forelock, and somewhat oblique violet eyes, which gave her face a resemblance to Chinese faces, and at the same time a certain expression of malice and wit. She had a strange way of bearing herself, which consisted in thrusting back her shoulders and pushing forward her body; in consequence of this, Bukatski said of her that she carried her bust *en offrande.*

Almost immediately she told Marynia that, as they were sitting in the same studio, they ought to consider each other as colleagues; and told Pan Stanislav that she remembered him, from the ball at Ostend, as a good dancer and *causeur*, and therefore that she would not delay in taking advantage of that knowledge now. To both she said that it was very agreeable to her, that she was delighted with Rome, that she was reading "Cosmopolis," that she was in love with the Villa Doria, with the view from the Pincian, that she hoped to see the catacombs in company with them, and that she knew the works of Rossi, in Allard's translations. Then, pressing Svirski's hand, and smiling coquettishly at Pan Stanislav, she went out, declaring that she gave way to one worthier than herself, and left the impression of a whirlwind, a Chinese woman, and a flower. Pan Osnovski, a very young man, with a light blond face without significance, but kindly, followed her, and hardly had he been able to put in a word.

Svirski drew a deep breath.

"Oh, she is a storm!" said he; "I have a thousand difficulties in keeping her at rest two minutes."

"But what an interesting face!" said Marynia. "Is it permitted to look at the portrait?"

"It lacks little of being finished; you may look at it."

Marynia and Pan Stanislav approached the portrait, and could express admiration without excess of politeness. That head, painted in water-colors, had the strength and warmth of an oil painting, and at the same time the whole spiritual essence of Pani Osnovski was in it. Svirski listened to the praises calmly; it was clear that he was pleased with his work. He covered the picture, and carried it to a dark corner of the studio, seated Marynia in an armchair already in position, and began to study her.

His persistent gaze confused her somewhat,—her cheeks began to flush; but he smiled with pleasure, muttering,—

"Yes; this is another type,—earth and heaven!"

At moments he closed one eye, which confused Marynia still more; at moments he approached the cardboard, and again drew back, and again studied her; and again he said, as if to himself,—

"In the other case, one had to bring out the devil, but here womanliness."

"As you have seen that immediately, I feel sure of a masterpiece," said Pan Stanislav.

All at once Svirski stopped looking at the paper and at Marynia, and, turning to Pan Stanislav, smiled joyously, showing his sound teeth.

"Yes, womanliness! and her own womanliness, that is the main characteristic of the face."

"And seize it, as you seized the devil in the other one."

"Stas!" exclaimed Marynia.

"It is not I who invented that, but Pan Svirski."

"If you wish, we will say imp, not devil,—a comely imp, but a dangerous one. While painting, I observe various things. That is a curious type,—Pani Osnovski."

"Why?"

"Have you observed her husband?"

"Somehow I was so occupied with her that I had no time."

"There it is: she hides him in such a degree that he is hardly visible; and, what is worse, she herself does not see him. At the same time he is one of the most worthy men in the world, uncommonly well-bred, considerate to others in an unheard-of degree, very rich, and not at all stupid. Moreover, he loves her to distraction."

Here Svirski began to paint, and repeated, as if in forgetfulness, —

"Lo-ves her to dis-trac-tion. Be pleased to arrange your hair a little about the ear. If your husband is a talker, he will be in despair, for Bukatski declares that when I begin work my lips never close, and that I let no one have a word. She, do you see, may be thus far as pure as a tear, but she is a coquette. She has an icy heart with a fiery head. A dangerous species, — oh, dangerous! She devours books by whole dozens, — naturally French books. She learns psychology in them, learns of feminine temperaments, of the enigma of woman, seeks enigmas in herself, which do not exist at all in her, discovers aspirations of which yesterday she knew nothing. She is depraving herself mentally; this mental depravation she considers wisdom, and makes no account of her husband."

"But you are a terrible man," remarked Marynia.

"My wife will hide to-morrow from fear, when the hour for sitting comes," said Pan Stanislav.

"Let her not hide; hers is a different type. Osnovski is not at all dull; but people, and especially, with your permission, women, are so unwise, that if a man's cleverness does not hit them on the head, if a man lacks confidence in himself, if he does not scratch like a cat and cut like a knife, they do not value him. As God lives, I have seen this in life a hundred times."

After a while he closed one eye again, gazed at Marynia, and continued, —

"In general, how foolish human society is! More than once have I put to myself this question: Why is honesty of character, heart, and such a thing as kindness, less valued than what is called mind? Why, in social life, are two categories pre-eminent, wise and foolish? It is not the custom, for example, to say, virtuous and unvirtuous; to such a degree is it not the custom, that the very expressions would seem ridiculous."

"Because," said Pan Stanislav, "mind is the lantern with which virtue and kindness and heart must light the way for themselves, otherwise they might break their noses, or, what is worse, break the noses of other people."

Marynia did not utter, it is true, a single word; but in her face it was possible to read distinctly, "How wise this Stas is — terribly wise!"

"Wise Stas" added meanwhile, —

"I am not speaking of Osnovski now, for I do not know him."

"Osnovski," said Svirski, "loves his wife as his wife, as his child, and as his happiness; but she has her head turned, God knows with what, and does not repay him in kind. Women interest me, as an unmarried man, immensely; more than once have I talked whole days about women, especially with Bukatski, when they interested him more than they do now. Bukatski divides women into plebeian souls, by which he means poor and low spirits, and into patrician souls, — that is, natures ennobled, full of the higher aspirations, and resting on principles, not phrases. There is a certain justice in this, but I prefer my division, which is simply into grateful and ungrateful hearts."

Here he withdrew from the sketch for a moment, half closed his eyes, then, taking a small mirror, placed it toward the picture, and began to look at the reflection.

"You ask what I mean by grateful and ungrateful hearts," said he, turning to Marynia, though she had not asked about anything. "A grateful heart is one which feels when it is loved, and is moved by love; and in return for the loving, loves more and more, yields itself more and more, prizes the loving, and honors it. The ungrateful heart gets all it can from the love given; and the more certain it feels of this love, the less it esteems it, the more it disregards and tramples it. It is enough to love a woman with an ungrateful heart, to make her cease loving. The fisherman is not concerned for the fish in the net; therefore Pani Osnovski does not care for Pan Osnovski. In the essence of the argument this is the rudest form of egotism in existence, — it is simply African; and therefore God guard Osnovski, and may the Evil One take her, with her Chinese eyes of violet color, and her frizzled forelock! To paint such a woman is pleasant, but to marry — we are not such fools. Will you believe it, I am in so much dread of an ungrateful heart that I have not married so far, though my fortieth year has sounded distinctly?"

"But it is so easy to recognize such a heart," said Marynia.

"May the Evil One take what is bad!" answered Svirski. "Not so easy, especially when a man has lost sense and reason."

Bending his athletic form, he looked at the sketch some time, and said,—

"Well, enough for to-day. As it is, I have talked so continuously that flies must have dropped from the walls. To-morrow, if you hear too much, just clap your hands. I do not talk so with Pani Osnovski, because she herself likes to talk. But how many titles of books have I heard? Enough of this! I wanted to say something more, but have forgotten. Ah! this is it,—you have a grateful heart."

Pan Stanislav laughed, and invited Svirski to dinner, promising him the society of Bukatski and Vaskovski.

"With great delight," answered Svirski; "I am as much alone here as a wild beast. As the weather is clear and the moon full, we will go later to see the Colosseum by moonlight."

The dinner took place, however, without Bukatski's mental hobbies, for he felt out of health, and wrote that he could not come. But Svirski and Vaskovski suited each other excellently, and became friends right away. Only while he was working did Svirski let no one have a word; in general, he liked to hear others, knew how to listen, and, though the professor and his views seemed to him comical sometimes, so much sincerity and kindness was evident in the old man that it would have been difficult for him not to win people. His mystic face and the expression of his eyes struck the artist. He sketched him a little in his mind; and, while listening to his talk about the Aryans, he thought how that head would look if all that was in it were brought out distinctly.

Toward the end of the dinner the professor asked Marynia if she would like to see the Pope. He said that in three days a Belgian pilgrimage was to arrive, and that she might join it. Svirski, who knew all Rome and all the monsignores, guaranteed to effect this with ease. When he heard this, the professor looked at him, and inquired,—

"Then you are almost a Roman?"

"Of sixteen years' standing."

"Is it possible!"

Here the professor was somewhat confused, fearing lest he had committed some indiscretion, but still wishing to know what to think of a man so sympathetic, he overcame his timidity, and inquired, —

"But of the Quirinal, or the Vatican?"

"From Pognembin," answered Svirski, frowning slightly.

The end of the dinner interrupted further explanations and converse. Marynia could scarcely sit still at the thought that she would see the Capitol, the Forum, and the Colosseum by moonlight. In fact, somewhat later they were driving toward the ruins along the Corso, which was lighted by electricity.

The night was calm and warm. Around the Forum and Colosseum the place was completely deserted; as, for that matter, it is in the day sometimes. Near the church of Santa Maria Liberatrice some person in an open window was playing on a flute, and one could hear every note in the stillness. On the front of the Forum a deep shadow fell from the height of the Capitol and its edifices; but farther on it was flooded with clear, greenish light, as was also the Colosseum, which seemed silver. When the carriage halted at the arches of the gigantic circus, Pan Stanislav, Svirski, and Vaskovski entered the interior, and pushed toward the centre of the arena, avoiding the fragments of columns, friezes, piles of bricks, stones, and bases of columns standing here and there, and fragments piled up near the arches. Under the influence of silence and loneliness, words did not rise to their lips. Through the arched entrances came to the interior sheaves of moonlight, which seemed to rest quietly on the floor of the arena, on the opposite walls, on the indentations, on openings in the walls, on breaks, on the silvered mosses and ivy, covering the ruin here and there. Other parts of the building, sunk in impenetrable darkness, produced the impression of black and mysterious gulleys. From the low-placed cunicula came the stern breath of desolation. Reality was lost amidst that labyrinth and confusion of walls, arches, bright spots, bright stripes, and deep shadows. The colossal ruin seemed to lose its real existence, and to become a dream vision, or rather, a kind of wonderful impression composed of silence, night, the moon, sadness, and the remembrance of a past, mighty, but full of blood and suffering.

Svirski began to speak first, and in a subdued voice, —

"What pain, what tears, were here! what a measureless tragedy! Let people say what they please, there is something beyond human in Christianity; and that thought cannot be avoided."

Here he turned to Marynia, and continued, —

"Imagine that might: a whole world, millions of people, iron laws, power unequalled before or since, an organization such as has never been elsewhere, greatness, glory, hundreds of legions, a gigantic city, possessing the world, — and that Palatine hill over there, possessing the city; it would seem that no earthly power could overturn it. Meanwhile two Jews come, — Peter and Paul, not with arms, but a word; and see, here is a ruin, on the Palatine a ruin, in the Forum a ruin, and above the city crosses, crosses, crosses and crosses."

Again there was silence; but from the direction of Santa Maria Liberatrice the sound of the flute came continually.

After a while Vaskovski said, pointing to the arena, —

"There was a cross here, too, but they have borne it away."

Pan Stanislav was thinking, however, of Svirski's words; for him they had a more vital interest than they could have for a man who had finished the spiritual struggle with himself. At last he said, following his own course of thought, —

"Yes, there is something beyond human in this; some truth shines into the eyes here, like that moon."

They were going slowly toward the entrance, when a carriage rattled outside. Then in the dark passage leading to the centre of the circus, steps were heard; two tall figures issued from the shade into the light. One of these, dressed in gray stuff, which gleamed like steel in the moonlight, approached a number of steps to distinguish the visitors better, and said all at once, —

"Good-evening! The night is so beautiful that we, too, came to the Colosseum. What a night!"

Pan Stanislav recognized the voice of Pani Osnovski.

Giving her hand, she spoke with a voice as soft as the sound of that flute which came from the direction of the church, —

"I shall begin to believe in presentiments, for really something told me that here I should find acquaintances. How beautiful the night is!"

## CHAPTER XXXIV.

On returning to the hotel, Pan Stanislav and Marynia were surprised somewhat to find the Osnovskis' cards; and their astonishment rose from this, that, being newly married, it was their duty to make the first visit. For this unusual politeness it was needful to answer with equal politeness, hence they returned the visit on the following day. Bukatski, who saw them before they made it, though he was very unwell, and could barely drag his feet along, brought himself still to one of his usual witticisms, and said to Pan Stanislav, when they were alone for a moment, —

"She will play the coquette; but if thou suppose that she will fall in love with thee, thou art mistaken. She is a little like a razor, — she needs a strap to sharpen herself; in the best event, thou wilt be a strap for her."

"First, I do not wish to be her strap," answered Pan Stanislav; "and second, it is too early."

"Too early? That means that thou art reserving the future for thyself."

"No; it means that I am thinking of something else, and also that I love my Marynia more and more. And when that ends, too early will be too late, and that Pani Osnovski might dent, but not sharpen herself, on me."

And Pan Stanislav, in saying this, was sincere: he had his thoughts occupied really with something else; he was too honorable to betray his wife at any time, but even if not, it was too early to begin.

He was so greatly sure of his strength that he felt a certain readiness to expose himself to trial. In other words, it would have given the man a kind of pleasure if Pani Osnovski had dented herself on him.

After lunch he went with Marynia to sit to Svirski; the sitting, however, was short, since the artist was judge in some exhibition, and had to hasten to a meeting. They returned home, and Pan Osnovski came to them a quarter of an hour later.

Pan Stanislav, after his conversation with Svirski, had a kind of compassion for Osnovski, but also a sort of small opinion. Marynia, however, felt for him a living sympathy; she was won by what she had heard of his kindness and delicacy, as well as his attachment to his wife. It seemed to her now that all these qualities were as if written on his face, — a face by no means ugly, though it had pimples here and there.

After the greeting, Osnovski began to speak with the confident freedom of a man accustomed to good society:

"I come at the instance of my wife with a proposal. Praise to God, visiting ceremonies are ended between us, though abroad it is not worth while to reckon too precisely in this matter. The affair is this: We are going to St. Paul's to-day, and then to the Three Fountains. That is outside the city; there is an interesting cloister in the place, and a beautiful view. It would be very agreeable to us if you would consent to make the trip in our company."

Marynia was always ready for every trip, especially in company, and with pleasant conversation; in view of this she looked at her husband, waiting for what he would say. Pan Stanislav saw that she wished to go, and, besides, he thought in his soul, "If the other wants to dent herself, let her do it." And he answered, —

"I would consent willingly, but this depends on my superior power."

His "superior power" was not sure yet whether the obedient subordinate meant that really; but, seeing on his face a smile and good-humor, she made bold to say at last, —

"With much thankfulness; but shall we not cause trouble?"

"Not trouble, but pleasure," answered Osnovski. "In that event the matter is ended. We 'll be here in a quarter of an hour."

In fact, they set out a quarter of an hour later. Pani Osnovski's Chinese eyes were full of satisfaction and repose. Wearing an iris-colored robe, in which she might pass for the eighth wonder of the world, she looked really like a rusalka.[1] And before they had reached St. Paul's, Pan Stanislav did not know how Pani Osnovski, who had not spoken on this subject to him, had been able somehow to say to him, or at least to give him to understand, more or less as follows: "Thy wife is a pleasant little woman from the country; of my husband nothing need be said.

[1] River-maiden among the Slavs.

We two only are able to understand each other and share impressions."

But he resolved to torment her. When they arrived at St. Paul's, which Pani Osnovski did not mention otherwise than as "San Poolo fuori le Mura,"[1] her husband wished to stop the carriage, but she said, —

"We will stop when returning, for we shall know then how much time is left for this place; but now we'll go straight to the Three Fountains."

Turning to Pan Stanislav, she continued, "There are in this famous place various things, about which I should like to ask you."

"Then you will do badly, for I know nothing at all of these matters."

It appeared soon, on passing various monuments, that of the whole party Pan Osnovski knew most. The poor man had been studying the guide-books from morning till evening, so that he might be a guide for his wife, and also to please her with his knowledge. But she cared nothing for explanations which her husband could give, precisely because they came from him. The insolent self-assurance with which Pan Stanislav had confessed that he had no idea of antiquities was more to her taste.

Beyond St. Paul's opened out a view on the Campagna with its aqueducts, which seemed to run toward the city in haste, and on the Alban hills, veiled, as they were, with the blue haze of distance, — a view at once calm and bright. Pani Osnovski gazed for some time with a dreamy look, and then inquired, —

"Have you been in Albani or Nemi?"

"No," answered Pan Stanislav; "sitting to Svirski breaks the day so for us that we cannot make long excursions till the portrait is finished."

"We have been there; but when you are going, take me with you, take me with you! Is it agreed? Will you permit?" added she, turning to Marynia. "I shall be a fifth wheel to some extent, but never mind. Besides, I shall sit quietly, very quietly, in a corner of the carriage, and not give out one mru mru! Is it agreed?"

"Oi! little one, little one," said Pan Osnovski.

But she continued, "My husband will not believe that I am in love with Nemi; but I am. When I was there, it seemed to me that Christianity had not reached the place

[1] Thus printed to show her style of Italian.

yet; that in the night certain priests come out and celebrate pagan rites on the lake. Silence and mystery! there you have Nemi. Will you believe that when I was there the wish came to me to be a hermit, and it has not left me to this moment? I would build a cell on the bank of the lake for myself, and wear a robe long and gray, like the habit of Saint Francis of Assisi, and go barefoot. What would I give to be a hermit! I see myself at the lake—"

"Anetka,[1] but what would become of me?" inquired Osnovski, half in jest, half in earnest.

"Oh, thou wouldst console thyself," said she, curtly.

"Thou wouldst be a hermitess," thought Pan Stanislav, "if on the other side of the lake there were a couple of dozen dandies gazing through glasses to see what the hermitess was doing, and how she looked."

He was too well-bred to tell her this directly; but he told her something similar, and which could be understood.

"Naturally," said she, laughing; "I should live by alms, and should have to see people sometimes; if you came to Nemi, I should come to you too and repeat in a very low voice, 'Un soldo! un soldo!'"

Saying this, she stretched her small hands to him, and shook them, repeating humbly,—

"Un soldo per la povera! un soldo!"

And she looked into his eyes.

Pan Osnovski spoke meanwhile to Marynia.

"This is called Three Fountains," said he, "for there are three springs here. Saint Paul's head was cut off at this place; and there is a tradition that the head jumped three times, and that on those places springs burst forth. The place belongs now to the Trappists. Formerly people could not pass a night here, there was such fever; now there is less, for they have planted a whole forest of eucalyptuses on the hills. Oh, we can see it already."

But Pani Osnovski, bending back somewhat, half closed her eyes for a moment, and said to Pan Stanislav,—

"This Roman air intoxicates me. I am as if beside myself. At home I cannot force from life more than it gives me; but here I am demoralized, I feel that something is wanting to me. Do I know what? Here one feels something, divines something, yearns for something. Maybe that is bad. Maybe it is not right for me to say this. But I say always what passes through my mind.

[1] A diminutive of Aneta.

At home, when a child, they called me Little Sincerity. I shall beg my husband to take me hence. It may be better to live in my own narrow shell, like a nut, or a snail."

"It may be pleasant in shells for nuts or snails," answered Pan Stanislav, with gravity, "but not for birds, and besides birds of paradise, of which there is a tradition that they have no legs and can never rest, but must fly and fly."

"What a beautiful tradition!" exclaimed Pani Osnovski. And, raising her hands, she began to move them, imitating the motion of wings, and repeating, —

"This way, forever through the air."

The comparison flattered her, though she was astonished that Pan Stanislav had uttered it with a serious voice, but with an inattentive and, as it were, ironical face. He began to interest her, for he seemed very intelligent, and more difficult to master than she had expected.

Meanwhile they arrived at Three Fountains. They visited the garden, the church, and the chapel, in the basement of which three springs were flowing. Pan Osnovski explained, in his kind, somewhat monotonous voice, what he had read previously. Marynia listened with interest; but Pan Stanislav thought, —

"Still to live three hundred and sixty-five days in a year with him, must be a little tiresome."

That justified Pani Osnovski in his eyes for the moment; she, taking upon herself now the new rôle of bird of paradise, did not rest for a moment, not merely on the ground, but on any subject. First she drank eucalyptus liquor, which the cloister prepared as a means against fever; then she declared decisively that if she were a man she would be a Trappist. Later, however, she remembered that her sailing career would be agreeable "ever between sea and sky, as if living in endlessness;" at last the wish to become a great, a very great writer, gained the day against everything else, — a writer describing the minutest movements of the soul, half-conscious feelings, desires incompletely defined, all forms, all colors, all shades. The party learned also, as a secret, that she was writing her memoirs, which "that honest Yozio" considers a masterpiece; but she knows that that is nothing, she has not the least pretensions, and she ridicules Yozio and the memoirs.

"Yozio" looks at her with loving eyes, and with great affection on his pimpled face, and says with a protest, —

"As to the memoirs, I beg pardon greatly."

They drove away about sundown. There were long shadows from the trees; the sun was large and red. The distant aqueducts and the Alban hills were gleaming in rose-color. They were halfway when the "Angelus" was sounded in the tower of St. Paul's, and immediately after were heard a second, a third, a tenth. Each church gave the signal to the succeeding one; and such a mighty chorus was formed as if the whole air were ringing, as if the "Angelus" had been sounded not merely by the city, but the whole region, the plains, and the mountains.

Pan Stanislav looked on Marynia's face, lighted by the golden gleams. There was great calm in it and attention. It was evident that she was repeating the "Angelus" now, as she had repeated it in Kremen, when it was sounded in Vantory. Always and everywhere the same. Pan Stanislav remembered again the "service of God." It seemed to him more simple and pacifying than ever. But now, while approaching the city, he understood the permanence, the vitality, the immensity, of those beliefs. "All this," thought he, "has endured thus for a thousand and a half of years; and the strength and certainty of this city is only in those towers, those bells, that permanence of the cross, which endures and endures." Again Svirski's words came to him: "Here a ruin, on the Palatine a ruin, in the Forum a ruin, but over the city crosses, crosses, crosses and crosses." It seemed to him beyond a doubt that in that very permanence there is something superhuman. Meanwhile the bells sounded, and the heavens above the city were covered with twilight. Under the impression produced by the praying Marynia, and the bells, and that vesper feeling, which seemed to hover over the city and the whole land, the following thought began to take form in Pan Stanislav, who had much mental directness: "What an idiot and vain fool should I be, in view of the needs of faith and that feeling of God, were I to seek some special forms of love and reverence of my own, instead of accepting those which Marynia calls 'service of God,' and which still must be the best, since the world has lived nearly two thousand years in them!" Then the reasoning side of this thought struck him as a practical man, and he continued to himself, almost joyously: "On one side the traditions of a thousand years, the life of God knows how many generations and how many societies, for which there was and is delight in those forms, the authority for God knows how many persons who consider them as the only forms; on the other side, who? I, a partner in the commission house of Bigiel and Polanyetski; and I had the pretension to think out something better into which the Lord God would fit Himself more conveniently. For this it is needful at least to be a fool! I, besides, am a man sincere with myself; and I could not endure it if from time to time the thought came to me, — I am a fool. But my mother believed in this, and my wife believes; and I have never seen greater peace in any one than in them."

Here he looked at Marynia once and a second time; she had finished evidently her "Angelus," for she smiled at him in answer, and inquired, —

"Why so silent?"

"We are all silent," he answered.

And so it was, but for various reasons. While Pan Stanislav was occupied with his thoughts, Pani Osnovski attacked him a number of times with her eyes and her words. He answered her words with something disconnected, and did not notice her glances in any way. He simply offended her: she might have forgiven him, she might have been pleased even, if to her statement that she wished to be a nun, he had answered with impudence concealed in polished words; but he wounded her mortally when he ceased to notice her, and in punishment she ceased also to notice him.

But as a person of good breeding she became all the politer to Marynia. She inquired touching her plans on the following day; and, learning that they were to be at the Vatican, she announced that she and her husband had tickets of admission, and would use the opportunity also.

"You know the dress?" inquired she. "A black robe, and black lace on the head. One looks a little old in them, but no matter."

"I know; Pan Svirski forewarned me," answered Marynia.

"Pan Svirski always talks of you to me when I am sitting to him. He has great regard for you."

"And I for him."

During this conversation they arrived at the hotel. Pan Stanislav received such a slight and cool pressure of the hand from the fair lady that, though his head was occupied with something else, he noticed it.

"Is that a new method," thought he, "or have I said something that displeased her?"

"What dost thou think of Pani Osnovski?" asked he of Marynia in the evening.

"I think that Pan Svirski may be right in some measure."

And Pan Stanislav answered: "She is writing at this moment 'memoirs,' which 'Yozio' considers a masterpiece."

## CHAPTER XXXV.

NEXT morning when Marynia came out to her husband he hardly knew her. Dressed in black, and with a black lace veil on her head, she seemed taller, more slender, darker, and older. But he was pleased by a certain solemnity in her which recalled the ceremony of their marriage. Half an hour later they started. On the road Marynia confessed to fear, and a beating of the heart. He pacified her playfully, though he, too, was moved somewhat; and when, after a short drive, they entered the gigantic half-circle in front of St. Peter's, he felt also that his pulse was not beating as every day, and, besides, he had a strange feeling of being smaller than usual. Near the steps, where stood a number of Swiss guards, arrayed in the splendid uniform invented by Michael Angelo, they found Svirski, who led them up with a throng of people, mostly Belgians. Marynia, who was somewhat dazed, did not know herself when she entered a very spacious hall, in which the throng was still denser, excepting on a space in the centre, where the Swiss guards were posted in lines, and kept a broad passage open. The crowd, among which the French and Flemish languages were to be heard, whispered in low voices, and turned their heads and eyes toward a passage, in which, from time to time, appeared, through the adjoining hall, forms in remarkable costumes, which reminded Pan Stanislav of galleries in Antwerp or Brussels. It seemed to him that the Middle Ages were rising from the dead: now it was some knight of those ages, in a helmet, different indeed from helmets on the ancient portraits, but with steel on his breast; now a herald in a short red dalmatica, and with a red cap on his head; at times through the open door appeared purple cardinals, or violet bishops, ostrich feathers, lace on black velvet, and heads immensely venerable, white hair and faces, as if from a sarcophagus. But it was evident that the glances of the throng were falling on those peculiar dresses and colors and faces, as if, in passing, that their eyes were waiting for something beyond, something higher, some other heart; it was clear that in people's minds attention was fixed as was feeling in their souls, in waiting for a moment which comes once in a lifetime, and is memorable ever after. Pan Stanislav, holding Marynia by the hand, so as not to lose her in the throng, felt that hand tremble from emotion; as to him, in the midst of those silent crowds and beating hearts, before that historical dignity of former ages rising from the dead, as it were, in the midst of that attention and expectation, he felt a second time the wonderful impression of becoming smaller and smaller, till he was the smallest that he had ever been in life.

At that moment a low and rather panting voice whispered near them,—

"I have been looking for you, and found you with difficulty. The ceremony will begin at once, it seems."

But it was not to begin at once. The monsignor acquaintance greeted Svirski meanwhile, and, speaking a few words to him, conducted the whole party politely to the adjoining hall, which was fitted in crimson damask. Pan Stanislav saw with astonishment that this hall, too, was full of people, with the exception of one end, which was reserved by a guard of honor, and in which was an armchair on an elevation, and before it a number of prelates and bishops conversing confidentially. Here expectation and attention were more expressly visible. It was evident that people were holding their breath; and all faces had a solemn, mysterious expression. The azure clearness of the day, mingled with the purple reflections of the tapestry, filled that hall with a kind of unusual light, in which the rays of the sun, breaking in here and there through the window-panes, appeared very ruddy and of a deeper red.

They waited some time yet; at last, in the first hall a murmur was heard, then a muttering, then a shout, and, finally, in the open side door appeared a white figure, borne by the noble guard. Marynia's hand pressed Pan Stanislav's nervously; he returned the pressure; and swift impressions, merged in one general feeling of the exceptional and solemn import of the moment, flashed through their minds, as during the ceremony of their marriage.

One of the cardinals began to speak, but Pan Stanislav neither heard nor understood what he said. His eyes, his thoughts, his whole soul, were with the figure clothed in white. Nothing in it escaped his attention,—its unparalleled emaciation, its frailness, its thinness, and its face as pale, and at the same time as transparent, as faces of the dead are. There was in it something which had no physical strength, or in every case it seemed to him simply half body, half apparition, — as it were, a light shining through alabaster; a spirit, fixed in some transparent matter; an intermediate link between two worlds; a link human yet, though already preterhuman, earthly so far, but also above earthly things. And through a marvellous antithesis the matter in it seemed to be something apparitional, and the spirit something material.

Afterward, when people began to approach it for a blessing; when Pan Stanislav saw his Marynia at its feet; when he felt that to those knees, already half empyrean, one might still incline as to those of a father, — an emotion surpassing everything seized him; his eyes were as if mist-covered; never in life had he felt himself such a small grain of sand, but at the same time he felt himself a grain of sand in which the grateful heart of a little child was throbbing.

After they had gone out, all were silent. Marynia had eyes as if roused from sleep; Vaskovski's hands were trembling. Bukatski dragged himself in to lunch; but, being ill, he could not excite conversation in any one. Svirski, strange to say, talked little while Marynia was sitting, and returned continually to the same subject; from time to time he repeated, —

"Yes, yes; whoever has not seen that can have no conception of it. That will remain."

In the evening Pan Stanislav and Marynia went to see the sunset from Trinità dei Monti. The day ended very beautifully. The whole city was buried in a kind of hazy golden gleam; under their feet, far down in the valley, on the Piazza di Spagna, darkness was beginning, but a darkness yet lighted, in the mild tones of which irises and white lilies were visible among the flowers set out on both sides of the Via Condotti. In the whole picture there was great and undisturbed repose, — a kind of soothing announcement of night and sleep. Then the Piazza di Spagna began to sink more and more in the shade, but the Trinità was shining continually in purple.

Pan Stanislav and Marynia felt this calmness reflected in themselves; they descended the giant stairs then with a wonderful feeling of peace in their souls. All the impressions of the day settled down in them in lines as great and calm as those twilight belts, which were still shining above them.

"Knowest thou," said Pan Stanislav, "what I remember yet from childhood's years? That with us at home they always said the evening rosary together." And he looked with an inquiring glance into Marynia's eyes.

"Oh, my Stas!" said she, with a voice trembling from emotion, "I did not dare to mention this — my best."

"'Service of God,' — dost thou remember?"

But she had said that formerly with such simplicity, and as a thing so self-evident, that she remembered nothing whatever about it.

## CHAPTER XXXVI.

But Pan Stanislav was in permanent disfavor with Pani Osnovski. Meeting him at Svirski's, between one sitting and another, she spoke to him only in so far as good breeding and politeness demanded. He saw this perfectly, and asked himself sometimes, "What does that woman want of me?" but troubled himself little. He would have troubled himself still less if "that woman," instead of being eight and twenty, had been eight and fifty years of age; if she had been without those violet eyes and those cherry lips. And such is human nature that, in spite of the fact that he wanted nothing of her, and expected nothing, he could not refrain from thinking what might happen should he strive really for her favor, and how far would she be capable of going.

They had another trip of four to the catacombs of St. Calixtus, for Pan Stanislav wished to repay politeness with politeness, — that is, a carriage with a carriage. But this trip did not bring reconciliation; they only conversed so far as not to call attention to themselves. At last this began to anger Pan Stanislav. In fact, Pani Osnovski's bearing developed a special relation between them, unpleasant in a way, but known only to them, hence something between them exclusively, — a kind of secret, to which no one else was admitted. Pan Stanislav considered that all this would end with the work on her portrait; but though the face had been finished some time, there remained many little details, for which the presence of the charming model was indispensable. Even for the simple reason that Svirski did not wish to lose time, it happened that when Pan Stanislav and his wife came, the Osnovskis were in the studio. Sometimes they stopped a little for greeting and a short talk touching yesterday's impressions; sometimes Osnovski was sent by his wife on an errand, or for some news. In that event he went out first, leaving the carriage for her before the studio.

And it happened once that when Marynia had taken her place for a sitting, Pani Osnovski had not gone yet; after a while, learning that Marynia had been at the theatre the evening before, she, while putting on her hat and gloves before the mirror, inquired about singers and the opera, then, turning to Pan Stanislav, she said, —

"And now, I pray you, conduct me to the carriage."

She threw on her wrap, and began to look for the ribbons sewn behind to the lining, so as to fasten it around her waist, but she stopped suddenly at the entrance, —

"I cannot find the ribbons because I have my gloves on; take pity on me."

Pan Stanislav had to look for the ribbons, but in doing so he was forced to put his arm almost around her; after a moment the brewing of desire poured about him, all the more since she bent toward him, and the warmth of her face and body struck him.

"But why are you angry with me?" inquired she, in an undertone; "that is bad. I am in such need of friendly souls. What have I done to you?"

He found the ribbons, recovered himself, and with that somewhat coarse satisfaction of a rude man, who desires to use his triumph, and to signify that he has not yielded, answered simply, with an impertinence, —

"You have done nothing to me, and you can do nothing."

But she repulsed the impoliteness, as if it were a ball at tennis.

"Because sometimes I notice persons so little that I hardly see them."

They went in silence to the carriage.

"But is it that way?" thought Pan Stanislav, returning to the studio; "a man might advance there as far as he pleased;" and a quiver passed through him. "As far as he pleased," repeated he.

Herewith he was not conscious that he had made such a mistake as is made daily by dozens of men who are lovers of hunting in other men's grounds. Pani Osnovski was a coquette: she had a dry heart, and her thought was dishonorable already; but she was hundreds of miles yet from complete physical fall.

Meanwhile Pan Stanislav returned to the studio feeling that he had made an immense sacrifice for Marynia, and with a certain regret in his heart, first, because she would not know what had happened, and second, if she should know, she would consider his action as perfectly simple. This feeling angered him; and when he looked at her, at her clear eyes, her calm face, and her fair, honest beauty, a comparison of those two women urged itself into his mind in spite of him, and in his soul he said, —

"Ah, Marynia! such as she would rather sink through the earth; of her it is possible to be certain."

And — singular thing — there was in this an undoubted recognition, but there was also a shade of regret, and, as it were, of irritation, that that was a woman so greatly his own that he did not feel bound to a continual admiration of her worthiness.

And for the rest of the sitting he turned his thought to Pani Osnovski. He supposed that in future she would simply cease to give her hand to him, and it turned out that he was mistaken again. On the contrary, wishing to show that she attached no importance to him or to his words, she was more polite to him than hitherto. Pan Osnovski, however, had an offended look, and became more and more icy every day toward him. This was caused, undoubtedly, by conversations with "Anetka."

A few days later, however, impressions of another sort effaced that adventure from Pan Stanislav's mind. Bukatski had long been ill; he complained more and more of a pain in the back of his head, and a strange feeling of separating from his own muscles. His humor revived still at moments, but it shot up and went out like fireworks. He came to the *table d'hôte* more rarely. At last Pan Stanislav received his card one morning; on it these words were written with a very uncertain hand, —

My Dear, — After to-night it seems that I am about to get on horseback. If thou wish to see my departure, come, especially in lack of anything better to do.

Pan Stanislav hid the card from Marynia, but went straightway. He found Bukatski in bed, and a doctor with him, whom Bukatski sent away that moment.

"Thou hast frightened me terribly," said Pan Stanislav. "What ails thee?"

"Nothing great, — a little paralysis of the lower part of the body."

"Have the fear of God!"

"Thou speakest wisely, if there were time for it; but now I have no power in my left arm, in my left leg, and I cannot rise. Thus did I wake this morning. I thought that I had lost speech, too, and began to declaim to myself,

'Per me si va;' but, as thou seest, I have not lost speech. My tongue remained, and now I am trying to find calmness of thought."

"But art thou sure that it is paralysis? It may be a temporary numbness."

"What is life?—Ah, only a moment," Bukatski began to declaim; "I cannot move, and that is the end, or, if thou prefer, the beginning."

"That would be a terrible thing, but I do not believe it; any one may be benumbed for a time."

"There are moments in life which are somewhat bitter, as the carp said when the cook was scraping his scales off with a knife. I confess that at first terror took hold of me. Hast thou ever felt the hair rising on thy head? It is not to be reckoned altogether among feelings of delight. But I have recovered my balance, and now, at the end of three hours, it seems to me that I have lived ten years with my paralysis. It is a question of habit! as the mushroom said when in the frying-pan. I am chatting much, for I haven't much time. Dost thou know, my dear friend, that I shall die in a couple of days?"

"Indeed, thou art chatting! Paralyzed people live thirty years."

"Even forty," answered Bukatski. "Paralysis in that case is a luxury which some may permit themselves, but not men like me. For a strong man, who has a good neck, good shoulders, good breast, and proper legs, it may be even a species of rest, a kind of vacation after a frolicsome youth, and an opportunity for meditation; but for me! Dost remember how thou wert laughing at my legs? Well, I tell thee that they were elephantine at that time if compared with what they are to-day. It is not true that every man is a clod; I am only a line,—I am not joking,—and, moreover, a line vanishing *in infinity.*"

Pan Stanislav began to shrug his shoulders, to contradict, and to quote known examples; but Bukatski resisted.

"Stop! I feel and know that in a couple of days paralysis of the brain will set in. I have been expecting this a whole year, but told no one, and for a year have been reading books on medicine. A second attack will come, and that will be final."

Here he was silent, but after a time continued,—

"And, believe me, I do not like this. Think of it: I am as much alone as a finger cut off from its hand; I have no one. Here, and even in Warsaw, only people who are paid would take care of me. Life is terribly wretched when a man is without power of movement, and without a living soul who is related. When I lose speech, as I have lost power of motion, any woman in attendance, or any man, may strike me on the face as much as she or he pleases. But thou must know one thing. I feared paralysis at the first moment; but in my weak body there is a brave spirit. Remember what I said to thee, — that I fear not death; and I do not fear it."

Here there gleamed in Bukatski's eyes a certain pale reflection of daring and energy, hidden somewhere in the bottom of that disjointed and softened soul.

But Pan Stanislav, who had a good heart, put his hand on the palm already paralyzed, and said, with great feeling, —

"My Adzia! But do not suppose that we will leave thee thus, desert thee as thou art; and do not say that thou hast no one. Thou hast me, and besides me, my wife, and Svirski, Vaskovski, and the Bigiels. For us thou art not a stranger. I will take thee to Warsaw, I will put thee in the hospital, and we will care for thee, and no attendant will strike thee on the face, — first, because I should break the bones of such a person; secondly, we have Sisters of Charity, and among them is Pani Emilia."

Bukatski was silent, and grew pale a little; he was more moved than he wished to show. A shadow passed over his eyes.

"Thou art a good fellow," said he, after a prolonged silence. "Thou knowest not what a miracle thou hast worked, for thou hast brought it about that I wish something yet. Yes; I should like wonderfully to go to Warsaw, to be among you all. I should be immensely pleased there."

"Here thou must go at once to some hospital, and be under constant care. Svirski must know where the best one is. Yield thyself to me, wilt thou? Let me arrange for thee."

"Do what may please thee," answered Bukatski, whom consolation began to enter now, in view of the new plans and the energy of his friend.

Pan Stanislav wrote to Svirski and to Vaskovski, and sent out messengers immediately. Half an hour later both appeared, Svirski with a famous local physician. Before mid-day Bukatski found himself in a hospital, in a well-lighted and cheerful chamber.

"What a pleasant and warm tone!" said he, looking at the golden color, and the walls and ceiling. "This is nice." Then, turning to Pan Stanislav, he said, "Come to me in the evening, but go now to thy wife."

Pan Stanislav took farewell of him, and went out. When he reached home he told Marynia the whole story cautiously, for he did not wish to frighten her with sudden news, giving the idea that he was in a dangerous condition. Marynia begged him to take her to Bukatski, if not in the evening, in the morning early, which he promised to do. They went immediately after lunch, for that day there was no sitting in the studio.

But before they arrived, Vaskovski was there, and he did not leave Bukatski for a moment. When the patient had settled himself well in the new bed, the old man told him how once he had thought himself dying, but after confession and receiving the sacraments, he grew better, as if by a miracle.

"A well-known method, dear professor," said Bukatski, with a smile; "I divine what thy object is."

The professor was as confused as if caught in some evil deed, and crossed his hands.

"I will lay a wager that it would help thee," said he.

Bukatski answered with a gleam of his former humor, "Very well. In a couple of days I shall convince myself, on the other side of the river, how much it will help me."

The arrival of Marynia pleased him, all the more that it was unexpected. He said that he had not thought to see any woman on this side of the river, and, moreover, one of his own. Therewith he began to scold them all a little, but with evident emotion.

"What sentimentalists they are!" said he. "It is simply a judgment to be occupied with such a skeleton grandfather as I am. Ye will never have reason. What is this for? What good in it? See, even before death, I am forced to be grateful; and I am sincerely, very sincerely grateful."

But Marynia did not let him talk about death; on the contrary, she said with great firmness that he must go to Warsaw, and be among his friends. She spoke of this as a thing the execution of which was not subject to the least doubt, and she succeeded gradually in convincing Bukatski of it. She told him how to prepare, and at last he listened to her eagerly. His thoughts passed into a certain condition of yielding, in which they let themselves be led. He felt like a child, and, besides, a poor child.

That same day Osnovski visited him, and also showed as much interest and feeling as if he had been his own brother. Bukatski had out and out not expected all this, and had not counted on anything similar. Therefore, when later in the evening Pan Stanislav came a second time, and no others were present, he said to him, —

"I tell thee sincerely that never have I felt with such clearness that I made life a stupid farce, that I have wasted it like a dog." And soon after he added, "And if I had found a real pleasure in that method by which I was living; but I had not even that satisfaction. How stupid is our epoch! A man makes two of himself; all that is best in him he hides away, shuts in somewhere in corners, and becomes a kind of ape. He rather persuades himself of the uselessness of life than feels it. How wonderful this is! One thing consoles me, — that in truth death is the only thing real in life, though, on the other hand, this again is not a reason why, before it comes, we should say of it as a fool says of wine, that it is vinegar."

"My dear friend," answered Pan Stanislav, "thou hast always tortured thyself with this endless winding of thought around some bobbin. Do not do that at present."

"Thou art right. But I am unable not to think that while I was walking around and was well in a fashion, I jeered at life; and now — I tell thee as a secret — I want to live longer."

"Thou wilt live longer."

"Give me peace. Thy wife was persuading me of that, but now again I do not believe it. And it is painful to me, — I have thrown myself away. But hear why I wanted to speak with thee. I know not whether any account is waiting for me; I say sincerely that I know not, but still I feel a kind of strange alarm, as if I were afraid. And I will tell thee something: during life I did nothing for my fellows, and I was able! I was able! In presence of this thought fear seizes me; I give thee my word! That is an unworthy thing. I did nothing; I ate bread without paying for it, and now — death. If there are any whips beyond, and if they are waiting for me, it is to punish that; and listen, Stas, it is painful to me."

Here, although he spoke with the careless tone usual to him, his face expressed real dread, his lips grew pale somewhat, and on his forehead drops of sweat appeared.

"But stop!" said Pan Stanislav; "see what comes to his head. Thou art injuring thyself."

But Bukatski spoke on: "Listen! wait! I have property which is rather considerable; let even that do something for me. I will leave thee a part of it, and do thou use the remainder for something useful. Thou art practical, so is Bigiel. Think of something, thou and he, for I do not believe that I shall have time. Wilt thou do this?"

"That, and thy every wish."

"I thank thee. How wonderful are fears and reproaches of this kind! And still I cannot escape a feeling of guilt. The conditions are such that I am not right! One should do something honorable even just before death. But it is no joke,—death. If that were something visible, but it is so dark. And one must decay, corrupt, and rot *in the dark.* Art thou a believer?"

"Yes."

"But I, neither yes nor no. I amused myself with Nirvana, as with other things. Dost thou know, were it not for the feeling of guilt, I should be more at rest? I had no idea that this would pain me so; I have the impression that I am a bee which has robbed its hive, and that is a low thing. But at least my property will remain after me. This is true, is it not? I have spent a little, but very little, on pictures, which will remain, too; is n't this true? But now, how I should like to live longer, even a year, even long enough not to die here!"

He meditated a while, and then said,—

"I understand one thing now: life may be bad, for a man may order it foolishly; but existence is good."

Pan Stanislav went away late in the night. Through the following week the health of the patient was wavering. The doctors were unable to foresee anything; they judged, however, that a journey was not dangerous in any case. Svirski and Vaskovski volunteered to go to Warsaw with the sick man, who was yearning for home more and more, and who mentioned Pani Emilia, the Sister of Charity, almost daily. But on the eve of the day on which he was to go, he lost speech suddenly. Pan Stanislav's heart was bleeding when he looked at his eyes, in which at moments a terrible alarm was depicted, and at moments a kind of great, silent prayer. He tried to write, but could not. In the evening came paralysis of the brain, and he died.

They buried him in the Campo Santo temporarily. Pan Stanislav thought that his looks uttered a prayer to be carried to his own country, and Svirski confirmed that thought.

Thus vanished that bubble which gleamed sometimes with the colors of the rainbow, but was as empty and evanescent as any bubble.

Pan Stanislav was sincerely afflicted by his death, and meditated afterward for whole hours on that strange life. He did not share these thoughts with Marynia, for somehow it had not become a custom with him yet to confide to her anything that took place in his mind. Finally, as happens often with people who are thinking of the dead, he drew from these thoughts various conclusions to his own advantage.

"Bukatski," said he to himself, "was never able to come to harmony with his own mind: he lacked the understanding of life; he could not fix his position in that forest, and he travelled always according to the fancy of the moment. But if he had felt contented with that system, if he had squeezed something out of life, I should own that he had sense. But it was unpleasant for him. It is really a foolish thing to persuade one's self, before death comes, that wine is vinegar. But I look at matters more clearly, and, besides, I have been far more sincere with myself. Happen what may, I am almost perfectly in order with God and with life."

There was truth in this, but there was also illusion. Pan Stanislav was not in order with his own wife. He judged that if he gave her protection, bread, good treatment, and put kisses on her lips from time to time, he was discharging all possible duties assumed with regard to her. Meanwhile their relations began to be more definitely of this sort,— that he only deigned to love and receive love. In the course of his observations of life this strange phenomenon had struck him more than once, — that when, for example, a man well-known for honor does some noble deed, people wave their hands as if with a certain indifference, saying, "Oh, that is Pan X——; from him this is perfectly natural!" When, however, some rogue chanced to do something honorable, these same people said with great recognition, "But there is something in the man." A hundred times Pan Stanislav observed that a copper from a miser made more impression than a ducat from a generous giver. He did not notice, however, that with Marynia he followed the same method of judgment and recognition. She gave him all her being, all her soul. "Ah, Marynia! that is natural!" and he waved his hand too. Had her love not been so generous, had it come to him with supreme difficulty, with the conviction that it was a treasure, and given as such, with the conviction that she was a divinity demanding a bowed head and honor, Pan Stanislav would have received it with a bowed head, and would have rendered the honor. Such is the general human heart; and only the choicest natures, woven from rays, have power to rise above this level. Marynia had given Pan Stanislav her love as his right. She considered his love as happiness, and he gave it as happiness; he felt himself the idol on the altar. One ray of his fell on the heart of the woman and illumined it: the divinity kept the rest of the rays for itself; taking all, it gave only a part. In his love there was not that fear which flows from honor, and there was not that which in every fondling says to the woman beloved, "at thy feet."

But they did not understand this yet, either of them.

## CHAPTER XXXVII.

"I do not ask if thou art happy," said Bigiel to Pan Stanislav after his return to Warsaw; "with such a person as thy wife it is not possible to be unhappy."

"True," answered Pan Stanislav; "Marynia is such an honest little woman that it would be hard to find a better." Then, turning to Pani Bigiel, he said, —

"We are both happy, and it cannot be otherwise. You remember, dear lady, our former conversations about love and marriage? You remember how I feared to meet a woman who would try to hide the world from her husband with herself, to occupy all his thoughts, all his feelings, to be the single object of his life? You remember how I proved to you and Pani Emilia that love for a woman could not and should not in any case be for a man everything; that beyond it there are other questions in the world?"

"Yes; but I remember also how I told you that domestic occupations do not hinder me in any way from loving my children; for I know in some fashion, as it seems to me, that these things are not like boxes, for example, of which, when you have put a certain number on a table, there is no room for others."

"My wife is right now," said Bigiel. "I have noticed that people often deceive themselves when they transfer feelings or ideas into material conditions. When it is a question of feelings or ideas, space is not to be considered."

"Oh, stop! Thou art conquered to the country," said Pan Stanislav, humorously.

"But if the position is pleasant for me?" said Bigiel, promptly. "Moreover, thou, too, wilt be conquered."

"I?"

"Yes; with honesty, kindness, and heart."

"That is something different. It is possible to be conquered, and not be a slipper. Do not hinder me in praising Marynia; I have succeeded in a way that could not be improved, and specially for this reason, — that she is satisfied with the feeling which I have for her, and has no wish to be my exclusive idol. For this I love her. God has guarded me from a wife demanding devotion of the whole soul, whole mind, whole existence; and I thank Him sincerely, since I could not endure such a woman. I understand more easily that all may be given of free will, and when not demanded."

"Believe me, Pan Stanislav," answered Pani Bigiel, "that in this regard we are all equally demanding; but at first we take frequently that part for the whole which they give us, and then —"

"And then what?" interrupted Pan Stanislav, rather jokingly.

"Then those who have real honesty in their hearts attain to something which for you is a word without meaning, but for us is often life's basis."

"What kind of talisman is that?"

"Resignation."

Pan Stanislav laughed, and added, "The late Bukatski used to say that women put on resignation frequently, as they do a hat, because it becomes them. A resignation hat, a veil of light melancholy, — are they ugly?"

"No, not ugly. Say what you please; they may be a dress, but in such a dress it is easier to reach heaven than in another."

"Then my Marynia is condemned to hell, for she will never wear that dress, I think. But you will see her in a moment, for she promised to come here after office hours. She is late, the loiterer; she ought to be here now."

"Her father is detaining her, I suppose. But you will stay to dine with us, will you not?"

"We will stay to dine. Agreed."

"And some one else has promised us to-day, so the society will only be increased. I will go now to tell them to prepare places for you."

Pani Bigiel went out; but Pan Stanislav asked Bigiel, —

"Whom hast thou at dinner?"

"Zavilovski, the future letter-writer of our house."

"Who is he?"

"That poet already famous."

"From Parnassus to the desk? How is that?"

"I do not remember, now, who said that society keeps its geniuses on diet. People say that this man is immensely capable, but he cannot earn bread with verses. Our Tsiskovski went to the insurance company; his place was left vacant, and Zavilovski applied. I had some scruples, but he told me that for him this place was a question of bread, and the chance of working. Besides, he pleased me, for he told me at once that he writes in three languages, but speaks well in none of them; and second, that he has not the least conception of mercantile correspondence."

"Oh, that is nonsense," answered Pan Stanislav; "he will learn in a week. But will he keep the place long, and will not the correspondence be neglected? Business with a poet!"

"If he is not right, we will part. But when he applied, I chose to give the place to him. In three days he is to begin. Meanwhile, I have advanced a month's salary; he needed it."

"Was he destitute?"

"It seems so. There is an old Zavilovski, — that one who has a daughter, a very wealthy man. I asked our Zavilovski if that was a relative of his; he said not, but blushed, so I think that the old man is his relative. But how it is with us? A balance in nothing. Some deny relationship because they are poor; others, because they are rich. All through some fancy, and because of that rascally pride. But he'll please thee; he pleased my wife."

"Who pleased thy wife?" asked Pani Bigiel, coming in.

"Zavilovski."

"For I read his beautiful verses entitled, 'On the Threshold.' At the same time he looks as if he were hiding something from people."

"He is hiding poverty, or rather, poverty was hiding him."

"No; he looks as if he had passed through some severe disappointment."

"Thou wert able to see in him a romance, and to tell me that he had suffered much. Thou wert offended when I put forth the hypothesis that it might be from worms in childhood, or scald-head. That was not poetical enough for her."

Pan Stanislav looked at his watch, and was a little impatient.

"Marynia is not coming," said he; "what a loiterer!"

But the "loiterer" came at that moment, or rather, drove up. The greeting was not effusive, for she had seen the Bigiels at the railway. Pan Stanislav told his wife that they would stay to dine, to which she agreed willingly, and fell to greeting the children, who rushed into the room in a swarm.

Now came Zavilovski, whom Bigiel presented to Pan Stanislav and Marynia. He was a man still young, — about seven or eight and twenty. Pan Stanislav, looking at him, considered that in every case his mien was not that of a man who had suffered much; he was merely ill at ease in a society with which he was more than half unacquainted. He had a nervous face, and a chin projecting prominently, like Wagner's, gladsome gray eyes, and a very delicate forehead, whiter than the rest of his face; on his forehead large veins formed the letter *Y*. He was, besides, rather tall and somewhat awkward.

"I have heard," said Pan Stanislav to him, "that in three days you will be our associate."

"Yes, Pan Principal," answered the young man; "or rather, I shall serve in the office."

"But give peace to the 'principal,'" said Pan Stanislav, laughing. "With us it is not the custom to use the words 'grace,' or 'principal' unless perchance such a title would please my wife by giving her importance in her own eyes. But listen, Pani Principal*ess*," said he, turning to Marynia, "would it please thee to be called principal*ess*? It would be a new amusement."

Zavilovski was confused; but he laughed too, when Marynia answered, —

"No; for it seems to me that a principal*ess* ought to wear an enormous cap like this" (here she showed with her hands how big), "and I cannot endure caps."

It grew pleasanter for Zavilovski in the joyous kindness of those people; but he was confused again when Marynia said, —

"You are an old acquaintance of mine. I have read nothing of late, for we have just returned home; has anything appeared while we were gone?"

"No, Pani," answered he; "I occupy myself with that as Pan Bigiel does with music, — in free moments, and for my own amusement."

"I do not believe this," said Marynia.

And she was right not to believe, for it was not true at all. Zavilovksi's reply was lacking also in candor, for he wished to let it be known that he desired beyond all to pass as the correspondent of a commercial house, and to be considered an employee, not a poet. He gave a title to

Bigiel and Pan Stanislav, not through any feeling of inferiority, but to show that when he had undertaken office-work he considered it as good as any other, that he accommodated himself to his position, and would do so in the future. There was in this also something else. Zavilovski, though young, had observed how ridiculous people are, who, when they have written one or two little poems, pose as seers, and insist on being considered such. His great self-esteem trembled before the fear of the ridiculous; hence he fell into the opposite extreme, and was almost ashamed of his poetry. Recently, when suffering great want, this feeling became almost a deformity, and the least reference by any one to the fact that he was a poet brought him to suppressed anger.

But meanwhile he felt that he was illogical, since for him the simplest thing would have been not to write and publish poems; but he could not refrain. His head was not surrounded with an aureole yet, but a few gleams had touched it; these illuminated his forehead at one moment, and then died, in proportion as he created, or neglected. After each new poem the gleam began again to quiver; and Zavilovski, as capable as he was ambitious, valued in his heart those reflections of glory more than aught else on earth. But he wanted people to talk of him only among themselves, and not to his eyes. When he felt that they were beginning to forget him, he suffered secretly. There was in him, as it were, a dualism of self-love, which wanted glory, and at the same time rejected it through a certain shyness and pride, lest some one might say that too much had been given. And many contradictions besides inhered in him, as a man young and impressionable, who takes in and feels exceptionally, and who, amidst his feelings, is not able frequently to distinguish his own personal *I*. For this reason it is that artists in general seem often unnatural.

Now came dinner, during which conversation turned on Italy, and people whom the Polanyetskis had met there. Pan Stanislav spoke of Bukatski and his last moments, and also of the dead man's will, by which he became the heir to a fairly large sum of money. By far the greater part was to be used for public objects, and touching this he had to confer with Bigiel. They loved Bukatski, and remembered him with sympathy. Pani Bigiel had even tears in her eyes when Marynia stated that before death he had confessed; and that he died like a Christian. But this sympathy was of the kind that one might eat dinner with; and if Bukatski had, in truth, sighed sometimes for Nirvana, he had what he wanted at present, since he had become for people, even those near him, and who loved him, a memory as slight as it was unenduring. A week longer, a month, or a year, and his name would be a sound without an echo. He had not earned, in fact, the deep love of any one, and had not received it; his life flowed away from him in such fashion that after even a child like Litka, there remained not only a hundred times more sorrow, but also love and memorable traces. His life roused at first the curiosity of Zavilovski, who had not known him; but when he had heard all that Pan Stanislav narrated, he said, after thinking a while, "An additional copy." Bukatski, who joked at everything, would have been pained by such an epitaph.

Marynia, wishing to give a more cheerful turn to conversation, began to tell of the excursions they had made in Rome and the environs, either alone, with Svirski, or the Osnovskis. Bigiel, who was a classmate of Osnovski, and who from time to time saw him yet, said,—

"He has one love,—his wife; and one hatred,—his corpulence, or rather, his inclination to it. As to other things, he is the best man on earth."

"But he seems quite slender," said Marynia.

"Two years ago he was almost fat; but since he began to use a bicycle, fence, follow the Banting system, drink Karlsbad in summer, and go in winter to Italy or Egypt to perspire, he has made himself slender again. But I have not said truly that he has a hatred for corpulence; it is his wife who has, and he does this through regard for her. He dances whole nights, too, at balls, for the same reason."

"He is a *sclavus saltans*," said Pan Stanislav. "Svirski has told us of this already."

"I understand that it is possible to love a wife," said Bigiel; "it is possible to consider her, according to the saying, as the apple of the eye. Very well! But, as I love God, I have heard that he writes verses to his wife; that he opens books with his eyes closed, marks a verse with his finger, and divines to himself from what he reads whether he is loved. If it comes out badly, he falls into melancholy. He is in love like a student, —counts all her glances, strives to divine what this or that word is to mean, kisses not only her feet and hands, but when he thinks that no one is looking, he kisses her gloves. God knows what it is like! and that for whole years."

"How much in love!" said Marynia.

"Would it be to thy liking were I such?" asked Pan Stanislav.

She thought a while, and answered, "No; for in that case thou wouldst be another man."

"Oh, that is a Machiavelli," said Bigiel. "It would be worth while to write down such an answer, for that is at once a praise, and somewhat of a criticism, — a testimony that as it is, is best, and that it would be possible to wish for something still better. Manage this for thyself, man."

"I take it for praise," said Pan Stanislav, "though you" (here he turned to Pani Bigiel), "will say surely that it is resignation."

"The outside is love," answered Pani Bigiel, laughing; "resignation may come in time, as lining, if cold comes."

Zavilovski looked on Marynia with curiosity; she seemed to him comely, sympathetic, and her answer arrested his attention. He thought, however, that only a woman could speak so who was greatly in love, and one for whom there was never enough of feeling. He began to look at Pan Stanislav with a certain jealousy; and because he was a great hermit, the words of the song came at once to his head, "My neighbor has a darling wife."

Meanwhile, since he had been silent a whole hour, or had spoken a couple of words merely, it seemed to him that he ought to engage in the conversation somehow. But timidity restrained him, and, besides, a toothache, which, when the sharpest pain had passed, was felt yet at moments acutely enough. This pain had taken all his courage; but he rallied finally, and asked, —

"But Pani Osnovski?"

"Pani Osnovski," said Pan Stanislav, "has a husband who loves for two; therefore she has no need to fatigue herself, so Svirski, at least, insists. She has Chinese eyes; she is Aneta by name; has filling in her upper teeth, which is visible when she laughs much, therefore she prefers to smile; in general, she is like a turtle-dove, — she turns in a circle, and cries, 'Sugar! sugar!'"

"That is a malicious man," said Marynia. "She is beautiful, lively, witty; and Pan Svirski cannot know how much she loves her husband, for surely he has n't mentioned the matter to her. All these are simply suppositions."

Pan Stanislav thought two things: first, that they were not suppositions; and second, that he had a wife who was as naive as she was honest.

But Zavilovski said, —

"I am curious to know what would happen were she as much in love with him as he is with her."

"It would be the greatest double egotism that the world has ever witnessed," said Pan Stanislav. "They would be so occupied with each other that they would see no other thing or person on earth."

Zavilovski smiled, and said, "Light does not prevent heat; it produces it."

"Taking matters strictly, that is rather a poetical than a physical comparison," said Pan Stanislav.

But Zavilovski's answer pleased the two ladies, so both supported him ardently; and when Bigiel joined them, Pan Stanislav was outvoted.

After that they talked of Mashko and his wife. Bigiel said that Mashko had taken up an immense case against Panna Ploshovski's million-ruble will, in which a number of rather distant heirs appeared. Pan Plavitski had written of this to Marynia while she was in Italy; but, considering the whole affair such an illusion as were aforetime the millions resting on the marl of Kremen, she barely mentioned it to her husband, who waved his hand on the whole question at once. Now, as Mashko had taken up the affair, it seemed more important. Bigiel supposed that there must be some informality in the will, and declared that if Mashko won, he might stand on his feet right away, for he had stipulated an immense fee for himself. The whole affair roused Pan Stanislav's curiosity greatly.

"But Mashko has the elasticity of a cat," said he; "he always falls on his feet."

"And this time thou shouldst pray that he may not break his back," answered Bigiel; "for it is a question of no small amount, both for thee and thy father-in-law. Ploshov alone with all its farms is valued at seven hundred thousand rubles; and, besides, there is much ready money."

"That would be wonderful, such unexpected gain!" said Pan Stanislav.

But Marynia heard with pain that her father had indeed

appeared among the other heirs in the suit against the will. "Stas" was for her a rich man, and she had blind faith that he could make millions if he wished; her father had an income, and, besides, she had given him the life annuity from Magyerovka; hence poverty threatened no one. It would have been pleasant indeed for her to be able to buy Kremen, and take "Stas" there in summer, but not for money got in this way.

"I am only pained by this," said she, with great animation. "That money was bequeathed so honestly. It is not right to change the will of the dead; it is not right to take bread from the poor, or schools. Panna Ploshovski's brother's son shot himself; it may have been for her a question of saving his soul, of gaining God's mercy. This breaking of the will is not right. People should think and feel differently."

She grew even flushed somewhat.

"How determined she is!" said Pan Stanislav.

But she pushed forward her somewhat too wide mouth, and called out with the expression of a pouting child, —

"But say that I am right, Stas; say that I am right. 'T is thy duty to say so."

"Without doubt," answered Pan Stanislav; "but Mashko may win the case."

"I wish him to lose it."

"How determined she is!" repeated Pan Stanislav.

"And how honest, what a noble nature!" thought Zavilovski, framing in his plastic mind conceptions of goodness and nobility in the form of a woman with dark hair, blue eyes, a lithe form, and mouth a trifle too wide.

After dinner Bigiel and Pan Stanislav went for a cigar and black coffee to the office, where they had to hold meanwhile the first consultation concerning the objects for which Bukatski's property had been bequeathed. Zavilovski, as a non-smoker, remained with the ladies in the drawing-room. Then Marynia, who, as lady principal*ess*, felt it her duty to give courage to the future employee of the "house," approached him, and said, —

"I, as well as Pani Bigiel, wish that we should all consider one another as members of one great family; therefore I hope that you will count us too as your good acquaintances."

"With the greatest readiness, if you permit me," answered Zavilovski. "As it is, I would have testified my respect."

"I made the acquaintance of all the gentlemen in the office only at my wedding. We went abroad immediately after; but now it will come to a nearer acquaintance. My husband told me that he should like to have us meet one week at Pan Bigiel's, and the next week at our house. This is a very good plan, but I make one condition."

"What is that?" asked Pani Bigiel.

"Not to speak of any mercantile matter at those meetings. There will be a little music, for I hope that Pan Bigiel will attend to that; sometimes we 'll read something, like 'On the Threshold.'"

"Not in my presence," said Zavilovski, with a forced smile.

"Why not?" inquired she, looking at him with her usual simplicity. "We have spoken of you more than once in presence of people really friendly, and thought of you before it came to an acquaintance; and why should we not all the more now?"

Zavilovski felt wonderfully disarmed. It seemed to him that he had fallen among exceptional persons, or at least that Pani Polanyetski was an exceptional woman. The fear, which burned him like fire, that he might appear ridiculous with his poetry, his over-long neck, and his pointed elbows, began to decrease. He felt in a manner free in her presence. He felt that she said nothing for the mere purpose of talking, or for social reasons, but only that which flowed from her kindness and sensitiveness. At the same time her face and form delighted him, as they had delighted Svirski in Venice. And since he was accustomed to seek forms for all his impressions, he began to seek them for her too; and he felt that they ought to be not only sincere, but exquisite, charming, and complete, just as her own beauty was exquisite and complete. He recognized that he had a theme, and the artist within him was roused.

She began now to ask with great friendliness about his family relations; fortunately the appearance of Bigiel and Pan Stanislav in the drawing-room freed him from more positive answers, which would have been disagreeable. His father had been a noted gambler and roisterer on a time, and for a number of years had been suffering in an institution for the insane.

Music was to interrupt that dangerous conversation. Pan Stanislav had finished the discussion with Bigiel, who said, —

"That seems to me a perfect project, but it is necessary to think the matter over yet."

Then, leaning on his violin, he began to meditate really, and said at last, —

"A wonderful thing! When I play, it is as if there were nothing else in my head, but that is not true. A certain part of my brain is occupied with other things; and it is exactly then that the best thoughts come to me."

Saying this, he sat down, took the violoncello between his knees, closed his eyes, and began the "Spring Song."

Zavilovski went home that day enchanted with the people and their simplicity, with the "Spring Song," and especially with Pani Polanyetski.

She did not even suspect that in time she might enrich poetry with a new thrill.

# CHAPTER XXXVIII.

The Mashkos visited the Polanyetskis in a week after their return. She, in a gray robe, trimmed with marabout feathers of the same color, looked better than ever before. Inflammation of the eyes, from which she had suffered formerly, had disappeared. Her face had its usual indifferent, almost dreamy mildness, but at present this only enhanced her artistic expression. The former Panna Kraslavski was about five years older than Marynia; and before marriage the lady looked still older, but now it seemed as if she had grown young. Her slender form, really very graceful, was outlined in a closely fitting dress as firmly as a child's form. It was strange that Pan Stanislav, who did not like the lady, found in her something attractive, and whenever he looked at her said to himself, "But there is something in her." Even her monotonous and somewhat childlike voice had a certain charm for him. At present he said to himself plainly that she looked exceptionally charming, and had improved more than Marynia.

Mashko, on his part, had unfolded like a sunflower. Distinction was just beaming from him; and at her side self-confidence and pride were softened by affability. It seemed impossible that he could visit all his lands within one day, — in a word, he *pretended* more than ever. But he did not pretend love for his wife, since it was evident from every look of his that he felt it really. In truth, it would have been difficult to find a woman who could answer better to his idea of refinement, good taste, and the elegance of high society. Her indifference, her, as it were, frozen manner with people, he considered as something simply unapproachable. She never lost this "distinction" at any time, even when she was alone with him. And he, as a genuine parvenu who had won a princess, loved her precisely because she seemed a princess, and because he possessed her.

Marynia inquired where they had passed the honeymoon. Pani Mashko answered on "my husband's estate," in such a tone as if that "husband's estate" had been entailed during twenty generations; wherewith she added that they were not going abroad till next year, when her husband would finish certain affairs. Meanwhile they would go again to her "husband's estate" for the summer months.

"Do you like the country?" inquired Marynia.

"Mamma likes the country," answered Pani Mashko.

"And does Kremen please your mamma?"

"Yes. But the windows in the house are like those in a conservatory. So many panes!"

"That is somewhat needed," said Marynia; "for when one of those panes is broken, any glazier of the place can put in a new one, but for large panes it would be necessary to send to Warsaw."

"My husband says that he will build a new house."

Marynia sighs in secret, and the conversation is changed. Now they talk of mutual acquaintances. It appears that Pani Mashko had taken lessons in dancing once, together with "Anetka" Osnovski and her young relative, Lineta Castelli; that they are well acquainted; that Lineta is more beautiful than Anetka, and, besides, paints, and has a whole album of her own poems. Pani Mashko has heard that Anetka has returned already and that Lineta is to live in the same villa till June together with her aunt Bronich, "and that will be very pleasant, for they are so nice."

Pan Stanislav and Mashko make their way to the adjoining room, and talk over Panna Ploshovski's will.

"I can inform thee that I have sailed out very nearly," said Mashko. "I was almost over the precipice; but that action put me on my feet, by this alone, that I began it. For years there has not been such a one. The question is one of millions. Ploshovski himself was richer than his aunt; and before he shot himself, he willed his property to Pani Krovitski's mother, and when she did n't accept it, the whole fortune went to old Panna Ploshovski. Thou wilt understand now how much property the woman must have left."

"Bigiel mentioned something like seven hundred thousand rubles."

"Tell thy Bigiel, since he has such love for giving figures, that it is more than twice that amount. Well, in justice it should be said that I have strength to save myself, and that it is easier to throw me into water than to drown me. But I will tell thee something personal. Knowest thou whom I have to thank for this? Thy father-in-law. Once he mentioned the affair to me, but I waved my hand at it. Afterward I fell into the troubles of which I wrote thee. I had a knife at my throat. Well, three weeks since I chanced to meet Pan Plavitski, who mentioned among other persons Panna Ploshovski, and invented against her all that he could utter. Suddenly I slap my forehead. What have I to lose? Nothing. I ask Vyshynski, clerk of the court, to bring the will to me. I find informalities, — small ones, but they are there. In a week I have power of attorney from the heirs, and begin an action. And what shall I say? At a mere report of the fee which I am to get in case of success, confidence returns to people, patience returns to my creditors, credit returns to .me, and I am firm. Dost remember? there was a moment when I was lowering my tone, when through my head were passing village ideas of living by an ant-like industry, of limiting my style of living. Folly! That is difficult, my dear. Thou hast reproached me because I pretend; but with us pretence is needful. To-day I must give myself out as a man who is as sure of his property as he is of victory."

"Tell me sincerely, is this a good case?"

"How a good case?"

"Simply will it not be needful to pull the matter too much by the ears against justice?"

"Thou must know that in every case there is something to be said in its favor, and the honor of an advocate consists just in saying this something. In the present case the special questions are, who are to inherit, and is the will so drawn as to stand in law; and it was not I who made the law."

"Then thou hast hopes of gaining?"

"When it is a question of breaking a will, there are chances almost always, because generally the attack is conducted with a hundred times more energy than is the defence. Who will defend against me? Institutions; that is, bodies unwieldy by nature, of small self-help, whose representatives have no personal interest in the defence. They will find an advocate; well! but what will they give him, what can they give him? As much as is allowed by law; now that advocate will have more chances of profit in case I win, for that may depend on a personal bargain between him and me. In general, I tell thee that in legal actions, as in life, the side wins which has the greater wish to win."

"But public opinion will grind thee into bran, if thou

break such wills. My wife is interested a little, thou seest."

"How a little?" interrupted Mashko. "I shall be a genuine benefactor to both of you."

"Well, my wife is indignant, and opposed to the whole action."

"Thy wife is an exception."

"Not altogether; it is not to my taste either."

"What 's this? Have they made thee a sentimentalist also?"

"My dear friend, we have known each other a long time; use that language with some other man."

"Well, I will talk of opinions only. To begin with, I tell thee that a certain unpopularity for a man genuinely *comme il faut* rather helps than harms him; second, it is necessary to understand those matters. People would grind me into bran, as thou hast said, should I lose the case; but if I win, I shall be considered a strong head — and I shall win."

After a while he continued, "And from an economical point of view, what is the question? The money will remain in the country; and, as God lives, I do not know that it will be put to worse use. By aid of it a number of sickly children might be reared to imbecility and help dwarf the race, or a number of seamstresses might get sewing-machines, or a number of tens of old men and women live a couple of years longer; not much good could come to the country of that. Those are objects quite unproductive. We should study political economy some time. Finally, I will say in brief, that I had the knife at my throat. My first duty is to secure life to myself, my wife, and my coming family. If thou art ever in such a position as I was, thou 'lt understand me. I chose to sail out rather than drown; and such a right every man has. My wife, as I wrote thee, has a considerable income, but almost no property, or, at least, not much; besides, from that income she allows something to her father. I have increased the allowance, for he threatened to come here, and I did n't want that."

"So thou art sure, then, that Pan Kraslavski exists? Thou hast mentioned him, I remember."

"I have; and for that very reason I make no secret of the matter now. Besides, I know that people talk to the prejudice of my father-in-law and my wife, that they relate God knows what; hence I prefer to tell thee, as a friend, how things are. Pan Kraslavski lives in Bordeaux. He was an agent in selling sardines, and was earning good money, but he lost the position, for he took to drinking, and drinks absinthe; besides, he has created an illegal family. Those ladies send him three thousand francs yearly; but that sum does not suffice him, and, between remittance and remittance, need pinches the man. Because of this he drinks more, and torments those poor women with letters, threatening to publish in newspapers how they maltreat him; and they treat him better than he deserves. He wrote to me, too, immediately after my marriage, begging me to increase his allowance a thousand francs. Of course he informs me that those women have 'eaten him up;' that he has n't had a copper's worth of happiness in life; that their selfishness has gnawed him, and warns me against them." Here Mashko laughed. "But the beast has a nobleman's courage. Once, from want, he was going to sell handbills in the corridor of the theatre; but the authorities ordered him to don a kind of helmet, and he could not endure that. He wrote to me as follows: 'All would have gone well, sir, but for the helmet; when they gave me that, I could not.' He preferred death by hunger to wearing the helmet! My father-in-law pleases me! I was in Bordeaux on a time, but forget what manner of helmets are worn by the venders of handbills; but I should like to see such a helmet. Thou wilt understand, of course, that I preferred to add the thousand francs, if I could keep him far away, with his helmet and his absinthe. This is what pains me, however: people say that even here he was a sort of tipstaff, or notary; and that is a low fiction, for it is enough to open the first book on heraldry to see who the Kraslavskis were. Here connections are known; and the Kraslavskis are in no lack of them. The man fell; but the family was and is famous. Those ladies have dozens of relatives who are not so and so; and if I tell this whole story, I do so because I wish thee to know what the truth is."

But the truth touching the Kraslavskis concerned Pan Stanislav little; so he returned to the ladies, and all the more readily that Zavilovski had just come. Pan Stanislav had invited the young man to after-dinner tea, so as to show him photographs brought from Italy. In fact, piles of them were laid out on the table: but Zavilovski was holding in his hand the frame containing the photograph of Litka's head, and was so enchanted that immediately after they made him acquainted with Mashko, he looked again at the portrait, and continued to speak of it.

"I should have thought it the idea of an artist rather than a portrait of a living child. What a wonderful head! What an expression! Is this your sister?"

"No," answered Marynia; "that is a child no longer living."

In the eyes of Zavilovski, as a poet, that tragic shadow increased his sympathy and admiration for that truly angelic face. He looked at the photograph for some time in silence, now holding it away from his eyes, and now drawing it nearer.

"I asked if it was your sister," said he, "because there is something in the features, in the eyes rather; indeed, there is something."

Zavilovski seemed to speak sincerely; but Pan Stanislav had such a respect for the dead child, a respect almost religious, that, in spite of his recognition of Marynia's beauty, the comparison seemed to him a kind of profanation. Hence, taking the photograph from Zavilovski's hands, he put it back on the table, and began to speak with a certain harsh animation, —

"Not the least; not the least! There is not one trait in common. How is it possible to compare them! Not one trait in common."

This animation touched Marynia somewhat.

"I am of that opinion, too," said she.

But her opinion was not enough for him.

"Did you know Litka?" asked he, turning to Pani Mashko.

"I did."

"True; you saw her at the Bigiels'."

"I did."

"Well, there was n't a trace of likeness, was there?"

"No."

Zavilovski, who adored Marynia, looked at Pan Stanislav with a certain astonishment; then he glanced at the tall form of Pani Mashko, outlined through the gray robe, and thought, —

"How elegant she is!"

After a while the Mashkos rose to take farewell. Mashko, when kissing Marynia's hand at parting, said, —

"Perhaps I shall go to St. Petersburg soon; at that time remember my wife a little."

During tea Marynia reminded Zavilovski of his promise to bring at his first visit, and read to her, the variant of "On the Threshold;" he had grown so attached to the Polanyetskis already that he gave not only the variant, but another poem, which he had written earlier. It was evident that he was amazed himself at his own self-confidence and readiness; so that when he had finished reading, and heard the praises, which were really sincere, he said, —

"I declare truly that with you, after the third meeting, it seems as though we were acquainted from of old. So true is this that I am astonished."

Pan Stanislav remembered that once he had said something similar to Marynia in Kremen; but he received this now as if it included him also.

But Zavilovski had her only in mind; she simply delighted him with her straightforward kindness, and her face.

"That beast is really capable," said Pan Stanislav, when Zavilovski had gone. "Hast thou noticed that he is changed a little in the face?"

"He has cut his hair," answered Marynia.

"Ah, ha! and his chin sticks out a trifle more."

Thus speaking, Pan Stanislav rose and began to put away the photographs on the shelves above the table; finally, he took Litka's portrait, and said, —

"I will take this to my study."

"But thou hast that one there with the birches, colored."

"True; but I do not want this here so much in view. Every one makes remarks, and sometimes that angers me. Wilt thou permit?"

"Very well, my Stas," answered Marynia.

## CHAPTER XXXIX.

Bigiel persuaded Pan Stanislav emphatically not to extend the house, and not to throw himself too hurriedly into undertakings of various sorts. "We have created," said he, "an honorable mercantile firm of a kind rare in this country; hence we are useful." He maintained that from gratitude alone they ought to continue a business through which they had almost doubled their property. At the same time he expressed the conviction that they would show more sense if at this juncture specially they managed matters with care and solidly, and that their first bold speculation, though it had been fortunate, should not only not entice them to others, but should be the last.

Pan Stanislav agreed that it was necessary to show moderation, especially in success; but he complained that he could not find a career in the house, and that he wanted to produce something. He had common-sense enough not to think yet of a factory on his own capital. "I do not wish to carry on a small one," said he, "since a large one producing *en gros* attracts me, and I have not capital for it; one with shares, I should be working not for myself, but for others." He understood, too, that it was not easy to find shareholders among the local elements, and he did not want strangers; he knew, moreover, that he could not rouse confidence in them, and that his name alone would be a hindrance. Bigiel, for whom it was a question of the "house," was sincerely pleased with this sobriety of view.

In Pan Stanislav was roused still another desire, which is as old as man, — the desire of possession. After the lucky grain speculation and the will of Bukatski, he was quite wealthy; but with all his real sobriety, he had a certain strange feeling that that wealth, consisting even of the most reliable securities shut up in fire-proof safes, was just paper, and would remain so till he owned something real, of which he could say, "This is mine." That strange desire was seizing him with growing force. For him it was not a question of anything great, but of some corner of his own, where he might feel at home. He tried to philosophize over this, and to explain to Bigiel that such a desire of ownership must be some inborn passion which might be repressed, but which, in riper age, would appear with new strength. Bigiel acknowledged that that might be true, and said, —

"That is proper. Thou art married, hence hast the wish to have thy own hearth, not a hired one; and since thou hast the means, then make such a hearth for thyself."

Pan Stanislav had been thinking for some time of building a large house in the city, — a house which would satisfy his desire of ownership, and also bring income. But one day he noted a bad side in this practical project,— namely, it had no charm. It is necessary to love that something of which he said, "It is mine;" and how love a brick building, in which any one may live who will hire lodgings. At first he was ashamed of this thought, for it seemed sentimental; but afterward he said to himself, "No; since I have means, it is not only not sentimental to use them in a way which will assure satisfaction, but a proof of judgment." He was more attracted by the thought of a smaller house in the city, or outside the city, —one in which only he and his wife would live. But he wanted with it even a piece of land on which something would grow; he felt, for example, that the sight of trees growing in his garden or before his house, on his land, would cause him great pleasure; he was astonished himself that this was so, but it was. At last he came to the conviction that it would be more agreeable to have some little place near the city, something in the style of that summer house which Bigiel owned, but with a piece of land, a piece of forest, some acres of garden, finally, with grounds, and with a stork's nest somewhere on an old linden-tree.

"Since I have means to get it, I prefer it to be thus, not otherwise, —that is, to be beautiful, not ugly," said he.

And he began to consider the affair on every side. He understood that since it was a question of a nest in which he was to live out his life, he ought to select with care; hence he did not hurry. Meanwhile meditation over this occupied all his hours free from counting-house toil, and caused him real pleasure. Various people learned soon that Pan Stanislav was seeking to buy with ready money; hence propositions came from various sides, often strange, but at times attractive. On occasions he had to drive to villas in the city, or outside it. Frequently, after his return from the counting-house, or after dinner, Pan Stanislav shut himself in with plans, with papers, and came out only in the evening. In those days Marynia had much leisure. She noted at last that something occupied him unusually, and tried to learn what it was by questioning; but he answered, —

"My child, when there is a result, I will tell thee; but while I know nothing, it would be difficult to talk about nothing. That is so opposed to my nature."

She learned at last what the question was from Pani Bigiel, who had learned it from her husband, to whose nature it was not repugnant to speak with his wife about all undertakings and plans for the future. For Marynia it would have been also immensely agreeable to speak with her husband of everything, and especially of the chance of a nest. Her eyes laughed at the very thought of that; but since "Stas's" disposition stood in the way, she preferred through delicacy not to inquire.

He had no ill-will in this, but simply it did not occur to him to initiate her into any affair in which there was a question of money. It might have been otherwise had she brought him a considerable dower, or had he been forced to manage her property. In such affairs he was very scrupulous. But since he was managing only his own, he did not feel now any more than in his past unmarried years any need of confessing, especially while nothing was determined. With Bigiel alone did he talk, because he was accustomed to talk with him of business.

With his wife he spoke of things which, according to him, "pertained to her;" hence, among other things, of the acquaintances which they should make. Toward the end of his single life he had been scarcely anywhere; but he felt that at present he could not act thus. They returned, therefore, visits to the Mashkos; and on a certain evening they began to consider whether they ought to visit the Osnovskis, who had returned from abroad, and would remain in Warsaw till the middle of June. Marynia said that they ought, because they should see them at Pani Mashko's; and she wished to make a visit, for she liked Pan Osnovski, who had moved her sympathy. Pan Stanislav seemed less willing, and the decision was according to his wish at first; but some days later the Osnovskis met Marynia and greeted her so cordially, Pani Osnovski repeated so often, "We Roman women," and both put such emphasis on the hope of seeing and meeting her, that it was not possible to avoid the visit.

When the visit was made, politeness was shown first of all to Marynia. The husband vied with his wife in this regard. Like well-bred people, they were faultlessly polite to Pan Stanislav, but colder. He understood that Marynia played the first, and he only the second rôle, and that irritated him a little. Pan Osnovski, for that matter, had no need to make an effort in being polite to Marynia; for, feeling that she had for him earnest sympathy, he repaid her with interest, though, in general, to act thus was not his habit.

He seemed to her more in love with his wife than ever. It was evident that his heart beat with more life when he was looking at her. When speaking to her, he seemed to offer his expressions with a certain fear, as it were, lest he might offend her with something. Pan Stanislav looked on with a kind of pity; but the sight was also touching. In his struggle with corpulence, however, Pan Osnovski had gained such a crushing victory that his clothing seemed too large for him. The pimples on his blond face had vanished, and, in general, he was more presentable than he had been.

But the lady had, as ever, her incomparable, sloping violet eyes, and thoughts, which, like birds of paradise, were playing in the air continually.

The Polanyetskis made new acquaintances at the Osnovskis, — namely, Pani Bronich and her sister's daughter, Panna Castelli; these ladies had arrived for the "summer carnival" in Warsaw, and were living in the same villa, which the late Pan Bronich had sold to the Osnovskis, with the reservation of one pavilion for his wife. Pani Bronich was a widow after Pan Bronich, whom she mentioned as the last relative of the Princes Ostrogski, and as the last descendant of Rurik. She was known in the city also under the title of "Sweetness;" for this name she was indebted to the fact that, when talking, especially to persons whom she needed, she became so pleasing that it seemed as if she were speaking through a lump of sugar held in her mouth. Marvels were told of her lies. Panna Castelli was the daughter of Pani Bronich's sister, who, in her day, to the great offence of her family and of society, married an Italian, a music-teacher, and died in labor, leaving a daughter. When, a year later, Pan

Castelli was drowned at Venice, in the Lido, Pani Bronich took her niece, and reared her.

Panna Lineta was a beauty, with very regular features, blue eyes, golden hair, and a complexion too fair, for it was almost like porcelain. Her eyelids were rather heavy; this gave her a dreamy look, but that dreaminess might seem also concentration. It might be supposed that she was a person who led an immensely developed inner life, and hence bore herself indifferently toward all that surrounded her. If any man had not come on that idea unaided, he might be sure that Pani Bronich would help him. Pani Osnovski, who had passed through the grades of enchantment over her cousin, said of Lineta's eyes, "They are as deep as lakes." The only question was what is at the bottom; and it was precisely this secret which gave her charm to the young lady.

The Osnovskis came with the intention of remaining in Warsaw; but Pani Aneta had not seen Rome in vain. "Art, and art!" said she to Pani Marynia; "I wish to know of nothing else." Her professed plan was to open an "Athenian" salon; but her secret one was to become the Beatrice of some Dante, the Laura of some Petrarch, or, at least, something in the nature of Vittoria Colonna for some Michael Angelo.

"We have a nice garden with the villa," said she. "The evenings will be beautiful, and we shall pass them in such Roman and Florentine conversations. You know" (here she raised her hands to the height of her shoulders, and began to move them), "the gray hour, a little twilight, a little moonlight, a few lamps, a few shadows from the trees; we shall sit and talk in an undertone about everything,—life, feelings, art. In truth, that is worth more than gossip! My Yozio, perhaps thou wilt be annoyed; but be not angry, do this for my sake, and, believe me, it will be very nice."

"But, my Anekta, can I be annoyed by what pleases thee?"

"Especially now, while Lineta is with us; she is an artist in every drop of her blood."

Here she turned to Lineta. "What fine thread is that head spinning now? What dost thou say of such Roman evenings?"

Lineta smiled dreamily; and the widow of "Rurik's last descendant" began to speak, with an expression of indescribable sweetness, to Pan Stanislav,—

"You do not know that Victor Hugo blessed her when she was yet a little girl."

"Then did you ladies know Victor Hugo?" asked Marynia.

"We? no! I would not know him for anything in the world; but once, when we were going through Passy, he stood on a balcony, and I know not whether through something prophetic, or through inspiration, the moment he set eyes on Lineta, he raised his hand and blessed her."

"Aunt!" said Panna Castelli.

"When it is true, my child; and what is true, is true! I called at once to her, 'See, see! he is raising his hand!' and Pan Tsardyn, the consul, who was sitting on the front seat, saw also that he raised his hand, and gave a blessing. I tell this freely, for perhaps the Lord God forgave him his sins, of which he had many, because of this blessing. He was of such perverse mind; and still, when he saw Lineta, he blessed her."

There was in the tale this much truth,—those ladies, while going through Passy, really saw Victor Hugo on a balcony. As to the blessing which they said he gave Lineta, malicious tongues in Warsaw declared that he raised his hand because he was yawning at the moment.

Meanwhile Pani Aneta continued,—

"We 'll make for ourselves here a little Italy; and should the attempt fail, next winter we 'll escape to the great one. It has entered my head already to open a house in Rome. Meantime Yozio has bought a number of nice copies of statues and paintings. That was so worthy on his part, for he does n't care much about them; he did this only for me. There are very good things among them; for Yozio had the wit not to trust himself, and begged the aid of Pan Svirski. It is a pity that they are not here; it is a pity, too, that Pan Bukatski died, as it were, through perversity, for he would have been useful. At times he was very nice; he had a certain subtlety, snake-like, and that in conversation, gives life. But" (here she turned to Marynia) "do you know that you have conquered Pan Svirski utterly? After you had left Rome, he talked of no one else, and he has begun a Madonna with your features. You 'll become a Fornarina! Evidently you have luck with artists; and when my Florentine evenings begin, Lineta and I must be careful,—if not, we shall go to the corner."

But Pani Bronich, casting hostile glances at Marynia. said.—

"If it is a question of faces which make an impression on artists, I'll tell the company what happened once in Nice."

"Aunt!" interrupted Panna Castelli.

"But if it is true, my child; and what's true, is true! A year ago — no! two years ago — Oh, how time flies! —"

But Pani Aneta, who had heard more than once, surely, what had happened at Nice, began to inquire of Marynia, —

"But have you many acquaintances in the world of artists?"

"My husband has," answered Marynia, "I have not; but we know Pan Zavilovski."

Pani Aneta fell into real enthusiasm at this news. It was her dream to know Zavilovski, and let "Yozio" say if it was not her dream. Not long before, she and Lineta had read his verses entitled "Ex imo;" and Lineta, who, at times, knows how to describe an impression with one word, as no one else can, said, — what is it that she said so characteristic?

"That there was in that something bronze-like," added Pani Bronich.

"Yes, something bronze-like; I imagined to myself also Pan Zavilovski as something cast. How does he look in reality?"

"He is short, fat, fifty years old," said Pan Stanislav, "and has no hair on his head."

At this the faces of Pani Aneta and Lineta took on such an expression of disenchantment that Marynia laughed, and said, —

"Do not believe him, ladies; he is malicious, and likes to torment. Pan Zavilovski is young, somewhat shy, a little like Wagner."

"That means that he has a chin like Punch," added Pan Stanislav.

But Pani Aneta paid no heed to Pan Stanislav's words, and obtained from Marynia a promise to make her acquainted with Pan Zavilovski, and soon, "very soon, for summer is at the girdle!"

"We will try to make it pleasant for him among us, and that he should n't be shy; though, if he is a little shy, that is no harm, for he ought to be, and, like an eagle in a cage, withdraw when people approach him. But we will come to an understanding with Lineta; she, too, is wrapped up in herself, and is as mysterious as a sphinx."

"It seems to me that every uncommon soul—" began Aunt Sweetness.

But the Polanyetskis rose to go. In the entrance they met the wonderful Kopovski, whose shoes the servants were dusting, and who was arranging meanwhile the hair on his statuesque head, which was as solid as marble. When outside, Pan Stanislav remarked,—

"He, too, will be useful for their 'Florentine' evenings; he, too, is a sphinx."

"If he were to stand in a niche," said Marynia. "But what beautiful women they are!"

"It is a wonderful thing," answered Pan Stanislav, "though Pani Osnovski is good-looking, I, for example, prefer Pani Mashko as a beauty. As to Castelli, she is, in truth, beautiful, though too tall. Hast thou noticed how they speak of her all the time, but she not a word?"

"She has a very intelligent opinion," answered Marynia, "but is, perhaps, a little timid, like poor Zavilovski."

"It is necessary to think of arranging for that acquaintance."

But an accident disturbed these plans of making the acquaintance. Marynia, on the day following this visit, slipped on the stone stairs, and struck her knee against the step with such violence that she had to lie in bed several days. Pan Stanislav, on returning from the office, learned what had happened. Alarmed at first, then pacified by the doctor, he upbraided his wife rather sharply.

"Thou shouldst remember that it may be a question not of thee alone," said he.

She suffered severely from the fall and from these words, which seemed to her too unsparing; for she considered that with him it should above all be a question of her, especially as other fears were baseless so far. Aside from this, he showed great attention; neither on the next nor the following day did he go to the counting-house, but remained to take care of her. In the forenoon he read to her; after lunch, he worked in the adjoining room with open doors, so that she might call him at any moment. Affected by this care, she thanked him very warmly; in return he kissed her, and said,—

"My child, it is a simple duty. Thou seest that even strangers inquire about thee daily."

In fact, strangers did inquire daily. Zavilovski inquired in the counting-house, "How does the lady feel?" Pani

Bigiel came in the forenoon, and Bigiel in the evening; without going to the chamber of the sick woman, he played on the piano in the next room to entertain her. The Mashkos and Pani Bronich left cards twice. Pani Osnovski, leaving her husband in the carriage below, broke into Marynia a little by violence, and sat with her about two hours, talking, with her usual gift of jumping from subject to subject, of Rome, of her intended evenings, of Svirski, of her husband, of Lineta, and of Zavilovski, who did n't let her sleep. Toward the end of the visit, she declared that they ought to say *thou* to each other, and that she invited Marynia to give aid in one plan: "that is, not a plan, but a conspiracy;" or, rather, in a certain thing which had so struck into her head that it was burning, and burning to such a degree that her whole head was on fire.

"That Zavilovski has so stuck in my mind that Yozio has begun to be jealous of him; but in the end of the affair, Yozio, poor fellow, does n't know himself what to think. I am sure that he and Lineta are created for each other, — not Yozio and Lineta, but Zavilovski and Lineta. That poetry, that poetry! And don't laugh, Marynia; don't think me moonstruck. Thou dost not know Lineta. She needs some uncommon man. She would n't marry Kopovski for anything, though Kopovski looks like an archangel. Such a face as Kopovski has, I have never seen in life. In Italy, perhaps, in some picture, and even then not. Knowest thou what Lineta says of him? — 'C'est un imbécile.' But still she looks at him. Think how beautiful that would be, if they should become acquainted, and love, and take each other, — that is, not Kopovski and Lineta, but Zavilovski and Lineta. That would be a couple! Lineta, with her aspirations, whom can she find? Where is there a man for her? What we have seen, that we have seen. I imagine how they would live. It is so wearisome in the world that when it is possible to have such a plan, it is worth while to work for it. Moreover, I know that that will succeed without difficulty, for Aunt Bronich is wringing her hands, — where can she find a husband for Lineta? I am afraid that I have worn thee out, and surely I have tormented thee; but it is so nice to talk, especially when one is making some plan."

In fact, Marynia felt, as it were, a turning of the head after Pani Aneta had gone. Still when Pan Stanislav came in, she told him of the plans prepared against Zavilovski, and, laughing a little at the eagerness of Pani Aneta, said at last, —

"She must have a good heart, and she pleases me; but what an enthusiast! What is there that does n't rush through her head?"

"She is impetuous, but no enthusiast," answered Pan Stanislav; "and see what the difference is, — enthusiasm comes almost always from the warmth of a good heart, while impetuousness frequently agrees with a dry heart, and often comes even from this, that the head is hot, and the heart is asleep."

"Thou hast no liking for Pani Aneta," said Marynia.

Pan Stanislav did not indeed like her; but this time, instead of confirming or contradicting, he looked at his wife with a certain curiosity, and that moment her beauty struck him, — her hair flowing in disorder on the pillow, and her small face coming out of the dark waves, just like a flower. Her eyes seemed bluer than usual; through her open mouth was to be seen the row of small white teeth. Pan Stanislav approached her, and said in an undertone, —

"How beautiful thou art to-day!"

And, bending over her, with changed face, he fell to kissing her eyes and mouth.

But every kiss moved her, and each movement caused pain. It was disagreeable, besides, that he had noticed her beauty as if by accident; his expression of face was distasteful to her, and his inattention; therefore she turned away her head.

"Stas, do not kiss me so roughly; thou knowest that I am suffering."

Then he stood erect, and said with suppressed anger, —

"True; I beg pardon."

And he went to his room to examine the plan of a certain summer house with a garden, which had been sent to him that morning.

## CHAPTER XL.

But Marynia's illness was not lasting, and a week later she and her husband were able to visit the Bigiels, who had moved to their summer residence; for the weather, notwithstanding the early season, was fine, and in the city summer heats were almost beginning. Zavilovski, who had grown accustomed to them, went also, taking an immense kite, which he was to fly in company with Pan Stanislav and the children. The Bigiels, too, liked Zavilovski, since he was simple, and, except his shyness, a pleasant man, on occasions even childlike. Pani Bigiel maintained, moreover, that he had a peculiar head; which was in so far true, that he had a scar on his eyelid, and that his prominent chin gave him an expression of energy which was contradicted utterly by his upper face, which was delicate, almost feminine. At first Pani Bigiel sought in him an original; but he mastered everything, and therefore himself, too quickly. He was simply a great enthusiast of unequal temper, because he was timid; and he was not without hidden pride.

At dinner they mentioned the Osnovskis to him, and the projected Athenian-Roman-Florentine evenings, Panna Castelli, and the curiosity which he had roused in the ladies. When he heard this, he said, —

"Oh, it is well to know that; I shall not go there now for anything in the world."

"You will make their acquaintance first at our house," said Marynia.

"I shall escape from the entrance," said he, clasping his hands.

"Why?" asked Pan Stanislav. "It is needful to have the courage not only of one's convictions, but of one's verses."

"Evidently," said Pani Bigiel. "What is there to be ashamed of? I should look people in the eyes boldly and say: I write; yes, I write."

"I write; yes, I write," repeated Zavilovski, raising his head and laughing.

But Marynia continued: "You will make their acquaintance at our house; then you will leave your card with them, and after that we will visit them some evening."

"I cannot hide my head in snow," said he, "because there is none; but I'll find some place of hiding."

"But if I entreat you greatly?"

"Then I will go," answered Zavilovski, after a while, blushing slightly; and he looked at her.

Her face, somewhat pale after protracted lying in bed, had become more delicate, and looked like the face of a maiden of sixteen. She seemed so wonderful to the young man that he could refuse her nothing.

In the evening, Pan Stanislav was to take him back to the city; but before that Marynia said to him, —

"Now you must be constrained, for you have not seen Panna Lineta Castelli; but as soon as you have seen her, you will fall in love."

"I, Pani?" cried Zavilovski, putting his hand on his breast; "I, with Panna Castelli?"

And there was so much sincerity in his question that he was confused again; but this time Marynia herself was confused somewhat.

Meantime Pan Stanislav has finished his conversation with Bigiel about the dangers of investing capital in land, and they drive away. Marynia remembers how once she returned with her father, Pani Emilia, Litka, and Pan Stanislav from the Bigiels, in a moonlight night such as this; how "Pan Stanislav" was in love with her then; how unhappy he was; how severe she was with him; and her heart begins to beat with pity for that "Pan Stanislav," who suffered so much on a time. She wants to nestle up to him and implore pardon for those evil moments of the past; and but for the presence of Zavilovski, she would do so.

But that old-time Pan Stanislav is sitting there calm and self-confident at her side, and smoking his cigar. Moreover, she is his; he has taken her and has her; all is over.

"Of what art thou thinking, Stas?" inquired she.

"Of the business of which I was talking with Bigiel."

And, shaking the ashes from his cigar, he replaced it in his mouth, and drew so vigorously that a ruddy gleam lighted his mustache and a part of his face.

Zavilovski, looking at Marynia's face, thought in his young soul that if she were his wife he would not smoke a cigar, nor think of business of which he had been talking with Bigiel, but might kneel before her and adore her on his knees.

And gradually, under the influence of the night and that sweet womanly face, which he glorified, exaltation possessed him. After a time he began to declaim, at first in silence, as if to himself, then more audibly, his verses entitled, "Snows on the Mountains." There was in that poem, as it were, an immense yearning for something unapproachable and immaculate. Zavilovski himself did not know when they arrived in the city, and when lamps began to gleam on both sides of the street. At Pan Stanislav's house Marynia said, —

"To-morrow, then, to a five o'clock."

"Yes," answered he, kissing her hand.

Marynia was sunk somewhat in revery under the influence of the ride, the night, and maybe the verses. But from the time of their stay in Rome, she and her husband had repeated the rosary together. And after these prayers a great tenderness possessed her suddenly, — as it were, an influx of feeling, hidden for a time by other impressions. Approaching him, she put her arms around his neck, and whispered, —

"My Stas, but we feel so pleasant together, do we not?"

He drew her toward him, and answered with a certain careless boastfulness, —

"But do I complain?"

And it did not occur to him that there was in her question something like a shade of doubt and sorrow, which she did not like to admit to her soul, and desired him to calm and convince her.

Next morning in the office Zavilovski gave Pan Stanislav a cutting from some paper of "Snows on the Mountains;" he read it during dinner, but with the sound of forks the verses seemed less beautiful than amid the night stillness and in moonlight.

"Zavilovski told me," said Pan Stanislav, "that a volume would be issued soon; but he has promised to collect first everything printed in various journals, and bring it to thee."

"No," said Marynia; "he should keep them for Lineta."

"Ah, they are to meet to-morrow for the first time. Ye wish absolutely to make an epoch in Zavilovski's life?"

"We do," answered Marynia, with decisiveness. "Aneta astonished me at first; but why not?"

Indeed, the meeting took place. The Osnovskis, Pani Bronich, and Panna Castelli came very punctually at five; Zavilovski had come still earlier, to avoid entering a room in presence of a whole society. But as it was he was not only frightened, but more awkward than usual, and never had his legs seemed so long to him. There was, however, a certain distinction even in his awkwardness; and Pani Aneta was able to see that. The first scenes of the human comedy began, in which those ladies, as well-bred persons, guarding against every rudeness and staring at Zavilovski, did not, however, do anything else; he, feigning not to see this, was not thinking of anything else than how they were looking at him and judging him. This caused him great constraint, which he strove to hide by artificial freedom; he had so much self-love, however, that he was interested in having the judgment favorable. But the ladies were so attuned previously that the decision could not be unfavorable; and even had Zavilovski turned out flat and dull it would have been taken for wisdom and poetic originality. More indifferent was the bearing of Lineta, who was somewhat astonished that for the moment, not she was the sun, and Zavilovski the moon, but the contrary. The first impression which he made on her was: "What comparison with that stupid Kopovski!"

And the incomparable, wonderful face of that "stupid" stood before her eyes as if living; therefore her lids became dreamier still, and the expression of her face called to mind a sphinx in porcelain more than ever. She is irritated, however, that Zavilovski turns almost no attention to her form of a Juno, nor to that something "mysterious and poetic," which, as Pani Bronich insists, fetters one from the first glance. She begins to observe him gradually; and, having, besides her poetic inclination, the sense of social observation developed powerfully, she sees that he has much expression indeed, but that his coat fits badly, that he dresses, of course, at a poor tailor's, and that the pin in his cravat is *mauvais genre* simply. Meanwhile he casts occasional glances at Marynia, as the one near and friendly soul, and converses with Pani Aneta, who considers it as the highest tact not to mention poetry on first acquaintance, and, knowing that Zavilovski had passed the early years of his childhood in the country, begins to chatter about her inclinations for rural life. Her husband prefers the city always, having his friends and pleasures in the city, but as to her! — "Oh, I am sincere, and I confess at once that I cannot endure land management and accounts; for this I have been scolded more than once. Besides, I am a trifle lazy; therefore I should like work in which I could be lazy. What should I like, then?"

Here she spreads out her extended fingers so as to count more easily the occupations which would suit her taste:

"First, I should like to herd geese!"

Zavilovski laughs; she seems to him natural, and, besides, the picture of Pani Osnovski herding geese amuses him.

Her violet eyes begin to laugh also; and she falls into the tone of a free and joyous maiden, who talks of everything which runs through her head.

"And you would like that?" inquires she of Zavilovski.

"Passionately."

"Ah, you see! What else? I should like to be a fisherman. The morning dawn must be reflected beautifully in the water. Then the damp nets before the cottage, with films of water between the meshes of the net. If not a fisherman, I should like to be at least a heron, and meditate in the water on one leg, or a lapwing in the fields. But no! the lapwing is a sad kind of bird, as if in mourning."

Here she turned to Panna Castelli, —

"Lineta, what wouldst thou like to be in the country?"

Panna Lineta raised her lids, and answered after a while, —

"A spider-web."

The imagination of Zavilovski as a poet was touched by this answer. Suddenly a great yellow sweep of stubble stood before his eyes, with silver threads floating in the calm blue and in the sun.

"Ah, what a pretty picture!" said he.

He looked more carefully at Lineta; and she smiled, as if in thankfulness that he had felt the beauty of the image.

But at that moment the Bigiels came. Pani Bronich took Zavilovski into her sphere of influence, and so hemmed him in with her chair that he had no chance to escape. It was easy to divine the subject of their dialogue, for Zavilovski raised his eyes from time to time to Lineta, as if to convince himself that he was looking at that about which he was hearing. At last, though the conversation was conducted in subdued tones, those present heard these words, spoken as if through sugar, —

"Do you know that Napoleon — that is, I wanted to say Victor Hugo — blessed her?"

In general, Zavilovski had heard so many uncommon things that he might look at Lineta with a certain curiosity. She had been, according to those narratives, the most marvellous child in the world, always very gentle, and not strong. At ten years she had been very ill; sea air was prescribed, and those ladies dwelt a long time on Stromboli.

"The child looked at the volcano, at the sea, and clapped her little hands, repeating, 'Beautiful, beautiful!' We went there by chance, wandered in on a hired yacht, without object; it was difficult to stay long, for that is an empty island. There was no proper place to live in, and not much to eat; but she, as if with foreknowledge that she would regain her health there, would not leave for anything. In fact, in a month, and if not in a month, in two, she began to be herself, and see what a reed she is."

In fact, Lineta, though shapely and not too large, in stature was somewhat taller than Pani Aneta. Zavilovski looked at her with growing interest. Before the guests separated, when he was freed at last from imprisonment, he approached her, and said, —

"I have never seen a volcano, and I have no idea what impression it may make."

"I know only Vesuvius," answered she; "but when I saw it there was no eruption."

"But Stromboli?"

"I do not know it."

"Then I have heard incorrectly, for — your aunt —"

"Yes," answered Lineta, "I don't remember; I was small, I suppose."

And on her face displeasure and confusion were reflected.

Before she took leave, Pani Aneta, without destroying her rôle of charming prattler, invited Zavilovski for some evening, "without ceremony and without a dress-coat, for such a spring might be considered summer, and in summer freedom is the most agreeable. That such a man as you does not like new acquaintances, I know, but for that there is a simple remedy: consider us old acquaintances. We are alone most generally. Lineta reads something, or tells what passes through her head; and such various things pass through her head that it is worth while to hear her, especially for a person who beyond others is in a position to feel and understand her."

Panna Lineta pressed his hand at parting with unusual heartiness, as if confirming the fact that they could and should understand each other. Zavilovski, unused to society, was a little dazed by the words, the rustle of the robes, the eyes of those ladies, and by the odor of iris which they left behind. He felt besides some weariness, for that conversation, though free and apparently natural, lacked the repose which was always found in the words of Pani Polanyetski and Pani Bigiel. For a time there remained with him the impression of a disordered dream.

The Bigiels were to stay to dinner. Pan Stanislav therefore kept Zavilovski. They began to talk of the ladies.

"Well, and Panna Castelli?" asked Marynia.

"They have much imagination," answered Zavilovski, after a moment's hesitation. "Have you noticed how easy it is for them to speak in images?"

"But really, what an interesting young lady Lineta is!"

Lineta had not made a great impression on Pan Stanislav; besides, he was hungry and in a hurry for dinner, so he said somewhat impatiently, —

"What do you see in her? Interesting until she becomes an every-day subject."

"No; Lineta will not become an every-day person," said Marynia. "Only those ordinary, simple beings become every-day subjects who know how to do nothing but love."

To Zavilovski, who looked at her that moment, it seemed that he detected a shade of sadness. Perhaps, too, she was weak, for her face had lily tones.

"Are you wearied?" inquired he.

"A little," answered she, smiling.

His young, impressionable heart beat with great sympathy for her. "She is in truth a lily," thought he; and in comparison with her sweet charm Pani Osnovski stood before him as a chattering nut-cracker, and Panna Castelli as the inanimate head of a statue. At first, after sight of Marynia, he was dreaming of a woman like her; this evening he began to dream, not of one like her, but of her. And since he was quickly aware of everything that happened in him, he noticed that she was beginning to be a "field flower," but a beloved one.

Pan Stanislav, meeting him next day in the counting-room, asked, —

"Well, did the dreamy queen come to you in a vision?"

"No," answered Zavilovski, blushing.

Pan Stanislav, seeing that blush, laughed, and said,—

"Ha! it's difficult! Every one must pass that; I, too have passed it."

## CHAPTER XLI.

MARYNIA did not complain even to herself of her husband. So far there had not been the least misunderstanding between them. But she was forced to confess that genuine, very great happiness, and especially very great love, such as she had imagined when Pan Stanislav was her betrothed, she had imagined as different. Of this each day convinced her: her hopes had been of one kind; reality proved to be of another. Marynia's honest nature did not rebel against this reality; but a shade of sadness came over her, and the feeling that that shade might in time be the basis of her life. With a soul full of good-will, she tried to explain to herself at the beginning that those were her own fancies. What was lacking to her, and in what could Pan Stanislav have disappointed her? He had never caused her pain purposely; as often as it occurred to him that a given thing might please her, he tried to obtain it; he was liberal, careful of her health; at times he covered her face and hands with kisses,—in a word, he was rather kind than ill-natured. Still there was something lacking. It was difficult for Marynia to describe this in one word, or in many; but her mind was too clear not to understand what her heart felt every day more distinctly, every day with more sadness. Something was wanting! After a great and solemn holiday of love, a series of common days had set in, and she regretted the holiday; she would have it last all her life; she saw now, with sorrow, that to her husband this common life seemed precisely what was normal and wished for. It was not bad, such as it was; but it was not that high happiness which "such a man" should be able to feel, create, and impart. But there was a question of other things also. She felt, for example, that she was more his than he was hers; and that though she gave him her whole soul, he returned to her only that part of his which he had designed in advance for home use. It is true that she said to herself, "He is a man; besides me he has a whole world of work and thought." But she had hoped once that he would take her by the hand and lead her into that world,—that in the house, at least, he would share it with her; at present she could not even flatter herself that he would do so. And the reality was worse than she had imagined. Pan Stanislav, as he expressed himself, took her, and had her; and when their mutual feeling became at the same time a simple mutual obligation, he judged that it was not needful otherwise to care for her, or otherwise to be occupied with her than with any duty of every-day life. It did not come to his head simply that to such a fire it was not enough to bring common fuel, such as is put in a chimney, but that there was need to sprinkle on it frankincense and myrrh, such as is sprinkled before an altar. If a man were to tell him something like this, he would shrug his shoulders, and look on him as a sentimentalist. Hence there was in him the carefulness of a husband, perhaps, but not the anxiety of a lover, — concern, watching, or awe of that kind which, in the lower circles of earthly feelings, corresponds to fear of God in religion. On a time when, after the sale of Kremen, Marynia was indifferent to him, he felt and passed through all this; but now, and even beginning with Litka's death, when he received the assurance that she was his property, he thought no more of her than was necessary to think of property. His feeling, resting preeminently on her physical charm, possessed what it wanted, and was at rest; while time could only vulgarize, cool, and dull it.

Even now, though still vivid, it lacks the alert and careful tenderness which existed, for example, in his feeling for Litka. And Marynia noticed this. Why was it so? To this she could not answer; but still she saw clearly that she was for this man, to whom she wished to be everything, something more common and less esteemed than the dead Litka.

It did not occur to her, and she could not imagine by any means, that the only reason was this, — that that child was not his, while she had given him soul and body. She judged that the more she gave, the more she ought to receive and have. But time brought her in this regard many disappointments. She could not but notice, too, that all are under a certain charm of hers; that all value her, praise her; that Svirski, Bigiel, Zavilovski, and even Pan Osnovski, look on her, not only with admiration, but with enthusiasm almost; while "Stas" regards her distinguishing traits less than any man. It had not occurred to her for a moment that he could be incapable of seeing in her and valuing that which others saw and valued so easily. What was the cause, then, of this? These questions tormented her night and day now. She saw that Pan Stanislav feigned to have in all cases a character somewhat colder and more serious than he had in reality, but to her this did not seem a sufficient answer. Unfortunately only one answer remained: "He does not love me as he might, and therefore does not value me as others do." There was in this as much truth as disappointment and sadness.

The instinct of a woman, which, in these cases, never deceives her, warned Marynia that she had made an uncommon impression on Zavilovski; that that impression increased with every meeting. And this thought did not make her indignant; she did not burst out with the angry question, "How dare he?" since, for that matter, he had not dared anything, — on the contrary, it gave her a certain comfort, certain confidence in her own charm, which at moments she had begun to lose, but withal it roused the greater sorrow that such honor, such enthusiasm, should be shown her by some stranger, and not by "Stas." As to Zavilovski, she felt nothing for him save a great sympathy and good-will; hence her thoughts remained pure. She was incapable of amusing herself through vanity by the suffering of another; and for that reason, not wishing him to go too far, she associated herself willingly with the plan of Pani Aneta of bringing him into more intimate relations with Panna Castelli, though that plan seemed to her as abrupt as it was unintelligible. Moreover, her heart and mind were occupied thoroughly with the questions: Why does that kind, wise, beloved "Stas" not go to the heights with her? why does he not value her as he might? why does he only love her, but is not in love with her? why does he consider her love as something belonging to him, but not as something precious? whence is this, and where lies the cause of it?

Every common, selfish nature would have found all the fault in him; Marynia found it in herself. It is true that she made the discovery through foreign aid; but she was always so eager to remove from "Stas" every responsibility, and take it on herself, that though it caused fear, this discovery brought her delight almost.

Once, on an afternoon, she was sitting by herself, with her hands on her knees, lost in thoughts and questions to which she could find no answer, when the door opened, and in it appeared the white head-dress and dark robe of a Sister of Charity.

"Emilka!" cried Marynia, with delight.

"Yes; it is I," said the Sister. "This is a free day for me, and I wished to visit thee. Where is Pan Stanislav?"

"Stas is at the Mashkos, but he will return soon. Ah, how glad he will be! Sit down and rest."

Pani Emilia sat down and began to talk. "I should run in oftener," said she, "but I have no time. Since this is a free day, I was at Litka's. If you could see how green the place is, and what birds are there!"

"We were there a few days ago. All is blooming; and such rest! What a pity that Stas is not at home!"

"True; besides, he has a number of Litka's letters. I should like to ask him to lend them to me. Next week I 'll run in again and return them."

Pani Emilia spoke calmly of Litka now. Maybe it was because there remained of herself only the shadow of a living person, which was soon to be blown away; but for the time there was in it undisturbed calm. Her mind was not absorbed so exclusively now by misfortune, and that previous indifference to everything not Litka had passed. Having become a Sister of Charity, she appeared again among people, and had learned to feel everything which made their fortune or misfortune, their joy or their sorrow, or even pleasure or suffering.

"But how nice it is in this house! After our naked walls, everything here seems so rich to me. Pan Stanislav was very indolent at one time: he visited the Bigiels and us, never wished to be elsewhere; but now I suppose he bestirs himself, and you receive many people?"

"No," answered Marynia; "we visit only the Mashkos, Pani Bronich, and the Osnovskis."

"But wait! I know Pani Osnovski; I knew her before she was married. I knew the Broniches, too, and their niece; but she had not grown up then. Pan Bronich died two years ago. Thou seest how I know every one."

Marynia began to laugh. "Really, more people than I do. I made the acquaintance of the Osnovskis in Rome only."

"But I lived so many years in Warsaw, and everything came to my ears. I was in the house apparently, but the world occupied me. So frivolous was I in those days! For that matter, thy present Pan Stas knew Pani Osnovski."

"He told me so."

"They met at public balls. At that time she was to marry Pan Kopovski. There were tears and despair, for her father opposed it. But she succeeded well, did she not? Pan Osnovski was always a very good man."

"And to her he is the very best. But I did not know that she was to marry Kopovski; and that astonishes me, she is so intelligent."

"Praise to God, she is happy, if she would think so! Happiness is a rare thing, and should be used well. I have learned now to look at the world quite impartially, as only those can who expect nothing for themselves from it; and knowest thou what comes more than once to my head? That happiness is like eyes, — any little mote, and at once tears will follow."

Marynia laughed a little sadly, and said, —

"Oi! that 's a great truth."

A moment of silence ensued; then Pani Emilia, looking attentively at Marynia, laid her transparent hand on her hand mildly, and asked, —

"But thou, Marynia, art happy, art thou not?"

Such a desire to weep seized Marynia on a sudden that she resisted it only with the utmost effort; that lasted, however, one twinkle. Her whole honest soul trembled suddenly at the thought that her tears or sorrow would be a kind of complaint against her husband; therefore she mastered her emotion by strength of will, and said, —

"If only Stas is happy!" And she raised her eyes, now perfectly calm, to Pani Emilia, who said, —

"Litka will obtain that for thee. I inquired only because thou wert in appearance somehow gloomy, as I entered. But I know best how he loved thee, and how unhappy he was when thou wert angry with him because of Kremen."

Marynia's face was bright with a smile. So pleasant to her was every word of his former love that she was ready to listen to that kind of narrative, even if it went on forever.

Pani Emilia continued, while touching her hand: "But thou, ugly child, wert so cruel as neither to value nor regard his true attachment, and I was angry at times with thee. At times I feared for the honest Pan Stanislav;

I was afraid that he would grow sick of life, lose his mind, or become misanthropic. For seest thou when one wrinkle is made in the depth of the heart, it may not be smoothed for a lifetime."

Marynia raised her head, and began to blink as if some light had struck her eyes suddenly.

"Emilka, Emilka!" cried she, "how wise thy discourse is!"

Pani Emilia was called now "Sister Aniela;" but Marynia always gave her her old name.

"What! wise? I am just talking of old times. But Litka will implore for thee happiness, which God will grant, for thou and Stas deserve it, both of you."

And she made ready to go. Marynia tried to detain her till "Stas" came, but in vain, for work was awaiting her in the institution. She chatted, however, at the door, fifteen minutes longer, in the manner of women; at last she went away, promising to visit them again the coming week.

Marynia returned to her armchair at the window, and, resting her head on her hand, fell to meditating on Pani Emilia's words; after a while she said, in an undertone, —

"The fault is mine."

It seemed to her that she had the key to the enigma, — she had not known how to respect a power so true and so mighty as love is. And now, in her terrified heart, that love seemed a kind of offended divinity which punishes. In the old time Pan Stanislav had been on his knees in her presence. As often as they met, he had looked into her eyes, watching for forgiveness from her heart, and from those memories, pleasant, departed, but dear, which connected them. If at that time she had brought herself to straightforwardness, to magnanimity; if she had extended her hands to him, as her secret feeling commanded, — he would have been grateful all his life, he would have honored her, he would have honored and loved with the greater tenderness, the more he felt his own fault and her goodness. But she had preferred to swaddle and nurse her feeling of offence, and coquet at the same time with Mashko. When it was necessary to forget, she would not forget; when it was necessary to forgive, she would not forgive. She preferred to suffer herself, provided he suffered also. She had given her hand to Pan Stanislav when she could not do otherwise, when not to give it would have been simply dishonorable and stupid stubbornness. That stifled love, it is true, rose up in its whole irrepressible might then, and she loved, heart and soul, but too late. Love had been injured; something had broken, something had perished. In his heart there had come an ill-omened wrinkle like that of which Pani Emilia had spoken; and now she, Marynia, was harvesting only what she had sown with her own hand.

He is not guilty of anything in this case, and if any one has spoiled another's life, it is not he who has spoiled her life; it is she who has spoiled his.

Such a terror possessed her at this thought, and such sorrow, that for a moment she looked at the future with perfect amazement. And she wished to weep, too, and weep like a little child. If Pani Emilia had not gone, she would have done so on her shoulder. She was so penetrated with the weight of her own offences that if at that moment some one had come and tried to free her of this weight, if this one had said to her, "Thou art as guilty as a dove," she would have considered the speech dishonest. The most terrible point in her mental conflict was this,—that at the first moment the loss seemed irreparable, and that in the future it might be only worse and worse, because "Stas" would love her less and less, and would have the right to love her less and less,—in one word, she saw no consolation before her.

Logic said this to her: "To-day it is good in comparison with what it may be to-morrow; after to-morrow, a month, or a year. And here it is a question of a lifetime!"

And she began to exert her poor tortured head to discover, if not a road, at least some path, by which it would be possible to issue from those snares of unhappiness. At last, after a long effort, after God knows how many swallowed tears, it seems to her that she sees a light, and that that light, in proportion as she looks at it, increases.

There is, however, something mightier than the logic of misfortune, mightier than committed offences, mightier than an offended divinity, which knows nothing but vengeance,—and this is the mercy of God.

She has offended; therefore she ought to correct herself. It is needful, then, to love "Stas," so that he may find all which has perished in his heart; it is needful to have patience, and not only not to complain of her present lot, but to thank God and "Stas" that it is such as it is. If greater griefs and difficulties should come, it is necessary to hide them in her heart in silence, and endure long, very long, even whole years, till the mercy of God comes.

The path began to change then into a highway. "I shall not go astray," said Marynia to herself. She wanted to weep from great joy then; but she judged that she could not permit that. Besides, "Stas" might return at any moment, and he must find her with dry eyes.

In fact, he returned soon. Marynia wished at the first moment to throw herself on his neck, but she felt such guilt in reference to him that some sudden timidity stopped her; and he, kissing her on the forehead, inquired, —

"Was any one here?"

"Emilia was, but she could not stay longer. She will come next week."

He was irritated at this.

"But, my God! thou knowest that it is such a pleasure for me to see her; why not let me know? Why didst thou not think of me, knowing where I was?"

She, like a child explaining itself, spoke with a voice in which tears were trembling, but in which there was at the same time a certain trust, —

"No, Stas, on the contrary, as I love, I was thinking all the time of thee."

## CHAPTER XLII.

"But you see I was there," said Zavilovski, joyously, at the Bigiels'. "They looked on me somewhat as they might on a panther, or a wolf, but I turned out a very tame creature; I tore no one, killed no one, answered with more or less presence of mind. No; I have long since considered that it is easier to live with people than it seems, and only in the first moments have I a wish always to run away. But those ladies are indeed very free."

"I beg you not to put us off, but tell exactly how it was," said Pani Bigiel.

"How it was? Well, first, I entered the inclosure of the villa, and did not know what to do further, or where the Osnovskis lived, or Pani Bronich; whether to pay them a visit at once, or whether it was necessary to visit both separately."

"Separately," said Pan Stanislav; "Pani Bronich has separate apartments, though they have one drawing-room, which they use in common."

"Well, I found all in that drawing-room; and Pani Osnovski first brought me out of trouble, for she said that she would share me with Pani Bronich, and that I should make two visits at one time. I found Pani Mashko there and Pan Kopovski; and he is such a man, so beautiful that he ought to have on his head one of those velvet-crowned caps which jewellers wear. Who is Kopovski?"

"An idiot!" answered Pan Stanislav. "In that is contained his name, his manner of life, his occupation, and personal marks. Another description of the man would not be needed even in a passport."

"Now I understand," said Zavilovski; "and certain words which I heard have become clear for me. That gentleman was sitting, and the young ladies were painting him. Pani Osnovski, his full face in oil; Panna Castelli, his profile in water-colors. Both had print skirts over their dresses, and both were beautiful. Evidently Pani Osnovski is just beginning to paint, but Panna Castelli has had much practice."

"Of what did they talk?"

Zavilovski turned to Marynia. "First, those ladies asked about your health; I told them that you looked better and better."

He did not say, however, that on that occasion he had blushed like a student, and that at present he consoled himself only with the thought that all had been so occupied in painting that they did not notice him, in which he was mistaken. He was confused now a little, and, wishing to hide this, continued, —

"Later we spoke of painting, of course, and portraits. I observed that Panna Castelli took something from the head of Kopovski; she answered me, —

" 'It is not I, but nature.'

"She is a witty young lady; she said this in a perfectly audible voice. I began to laugh, all the others too, and with us Kopovski himself. He must have an accommodating character. He declared later on that if he looked worse to-day than usual, it was because he had not slept enough, and that he was in a hurry for the embraces of Orpheus."

"Orpheus?"

"That 's what he said. Pan Osnovski corrected him without ceremony; but he did not agree to the correction, saying Orpheus at least ten times, and that he remembered well. Those ladies amused themselves a little with him, but he is such a fine-looking fellow that they are glad to paint him. But what an artist Panna Castelli is! When she went to showing me various plain surfaces with the brush, and lines on the portraits of Pan Kopovski, which she had begun, she touched colors, 'What a line that is! and what tones these are!' I must do her the justice to say that she looked at the time like one of the Muses. She told me that it pleases her beyond everything to paint portraits, and that she meditates on a face to begin with, as on a model, and that she dreams of those heads in which there is anything uncommon."

"Oh, ho ! and you will appear to her in a dream first, and then sit for her, I am sure," said Marynia. "And that will be well."

Zavilovski added with a voice somewhat uncertain, —

"She told me, it is true, that that is a tribute which she likes and extorts from good acquaintances; she did not turn to me, however, directly, with this request. Had it not been for Pani Bronich, there would have been no talk of it."

"Pani Bronich saved the Muse the trouble," said Pan Stanislav.

"But that will be well," said Marynia.

"Why?" inquired Zavilovski; and he looked at her with a glance at once submissive and alarmed. The idea that she might push him to another woman purposely, because she divined what was passing in his heart, attracted him, and at the same time filled him with fear.

"Because," answered Marynia, "I, indeed, am almost unacquainted with Panna Lineta, and judge only from my first impressions and from what I hear of her; but it seems to me that hers is an uncommon nature, and that there is something deep in her heart. It is well, then, that you should become acquainted."

"I also judge from first impressions," answered Zavilovski, quieted; "and it is true that Pani Castelli seems to me less shallow than Pani Osnovski. In general, those are beautiful and pleasant ladies; but — maybe I cannot define it, because I am not acquainted enough with society — but, coming away from them, I had a feeling as if I had been travelling on the railway with exceedingly charming foreign ladies, who amused themselves by conversing very wittily — but nothing more. Something foreign is felt in them. Pani Osnovski, for example, is exactly like an orchid, — a flower very peculiar and beautiful, but a kind of foreign flower. Panna Castelli is also that way, and in her there is nothing homelike. With them there is no feeling that one grew up on the same field, under the same rain and same sunshine."

"What intuition this poet has!" said Pan Stanislav.

Zavilovski became so animated that on his delicate forehead the veins in the form of the letter *Y* became outlined more distinctly. He felt that his blame of those ladies was also praise for Marynia, and that made him eloquent.

"Besides," continued he, "there exists a certain instinct which divines the real good wishes of people; it is not divined in that house. They are pleasant, agreeable, but their society has the appearance of form only; therefore I think that an earnest man, who becomes attached to people easily, might experience there many deceptions. It is a bitter and humiliating thing to mistake social tares for wheat. As to me, that is just why I fear people; for though Pan Stanislav says that I have intuition, I know well that at the root of the matter I am simple. And such things pain me tremendously. Simply my nerves cannot endure them. I remember that when still a child I noticed how people acted toward me in one way before my parents, and in another when my parents were absent; that was one of the great vexations of my childhood. It seemed to me contemptible, and pained me, as if I myself had done something contemptible."

"Because you have an honest nature," said Pani Bigiel.

He stretched forth his long arms, with which he gesticulated, when, forgetting his timidity, he spoke freely, and said, —

"O sincerity! in art and in life, that is the one thing!"

But Marynia began, in defence of those ladies: "People, and especially men, are frequently unjust, and take their own judgments, or even suppositions, for reality. As to Pani Osnovski and Lineta, how is it possible to suspect them of insincerity? They are joyful, kind, cordial, and whence should that come if not from good hearts?" Then, turning to Zavilovski, she began at him, partly in earnest, partly in jest, "You have not such an honest nature as Pani Bigiel says, for those ladies praise you, and you criticise them —"

But Pan Stanislav interrupted her with his usual vivacity: "Oh, thou art an innocent, and measurest all things with thy own measure. Wilt thou understand this, that petty cordiality and kindness may flow also from selfishness, which likes to be cosey and comfortable.

"If you," said he, turning to Zavilovski, "pay such homage to sincerity, it is sitting before you! You have here a real type of it."

"I know that! I know that!" said Zavilovski, with warmth.

"But is it thy wish to have me otherwise?" inquired Marynia, laughing.

He laughed also, and answered: "No, I would not. But, by the way, what a happiness it is that thou art not too small, and hast no need of heels; for shouldst thou wear them, chronic inflammation of the conscience would strike thee for deceiving people."

Marynia, seeing that Zavilovski's eyes were turned toward her feet, hid them under the table involuntarily, and, changing the subject, said, —

"But your volume is coming out these days, I think?"

"It would have been published already, but I added one poem; that causes delay."

"And may we know what the poem is called?"

"Lilia" (Lily).

"Is it not Lilia-Lineta?"

"No; it is not Lilia-Lineta."

Marynia's face grew serious. For her, it was easy to divine from the answer that the poem was to her and about her; hence she felt a sudden vexation, because she alone and one other, Zavilovski, knew this, and that there had arisen between them, for this cause, a sort of secret known to them only. This seemed to her not in accord with that honesty of hers mentioned a moment earlier, and a kind of sin against "Stas." For the first time, she saw the mental trouble into which a woman may fall, even though she be most in love with her husband and most innocent, if only the not indifferent look of another man fall on her. It seemed to her impossible, in any case, to lead her husband into the secret of her supposition. For the first time, she was seized by a certain anger at Zavilovski, who felt this straightway with his nerves of an artist, just as the barometer reflects a change of atmosphere; and, being a man without experience, he took the matter tragically. He imagined that Marynia would close her doors on him, would hate him, that he would not be able to see her; and the world appeared in mourning colors all at once to him. In his artistic nature there existed a real mixture of selfishness and fantasy with genuine tenderness, well-nigh feminine, which demanded love and warmth. Having become acquainted with Marynia, he cleaved to her with the selfishness of a sybarite, to whom such a feeling is precious, and who thinks of nothing else; next, his fancy raised her to poetic heights, and enhanced her charm a hundredfold, made her a being almost beyond the earth; and, finally, his native sensitiveness, to which loneliness and the want of a near heart caused actual pain, was so moved by the goodness with which he was received, that from all this was produced something having every appearance of love. A physical basis was lacking to this feeling, however. Besides his capacity for impulses, as ideal as the soul itself is, Zavilovski, like most artists, had the thoughts of a satyr. Those thoughts were sleeping at that time. He arrayed Marynia in so many glories and so much sacredness that he did not desire her; and if, against every likelihood, she were to cast herself on his neck unexpectedly, she would cease to be for him æsthetically that which she was, and which he wished her to be in future, — that is, a stainless being. All the more, therefore, did he judge that he could permit himself such a feeling, and all the more was he grieved now to part with that intoxication which had lulled his thought in such a beautiful manner, and filled the void of his life. It had been so pleasant for him, on returning home, to have a womanly figure at whose feet he had placed his soul, — to have one of whom to dream, and to whom he might write verses. Now he understands that if she discovers definitely what is taking place in him, if he does not succeed in hiding this better than hitherto, their relations cannot endure, and the former void, more painful than ever, will surround him a second time. He began then to think how he was to escape this, and how, not only not to lose anything of what he had enjoyed so far, but to see Marynia still oftener. In his quick imagination, there was no lack of methods. When he had made a hasty review, he found and chose one which, as it seemed to him, led directly to his object.

"I will fall in love, as it were, with Panna Castelli," said he to himself, "and will confess to Pani Polanyetski my torments. That not only will not separate us, but will bring us nearer. I will make her my patroness."

And straightway he begins to arrange the thing as if he were arranging objects. He imagines that he is in love with that "dreamy queen;" that he is unhappy, and that he will confess his secret to Marynia, who will listen to him willingly, with eyes moist from pity, and, like a real sister, will place her hand on his head. This play of fancy seemed to him so actual, and his sensitiveness was so great, that he composed expressions with which he would confess to Marynia; he found simple and touching ones, and he did this with such occupation that he himself was moved sincerely.

Marynia, returning home with her husband, thought of that poem entitled "Lilia," which had delayed the issue of the book. Like a real woman, she was somewhat curious about it, and feared it a little. She feared too in general the difficulty which the future might bring in the relation with Zavilovski. And under the influence of these fears she said, —

"Knowest thou of what I am thinking? That Lineta would be a great prize for Zavilovski."

"Tell me," answered Pan Stanislav, "what shot this Zavilovski and that girl into thy head."

"I, my Stas, am not a matchmaker, I say only that it would not be bad. Aneta Osnovski is rather a hot head, it is true; but she is so lively, such a fire spark."

"Abrupt, not lively; but believe me that she is not so simple as she seems, and that she has her own little personal plan in everything. Sometimes I think that Panna Lineta concerns her as much as she does me, and that at the root of all this something else is hidden."

"What could it be?"

"I don't know, and I don't know, perhaps, because I don't care much. In general, I have no faith in those women."

Their conversation was interrupted by Mashko, who was just driving in by the road before their house; and, seeing them, he hastened to greet Marynia, and said then to Pan Stanislav, —

"It is well that we have met, for to-morrow I am going away for a couple of days, and to-day is my time for payment, so I bring thee the money."

"I have just been at your father's," said he, turning to Marynia. "Pan Plavitski seems in perfect health; but he told me that he yearns for the country and land management, therefore he is thinking whether to buy some little place near the city, or not. I told him that if we win the will case he can stay at Ploshov."

Marynia did not like this conversation, in which there was evident, moreover, a slight irony; hence she did not wish to continue it. After a while Pan Stanislav took Mashko to his study, —

"Then is all going well?" asked he.

"Here is the instalment due on my debt," answered Mashko; "be so kind as to give a receipt."

Pan Stanislav sat down at his desk, and wrote a receipt.

"But now there is another affair," continued Mashko: "I sold some oak in Kremen once, on condition that I might redeem it, returning the price and a stipulated interest. Here is the price and the interest. I trust that thou hast nothing to add; I can only thank thee for a real service rendered, and shouldst thou ever need something of me, I beg thee, — without any ceremony, I beg thee to come to me, service for service. As is known to thee, I like to be grateful."

"This monkey is beginning to patronize me," thought

Pan Stanislav. And if he had not been in his own house, he might have uttered the silent remark aloud; but he restrained himself and said, —

"I have nothing to add; such was the contract. Besides, I have never considered that as business."

"All the more do I esteem it," answered Mashko, kindly.

"Well, what is to be heard in general?" inquired Pan Stanislav. "Thou art moving with all sails, I see. How is it with the will?"

"On behalf of the benevolent institutions a young little advocate is appearing named Sledz (herring). A nice name, is n't it? If I should call a cat by that name, she would miau for three days. But I'll pepper that herring and eat him. As to the lawsuit? It stands this way, that at the end of it I shall be able to withdraw from law in all likelihood, which, moreover, is not an occupation befitting me — and I will settle in Kremen permanently."

"With ready money in thy pocket?"

"With ready money in my pocket, and in plenty. I have enough of law. Of course, whoso came from the country is drawn to it. That is inherited with the blood. But enough of this matter, for the present. To-morrow, as I told thee, I am going away; and I recommend my wife to thee, all the more that Pani Kraslavski has gone just now to an oculist in Vienna. I am going besides to the Osnovskis' to ask them too to remember her."

"Of course we shall think of her," said Pan Stanislav. Then the conversation with Marynia occurred to him, and he asked, —

"Thy acquaintance with the Osnovskis is of long standing?"

"Rather long, though my wife knows them better. He is a very rich man; he had one sister who died, and a miserly uncle, after whom he received a great fortune. As to her, what shall I say to thee? she read when still unmarried all that came to her hand; she had pretensions to wit, to art, — in a word, to everything to which one may pretend, — and in her way fell in love with Kopovski: here she is for thee *in toto*."

"And Pani Bronich and Panna Castelli?"

"Panna Castelli pleases women rather than men; moreover, I know nothing of her, except that it is said that this same Kopovski tried for her, or is trying now, but Pani Bronich —"

Here Mashko began to laugh. "Pani Bronich the Khedive conducted in person over the pyramid of Cheops; the late Alphonso of Spain said every day to her in Cannes, 'Bon jour, Madame la Comtesse.' In the year 56, Musset wrote verses in her album, and Moltke sat with her on a trunk in Karlsbad, — in one word, she has been at every coronation. Now, since Panni Castelli has grown up, or rather luxuriated up to five feet and some inches, Aunt 'Sweetness' makes those imaginary journeys, not on her own account, but her niece's, in which for some time past Pani Osnovski helps her so zealously that it is difficult to understand what her object is. This is all, unless it is thy wish to know something of the late Pan Bronich, who died six years ago, it is unknown of what disease, for Pani Bronich finds a new one every day for him, adding, besides, that he was the last of the descendants of Rurik, not stating, however, that the second last descendant — that is, his father — was manager for the Rdultovskis, and made his property out of them. Well, I have finished, — 'Vanity fair!' Be well, keep well, and in case of need count on me. If I were sure that such a need would come quickly, I would make thee promise to turn to no one but me. Till we meet!"

When he had said this, Mashko pressed his friend's hand with indescribable kindness; and when he had gone, Pan Stanislav, shrugging his shoulders, said, —

"Such a clever man apparently, and does n't see the very same vanity in himself that he is laughing at in others! How different he was such a little while ago! He had almost ceased to pretend; but when trouble passed, the devil gained the upper hand."

Here he remembered what Vaskovski had said once about vanity and playing a comedy; then he thought, —

"And still such people have success in this country."

## CHAPTER XLIII.

Pani Osnovski forgot her "Florentine-Roman" evenings so thoroughly that she was astonished when her husband reminded her once of them. Such evenings are not even in her head now; she has other occupations, which she calls "taming the eagle." If any one does not see that the *eagle* and Lineta are created for each other, then, with permission of my husband and lord, he has very short sight; but there is no help for that. In general, men fail to understand many things, for they lack perception. Zavilovski may be an exception in this regard; but if Marynia Polanyetski would tell him, through friendship, to dress with more care and let his beard grow, it would be perfect! "Castelka"[1] is so thoroughly æsthetic that the least thing offends her, though on the other hand he carries her away, — nay, more, he hypnotizes her simply. And with her nature that is not wonderful.

Pan Osnovski listened to this chattering, and, dissolving from ecstasy, watched the opportunity to seize his wife's hands, and cover them, and her arms to the elbow, with kisses; once, however, he put the perfectly natural question, which Pan Stanislav too had put to Marynia, —

"Tell me what concern thou hast in this?"

But Pani Aneta said coquettishly, —

"*La reine s'amuse!* It is not a trick to write books. If there be only a little talent, that 's enough; but to bring into life that which is described in books is a far greater trick, and, besides, what amusement!"

And after a while she added, —

"I may have some personal object; and if I have, let Yozio guess it."

"I 'll tell it in thy ear," answered Osnovski.

She put out her ear with a cunning mien, blinking her violet eyes with curiosity. But Osnovski only brought his lips to her ear to kiss it; for the whole secret he repeated simply, —

"*La reine s'amuse!*"

[1] Familiar for Castelli.

And there was truth in this. Pani Aneta might have her own personal object in bringing Zavilovski near "Castelka;" but in its own way that development of a romance in life and the rôle of a little Providence occupied and amused her immensely.

With these providential intentions she ran in often to Marynia, to learn something of the "eagle," and returned in good spirits usually. Zavilovski, wishing to lull Marynia's suspicions, spoke more and more of Lineta; his diplomacy turned out so effectual that once, when Pani Aneta inquired of Marynia directly if Zavilovski were not in love with her, she answered, laughing, —

"We must confess that he is in love, my Anetka, but not with me, nor with thee. The apple is adjudged to Lineta, and nothing is left to us but to cry or be comforted."

On the other hand, feelings and thoughts were talked into and attributed continually to Lineta which self-love itself would not let her deny. From morning till evening she heard that this "eagle" of wide wings was in love with her; that he was at her feet; and that such a chosen one, such an exceptional being, as she was, could not be indifferent to this. It flattered her also too much to make it possible for her to be indifferent. While painting Kopovski, she admired always, it is true, the "splendid plain surfaces" on his face, and liked him because he offered her a field for various *successes*, which were repeated later as proofs of her wit and cleverness; she liked him for various reasons. Zavilovski, too, was not an ill-looking man, though he did not wear a beard, and did not dress with due care. Besides, so much was said of his wings, and of this, — that a soul such as hers should understand him. All said this, not Pani Aneta only. Pani Bronich, who, on a time, did not understand how any one could avoid falling in love with herself, transferred later on to her niece this happy self-confidence, and accepted the views of Pani Aneta, ornamenting at the same time the canvas of reality with flowers from her own mind. At last Pan Osnovski, too, joined the chorus. Out of love for his wife, he loved "Castelka" and Pani Bronich, and was ready to love whatever had remote or near relation to "Anetka," hence he took the matter seriously. Zavilovski was for him sympathetic; the information which he collected touching him was favorable. In general, he learned only that he was misanthropic, ambitious, and pursued stubbornly whatever he aimed at; besides, he was secretive, and greatly gifted. Since all this pleased the ladies, Osnovski began to think with perfect seriousness "if that were not well." Zavilovski justified so far the serious view of affairs,—he had begun for some time to visit more frequently the "common drawing-room," and to speak oftener with Lineta. The first, it is true, he did always at the cordial invitation of Pani Aneta, but the other flowed from his will. Pani Aneta noticed, also, that his glance rested more and more on the golden hair and the dreamy lids of "Castelka," and his eyes followed her when she passed through the drawing-room. Indeed, he began to survey her more carefully, a little through diplomacy, a little through curiosity.

The affair became much more important when the first volume of his poetry was issued. The poems had won attention already and were much spoken of; but the effect was weakened through this,—that they had appeared at considerable intervals, and unconnected. Now the book struck people's eyes; it was brilliant, strong, sincere. The language had freshness and metallic weight, but still bent obediently, and assumed the most subtile forms. The impression increased. Soon the murmur of praise changed to a roar filled with admiration. With the exaggeration usual in such cases, the work was exalted above its value, and in the young poet people began to foresee the coming heir of great glory and authority; his name passed from newspaper offices to publicity. People spoke of him everywhere, were occupied with him, sought him; curiosity became the greater that he was little known personally. The old rich Zavilovski, Panna Helena's father, who said that the two greatest plagues existing were perhaps the gout and poor relatives, repeated now to every one who asked him, "*Mais oui, mais oui,—c'est mon cousin;*" and such testimony had also its social weight for many persons, and, among others, weight of first order for Pani Bronich. Pani Aneta and Lineta ceased even to suffer because of the pin of "poor taste" in Zavilovski's necktie, for now everything about him might pass as original. She was pained yet that his name was Ignatsi. They would have preferred another more in keeping with his fame and his poetry; but when Osnovski, who from Metz had brought home a little Latin, explained to them that it meant "fiery," they answered that if that were true, it was another thing; and they were reconciled with Ignatsi.

Sincere and great joy reigned at Bigiel's, at Pan Stanislav's, and in the counting-house, because the book had won such fame; they were not envious in the counting-house. The old cashier, the agent, and the second book-keeper were proud of their colleague, as if his glory had brightened the counting-house also. The cashier even said, "But we have shown the world what our style is!" Bigiel was thinking for two days whether in view of all this Zavilovski should remain in a modest position in the house of Polanyetski and Bigiel; but Zavilovski, when questioned by him, answered, —

"This is very good of you, kind sir. Because people are talking a little about me, you want to take my morsel of bread from me, and my pleasant associates. I found no publishers; and had it not been for your book-keeper, I could not have published the volume."

To such an argument there was no answer, and Zavilovski remained in the counting-house. But he was a more frequent guest both at Bigiel's and at Pan Stanislav's. At the Osnovskis' he had not shown himself for a whole week after the volume was published, just as if something had happened. But Pani Bigiel and Marynia persuaded him to go; he had a secret desire, too, — hence one evening he went.

But he found the company just going to the theatre. They wished to remain at home absolutely, but he would not consent; and to the evident delight of Pani Osnovski and Lineta, it ended in this, — that he went with them. "Let Yozio buy a ticket for a chair if he wishes." And Yozio took a ticket for a chair. During the play Zavilovski sat in the front of the box with Lineta, for Pani Aneta had insisted that Pani Bronich and she would play "mother" for them. "You two can say what you please; and if any one comes, I will so stun him that he 'll not have power to trouble you." The eyes of people were turned frequently to that box when it was known who were sitting there, and Lineta felt that a kind of halo surrounded her; she felt that people not only were looking at him, but at the same time inquiring, "Whose is that head with golden hair and dreamy lids, to whom he is inclining and speaking?" She, on her part, looking at him sometimes, said to herself, "Were it not for the too prominent chin, he would be perfectly good-looking; his profile is very delicate, and a beard might cover his chin." Pani Aneta carried out her promise nobly; and when Kopovski appeared, she occupied him so much that he could barely greet Lineta, and say to Zavilovski,—

"Ah, you write verses!"

After this happy discovery he succeeded in adding, but rather as a monologue, "I should like verses immensely; but, a wonderful thing, the moment I read them I think of something else right away."

Lineta, turning her face, cast a long glance at him; and it is unknown which was stronger in this glance, the maliciousness of the woman, or the sudden admiration of the artist, for that head without brains, which, issuing from the depth of the box, seemed, on the red background of the wall, like some masterly thought of an artist.

After the theatre, Pani Aneta would not let Zavilovski go home; and all went to drink tea. Hardly had they reached the house, when Pani Bronich began to make reproaches.

"You are an evil man; and if anything happens to Lineta, it will be on your conscience. The child does n't eat, does n't sleep; she only reads you, and reads."

Pani Aneta added immediately,—

"True! I, too, have cause of complaint: she seized your book, and will not give it to any one for an instant; and when we are angry, do you know what she answers? 'This is mine! this is mine!'"

And Lineta, though she had not the book in her hands at that moment, pressed them to her bosom, as if to defend something, and said in a low, soft voice,—

"For it is mine, mine!"

Zavilovski looked at her and felt that something had, as it were, thrilled in him. But on returning home late he passed by Pan Stanislav's windows, in which light was still shining. After the theatre and conversation at the Osnovskis' he felt a certain turning of the head. Now the sight of those windows brought him to himself; he felt suddenly such a pleasant impression as one experiences on thinking of something very good and very dear. His immense, pure homage for Marynia arose in him with its former power: he was possessed by that kind of mild exaltation in which the desires fall asleep, and a man becomes almost entirely a spirit; and he returned home, muttering passages from the poem "Lilia," the most full of exaltation of any which he had written in his life yet.

There was light at Pan Stanislav's because something had happened, which seemed to Marynia that mercy of God expected and hoped for.

In the evening, after tea, she was sitting breaking her head, as usual, over daily accounts, when she put the pencil down on a sudden. After a while she grew pale, but her face became clear; and she said, with a voice slightly changed, —

"Stas!"

Her voice surprised him somewhat; therefore he approached her, and asked, —

"What is the matter? Thou art a little pale."

"Come nearer; I'll tell thee something."

And, taking his head with her hands, she whispered into his ear, and he listened; then, kissing her on the forehead, he said, —

"Only be not excited, lest thou hurt thyself."

But in his words emotion was evident. He walked through the room, looked at her a while, kissed her again on the forehead; at last he said, —

"Usually people wish a son first, but remember that it be a daughter. We 'll call her Litka."

Neither of them could sleep that night for a long time, and that was why Zavilovski saw light in the windows.

## CHAPTER XLIV.

In a week, when probability had become certainty, Pan Stanislav gave the news to the Bigiels. Pani Bigiel flew the same day to Marynia, who fell to weeping with gladness on her honest shoulders.

"It seems to me," said she, "that Stas will love me more now."

"How more?"

"I wished to say still more," answered Marynia. "Seest thou, for that matter, I have never enough."

"He would have to settle with me if there were not enough."

The tears dried on Marynia's sweet face, and only a smile remained. After a time she clasped her hands, as if in prayer, and said,—

"Oh, my God, if it is only a daughter! for Stas wants a daughter."

"And what wouldst thou like?"

"I—but don't tell Stas—I should like a son; but let it be a daughter."

Then she grew thoughtful, and asked,—

"But there is no help, is there?"

"There is not," answered Pani Bigiel, laughing; "for that they have not found yet any remedy."

Bigiel, on his part, gave the news to every one whom he met; and in the counting-house he said, in Pan Stanislav's presence, with a certain unction in his voice,—

"Well, gentlemen, it seems that the house will be increased by one member."

The employees turned inquiring glances on him; he added,—

"Thanks to Pan and Pani Polanyetski."

Then all hurried to Pan Stanislav with good wishes, excepting Zavilovski, who, bending over his desk, began to look diligently at columns of figures; and only after a while, when he felt that his conduct might arrest attention, did he turn with a changed face to Pan Stanislav, and, pressing his hand, repeat, "I congratulate, I congratulate!"

It seemed to him then that he was ridiculous, that something had fallen on his head; that he felt empty, boundlessly stupid; and that the whole world was fabulously trivial. The worst, however, was the feeling of his own ridiculousness; for the affair was so natural and easily foreseen that even such a man as Kopovski might foresee it. At the same time, he, an intelligent man, writing poetry, pervaded with enthusiasm, grasping everything which happened around, slipped into such an illusion that it seemed to him then as if a thunderbolt had struck him. What overpowering ridiculousness! But he had made the acquaintance of Marynia as Pani Polanyetski, and imagined to himself unconsciously that she had always been, and would be, Pani Polanyetski in the future as she was in the present, and simply it had not occurred to him that any change might supervene. And behold, observing lily tones once on her face, he called her Lily, and wrote lily verses to her. And now that lost sense, which to vexation adds something of ridicule, whispered in his ear, "Ah, a pretty lily!" And Zavilovski felt more and more crushed, more and more ridiculous; he wrote verses, but Pan Stanislav did not write any. In that apposition there was a gnawing bitterness, and something idiotic; he took deep draughts from that cup, so as not to lose one drop in the drinking. If his feelings had been betrayed; if he had made them known to Marynia; if she had repulsed him with utter contempt, and Pan Stanislav had thrown him downstairs,—there would have been something in that like a drama. But such an ending,—"such flatness!" He had a nature feeling everything ten times more keenly than common men; hence the position seemed to him simply unendurable, and those office hours, which he had to sit out yet, a torture. His feeling for Marynia had not sunk in his heart deeply; but it occupied his imagination altogether. Reality now struck its palm on his head without mercy; the blow seemed to him not only painful and heavy, but also given sneeringly. The desperate thought came to his head to seize his cap, go out, and never come back again. Fortunately, the usual hour for ending work came at last, and all began to separate.

Zavilovski, while passing through the corridor, where, at a hat-rack, a mirror was fixed, saw his projecting chin and tall form in it, and said to himself, "Thus looks an idiot." He did not go to dine that day with the second book-keeper, as usual; he would have been even glad to flee from his own person. Meanwhile he shut himself in at home, and with the exaggeration of a genuine artist, heightened to impossible limits his misfortune and ridiculous position. After some days he grew calm, however; he felt only a strange void in his heart, — precisely as if it were a dwelling vacated by some one. He did not show himself at Pan Stanislav's for a fortnight; but at the end of that time he saw Marynia at the Bigiels', and was astonished.

She seemed to him almost ugly. That was by no means his prejudice, for, though it was difficult to notice a change in her form, still she had changed greatly. Her lips were swollen; there were pimples on her forehead; and she had lost freshness of color. She was calm, however, but somewhat melancholy, as if some disappointment had met her. Zavilovski, who, in truth, had a good heart, was moved greatly by her ugliness. Before, it seemed to him that he would disregard her; now that seemed to him stupid.

But her face only had changed, not her kindness or good-will. Nay, feeling safe now from superfluous enthusiasms on his part, she showed him more cordiality than ever. She asked with great interest about Lineta; and when she found that a subject on which he, too, spoke willingly, she began to laugh with her former laughter, full of indescribable sweetness, and said almost joyously, —

"Well, well! People wonder there why you have not visited them for so long a time; and do you know what Aneta and Pani Bronich told me? They told me — "

But here she stopped, and after a while said, —

"No; I cannot tell this aloud. Let us walk in the garden a little."

And she rose, but not with sufficient care, so that, stumbling at the first step, she almost fell.

"Be careful!" cried Pan Stanislav, impatiently.

She looked at him with submission, almost with fear.

"Stas," said she, blushing, "as I love thee, that was inadvertent."

"But do not frighten her so," said Pani Bigiel, quickly.

It was so evident that Pan Stanislav cared more at that moment for the coming child than Marynia, that even Zavilovski understood it.

As to Marynia, this was known to her long before that day; she had passed through a whole mental battle with herself just because of it. Of that battle she had not spoken to any one; and it was the more difficult, the more the state of her health advised against excitement, unquiet, and an inclination to gloomy brooding. She had passed through grievous hours before she said to herself, "It must be as it is."

Pan Stanislav would have been simply astonished had any one told him that he did not love, and especially that he did not value, his wife as duty demanded. He loved her in his own way, and judged at once that, if ever, it was then that the child should be for both a question beyond every other. Vivacious and impulsive by nature, he pushed this care at moments too far, but he did not account this to himself as a fault; he did not even stop to think of what might take place in the soul of Marynia. It seemed to him that among other duties of hers one of the first was the duty of giving him children; that it was a simple thing, therefore, that she should accomplish this. Hence he was thankful to her, and imagined that, being careful of a child, he was by that very act careful of her, and careful in a degree that few husbands are. If he had considered it proper to call himself to account touching his treatment of her, he would have considered it a thing perfectly natural also that her charm, purely feminine, attracted him now less than it had hitherto. With each day she became uglier, and offended his æsthetic sense sometimes; he fancied that, concealing this from her, and trying to show her sympathy, he was as delicate as a man could well be to a woman.

She, on her part, had the impression that the hope on which she had counted most had deceived her; she felt that she had descended to the second place, that she would descend more and more. And in spite of all her affection for her husband, in spite of the treasures of tenderness which were collecting in her for the future child, rebellion and regret seized her soul at the first moment. But this did not last long; she battled with these feelings also, and conquered. She said to herself that here it was no one's fault; life is such that this issues from the natural condition of things, which, again, is a result of God's will. Then she began to accuse herself of selfishness, and crush herself with the weight of this thought: Has she a right to think of herself, not of "Stas," and not of her future child? What can she bring against "Stas"? What is there wonderful in this, that he, who had loved even a strange child so much, has his soul occupied now, above all, with his own; that his heart beats first for it? Is there not an offence against God in this, — that she permits herself to bring forward first of all rights of her own, happiness of her own, she, who has offended so much? Who is she, and what right has she to an exceptional fate? And she was ready to beat her breast. The rebellion passed; there remained only somewhere in the very depths of her heart a little regret that life is so strange, and that every new feeling, instead of strengthening a previous one, pushes it into the depths. But when that sorrow went from her heart to her eyes, under the form of tears, or began to quiver on her lips, she did not let it have such an escape.

"I shall be calm in a moment," thought she, in her soul. "Such it is, such it will be, and such is right; for such is life, and such is God's will, with which we must be reconciled." And at last she was reconciled.

By degrees she found repose even, not giving an account to herself that the basis of this was resignation and sadness. It was sadness, however, which smiled. Being young, it was almost bitter at times to her, when all at once, in the eyes of her husband, or of even some stranger, she read clearly, "Oh, how ugly thou hast grown!" But because Pani Bigiel had said that "afterward" she would be more beautiful than ever, she said in her soul to them, "Wait!" — and that was her solace.

She answered also something similar to Zavilovski. She was at once glad, and not glad, of the impression she had made on him; for if on the one hand her self-love had suffered a little, on the other she felt perfectly safe, and could speak with him freely. She wished to speak, and speak with full seriousness, for a few days before, Pani Aneta had told her directly that "The Column" was in love to the ears, and that Zavilovski had every chance with her.

This forging the iron while hot disquieted her somewhat; she could not understand why it was so, even taking into consideration the innate impetuosity of Pani Aneta. For Zavilovski, who had become somehow the Benjamin of both houses, she, as well as the Bigiels and Pan Stanislav, had great friendship; and, besides, she was grateful to him, for, be things as they might, he had appreciated her. He had known her truly, hence she would help him with gladness in that which seemed to her a great opportunity; but she thought also, "Suppose it should be bad for him." She feared responsibility a little, and her own previous diplomacy. Now, therefore, she wishes to learn first what he thinks really, and then give him to understand how things are, and finally advise him to examine and weigh with due care in the given case.

"They are wondering there, because you have not called for a long time," said she, when they had gone to the garden.

"What did Pani Osnovski say?" inquired Zavilovski.

"I will tell you only one thing, though I am not sure that I ought to repeat it. Pani Aneta told me — that — but no! First, I must learn why you have not called there this long time."

"I was not well, and I had a disappointment. I made no visits; I could not! You have stopped talking."

"Yes, for I wished to know if you were not angry at those ladies for some cause. Pani Aneta told me that Lineta supposed you were, and that she saw tears in her eyes a number of times, for that reason."

Zavilovski blushed; on his young and impressionable face real tenderness was reflected.

"Ah, my God!" answered he; "I angry, and at a lady like Panna Lineta? Could she offend any one?"

"I repeat what was said to me, though Pani Aneta is so impulsive that I dare not guarantee all she says to be accurate. I know that she is not lying; but, as you understand, very impulsive people see things sometimes as if through a magnifying-glass. Satisfy yourself. Lineta seems to me agreeable, very uncommon, and very kind — but judge for yourself; you have such power of observation."

"That she is kind and uncommon is undoubted. You remember how I said that they produced the impression of foreign women; that is not true altogether. Pani Osnovski may, but not Panna Lineta."

"You must look yourself, and look again," said Marynia. "You understand that I persuade you to nothing. I should have a little fear, even of Stas, who does not like those ladies. But I say sincerely that when I heard of Lineta's tears, my heart was touched. The poor girl!"

"I cannot even tell you how the very thought of that stirs me," replied Zavilovski.

Further conversation was interrupted by the coming of Pan Stanislav, who said, —

"Well? always matchmakers! But these women are incurable. Knowest thou, Marynia, what I will tell thee? I should be most happy wert thou to refrain from such matters."

Marynia began to explain; but he turned to Zavilovski, and said, —

"I enter into nothing in this case, and know only this, — that I have not the least faith in those ladies."

Zavilovski went home full of dreams. All the strings of his imagination had been stirred and sounded, so that the wished-for sleep fled from him. He did not light a lamp, so that nothing might prevent him from playing on those quivering strings; he sat in the moonlight and mused, or rather, created. He was not in love yet; but a great tenderness had possessed him at thought of Lineta, and he arranged images as if he loved already. He saw her as distinctly as though she were before him; he saw her dreamy eyes, and her golden head, bending, like a cut flower, till it reached his breast. And now it seems to him that he is placing his fingers on her temples, and that he is feeling the satin touch of her hair, and, bending her head back a little, he looks to see if the fondling has not dried her tears; and her eyes laugh at him, like the sky still wet from rain, but sunny. Imagination moves his senses. He thinks that he is confessing his love to her; that he presses her to his bosom, and feels her heart beating; that he kneels with his head on her knees, from which comes warmth through the silk garment to his face. And he began in reality to shiver. Hitherto she had been for him an image; now he feels her for the first time as a woman. There is not in him even one thought which is not on her; and he so forgets himself in her that he loses consciousness of where he is, and what is happening within him.

Some kind of hoarse singing on the street roused him; then he lighted a lamp, and began to think more soberly. A kind of alarm seized him now, because one thing seemed undoubted, — if he did not cease to visit Pani Bronich and the Osnovskis altogether, he would fall in love with that maiden past memory.

"I must choose, then," said he to himself.

And next day he went to see her, for he had begun to

yearn; and that same night he tried to write a poem with the title of "Spider-web."

He dared not go to Pani Bronich herself, so he waited till the hour when he could find all at tea, in the common drawing-room. Pani Aneta received him with uncommon cordiality, and outbursts of joyous laughter; but he, after greeting her, began to look at Lineta's face, and his heart beat with more force when he saw in her a great and deep joy.

"Do you know what?" cried Pani Aneta, with her usual vivacity. "Our 'Poplar' likes beards so much that I thought this of you: 'he is letting his beard grow, and does not show himself.'"

"No, no!" said the "Poplar," "stay as you were when I made your acquaintance."

But Pan Osnovski put his arm around Zavilovski, and said, in that pleasant tone of a man of good breeding, who knows how to bring people at once to more intimate and cordial relations, —

"Did Pan Ignas hide himself from us? Well, I have means to compel him. Let Lineta begin his portrait, then he must come to us daily."

Pani Aneta clapped her hands.

"How clever that Yozio is, wonderfully clever!"

His face was radiant because he had said a thing pleasing to his wife, and he repeated, —

"Of course, my Anetka, of course."

"I have promised already to paint it," said Lineta, with a soft voice, "but I was afraid to be urgent."

"Whenever you command," answered Pan Ignas.

"The days are so long now that about four, after Pan Kopovski; for that matter, I shall finish soon with that insufferable Kopovski."

"Do you know what she said about Pan Kopovski?" began Pani Aneta.

But Lineta would not permit her to say this for anything; she was prevented, moreover, by Pan Plavitski, who came in at that moment, and broke up the conversation. Pan Plavitski, on making the acquaintance of Pani Aneta at Marynia's, lost his head for her, and acknowledged this openly; on her part, she coquetted with him unsparingly, to the great delight of herself and of others.

"Let papa sit near me here," said she; "we will be happy side by side, won't we?"

"As in heaven! as in heaven!" replied Plavitski, stroking his knees with his palms time after time, and thrusting out the tip of his tongue from enjoyment.

Zavilovski drew up to Lineta and said, —

"I am so happy to be able to come every day. But shall I not occupy your time, really?"

"Of course you will occupy it," answered she, looking him in the eyes; "but you will occupy it as no one else can. I was really too timid to urge, because I am afraid of you."

Then he looked into the depth of her eyes, and answered with emphasis, —

"Be not afraid."

Lineta dropped her eyelids, and a moment of rather awkward suspense followed; then the lady inquired, in a voice somewhat lowered, —

"Why did you not come for such a long time?"

He had it on his tongue to say, "I was afraid," but he had not the daring to push matters that far; hence he answered, —

"I was writing."

"A poem?"

"Yes, called 'Spider-web;' I will bring it to-morrow. You remember that when I made your acquaintance, you said that you would like to be a spider-web. I remembered that; and since then I see continually such a snowy thread sporting in the air."

"It sports, but not with its own power," answered Lineta, "and cannot soar unless —"

"What? Why do you not finish?"

"Unless it winds around the wing of a Soarer."

When she had said this, she rose quickly and went to help Osnovski, who was opening the window.

Zavilovski remained alone with mist in his eyes. It seemed to him that he heard the throbbing of his temples. The honeyed voice of Pani Bronich first brought him to his senses, —

"A couple of days ago old Pan Zavilovski told me that you and he are related; but that you are not willing to visit him, and that he cannot visit you, since he has the gout. Why not visit him? He is a man of such distinction, and so pleasant. Go to him; it is even a disappointment to him that you do not go. Go to visit him."

"Very well; I can go," answered Zavilovski, who was ready that moment to agree to anything.

"How kind and good you must be! You will see your cousin, Panna Helena. But don't fall in love with her, for she too is very distinguished."

"No, there is no danger," said Zavilovski, laughing.

"They say besides that she was in love with Ploshovski, who shot himself, and that she wears eternal mourning in her heart for him. But when will you go?"

"To-morrow, or the day after. When you like."

"You see, they are going away. The summer is at our girdles! Where will you be in the summer?"

"I do not know. And you?"

Lineta, who during this time had returned and sat down not far away, stopped her conversation with Kopovski, and, hearing Pan Ignas's question, replied, —

"We have no plan yet."

"We were going to Scheveningen," said Pani Bronich, "but it is difficult with Lineta." And after a while she added in a lower voice: "She is always so surrounded by people; she has such success in society that you would not believe it. Though why should you not? It is enough to look at her. My late husband foretold this when she was twelve years of age. 'Look,' said he, 'what trouble there will be when she grows up.' And there is trouble, there is! My husband foresaw many things. But have I told you that he was the last of the Rur— Ah, yes! I have told you. We had no children of our own, for the first one didn't come to birth, and my husband was fourteen years older than I; later on he was to me more, — a father."

"How can that concern me?" thought Pan Ignas. But Pani Bronich continued, —

"My late husband always grieved over this, that he had no son. That is, there was a son, but he came halfway too early" (here tears quivered in the voice of Pani Bronich). "We kept him some time in spirits. And, if you will believe it, when there was fair weather he rose, and when there was rain he sank down. Ah, what a gloomy remembrance! How much my husband suffered because he was to die, — the last of the Rur —. But a truce to this; 't is enough that at last he was as attached to Lineta as to a relative, — and surely she was his nearest relative, — and what remains after us will be hers. Maybe for that reason people surround her so. Though — no! I do not wonder at them. If you knew what a torment that is to her, and to me. Two years ago, in Nice, a Portuguese, Count Jao Colimaçao, a relative of the Alcantaras, so lost his head as to rouse people's laughter. Or that Greek of last year, in Ostend! — the son of a banker, from Marseilles, a millionnaire. What was his name? Lineta, what was the name of that Greek millionnaire, that one who, thou knowest?"

"Aunt!" said Lineta, with evident displeasure.

But the aunt was in full career already, like a train with full steam.

"Ah, ha! I recollect," said she, — "Kanafaropulos, Secretary of the French Embassy in Brussels."

Lineta rose and went to Pani Aneta, who was talking at the principal table with Plavitski. The aunt, following her with her eyes, said, —

"The child is angry. She hates tremendously to have any one speak of her successes; but I cannot resist. Do you understand me? See how tall she is! How splendidly she has grown! Anetka calls her sometimes the column, and sometimes the poplar; and really, she is a poplar. What wonder that people's eyes gaze at her! I have n't mentioned yet Pan Ufinski. That's our great friend. My late husband loved him immensely. But you must have heard of Pan Ufinski? That man who cuts silhouettes out of paper. The whole world knows him. I don't know at how many courts he has cut silhouettes; the last time he cut out the Prince of Wales. There was also a Hungarian."

Osnovski, who sat near by amusing himself with a pencil at his watch-chain, now drawing it out, now pushing it back, grew impatient at last, and said, —

"A couple of more such, dear aunt, and there would be a masquerade ball."

"Precisely, precisely!" answered Pani Bronich. "If I mention them, it is because Lineta does n't wish to hear of any one. She is such a chauviniste! You have no idea what a chauviniste that child is."

"God give her health!" said Pan Ignas.

Then he rose to take farewell. At parting, he held for some time the hand of Lineta, who answered also with an equally prolonged pressure.

"Till to-morrow," said he, looking into her eyes.

"Till to-morrow — after Pan Kopovski. And do not forget 'Spider-web.'"

"No, I will not forget — ever," answered Zavilovski, with a voice somewhat moved.

He went out with Plavitski; but they had scarcely found themselves on the street, when the old man, tapped him lightly on the arm, and stopping, said, —

"Young man, do you know that I shall soon be a grandfather?"

"I know."

"Yes, yes!" repeated Plavitski with a smile of delight, "and in addition to that, I will tell you only this much: there is nothing to surpass young married women!"

And, laughing, he began to clap Pan Ignas time after time on the shoulder; then he put the ends of his fingers to his lips, took farewell, and walked off.

But his voice, slightly quivering, came to Pan Ignas from a distance, —

"There is nothing to surpass young married women." Noise on the street drowned the rest.

## CHAPTER XLV.

FROM that time Pan Ignas went every day to Aunt Bronich's. He found Kopovski there frequently, for toward the end something had been spoiled in the portrait of "Antinous." Lineta said that she had not been able to bring everything out of that face yet; that the expression in the picture was not perhaps what it should be,—in a word, she needed time for reflection. With Pan Ignas her work went more easily.

"With such a head as Pan Kopovski's," said she once, "it is enough to change the least line, it is enough to have the light wrong, to ruin everything. While with Pan Zavilovski one must seize first of all the character."

On hearing this, both were satisfied. Kopovski declared even that it was not his fault; that God had created him so. Pani Bronich said later on that Lineta had said apropos of that: "God created him; the Son of God redeemed him; but the Holy Ghost forgot to illuminate him." That witticism on poor Kopovski was repeated throughout Warsaw.

Pan Ignas liked him well enough. After a few meetings he seemed to him so unfathomably stupid that it did not occur to him that any one could be jealous of the man. On the contrary, it was always pleasant to look at him. Those ladies too liked him, though they permitted themselves to jest with him; and sometimes he served them simply as a ball, which they tossed from hand to hand. Kopovski's stupidity was not gloomy, however, nor suspicious. He possessed a uniform temper and a smile really wonderful; of this last he was aware, perhaps, hence he preferred to smile rather than frown. He was well-bred, accustomed to society, and dressed excellently; in this regard he might have served as a model to Pan Ignas.

From time to time he put astonishing questions, which filled the young ladies with merriment. Once, hearing Pani Bronich talk of poetic inspirations, he asked Pan Ignas, "If anything was taken for it or not," and at the first moment confused him, for Pan Ignas did not know what to answer.

Another time Pani Aneta said to him, —

"Have you ever written poetry? Make some rhyme, then."

Kopovski asked time till next day; but next day he had forgotten the request, or could not make the verses. The ladies were too well-bred to remind him of his promise. It was always so agreeable to look at him that they did not wish to cause him unpleasantness.

Meanwhile spring ended, and the races began. Pan Ignas was invited for the whole time of their continuance to the carriage of the Osnovskis. They gave him a place opposite Lineta; and he admired her with all his soul. In bright dresses, in bright hats, with laughter in her dreamy eyes, with her calm face flushing somewhat under the breath of fresh breezes, she seemed to him spring and paradise. Returning home, he had his eyes full of her, his mind and his heart full. In that world in which they lived, in the society of those young men, who came up to the carriage to entertain the ladies, he was not at home, but the sight of Lineta recompensed him for everything. Under the influence of sunny days, fair weather, broad summer breezes, and that youthful maiden, who began to be dear to him, he lived, as it were, in a continuous intoxication; he felt youth and power in himself. In his face there was at times something truly eagle-like. At moments it seemed to him that he was a ringing bell, sounding and sounding, heralding the delight of life, the delight of love, the delight of happiness, — a great jubilee of loving.

He wrote much, and more easily than ever before; there was besides in his verses that which recalled the fresh odor of newly ploughed fields, the vigor of young leaves, the sound of wings of birds flying on to fallow land to the immense breadth of plains and meadows. He felt his own power, and ceased to be timid about poetry even before strangers, for he understood that there was something about him, something within him, and that he had something to lay at the feet of a loved one.

Pan Stanislav, who, in spite of his mercantile life, had an irrestrainable passion for horses, and never neglected the races, saw Pan Ignas every day with the Osnovskis and Panna Castelli, and gazing at the latter as at a rainbow; when he teased him in the counting-house for being in love, the young poet answered, —

"It is not I, but my eyes. The Osnovskis will go soon, those ladies too; and all will disappear like a dream."

But he did not speak truth, for he did not believe that all could disappear like a dream. On the contrary, he felt that for him a new life had begun, which with the departure of Panna Lineta might be broken.

"And where are Pani Bronich and Panna Castelli going?" continued Pan Stanislav.

"For the rest of June and during July they will remain with the Osnovskis, and then go, as they say, to Scheveningen; but this is not certain yet."

"Osnovski's Prytulov is fifteen miles from Warsaw," said Pan Stanislav.

For some days Pan Ignas had been asking himself, with heart beating, whether they would invite him or not; but when they invited him, and besides very cordially, he did not promise to go, and with all his expressions of gratitude held back, excusing himself with the plea of occupation and lack of time. Lineta, who was sitting apart, heard him, and raised her golden brows. When he was going, she approached him and asked, —

"Why will you not come to Prytulov?"

He, seeing that no one could hear them, said, looking into her eyes, —

"I am afraid."

She began to laugh, and inquired, repeating Kopovski's words, —

"Is it necessary to take anything for that?"

"It is," answered he, with a voice somewhat trembling; "I need to take the word, come, from you!"

She hesitated a moment; perhaps she did not dare to tell him directly in that form which he required, but she blushed suddenly and whispered, —

"Come."

Then she fled, as if ashamed of those colors on her face, which, in spite of the darkness, were increasingly evident.

On the way home it seemed to Pan Ignas that a shower of stars was raining down on him.

The departure of the Osnovskis was to take place in ten days only. Up to that time, the painting of portraits was to continue its usual course, and to go on in the same fashion till the last day, for Lineta did not wish to lose time. Pani Aneta persuaded her to paint Pan Ignas exclusively, since Kopovski would need only as many sittings as could be arranged in Prytulov just before their departure for Scheweningen. For Pan Ignas those sittings had become the first need of his life, as it were; and if by chance there was any interruption, he looked on that day as lost. Pani Bronich was present at the sittings most frequently. But he divined in her a friendly soul; and at last the manner in which she spoke of Lineta began to please him. They both just composed hymns in honor of Lineta, whom in confidential conversation Pani Bronich called "Nitechka."[1] This name pleased Pan Ignas the more clearly he felt how that "Nitechka" (thread) was winding around his heart.

Frequently, however, it seemed to him that Pani Bronich was narrating improbable things. It was easy to believe that Lineta was and could be Svirski's most capable pupil; that Svirski might have called her "La Perla;" that he might have fallen in love with her, as Pani Bronich gave one to understand. But that Svirski, known in all Europe, and rewarded with gold medals at all the exhibitions, could declare with tears, while looking at some sketch of hers, that saving technique, he ought rather to take lessons of her, of this even Pan Ignas permitted himself to doubt. And somewhere, in some corner of his soul, in which there was hidden yet a small dose of sobriety, he wondered that Panna "Nitechka" did not contradict directly, but limited herself to her words usual on such occasions: "Aunt! thou knowest that I do not wish you to repeat such things."

But at last he lost even those final gleams of sobriety, and began to have feelings of tenderness even over the late Bronich, and almost fell in love with Pani Bronich, for this alone, — that he could talk with her from morning till night of Lineta.

In consequence of this repeated insistence of Pani Bronich, he visited also, at this time, old Pan Zavilovski, that Crœsus, at whose house he had never been before. The old noble, with milk-white mustaches, a ruddy complexion, and gray hair closely trimmed, received him with his foot in an armchair, and with that peculiar great-lord familiarity of a man accustomed to this, — that people count more with him than he with them.

"I beg pardon for not standing," said he, "but the gout is no joke. Ha, what is to be done! An inheritance! It seems that this will be attached to the name for the ages of ages. But hast thou not a twist in thy thumb sometimes?"

[1] "Nitechka" (little thread) is the diminutive of "Nitka," itself a diminutive of "Nits," which means thread.

"No," answered Pan Ignas, who was a little astonished, as well at the manner of reception as that the old noble said *thou* to him from the first moment.

"Wait; old age will come."

Then, calling his daughter, he presented Pan Ignas to her, and began to speak of the family, explaining to the young man how they were related. At last he said, —

"Well, I have not written verses, for I am too dull; but I must tell thee that thou hast written them for me, and that I was not ashamed, though I read my name under the verses."

But the visit was not to end successfully. Panna Zavilovski, a person of thirty years, good-looking, but, as it were, untimely faded and gloomy, wishing to take some part in the conversation, began to inquire of her "cousin" whom he knew, and where he visited. To every name mentioned, the old noble appended, in one or two words, his opinion. At mention of Pan Stanislav, he said, "Good blood!" at Bigiel's, he inquired, "How?" and when the name was repeated, he said, "*Connais pas;*" Pani Aneta he outlined with the phrase, "Crested lark!" at mention of Pani Bronich he muttered, "Babbler;" at last, when the young man named, with a certain confusion, Panna Castelli, the noble, whose leg twitched evidently at that moment, twisted his face terribly, and exclaimed, "Ei! a Venetian *half-devil!*"

At this, it grew dark in the eyes of Pan Ignas, who, notwithstanding his shyness, was impulsive; his lower jaw came forward more than ever, and, rising, he measured with a glance the old man from his aching foot to his crown, and said, —

"You have a way of giving sharp judgments, which does not suit me; therefore it is pleasant to take farewell."

And, bowing, he took his hat and departed.

Old Pan Zavilovski, who permitted himself everything, and to whom everything was forgiven, looked at his daughter some time with amazement, and only after long silence exclaimed, —

"What! has he gone mad?"

The young man did not tell Pani Bronich what had happened. He said merely that he had made a visit, and that father and daughter alike did not please him. She learned everything, however, from the old man himself, who, for that matter, did not call Lineta anything but "Venetian half-devil," even to her eyes.

"But to make the matter perfect, you have sent me a full devil," said he; "it is well that he did not break my head."

Still in his voice one might note a species of satisfaction that it was a *Zavilovski* who had shown himsef so resolute; but Pani Bronich did not note it. She took the affair somewhat to heart, and, to the great astonishment of the "full-devil," said to him, —

"He is wild about Lineta, and with him this is a sort of term of tenderness; besides, one should forgive a man much who has such a position, and in this age. It must be that you have n't read Krashevski's novel, 'Venetian Half-Devil.' This is a title in which there is a certain poetry ever since that author used it. When the old man grows good-natured, write him a couple of words, will you not? Such relations should be kept up."

"Pani," answered Pan Ignas, "I would not write to him for anything in the world."

"Even if some one besides me should ask?"

"That is — again, I am not a stone."

Lineta laughed when she heard these words. In secret she was pleased that Pan Ignas, at one word touching her which to him seemed offensive, sprang up as if he had heard a blasphemy. So that during the sitting, when for a while they were alone, she said, —

"It is wonderful how little I believe in the sincerity of people. So difficult is it for me to believe that any one, except aunt, should wish me well really."

"Why?"

"I don't know. I cannot explain it to myself."

"But, for example, the Osnovskis? Pani Aneta?"

"Pani Aneta?" repeated Lineta.

And she began to paint diligently, as if she had forgotten the question.

"But I?" asked Pan Ignas, in a lower voice.

"You — yes. You, I am sure, would not let any one speak ill of me. I feel that you are sincerely well-wishing, though I know not why, for in general I am of so little worth."

"You of little worth!" cried Pan Ignas, springing up. "Remember that, in truth, I will let no one speak ill of you, not even you yourself."

Lineta laughed and said, —

"Very well; but sit down, for I cannot paint."

He sat down; but he looked at her with a gaze so full of love and enchantment that it began to confuse her.

"What a disobedient model!" said she; "turn your head to the right a little, and do not look at me."

"I cannot! I cannot!" answered Pan Ignas.

"And I, in truth, cannot paint, for the head was begun in another position. Wait!"

Then she approached him, and, taking his temples with her fingers, turned his head toward the right slightly. His heart began to beat like a hammer; everything went around in his eyes; and, holding the hand of Lineta, he pressed her warm palm to his lips, and made no answer, — he only pressed it more firmly.

"Talk with aunt," said she, hurriedly. "We are going to-morrow."

They could not say more, for that moment Osnovski, Kopovski, and Pani Aneta, who had been sitting in the drawing-room adjoining, came into the studio.

Pani Aneta, seeing Lineta's blushing cheeks, looked quickly at Pan Ignas, and asked, —

"How is it going with you to-day?"

"Where is aunt?" inquired Lineta.

"She went out to make visits."

"Long since?"

"A few minutes ago. How has it gone with you?"

"Well; but enough for to-day."

Lineta put down her brush, and after a moment went to wash her hands. Pan Ignas remained there, answering, with more or less presence of mind, questions put to him; but he wanted to go. He feared the conversation with Pani Bronich, and, with the habit of cowards, he wished to defer it till the morrow; he wanted, besides, to remain a while with his own thoughts, to arrange them, to estimate better the significance of what had happened. For at that moment he had in his head merely a certain chaos of indefinite thoughts; he understood that something unparalleled had happened, — something from which a new epoch in life would begin. At the very thought of this, a quiver of happiness passed through him, but also a quiver of fear, for he felt that now it was too late to withdraw; through love, through confession, through declaration to the lady and to her family, he must advance to the altar. He desired this with his whole soul; but he was so accustomed to consider everything that was happiness as a poetic imagining, as something belonging exclusively to the world of thought, art, and dreams, that he almost lacked daring to believe that Lineta could become his wife really. Meanwhile he had barely endurance to sit out the time; and when Lineta returned, he rose to take leave.

She gave him her hand, cooled by fresh water, and said,—

"Will you not wait for aunt?"

"I must go; and to-morrow I will take farewell of you and Pani Bronich."

"Then till our next meeting!"

This farewell seemed to Pan Ignas, after what had happened, so inappropriate and cold that despair seized him; but he had not the daring to part before people otherwise, all the more that Pani Aneta was looking at him with uncommon attention.

"Wait! I have something to do in the city; we'll go together," said Osnovski, as he was going out.

And they went together; but barely were they outside the gate of the villa, when Pan Osnovski stopped, and put his hand on the poet's arm.

"Pan Ignas, have you not quarrelled a little with Lineta?"

Pan Ignas looked at him with great eyes.

"I? with Panna Lineta?"

"Yes, for you parted somehow coldly. I thought you were as far, at least, as hand-kissing."

Pan Ignas's eyes grew still larger; Osnovski laughed, and said, —

"Well, I'll tell you the truth. My wife, as a woman who is curious, looked at you, and said that something had happened. My Pan Ignas, you have in me a great friend, who, besides, knows what it is to love. I can say to you only one thing, — God grant you to be as happy as I am!"

When he had said this, he began to shake his guest's hand; and Pan Ignas, though confused to the highest degree, was barely able to refrain from falling on his neck.

"Have you really some work to-day? Why did you go?"

"I will tell you sincerely. I wanted to collect my thoughts, and, besides, fear of Pani Bronich seized me."

"Then you do not know aunt? Her head, too, is warm with the question. Come with me a bit of the road, and then go back without ceremony. On the way you will collect your thoughts; by that time Pani Bronich will be at home, and you will tell her your little story, at which she will weep. Nothing else threatens you. Remember, too, that if you are fortunate you are to thank mainly my Aneta, for, as God lives, she has filled Castelka's head, as your own sister might. She has such an impetuous head, and at the same time such an honest heart. Equally good women there may be, but a better there is not on earth. It seemed to us a little that that fool Kopovski was inclined to Castelka, and Aneta was tremendously angry. They like Kopovski; but to let her marry such a man — that would be too much."

Thus talking, he took Pan Ignas by the hand, and after a moment, continued, "We are to be relatives soon; let us drop ceremony and say *thou* to each other. I must tell thee further: I have no doubt Castelka loves thee with her whole heart, for she is a true woman also. Besides, they have turned her head with thee greatly; but she is so young yet that I tell thee to throw fuel on the fire — throw it! Dost understand? What is begun should become rooted; this can happen easily, for hers is really an uncommon nature. Do not think that I wish to forewarn or to frighten thee. No; it is a question only of making things permanent. That she loves thee is not subject to doubt. If thy eyes had but seen her when she was carrying thy book around, or what happened when she and thou were returning from the theatre. A stupid thought came to my head then. I spoke of having heard that old Zavilovski wished to make thy acquaintance because he had planned to marry thee to his daughter, so that his property might not leave the name; and imagine to thyself, that poor girl, when she heard this, became as pale as paper, so that I was frightened, and took back my words in all haste. What is thy answer to this?"

Pan Ignas wanted to laugh and to weep; but he merely pressed to his side, and pressed with all his force, Osnovski's hand, which he held under his arm, and said, after a while,—

"I am not worthy of her, no."

"Well, and after that 'no' perhaps thou wilt say, 'No, I do not love her properly.'"

"That may be true," answered Pan Ignas, raising his eyes.

"Well, go back now, and tell thy little story to Aunt Bronich. Do not fear being too pathetic; she likes that. Till we meet again, Ignas! I shall be back myself in an hour or so, and we shall have a betrothal evening."

They pressed each other's hands, and Osnovski said, with a feeling which was quite brotherly, —

"I repeat once more: God grant thee to find in Castelka such a wife as my Anetka!"

On the way back Pan Ignas thought that Osnovski was an angel, Pani Osnovski another, Pani Bronich a third, and Lineta, soaring above them all on the wings of an archangel, something divine and sacred. He understood at that moment that a heart might love to pain. In his soul he was kneeling at her knees, bowing to the earth at her feet; he loved her, deified her, and to all these feelings, which were playing in him one great hymn, as it were, to greet the dawn, was joined a feeling of such tenderness, as if that magnified woman was also a little child, alone, and wonderfully loved, but a little thing, needing care. He recalled Osnovski's story of how she had grown pale when they told her that there was a plan to marry him to another; and in his soul he repeated, "Ah, but thou art mine, thou art mine!" He grew tender beyond measure, and gratitude so filled his heart that it seemed to him that he could not repay her in a lifetime for that one moment of paleness. He felt happier than ever before; and at moments the immensity of this happiness almost frightened him. Hitherto he had been a theoretical pessimist, but now reality gave the lie to those passing theories with such power that it was hard for him to believe that he could have deceived himself to such a degree.

Meanwhile he was returning to the villa, inhaling along the way the odor of blooming jasmines, and having some species of dim feeling that that intoxicating odor was nothing external, but simply a part and component of his happiness. "What people! what a house! what a family!" said he to himself; "only among them could my White One be reared!" Then he looked on the sun, setting in calmness; he looked at the golden curtains of evening, bordered with purple; and that calmness began to possess him. In those immense lights he felt boundless love and kindness, which look on the world, cherish, and bless it. He did not pray in words, it is true; but everything was singing one thanksgiving prayer in his soul.

At the gate of the villa he recovered as if from a dream; he saw an old serving-man of the Osnovskis, who was looking at the passing carriages.

"Good-evening, Stanislav," said he; "but has not Pani Bronich returned?"

"I am just looking, but I do not see her."

"Are the ladies in the drawing-room yet?"

"They are; and Pan Kopovski, too."

"But who will open for me?"

"The door is open. I 've come out only this minute."

Pan Ignas went up; but, finding no one in the common drawing-room, he went to the studio. There, too, he found no one; but in the adjoining smaller chamber certain low voices reached him through the portière dividing that room from the studio. Thinking to find there both ladies and Kopovski, he drew aside the portière slightly, and, looking in, was stupefied.

Lineta was not in the room; but Kopovski was kneeling before Pani Osnovski, who, holding her hands thrust into his abundant hair, was bending his head back, inclining her face at the same time, as if to place a kiss on his forehead.

"Anetka, if thou love me—" said Kopovski, with a voice stifled from passion.

"I love—but no! I don't want that," answered Pani Osnovski, pushing him away somewhat.

Pan Ignas dropped the portière with an involuntary movement; for a moment he stood before it as if his feet had grown leaden. Finally, without giving himself a clear account of what he was doing, he passed through the studio, where the sound of his steps was deadened on the thick carpet, as it had been when he entered; he passed the main drawing-room, the entrance, the front steps, and came to himself at the gate of the villa.

"Is the serene lord going out?" inquired the old serving-man.

"Yes," answered Pan Ignas.

He walked away as quickly as if escaping from something. After a time, however, he stopped, and said aloud to himself,—

"Why have I not gone mad?"

And suddenly madness seemed to him possible, for he felt that he was losing the thread of his thoughts; that he could not give himself an account of anything; that he understood nothing, believed nothing. Something began to tear in him, fall away. How was it? That house which a moment before he thought to be some kind of blessed retreat of exceptional souls, conceals the usual falsehood, the usual wickedness, the usual vileness of life, — a wretched and shameful comedy. And his Lineta, his White One, is breathing such an atmosphere, living in such an environment, existing with such beings! Here Osnovski's words occurred to him: "God grant thee to find in Castelka such a wife as I have in my Anetka!" "I thank thee," thought Pan Ignas, and he began to laugh, in spite of himself. Neither evil nor vileness were to him a novelty: he had seen them, and he knew that they existed; but for the first time life showed them to him with such a merciless irony, as that through which Pan Osnovski, — a man who had shown him the heart of a brother; a man honest, just, kind as few people in the world are — turned out to be also a fool, a kind of exalted idiot, exalted through his faith and his feeling; an idiot through a woman. And for the first time, too, he saw clearly what a bad and contemptible woman may make of a man, without any fault of his. On a sudden new, dreadful horizons of life opened before him, — whole regions, the existence of which he had not suspected; he had understood before that an evil woman, like a vampire, may suck the life out of a man, and kill him, and that seemed to him demonic, but he had not imagined that she could make a fool of him also. He could not master that thought. But still, Osnovski was ridiculous when he wished him to be as happy with his future wife as he with Anetka; there was no help for this case either. One should not so love as to grow blind to that degree.

Here his thoughts passed to Lineta. At the first moment he had a feeling that from that vileness in the house of the Osnovskis, and from that doubt which was born in his heart, a certain shadow fell on her also. After a while he began, however, to cast out that feeling as though it were profanation, treason against innocence, treason against a being as pure as she was beloved, and defiling in thought her and her angelic plumage. Indignation at himself seized him. "Does such a dove even think evil?" asked he, in his soul. And his love rose still more at the thought that "such a super-pure child" must come in contact with such depravity. He would take her with the utmost haste possible from Pani Osnovski's, guard her from that woman's influence, seize her in his arms, and bear her from that house, in which her innocent eyes might be opened on evil and depravity. A certain demon whispered at moments to his ear, it is true, that Osnovski, too, believes as he does, and that he would give his own blood in pledge for his wife's honesty; he too would count every doubt a profanation of her sacredness. But Pan Ignas drove away those whisperings with dread. "It is enough to look into her eyes," said he; and at the mere thought of those eyes, he was ready to beat his own breast, as if he had sinned most grievously. He was also angry at himself because he had come out, because he had not waited for Pani Bronich, and had not strengthened himself with the sight of Lineta. He remembered now how he had pressed her hand to his lips; how she, changing from emotion, said to him, "Speak with aunt." How much angelic simplicity and purity there was in those words! what honesty of a soul, which, loving, wishes to be free to love before the whole world! Pan Ignas, when he thought of this, was seized by a desire to return; but he felt that he was too much excited, and that he could not explain his former presence if the servant should mention it.

Then again the picture rose before his eyes of Kopovski kneeling to Pani Osnovski; and he fell to inquiring of himself what he was to do in view of this, and how he was to act. Warn Osnovski? he rejected this thought at once with indignation. Shut himself in with Pani Osnovski, and give her a sermon, eye to eye? She would show him the door. After a time it came to his head to threaten Kopovski, and force from him a promise to cease visiting the Osnovskis. But soon he saw that that, too, was useless. Kopovski, if he had even a small share of courage, would give him the lie, challenge him; in such a case he would have to be silent, and people would think that the scandal rose because of Panna Castelli. Pan Ignas was sorry for Osnovski; he had conceived for the man a true friendship, and, on the other hand, he was too young to be reconciled at once with the thought that evil and human crookedness were to continue unpunished. Ah! but if at that juncture he could have counselled with some one, — for instance, with Pan Stanislav or Marynia. But that could not be. And after long thought he resolved to bury all in himself, and be silent.

At the same time, from the passionate prayer of Kopovski and the answer of Pani Aneta, he inferred that the evil might not have passed yet into complete fall. He did not know women; but he had read no little about them. He knew that there exists some for whom the form of evil has more charm than the substance; that there are women devoid of moral sense, but also of passion, who have just as much desire for a prohibited adventure as they have repugnance to complete fall, — in a word, those who are incapable of loving anybody, who deceive their lovers as well as their husbands. He recalled the words of a certain Frenchman: "If Eve had been Polish, she would have plucked the apple, but not eaten it." A similar type seemed to him Pani Aneta; vice might be in her as superficial as virtue, and in such case the forbidden relation might annoy her very soon, especially with a man like Kopovski.

Here, however, Pan Ignas lost the basis of reasoning and the key to the soul of Pani Aneta. He would have understood relations with any other man more readily than with Kopovski, — that archangel with the brains of an idiot. "A poodle understands more of what is said to him," thought Pan Ignas; "and a woman with such aspirations to reason, to science, to art, to the understanding of every thought and feeling, could lower herself for such a head!" He could not explain this to himself, even with what he had read about women.

And still reality said more definitely than all books that it was so. Suddenly Pan Ignas remembered what Osnovski had said to him about their fear lest that fool might have plans against Castelka, that the mention of this had angered Pani Aneta immensely, and that she filled Lineta's head with feeling for another. So then, for Pani Aneta the question consisted in this, that Kopovski should not pay court to Lineta. She wanted to save him for herself. Here Pan Ignas shivered all at once, for the thought struck him, that if that were true, Kopovski must have had some chance of success; and again a shadow pursued the bright form of Lineta. If that were true, she would fall in his eyes to the level of Pani Aneta. After a time he felt bitterness in his mouth and fire in his brain. Anger sprang upon him, like a tempest; he could not forgive her this, and the very suspicion would have poisoned him. Halting again on the street, he felt that he must throttle that thought in himself, or go mad from it.

In fact, he put it down so effectively that he recognized himself as the lowest fool for this alone, — that the thought could come to him. That Lineta was incapable of loving Kopovski was shown best by this, — that she had fallen in love with him, Pan Ignas; and the fears and suspicions of Pani Aneta flowed only from the self-love of a vain woman, who was afraid that another might be recognized as more attractive and beautiful than she was. Pan Ignas had the feeling of having pushed from his breast a stone, which had oppressed him. He began then in spirit to implore on his knees pardon of the unspotted one; and thenceforth his thoughts touching her were full of love, homage, and contrition.

Now he made the remark to himself that evil, though committed by another, bears evil; how many foul thoughts had passed through his mind only because he had seen a fool at the feet of a giddy head! He noted that consideration down in his memory.

When near his lodgings he met Pan Stanislav with Pani Mashko on his arm; and that day had so poisoned him that a sudden suspicion flashed through his mind. But Pan Stanislav recognized him in the light of the moon and a lamp, and had no desire to hide evidently, for he stopped him.

"Good-evening," said he. "Why home so early to-day?"

"I was at Pani Bronich's, and I am just strolling about, for the evening is beautiful."

"Then step in to us. As soon as I conduct this lady home, I will return. My wife has not seen you this long time."

"I will go," said Pan Ignas.

And a desire to see Pani Marynia had seized him really. So many thoughts and feelings had rushed through him that he was weary; and he knew that the calm and kind face of Marynia would act on him soothingly.

Soon he rang the bell at Pan Stanislav's. When he had entered, he explained, after the greeting, that he came at the request of her husband, to which she answered, —

"Of course! I am very glad. My husband at this

moment is escorting home Pani Mashko, who visited me, but he will return to tea. The Bigiels will be here surely, and perhaps my father will come, if he has not gone to the theatre."

Then she indicated a place at the table to him, and, straightening the lamp shade, began on the work with which she was occupied previously, — making little rosettes of narrow red and blue ribbons, of which there was a pile lying before her.

"What are you making?" asked Pan Ignas.

"Rosettes. They are sewed to various costumes."

After a while she added, —

"But this is far more interesting, — what are you doing? Do you know that all Warsaw is marrying you to Lineta Castelli? They have seen you both in the theatre, at the races; they see you at the promenades; and it is impossible to persuade them that the affair is not decided already."

"Since I have spoken with you so openly, I will tell you now that it is almost decided."

Marynia raised to him eyes enlivened with a smile and with curiosity.

"Is that true? Ah, that is a perfect piece of news! May God give you such happiness as we wish you!"

Then she stretched her hand to him, and afterward inquired with roused curiosity, —

"Have you spoken with Lineta?"

Pan Ignas told her how it was, and acknowledged his conversation with Lineta and with Osnovski; then, letting himself be borne away in the narrative, he confessed everything that had happened to him — how, from the beginning, he had observed, criticised, and struggled with himself; how he had not dared to hope; how he had tried to drive that feeling from his head, or rather, from his heart, and how he could not resist it. He assured her that he had promised himself a number of times to cut short the acquaintance and the visits, but strength failed him each time; each time he saw with amazement that the whole world, the whole object of his life, was there; that without her, without Lineta, he would not know what to do with his life — and he went back to her.

Pan Ignas had not observed himself less truthfully, but he criticised and struggled less than he said. He spoke sincerely, however. He added at the end that he knew with certainty that he loved, not his own feelings involved in Lineta, but Lineta herself, for herself, and that she was the dearest person on earth to him.

"Think," said he, "others have families, mothers, sisters, brothers; I, except my unfortunate father, have no one, and therefore my love for the whole world is centred in her."

"True," said Marynia; "that had to come."

"This seems a dream to me," continued he; "it cannot find place in my head that she will be my wife really. At times it seems to me that this cannot happen; that something will intervene; that all will be lost."

In fact, this feeling was strengthened in him by exaltation, to which he was more inclined than other men, and at last he began to tremble nervously; then he covered his eyes with his hands, and said, —

"You see I must shield my eyes to imagine this properly. Such happiness! such fabulous happiness! What does a man seek in life, and in marriage? Just that, and in its own course that exceeds his strength. I do not know whether I am so weak or what? but I say sincerely that at times breath fails me."

Marynia placed her rosette on the table, and, putting her hands on it, looked at him for a while, then said, —

"You are a poet, and are carried away too much; you should look more calmly. Listen to what I will tell you. I have a little book from my mother, in which, while she was sick and without hope of recovery, she wrote for me what she thought was good. About marriage she wrote down something which later I have not heard from any one, and have not read in any book, — that is, that one should not marry to be happy, but to accomplish those duties which God imposes at marriage; and that happiness is only an addition, a gift of God. You see how simple this is; and still it is true that not only have I not heard it since, but I have not seen any woman or any man about to marry who thought more of duty than of happiness. Remember this, and repeat it to Lineta, — will you?"

Pan Ignas looked at her with atonishment.

"Do you know this is so simple that really it will never come to any one's mind?"

She laughed a little sadly, and, taking her rosette, began again to sew. After a while she repeated, —

"Tell that to Lineta."

And she sewed on, drawing out with quick movement her somewhat thin hand, together with the needle.

"You will understand that if one has such a principle in the heart, one has perpetual peace, more joyous, or sadder, as God grants, but still deep. But without that there is only a kind of feverish happiness, and deceptions always at hand, even if only for this reason, — that happiness may be different from what we imagine it." And she sewed on.

He looked at her inclined head, at her moving hand, at her work; he heard her voice; and it seemed to him that that peace of which she had spoken was floating above her, was filling the whole atmosphere, was suspended above the table, was burning mildly in the lamp, and finally, was entering him.

He was so occupied with himself, with his love, that it did not even occur to him that her heart could be sad. Meanwhile he was penetrated, as it were, by a double astonishment: first, that these truths which she had told him were such an *a*, *b*, *c*, that they ought to lie on the very surface of every thought; and second, that in spite of this, his own thought had not worked them out of itself, or, at least, had not looked at them. "What is that," thought he, "our wisdom, bookish in comparison with that simple wisdom of an honest woman's heart?" Then, recalling Pani Aneta, and looking at Marynia, he began this monologue in his soul, "That woman and this woman!" And suddenly there came to him immense solace; all his disturbed thoughts settled down to their level. He felt that he was resting while looking at that noble woman. "In Lineta," said he to himself, "there is the same calmness, the same simplicity, and the same honesty."

Now Pan Stanislav came, a little later the Bigiels, after which the violoncello was brought. At tea Pan Stanislav spoke of Mashko. Mashko conducted the suit against the will with all energy, and it advanced, though there were difficulties at every step. The advocate on the side of the benevolent institutions — that young Sledz (herring), whom Mashko promised to sprinkle with pepper, cover with oil, and swallow — turned out not to be so easily eaten as had seemed. Pan Stanislav heard that he was a man cool, resolute, and at the same time a skilled lawyer.

"What is amusing, withal," said he, "is, that Mashko, as Mashko, considers himself a kind of patrician, who is fighting with a plebeian, and says this will be a test of whose blood is thicker. It is a pity that Bukatski is not living; this would give him amusement."

"But is Mashko in St. Petersburg all this time?" asked Bigiel.

"He returns to-day; for that reason she could not stay for the evening," answered Pan Stanislav; after a while he added, "I had in my time a prejudice against her; but I have convinced myself that she is not a bad woman, and, besides, is poor."

"How poor? Mashko has n't lost the case yet," said Pani Bigiel.

"But he is always from home. Pani Mashko's mother is in an optical hospital in Vienna, and will lose her eyes, perhaps. Pani Mashko is alone whole days, like a hermitess. I say that I had a prejudice against her, but now I am sorry for her."

"It is true," said Marynia, "that since marriage she has become far more sympathetic."

"Yes," answered Pan Stanislav; "and besides she has lost no charm. Red eyes injured her formerly; but now the redness has vanished, and she is as maiden-like as ever."

"But it is unknown whether Mashko is equally pleased with that," remarked Bigiel.

Marynia was anxious to tell those present the news about Pan Ignas; but since he was not betrothed yet officially, she did not know that it might be mentioned. When, however, after tea, Pani Bigiel began to inquire of him how the matter stood, he himself said that it was as good as finished, and Marynia put in her word announcing that the matter stood in this form, — that they might congratulate Pan Ignas. All began then to press his hand with that true friendship which they had for him, and genuine gladness possessed all. Bigiel, from delight, kissed Pani Bigiel; Pan Stanislav commanded to bring glasses and a bottle of champagne, to drink the health of the "most splendid couple" in Warsaw; Pani Bigiel began to joke with Pan Ignas, predicting what the housekeeping of a poet and an artist would be. He laughed; but was really moved by this, that his dreams were beginning to be real.

A little later, Pan Stanislav punched him, and said, —

"The happiness of God, but I will give you one advice: what you have in poetry, put into *business,* into work;

be a realist in life, and remember that marriage is no romance."

But he did not finish, for Marynia put her hand suddenly over his mouth, and said, laughing, "Silence, thou wise head!"

And then to Pan Ignas, "Don't listen to this grave pate: make no theories beforehand for yourself; only love."

"True, Pani, true," answered Pan Ignas.

"In that case, buy a harp for yourself," added Pan Stanislav, jeeringly.

At mention of the harp, Bigiel seized his violoncello, saying that they ought to end such an evening with music. Marynia sat at the piano, and they began one of Handel's serenades. Pan Ignas had the impression that the soul was going out of him. He took those mild tones into himself, and was flying amid the night, lulling Lineta to sleep with them. Late in the evening, he came out, as if strengthened with the sight of those worthy people.

## CHAPTER XLVI.

Marynia had such peace "as God gave," but really deep. A great aid to finding it was that voice from beyond the grave, — the little book, yellowed by years, in which she read "that a woman should not marry to be happy, but to fulfil the duties which God imposes on her then." Marynia, who looked frequently into this little book, had read more than once those lines before that; but real meaning they had taken on for her only of late, in that spiritual process through which she had passed after her return from Italy. It ended in this way, that she was not only reconciled with fate, but at present she did not admit even the thought that she was unhappy. She repeated to herself that it was a happiness different, it is true, from what she had imagined, but none the less real. It is certain that, if God had given her the power of arranging people's hearts, she would have wished "Stas" to show her, not more honor, but more of that tenderness of which he was capable, and which he had shown in her time to Litka; that his feeling for her might be less sober, and have in it a certain kernel of poetry which her own love had. But, on the other hand, she cherished always somewhere, in some little corner of her heart, — first, the hope that that might come to pass; and, second, she thought in her soul that, even if it did not, then, as matters stood, she ought to thank God for having given her a brave and honest man, whom she could not only love, but esteem. More than once she stopped to compare him with others, and could not find any one to sustain the comparison. Bigiel was worthy, but he had not that dash; Osnovski, with all his goodness, lacked practical knowledge of life and work; Mashko was a person a hundred times lower in everything; Pan Ignas seemed to her rather a genial child than a man, — in a word, from every comparison "Stas" came out always victorious, and the one result was that she felt for him an increasing trust as to vital questions, and loved him more and more. At the same time, while denying herself, subjecting to him her own *I*, bringing in sacrifice her imaginings and her selfishness, she had the feeling that she was developing more and more in a spiritual sense, that she was perfecting herself, that she was becoming better, that she was not descending to any level, but rising to some height, whence the soul would be nearer to God; and all at once she saw that in such a feeling lies the whole world of happiness. Pan Stanislav at that time was away from home often, therefore she was alone frequently; and, more than once, she reasoned with the great simplicity of an honest woman: "People should strive to be better and better; but if I am not worse than I was, it is well. Were it otherwise, maybe I should be spoiled." She did not come, however, to the thought that there was more wisdom in this than in all the ideas and talks of Pani Osnovski. It seemed to her natural, too, that she had less charm at that time for "Stas" than formerly. Looking into her mirror, she said to herself: "Well, the eyes do not change, but what a figure! what a face! If I were Stas, I would run out of the house!" And she thought an untruth, for she would not have run out; but it seemed to her that in this way she was increasing "Stas's" merit. She got comfort, too, from Pani Bigiel, who said that afterward she would be fairer than ever, "just like some young girl." And, at times, joy and thankfulness rose in her heart, because all is so wisely arranged; and if, at first, one is a little uglier and must suffer a little, not only does all return, but, as a reward, there is a beloved "bobo" which attaches one to life, and creates a new bond between wife and husband. In this way, she had times, not only of peace, but simply of joyfulness, and sometimes she said to Pani Bigiel, —

"Dost thou know what I think? — it is possible to be happy always, only we must fear God."

"What has one to do with the other?" asked Pani Bigiel, who from her husband had gained a love of clear thinking.

"This," answered Marynia, — "that we should rest with what He gives us, and not importune Him, because He has n't given that which seems to us better."

Then she added joyously, "We must n't tease for happiness." And both began to laugh.

Frequently, too, in the tenderness almost exaggerated which Pan Stanislav showed his wife, it was clearly evident that he was thinking chiefly of the child; but Marynia did not take that ill of him now. In truth, she never had; but at present she was willing to count it a merit in him, for she thought it the duty of both to care above all for the child, as for their future mutual love. Yielding up daily in this way something of her own care for self, she gained more and more peace, more and more calmness; these feelings were reflected in her eyes, which were more beautiful than ever. Her main anxiety now was that it should be a daughter. She was ready even in this to yield to the will of God, but she feared "Stas" a little; and one day she asked him in jest, —

"Stas, and thou wilt not kill me if it is a son?"

"No," answered he, laughing and kissing her hand; "but I should prefer a daughter."

"But I have heard from Pani Bigiel that men always prefer sons."

"But I am such a man that I prefer a daughter."

Not always, however, were her thoughts so joyous. At times it came to her head that she might die, for she knew that death happens in such cases; and she prayed earnestly that it should not happen, for first she feared it, second, she would be sorry to go away, even to heaven, when she had such a prospect of loving, and finally she imagined to herself that "Stas" would mourn for her immensely. And at that thought she grew as tender over him as if he had been at that moment a man more deserving of pity than all other unfortunates living. Never had she spoken to him of this, though it seemed to her that sometimes he had feared it.

But she deceived herself thoroughly. The doctor, who came to Marynia weekly, assured both her and her husband after each visit that all was and would be most regular; hence Pan Stanislav had no fear for his wife's future. The cause of his alarm was something quite different, which happily for herself Marynia had not suspected, and which Pan Stanislav himself had not dared even to name in his own mind. For some time something had begun to go wrong in his life calculations, of which he had been so proud, and which had given him such internal security. A little while before he had considered that his theories of life were like a house built of firm timbers, resting on solid foundations. In his soul he was proud of that house, and in secret exalted himself above those who had not the skill to build anything like it. Speaking briefly, he thought himself a better life architect than others. He judged that the labor was finished from foundation to summit, only go in, live, and rest there. He forgot that a human soul, like a bird when it has soared to a given height, not only is not free to rest, but must work its wings hard to support itself, otherwise the very first temptation will bring it to the earth again.

The worse and vainer the temptation, the more was he enraged at himself because he gave way to it. A mean desire, a low object, — he had not even anything to explain to himself; and still the walls of his house had begun to crack. Pan Stanislav was a religious man now, and that from conviction; he was too sincere with himself to enter into a compromise with his own principles, and say to himself that such things happen even to the firmest of believers. No! He was by nature a man rather unsparing, and logic said to him "either, or;" hence he felt that speaking thus it spoke justly. Hitherto he had not given way to temptation; but still he was angry because he was tempted, for temptation brought him to doubt his own character. Considering himself as better than others, he stood suddenly in face of the question, was he not worse than others, for not only had temptation attacked him, but he felt that in a given case he might yield to it.

More than once, while looking at Pani Osnovski, he repeated to himself the opinion of Confucius: "An ordinary woman has as much reason as a hen; an extraordinary woman as much as two hens." In view of Pani Mashko, it occurred to him that there are women with reference to whom this Chinese truth, which makes one indignant, is flattery. Had it been at least possible to say of Pani Mashko that she was honestly stupid, it would become a certain individual trait of hers; but she was not. A few, or a few tens of formulas had made of her a polite nonentity. Just as two or three hundred phrases make up the whole language of the inhabitants of New Guinea, and satisfy all their wants, so those formulas satified Pani Mashko as to social relations, thoughts, and life. For that matter, she was as completely passive within that shade of automatic dignity which narrowness of mind produces, and a blind faith that if proper formalities are observed, there can be no error. Pan Stanislav knew her as such, and as such ridiculed her more than once while she was unmarried. He called her a puppet, a manikin; he felt enraged at her because of that doctor who had perished for her in some place where pepper grows; he disregarded her and did not like her. But even then, as often as he saw her, whether at the Bigiels', or when on Mashko's business he went to Pani Kraslavski, he always returned under the physical impression which she made on him, of which he gave himself an account. That quenched face, that passive, vegetable calm of expression, that coldness of bearing, that frequent reddening of the eyes, that slender form, had in them something which affected him unusually. He explained that to himself then by some law of natural selection; and when he had outlined the thing technically, he stopped there, for the impression which Marynia had made on him was still greater, hence he had followed it. At present, however, Marynia was his, and he had grown used to her beauty, which, moreover, had disappeared for a period. It so happened that because of Mashko's frequent journeys, he saw Pani Mashko almost daily, in consequence of which former impressions not only revived, but, in the conditions in which Pan Stanislav found himself with reference to Marynia, they revived with unexpected vigor. And it happened finally that he who would not consent to be in leading strings for the ten times more beautiful and charming Pani Osnovski; he, who had resisted her Roman fantasies; he, who had looked on himself as a man of principles, stronger in character and firmer in mind than most people,—saw now that if Pani Mashko wished to push that edifice with her foot, all its bindings might be loosened, and the ceiling tumble on his head. Of a certainty, he would not cease to love his wife, for he was sincerely and profoundly attached to her; but he felt that he might be in a condition to betray her,—and then not only her, but himself, his principles, his conceptions of what an honest and a moral man should be. With a certain terror as well as anger, he found in himself not merely the human beast, but a weak beast. He was alarmed by this, he rebelled against this weakness; but still he could not overcome it. It was a simple thing in view of this, not to see Pani Mashko, or to see her as seldom as possible; meanwhile he was finding reasons to see her the oftenest possible. At first he wanted to lull himself with these reasons; but, in view of his innate consistency, that was impossible, and it ended with this, that he merely invented them. Straightway, he deceived with them his wife, and whomever he wished. When in company with Pani Mashko, he could not refrain from looking at her, from embracing with his glance her face and whole person. A sickly curiosity seized him as to how she would bear herself in case he appeared before her with what was happening within him. What would she say then? And he took pleasure in spite of himself in supposing that she would bear herself with perfect passiveness. He despised her beforehand for this; but she became the more desired by him thereby. In himself he discovered whole mountains of depravity, which he referred to long stay in foreign countries; and, having considered himself up to that time a fresh and healthy nature, he began to grow alarmed. Had he not been deceived in himself, and was not that wonderful impression produced on him by a being so little attractive the appearance of some neurosis consuming him without his knowledge? It had not occurred to him that there might exist even such conditions in which the soul of a man simply despises a woman, but the human beast longs for her.

In her, instinct had taken the place of mental keenness; besides, she was not so naive as not to know what his glance meant as it slipped over her form, or what his eyes said when talking, especially when they were alone, and he looked into her face with a certain persistence. At first she felt a kind of satisfaction for her self-love, which it is difficult for even an honest woman to resist when she sees the impression produced by her; when she feels herself distinguished, desired beyond others, — in a word, victorious. Besides, she was ready not to recognize and not to see the danger, just as a partridge does not wish to see it, when it hides its head in the snow, on feeling the hawk circling above it. For Pani Mashko appearances were this snow; and Pan Stanislav felt that. He knew also from his experience as a single man that there are women for whom it is a question above all of preserving certain, frequently even strange, appearances. He remembered some who burst out in indignation when he said to them in Polish that which they heard in French with a smile; he had met even those who were unapproachably firm at home and in the city, and so free in summer residences, at watering, or bathing places, and others who endured an attempt, but could not endure words, and others for whom the decisive thing was light or darkness. In all places where virtue did not come from the soul, and from principles ingrafted like vaccination into the blood, resistance or fall depended on accident or surroundings, or external, frequently favoring circumstances, personal ideas of polite appearances. He judged that it might be thus with Pani Mashko; and if hitherto he had not entered the road of testing and trying, it was simply because he was battling with himself, because he did not wish to give way, and, despising her in the bottom of his soul, he wished to escape the position of despising himself. Attachment to Marynia restrained him too, and sympathy, as it were, mingled with respect for her condition and gratitude to her, and the hope of fatherhood, which moved him, and a remembrance of the shortness of the time which they had lived together, and honesty, and a religious feeling. These were chains, as it were, at which the human beast was still tugging.

They did not hold, however, with equal strength always. Once, and, namely, that evening on which Pan Ignas had met them, he had almost betrayed himself. At the thought that Mashko was returning and that Pani Mashko was hastening home, therefore, a low, purely physical jealousy seized him; and he said with a certain anger, repressed, but visible, —

"True! I understand your haste! Ulysses is coming, and Penelope must be at home, but — "

Here he felt a desire to curse.

"But what?" inquired Pani Mashko.

Pan Stanislav answered without any hesitation, —

"Just to-day I wished to detain you longer."

"It is not proper," answered she briefly, with a voice as thin as though strained through a sieve.

And in that, "It is not proper," was her whole soul.

He returned, cursing earnestly her and himself. When he reached home he found in the clear, peaceful room Marynia and Pan Ignas, she proving to the poet that when they marry, people should not look for some imagined happiness, but the duties which God imposes at that time.

## CHAPTER XLVII.

"WHAT is Pani Osnovski to me, and what are all her affairs to me?" said Pan Ignas to himself next morning on the way to Pani Bronich's: "I am not going to marry her, but *my own one.* Why did I so tear and torment myself yesterday?"

And when he had said this "to his lofty soul," he began to think only of what he would say to Pani Bronich; for in spite of Osnovski's assurances, in spite of every hope that that conversation would be merely a certain form for observance, in spite of his confidence in Lineta's heart and the kindness of Pani Bronich, the "lofty soul" was in fear.

He found aunt and niece together; and, emboldened by yesterday, he pressed to his lips the hand of the young lady, who said, blushing slightly, —

"But I will run away."

"Nitechka, stop!" said Pani Bronich.

"No," answered she; "I fear this gentleman, and I fear aunt."

Thus speaking, she began to rub her golden head, like a petted kitten, against the shoulder of Pani Bronich, saying, —

"Do not wrong him aunt; do not wrong him."

And looking at him, she ran away really. Pan Ignas, from emotion and excess of love, was as pale as linen; Pani Bronich had tears on her lids. And, seeing that his throat was so pressed that it would have been easier for him to cry than to talk, she said, —

"I know why you have come. I have noticed this long time what was passing between you, my children."

Pan Ignas seized her hands, and began to press them to his lips one after the other; she on her part continued, —

"Oh, I myself have felt too much in life not to know real feelings; I will say more: it is my specialty. Women live only by the heart, and they know how to divine hearts. I know that you love Nitechka truly; and I am certain that if she did not love you, or if I should refuse her to you, you would not survive. Is it not true?"

Here she gazed at him with an inquiring glance, and he said with effort, —

"Beyond doubt! I know not what would happen to me."

"I guessed that at once," answered she, with radiant face. "Ah, my dear friend, a look is enough for me; but I shall not be an evil spirit as your genius. No, I shall not, I cannot be that. Whom shall I find for Nitechka? Where a man worthy of her? Who would have in him all that she loves and esteems chiefly? I cannot give her to Kopovski, and I will not. You perhaps do not know Nitechka as I do; but I cannot and will not give her."

In spite of all his emotion, that energy with which Pani Bronich refused "Nitechka's" hand to Kopovski astonished Pan Ignas, just as if he had declared for Kopovski, not for himself; and the aunt continued, moved, but evidently enjoying her own words and delighted with the position, —

"No! there can be no talk of Kopovski. You alone can make Nitechka happy. You alone can give her what she needs. I knew yesterday that you would talk with me today. I did not close an eye the whole night. Do not wonder at that. Here it is a question of Nitechka, and I was hesitating yet; therefore fear seized me in view of today's conversation, for I knew in advance that I would not resist you, that you would bear me away with your feeling and your eloquence, as yesterday you bore away Nitechka."

Pan Ignas, who neither yesterday nor to-day was able to buzz out one word, could not explain somehow to himself in what specially lay the power of his eloquence, or when he had time to exhibit it; but Pani Bronich did not permit him to hesitate longer on this question.

"And do you know what I did? This is what I do always in life's most serious moments. Speaking yesterday with Nitechka, I went early this morning to the grave of my husband. He is lying here in Warsaw — I know not whether I have told you that he was the last descendant of Rurik — Ah, yes, I have! Oh, dear friend, what a refuge for me that grave is; and how many good inspirations I have brought from it! Whether it was a question of the education of Nitechka, or of some journey, or of investing capital which my husband left me, or of a loan which some one of my relatives or acquaintances wished to make, I went there directly at all times. And will you believe me? More than once a mortgage is offered: it seems a good one; the business is perfect; more than once my heart even commands me to give or to lend, — but my husband, there in the depth of his eternal rest, answers: 'Do not give,' and I give not. And never has evil resulted. Oh, my dear, you who feel and understand everything, you will understand how to-day I prayed, how I asked with all the powers of my soul, 'Give Nitechka, or not give Nitechka?'"

Here she seized Pan Ignas's temples with her hands, and said through her tears, —

"But my Teodor answered, 'Give;' therefore I give her to thee, and my blessing besides."

Tears quenched indeed further conversation in Pani Bronich. Pan Ignas knelt before her; "Nitechka," who came in, as if at a fixed moment, dropped on her knees at his side; Pani Bronich stretched her hands and said sobbing, —

"She is thine, thine! I give her to thee; I and Teodor give her."

Then the three rose. Aunt Bronich covered her eyes with her handkerchief, and remained some time without motion; gradually, however, she slipped away the handkerchief, looking from one side at the two young people. Suddenly she laughed, and, threatening with her finger, said, —

"Oi! I know what you would like now, — you would like to be alone. Surely you have something to say to each other. Is it not true?"

And she went out. Pan Ignas took Lineta's hands that moment, and looked into her eyes with intoxication.

They sat down; and she, leaving her hands in his, rested her temple on his shoulder. It was like a song without words. Pan Ignas inclined his head toward her bright face. Lineta closed her eyes; but he was too young and too timid, he respected too much and he loved, hence he did not venture yet to touch her lips with his. He only kissed her golden hair, and even that caused the room in which they were sitting to spin with him; the world began to whirl round. Then all vanished from his eyes; he lost memory of where he was, and what was happening; he heard only the beating of his own heart; he felt the odor of the silken hair, which brushed his lips, and it seemed to him that in that was the universe.

But that was only a dream from which he had to wake.

After a certain time the aunt began to open the door gently, as if wishing to lose the least possible of the romance, in which, with Teodor's aid, she was playing the rôle of guardian spirit; in the adjoining chamber were heard the voices of the Osnovskis; and a moment later Lineta found herself in the arms of her aunt, from which she passed into the embraces of Pani Aneta. Osnovski, pressing Ignas's hands with all his power, said, —

"But what a joy in the house, what a joy! for we have all fallen in love with thee, — I, and aunt, and Anetka, not to speak of this little one."

Then he turned to his wife and said, —

"Knowest, Anetka, what I wished Ignas, even yesterday? that they should be to each other as we are." And, seizing her hands, he began to kiss them with vehemence.

Pan Ignas, though he knew not in general what was happening to him, found still presence of mind enough to look into the face of Pani Aneta; but she answered joyously, withdrawing her hands from her husband, —

"No, they will be happier; for Castelka is not such a giddy thing as I, and Pan Ignas will not kiss her hands so stubbornly before people. But, Yozio, let me go!"

"Let him only love her as I thee, my treasure, my child," answered the radiant Yozio.

Pan Ignas stayed at Pani Bronich's till evening, and did not go to the counting-house. After lunch he drove out in the carriage with the aunt and Lineta, for Pani Bronich wanted absolutely to show them to society. But their drive in the Alley was not a success altogether, because of a sudden hard shower, which scattered the carriages. On their return, Pan Osnovski, good as he ever was, made a new proposition which delighted Pan Ignas.

"Prytulov will not escape us," said he. "We live here as if we were half in the country; and since we have remained till the end of June, we may stay a couple of days longer. Let that loving couple exchange rings before our departure, and at the same time let it be free to Aneta and me to give them a betrothal party. Is it well, aunt? I see that they have nothing against it, and surely it will be agreeable for Ignas to have at the betrothal his friends the Polanyetskis and the Bigiels. It is true that we do not visit the latter, but that is nothing! We will visit them to-morrow, and the affair will be settled. Is it well, Ignas; is it well. aunt?"

Ignas was evidently in the seventh heaven; as to aunt, she didn't know indeed what Teodor's opinion would be in this matter, and she began to hesitate. But she might inquire of Teodor yet; and then she remembered that he had answered, "Give," with such a great voice from his place of eternal rest that it was impossible to doubt his good wishes, — hence she agreed at last to everything.

After dinner Kopovski, the almost daily guest, came; and it turned out that he was the only being in the villa to whom news of the feelings and betrothal of the young couple did not cause delight. For a time his face expressed indescribable astonishment; at last he said, —

"I never should have guessed that Panna Lineta would marry Pan Ignas."

Osnovski pushed Pan Ignas with his elbow, blinked, and whispered, with a very cunning mien, —

"Hast noticed? I told thee yesterday that he was making up to Castelka."

Pan Ignas left the villa of the Osnovskis late in the evening. When he reached home he did not betake himself to verses, however, though it seemed to him then that he was a kind of harp, the strings of which played of themselves, but to the counting-house, to unfinished correspondence and accounts.

At the counting-house all were so pleased with this that when the Bigiels returned the visit of the Osnovskis, and at the same time made the first visit to Pani Bronich, Bigiel said, —

"The worth of Pan Zavilovski's poetry is known to you ladies, but perhaps you do not know how conscientious a man he is. I say this because that is a rare quality among us. Since he remained all day with you here, and could not be at the counting-house, he asked to have it opened by the guard in the night; he took home the books and papers in his charge, and did what pertained to him. It is pleasant to think that one has to do with such a man, for such a man may be trusted."

Here, however, the honorable partner of the house of Bigiel and Polanyetski was astonished that such high praise from his lips made so little impression, and that Pani Bronich, instead of showing gladness, replied, —

"Ah, we hope that in future Pan Zavilovski will be able to give himself to labor more in accordance with his powers and position."

In general, the impression which both sides brought away from their acquaintance showed that somehow they were not at home with each other. Lineta pleased the Bigiels, it is true; but he, in going away, whispered to his wife, "How comfortably they live for themselves in this place!" He had a feeling that the spirit of that whole villa was a sort of unbroken holiday, or idling; but he was not able at once to express that idea, for he had not the gift of ready utterance.

But Pani Bronich, after their departure, said to "Nitechka,"—

"Of course, of course! They must be excellent people —true, perfect people! I am certain—yes, certain—"

And somehow she did not finish her thought; but "Nitechka" must have understood her, however, for she said,—

"But they are no relatives of his."

A few days later the relatives, too, made themselves heard. Pan Ignas, who, in spite of the wishes of Pani Bigiel, had not gone yet with excuses to old Zavilovski, received the following letter from him,—

Pan Wildcat!—Thou hast scratched me undeservedly, for I had no wish to offend thee; and if I say always what I think, it is permitted me because I am old. They must have told thee, too, that I never name, even to her eyes, thy young lady otherwise than Venetian half-devil. But how was I to know that thou wert in love and about to marry? I heard of this only yesterday, and only now do I understand why thou didst spring out of my sight; but since I prefer water-burners to dullards, and since through this devil of a gout I cannot go myself to thee to congratulate, do thou come to the old man, who is more thy well-wisher than seems to thee.

After this letter Pan Ignas went that same day, and was received cordially, though with scolding, but so kindly that this time the old truth-teller pleased him, and he felt in him really a relative.

"May God and the Most Holy Lady bless thee!" said the old man. "I know thee little; but I have heard such things of thee that I should be glad to hear the like touching all Zavilovskis."

And he pressed his hand; then, turning to his daughter, he said,—

"He 's a genial rascal, is n't he?"

And at parting he inquired,—

"But 'Teodor,' did n't he trouble thee too much? Hei?"

Pan Ignas, who, as an artist, possessed in a high degree the sense of the ridiculous, and to whom in his soul that Teodor, too, seemed comical, laughed and answered, —

"No. On the contrary, he was on my side."

The old man began to shake his head.

"That is a devil of an accommodating Teodor! Be on the lookout for him; he is a rogue."

Pani Bronich had so much genuine respect for the property and social position of old Zavilovski that she visited him next day, and began almost to thank him for his cordial reception of his relative; but the old man grew angry unexpectedly.

"Do you think that I am some empty talker?" asked he. "You have heard from me that poor relatives are a plague; and you think that I take it ill of them that they are poor. No, you do not know me! But, know this, when a noble loses everything, and is poor, he becomes almost always a sort of shabby fellow. Such is our character, or rather, its weakness. But this Ignas, as I hear from every side, is a man of honor, though poor; and therefore I love him."

"And I love him," answered Pani Bronich. "But you will be at the betrothal?"

"*C'est décidé.* Even though I had to be carried."

Pani Bronich returned radiant, and at lunch could not restrain herself from expressing suppositions which her active fancy had begun to create.

"Pan Zavilovski," said she, "is a man of millions, and greatly attached to the name. I should not be astonished at all were he to make our Ignas his heir, if not of the chief, of a considerable part of his property, or if he were to entail some of his estates in Poznan on him. I should not be surprised at all."

No one contradicted her, for events like that in the world had been seen; therefore after lunch, Pani Bronich, embracing Nitechka, whispered in her ear, —

"Oi, thou, thou, future heiress!"

But in the evening she said to Pan Ignas, —

"Be not astonished if I so mix up in everything, but I am your mamma. So mamma is immensely curious to know what kind of ring you are preparing for Nitechka? It will be something beautiful, of course. There will be so many people at the betrothal. And, besides, you have no idea what a fastidious girl! She is so æsthetic even in trifles; and she has her own taste, but what a taste! ho, ho!"

"I should like," answered Pan Ignas, "the stones to be of colors denoting faith, hope, and love, for in her is my faith, my hope, and my love."

"A very pretty idea! have you said this to Nitechka? Do you know what? Let there be a pearl in the middle, as a sign that she is a pearl. Symbols are in fashion now. Have I told you that Pan Svirski, when he gave her lessons, called her 'La Perla'? Ah, yes, I did. You do not know Pan Svirski? He, too — Yozio Osnovksi told me that he would come to-morrow. Well, then, a sapphire, a ruby, an emerald, and in the middle a pearl? Oh, yes! Pan Svirski, too — Will you be at the funeral?"

"Whose funeral?"

"Pan Bukatski's. Yozio Osnovski told me that Pan Svirski brought home his body."

"I did not know him; I have never seen him in my life."

"That is better; Nitechka would prefer that you had not known him. God in His mercy forgive him in spite of this, — that for me he was never a sympathetic person, and Nitechka could not endure him. But the little one will be glad of the ring; and when she is glad, I am glad."

The "Little One" was glad not only of the ring, but of life in general. The rôle of an affianced assumed for her increasing charm. Beautiful nights came, very clear, during which she and Pan Ignas sat together on the balcony. Nestling up to each other, they looked at the quivering of light on the leaves, or lost their gaze in the silver dust of the Milky Way, and the swarms of stars. From the acacia, growing under the balcony, there rose a strong and intoxicating odor, as from a great censer. Their powers seemed to go to sleep in them; their souls, lulled by silence, turned into clear light, were scattered in some way amidst the depth of night, and were melted into unity with the soft moonlight; and so the two, sitting hand in hand, half in oblivion, half in sleep, lost well-nigh the feeling of separate existence and life, preserving a mere semi-consciousness of some sort of general bliss and general "exaltation of hearts."

Pan Ignas, when he woke and returned to real life, understood that moments like those, in which hearts melt in that pantheism of love, and beat with the same pulsation with which everything quivers that loves, unites, and harmonizes in the universe, form the highest happiness which love has the power to give, and so immeasurable that were they to continue they would of necessity destroy man's individuality. But, having the soul of an idealist, he thought that when death comes and frees the human monad from matter, those moments change into eternity; and in that way he imagined heaven, in which nothing is swallowed up, but everything simply united and attuned in universal harmony.

Lineta, it is true, could not move with his flight; but she felt a certain turning of the head, as it were, a kind of intoxication from his flight, and she felt herself happy also. A woman even incapable of loving a man is still fond of her love, or, at least, of herself, and her rôle in it; and, therefore, most frequently she crosses the threshold of betrothal with delight, feeling at the same time gratitude to the man who opens before her a new horizon of life. Besides, they had talked love into Lineta so mightily that at last she believed in it.

And once, when Pan Ignas asked her if she was sure of herself and her heart, she gave him both hands, as if with effusion, and said, —

"Oh, truly; now I know that I love."

He pressed her slender fingers to his lips, to his forehead, and his eyes, as something sacred; but he was disquieted by her words, and asked, —

"Why 'now' for the first time, Nitechka? Or has there been a moment in which thou hast thought that thou couldst not love me?"

Lineta raised her blue eyes and thought a moment; after a while, in the corners of her mouth and in the dimples of her cheeks, a smile began to gather.

"No," said she; "but I am a great coward, so I was afraid. I understand that to love you is another thing from loving the first comer." And suddenly she began to laugh. "Oh, to love Pan Kopovski would be as simple as *bon jour;* but you — maybe I cannot express it well, but more than once it seemed to me that that is like going up on some mountain or some tower. When once at the top, a whole world is visible; but before that one must go and go, and toil, and I am so lazy."

Pan Ignas, who was tall and bony, straightened himself, and said, —

"When my dear, lazy one is tired, I 'll take her in my arms, like a child, and carry her even to the highest."

"And I will shrink up and make myself the smallest," answered Lineta, closing her arms, and entering into the rôle of a little child.

Pan Ignas knelt before her, and began to kiss the hem of her dress.

But there were little clouds, too, on that sky; the betrothed were not the cause, however. It seemed to the young man at times that his feelings were too much observed, and that Pani Bronich and Pani Aneta examined too closely whether he loves, and how he loves. He explained this, it is true, by the curiosity of women, and, in general, by the attention which love excites in them; but he would have preferred more freedom, and would have preferred that they would not help him to love. His feelings he considered as sacred, and for him it was painful to make an exhibition of them for uninvited eyes; at the same time every movement and word of his was scrutinized. He supposed also that there must be female sessions, in which Pani Bronich and Pani Aneta gave their "approbatur;" and that thought angered him, for he judged that neither was in a situation to understand his feelings.

It angered him also that Kopovski was invited to Prytulov, and that he went there in company with all; but in this case it was for him a question only of Osnovski, whom he loved sincerely. The pretext for the invitation was the portrait not finished yet by Lineta. Pan Ignas understood now clearly that everything took place at the word of Pani Aneta, who knew exactly how to suggest her own wishes to people as their own. At times even it came to his head to ask Lineta to abandon the portrait; but he knew that he would trouble her, as an artist, with that request, and, besides, he feared lest people might suspect him of being jealous of a fop, like "Koposio." [1]

[1] Nickname for Kopovski.

## CHAPTER XLVIII.

Svirski had come indeed from Italy with Bukatski's body; and he went at once on the following day to Pan Stanislav's. He met only Marynia, however, for her husband had gone outside the city to look at some residence which had been offered for sale. The artist found Marynia so changed that he recognized her with difficulty; but since he had liked her greatly in Rome, he was all the more moved at sight of her now. At times, besides, she seemed to him so touching and so beautiful in her way, with the aureole of future maternity, and besides she had brought to him so many artistic comparisons, with so many "types of various Italian schools," that, following his habit, he began to confess his enthusiasm audibly. She laughed at his originality; but still it gave her comfort in her trouble, and she was glad that he came,—first, because she felt a sincere sympathy with that robust and wholesome nature; and second, she was certain that he would be enthusiastic about her in presence of "Stas," and thus raise her in the eyes of her husband.

He sat rather long, wishing to await the return of Pan Stanislav; he, however, returned only late in the evening. Meanwhile there was a visit from Pan Ignas, who, needing some one now before whom to pour out his overflowing happiness, visited her rather often. For a while he and Svirski looked at each other with a certain caution, as happens usually with men of distinction, who fear each other's large pretensions, but who come together the more readily when each sees that the other is simple. So did it happen with these men. Marynia, too, helped to break the ice by presenting Pan Ignas as the betrothed of Panna Castelli, who was known to Svirski.

"Indeed," said Svirski, "I know her perfectly; she is my pupil!"

Then, pressing the hand of Pan Ignas, he said,—

"Your betrothed has Titian hair; she is a little tall, but you are tall, too. Such a pose of head as she has one might look for with a candle. You must have noticed that there is something swan-like in her movements; I have even called her 'The Swan.'"

Pan Ignas laughed as sincerely and joyously as a man does when people praise that which he loves most in life, and said with a shade of boastfulness,—

"'La Perla,' do you remember?"

Svirski looked at him with a certain surprise.

"There is such a picture by Raphael in Madrid, in the Museum del Prado," answered he. "Why do you mention 'La Perla'?"

"It seems to me that I heard of it from those ladies," said Pan Ignas, beaten from the track somewhat.

"It may be, for I have a copy of my own making in my studio Via Margutta."

Pan Ignas said in spirit that there was need to be more guarded in repeating words from Pani Bronich; and after a time he rose to depart, for he was going to his betrothed for the evening. Svirski soon followed, leaving with Marynia the address of his Warsaw studio, and begging that Pan Stanislav would meet him in the matter of the funeral as soon as possible.

In fact, Pan Stanislav went to him next morning. Svirski's studio was a kind of glass hall, attached, like the nest of a swallow, to the roof of one in a number of many storied houses, and visitors had to reach him by separate stairs winding like those in a tower. But the artist had perfect freedom there, and did not close his door evidently, for Pan Stanislav, in ascending, heard a dull sound of iron, and a bass voice singing,—

"Spring blows on the world warmly;
Hawthorns and cresses are blooming.
I am singing and not sobbing,
For I have ceased to love thee too!
Hu-ha-hu!"

"Well," thought Pan Stanislav, stopping to catch breath, "he has a bass, a real, a true bass; but what is he making such a noise with?"

When he had passed the rest of the steps, however, and then the narrow corridor, he understood the reason, for he saw through the open doors Svirski, dressed to his waist in a single knitted shirt, through which was seen his Herculean torso; and in his hands were dumb-bells.

"Oh, how are you?" he called out, putting down the

dumb-bells in presence of his guest. "I beg pardon that I am not dressed, but I was working a little with the dumb-bells. Yesterday I was at your house, but found only Pani Polanyetski. Well, I brought our poor Bukatski. Is the little house ready for him?"

Pan Stanislav pressed his hand. "The grave is ready these two weeks, and the cross is set up. We greet you cordially in Warsaw. My wife told me that the body is in Povanzki already."

"It is now in the crypt of the church. To-morrow we 'll put it away."

"Well, to-day I will speak to the priest and notify acquaintances. What is Professor Vaskovski doing?"

"He was to write you. The heat drove him out of Rome; and do you know where he went? Among the youngest of the Aryans. He said that the journey would occupy two months. He wishes to convince himself as to how far they are ready for his historical mission; he has gone through Ancona to Fiume, and then farther and farther."

"The poor professor! I fear that new disillusions are waiting for him."

"That may be. People laugh at him. I do not know how far the youngest of the Aryans are fitted to carry out his idea; but the idea itself, as God lives, is so uncommon, so Christian, and honest, that the man had to be a Vaskovski to come to it. Permit me to dress. The heat here is almost as in Italy, and it is better to exercise in a single shirt."

"But best not to exercise at all in such heat."

Here Pan Stanislav looked at Svirski's arms and said, —

"But you might show those for money."

"Well; not bad biceps! But look at these deltoids. That is my vanity. Bukatski insisted that any one might say that I paint like an idiot; but that it was not permitted any one to say that I could not raise a hundred kilograms with one hand, or that I could n't hit ten flies with ten shots."

"And such a man will not leave his biceps nor his deltoids to posterity."

"Ha! what 's to be done? I fear an ungrateful heart; as I love God, I fear it so much. Find me a woman like Pani Polanyetski, and I will not hesitate a day. But what should I wish you, — a son or a daughter?"

"A daughter, a daughter! Let there be sons; but the first must be a daughter!"

"And when do you expect her?"

"In December, it would seem."

"God grant happily! The lady, however, is healthy, so there is no fear."

"She has changed greatly, has she not?"

"She is different from what she was, but God grant the most beautiful to look so. What an expression! A pure Botticelli. I give my word! Do you remember that portrait of his in the Villa Borghese? Madonna col Bambino e angeli. There is one head of an angel, a little inclined, dressed in a lily, just like the lady, the very same expression. Yesterday that struck me so much that I was moved by it."

Then he went behind the screen to put on his shirt, and from behind the screen he said, —

"You ask why I don't marry. Do you know why? I remember sometimes that Bukatski said the same thing. I have a sharp tongue and strong biceps, but a soft heart; so stupid is it that if I had such a wife as you have, and she were in that condition, as God lives, I should n't know whether to walk on my knees before her, or to beat the floor with my forehead, or to put her on a table, in a corner somewhere, and adore her with upraised hands."

"Ai!" said Pan Stanislav, laughing, "that only seems so before marriage; but afterward habituation itself destroys excess of feeling."

"I don't know. Maybe I 'm so stupid —"

"Do you know what? When my Marynia is free, she must find for thee just such a wife as she herself is."

"Agreed!" thundered Svirski, from behind the screen. "Verbum! I give myself into her hands; and when she says 'marry,' I will marry with closed eyes."

And appearing, still without a coat, he began to repeat, "Agreed, agreed! without joking. If the lady wishes."

"Women always like that," answered Pan Stanislav. "Have you seen, for instance, what that Pani Osnovski did to marry our Pan Ignas to Panna Castelli? And Marynia helped her as much as I permitted; she kept her ears open. For women that is play."

"I made the acquaintance of that Pan Ignas at your house yesterday. He is an immensely nice fellow; simply a genial head. It is enough to look at him. What a profile, and what a woman-like forehead! and with that insolent jaw! His shanks are too long, and his knees must be badly cut, but his head is splendid."

"He is the Benjamin of our counting-house. Indeed, we love him surpassingly; his is an honest nature."

"Ah! he is your employee? But I thought he was of those rich Zavilovskis; I have seen abroad often enough a certain old original, a rich man."

"That is a relative of his," said Pan Stanislav; "but our Zavilovski has n't a smashed copper."

"Well," said Svirski, beginning to laugh, "old Zavilovski with his daughter, the only heiress of millions, a splendid figure! In Florence and Rome half a dozen ruined Italian princes were dangling around this young lady; but the old man declared that he would n't give his daughter to a foreigner, 'for,' said he, 'they are a race of jesters.' Imagine to yourself, he considers us the first race on earth, and among us, of course, the Zavilovskis; and once he showed that in this way: 'Let them say what they like,' said he; 'I have travelled enough through the world, and how many Germans, Italians, Englishmen, and Frenchmen have cleaned boots for me? but I,' said he, 'have never cleaned boots for any man, and I will not.'"

"Good!" answered Pan Stanislav, laughing; "he thinks boot-cleaning not a question of position in the world, but of nationality."

"Yes, it seems to him that the Lord God created other 'nations' exclusively so that a nobleman from Kutno may have some one to clean his boots whenever he chooses to go abroad. But does n't he turn up his nose at the marriage of the young man? for I know that he thinks the Broniches of small account."

"Maybe he turns up his nose; but he has become acquainted with our Pan Ignas not long since. They had not met before, for ours is a proud soul, and would not seek the old man first."

"I like him for that. I hope he has chosen well, for —"

"What! do you know Panna Castelli? What kind of a person is she?"

"I know Panna Castelli; but, you see, I am no judge of young ladies. Ba! if I knew them, I would not have waited for the fortieth year as a single man. They are all good, and all please me; but since I have seen, as married women, a few of those who pleased me, I do not believe in any. And that makes me angry; for if I had no wish to marry — well, I should say, leave the matter! but I have the wish. What can I know? I know that each woman has a corset; but what sort of a heart is inside it? The deuce knows! I was in love with Panna Castelli; but for that matter I was in love with all whom I met. With her, perhaps, even more than with others."

"And how is it that a wife did not come to your head?"

"Ah, the devil did n't come to my head! But at that time I had n't the money that I have to-day, nor the reputation. I was working for something then; and believe me that no people are so shy of workers as the children of workers. I was afraid that Pan Bronich or Pani Bronich might object, and I was not sure of the lady; therefore I left them in peace."

"Pan Ignas has no money."

"But he has reputation, and, besides, there is old Zavilovski; and a connection like that is no joke. Who among us has not heard of the old man? Besides, as to me, to tell the truth, I disliked the Broniches to the degree that at last I turned from them."

"You knew the late Pan Bronich, then? Be not astonished that I ask, for with me it is a question of our Pan Ignas."

"Whom have I not known? I knew also Pani Bronich's sister, — Pani Castelli. For that matter I have been twenty-four years in Italy, and am about forty, — that is said for roundness. In fact, I am forty-five. I knew Pan Castelli, too, who was a good enough man; I knew all. What shall I say to you? Pani Castelli was an enthusiast, and distinguished by wearing short hair; she was always unwashed, and had neuralgia in the face. As to Pani Bronich, you know her."

"But who was Pan Bronich?"

"'Teodor'? Pan Bronich was a double fool, — first, because he was a fool; and second, because he did n't know himself as one. But I am silent, for '*de mortuis nil nisi bonum.*' He was as fat as she is thin; he weighed more than a hundred and fifty kilograms, perhaps, and had fish eyes. In general, they were people vain beyond everything. But why expatiate? When a man lives a while in the world, and sees many people, and talks with them, as I do while painting, he convinces himself that there is really a high society, which rests on tradition, and besides that a *canaille*, which, having a little money, apes great society. The late Bronich and his present widow always seemed to me of that race; therefore I chose to keep them at a distance. If Bukatski were alive, he would let out his tongue now at their expense. He knew that I was in love with Panna Castelli; and how he ridiculed me, may the Lord not remember it against him! And who knows whether he did not speak justly? for what Panna Lineta is will be shown later."

"It concerns me most of all to learn something of her."

"They are good, all good; but I am afraid of them and their goodness, — unless your wife would go security for some of them."

At this point the conversation stopped, and they began to talk of Bukatski, or rather, of his burial of the day following, for which Pan Stanislav had made previously all preparations.

On the way from Svirski's he spoke to the priest again, and then informed acquaintances of the hour on the morrow.

The church ceremony of burial had taken place at Rome in its own time, so Pan Stanislav, as a man of religious feeling, invited a few priests to join their prayers to the prayers of laymen; he did this also through attachment and gratitude to Bukatski, who had left him a considerable part of his property.

Besides the Polanyetskis came the Mashkos, the Osnovskis, the Bigiels, Svirski, Pan Plavitski, and Pani Emilia, who wished at the same time to visit Litka. The day was a genuine summer one, sunny and warm; the cemetery had a different seeming altogether from what it had during Pan Stanislav's former visits. The great healthy trees formed a kind of thick, dense curtain composed of dark and bright leaves, covering with a deep green shade the white and gray monuments. In places the cemetery seemed simply a forest full of gloom and coolness. On certain graves was quivering a shining network of sunbeams, which had filtered in through the leaves of acacias, poplars, hornbeams, birch, and lindens; some crosses, nestling in a thick growth, seemed as if dreaming in cool air above the graves. In the branches and among the leaves were swarms of small birds, calling out from every side with an unceasing twitter, which was mild, and, as it were, low purposely, so as not to rouse the sleepers.

29

Svirski, Mashko, Polanyetski, and Osnovski took on their shoulders the narrow coffin containing the remains of Bukatski, and bore it to the tomb. The priests, in white surplices now gleaming in the sun, now in the shade, walked in front of the coffin; behind it the young women, dressed in black; and all the company went slowly through the shady alleys, silently, calmly, without sobs or tears, which usually accompany a coffin. They moved only with dignity and sadness, which were on their faces as the shadow of the trees on the graves. There was, however, in all this a certain poetry filled with melancholy; and the impressionable soul of Bukatski would have felt the charm of that mourning picture.

In this way they arrived at the tomb, which had the form of a sarcophagus, and was entirely above ground, for Bukatski during life told Svirski that he did not wish to lie in a cellar. The coffin was pushed in easily through the iron door; the women raised their eyes then; their lips muttered prayers; and after a time Bukatski was left to the solitude of the cemetery, the rustling trees, the twitter of birds, and the mercy of God.

Pani Emilia and Pan Stanislav went then to Litka; while the rest of the company waited in the carriages before the church, for thus Pani Aneta had wished.

Pan Stanislav had a chance to convince himself, at Litka's grave, how in his soul that child once so beloved had gone into the blue distance and become a shade. Formerly when he visited her grave he rebelled against death, and with all the passion of fresh sorrow was unreconciled to it. To-day it seemed to him well-nigh natural that she was lying in the shadow of those trees, in that cemetery; he had the feeling almost that it must end thus. She had ceased all but completely to be for him a real being, and had become merely a sweet inhabitant of his memory, a sigh, a ray, simply one of that kind of reminiscences which is left by music.

And he would have grown indignant at himself, perhaps, were it not that he saw Pani Emilia rise after her finished prayer with a serene face, with an expression of great tenderness in her eyes, but without tears. He noticed, however, that she looked as sick people look, that she rose from her knees with difficulty, and that in walking she leaned on a stick. In fact, she was at the beginning of a sore disease of the loins, which later on confined her for years to the bed, and only left her at the coffin.

Before the cemetery gate the Osnovskis were waiting for them; Pani Aneta invited them to a betrothal party on the morrow, and then those "who were kind" to Prytulov

Svirski sat with Pani Emilia in Pan Stanislav's carriage, and for some time was collecting his impressions in silence; but at last he said, —

"How wonderful this is! To-day at a funeral, to-morrow at a betrothal; what death reaps, love sows, — and that is life!"

## CHAPTER XLIX.

PAN IGNAS wished the betrothal to be not in the evening before people, but earlier; and his wish was gratified all the more, since Lineta, who wished to show herself to people as already betrothed, supported him before Aunt Bronich. They felt freer thus; and when people began to assemble they appeared as a young couple. The light of happiness shone from Lineta. She found a charm in that rôle of betrothed; and the rôle added charm to her. In her slender form there was something winged. Her eyelids did not fall to-day sleepily over her eyes; those eyes were full of light, her lips of smiles, her face was in blushes. She was so beautiful that Svirski, seeing her, could not refrain from quiet sighs for the lost paradise, and found calmness for his soul only when he remembered his favorite song, —

"I am singing and not sobbing,
For I have ceased to love thee too!
Hu-ha-hu!"

For that matter her beauty struck every one that day. Old Zavilovski, who had himself brought in his chair to the drawing-room, held her hands and gazed at her for a time; then, looking around at his daughter, he said, —

"Well, such a Venetian half-devil can turn the head, she can, and especially the head of a poet, for in the heads of those gentlemen is fiu, fiu! as people say."

Then he turned to the young man and asked, —

"Well, wilt thou break my neck to-day because I said Venetian half-devil to thee?"

Pan Ignas laughed, and, bending his head, kissed the old man's shoulder. "No; I could not break any one's neck to-day."

"Well," said the old man, evidently rejoiced at those marks of honor, "may God and the Most Holy Lady bless you both! I say the Most Holy Lady, for her protection is the basis."

When he had said this, he began to search behind in the chair, and, drawing forth a large jewel-case, said to Lineta,—

"This is from the family of the Zavilovskis; God grant thee to wear it long!"

Lineta, taking the box, bent her charming figure to kiss him on the shoulder; he embraced her neck, and said to the bridegroom, —

"But thou might come."

And he kissed both on the forehead, and said, with greater emotion than he wished to show, —

"Now love and revere each other, like honest people."

Lineta opened the case, in which on a sapphire-colored satin cushion gleamed a splendid *rivière* of diamonds. The old man said once more with emphasis, "From the family of the Zavilovskis," wishing evidently to show that the young lady who married a Zavilovski, even without property, was not doing badly. But no one heard him, for the heads of the ladies — of Lineta, Pani Aneta, Pani Mashko, Pani Bronich and even Marynia — bent over the flashing stones; and breath was stopped in their mouths for a time, till at last a murmur of admiration and praise broke the silence.

"It is not a question of diamonds!" cried Pani Bronich, casting herself almost into the arms of old Zavilovski, "but as the gift, so the heart."

"Do not mention it Pani; do not mention it!" said the old man, warding her off.

Now the society broke into pairs or small groups; the betrothed were so occupied with each other that the whole world vanished from before them. Osnovski and Svirski went up to Marynia and Pani Bigiel. Kopovski undertook to entertain the lady of the house; Pan Stanislav was occupied with Pani Mashko. As to Mashko himself, he was anxious evidently to make a nearer acquaintance with the Crœsus, for he so fenced him off with his armchair that no one could approach him, and began then to talk of remote times and the present, which, as he divined easily, had become a favorite theme for the old man.

But he was too keen-witted to be of Zavilovski's opinion in all things. Moreover, the old man did not attack recent times always; nay, he admired them in part. He acknowledged that in many regards they were moving toward the better; still he could not take them in. But Mashko explained to him that everything must change on earth; hence nobles, as well as other strata of society.

"I, respected sir," said he, "hold to the land through a certain inherited instinct, — through that something which attracts to land the man who came from it; but, while managing my own property, I am an advocate, and I am one on principle. We should have our own people in that department; if we do not, we shall be at the mercy of men coming from other spheres, and often directly opposed to us. And I must render our landholders this justice, that for the greater part they understand this well, and choose to confide their business to me rather than to others. Some think it even a duty."

"The bar has been filled from our ranks at all times," answered Pan Zavilovski; "but will the noble succeed in other branches? As God lives, I cannot tell. I hear, and hear that we ought to undertake everything; but people forget that to undertake and to succeed are quite different. Show me the man who has succeeded."

"Here he is, respected sir, Pan Polanyetski: he in a commission house has made quite a large property; and what he has is in ready cash, so that he could put it all on the table to-morrow. He will not deny that my counsels have been of profit to him frequently; but what he has made, he has made through commerce, mainly in grain."

"Indeed, indeed!" said the old noble, gazing at Pan Stanislav, and staring from wonder, "has he really made property? Is it possible? Is he of the real Polanyetskis? That 's a good family."

"And that stalwart man with brown hair?"

"Is Svirski the artist."

"I know him, for I saw him abroad; and the Svirskis did not make fires as an occupation."

"But he can only paint money, for he has n't made any."

"He has n't!" said Mashko, in a confidential tone. "Not one big estate in Podolia will give as much income as aquarelles give him."

"What is that?"

"Pictures in water-colors."

"Is it possible? not even oil paintings! And he too—? Ha! then, perhaps, my relative will make something at verses. Let him write; let him write. I will not take it ill of him. Pan Zygmund was a noble, and he wrote, and not for display. Pan Adam was a noble also; but he is famous,—more famous than that brawler who has worked with democracy— What 's his name? Never mind! You say that times are changing. Hm, are they? Let them change for themselves, if only with God's help, for the better."

"The main thing," said Mashko, "is not to shut up a man's power in his head, nor capital in chests; whoever does that, simply sins against society."

"Well, but with permission! How do you understand this, — Am I not free to close with a key what belongs to me; must I leave my chests open to a robber?"

Mashko smiled with a shade of loftiness, and, putting his hand on the arm of the chair, said, —

"That is not the question, respected sir." And then he began to explain the principles of political economy to Pan Zavilovski; the old noble listened, nodding his head, and repeating from time to time, —

"Indeed! that is something new! but I managed without it."

Pani Bronich followed the betrothed with eyes full of emotion, and at the same time told Plavitski (who on his part was following Pani Aneta with eyes not less full of emotion) about the years of her youth, her life with Teodor, and the misfortune which met them because of the untimely arrival in the world of their only descendant, and Plavitski listened with distraction; but, moved at last by her own narrative, she said with a somewhat quivering voice, —

"So all my love, hope, and faith are in Lineta. You will understand this, for you too have a daughter. And as to Lolo, just think what a blessing that child would have been had he lived, since even dead he rendered us so much service —"

"Immensely touching, immensely touching!" interrupted Plavitski.

"Oh, it is true," continued Pani Bronich. "How often in harvest time did my husband run with the cry, 'Lolo monte!' and send out all his laboring men to the field. With others, wheat sprouted in the shocks, with us, never. Oh, true! And the loss was the greater in this, that that was our last hope. My husband was a man in years, and I can say that for me he was the best of protectors; but after this misfortune, only a protector."

"Here I cease to understand him," said Plavitski. "Ha, ha! I fail altogether to understand him."

And, opening his mouth, he looked roguishly at Pani Bronich; she slapped him lightly with her fan, and said, —

"These men are detestable; for them there is nothing sacred."

"Who is that, a real Perugino,--that pale lady, with whom your husband is talking?" asked Svirski now of Marynia.

"An acquaintance of ours, Pani Mashko. Have you not been presented to her?"

"Yes; I became acquainted with her yesterday at the funeral, but forget her name. I know that she is the wife of that gentleman who is talking with old Pan Zavilovski. A pure Vannuci! The same quietism, and a little yellowish; but she has very beautiful lines in her form."

And looking a little longer he added,—

"A quenched face, but uncommon lines in the whole figure. As it were slender; look at the outline of her arms and shoulders."

But Marynia was not looking at the outlines of the arms and shoulders of Pani Mashko, but at her husband; and on her face alarm was reflected on a sudden. Pan Stanislav was just inclining toward Pani Mashko and telling her something which Marynia could not hear, for they were sitting at a distance; but it seemed to her that at times he gazed into that quenched face and those pale eyes with the same kind of look with which during their journey after marriage he had gazed at her sometimes. Ah, she knew that look! And her heart began now to beat, as if feeling some great danger. But immediately she said to herself, "That cannot be! That would be unworthy of Stas." Still she could not refrain from looking at them. Pan Stanislav was telling something very vivaciously, which Pani Mashko listened to with her usual indifference. Marynia thought again: "Something only seemed to me! He is speaking vivaciously as usual, but nothing more." The remnant of her doubt was destroyed by Svirski, who, either because he noticed her alarm and inquiring glance, or because he did not notice the expression on Pan Stanislav's face, said,—

"With all this she says nothing. Your husband must keep up the conversation, and he looks at once weary and angry."

Marynia's face grew radiant in one instant. "Oh, you are right! Stas is annoyed a little, surely; and the moment he is annoyed he is angry."

And she fell into perfect good-humor. She would have been glad to give a *rivière* of diamonds, like that which Pan Zavilovski had brought to Lineta, to make "Stas" approach at that moment, to say something herself to him, and hear a kind word from him. In fact, a few minutes later her wish was accomplished, for Osnovski approached Pani Mashko; Pan Stanislav rose, and, saying a word or two on the way to Pani Aneta, who was talking to Kopovski, sat down at last by his wife.

"Dost wish to tell me something?" he inquired.

"How wonderful it is, Stas, for I called to thee that moment, but only in mind; still thou hast felt and art here with me."

"See what a husband I am," answered he, with a smile. "But the reason is really very simple: I noticed thee looking at me; I was afraid that something might have happened, and I came."

"I was looking, for I wanted something."

"And I came, for I wanted something. How dost thou feel? Tell the truth! Perhaps thou hast a wish to go home?"

"No, Stas, as I love thee, I am perfectly comfortable. I was talking with Pan Svirski of Pani Mashko, and was entertained well."

"I guessed that you were gossiping about her. This artist says himself that he has an evil tongue."

"On the contrary," answered Svirski, "I was only admiring her form. The turn for my tongue may come later."

"Oh, that is true," said Pan Stanislav; "Pani Osnovski says that she has indeed a bad figure, and that is proof that she has a good one. But, Marynia, I will tell thee something of Pani Osnovski." Here he bent toward his wife, and whispered, "Knowest what I heard from Kopovski's lips when I was coming to thee?"

"What was it? Something amusing?"

"Just as one thinks: I heard him say *thou* to Pani Aneta."

"Stas!"

"As I love thee, he did. He said to her, 'Thou art always so.'"

"Maybe he was quoting some other person's words."

"I don't know. Maybe he was; maybe he was n't. Besides, they may have been in love sometime."

"Fi! Be ashamed."

"Say that to them — or rather to Pani Aneta."

Marynia, who knew perfectly well that unfaithfulness exists, but looking on it rather as some French literary theory, — she had not even imagined that one might meet such a thing at every step and in practice, — began to look now at Pani Aneta with wonder, and at the same time with the immense curiosity with which honest women look at those who have had boldness to leave the high-road for by-paths. She had too truthful a nature, however, to believe in evil immediately, and she did not; and somehow it would not find a place in her head that really there could be anything between those two, if only because of the unheard-of stupidity of Kopovski. She noticed, however, that they were talking with unusual vivacity.

But they, sitting somewhat apart between a great porcelain vase and the piano, had not only been talking, but arguing for a quarter of an hour.

"I fear that he has heard something," said Pani Aneta, with a certain alarm, after Pan Stanislav had passed. "Thou art never careful."

"Yes, it is always my fault! But who is forever repeating, 'Be careful'?"

In this regard both were truly worthy of each other, since he could foresee nothing because of his dulness, and she was foolhardy to recklessness. Two persons knew their secret now; others might divine it. One needed all the infatuation of Osnovski not to infer anything. But it was on that that she reckoned.

Meanwhile Kopovski looked at Pan Stanislav and said, —

"He has heard nothing."

Then he returned to the conversation which they had begun; but now he spoke in lower tones and in French, —

"Didst thou love me, thou wouldst be different; but since thou dost not love, what harm could that be to thee?"

Then he turned on her his wonderful eyes without mind, while she answered impatiently, —

"Whether I love, or love not, Castelka never! Dost understand? Never! I would prefer any other to her, though, if thou wert in love with me really, thou wouldst not think of marriage."

"I would not think of it, if thou wert different."

"Be patient."

"Yes! till death? If I married Castelka, we should then be near really."

"Never! I repeat to thee."

"Well, but why?"

"Thou wouldst not understand it. Besides, Castelka is betrothed; it is too bad to lose time in discussing this."

"Thou thyself hast commanded me to pay court to her, and now art casting reproaches. At first I thought of nothing; but afterward she pleased me,—I do not deny this. She pleases all; and, besides, she is a good match."

Pani Aneta began to pull at the end of her handkerchief.

"And thou hast the boldness to say to my eyes that she pleased thee," said she at last. "Is it I, or she?"

"Thou, but thee I cannot marry; her I could, for I saw well that I pleased her."

"If thou wert better acquainted with women, thou wouldst be glad that I did not let it go to marriage. Thou dost not know her. She is just like a stick, and, besides, is malicious in character. Dost thou not understand that I told thee to pay court to her out of regard to people, and to Yozio? Otherwise, how explain thy daily visits?"

"I could understand, wert thou other than thou art."

"Do not oppose me. I have fixed all, as thou seest, to keep thy portrait from being finished, and give thee a chance to visit Prytulov. Steftsia Ratkovski, a distant relative of Yozio's, will be there soon. Dost understand? Thou must pretend that she pleases thee; and I will talk what I like into Yozio. In this way thou wilt be able to stop at Prytulov. I have written to Panna Ratkovski already. She is not a beauty, but agreeable."

"Always pretence, and nothing for it."

"Suppose I should say to thee: Don't come."

"Anetka!"

"Then be patient. I cannot be angry long with thee. But now go thy way. Amuse Pani Mashko."

And a moment later Pani Aneta was alone. Her eyes followed Kopovski a while with the remnant of her anger, but also with a certain tenderness. In the white cravat, with his dark tint of face, he was so killingly beautiful that she could not gaze at him sufficiently. Lineta was now the betrothed of another; still the thought seemed unendurable that that daily rival of hers might possess him, if not as husband, as lover. Pani Aneta, in telling Kopovski that she would yield him to any other rather than to Castelka, told the pure truth. That was for her a question, at once of an immense weakness for that dull Endymion, and a question of self-love. Her nerves simply could not agree to it. Certain inclinations of the senses, which she herself looked on as lofty, and rising from a Grecian nature, but which at the root of the matter were common, took the place in her of morality and conscience. By virtue of these inclinations, she fell under the irresistible charm of Kopovski; but having not only a heated head, but a temperament of fishy coldness, she preferred, as Pan Ignas divined intuitively, the play with evil to evil itself. Holding, in her way, to the principle, "If not I, then no one!" she was ready to push matters to the utmost to prevent the marriage of Kopovski to Lineta, the more since she saw that Lineta, in spite of all her "words" about Kopovski, in spite of the irony with which she had mentioned him and her jests about the man, was also under the charm of his exceptional beauty; that all those jests were simply self-provocation, under which was concealed an attraction; and that, in general, the source of her pleasure and Lineta's was the same. But she did not observe that, for this reason, she at the bottom of her soul had contempt for Lineta.

She knew that Lineta, through very vanity, would not oppose her persuasion, and the homages of a man with a famous name. In this way, she had retained Kopovski, and, besides, had produced for herself a splendid spectacle, on which women, who are more eager for impressions than feelings, look always with greediness. Besides, if that famous Pan Ignas, when his wife becomes an every-day object, should look somewhere for a Beatrice, he might find her. Little is denied men who have power to hand down, to the memory of mankind and the homage of ages, the name of a loved one. These plans for the future Pani Aneta had not outlined hitherto expressly; but she had, as it were, a misty feeling that her triumph would in that case be perfect.

Moreover, she had triumphed even now, for all had gone as she wished. Still Kopovski made her angry. She had considered him as almost her property. Meanwhile, she saw that, so far as he was able to understand anything, he understood this, that the head does not ache from abundance, and that Aneta might not hinder Lineta. That roused her so keenly that at moments she was thinking how to torment him in return. Meanwhile, she was glad that Lineta paraded herself as being in love really, soul and heart, with Pan Ignas, which for Kopovski was at once both a riddle and a torture.

These thoughts flew through her head like lightning, and flew all of them in the short time that she was alone.

At last she was interrupted by the serving of supper. Osnovski, who desired that his wife should be surrounded by such homage from every one as he himself gave, and to whom it seemed that what he had said to Pan Ignas about his married life was very appropriate, had the unhappy thought to repeat at the first toast the wish that Pan Ignas might be as happy with Lineta as he with his wife. Hereupon, the eyes of Pan Ignas and Pan Stanislav turned involuntarily to Pani Osnovski, who looked quickly at Pan Stanislav, and doubts on both sides disappeared in one instant; that is, she gained the perfect certainty that Pan Stanislav had heard them, and he, that Kopovski had not quoted the words of another, but had said *thou* in direct speech to the lady. Pani Aneta had guessed even that Pan Stanislav must have spoken of that to Marynia, for she had seen how, after he had passed, both had talked and looked a certain time at her with great curiosity. The thought filled her with anger and a desire of revenge, so that she listened without attention to the further toasts, which were given by her husband, by Pan Ignas, by Plavitski, and at last by Pan Bigiel.

But, after supper, it came to her head all at once to arrange a dancing-party; and "Yozio," obedient as ever to each beck of hers, and, besides, excited after feasting, supported the thought enthusiastically. Marynia could not dance, but besides her there were five youthful ladies, — Lineta, Pani Osnovski, Pani Bigiel, Pani Mashko, and Panna Zavilovski. The last declared, it is true, that she did not dance; but, since people said that she neither danced, talked, ate, nor drank, her refusal did not stop the readiness of others. Osnovski, who was in splendid feeling, declared that Ignas should take Lineta in his arms, for surely he had not dared to do so thus far.

It turned out, however, that Pan Ignas could not avail himself of Pan Osnovski's friendly wishes, for he had never danced in his life, and had not the least knowledge of dancing, which not only astonished Pani Bronich and Lineta, but offended them somewhat. Kopovski, on the other hand, possessed this art in a high degree; hence he began the dance with Lineta, as the heroine of the evening. They were a splendid pair, and eyes followed them involuntarily. Pan Ignas was forced to see her golden head incline toward Kopovski's shoulder, to see their bosoms near each other, to see both whirling to the time of Bigiel's waltz, joined in the harmony of movement, blending, as it were, into one tune and one unity. Even from looking at all this, he grew angry, for he understood that there was a thing which he did not know, which would connect Lineta with others and disconnect her with him. Besides, people about him mentioned the beauty of the dancing couple; and Svirski, sitting near him, said, —

"What a beautiful man! If there were male houris, as there are female, he might be a houri in a Mussulman paradise for women."

They waltzed long; and there was in the tones of the music, as in their movements, something, as it were, intoxicating, a kind of dizzy faintness, which incensed Pan Ignas still more, for he recalled Byron's verses on waltzing, — verses as cynical as they are truthful. At last, he said to himself, with complete impatience: "When will that ass let her go?" He feared, too, that Kopovski might tire her too much.

The "ass" let her go at last at the other end of the hall, and straightway took Pani Aneta. But Lineta ran up to her betrothed, and, sitting down at his side, said,

"He dances well, but he likes to exhibit his skill, for he has nothing else. He kept me too long. I have lost breath a little, and my heart is beating. If you could put your hand there and feel how it beats — but it is not proper to do so. How wonderful, too, for it is your property."

"My property!" said Pan Ignas, holding out his hand to her. "Do not say 'your' to me to-day, Lineta."

"Thy property," she whispered, and she did not ward off his hand, she only let it drop down a little on her robe, so that people might not notice it.

"I was jealous of him," said Pan Ignas, pressing her fingers passionately.

"Dost wish I will dance no more to-day? I like to dance, but I prefer to be near thee."

"My worshipped one!"

"I am a stupid society girl, but I want to be worthy of thee. As thou seest, I love music greatly, — even waltzes and polkas. Somehow they act on me wonderfully. How well this Pan Bigiel plays! But I know that there are things higher than waltzes. Hold my handkerchief, and drop my hand for a moment. It is thy hand, but I must arrange my hair. It is time to dance; to dance is not wrong, is it? But if thou wish, I will not dance, for I am an obedient creature. I will learn to read in thy eyes, and afterward shall be like water, which reflects both clouds and clear weather. So pleasant is it for me near thee! See how perfectly those people dance!"

Words failed Pan Ignas; only in one way could he have shown what he felt, — by kneeling before her. But she pointed out Pan Stanislav, who was dancing with Pani Mashko, and admired them heartily.

"Really he dances better than Pan Kopovski," said she, with gleaming eyes; "and she, how graceful! Oh, I should like to dance even once with him — if thou permit."

Pan Ignas, in whom Pan Stanislav did not rouse the least jealousy, said, —

"My treasure, as often as may please thee. I will send him at once to thee."

"Oh, how perfectly he dances! how perfectly! And this waltz, it is like some delightful shiver. They are sailing, not dancing."

Of this opinion, too, was Marynia, who, following the couple with her eyes, experienced a still greater feeling of bitterness than Pan Ignas a little while earlier; for it seemed a number of times to her that Pan Stanislav had looked again on Pani Mashko with that expression with which he had looked when Svirski supposed that either he was annoyed, or was angry. But now such a supposition was impossible. At moments both dancers passed near her; and then she saw distinctly how his arm embraced firmly Pani Mashko's waist, how his breath swept around her neck, how his nostrils were dilated, how his glances slipped over her naked bosom. That might be invisible for others, but not for Marynia, who could read in his face as in a book. And all at once the light of the lamps became dark in her eyes; she understood that it was one thing not to be happy, and another to be unhappy. This lasted briefly, — as briefly as one tact of the waltz, or one instant in which a heart that is straitened ceases to beat; but it sufficed for the feeling that life in the future might be embroiled, and present love changed into a bitter and contemptuous sorrow. And that feeling filled her with terror. Before her was drawn aside, as it were, a curtain, behind which appeared unexpectedly all the sham of life, all the wretchedness and meanness of human nature. Nothing had happened yet, absolutely nothing; but a vision came to Marynia, in which she saw that there might be a time when her confidence in her husband would vanish like smoke.

She tried, however, to ward away doubts; she wished to talk into herself that he was under the influence of the dance, not of his partner; she preferred not to believe her eyes. Shame seized her for that "Stas" of whom she had been so proud up to that time; and she struggled with all her strength against that feeling, understanding that it was a question of enormous importance, and that from that little thing, and from that fault of his, hitherto almost nothing, might flow results which would act on their whole future.

At that moment was heard near her the jesting voice of Pani Aneta.

"Ah, Marynia, nature has created, as it were, purposely, thy husband and Pani Mashko to waltz with each other. What a pair!"

"Yes," answered Marynia, with an effort.

And Pani Aneta twittered on: "Perfectly fitted for each other. It is true that in thy place I should be a little jealous; but thou, art thou jealous? No? I am outspoken, and confess freely that I should be; at least, it was so with me once. I know, for that matter, that Yozio loves me; but these men, even while loving, have their little fancies. Their heads do not ache the least on that score; and that our hearts ache, they do not see, or do not wish to see. The best of them are not different. Yozio? true! he is a model husband; and dost thou think that I do not know him? Now, when I have grown used to him, laughter seizes me often, for they are all so awkward! I know the minute that Yozio is beginning to be giddy; and knowest thou what my sign is?"

Marynia was looking continually at her husband, who had ceased now to dance with Pani Mashko, and had taken Lineta. She felt great relief all at once, for it seemed to her that "Stas," while dancing with Lineta, had the same expression of face. Her suspicions began to fade; and she thought at once that she had judged him unjustly, that she herself was not good. She had never seen him dancing before; and the thought came to her head that perhaps he danced that way always.

Then Pani Aneta repeated, "Dost know how I discover when Yozio is beginning to play pranks?"

"How?" inquired Marynia, with more liveliness.

"I will teach thee the method. Here it is: the moment he has an unclean conscience, he puts suspicion on others, and shares these suspicions with me, so as to turn attention from himself. Dear Yozio! that is their method. How they lie, even the best of them!"

When she had said this, she went away, with the conviction that on the society chessboard she had made a very clever move; and it was clever. In Marynia's head a kind of chaos now rose; she knew not what to think at last of all this. Great physical weariness seized her also. "I am not well," said she to herself; "I am excited, and God knows what may seem to me." And the feeling of weariness increased in her every moment. That whole evening seemed a fever dream. Pan Stanislav had mentioned Pani Aneta as a faith-breaking woman; Pani Aneta had said the same of all husbands. Pan Stanislav had been looking with dishonest eyes on Pani Mashko, and Pani Aneta had said *thou* to Kopovski. To this was added the dancing couples, the monotonous tact of the waltz, the heads of the lovers, and finally, a storm, which was heard out of doors. What a mixture of impressions! what a phantasmagoria! "I am not well," repeated Marynia in her mind. But she felt also that peace was leaving her, and that this was the unhappy evening of her life. She wished greatly to go home, but, as if to spite her, there was a pouring rain. "Let us go home! let us go home!" If "Stas" should say some good and cordial word besides. Let him only not speak of Pani Aneta or Pani Mashko; let him speak of something that related to him and her, and was dear to them.

"Oh, how tired I am!"

At that moment Pan Stanislav came to her; and at sight of her poor, pale face, he felt a sudden sympathy, to which his heart, kind in itself, yielded easily.

"My poor dear," said he, "it is time for thee to go to bed; only let the rain pass a little. Thou art not afraid of thunder?"

"No; sit near me."

"The summer shower will pass soon. How sleepy thou art!"

"Perhaps I ought not to have come, Stas. I have great need of rest."

He had a conscience which was not too clear, and was

angry at himself. But it had not come to his mind that what she was saying of rest might relate to him and his attempts and conduct with Pani Mashko; but he felt all at once that if she had suspected, her peace would be ruined forever through his fault, and since he was not a spoiled man, fear and compunction possessed him.

"To the deuce with all dances!" said he. "I will stay at home, and take care of that which belongs to me."

And he said this so sincerely that a shadow of doubt could not pass through her head, for she knew him perfectly. Hence a feeling of immense relief came upon her.

"When thou art with me," said she, "I feel less tired right away. A moment ago I felt ill somehow. Aneta sat near me; but what can I care for her? When out of health, one needs a person who is near, who is one's own, and reliable. Perhaps thou wilt scold me for what I say, since it is strange to say such things at a party, among strangers, and so long after marriage. I understand myself that it is somewhat strange; but I need thee really, for I love thee much."

"And I love thee, dear being," answered Pan Stanislav who felt then that love for her could alone be honest and peaceful.

Meanwhile the rain decreased; but there was lightning yet, so that the windows of the villa were bright blue every moment. Bigiel, who, after the dancing, had played a prelude of Chopin's, was talking now with Lineta and Pan Ignas about music, and, defending his idea firmly, said, —

"That Bukatski invented various kinds and types of women; and I have my musical criterion. There are women who love music with their souls, and there are others who love it with their skin, — these last I fear."

A quarter of an hour later the short summer storm had passed by, and the sky had cleared perfectly; the guests began to prepare for home. But Zavilovski remained longer than others, so that he might be the last to say good-night to Lineta.

Out of fear for Marynia, Pan Stanislav gave command to drive the carriage at a walk. The picture of her husband dancing with Pani Mashko was moving in her tortured head continually. Pani Aneta's words, "Oh, how they lie! even the best of them," were sounding in her ears. But Pan Stanislav supported her meanwhile with his arm, and held her resting against him during the whole way; hence her disquiet disappeared gradually. She wished from her soul to put some kind of question to him, from which he might suspect her fears and pacify her. But after a while she thought: "If he did not love me, he would not show anxiety; he could be cruel more readily than pretend. I will not ask him to-day about anything." Pan Stanislav, on his part, evidently under the influence of the thought which moved in his head, and under the impression that she alone might be his right love and true happiness, bent down and kissed her face lightly.

"I will not ask him about anything to-morrow either," thought Marynia, resting her head on his shoulder. And after a while she thought again, "I will never tell him anything." And fatigue, both physical and mental, began to overpower her, so that before they reached home her eyes were closed, and she had fallen asleep on his arm.

Pani Bronich was sitting, meanwhile, in the drawing-room, looking toward the glass door of the balcony, to which the betrothed had gone out for a moment to breathe the air freshened by rain, and say good-night to each other without witnesses. After the storm the night had become very clear, giving out the odor of wet leaves; it was full of stars, which were as if they had bathed in the rain, and were smiling through tears. The two young people stood some time in silence, and then began to say that they loved each other with all their souls; and at last Pan Ignas stretched forth his hand, on which a ring was glittering, and said, —

"My greatly beloved! I look at this ring, and cannot look at it sufficiently. To this moment it has seemed to me that all this is a dream, and only now do I dare to think that thou wilt be mine really."

Then Lineta placed the palm of her hand on his, so that the two rings were side by side; and she said, with a voice of dreamy exaltation, —

"Yes; the former Lineta is no longer in existence, only thy betrothed. Now we must belong with our whole lives to each other; and it is a marvel to me that there should be such power in these little rings, as if something holy were in them."

Pan Ignas's heart was overflowing with happiness, calm, and sweetness.

"Yes," said he; "for in the ring is the soul, which

yields itself, and in return receives another. In such a golden promise is ingrafted everything which in a man says, 'I wish, I love, and promise.'"

Lineta repeated like a faint echo, "I wish, I love, and promise."

Next he embraced her and held her long at his breast, and then began to take farewell. But, borne away by the might of love and the impulse of his soul, he made of that farewell a sort of religious act of adoration and honor. So he gave good-night to those blessed hands which had given him so much happiness, and good-night to that heart which loved him, and good-night to the lips which had confessed love, and good-night to the clear eyes through which mutuality gazed forth at the poet; and at last the soul went out of him, and changed itself, as it were, into a shining circle, around that head which was dearest in the world and worshipped.

"Good-night!"

After a while Pani Bronich and Lineta were alone in the drawing-room.

"Art wearied, child?" inquired Pani Bronich, looking at Lineta's face, which was as if roused from sleep.

And Lineta answered, —

"Ah, aunt, I am returning from the stars, and that's such a long journey."

## CHAPTER L.

Pan Ignas could say to himself that sometimes a lucky star shines even for poets. It is true that since the day of his betrothal to Lineta it had occurred to him frequently that there would be need now to think of means to furnish a house, and meet the expenses, as well of a marriage as a wedding; but, being first of all in love, and not having in general a clear understanding of such matters, he represented all this to himself only as some kind of new difficulty to be overcome. He had conquered so many of these in his life that, trusting in his power, he thought that he would conquer this too; but he had not thought over the means so far.

Others, however, were thinking for him. Old Zavilovski, in whom, with all his esteem for geniuses, nothing could shake the belief that every poet must have "fiu, fiu" in his head, invited Pan Stanislav to a personal consultation, and said, —

"I will say openly that this youngster has pleased me, though his father was, with permission, a great roisterer; nothing for him but cards and women and horses. He came to grief in his time. But the son is not like the father; he has brought to the name not discredit, but honor. Well, others have not accustomed me much to this; but the Lord God grant that I shall not forget the man. I should like, however, to do something for him at once; for though a distant relative, he is a relative, and the name is the same, — that is the main thing."

"We have been thinking of this," said Pan Stanislav, "but the thing is difficult. If aid be spoken of, he is so sensitive that one may make the impatient fellow angry."

"Indeed! How stubborn he is!" said Zavilovski, with evident pleasure.

"True! He has kept books and written letters for our house a short time. But we have conceived a real liking for him; therefore my partner and I have offered him credit ourselves. 'Take a few thousand rubles,' said we, 'for expenses and furnishing a house, and return them to us in the course of three years from thy salary.' He would not: he said that he had trust in his betrothed; she would accommodate herself to him, he felt sure, and he did not want the money. Osnovski, too, wanted to offer aid, but we stopped him, knowing that it was useless. Your project will be difficult."

"Maybe, then, he has something?"

"He has, and he has n't. We have just learned that some thousands of rubles came to him from his mother; but with the interest he supports his father in an insane asylum, and considers the capital as inviolable. That he takes nothing from it, is certain, for before he began with us, he suffered such poverty that he was simply dying of hunger, and he did n't touch a copper. Such is his character. And you will understand why we esteem him. He is writing something, it seems, and thinks that he will meet the expense of first housekeeping with it. Maybe he will; his name means much at present."

"Pears on willows!" said Pan Zavilovski. "You tell me that his name means much — does it? But that 's pears on willows!"

"Not necessarily; only it will not come quickly."

"Well, he was ceremonious with you because you were strangers, but I am a relative."

"We are strangers, but older acquaintances than you, and we know him better."

Zavilovski, unaccustomed to contradiction, began to move his white mustaches, and pant from displeasure. For the first time in his life he had to trouble himself about the question, would the man to whom he wished to give money be pleased to accept it? This astonished, pleased, and angered him all at once; he recalled, then, something which he did not mention to Pan Stanislav, and this was it, — how many times had he paid notes for the father of the young man? — and what notes! But see, the apple has fallen so far from the tree that now there is a new and unexpected trouble.

"Well," said he, after a while, "may the merciful God grant the young generation to change; for now, O devil, do not go even near them!"

Here his face grew bright all at once with an immense honest pleasure. The inexhaustible optimism, lying at the bottom of his soul, when it found a real cause to justify itself, filled his heart with glad visions.

"Bite him now, lord devil," said he, "for the beast is

as if of stone! — a capable rascal! resolute in work, and character; that is what it is, — character."

Here he stared, and, shaking his head, fixed his lips as a sign of wonder, as if to whistle, and after a moment, added, —

"Indeed! and that in a noble! As God lives, I did n't expect it."

But talking in this way he deceived himself, for all his life he had expected everything.

"It seems, then," said Pan Stanislav, "that there is no help but this, Panna Castelli must accommodate herself to him."

But the old noble made a wry face all at once. "That is talk! tfu! Will she accommodate, or will she not? the deuce knows her! She is young; and as she is young, maybe she is ready for everything; but who will give assurance, and for how long? Besides, there is her aunt and that accommodating dead man; when he shouts from under the ground, go and talk with him. As God is true, I esteem people who have acquired property; but when any one has crept out of a cottage, and not a mansion, and pretends that he lived always in palaces, he wants palaces. And so it was with old Bronich. Neither of them was lacking in vanity; the young woman was reared in such a school, — nothing but comfort and abundance. Ignas does not know them in that respect — and you do not. Such a woman as this" (here he pointed to his daughter) "would go to a garret even, once she had given her word; but that other one, she may not go easily."

"I do not know them," said Pan Stanislav, "though I have heard various reports; but through good-will for Ignas, I should like to know definitely what to think of them."

"What to think of them! I have known them a long time, and I, too, do not know much. Well, judging from what Bronich herself says, the women are saints, the most worthy. And pious! Ha! they should be canonized while living! But you see it is this way, — there are women among us who bear God and the commands of faith in their hearts, and there are such, too, who make of our Catholic religion, Catholic amusement; and such talk the loudest, and grow up where no one sowed them. That 's what the case is."

"Ah, how truly you have spoken!" said Pan Stanislav,

"Well, is it not true?" inquired Zavilovski. "I have seen various things in life; but let us return to the question. Have you any method to make this wild cat accept aid, or not?"

"It is necessary to think of something; but at this moment nothing occurs to me."

Thereupon Panna Helena Zavilovski, who, occupied with embroidery on canvas, was silent up to that moment as if not hearing the conversation, raised her steel cold eyes suddenly, and said, —

"There is a very simple method."

The old noble looked at her.

"See, she has found it! What is this simple method?"

"Let papa deposit sufficient capital for Pan Ignas's father."

"It would be better for thee not to give that advice; I have done enough in my life for Pan Ignas's father, though I had no wish to see him, and prefer now to do something for Pan Ignas himself."

"I know; but if his father has an income assured till his death, Pan Ignas will be able to command that which he has from his mother."

"As God is dear to me, that is true!" said Pan Zavilovski, with astonishment. "See! we have both been breaking our heads for nothing, and she has discovered it. True, as God is dear to me!"

"You are perfectly right," said Pan Stanislav, looking at her with curiosity.

But she had inclined to the embroidery her face, which was without expression of interest, and, as it were, faded before its time.

The news of such a turn of affairs pleased Marynia and Pani Bigiel greatly, and gave at the same time occasion to speak of Panna Helena. Formerly she was considered a cold young lady, who placed form above everything; but it was said that later a way was broken through that coldness to her heart by great feeling, which, turning into a tragedy, turned also that society young lady into a strange woman, separated from people, confined to herself, jealous of her suffering. Some exalted her great benevolence; but if she was really benevolent, she did her good work so secretly that no one knew anything definite. It was difficult, also, for any one to approach her, for her indifference was greatly like pride. Men declared that in her manner there was something simply contemptuous, just as if she could not forgive them for living.

Pan Ignas had been in Prytulov, and returned only the week following the old man's talk with Pan Stanislav,—that is, when the noble had deposited in the name of his father twice the amount of capital which had served so far to pay his expenses at the asylum. When he learned of this, Pan Ignas rushed off to thank the old man, and to save himself from accepting it; but Zavilovski, feeling firm ground under his feet, grumbled him out of his position.

"But what hast thou to say?" asked he. "I have done nothing for thee; I have given thee nothing. Thou hast no right to receive or not to receive; and that it pleased me to go to the aid of a sick relative is a kind of act permitted to every man."

In fact, there was nothing to answer; hence the matter ended in embraces and emotion, in which these two men, strangers a short time before, felt that they were real relatives.

Even Panna Helena herself showed "Pan Ignas" good-will. As to old Zavilovski, he, grieving in secret over this, that he had no son, took to loving the young man heartily. A week later, Pani Bronich, who had visited Warsaw on some little business, went to Yasmen to learn what was to be heard about the gout, and to speak of the young couple. When she repeated a number of times, to the greater praise of "Nitechka," that she was marrying a man without property, the old noble grew impatient, and cried, —

"What do you say to me? God knows who makes the better match, even with regard to property, omitting mention of other things."

And Pani Bronich, who moreover endured all from the old truth-teller, endured smoothly even the mention of "other things." Nay, a half an hour later, she spread the wings of her imagination sufficiently. Visiting the Polanyetskis on the way, she told them that Pan Zavilovski had given her a formal promise to make an entail for "that dear, dear Ignas," with an irrepressible motherly feeling that at times he took the place of Lolo in her heart. Finally, she expressed the firm conviction that Teodor would have loved him no less than she, and that thereby sorrow for Lolo would have been less painful to both of them.

Pan Ignas did not know that he had taken the place of Lolo in Pani Bronich's heart, nor did he know of the entail discovered for him, but he noticed that his relations with people had begun already to change. The news of that entail must have spread through the city with lightning-like swiftness, for his acquaintances greeted him in some fashion differently; and even his colleagues of the bureau, honest people, began to be less familiar. When he returned from Prytulov, he had to visit all persons who had been present at the betrothal party at the Osnovskis'; and the quickness with which the visit was returned by such a man as Mashko, for example, testified also to the change in his relations. In the first period of their acquaintance, Mashko treated him somewhat condescendingly. Now he had not ceased, it is true, to be patronizing, but there was so much kindness and friendly confidence in his manner, such a feeling for poetry even. No! Mashko had nothing against poetry; he would have preferred, perhaps, if Pan Ignas's verses were more in the spirit of safely thinking people; but in general he was reconciled to the existence of poetry, and even praised it. His favorable inclination both to poetry and the poet were evident from his look, his smile, and the frequent repetition, "but of course, — of course, — but very!" Pan Ignas, who was in many regards naive, but at the same exceptionally intelligent, still understood that in all this there was some pretence, hence he thought: "Why does this, as it were, thinking man pose in such style that it is evident?"

And that same day he raised this question in a talk with the Polanyetskis; at their house it was that he had made Mashko's acquaintance.

"Were I to pose," said he, "I should try so to pose that people could not recognize it."

"Those who pose," answered Pan Stanislav, "count on this, that, though people notice the posing, still, through slothfulness or a lack of civic courage, they will agree to that which the pose is intended to express. Moreover, the thing is difficult. Have you noticed that women who use rouge lose gradually the sense of measure? It is the same with posing. The most intelligent lose this sense of measure."

"True," answered Pan Ignas, "as it is true also that one can reproach people with everything."

"As to Mashko," continued Pan Stanislav, "he knows,

besides, that you are marrying a lady who passes for wealthy; he knows that you are a favorite with Pan Zavilovski, and perhaps he would like to approach him through your favor. Mashko must think of the future; for they tell me that the action to break the will, on which his fate depends, is not very favorable."

Such was the case really. The young advocate who had appeared in defence of the will had shown much energy, adroitness, and persistence.

Here ceased their conversation about Mashko, for Pani Marynia had begun to inquire about Prytulov and its inhabitants, — a subject which for Pan Ignas was inexhaustible. In his expressive narrative, the residence at Prytulov appeared, with its lindens along the road, then its shady garden, ponds, reeds, alders, and on the horizon a belt of pine-wood. Kremen, which had faded in Marynia's memory, stood before her now as if present; and, in that momentary revival of homesickness, she thought that sometime she would beg "Stas" to take her even to Vantory, to that little church in which she was baptized, and where her mother was buried. Maybe Pan Stanislav remembered Kremen at that moment, for, waving his hand, he said, —

"It is always the same in the country. I remember Bukatski's statement, that he loved the country passionately, but on condition 'that there should be a perfect cook in the house, a big library, beautiful and intelligent women, and no obligation to stay longer than two days in a twelvemonth.' And I understand him."

"But still," said Marynia, "it is thy wish to have a piece of land of thy own near the city."

"To live in our own place in summer, and not with the Bigiels, as we must this year."

"But in me," said Pan Ignas, "certain field instincts revive the moment I am in the country. For that matter, my betrothed does not like the city, and that is enough for me."

"Does Lineta dislike the city really?" inquired Marynia, with interest.

"Yes, for she is a born artist. I gaze on nature too, and feel it; but she shows me things which I should not notice myself. A couple of days ago, we all went into the forest, where she showed me ferns in the sun, for instance. They are so delicate! She taught me also that the trunks of pine-trees, especially in the evening light, have a violet tone. She opens my eyes to colors which I have not seen hitherto, and, like a kind of enchantress going through the forest, discloses new worlds to me."

Pan Stanislav thought that all this might be a proof of artistic sense, but also it might be an expression of the fashion, and of that universal love for painting color which people talk into themselves, and in which any young lady at present may be occupied, not from love of art, but for show. He had not occupied himself with painting; but he noticed that, for society geese, it had become of late a merchandise, exhibited willingly in Vanity Fair, or, in other words, a means to show artistic culture and an artistic soul.

But he kept these thoughts to himself; and Pan Ignas talked on, —

"Besides, she loves village children immensely. She says that they are such perfect models, and less vulgarized than the little Italians. When there is good weather, we are all day in the fresh air, and we have become sunburnt, both of us. I am learning to play tennis, and make great progress. It is very easy, but goes hard at first. Osnovski plays passionately, so as not to grow fat. It is difficult to tell what a kind and high-minded person that man is."

Pan Stanislav, who during his stay in Belgium had played tennis no less passionately than Osnovski, began to boast of his skill, and said, —

"If I had been there, I should have shown you how to play tennis."

"Me you might," answered Pan Ignas; "but they play perfectly, especially Kopovski."

"Ah, is Kopovski in Prytulov?" asked Pan Stanislav.

"He is," said Pan Ignas.

And suddenly they looked into each other's eyes. In one instant each divined that the other knew something; and they stopped talking. A moment of silence and even of awkwardness ensued, for Pani Marynia blushed unexpectedly; and not being able to hide this, she blushed still more deeply.

Pan Ignas, who had thought that he was the exclusive possessor of the secret, was astonished at seeing her blush, and was confused too; then, wishing to cover the confusion with talk, he went on hurriedly, —

"Yes; Kopovski is in Prytulov. Osnovski invited him, so that Lineta might finish his portraits, for later on there will be no time. Besides, there is a relative of Osnovski's there also, Panna Ratkovski; and I think that Kopovski is courting her. She is a pleasing and quiet young lady. In August we are all going to Scheveningen, for those ladies do not like Ostend. If Pan Zavilovski had not come with such cordial assistance to my father, I should not have been able to go; but now my hands are free."

When he had said this, he began to talk with Pan Stanislav about his position in the counting-house, which he did not wish to leave. On the contrary, he asked a leave of some months, in view of exceptional circumstances; then he took farewell and went out, for he was in a hurry to write to his betrothed. In a couple of days he was to go to Prytulov again; but meanwhile he wrote sometimes even twice a day. And on the way to his lodgings he composed to himself the words of the letter, for he knew that Lineta would read it in company with Pani Bronich; that both would seek in it not only heart but wings; and that the most beautiful passages would be read in secret to Pani Aneta, Pan Osnovski, and even Panna Ratkovski. But he did not take this ill of his beloved "Nitechka,"—nay, he was thankful to her that she was proud of him; and he used all his power to answer to her lofty idea of him. The thought did not anger him either, that people would know how he loved her. "Let them know that she was loved as no one else in the world."

He thought then a little of Marynia too. Her blushes moved him, for he saw in them a proof of a most pure nature, which not only was incapable of evil itself, but which was even ashamed, offended, and alarmed by evil in others. And, comparing her with Pani Aneta, he understood what a precipice divided those women, apparently near each other by social position and mental level.

When Pan Ignas had gone, Pan Stanislav said,—

"Hast thou seen that Zavilovski must have noticed something? Now I have no doubt. That Osnovski is blind, blind!"

"Just his blindness should restrain and hold her back," said Marynia. "That would be terrible."

"That is not 'would be,' it is terrible. Thou seest, noble souls pay for confidence with gratitude; mean ones, with contempt."

## CHAPTER LI.

These words were a great consolation to Marynia, for, remembering her previous alarms, she thought at once that Pan Stanislav would not have said anything like them had he been capable of betraying her confidence; for she did not suppose that a man can have one measure for his neighbors and another for himself, and that in life these different measures meet at every step. She said to herself that to restrain her husband from everything, it was enough to show perfect trust in him; and she thought now with less fear of the nearness of Pani Kraslavski's country house to the house of the Bigiels, in which she and her husband were to pass the summer. It was easy to divine that Pani Mashko, who had moved already into her mother's house, would be a frequent guest at the Bigiels' from very tedium. Mashko did not send her to Kremen, for he did not wish to be separated from her during summer. From Warsaw, where he had to be on business, it was easy to go every day to Pani Kraslavski's villa, one hour's ride from the city barrier, while to distant Kremen such journeys were not possible. To Mashko, really in love with his wife, her presence was requisite to give him strength, for trying times had come again. The case against the will was not lost yet by any means; but it had taken a turn which was unfavorable, since the defence was very vigorous. It had begun to drag, so people began to doubt; and for Mashko doubt approached defeat. His credit, almost fallen at the opening of the case, had bloomed forth like an apple-tree in spring, but was beginning now to waver a second time. Sledz (the opposing advocate), hostile personally to Mashko, and in general a man of strong will, not only did not cease to spread news of the evil plight of his opponent, but strove that doubts as to the favorable issue of the will case should make their way into the press. A merciless legal and personal warfare set in. Mashko strove with every effort to lame his enemy; and when they met, he bore himself defiantly. This brought no advantage, however. Credit became more and more difficult; and creditors, though so far paid regularly, lost confidence. Again a feverish hunt began for money, to stop one debt with another, and uphold the opinion of ready solvency. Mashko exhibited such intelligence and energy in this struggle that, had it not been for the fundamental error in his life relations, he would have advanced to fame and great prosperity.

The breaking of the will might save all, but to break the will it was needful to wait; meanwhile to mend threads breaking here and there was difficult as well as humiliating. It came to this, that in two weeks after the Polanyetskis had moved to Bigiel's, when the Mashkos came to them with a visit, Mashko was forced to ask of Pan Stanislav a "friendly service;" that is, his signature to a note for a few thousand rubles.

Pan Stanislav was by nature an obliging man and inclined to be liberal, but he had his theory, which in money affairs enjoined on him to be difficult, hence he refused his signature; but to make up he treated Mashko to his views on money questions between friends, —

"When it is a question not of a mutually profitable affair," said he to him, "but of a personal service, I refuse on principle to sign; but I will oblige with ready money as far as an acquaintance or a friend may need it in temporary embarrassment, but not in a desperate position. In this last case I prefer to keep my service till later."

"That means," answered Mashko, dryly, "that thou art giving me a small hope of support when I am bankrupt."

"No; it means that should a catastrophe come, and thou borrow of me, thou 'lt be able to keep the loan, or begin something anew with that capital. At present thou wilt throw it into the gulf, with loss to me, without profit to thyself."

Mashko was offended.

"My dear friend," said he, "thou seest my position in a worse light than I myself see it, and than it is in reality. It is merely a temporary trouble, and a small one. I esteem thy good wishes, but this very day I would not give my prospects for thy actual property. Now I have one other friendly request; namely, that we speak no more of this."

And they went to the ladies, — Mashko angry at himself for having made the request, and Pan Stanislav for having refused it. His theory, that in money questions it was proper to be unaccommodating, caused him such bitter moments more than once, not to mention the harm which it had done him in life.

When with the ladies his ill-humor increased because of the contrast between Pani Mashko and Marynia. To Mashko's intense disappointment nothing announced that Pani Mashko was to be a mother. On the contrary, she preserved all the slenderness of maiden forms; and now, especially in her muslin summer robes, she looked, near Marynia, who was greatly changed and unwieldy, not only like a maiden, but younger than her neighbor by some years. Pan Stanislav, to whom it had seemed that the strange attraction which she exercised on him was overcome, felt suddenly that it was not, and that because of their living near each other, and of his seeing her frequently, he would yield more and more to her physical charm.

Still his relations with his wife had become warmer since Pan Ignas's betrothal evening, and Marynia was in better spirits than before; so now after the Mashkos had gone, she, seeing that the men had parted more coolly than usual and that in general Pan Stanislav was ill-humored, inquired if they had not quarrelled.

Pan Stanislav had not the habit of talking with her about business; but at this moment he was dissatisfied with himself, and felt that need of telling what troubled his mind which a man who is somewhat egotistical feels when he is sure that he will find sympathy in a heart devoted to him. Therefore he said, —

"I refused Mashko a loan; and I tell thee sincerely that it pains me now that I did so. He has certain chances of success yet; but his position is such that before he reaches his object he may be ruined by any obstacle. Of course we have never been in friendship; I almost do not like him. He irritates, he angers me; still life brings us together constantly, and he rendered us once a great service. It is true that I have rendered him services too; but now he has a knife at his throat again."

Marynia heard these words with pleasure, for she thought that if "Stas" were really under the charm of Pani Mashko, he would not have refused the loan, and second, she saw in his sorrow the proof of a good heart. She too was sorry for their neighbor, but as she had brought her husband hardly any dower, she did not venture to ask "Stas" directly to assist Mashko, she merely inquired, —

"But dost thou think that the loan would be lost?"

"Perhaps so, perhaps not," answered Pan Stanislav. Then with a certain boastfulness: "I can refuse. Bigiel has a softer heart."

"But don't say that. Thou art so kind. The best proof is this, that the present matter is so disagreeable to thee."

"Naturally it cannot be agreeable to think that a man, though a stranger, is squirming like a snake because of a few thousand rubles. I know what the question is. Mashko has given to-morrow as the last day of payment. Hitherto he has sought money everywhere, but sought guardedly, not wishing to make a noise and alarm his creditors; and in straits he relied on me. So thou seest, he will not pay to-morrow. I will suppose that in a few days he will find money as much as he needs; but meanwhile the opinion of his accuracy will be shaken, and in the position in which he is anything may be ruin for him."

Marynia looked at her husband; at last she said with a certain timidity, —

"And would this be really difficult for thee?"

"If thou wish the truth, not at all. I have even a check-book here with me; I took it to give earnest-money, if I found a place to buy. Oh, interest in a former adorer and sympathy for him give me something to think of," said he, laughing.

Marynia laughed too, for she was glad that she had brightened her husband's face; but, shaking her charming head, she said, —

"No! not sympathy for an adorer, but vile egotism, for I think to myself, are the two thousand rubles worth the sorrow of my husband?"

Pan Stanislav began to smooth her hair with his hand.

"But thou," said he, "art an honest little woman to thy bones."

Then he said, "Well, now, decide; one, two, three! to give?"

She made no answer, but began to wink her eyes like a petted child, as a sign to give. Both became joyous at once; but Pan Stanislav pretended to complain and mutter.

"See what it is to be under the slipper. Drag on through the night, man, and beg Pan Mashko to take thy money, because it pleases that fondled figure there."

And her heart was overflowing with delight, simply that he called her a "fondled figure." All her former sorrows and alarms vanished as if enchanted by those words. Her radiant eyes looked at her husband with indescribable love. After a while she inquired, —

"Is it necessary to go there right away?"

"Of course. Mashko will go to the city at eight in the morning, and be flying all day."

"Then give order to make Bigiel's horse ready."

"No! The moon is shining, and it is not far; I'll go on foot."

Thus saying, he took farewell of Marynia, and, seizing his check-book, went out. On the road he thought,—

"But Marynia might be applied to a wound. She is such a golden woman that though at times a man might like to play some prank, he simply has n't the heart for it. God has given me a wife of the kind of which there are few on earth."

And he felt at the moment that he loved her in truth. He felt also that love alone in itself, as a mutual attraction between persons of different sexes, is not happiness yet, and if ill directed may be even a misfortune; but that, on the other hand, the imagination of people cannot dream out a truer happiness on earth than great and honest love in marriage. "There is nothing superior to that," said Pan Stanislav to himself; "and to think that it lies at hand; that it is accessible to each one; that it is simply an affair of good and honest will; and that people trample on that ready treasure and sacrifice their peace for disturbance, and their honor for dishonor."

Thus meditating, he went to the villa of the Mashkos, the windows of which were shining like lanterns on the dark ground of the forest. When he had passed through the gate to the yard lighted by the moon, and had drawn near the porch, he saw, through the window of the room next the entrance, Mashko and his wife, sitting on a low sofa formed like a figure eight, near which was a small table and a lamp. Mashko was embracing his wife with one arm; with his other hand he held her hand, which he raised to his lips, and then lowered, as if thanking her. All at once he embraced the young woman, with both arms drew her toward him, and inclining, began to kiss her mouth passionately; she, with hands dropped without control on her knees, not returning his fondling, but also not refusing, yielded as passively as if she had been deprived of blood and will. For a time Pan Stanislav saw only the top of

Mashko's head, his long side whiskers moving from the kissing; and at sight of that the blood rushed to his head. And he was dashed with just such a flood of desire as when looking for the ribbons of Pani Osnovski's mantle (in Rome), and the more burning that it was strengthened by a whole series of temptations. This purely physical attraction, surprising to Pan Stanislav himself, and with which he had struggled long, revived now with irresistible force. In a twinkle were roused in him the wild instincts of the primitive man, who, when he sees the woman desired in the embrace of another, is enraged and ready to fight to the death for her with the fortunate rival. Together with desire, jealousy burned him, — an unjust, a pitiful, and the lowest of all kinds of jealousy, because purely physical, but still so unbridled that he, who the moment before had understood that only honest love for a wife might be real happiness, was ready to trample that happiness and that love, if he could trample Mashko, and seize himself in his arms that slender body of a woman, and cover with kisses that face of a puppet, without mind, and less beautiful than the face of his own wife.

That sight beyond the window not only excited him, but he could not suffer it; hence he sprang to the door and pulled the bell feverishly. The thought that that sound, heard on a sudden in the silence, would stop that fondling of husband and wife roused a savage and malicious delight in him. When the servant opened the door, Pan Stanislav gave command to announce him, and endeavored to calm himself and compose somehow that which he had to tell Mashko.

After a while Mashko came out with a face somewhat astonished, —

"Pardon that I come so late, but my wife scolded me because I refused thee a service; and since I knew that thou wilt go early in the morning, I have come to settle the business to-night."

On Mashko's face a secret joy was reflected. He divined straightway that such a late visit from his neighbor had relation to their previous talk; he did not hope, however, that the affair would go so smoothly and at once.

"I beg thee," said he. "My wife is not sleeping yet."

And he brought him into that room the interior of which Pan Stanislav had seen the minute before. Pani Mashko was sitting on the same sofa; in her hand she held a book and a paper-knife, which evidently she had taken from the table that moment. Her quenched face seemed calm, but traces of the fresh kisses were evident on her cheeks; her lips were moist, her eyes misty. The blood seethed up again in Pan Stanislav; and in spite of all efforts to keep himself indifferent, he so pressed the hand given him that Pani Mashko's lips contracted as if from pain.

But when he touched her hand, a shiver ran through him from feet to crown. There was in that very giving of her hand something so passive that it ran through his head involuntarily that that woman was not capable of resisting any man who had the courage and daring to attack her directly.

Meanwhile Mashko said, —

"Imagine to thyself, we have both raised a storm, — thou for refusing me a service, and I for requesting it. Thou hast an honest wife, but mine is no worse. Thine took me into her protection, and mine thee. I revealed to her plainly my temporary trouble, and she scolded me for not having done so before. Evidently she did not speak to me as a lawyer, for of that she has no idea; but in the end of ends she said that Pan Polanyetski refused me justly; that one should give some security to a creditor; and this security she is ready to give with her life annuity, and in general with all that she has. I was just thanking her when you came." Here Mashko laid his hand on Pan Stanislav's arm.

"My dear friend, I agree with thee that thy wife is the best person on earth; and I agree all the more that I have fresh proof of it, on condition, however, that thou assure me that mine is no worse. It ought not to surprise thee, then, that I hide my troubles from her, for, as God is true, I am always ready to share the good with such a beloved one, but the evil, especially the temporary, to keep for myself; and if thou knew her as I do, this would be no wonder to thee."

Pan Stanislav, who, despite all the temptation which Pani Mashko was for him, entertained by no means a high opinion of the woman, and had not considered her in the least as capable of sacrifice, thought, —

"She is, in truth, a good woman; and I was mistaken, or Mashko has lied to her, so that she really considers his position as brilliant, and this trouble as purely a passing one." And he said aloud to her, —

"I am an accurate man in business; but for whom do you hold me, when you think that I would ask security on your property? I refused simply through sloth, and I am terribly ashamed of it; I refused to avoid going at a given time to Warsaw for a new supply. In summer a man becomes lazy and egotistical. But the question is a small one; and to a man like your husband, who is occupied in property, such troubles happen daily. Not infrequently loans are needed only because one's own money cannot be raised at a given moment."

"Just that has happened to me," answered Mashko, satisfied, evidently, that Pan Stanislav had presented affairs to his wife in this manner.

"Mamma occupied herself with business, therefore I have no knowledge of it," put in Pani Mashko; "but I thank you."

Pan Stanislav began to laugh. "Finally, what do I want of your security? Suppose for a moment that you will be bankrupt, and I will suppose so just because nothing similar threatens you; can you imagine me in such an event bringing an action against you, and taking your income?"

"No," said Pani Mashko.

Pan Stanislav raised her hand to his lips, but with all the seeming of society politeness; he pressed his lips to it with all his force, and at the same time there was in the look that he gave her such passion that no declaration in words could have said more.

She did not wish to betray that she understood, though she understood well that the show of politeness was for her husband, and the power of the kiss for herself. She understood, also, that she pleased Pan Stanislav, that her beauty attracted him; still better, however, she understood that she was triumphing over Marynia, of whose beauty, while still unmarried, she was jealous, hence, first of all, she felt her self-love deeply satisfied. For that matter she had noticed for a long time that Pan Stanislav was ardent in her presence; hers was not a nature either so honest or so delicate that that action could offend or pain her. On the contrary, it roused in her curiosity, interest, and vanity. Instinct warned her, it is true, that he is an insolent man, who, at a given moment, is ready to push matters too far, — and that thought filled her at times with alarm; but since nothing similar had happened yet, the very fear had a charm for her.

Meanwhile she said to Pan Stanislav, —

"Mamma mentions you always as a man to be relied on in every case."

She said this with her usual thin voice, which Pan Stanislav had laughed at before more than once; but now everything in her became more attractive thereby, and hence, looking her fixedly in the eyes, he said, —

"Think the same of me."

"Have mutual confidence in each other," put in Mashko, jestingly; "but I will go to my study to prepare what is needed, and in a moment we will finish the matter."

Pani Mashko and her guest were left alone. On her face a certain trouble was apparent. To hide this she began to straighten the shade on the lamp; but he approached her quickly, and began, —

"I shall be happy if you think the same of me. I am a man greatly devoted to you; I should be glad to have even your friendship. Can I rely on it?"

"You can."

"I thank you."

When he had said this, he extended his hand to her, for all that he had said was directed only to this, to get possession of her hand. In fact, Pani Mashko did not dare to refuse it; and he, seizing it, pressed it to his lips a second time, but this time he did not stop with one kiss, — he fell to devouring it almost. It grew dark in his eyes. A moment more, and in his madness he would have seized and drawn that desired one toward him. Meanwhile, however, Mashko's squeaking boots were heard in the adjoining room; hearing which, Pani Mashko began to speak first, hurriedly, —

"My husband is coming."

At that moment Mashko opened the door, and said, —

"I beg thee."

Then, turning to his wife, he added, —

"Give command at once to bring tea; we will return soon."

In fact, the business did not occupy much time, for Pan Stanislav filled out a check, and that was the end. But Mashko treated him to a cigar, and asked him to sit down, for he wished to talk.

"New troubles are rolling on to me," said he; "but I shall wade out. More than once I have had to do with greater ones. It is only a question of this, — that the sun should get ahead of the dew, and that I should open some new credit for myself, or some new source of income, before the conclusion of the will case, and in support of it."

Pan Stanislav, all roused up internally, listened to this beginning of confidences with inattention, and chewed his cigar impatiently. On a sudden, however, the dishonest thought came to him that, were Mashko to be ruined utterly, his wife would be a still easier prey; hence he asked dryly, —

"Hast thought of this, what thou art to do should the case be lost?"

"I shall not lose it."

"Everything may happen; thou knowest that best thyself."

"I do not wish to think of it."

"Still it 's thy duty," said Pan Stanislav, with an accent of a certain pleasure, which Mashko did not notice. "What wilt thou do in such a case?"

Mashko rested his arms on his knees, and looking gloomily on the floor, said, —

"In such a case I shall have to leave Warsaw."

A moment of silence came. The young advocate's face became gloomier and gloomier; at last he grew thoughtful, and said, —

"Once, in my best days, I knew Baron Hirsh, in Paris. We met a number of times, and once we took part in some affair of honor. Sometimes now, when doubts come upon me, I remember him; he has withdrawn, apparently, from business, but really has much on hand, especially in the East. I know men who have made fortunes by him, for the field there is open at every step."

"Dost think it possible to go to him?"

"Yes; but besides that I can shoot into my forehead."

But Pan Stanislav did not take this threat seriously. From that short conversation he convinced himself of two things: first, that Mashko, in spite of apparent confidence, thought often of possible ruin; and second, that in such an event he had a plan, fantastic, it may be, but ready.

Mashko shook himself suddenly out of his gloomy visions, and said, —

"My strength has lain always in this, — that I never think of two things at once. Therefore I am thinking only of the will case. That scoundrel will do everything to ruin me in public opinion, I know that; but I sneer at public opinion, and care only for the court. Should I fail before the decision, that might have a bad influence, perhaps. Dost understand? They would consider the whole case then as the despairing effort of a drowning man, who grasps at what he can. I have no wish for that position; therefore I must seem to be a man standing on firm feet. This is a sad necessity, and I am not free now to be even economical. I cannot diminish my scale of living. As thou seest me, I have troubles to my ears; as for that matter, who knows it better than thou, who art giving me a loan? And still, as late as yesterday, I was buying Vyborz, a considerable property in Ravsk, simply to throw dust in the eyes of my creditors and opponents. Tell me, dost thou know old Zavilovski well?"

"Not long. I made his acquaintance through the young man."

"But thou hast pleased him, for he has immense admiration for men with noble names who make property. I know that he is his own agent; but he is growing old, and the gout is annoying him. I have put several thoughts before him; therefore, if he asks thee about anything, recommend me. Understand that I do not wish to get at his money chest, though, as agent, I should have some income, which would be greatly to my hand; but the main question for me is that it should become noised abroad that I am the agent of such a millionnaire. Is it true that he intends to create an entail for the young man out of his estates in Poznan?"

"So Pani Bronich says."

"That would be a proof that it is not true; but all things are possible. In every case the young man, too, will receive with his wife a certain dower; and, being a poet, he has not the least idea, surely, how to handle such matters. I might serve him, too, with advice and aid."

"I must refuse you decisively in his name, for we have engaged to occupy ourselves with his interests in future, — that is, my partner and I."

"It is not a question with me of his interest either," said Mashko, frowning slightly, "but that I might tell people that I am Zavilovski's agent; for, dost understand, before it is known which Zavilovski, my credit can only gain by it?"

"Thou knowest that I never look into other men's business; but I tell thee sincerely that for me it would be a terrible thing to exist in this way only on credit."

"Ask the greatest millionnaires on earth if they made fortunes on another basis."

"And ask all bankrupts if they did not fail from that cause."

"As to me, the future will show."

"It will," said Pan Stanislav, rising.

Mashko thanked him once more for the loan; and both went to tea to the lady, who inquired, —

"Well, the business is finished?"

Pan Stanislav, whom her appearance roused again, and who remembered suddenly that a little while before she said to him, "My husband is coming!" as if half guilty, answered her without reference to Mashko, —

"Between your husband and me it is, but between us two — not yet."

Pani Mashko, though she had cool blood, was still confused, as if frightened at his daring; and Mashko asked, —

"How is that?"

"This way," answered Pan Stanislav: "that the lady thought me capable of asking her property in pledge, and I cannot pardon her that yet."

Pani Mashko looked at him with her indefinite gray eyes, as if with a certain admiration. His boldness had imposed on her, and the presence of mind with which he was able to give a polite society turn to his words. He seemed to her also at that moment a fine-looking man, beyond comparison better-looking than Mashko.

"I beg pardon," said she.

"That will not be given easily. You do not know what a stubborn and vengeful man I am."

Then she answered with a certain coquetry, like a person conscious of her charm and her power, —

"I don't believe that."

He sat near her; and taking, with a somewhat uncertain hand, the cup, he began to stir the tea with the spoon. Greater and greater alarm seized him. More than once before he had called Pani Mashko, while unmarried, a fish; but now he felt warmth passing through her light garments from her body, and felt as if some one were scattering sparks on him. Again he remembered her words, "My husband is coming;" and waves of blood rushed to his heart, for it seemed to him that only a woman could speak thus who was prepared and ready for everything. Some voice in his soul said, "That is only a question of opportunity;" and at this thought his unbridled desire was turned at once to unbridled delight. He ceased altogether to control himself. Soon he began to seek her foot with his; but suddenly that act seemed to him passing rude and peasant-like. Finally he said to himself that since it was a question of opportunity only, he ought to know how to wait. He foresaw that the time would come, the opportunity be found.

Meanwhile his position was awkward; he had to keep up a conversation quite in disaccord with the state of his mind, and to answer Mashko, who asked about the future plans of Pan Ignas, and various things of like tenor. At last he rose to leave; but before going, he turned and said to Mashko, —

"Some dogs attacked me on the way, and I forgot my cane; lend me thine."

No dogs had attacked, but with him it was a question of remaining even one minute alone with the young woman, so that when Mashko went out he approached her quickly, and said, with a sort of stifled and unnatural voice, —

"You see what is taking place with me?"

She saw, indeed, his excitement, his eyes glittering with desire, and his distended nostrils. Alarm and fear seized her at once; but he remembered only her words, "My husband is coming," and one feeling, described by the words, "let happen what may," made the man, who, a moment before, said to himself that he ought to know how to wait, put everything on one card in the twinkle of an eye, and whisper, —

"I love you."

She stood before him with downcast eyes, as if stunned, and turned into a pillar under the influence of those words, from which simple infidelity must begin, and then a new epoch in life. She turned her head away slightly, as if to avoid his gaze. Silence followed, broken only by the somewhat panting breath of Pan Stanislav. But in the next room Mashko's squeaking boots were heard.

"Till to-morrow," said Pan Stanislav.

And in that whisper there was something almost commanding. Pani Mashko stood all this time with downcast eyes, motionless as a statue.

"Here is the cane," said Mashko. "To-morrow morning I go to the city, and return only in the evening. If the weather is good, maybe thou and Pani Polanyetski would like to visit my hermitess."

"Good-night," said Pan Stanislav.

And after a while he found himself on the empty road, which was lighted by the moon. It seemed to him that he had sprung out of a flame. The calm of the night and the forest was in such contrast to his tempest that it struck him like something uncommon. The first impression which he was able to note was the feeling that his internal conflict was closed, his hesitations ended; that the bridges were burned, and all was over. Some internal voice began to shout in his soul that first of all it had transpired that he was a wretch; but in this thought precisely there was a kind of desperate solace, for he said to himself if it were true, he must come to terms with himself as with a wretch, and in that event "let everything perish, and let the devils take all." In every case a wretch will not need to fight with his own inclinations, and may indulge himself. Yes, all is over, and the bridges are burned! He will be false to Marynia, trample her heart, trample honesty, trample the principles on which he built his life; but in return he will have Pani Mashko. Now one of two, either she will complain of him to her husband, and to-morrow there will be a duel,—if so be, let it come,—or she will be silent, and in that case will be his partner. To-morrow Mashko will go to Warsaw; and he, Pan Stanislav, will gain all that he desires, even if the world had to sink the next moment. If she will not expose him, it is better for her not to try resistance. He imagined even that she would not try, or if she did, she would do so only to preserve appearances. And it began to seethe in him again; that helplessness of hers, which formerly roused so much contempt in him, had become now an additional charm. He imagined the morrow, and the passiveness of that woman. In spite of all his chaos of thought, he understood perfectly that just in that passiveness she would seek later on an excuse: she would say to herself that she was not a partaker in the guilt, because she was forced to it; and in this way she would calumniate God, her own conscience, and, if need be, her husband. And thinking thus, he despised her as much as he desired her; but he felt at the same time that he himself was not much worthier, and that by virtue of a certain selection, not only natural, but moral, they ought to belong to each other.

He understood, also, that for him it was too late to withdraw from that road, and that once those same lips of his, which had sworn faith and love to Marynia, had said to another woman, "I love!" the greatest evil was committed. The rest was simply a sequence, which it was not proper to reject, even for this reason, — that in every case it was a pleasure. He imagined that all must reason thus who throw honesty through the window, and resolve on deeds of vileness; and the reasoning seemed to him as exact as it was immoral. And the more soberly he reflected, the more he was astonished at his own degradation. He had seen much evil and hidden vileness in the world under the guise of refinement and polish. He knew that corruption had worked out for itself, somehow, under the influence of bad books, a right of citizenship; but he remembered that he was indignant at this, that he wished simplicity and strictness for the society in which he lived, in the conviction that only on such bases could social strength and permanence be developed. Nothing had roused in him so many fears for the future as that refined evil of the West sown on the wild Slav field, and growing up on it with a sickly bloom of dilettantism, license, weakness, and faithlessness. More than once, as he remembered, he had reproached with such sowings, at one time high financial spheres, at another aristocracy of birth; and more than once he had attacked them without mercy. Now he understood that whoso lives in an atmosphere filled with carbonic gas, must suffocate. In what was he better than others? Or rather, how much worse was he than those who, floating in corruption, as sticks float in water, do not, at least, amuse themselves with hypocrisy, nor deceive themselves, nor prescribe rules to others, nor erect ideals of a healthy man spiritually, an honest husband, an honest father, as a binding model. And he almost refused to believe that he was the man who once gave Pani Emilia ideal friendship, and promised faithfulness to Marynia, and who considered that he had a clear intellect and a character juster and stronger than others.

He stronger? His strength was only deception, coming from lack of temptation. If he had loved Pani Emilia with the ideal feeling of a brother: if he had resisted the coquetry of Pani Aneta, — it was only because they did not rouse in him that animal feeling which that puppet with her red eyes roused, she whom his soul rejected, but for whom his senses were striving this long time. He thought then, too, that his feeling for Marynia had never been honest, for at the basis of things it was not anything else than just such an animal attraction. Familiarity had dulled it; and, restrained by the condition of Marynia, he had turned to where he was able, and turned without restraint or scruple hardly half a year after his marriage.

And Pan Stanislav, who, on leaving Mashko's house, had the feeling that he was a wretch, thought all at once that he was more of a wretch than at first he had imagined, for he remembered now that he was to be a father.

At home, in Marynia's windows, the lights had not been extinguished; he would have given much to find her sleeping. It came to his mind, even, to walk on and not return till there was darkness in the chamber. But suddenly he saw her profile in the window. She must be looking for him; and, since it was clear in front of the house, she must have seen him, — hence he halted and went in.

She received him in a white night wrapper, and with unbound hair. There was in that unbound hair a certain calculated coquetry, for she knew that she had beautiful hair, and that he liked to fondle it.

"Why art thou not sleeping?" asked he, coming in.

She approached him, sleepy, but smiling, and said, —

"I was waiting for thee to say the evening prayer."

Since their stay in Rome they had prayed together; but at present the very thought of this seemed to him insupportable. Meanwhile Marynia inquired, —

"Well, Stas, art content that thou hast saved him? Thou art, I think."

"Yes," answered he.

"But she does not know of his position?"

"She does and does not. It is late. Let us go to sleep."

"Good-night. Dost thou know of what I have been thinking here alone? That thou art so good and honest."

And, extending her face to him, she put her arms around his neck; he kissed her, feeling at the same time the pure honesty of her kiss, and his own vileness, and the whole series of vilenesses which he would have to commit later on.

One of these he committed right there, kneeling down to the prayer, which Marynia repeated aloud. He could not avoid saying it; and in saying it, he merely played a pitiful comedy, for he could not pray.

After the prayer was finished and a second good-night given, he could not sleep. It seemed to him that, when coming from Mashko's, he had embraced with his mind his action and all its moral consequences. Meanwhile it turned out that he had not. It came to his head now that it is possible not to believe in God, but not permitted to make sport of Him. To commit, for example, a perfidy, to return home to-morrow, or the following day, after having committed adultery, and kneel down to prayer, that would be too much. He felt that it was necessary to choose either religious feeling and sincere faith, or Pani Mashko. To reconcile these was not possible. And all at once he saw that everything which he had worked out and elaborated in himself purposely for years, that all that immense calm, resulting from the solution of life's chief enigma, —in a word, that which composed the essence of his spiritual existence, — must be rejected outright. On the other hand, he understood equally well that, from to-morrow forward, he must give the lie to his own social principles, to his recognition of the family as the basis of social existence. It is not permitted to proclaim such principles, and seduce other men's wives in secret. It was necessary to choose here too. As to Marynia, perfidy against her had been committed already. With one sweep, then, his relations with God, with society, with his wife, had gone to ruin; the ceiling of that spiritual house, reared with great labor, and in which he had been dwelling, had tumbled on his head. And that chilling cold of evil filled him with wonder. He had not expected that, on cutting a single thread, the whole fabric would unravel so quickly; and with astonishment he asked himself how there can exist in the world opportunism of that kind, which reconciles faith-breaking in life with honesty and honor? For that is what is done. He knew many so-called decent people, married men, loving their wives, as it were, religious, — and at the same time pursuing every woman they met. These same men, who would account to their wives every deviation from duty as a crime, permitted themselves conjugal infidelity without a scruple. He remembered how one of his acquaintances, pushed to the wall on this point, wriggled out humorously with the well-known street witticism that he was not a Swedish match. Absolute infidelity was obliterated, and among men passed as something permitted, almost customary. That thought brought Pan Stanislav a moment of consolation, but a short one, for he was consistent, if not in his actions, at least in his reasoning. True! The world is not composed of thieves and hypocrites alone, but in great part of thoughtless and frivolous people; and this opportunism, reconciling adultery with honor and honesty, is nothing else than frivolity. For in what can custom excuse a man, who recognizes the immorality and stupidity of that custom? For a fool, infidelity may be a joke, thought Pan Stanislav; for a man who thinks seriously, it is scoundrelism, as much opposed to ethics as a crime, as the signing of other men's names to notes, as the breaking of an oath, as the breaking of a word, as swindling in trade, or in cards. Religion may forgive the sin of adultery as a momentary fall; but adultery which excuses itself beforehand, excludes religion, excludes society, excludes honesty, excludes honor. Pan Stanislav, who, in his reasonings with himself, was always consistent and in general utterly unsparing, did not withdraw before this last induction. But he was frightened when he saw the precipice. If he did not withdraw, he would break his neck; but at the same time he began to fret at his own weakness. He knew himself well enough, with sorrow and with contempt also for his own weakness; he knew in advance that when he should see Pani Mashko, the human beast would get the upper hand of his soul. To withdraw? But he had repeated that to himself, and determined it after every temptation; and afterward, in presence of each succeeding one, passion had run away with his will at breakneck speed, just as a wild horse runs away with a rider. At the very remembrance of this he wanted to curse. If he had been unhappy at home, if his passion had grown up on the ground of great love, he would have had some excuse for it; but he did not love Pani Mashko,— he only desired her. He could never give himself an account of this dualism in the nature of man, — he knew only that he desired and would desire after every meeting, after every thought of her.

There remained one escape, not to see her, — an impossible escape, not only with reference to relations of acquaintance of every kind, but even with reference to this, that then Marynia would begin to suspect something. Pan Stanislav did not even suppose that that had taken place already, and that she merely concealed from him her suffering; he gave account to himself, however, that if his treason should in any way come out, it would be a blow simply beyond the strength of that mild and trusting woman. And his reproaches increased still more. Great pity and compassion for her seized him, as well as increased contempt for himself. In spite of darkness, the blood rushed to his face when he remembered that the fatal words had fallen; that he had said, "I love," to Pani Mashko; that he had deceived and betrayed Marynia, that honest, truthful woman; and that he was capable of betraying her trust, and trampling on her heart.

For a while it seemed to him a pure impossibility; but his conscience answered him, Thou art capable! Still, in that sorrow and pity for her he found a kind of consolation, when he saw that his feeling for her was and is something more than animal attraction, and that there were in him certain attachments, flowing out of the community of life and mutual possession; from the marriage vow; from comradeship in good and evil fortune; from the great esteem and affection which in future was to be strengthened by a child. Never had he loved her more than in that moment of internal torture, and never had there risen in him greater tenderness. Day began to break; through the openings of the window the dawn was entering, and filled the chamber with a pale light, in which he could see indistinctly her dark head sunk in the pillow. His heart was filled with the feeling that that was his only and best treasure,— his greatly beloved comrade sleeping there, his best friend, his wife, and the future mother of his child. And no conclusions, no reasonings about religion and social unvirtue, filled him with such disgust for that unvirtue and for himself as the sight of that mild, sleeping face. The light through the openings entered more and more, and her head emerged more distinctly each moment from the shade. The half-circles of her eyelids were visible already on her cheeks; and Pan Stanislav, looking at her, began to say to himself, "Thy honesty will help me!" All at once better feelings gained the victory in him: the beast abandoned his soul; and a certain consolation seized him, for he thought that if he were such a wretch as he had imagined, he would have followed the voice of passion with a lighter heart, and would not have passed through such suffering.

He woke late in the morning, wearied and somewhat ill; he felt such dissatisfaction and exhaustion as he had never felt before. But by the light of day, and besides a rainy and gloomy day, the whole affair stood before him differently,— it seemed more sober, ordinary; the future did not appear to him so terrible, nor his fault so great. Everything grew smaller in his eyes; he began to think then principally of this, whether Pani Mashko had confessed all to her husband or not. At moments he had the feeling of a man who has crawled into a great and sore trouble needlessly. Gradually, however, this feeling was changed into an ever increasing and more vivid alarm. "The position is stupid," said he to himself. "Every reproach may be made against Mashko, but not this, that he is an incompetent or a coward; and he will not put such an insult as that into his pocket. Hence there will be an explanation, a scandal, perhaps a duel. May the thunderbolts shatter it! What a fatal history, if the thing reaches Marynia!" And he began to be angry with the whole world. Till then he had had perfect peace; he had cared for no one, counted with no one. To-day, however, he is turning to every side; in his head is the question, "Has she told; has she not told?" and from the morning he could not think of aught else. It went that far that finally he put to himself this question: "What the deuce! am I afraid of Mashko? I?" It was not Mashko whom he feared, but Marynia, which was in like manner something both new and astonishing, for a couple of days earlier he would have admitted anything rather than this, — that he would ever fear Marynia. And as midday approached, the affair, which seemed to him diminished in the morning, began again to increase in his eyes. At moments he strengthened himself with the hope that Pani Mashko would be silent; at moments he lost that hope. And then he felt that he would not dare to look into the eyes, not of Marynia, merely, but of any one; and he feared Bigiel, too, and Pani Bigiel, and Pani Emilia, Pan Ignas, — in a word, all his acquaintances. "See what it is to make a muddle!" thought he. "How much one stupidity costs!" His alarm increased to the degree that at last, under pretext of returning the cane, he sent a servant boy to Pani Mashko with a bow, and an inquiry as to her health.

The servant returned in half an hour. Pan Stanislav saw him through the window, and, going down hurriedly to meet him, learned that he had brought a note from Pani Mashko to Marynia. Taking the note, he gave it to Marynia; and his heart beat with still greater alarm while watching her face as she read it.

But Marynia, when she had finished, raised her calm eyes to him, and said, —

"Pani Mashko invites us to supper to-day — and the Bigiels also."

"A-a!" answered Pan Stanislav, drawing a full breath. And in his soul he added, "She has not told."

"We will go, shall we not?" asked Marynia.

"If thou wish — that is, go with the Bigiels, for after dinner I must go to the city. I must see Svirski; perhaps I shall bring him here."

"Then we may send an excuse?"

"No, no! go with the Bigiels. Maybe I shall call in on the way and explain to her; but even that is not necessary. Thou wilt explain for me." And he went out, for he needed to be alone with his thoughts.

"She has not told;" a feeling of relief and delight now possessed him. She had not told her husband; she was not offended; she had invited them. She has agreed, therefore, to everything; she is ready to go farther, and to go everywhere, whithersoever he may wish to lead her. What is that invitation itself, if not a wish to put him at ease, if not an answer to his, "Till to-morrow"? Now all depends on him alone; and shivers begin again to go from his feet to his head. There are no hindrances unless in himself. The fish has swallowed the hook. Temptations attacked him with new power, for uncertainty restrained them no longer. Yes, the fish had swallowed the hook; she had not resisted. Here a feeling of triumph seized him, and of satisfaction for his self-love; and at the same time, thinking of Pani Mashko, he began almost to beg pardon of her in his soul, because he had at moments been capable of doubting her, and thinking her an honest woman for even five minutes. Now, at least, he knew what to think of her, and he was thankful. After a while he laughed at his previous fears. In this way he rendered the first tribute due her, contempt. She had ceased to be for him something unattainable, something for which a battle between hope and fear is fought. In spite of himself, he imagined her now as something of his, as his own, always attractive, but for this very reason less valuable. The thought also caused him pleasure, that if he resisted temptation at present, it would be a pure merit. Now, when the doors stood open, he saw with wonder that the desire of resistance increased in him. Once more all that he had said during the sleepless night about faith-breaking flew through his mind. Once more his heart reminded him of Marynia, her justness, her honesty, her approaching motherhood, and that great peace, that real happiness, which he could find only near her; and in the end of all these considerations he decided to go to the city, and not be at Pani Mashko's.

After midday he gave command to bring the horses. When he was seated in Bigiel's carriage he bent over, embraced Marynia at parting, "Amuse thyself well," and drove away. His morning exhaustion had passed; he recovered even his humor, for he felt satisfied with himself. Confidence in his own power and character returned to him. Meanwhile, a certain exciting pleasure was caused in his mind by the thought of Pani Mashko's astonishment when she should learn that he had gone, and had no intention to visit her. He felt a certain need of revenge on the woman for the physical impression which she had produced on him. Since the coming of that note, which she had written to Marynia, his contempt for her had increased with such force that soon he began to think that he would be in a position to come off victorious, even should he visit her.

"And if I should go there, indeed, and give another meaning to yesterday's words," said he. But directly he thought, "I will not be a deceiver, at least, with reference to myself."

He was certain, however, that she would not be astonished at his coming. After what he had told her yesterday, she might suppose that he would find some excuse for visiting her before the arrival of Marynia and the Bigiels, or for remaining behind them.

But should she see him driving past, she might think that he feared her, or consider him a boor, or jester.

"There is no doubt," monologued he, further, "that a man who does not consider himself a fool, or a dolt, incapable of resisting any puppet, would go in and try to correct in some fashion yesterday's stupidity."

But at the same moment fear seized him. That same voice which yesterday evening shouted in his soul that he was a wretch, began to shout again with redoubled energy.

"I will not go in," thought Pan Stanislav. "To understand and to be able to refrain are two different matters."

Pani Kraslavski's villa was visible now in the distance.

Suddenly it flew into his head that Pani Mashko, through vexation and the feeling of being contemned, through offended self-love, through revenge, might tell Marynia something that would open her eyes. Maybe she would do that with one word, with one smile, giving even, it might be, to understand further, that certain insolent hopes of his had been shattered by her womanly honesty, and in that way explain his absence. Women rarely refuse themselves such small revenges, and still more rarely are they merciful one toward another.

"If I had the courage to go in—"

At that moment the carriage was even with the gate of the villa.

"Stop!" said Pan Stanislav to the driver.

He saw on the balcony Pani Mashko, who, however, withdrew at once.

He walked through the yard; the servant received him at the door.

"The lady is upstairs," said he.

Pan Stanislav felt that his legs were trembling under him, when he walked up the steps; meanwhile the following thoughts flew through his head,—

"He may permit himself everything who takes life lightly, but I do not take it lightly. If, after all that I have considered and thought over and said, I could not master myself, I should be the last among men." Now, standing at the door of the room pointed out by the servant, he inquired,—

"Is it permitted?"

"I beg," said the thin voice.

And after a while he found himself in Pani Mashko's boudoir.

"I have come in," said he, giving her his hand, "to explain that I cannot be at supper. I must go to the city."

Pani Mashko stood before him with head a little inclined, with drooping eyes, confused, full of evident fear, having in her posture and expression of face something of the resigned victim, which sees that the decisive moment has come, and that the misfortune must happen.

That state of mind came on Pan Stanislav, too, in one flash; hence, approaching her suddenly, he asked with stifled voice,—

"Are you afraid? Of what are you afraid?"

## CHAPTER LII.

Next morning Pani Polanyetski received a letter from her husband, stating that he would not return that day, for he was going to look at a place situated on the other side of the city. On the following day, however, he returned, and brought Svirski, who had promised Bigiel and Pan Stanislav before that he would visit them at their summer residence.

"Imagine to thyself," said Pan Stanislav, after greeting his wife, "that that Buchynek, which I have been looking at, lies next to old Zavilovski's Yasmen; when I learned that, I visited the old man, who is not feeling well, and in Yasmen I found Pan Svirski, unexpectedly. He helped me to look at Buchynek, and the house pleased him much. There is a nice garden, a large pond, and some forest. Once it was a considerable property; but the land has been sold away, so that little remains now with the residence."

"A pretty, very pretty place," said Svirski. "There is much shade, much air, and much quiet."

"Wilt thou buy it?" inquired Marynia.

"Perhaps. Meanwhile I should like to rent it. We could live there the rest of the summer, and satisfy ourselves as to whether it would suit us. The owner is so certain that a stay there will be agreeable to us that he agrees to rent it. I should have given him earnest-money at once, but I wished to know what thy thought would be."

Marynia was a little sorry to lose the society of the Bigiels; but, noticing that her husband was looking into her eyes earnestly, and that he had an evident wish that they should live the rest of the summer by themselves, she said that she would agree most willingly.

The Bigiels began to oppose, and offer a veto; but when Pan Stanislav represented to them that it was a question of trying a house in which he and Marynia would be likely to live every summer to the end of their lives, they had to confess that the reason was sufficient.

"To-morrow I will engage the place, and carry out all the furniture necessary from Warsaw, and we can move in the day after."

"That is just as if you wished to flee from us as soon as possible," said Pani Bigiel; "why such haste?"

"There is no trouble with packing," answered he, hurriedly; "and you know that I do not like delay."

Finally it was left in this way: that the Polanyetskis were to go to Buchynek in four days. Now dinner was served, during which Svirski told how Pan Stanislav had found him at Zavilovski's in Yasmen.

"Panna Helena wished me to paint her father's portrait," said he, "and to paint it in Yasmen. I went because I was eager for work, and, besides, the old man has an interesting head. But nothing could come of that. They are in a residence with walls two yards thick; for that reason there is poor light in the rooms. I would not paint under such conditions; and then another hindrance appeared, — the model was attacked by the gout. The doctor, whom they took with them to the country, told me that the old man's condition is not good, and may end badly."

"I am sorry for Pan Zavilovski," said Marynia, "for he seems a worthy man. And poor Panna Helena! In the event of his death she will be quite alone. And does he understand his own condition?"

"He does, and he does not; it is his way. He is always an original. Ask your husband how he received him."

Pan Stanislav laughed, and said, —

"On the way to Buchynek I learned that Yasmen was near, and I resolved to go there. Panna Helena took me to her father; but he was just finishing his rosary, and did not greet me till he had said the last 'Hail Mary.' Then he begged my pardon, and said thus: 'Those heavenly matadors in their own order; but with Her a man has more courage, and in old fashion, when She is merciful, all is well, for nothing is refused Her.'"

"What a type he is!" exclaimed Svirski.

The Bigiels laughed, but Marynia said that there was something affecting in such confidence. With this Svirski agreed, and Pan Stanislav continued, —

"Then he said that it was time for him to think of his will, and I did not oppose him, in usual fashion, for with me it is a question of our Pan Ignas. On the contrary, I told him that that was a purely legal matter, for which it was never too early, and that even young people ought to think of it."

"That is my opinion, too," put in Bigiel.

"We spoke also of Pan Ignas; the old man has come to love him heartily."

"Yes!" exclaimed Svirski. "When he learned that I had been in Prytulov, he began at once to inquire about him."

"Then have you been in Prytulov?" inquired Marynia.

"Four days. I like Osnovski immensely."

"And Pani Osnovski?"

"I gave my opinion in Rome of her, and, as I remember, let my tongue out like a scourge."

"I remember too. You were very wicked. How is it with the young couple?"

"Oh, nothing! They are happy. But Panna Ratkovski is there, — a very charming young lady. I lacked little of falling in love with her."

"There it is for you! But Stas told me that you are in love with all ladies."

"With all, and therefore always in love."

Bigiel, hearing this, stopped and said earnestly, —

"That is a good way never to marry."

"Unfortunately it is," said Svirski. Then, turning to Marynia, he said, "Pan Stanislav must have told you of our agreement, — that when you say to me 'marry,' I shall marry. That was the agreement with your husband; therefore I should wish you to see Panna Ratkovski. Her name is Stefania, which means the crowned. A pretty name, is it not? She is a calm kind of person, not bold, fearing Pani Aneta and Panna Castelli, but clearly honest. I had a proof of this. Whenever a young lady is in question, I observe everything and note it down in my memory. Once a beggar came to me in Prytulov with a face like that of some Egyptian hermit from Thebes. Pani Aneta and Panna Castelli rushed out at him with their cameras and photographed him, profile and full face, as much as was possible. But the old man wanted food, I think. He had come hoping for alms, but evidently he hated to ask. Peasants have that kind of feeling. Well, none of those ladies observed this, or at least did not note it; they treated him as a thing, till Panna Ratkovski told them that they were humiliating and hurting the old man. That is a small incident, but it shows heart and delicate feelings. That handsome Kopovski dangles about her; but she is not charmed with the man, like those ladies, who are occupied with him, who paint him, invent new costumes for him, hand him around, and almost carry him in their arms, like a doll. No; she told me herself that Kopovski annoys her; and that pleases me, too, for he has as much sense as the head of a walking-stick."

"As far as I have heard," said Bigiel, "Pan Kopovski needs money; and Panna Ratkovski is not rich. I know that her father, when dying, was in debt to a bank for a sum which, with interest, was due on the last day of last month."

"What is that to us?" interrupted Pani Bigiel.

"Thou art right, — that is not our affair."

"But how does Panna Ratkovski look?" inquired Marynia.

"Panna Ratkovski? She is not beautiful, but she has a sweet face, pale complexion, and dark eyes. You will see her, for those ladies expressed a wish to come here some day. And I persuaded them to it, for I want you to see her."

"Well," answered Marynia, laughing, "I shall see her, and declare my sentence. But if it be favorable?"

"I will propose; I give my word. In the worst case, I'll get a refusal. If you say 'no,' I'll go after ducks. At the end of July shooting is permitted."

"Oh, those plans are important!" said Pani Bigiel, — "a wife or ducks! Pan Ignas would not have spoken that way."

"Well, of what use is reason when one is in love?" said Marynia.

"You are right, and I envy him that very condition; not Panna Castelli, though I was in love with her once myself — oh, no! but just that condition in which one does not reason any longer."

"But what have you against Panna Castelli?"

"Nothing. I owe her gratitude, for — thanks to her — I had my time of illusions; therefore I shall never say an evil word of her, though some one is pulling me by the tongue greatly. So, ladies, do not pull me."

"On the contrary," said Pani Bigiel, "you must tell us of both. I will ask you only on the veranda, for I have directed to bring coffee there."

After a time they were on the veranda. The little Bigiels were running about in a many-colored crowd among the trees, circling about like bright butterflies. Bigiel placed cigars before Svirski. Marynia, taking advantage of the moment, went up to her husband, who was standing aside somewhat, and, raising her kindly eyes to him, asked:

"Why so silent, Stas?"

"I am tired. In the city there was heat, and in our house one might smother. I could n't sleep, for Buchynek got into my head."

"I, too, am curious about that Buchynek, dost thou know? In truth, I am curious. Thou hast done well to see the place and hire it; very well." And she looked at him with affection; but, seeing that he seemed really not himself, she said, —

"We will occupy Pan Svirski here, and do thou go and rest a while."

"No; I cannot sleep."

Meanwhile Svirski talked on. "There is no breeze," said he; "not a twig in motion. A genuine summer day! Have you noticed that in the season of heat, and in time of such calm, the whole world seems as if sunk in meditation. I remember that Bukatski found always in this something mystical, and said that he would like to die on such a sunny day, — to sit thus in an armchair, then fall asleep, and dissipate into light."

"Still, he did not die in summer," remarked Bigiel.

"No, but in spring, and in good weather. Besides, taking things in general, he did not suffer, and that is beyond all."

Here he was silent a while, and then added, —

"As to death, we may and should be reconciled to it, and death has never made me indignant; but why pain exists, that, as God lives, passes human understanding."

No one took up the consideration, so Svirski, shaking the ashes from his cigar, said, —

"But never mind that. After dinner, and with black coffee, it is possible to find a more agreeable subject."

"Tell us of Pan Ignas," said Pani Bigiel.

"He pleases me. In all that he does and says the lion's claw is evident, and, in general, his nature is uncommon, immensely vital. During those two days in Prytulov we became acquainted a little more nearly, and grew friendly. You have no idea how Osnovski has grown to like the man; and I told Osnovski openly that I feared that Pan Ignas might not be happy with those ladies."

"But why?" asked Marynia.

"That is difficult to say, since one has no facts; but it

is felt. Why? Because his nature is utterly different from theirs. You see, that all the loftier aspirations, which for Pan Ignas are the soul of his life, are for those ladies merely an ornament, — something like lace on a dress worn for guests, while on common days the person who owns it goes about in a dressing-gown; and that is a great difference. I fear lest they, instead of soaring with his flight, try to make him jog along by their side, at their own little goose-trot, and convert that which is in him into small change for their every-day social out-go. And there is something in him! I do not presuppose that catastrophes of any kind are to come, for I have not the right to refuse them ordinary petty honesty, but there may be non-happiness. I say only this much: you all know Pan Ignas, and you know that he is wonderfully simple; but still, according to me, his love for Castelka is too difficult and exclusive. He puts into it all his soul; and she is ready to give a little bit — so! The rest she would like to keep for social relations, for comforts, for toilets, for visits, for luxuries, for five o'clocks, for lawn-tennis with Kopovski, — in a word, for that mill in which life is ground into bran."

"This may not fit Panna Castelli, and if it does not, so much the better for Pan Ignas," said Bigiel; "but in general it is pointed."

"No," said Pani Bigiel, "that first of all is wicked; in truth, you hate women."

"I hate women!" exclaimed Svirski, raising his hands toward heaven.

"Do you not see that you are making Panna Castelli a common little goose?"

"I gave her lessons in painting, but I have never been occupied in her education."

Marynia, hearing all this, said, threatening Svirski, —

"It is wonderful that such a kind man should have such a wicked tongue."

"There is a certain justice in that," answered Svirski; "and more than once have I asked, am I really a kind man? But I think that I am. For there are people who calumniate their neighbors through a love for digging in the mud, and that is vile; there are others who do this through jealousy, and that is equally vile. Such a man as Bukatski talks even for a conceit; but I, first of all, am talkative; second, a human being, and especially a woman, interests me more than aught else in existence; and, finally, the shabbiness and flatness and petty vanities of human nature pain me terribly. And, as God lives, it is because I could wish that all women had wings; but since I see that many of them have only tails, I begin, from amazement alone, to shout in a heaven-piercing voice —"

"But why do you not shout in the same way against men?" inquired Pani Bigiel.

"Oh, let the men go! What do I care for them? Though, to speak seriously, we deserve perhaps to be shouted at more than the ladies."

Here Pani Bigiel and Marynia attacked the unfortunate artist; but he defended himself, and continued, —

"Well, ladies, take such a man as Pan Ignas, and such a woman as Panna Castelli: he has worked hard since his childhood; he has struggled with difficulties, thought hard, given something to the world already, — but what is she? A real canary in a cage. They give the bird water, sugar, and seed; it has only to clean its yellow plumage with its little bill, and twitter. Or is this not true? We work immensely, ladies. Civilization, science, art, bread, and all on which the world stands is absolutely our work. And that is a marvellous work. Oh, it is easy to talk of it, but difficult to do it. Is it right, or is it natural, that men push you aside from this work? I do not know, and at this moment it is not for me a question; but taking the world in general, only one thing has remained to you, — loving; therefore you should know, at least, how to love."

Here his dark face took on an expression of great mildness, and also, as it were, melancholy.

"Take me, for example; I am working apparently for this art of ours. Twenty-five years have I been daubing and daubing with a brush on paper or on canvas; and God alone knows how I slaved, how I toiled before I worked anything out of myself. Now I feel as much alone in the world as a finger. But what do I want? This, that the Lord God, for all this toil, might vouchsafe me some honest little woman, who would love me a little and be grateful for my affection."

"And why do you not marry?"

"Why?" answered Svirski, with a certain outburst. "Because I am afraid; because of you, one in ten knows how to love, though you have nothing else to do."

Further discourse was interrupted by the coming of Pan

Plavitski and Pani Mashko; she, in a dark blue foulard dress with white spots, looked from afar like a butterfly. Pan Plavitski looked like a butterfly also; and, approaching the veranda, he began to cry out, —

"I seized Pani Mashko, and brought her. Good-evening to the company; good-evening, Marynia! I was coming here to you on a droshky till I saw this lady standing out on the balcony; then I seized her, and we came on foot. I dismissed the droshky, thinking that you would send me home."

Those present began to greet Pani Mashko; and she, ruddy from the walk, fell to explaining joyously, while removing her hat from her ash-colored hair, that really Pan Plavitski had brought her away almost by force; for, awaiting the return of her husband, she did not like to leave home. Pan Plavitski pacified her by saying that her husband, not finding her at home, would guess where she was, and for the flight and the lonely walk he would not be angry, for that was not the city, where people raise scandal for any cause (here he smoothed his white shirt-front with the mien of a man who would not be at all astonished if scandal were roused touching him); "but the country has its own rights, and permits us to disregard etiquette."

When he had said this, he looked slyly at Pani Mashko, rubbed his hands, and added, —

"Ha, ha! the country has its rights; I said well, has its rights, and so there is no place for me like the country."

Pani Mashko laughed, feeling that the laugh was becoming, and that some one might admire her. But Bigiel, who, being himself a strict reasoner, demanded logic from all, turned to Plavitski, and said, —

"If there is no place like the country, why do you not move out of the city in summer?"

"How do you say?" asked Plavitski. "Why do I not move out? Because in the city, on one side of the street there is sun, and on the other shade. If I wish to warm myself, I walk in the sun; if it is hot for me, I walk in the shade. There is no place in summer like the city. I wanted to go to Karlsbad, but —"

Here he was silent for a moment; and, remembering only then that what he was giving to understand might expose a young woman to the evil tongues of people, he looked with a gloomy resignation on those present, and added, —

"Is it worth while to think of that pair of years left of my life, that are of no value to me, or to any one?"

"Here it is!" cried Marynia. "If papa will not go to Karlsbad, he will drink Millbrun with us in Buchynek."

"In what Buchynek?" asked Plavitski.

"True, we must announce *la grande nouvelle.*"

And she began to tell that Buchynek had been found and rented and probably would be bought; and that in three days she and her husband would move into that Buchynek for the whole summer.

Pani Mashko, hearing the narrative, raised her eyes to Pan Stanislav in wonder, and inquired, —

"Then are you really going to leave us?"

"Yes," answered he, with a trace of snappishness.

"A-a!"

And for a while she looked at him with the glance of a person who understands nothing and asks, "What does all this mean?" but, receiving no answer, she turned to Marynia and began an indifferent conversation. She was so instructed in the forms of society that only Pan Stanislav himself could perceive that the news about Buchynek had dulled her. But she had divined that her person might come into question, and that those sudden movings might be in connection with her. With every moment that truth stood before her with increasing clearness, and her cold face took on a still colder expression. Gradually a feeling of humiliation possessed her. It seemed to her that Pan Stanislav had done something directly opposed to what she had a right to expect of him; that he had committed a grave offence not only against her, but against all those observances which a man of a certain sphere owes to a woman. And her whole soul was occupied in this because it pained her more than his removal to Buchynek. In certain cases women demand more regard the less it belongs to them, and the more respect the less they are worthy of it, because they need it for their own self-deception, and often too because the infatuation, or delicacy, or comedian character in men gives women all they demand, at least for a season. Still, in this intention of moving in a few days to the opposite side of the city, was involved, as it were, a confession of breaking off relations which was worthy of a boor. Faith-breaking has its own style of *a posteriori* declaration, and has it always, for there is not on earth an example of a permanent relation resting on faithlessness. But this time the rudeness surpassed every measure, and the sowing had given an untimely, peculiar harvest. Pani Mashko's mind, though not very keen by nature, needed no extra effort to conclude that what had met her was contempt simply.

And at this very moment Pan Stanislav thought, "She must have a fabulous contempt for me."

It did not occur to them at the time that in the best event this contempt was a question of time merely. But Pani Mashko caught after one more hope, that this might be some misunderstanding, some momentary anger, some excitability of a fantastic man, some offence which she could not explain to herself, — in a word, something which might be less decisive than seemed apparent. One word thrown out in answer might explain everything yet. Judging that Pan Stanislav might feel the need of such a conversation, she determined to get it for him. Hence after tea she began to prepare for home, and, looking at Pan Stanislav, said, —

"Now I must request one of the gentlemen to conduct me."

Pan Stanislav rose. His tired, and at the same time angry face, seemed to say to her, "If 't is thy wish to have the pure truth, thou wilt have it;" but unexpectedly Bigiel changed the arrangement by saying, —

"The evening is so pleasant that we can all conduct you."

And they did. Plavitski, considering himself the lady's knight for that day, gave her his arm with great gallantry, and during the whole way entertained her with conversation; so that Pan Stanislav, who was conducting Pani Bigiel, had no chance to say one word except "good-night" at the gate.

That "good-night" was accompanied by a pressure of the hand which was a new inquiry — without an answer. Pan Stanislav, for that matter, was glad that he had not to give explanations. He could have given only unclear and disagreeable ones. Pani Mashko roused in him then as much mental distaste as physical attraction, and for both those reasons he considered that if he remained in Bigiel's house, she would be too near him. Moreover, he had sought Buchynek and found it chiefly because active natures, if confined too much, are forced instinctively to undertake and act even when that which they do is not in immediate connection with that which gives them pain. He had not the least feeling, however, that flight from danger was equivalent to a return to the road of honesty, or even led to it; it seemed to him then that it was too late for that, that honesty was a thing lost once and forever. "To flee," said he to himself; "there was a time to flee. At present flight is merely the egotism of a beast disturbed in one lair and seeking another." Having betrayed Marynia to begin with, he will betray Pani Mashko now out of fear that the relation with her may become too painful; and he will betray her in a manner as wretched as it is rude, by trampling on her. That is only a new meanness, which he permits himself like a desperado, in the conviction that, no matter how he may struggle, he will sink into the gulf ever deeper.

At the bottom of these thoughts was hidden, moreover, an immense amazement. If this had happened to some other man, who took life lightly, such a man might wave his hand and consider that one more amusing adventure had met him. Pan Stanislav understood that many would look on the affair in that way precisely. But he had worked out in himself principles, he had had them, and he fell from the whole height of them; hence his fall was the greater, hence he thought to himself, "That which I won, that to which I attained, is no protection whatever from anything. Though a man have what I had, he may break his neck as quickly as if he had nothing." And the position seemed to him simply beyond understanding. Why is this? What is the reason of it? To this question he had no answer; and, having doubted his own honesty and honor, he began now to doubt his own intellect, for he felt that he could grasp nothing, give no answer.

In general, he felt like a man lost in some mental wilderness; he could recover nothing, not even attachment to his wife. It seemed to him that, having lost in himself all human sides, he had lost at the same time the power and right to love her. With no less astonishment did he see that in the bottom of his heart he cherished a feeling of offence against her for his own fall. Up to that time he had not injured any one; hence he could not have known that usually a man has a feeling of offence and even hatred against a person whom he has wronged.

Meanwhile the society, after taking farewell of Pani Mashko, returned home. Marynia walked at her husband's side; but, supposing that he was occupied in calculations touching the purchase of the place, and remembering that he did not like to be interrupted in such cases, she did not break the silence. The evening was so warm that after returning they remained some time on the veranda. Bigiel tried to detain Svirski for the night, saying in jest that such a Hercules could not find room in his little brichka with Plavitski. Pan Stanislav, to whom the presence of any guest was convenient, supported Bigiel.

"Remain," said he. "I am going to the city to-morrow morning; we can go then together."

"But I am in a hurry to paint. To-morrow I wish to begin work early, and if I stay here there will be delay."

"Have you any work to be finished on time?" asked Marynia.

"No; but one's hand goes out of practice. Painting is a kind of work in which one is never permitted to rest. I have loitered much already, at one time in Prytulov, at another here; meanwhile my colors are drying."

Both ladies began to laugh; for that was said by a famous master, who ought to be free from fear that he would forget how to paint.

"It seems to people that when a man has reached a certain skill, he owns it," answered Svirski. "It is a wonderful thing, this human organism, which must either advance or fall back. I know not if this is so in everything, but in art it is not permitted to say to one's self, 'This is enough;' there is no leave to stop. If I cease to paint for a week, not only do I lose adroitness of hand, but I do not feel in power. The hand dulls,—that I can understand,—but the artistic sense dulls also; talent simply dulls. I used to think that this was the case only in my career, for in it technique has enormous significance; but, will you believe me, Snyatinski, who writes for the theatre, told me the same. And in literature like his, in what does technique consist, if not in this? Not to have any technique, or at least, to seem not to have it. Still, even Snyatinski says that he may not stop, and that he falls back or advances in proportion to his efforts. The services of art,—that sounds beautifully. Ah, what a dog service, in which there is never rest, never peace!—nothing but toil and terror. Is that the predestination of the whole race, or are we alone those tortured figures?"

Svirski, it is true, did not look like a tortured figure in any sense; he did not fall into a pathetic tone either, complaining of his occupation. But in his sweeping words there was a sincerity which gave them power. After a while he raised his fist; and, shaking it at the moon, which was showing itself just then above the forest, he cried out, half in joy, half in anger, —

"See that chubby face there! Once it learned to go around the earth, it was sure of its art. Oh, to have one moment like that in one's life!"

Marynia began to laugh, and, raising her eyes unwittingly in the direction of Svirski's hand, said, —

"Do not complain. It is not merely artists who are not free to stop; whether we work on a picture, or on ourselves, it is all one, we must work every hour, otherwise life is injured."

"There is immense need of work," interrupted Plavitski, with a sigh.

But Marynia continued, seeking a comparison with some effort, and raising her brows at the same time, —

"And you see, if any man were to say to himself, even for a moment, 'I am wise enough, and good enough,' that very saying would be neither good nor wise. Now it seems to me that we are all swimming across some deep place to a better shore; but whoso just wishes to rest and stops moving his hands, is drawn to the bottom by his own weight."

"Phrases!" exclaimed Pan Stanislav, on a sudden.

But she, pleased with the aptness of her comparison, answered, —

"No, Stas, as I love thee, they are not phrases."

"If God would grant me to hear such things always," said Svirski, with animation. "The lady is perfectly right."

Pan Stanislav, in reality, was also convinced that she was right; and, what was more, in that darkness, which surrounded him, something began to gleam like a lamp. He was just the man who had said to himself, "I am wise enough, I am good enough, — and I can rest;" he was just the man who had forgotten that there was need of continual effort; he had ceased to move his hands over the depth, and therefore his own weight took him down to the bottom. Such was the case! All these lofty religious and moral principles, which he had gained, he had enclosed in his soul, as a man encloses money in a chest, — and he made dead capital of them. He had them, but, as it were, hidden away. He fell into the blindness of the miser, who cheers himself with hoarded gold, but lives like a mendicant. He had them, but he did not live on them; and, trusting in his wealth, he imagined that his life accounts were closed, and that he might rest. But now a gray dawn, as it were, began in that night which surrounded his thoughts; and out of the darkness began to rise toward him a truth hazy, and as yet undefined, declaring that accounts of that sort could never be closed, and that life is an immense daily, ceaseless labor, which, as Marynia had said, ends only there, somewhere on the other and better shore.

## CHAPTER LIII.

"My dear Pan Ignas, why do you not dress like Pan Kopovski?" asked Pani Bronich. "Naturally, Nitechka values your poetry more than all costumes on earth; but you will not believe how æsthetic that child is, and what perfect knowledge she has in such matters. Yesterday, the poor dear came to me with such a pretty face that if you had seen her you would have melted. 'Aunt,' said she, 'why does Pan Ignas not have white flannel costumes in the morning? It is so elegant for all gentlemen to be in such costumes.' Have something like that made; she will be so glad. You see that Yozio Osnovski too has a flannel suit; he has even a number of them, through attention to Aneta. These are little things, I know; but they affect a woman greatly when she considers what they mean. You have no idea how she sees everything. In Scheveningen all wear such costumes till midday; and it would be disagreeable to her if any one should think that you did not belong to society which knows how to dress. You are so kind, you will buy such a costume; will you not? You will do that for her; and you will not take it ill of me that I speak of what Nitechka likes?"

"Oh," said Pan Ignas, "I'll do so, most willingly."

"How good you are! But, what else did I wish to say? Oh, yes! — and a nice yellow-leather travelling-case. My dear Pan Ignas, Nitechka loves immensely nice travelling-cases; and abroad, as a man looks, so is he valued. Yesterday — I will tell you this as a secret — we looked at Pan Kopovski's travelling-case. It is very nice, and in perfect taste, bought in Dresden. It pleased Nitechka much. Look at it, and buy one something in that style. I beg pardon of you for entering into this matter, but this is a trifle. You see, I know women in general, and I know Nitechka. There is no better way with her than to yield in little things. When it comes to great ones, she will give up everything. Besides, you have heard what chances of marriage she had, and still she chose you. Show her, then, gratitude even in small things. Have you not, as a student of character, noticed that natures capable of great sacrifice reserve themselves for exceptional occasions; but in every-day life they like to be gratified."

"Perhaps I have not thought of this so far."

"Oh, it is true beyond doubt, and that is just Nitechka's nature. But you are not in a position to know what kind of a nature she has, though you should know, for the reason that she chose you. But you men are not able to perceive so many shades of feeling. If it should come to some crisis, you would see that in her there is not one trace of selfishness. May the Lord God preserve her from every trial! but should it come to anything, you would see."

"I know that you esteem Panna Nitechka," said Pan Ignas, with certain animation; "but still you do not think so much good of her as I do."

"Ah, how I love you when you say things like that!" cried Pani Bronich, with delight. "My dear! But, if it is thus, then I will whisper still more in your ear: she loves passionately that gentlemen should wear black silk stockings; but remember that one look is enough for her to see what is silk and what is Scotch thread. My God! do not suppose that I wish to mix in everything. No one is able to keep away so well as I; but it is only a question of this, — that Nitechka should never think that you are not equal to others in any regard whatever. What 's to be done? You are marrying a real artist, who loves that everything around her should be beautiful. And, in truth, she will not be so poor as not to have a right to this. Will she?"

Pan Ignas took out his notebook, and said, —

"I will write down your orders, so as not to forget them."

There was a shade of irony in what he said. Pani Bronich, with her excess of words, her manner of talking, and especially her evident infatuation for things of exceptional superfluity, had made him impatient very often. Pan Ignas was offended by a certain parvenu element in her nature. Since he did not see what palaces she was building with the property of old Zavilovski, he was unable to understand that a sensitive woman could be so unceremonious with him in demands for "Nitechka" when it was a question of the style of their future life. He had supposed previously that it would be just the opposite, and that those ladies would be even over-scrupulous and delicate: this was his first disillusion. On the other hand, he was pained by the bad taste with which Pani Bronich mentioned almost daily the great matches which "Nitechka" might have made, and also her self-denials for his sake; these *self-denials* had not taken place yet. Pan Ignas did not over-estimate himself, but also he did not carry his head lower than was needful; and with that which was in him he considered himself not a worse, but a better match than such men as Kopovski, and the various Colimaçaos, Kanafaropuloses, and similar operatic lay figures. He was indignant at the very thought that they dared to compare these men with him, especially to his disadvantage. Having poetry and love in his soul, he judged that he had that which even princes of this world cannot command always. What his every-day life with Lineta would be, of that he had not thought much hitherto, or had thought in a general way only; but feeling strong, and being ready to seize every fate by the forelock, he trusted that it would be agreeable. To chaffer with this future he had no intention; and when Pani Bronich expressed wishes like these, he had to restrain himself from telling her that they seemed to him vulgar.

Svirski, when stopping at Prytulov, gave out once the striking opinion that love was not blind altogether, but only suffering from daltonism. Pan Ignas thought that the painter had Osnovski in mind, and did not suspect that he himself was a perfect example of a man subject to the infirmity mentioned. He was blind, however, only in reference to Lineta; except her he saw and observed everything with greater readiness than others. And certain observations filled him with astonishment. Omitting his observations on Pani Aneta, her Yozio, and Kopovski, he noticed, for example, that his own relations with Pani Bronich began to change; and from the time that he had become near to her, and she had grown accustomed to him, and confidential, as with a future relative, and the future husband of "Nitechka," she began to have less esteem for his person, his work, and his talent. To an ordinary eye this was invisible, perhaps, but to Pan Ignas it was clear, though he could not explain its origin. The future alone was to teach him that common natures, by contact with persons or things which are higher, lose esteem for them through this familiarity, as if showing involuntarily that whatever becomes near to them must thereby be infected with vulgarity and meanness, and cannot, for that very reason, continue lofty. Meanwhile Pani Bronich disenchanted him more and more. He was impatient at that convenient "Teodor," whose rôle it was to shield with his dignity from beyond the tomb every act of hers; he was amazed at that bird-like mobility of her mind which seized on the wing everything from the region of the good and the beautiful, and turned it at once into empty and meaningless phrases.

Besides, her enormous ill-will for people astonished him. Pani Bronich, almost servile in presence of old Zavilovski, spoke of him with animosity in private; Panna Helena she simply disliked; of Pani Kraslavski and Pani Mashko she spoke with endless irony; of the Bigiels, with contempt; more specially salt in her eye was Marynia. She listened to the praises rendered Marynia by Svirski, Pan Ignas, and Osnovski with the same impatience as if they had been detractions from Lineta. Pan Ignas convinced himself that, in truth, Pani Bronich cared for no one on earth except "Nitechka." But just this love made up in his mind for all her disagreeable peculiarities; he did not understand yet that such a feeling, when associated with hate and exclusiveness, instead of widening the heart, makes it narrow and dry, and is merely a two-headed selfishness, and that such selfishness may be as rude and harsh as if one-headed. Loving Lineta himself with his whole soul, and feeling better and kinder from the time that he had begun thus to love her, he considered that a person who loved really could not be evil at heart; and in the name of their common love, "Nitechka," he forgave Pani Bronich all her shortcomings.

But with reference to Lineta, that quick observer could not see anything. The strongest men make in love so many unhappy mistakes for one reason, — that they array the beloved in all their own sunbeams, not accounting to themselves afterward that this glory with which they are blinded has been put by themselves there. So it was with Pan Ignas. Lineta became accustomed more and more every day to him, and to her own rôle of betrothed. The thought that he had distinguished her, raised her above others, chosen her, loved her, from having been, as once, a continual living source of satisfaction to her vanity and pride, was beginning to lose the charm of novelty, and grow common. Everything which it was possible to win from it for her own personal glory had been won by the aid of Aunt Bronich. The admiration of people had been also "juggled out" of it, as Svirski said; and the statue was so near her eyes now that, instead of taking in the whole, she began to discover defects in the marble. At moments yet, under the influence of the opinion or admiration of others, she regained the recollection and knowledge of its proportions; but she was seized by a kind of astonishment that that man in love with her, looking into her eyes, and obedient to every beck of hers, was that Zavilovski over whom even Svirski loses his head, and whom such a man as Osnovski esteems as some precious public treasure. She could send him at any moment for fresh strawberries, if she wished, or for yarn; the knowledge of this caused her a certain pleasure, hence he was needed. She admired her own power in him, and sometimes she detailed to him impressions of this kind quite sincerely.

Once, when they went out to damp fields, Pan Ignas returned for her overshoes. Kneeling by an alder-tree, he put them on her feet, which he kissed. Then she, looking at that head bent to her feet, said,—

"People think you a great man, but you put on my overshoes."

Pan Ignas raised his eyes to her, and, amused by the comparison, answered joyously, without rising from his knees,—

"Because I love immensely."

"That is all right; but I am curious to know what people would say of it?"

And the last question seemed to occupy her most of all; but Pan Ignas quarrelled that moment with her because she said "you" to him, but he did not notice, however, that, in her "that is all right," there was that peculiar indifference with which things too familiar or less important are slipped over. With a similar half-attention she heard what he said then,—that not being vain, he considers himself a man like his fellows, but that he respects his career, and counts a life the greatest happiness in which it is possible to serve loftily, and love simply. In the feeling of this happiness he embraced her with his arm, so as to have his simple love as near his breast as possible. But when his prominent chin pushed forward still more, as happened whenever he spoke with enthusiasm, Lineta begged him to leave off the habit, as it made him look stern, and she liked joyous faces around her. While her hand was in now, she reminded him also that yesterday, when they were sailing over the pond, and he was tired after rowing, he breathed very loudly. She did not like to tell him then how that "acted on her nerves." Any little thing "acts on her nerves;" but nothing acts like some one who is tired, and breathes loudly near her.

Saying this, she took off her hat and began to fan her face. The breeze raised her bright hair; and in the green shade of the alder-trees, quivering in the sun, which shone in through the leaves, she looked like a vision. Pan Ignas delighted his eyes with her, and in her words admired, above all, the charm of a spoiled child. There was perhaps something more in them; but he neither sought nor found it, just because his love, with all its force, was simple.

Simplicity, however, does not exclude loftiness. Lineta had, in fact, clung like a spider-web to the wings of the bird, which, in spite of her, bore her to heights where one had to feel every movement with the heart, to divine all, to understand all, and where even the mind must exert itself to give expression to feeling. But Lineta was "so lazy,"—she had said so on a time to her soarer, who at present did not even suspect that those heights merely made her tired and dizzy, nothing more.

It happened to her now oftener and oftener to wake in the morning, and remember that she must meet her betrothed, that she must tune herself up to his high note; and this gave her the feeling that a child has, for whom a hard lesson is waiting. She had recited that lesson already; she had answered more or less everything which had been taught her; and she judged that her betrothed ought to give a vacation now. Finally, she had enough of all those uncommonnesses, both of herself and of others, those original sayings, those apt answers, with which she had campaigned in society so far. She felt, moreover, that the supply was exhausted, that the bottom of the well could be seen. There remained to her yet only certain artistic feelings, and that unendurable "Pan Ignas" might be satisfied, if from time to time she showed him now a broad field, now a bit of forest, now a strip of land with yellow grain, as if scattered in the light, and said, "Beautiful! beautiful!" That was easier. He, it is true, could not find words to express admiration of the artistic depth of soul hidden in such a single word as "beautiful;" but if that were true, what more did he want? and why, in conversation, in feelings, in method of loving, did he force her to those useless efforts? If he did not force her, if that came without his knowledge, so much the worse for him, that, being by nature so abrupt, he did not even know it. In such a case let him talk with Steftsia Ratkovski.

With "Koposio," on the other hand, there was no need of effort; his society was real rest for Lineta. The mere sight of him made her gladsome, called out a smile on her face, inclined her to jesting. It is true that Pan Stanislav had once in his life been jealous of Kopovski; but to Pan Ignas, a man who lived a mental life far more exclusively, and therefore measured everything with a measure purely mental, it did not even occur that a maiden so spiritualized and so "wise" as "Nitechka," could for a moment consider Kopovski as other than a subject for witticisms, which she permitted herself continually. Had not Pani Bronich, in spite of all her mental shallowness, grown indignant at the mere hint of giving Lineta to Kopovski? What Pan Ignas had seen between Kopovski and Pani Aneta was no lesson, for he considered his "Nitechka" as the opposite pole of Aneta. "Nitechka," besides, had chosen him, and he was the antithesis of Kopovski; that alone set aside every doubt. "Nitechka" amused herself with "Koposio," painted him, conversed with him, though Pan Ignas could not exhaust his astonishment at this, — how she could avoid falling asleep while he talked; she joked with him, she followed him with a look of amusement, — but only because she was a child yet, needing moments of amusement, and even of vanity. But no one saw better than she his whole measureless stupidity, and no one spoke of it more frequently. How often had she ridiculed it to Pan Ignas!

Not all eyes, however, looked at this amusement of hers in that way, and, above all, Pani Aneta looked at it differently; from time to time she told her husband directly that Castelli was coquetting with Kopovski; to "Yozio" himself this seemed at times to be true, and he had the wish to send Kopovski away from Prytulov politely. This Pani Aneta would not permit: "Since he is paying attention to Steftsia, we have no right to hinder that poor girl's fortune." Osnovski was sorry to lose that dear Steftsia on

Kopovski; but since, in fact, she had no property, and since Aneta wished the match, he would not oppose it.

But he was not able to control himself from astonishment and indignation at Castelka: "To have such a man as Ignas, and coquet with such a fool; to act so, a woman must be a soulless puppet surely." At first he could not understand it. On the hypothesis, however, that Aneta must have been mistaken, he began to observe the young lady diligently; and since, aside from his personal relation to his wife, he was not by any means dull-witted, he saw a number of things which, in view of his friendship for Pan Ignas, disquieted him greatly. He did not admit, it is true, that anything might take place to change the position; but he asked himself what Ignas's future would be with a woman who knew so little how to value him, and who was so slightly developed morally that she not only found pleasure in the society of such a brainless fop, but allowed herself to turn his head, and allure him.

"Anetka judges others by herself," thought Osnovski, "and has really deceived herself, ascribing certain deep feelings to Castelka. Castelka is a puppet; and, if spirits like Anetka and Ignas do not come, nothing rouses her." In this way that unfortunate man, affected with the daltonism of love, while discovering truth on one side, fell into greater and greater error on the other. On "Castelka," therefore, he looked more justly every day, and needed no excessive effort to convince himself that in the relations of that "ideal" "Nitechka" with Kopovski there were jests, it is true, there was much contradiction, teasing, even ridicule; but there was also such an irresistible weakness, and such an attraction, as women with the souls of milliners have for nice and nicely dressed young men. The phenomenal stupidity of Kopovski seemed to increase in country air; but as a recompense the sun gilded his delicate complexion, through which his eyes became more expressive, his teeth whiter, while the beard on his face was lighter, and gleamed like silk. Indeed, brightness shone not only from his youth and beauty, but also from his linen, from his neckties, from his exquisite and simple costumes. In the morning, dressed for lawn-tennis, in English flannel, he had in him the freshness of morning and the dreaminess of sleep. His slender, finished form appeared as if fondlingly through the soft cloth; and how could that bony Pan Ignas, with his insolent Wagner jaw and his long legs, be compared, in the eyes of those ladies, with that "mignon" who called to mind at once the gods of Greece and the fashion sheets, the glyptotheks of Italy and the *table d'hôtes* of Biarritz or Ostend. One should be such an original as that still-water Steftsia to insist, unless from malice, that he was an insufferable puppet. Castelka, it is true, laughed when Svirski said that Kopovski, especially when some question was put to him on a sudden, had an expression in which were evident the sixteen "quarterings" of stupidity in his escutcheon, both on the male and female side. In truth, he had a somewhat absent look, and, in general, could not understand at first what people said to him. But he was so joyous, he seemed so good-natured, and, in spite of a way of thinking which was not over elevated, he was so well-bred, beautiful, and fresh that everything might be forgiven him.

Pan Ignas deceived himself in thinking that only Pani Bronich was pining for things of external richness, and that his betrothed did not even know of those requests with which her aunt comes. Castelka did know of them. Having lost hope that "Pan Ignas" could ever be equal to Kopovski, she wanted at least that he should approach him. For things of external richness she had an inborn leaning, and "aunt," when begging Pan Ignas to buy this or that for himself, merely carried out Lineta's wishes. For her, really, one glance was enough to distinguish silk from Scotch thread, and all her soul was rushing instinctively to silk; for her Kopovski was among men what silk is among textures. Had it not been for Pani Aneta, who restrained the young man, and for the various lofty feelings which she had talked into Lineta, Lineta, without fail, would have married Kopovski. Osnosvki, knowing nothing of all this, was even astonished that that had not taken place; for he, in the end of his observations, had come to the conclusion that both for Lineta and Pan Ignas this would have been perhaps better.

One day he confided these thoughts to his wife, but she grew angry, and said, with great animation,—

"That did not happen, because it could not. No one is obliged to accommodate himself to Yozio's plans. I, first of all, saw that Castelka was coquetting with Kopovski. Who could know that she was such a nature? To be betrothed and to coquet with other men,—that passes human understanding. But she does it through vanity, and through spite against Steftsia Ratkovksi, and maybe to rouse jealousy in Pan Ignas. Who knows why? It is easy for Yozio to talk now, and to throw all the blame on me for having made this marriage; let Yozio remember better how many times he was enchanted with Castelka, how many times he said that hers was an uncommon nature, and that just such a one would make Pan Ignas happy. A pretty uncommon nature! Now she is coquetting with Kopovski, and if she were his betrothed she would coquet with Pan Ignas. Whoever is vain, will remain so forever. Yozio says that she was fitted for Kopovski; it was necessary to have that way of thinking at first, not at present, when she is the betrothed of Pan Ignas. But Yozio says this purposely to show me what a folly I committed in helping Pan Ignas."

And the whole affair was so turned by Pani Aneta that Pan Ignas and Castelka descended to the second place, but in the first appeared the cruelty and malice of Yozio. Osnovski, however, began to justify himself, and, opening his arms, said, —

"Anetka! How canst thou even suppose that I wanted to do anything disagreeable to thee? I know, besides, how honest and cordial thy wishes were; but terror takes hold of me when I think of the future of Ignas, for I love him. I should wish from the soul of my heart that God had given him such a person as thou art. My dearest little bird, thou knowest that I would rather lose my tongue than say one bitter thing to thee. I came to thee so just to talk and take counsel, for I know that in that dear head of thine there is always some cure for everything."

When he had said this, he began to kiss her hands and then her arms and face with great affection, and with increasing enthusiasm; but she turned her head aside, twisting away from his kisses, and saying, —

"Ah, how Yozio is sweating!"

He was, in fact, almost always in perspiration, for he played whole days at tennis, raced on horseback, rowed, wandered through fields and forests, to grow thin as far as was possible.

"Only tell me that thou art not angry," said he, dropping her hand, and looking into her eyes tenderly.

"Well, I am not; but what help can I give? Let them

go as quickly as possible to Scheveningen, and let Kopovski stay here with Steftsia."

"See, thou hast found a plan. Let them go at the beginning of August. But hast thou noticed that somehow Steftsia is not very — somehow Kopovski has not pleased her heart so far?"

"Steftsia is secretive as few are. Yozio does n't know women."

"Thou art right surely in that. But I even see that she does n't like Castelka. Maybe, also, she is angry in her heart with Kopovski, too."

"What!" inquired Aneta, with animation, "has Yozio seen anything with reference to Castelka?

Koposio laughs at her, for he has good teeth; but if I should see anything, he would n't be in Prytulov. Maybe, too, Castelka is coquetting with him, because such is her nature — without knowing it. That itself is bad, but that it should go as far as looking at each other seriously, I don't believe.

"But it is necessary to examine Koposio as to Steftsia. Knowest what, Yozio? I will go this very day with him on horseback to Lesnichovka, and I will talk with him rather seriously. Go thou in another direction!"

"Good, my child. But see, thy head is finding measures already!"

Going out, he stopped on the threshold, thought a while, and said, —

"But how wonderful all this is! and how it passes understanding! This Ignas catches everything on the wing; and at the same time he worships Castelka as if she were some divinity, and sees nothing and nothing."

In the afternoon, when Kopovski and Pani Aneta were riding along the shady road to the forest cottage, Pan Ignas followed them with his eyes, and looked at her figure on horseback, outlined in the well-fitting riding-dress. "She is shaped like a slender pitcher," thought he. "But how elegant and enticing she is! There is in this some irony of life, that that honest and kindly Osnovski divines nothing."

And truly there was irony of life in that, but not in that only.

## CHAPTER LIV.

SINCE the day when Pani Aneta and Kopovski made the trip to Lesnichovka, something had changed in the social relations of the dwellers in Prytulov. Pan Ignas looked, it is true, as formerly, into the eyes of his affianced, and was enchanted with her beyond measure; but in her intercourse with him and with others there was a certain light shade of ill-humor. Kopovski felt as if bound; he looked at Lineta by stealth only. He approached her hurriedly, and only in the absence of Pani Aneta; but he sat oftener near Panna Ratkovski, to whom he spoke, as it were, with his mind in another place. Pani Aneta was, moreover, more determined than usual; and, to the great satisfaction of "Yozio," she extended now such watchful care over every affair in Prytulov, that she took Kopovski aside twice for personal explanations. Lineta's glance did not follow Kopovski with that former half-gladsome, half-ironical freedom; but the cloudy eyes of Panna Ratkovski turned to Pan Ignas with a certain sympathy,—in one word, something had changed both in looks and relations.

But those were changes observable only to a very quick eye, and one accustomed to look at life of that kind, in which, for lack of greater objects and severe daily labor, the least shade of feelings and the most subtle movement of thoughts, and even dispositions, take on not only the form of far-reaching events, but frequently conceal the actual germs of such events in themselves. Externally life remained just the same it had been; that is, a kind of daily festival, a May day, country idleness, interwoven with love, æsthetic impressions, more or less witty conversations, and, finally, amusements. The arrangement of a whole series of these amusements, to fill out the day, was the sole occupation which weighed on their thoughts; and even this, for the greater part, Pan Osnovski took on himself as master of the house.

But on a certain day the uniform calm of that life was broken by a thunderbolt, under the form of two black-bordered envelopes addressed to Osnovski and Pan Ignas.

When they were brought in, the whole society was at after-dinner coffee; and the eyes of the ladies were turned with curiosity and alarm at the readers, who, taking cards from the unsealed envelopes, cried almost simultaneously,—

"Pan Zavilovski is dead!"

The news made a deep impression. Pani Bronich, as a person of the old school, and remembering those days when the coming of a courier in the country obliged the most sensitive ladies to faint, even before it was known what the courier had brought, fell into a kind of numbness, joined to loss of speech; Panna Ratkovski, who had spent some time at Pan Zavilovski's, and cherished great friendship for him and his daughter, grew pale in real earnest; Panna Lineta, seizing Pani Bronich's hand, tried to restore her to consciousness, whispering, "*Voyons, chère, tu n'es pas raisonnable!*" Pani Aneta, as if wishing to verify with her own eyes the substance of the announcement, took the card from her husband's hands, and read,—

"The respected Pan Eustachius Zavilovski departed this life on the 25th day of July. His grief-stricken daughter invites relatives and friends to the funeral, at the parish church in Yasmen, on the 28th day of the current month."

Then followed a moment of silence, which was broken by Pan Ignas.

"I knew him little," said he, "and was prepossessed against him once; but now I grieve for him sincerely, for I know that at heart he was a worthy man."

"And he loved thee sincerely," answered Osnovski. "I have proofs of that."

Pani Bronich, who, during this time, had recovered, declared that those proofs might appear now in their fulness, and that the heart of the deceased would very likely prove itself still greater than they imagined. "Pan Eustachius always loved Nitechka much, and such a man cannot be malicious." At times he had reminded her—that is, Pani Bronich—of Teodor, and therefore she had become so attached to him. He was, it is true, as abrupt on occasions as Teodor was gentle at all times; but both had that honesty of spirit which the Lord God is best able to value.

Then she turned to "Nitechka," reminding her that the least emotion would add to the sinking of her heart, and begging her to strive this time not to yield to innate sensitiveness. Pan Ignas, too, with the feeling that a common sorrow had struck him and Lineta for the first time, began to kiss her hands. This state of mind was broken by Kopovski, who said, as if in meditation on the transitory nature of human affairs, —

"I am curious to know what Panna Helena will do with the pipes left by her father."

In fact, the old noble's pipes were famous throughout the whole city. Through dislike for cigarettes and cigars, he had in his day made a great collection in his mansion for lovers of the pipe. Kopovski's anxiety about the pipes was not quieted, however, — first, because at that moment they brought Pan Ignas a letter from Pan Stanislav, containing also intelligence of the old man's decease, and an invitation to the funeral; secondly, because Osnovski began to advise with his wife about the trip to Yasmen.

It ended in this, — that all were to go at once to the city, where the ladies would set about buying various small articles of mourning, and on the second day, the day of the funeral, they would be in Yasmen. Thus did they do. Pan Ignas, immediately after their arrival, went to his lodgings to carry home things, and prepare a black suit for mourning; and then he went to the Polanyetskis, supposing that they, too, perhaps, had come in from the Bigiels. The servant informed him that his master had been there the day before, but had gone at once to Yasmen, near which place he had hired, or even bought, a house two weeks earlier.

Hearing this, he returned to Osnovski's villa to spend the evening with his betrothed.

At the entrance, the tones of a waltz by Strauss, coming from the depth of the house, astonished him. Meeting in the next salon Panna Ratkovski, he inquired who was playing.

"Lineta is playing with Pan Kopovski," answered she.

"Then Pan Kopovski is here?"

"He came a quarter of an hour since."

"And Pani and Pan Osnovski?"

They have not returned yet; Aneta is making purchases."

Pan Ignas, for the first time in his life, felt a certain dissatisfaction with Lineta. He understood that the deceased was nothing to her; still the moment for playing a four-handed waltz with Kopovski seemed inappropriate. He had a feeling that that showed want of taste. Pani Bronich, who did not lack society keenness, divined evidently that impression on his face.

"Nitechka was moved greatly, and worn out," said she; "and nothing calms her like music. I was much alarmed, for sinking of the heart had begun with her; and when Pan Kopovski came, I myself proposed that they play something."

They stopped playing; and Pan Ignas's unpleasant impression disappeared by degrees. There was for him in that villa a multitude of recent and precious remembrances. About dusk he took Lineta's arm, and they walked through the rooms. They stopped in various places; he called to mind something every moment.

"Dost remember," asked he, in the studio, "when painting, thou didst take me by the temple to turn my head aside, and for the first time in life I kissed thy hand; and thy words, 'Talk with aunt'?—I lost not only consciousness, but breath. Thou, my chosen, my dearest!"

And she answered,—

"And how pale thou wert then!"

"It is difficult not to be pale when the heart is dying in one from emotion; and I loved thee beyond memory."

Lineta raised her eyes, and said after a while,—

"How wonderful all this is!"

"What, Nitechka?"

"That it begins somehow, and begins as if it were a kind of trial, a kind of play; then one goes farther into it, and all at once the trap falls."

Pan Ignas pressed her arm to his bosom, and said,—

"Ah, yes! it has fallen! I have my bright maiden, and I won't let her go."

Then, walking on, they came to the great drawing-room. Pan Ignas pointed to the glass door, and said,—

"Our balcony, our acacia-tree."

It grew darker and darker. Objects in the room were sunk in shade; only here and there, on golden picture frames, gleamed points of light, like eyes of some kind gazing at the young couple.

"Dost thou love me?" asked Pan Ignas.

"Thou knowest."

"Say yes."

"Yes."

Then he pressed her arm more, and said with a voice changed through rising emotion,—

"Thou hast no idea, simply, how much happiness is in thee. I give thee my word; thou hast no idea. Thou knowest not how I love thee. I would give my life for thee. I would give the world for one hair of thine. Thou art my world, my life, my all. I should die without thee."

"Let us sit down," whispered Lineta; "I am so wearied."

They sat down, resting against each other, hidden in the dark. A moment of silence followed.

"What is the matter? Thou art trembling all over," whispered Lineta.

But she too, whether stirred by remembrances, or borne on by his feeling, or by nearness, began to breathe hurriedly, and, closing her eyes, was the first to put her lips forward toward his.

Meanwhile Kopovski was bored evidently in the adjoining room with Panna Ratkovski and Pani Bronich, for at that moment the tones of the waltz which he had played before with Lineta were heard.

When Pan Ignas returned to his own lodgings, the place seemed the picture of sadness and loneliness, a kind of objectless nomad dwelling, after which there will not be one memory; and he thought that that golden "Nitechka" had so wound herself around his heart that in truth he would not live without her, and could not.

The funeral, on the third day, was not numerously attended. The neighboring estates, as lying near the city, belonged for the greater part to rich people, who passed the summer season abroad; hence not many of Pan Zavilovski's acquaintances had remained in the city. But numerous throngs of villagers had assembled, who, crowding into the church, looked at the coffin as if with wonder that a man of such wealth, wading in property, in money and riches, was going into the ground like the first chance peasant who lived in a hut somewhere. Others looked with envy on the young lady to whom "so much wealth" was to fall. And such is human nature that not only peasants, but refined people, distant or near acquaintances of Pan Zavilovski, were unable even during the burial itself to refrain from thinking what that Panna Helena would do with those millions which were left her for the drying of tears. There were some too, who, supposing young Zavilovski as the last relative of that name, the heir of a considerable part of the property, gave themselves in secret the question whether that lucky poet, and millionnaire of the morrow, perhaps, would stop writing verses. And they thought, as if with a certain unexplained satisfaction, that he would probably.

But the chief attention was turned to Panna Helena. All wondered at the resignation with which she bore the loss, — the more painful, since after the death of her father she remained in the world all alone, without relatives nearer than the young poet, and even without friends, concerning whom she had long since ceased to busy herself. She walked after the coffin with a face over which tears were flowing, but which was calm, with that calmness usual to her, but somewhat lifeless and stony. On her return from the church, she spoke of the death of her father as if a number of months at least had passed since it happened. The ladies of Prytulov could not understand that an immense faith was speaking through her; and that in virtue of her faith, that death, in comparison with another, which she had survived, but which had rent her soul, seemed something that was sad, it is true, but at the same time a blessing, pressing out tears of sorrow, but not of despair. In fact, old Pan Zavilovski died very piously, though almost suddenly. From the time of his arrival in Yasmen, he had the habit of confessing twice a week; hence he did not lack religious consolation. He died with the rosary in his hand, in his armchair, having fallen previously into a light sleep, without any suffering; his usual pain having left him a few days before, so that he had even begun to gain the hope of a perfect return of health. Panna Helena, while speaking of this, in her low uniform voice, turned at last to Pan Ignas and said, —

"He mentioned you very often. Perhaps an hour before death he said that if you should come to Buchynek to Pan Polanyetski, to let him know, for he wished to see you without fail. Father loved and esteemed you greatly, greatly."

"Dear lady," said Pan Ignas, raising her hands to his lips, "I join you in mourning for him sincerely."

There was something noble and truthful, as well in his tones as in his words, therefore Panna Helena's eyes filled with tears; but the weeping of Pani Bronich was so loud that, had it not been for a flask of salts given her by Lineta, it would have passed into a nervous attack, very likely.

But Panna Helena, as if not hearing those sobs, thanked

Pan Stanislav for the aid which she had received from him, — he had occupied himself with those cares which the death of a near friend imposes, in addition to their misfortune, on those who are bereaved. He took all that on himself because of his active nature, and because at that juncture he seized every chance to occupy himself with something to deaden his thoughts, and escape from the torturing circle of his own meditations.

Marynia did not go to the grave, for her husband did not wish her exposed to crowding and fatigue, but she kept company with Panna Helena in the house, giving her consolation, as she could. Afterward she wished to take her, with the Prytulov ladies, to Buchynek, and even to keep her there a few days. Pan Stanislav supported this request; but as Panna Helena had her old governess at the mansion, she refused, assuring Marynia that in Yasmen it would not be disagreeable at all to her, and that she did not wish to leave it for the first days especially.

But the ladies from Prytulov, who, at the persuasion of Svirski, had intended to visit the Polanyetskis, went willingly with their acquaintances to Buchynek, — all the more since Pani Bronich desired to learn from Pan Stanislav nearer details touching the last moments of the deceased. Marynia, who had looked most curiously at Panna Ratkovski, took her in her carriage, and that happened which happens sometimes in society, — that the two youthful women felt at once an irrestrainable attraction to each other. In Panna Ratkovski's pensive eyes, in her expression, in her "retiring" face, as Svirski called it, there was something of such character that Marynia divined, at the first glance almost, a nature not bold, accustomed to retire into itself, delicate and sensitive. On the other hand, Panna Ratkovski had heard so much of Marynia from Pan Ignas, and heard because other ladies in Prytulov were not willing to lend their ears to praises of their neighbors, that, seeing in her eyes interest and sympathy, to which, in her poverty and loneliness, she was not accustomed, she nestled up with her whole heart to her. In this way they arrived at Buchynek as good friends, and Svirski, who was with Pan Stanislav, Osnovski, and Kopovski, arrived right after them; it did not need any great acuteness to divine that the judgment of Marynia would be for Panna Steftsia.

But he wished to hear it. Marynia began to show the

guests her new residence, which was to be her property, for Pan Stanislav had decided already to buy it. They looked specially at the garden, in which were growing uncommonly old white poplars. Svirski, taking advantage of this walk, gave his arm to Marynia; and on the way back to the house, when the party had scattered somewhat along all the paths, he asked with great precipitance, —

"Well, what is the first impression?"

"The best possible. Ah, what a good and sensitive child that must be! Try to know her."

"I? What for? I will propose this day. You think I will not do that? Upon my word, I will, to-day — and in Buchynek! I have no time for examination and meditation. In those affairs there must be a little daring. I will make a declaration this day, as true as I am here before you."

Marynia began to laugh, thinking that he was jesting; but he answered, —

"I am laughing, too, for there is nothing sad in this; it is no harm that this is a funeral day. I am not superstitious; or rather, I am, for I believe that nothing from your hand can be evil."

"But it is not from my hand; I only made her acquaintance to-day."

"It is all one to me. I have been afraid of women all my life; but of this one, somehow, I have no fear. She simply cannot be a thankless heart."

"I think, too, that she cannot."

"And do you see? this is my last chance. If she accepts me, I will carry her all my life, see?" (here he put his hand in the bosom of his coat); "if not, then —"

"Then what?"

"I 'll shut myself in, and for a whole week will paint from morning till night. I have said that I would go to shoot ducks — but no! This is more important than you think. I judge, however, that she ought to accept me. I know that she does not like that ladies' butterfly, that Kopovski; she is alone in the world, an orphan; she will do me a kindness, for which I shall be grateful all my days, because, really, I am a kind man — but I fear to grow embittered."

Marynia saw now, for the first time, that Svirski might speak seriously; and she answered, —

"You are, in truth, a kind man; hence you will never be embittered."

"On the contrary," answered he, with great animation, "it might end in that; I will be outspoken with you. Do you think that I am as happy as I seem? God knows that I am not. I have gained a little money and fame; that is true. But perhaps there has not been among men another who has so stretched forth his hands to a womanly ideal as I have. What is the result? I have met you, Pani Bigiel, maybe two or three others, worthy, true, sensible, pure as tears. Permit me! I do not wish to say pleasant things to you; but in what I say now I do not wish to announce a criticism, but to discover my suffering. I have seen among our women so much tinsel, so many common, frivolous natures, so much egotism, so much shallowness, so many thankless hearts, so many dolls from a picture, so many false aspirations, that from sight of them ten such men as I am might be embittered." After a while he added: "This child seems different; quiet, mild, and very honest. God grant that it come to pass; God grant her to want me!"

At the same time Pani Bronich, taking Pan Stanislav aside openly, spoke with uplifted eyes,—

"Oh, yes! he reminded me of my years of youth; and, as you see, in spite of this — that for a long time relations between us were broken — I preserved friendship for him to the end of his life. You must have heard! but no! you could not have heard, for I have never mentioned this to any one, that it depended on me alone — to be the mother of Helena. Now there is no longer any need to keep the secret. Twice he proposed to me, and twice I refused him. I respected and loved him always; but you will understand that when one is young, something else is sought for, — that is sought for which I found in my Teodor. Oh, that is true! Once he proposed in Ischia, a second time in Warsaw. He suffered much; but what could I do? Would you have acted otherwise if in my place? Tell me sincerely."

Pan Stanislav, not having the least desire to say, either sincerely or insincerely, how he would have acted in the position of Pani Bronich, replied,—

"Did you wish to ask me about something?"

"Yes, oh, yes! I wanted to ask you about his last moments. Helena said that he died suddenly; but you, who lived so near him, must have visited him, therefore you will remember what he said. Maybe you know what his last intentions and thoughts were? Personally I have not the least interest in the matter. My God! would it not be difficult to act more disinterestedly? You do not know Nitechka? But Pan Zavilovski gave me his word that he would leave Pan Ignas his estates in Poznan. If he did not keep his word, or if he did not try to keep it, may the Lord God forgive him, as I forgive him! Wealth, of course, amounts to nothing. Who has given a better example than Nitechka of disregard for wealth? Were it the opposite, she would not have refused such matches as the Marquis Jao Colimaçao, or Pan Kanafaropulos. You must have heard also of Pan Ufinski, — that same who, with his famous silhouettes, bought for himself a palace in Venice. His last work was to cut out the Prince of Wales. This very year he proposed to me for Nitechka. Oh, true! if any one has sought wealth, it is not we. But I should not wish Nitechka to think that she had made a sacrifice, for still, between us, she is making a sacrifice, and if considered in society fashion, a great sacrifice."

Pan Stanislav was an energetic man, angered by the last words of Pani Bronich, he answered, —

"I have not known either the Marquis Jao Colimaçao or Pan Kanafaropulos, but in this country they are rather fantastic names. I will suppose that Panna Castelli marries Pan Zavilovski out of love; in that case, every sacrifice is excluded. I am an outspoken man, and I say what I think. Whether Pan Ignas is a practical man is another question; but Pan Ignas does not know, and he does not want to ask, what Panna Castelli brings him. The ladies know perfectly what he brings, even from a society point of view."

"Oh, but you have not heard that the Castellis are descended from Marino Falieri."

"That is precisely what neither I nor any one else has heard. Let us suppose that for me and you such views have no meaning; but since you say, first, that, taking things from a society point of view, Panna Castelli is making a great sacrifice, I do not hesitate to deny that, and to say that, omitting Pan Ignas's talents and social position, the match is equal."

From his tone and face it was evident that if Pani Bronich would not stop at what he said, he was ready to speak more openly; but Pani Bronich, having evidently more than one arrow in her quiver, seized Pan Stanislav's hand, and, shaking it vigorously, exclaimed, —

"Oh, how honest you are, to take the part of Ignas so earnestly, and how I love him, as my own son! Whom have I in the world if not those two? And if I inquire whether you know of any arrangement made by Pan Zavilovski, I do so only through love for Pan Ignas. I know that old people like to put off and put off, just as if death let itself be delayed by that. Oh, death will not be delayed! no, no! Helena has no use for all those millions; but Ignas — he might then spread his wings really. For me and Nitechka the question beyond all questions is his talent. But if anything should come to pass — "

"What can I tell you?" said Pan Stanislav. "That Pan Zavilovski was thinking of Ignas is for me undoubted, and I tell you why. About ten days since, he gave command to bring some old arms to show them to me; thereupon he turned to his daughter, and I heard him say to her, 'These are not worth enumerating in the will; but after my death give them to Ignas, for you have no use for them.' From this I infer that either he made some will in favor of Ignas, or thought of it. Further I know nothing, for I made no inquiry of him. Should there be any new will, it will be known in a couple of days, and Panna Helena of a certainty will not hide it."

"Do you know that honest Helena well? But no, no! You do not know her as I know her, and I can be a surety for her. Never suspect her in my presence! Helena hide a will? Never, sir!"

"Let the lady be so kind as not to ascribe to me a thought which I have not, and from which I guard myself. The will can in no case be concealed, for it is made before witnesses."

"And do you see that it is not even possible to conceal it, for it is drawn up before witnesses? I was sure that it could not be concealed; but Pan Zavilovski loved Nitechka so much that even out of regard for her, he could not forget Ignas. He carried her in his arms when she was so big, see." Here Pani Bronich put one hand above the other, so as to give Pan Stanislav in that manner an idea of how big Lineta might have been at the time; but after a while she added, "And maybe she was n't even that big."

Then they returned to the rest of the company, who, having finished a survey of the garden, were assembling for dinner. Pan Stanislav, looking at the charming face of Lineta, thought that when Pan Zavilovski carried her in his arms, she might, in fact, have been a nice and pretty child. Suddenly he remembered Litka, whom he carried in his arms also, and inquired,—

"Then are you an old acquaintance of the deceased?"

"Oh—so," answered Lineta. "About four years. Aunt, how long is it since we became acquainted with Pan Zavilovski?"

"Of what is that dear head thinking?" exclaimed Pani Bronich. "Ah, my dear, what a happy age! and what a happy period!"

During this time Svirski, who was sitting near Panna Ratkovski, felt that it would not be so easy for him to carry out the promise given Marynia as it had seemed to him. Witnesses hindered him, and, still more, a certain alarm about the heart, joined to a loss of usual presence of mind and freedom. "To think," said he to himself, "that I am a greater coward than I supposed." And he did not succeed. He wanted at least to prepare the ground, and he talked of something different from what he wished; he noticed now that Panna Ratkovski had a beautiful neck, and pearl tones about her ears, and a very charming voice—but he noticed with astonishment that this made him still more timid. After lunch the whole company sat together as if through perversity. The ladies were wearied by the funeral; and when, an hour later, Pani Aneta announced that it was time to return, he felt at once a sensation of disappointment and relief.

"It is not my fault," thought he; "I had a fixed purpose."

But when the ladies were taking their places, the feeling of solace changed into sorrow for himself. He thought of his loneliness, and of this, that he had no one on whom to bestow his reputation or his property; he thought of his sympathy for Panna Ratkovski, of the confidence which she had roused in him, of the sincere feeling which he had conceived for her at the first glance,—and at the last moment he took courage.

Giving his arm to the young lady to conduct her to the carriage, he said,—

"Pan Osnovski has asked me to come again to Prytulov, and I will come, but with a brush and palette; I should like to have your head."

And he stopped, trying how to pass from that which he had said to that which he wished to say, and feeling at the same time that he needed to hurry immensely, for there was no time. But Panna Ratkovski, evidently unaccustomed to this, that any man should occupy himself with her, inquired with unfeigned astonishment, —

"Mine?"

"Permit me to be your echo," replied Svirski, hurriedly, and in a somewhat stifled voice, "and to repeat that word."

Panna Ratkovski looked at him as if not understanding what the question was; but at that moment Pani Aneta called her to the carriage, so Svirski had barely time to press her hand and say, —

"Till we meet again."

The carriage moved on. Her open parasol hid the face of Panna Ratkovski quickly; the artist followed with his eyes the departing ladies, and at last gave himself the question, —

"Have I made a declaration, or not?"

He was certain, however, that Panna Ratkovski would think, during the whole drive, of what he had told her. He thought, also, that he had answered adroitly, and that he had made good use of her question. In this regard he was satisfied; but at the same time he was astonished that he felt neither great joy nor fear, and that he had a certain dull feeling that something was lacking in the whole matter. It seemed to him that, in a moment so important, he was too little moved. And he returned from the gate to the house in thoughtfulness.

Marynia, who had seen the parting from a distance, had red ears from curiosity. Though her husband was not in the room at that moment, she dared not ask first; but Svirski read so clearly in her eyes the question, "Have you proposed?" that he laughed, and answered just as if she had inquired, —

"Yes, almost. Not completely; there was no chance for further conversation, so I could not receive an answer. I do not know even whether I was understood."

Marynia, not seeing in him that animation with which he had spoken to her before, and, ascribing this to alarm, wished to give him consolation, but the entrance of Pan Stanislav prevented her. Svirski too began to take farewell at once; but wishing evidently to satisfy her curiosity before he went away, he said, not regarding the presence of Pan Stanislav, —

"In every case I shall be in Prytulov to-morrow, or I shall write a letter; I hope that the answer will be favorable."

Then he kissed her hands with great friendship, and, after a while, found himself alone in his droshky, in clouds of yellow dust, and in his own thoughts.

As an artist he was so accustomed to seizing in artist fashion various details which intruded themselves on his eyes that he did so even now, but mechanically, without proper consciousness, as if only at the surface of his brain. But in the depth of it he was meditating on everything that had happened.

"What the devil, Svirski!" said he to himself; "what is happening to thee? Hast thou not passed twenty-five years so as to be able to jump over this ditch? Has not that happened for which thou wert eager this morning? Where is thy transport? thy delight? Why art thou not shouting, At last! Thou art about to marry! Dost understand, old man? At last! At last!"

But that was vain urging. The internal man remained cold. He understood that what had happened ought to be happiness; but he did not respond to it. Greater and greater astonishment was seizing him. He had acted, it seems, with all knowledge and will and choice. He was not a child, nor frivolous, nor a hysterical person, who knows not what he wants. Having reasoned out, finally, that it would be well, he had not changed his opinion. Panna Ratkovski, too, was ever that same retiring, "very reliable person;" why did the thought that she would be the "little woman," desired from of old, not warm him more vigorously? Why did hope, changed now almost into certainty, not turn into joy? And at the bottom of his soul there remained a certain feeling of disappointment.

"What I told her," thought he, "might be adroit, but it was dry. Let a thunderbolt strike me, if it was not, and, besides, it was unfinished. Simply I have no certainty yet, and I do not feel the thing as finished."

Here the impressions of an artist interrupted the thread of his thought. Sheep scattered on a sloping field visible from the road shaded by distance, and also bathed in the sunlight, seemed on the green background bright spots, with a strong tint of blue fringed with gold.

"Those sheep are sky blue, — impressionists are right in a small degree," muttered Svirski; "but may the devil take them! I am going to marry!"

And he returned to his meditations. Yes! The result did not answer to his hope and expectation. There are various thoughts which a man does not wish to confess to himself; there are feelings also which he does not wish to turn into definite thoughts. So it was with Svirski. He did not love Panna Ratkovski, and here was the direct answer to all the questions which he put to himself. But he dodged this answer as long as he could. He did not like to confess that he took that girl only because he had a great wish to marry. He wanted to explain to himself that he did not feel the affair finished, which was an evasion. He was not in love! Others reached love through a woman; but he wanted to fit a woman to his general internal demand for loving, — that is, he went by a road the reverse of the usual one. Others, having a divinity, built for it a church; he, having a church ready, was bringing into it a divinity, not because he had worshipped the divinity with all his power previously, but because it seemed to him not badly fitted for the architecture of the temple. And now he understood why he had shown so much ardor and resolution in the morning, but was so cold at that moment. By this was explained too the immense impetus in carrying out his plan, and the want of spiritual "halleluia," after it had been carried out.

Svirski's astonishment began to pass into sadness. He thought that he would have done better, perhaps, if, instead of thinking so much about a woman, instead of forming theories of what a woman ought to be, he had caught up the first girl who pleased his heart and senses. He understood now that a man loves the woman whom he does love, and that he does not fit to her any preconceived ideas, for ideas of love — like children — can be born only of a woman. All this was the more felt by him since he was conscious that he could love immensely; and he saw more and more positively that he was not loving as he might love. He remembered what in his time Pan Stanislav had told him in Rome of a certain young doctor, who, trampled by a thoughtless puppet, said: "I know what she is; but I cannot tear my soul from her." There was love strong as death; that man loved! It is unknown why Panna Castelli and Pan Ignas came at once to Svirski's mind; he remembered also Pan Ignas's face as he had seen it in Prytulov, lost in contemplation and, as it were, rapt into Heaven.

And again was roused in him the artist, who by whole years of custom takes the place of the man, even when the man is thinking of things the most personal. For a while he forgot himself and Panna Ratkovski, and thought of Pan Ignas's face, and of that which formed specially its most essential expression. Was it a certain concentrated exaltation? Yes! but there was something else which was still more essential.

And suddenly he trembled.

"A wonderful thing," thought he; "that is a tragic head."

## CHAPTER LV.

A FEW days later Pan Ignas was summoned by Pan Stanislav, and went to the city. The young man had a great desire to remain in Prytulov; but Panna Helena wished absolutely that he should be present at the opening of her father's will. He went, therefore, with Pan Stanislav and the grand-nephew of old Pan Zavilovski, — the advocate Kononovich, — for that purpose to Yasmen. But when Pan Ignas, during the two following days, in his letters to "Nitechka," poured forth on paper only his feelings, and made not the least reference to the will, Pani Bronich, whom such effusions had delighted up to that time, confessed now, as a secret, to Pani Aneta, that that was a stupid way of writing to a betrothed, and that there was *quelque chose de louche* in a silence which was as if designed. The first of those letters was sent, it is true, from the city, the second immediately after his arrival in Yasmen; the old lady insisted, however, that in every case Pan Ignas should have mentioned his hopes, at least, for by silence he showed "Nitechka" a lack of confidence, and simply offended her.

Osnovski insisted, on the contrary, that Pan Ignas was silent concerning his hopes through delicacy toward Lineta; and on this subject it came to a little dispute between him and Pani Bronich, who on that occasion uttered a psychic principle, that men in general have too weak a conception of two things: logic and delicacy. "Oh, that is true! As to logic, it is not your fault, perhaps; but you are that way, my Yozio, all of you." Not being able, however, to stay two days in one place, she went to the city on some plausible pretext, so as to find an informant in the question of the will.

Returning on the following day, she brought with her, first, Pani Mashko, whom she met at the Prytulov station, and who had been wishing for a long time to visit "that dear Anetka," and second, information that no new will of Pan Zavilovski had been found, and that the only and sole heiress of his immense property was Panna Helena. This news had been received in Prytulov already, by the third letter from Pan Ignas, which Lineta had received meanwhile; still its confirmation by Pani Bronich produced an uncommon impression, so that the arrival of Pani Mashko passed unobserved, as it were. This was all very strange. Those ladies had made the acquaintance of Pan Ignas as a man without property. Lineta became his betrothed when there were no hopes of a will. The affair had been arranged first under the influence of Pani Aneta, who was "firing the boilers, since there was need to move, and move quickly;" it took place under the influence of the general enthusiasm roused by Pan Ignas's poetry, under the influence of his fame; through the vanity of Pani Bronich and Lineta, which vanity felt not only satisfied, but borne away by this fact, that that famous and celebrated Zavilovski, who had turned all eyes to himself, was kneeling at the feet of no one else, but just "Nitechka." It took place, finally, for the sake of public opinion, which could not but glorify a young lady who had no thought for property, but only for that mental wealth which Pan Ignas possessed. It is true that, having begun in this way, everything went farther by the force too of that elemental rush, which, when once it has seized people, bears them on, without their will, as the currents of rivers bear objects swept away by them Be what might, Lineta became the betrothed of a man without property; and had it not been for those hopes which rose afterward, neither she nor Pani Bronich, nor any one else, could have or would have taken it ill of Pan Ignas that he had no inherited fortune. But such is human nature, that just because those hopes had risen, and by rising had made Pan Ignas an imposing match in the full measure, no one could help feeling a certain disappointment when they were blown apart now by the wind of reality. Some were grieved sincerely; others, like Kopovski and like Pani Mashko, who did not know herself why, felt a certain satisfaction at such a turn of affairs, but even such a true friend as Osnovski could not resist some feeling of disappointment.

Pan Ignas, in his last letter to Lineta, wrote among other things: "I should like to have wealth for thy sake; but what meaning has all wealth for me if compared with thee! I say sincerely that I have ceased to think of it; and I know that thou, whose feet walk not on the earth, art troubled no more than I am. And, as truly as I love thee, I am not troubled at all. These great assurances which I make are for me immensely sacred; hence thou must believe me. Various wants and lacks threaten people in life, but I tell thee this simply, I will not give thee to any one. Thou art my golden! my one dear child, and lady."

Lineta showed this letter to Pani Aneta, to Panna Ratkovski, and on the arrival of her aunt, to her aunt, of course. Pan Ignas had, indeed, not deceived himself as to her in this regard at least, that if in all Prytulov there was no talk of anything but old Pan Zavilovski's will, Lineta would be silent amid those conversations and regrets. It may be that her eyes assumed to a certain degree their former dreamy expression; maybe at the very corners of her mouth, when people spoke of Pan Ignas, something like a minute wrinkle of contempt might be gathered; maybe, finally, she talked very much with "aunt" evenings, when, after the general good-night, they went to their own rooms; but like a person who "does not walk on the earth," never did she raise her voice in this question before people.

"Koposio," once on a time, when they were left alone for a minute, began to talk with her about it; but she put her finger first to her own lips, and then pointed from a distance toward his lips, in sign that she did not wish such conversation. What is more, even Pani Bronich spoke before her little and guardedly concerning her disappointment. But when "Nitechka" was not in the room, the old woman could not stop the flow to her mouth of that bitterness which had risen in her heart; this flow carried her a number of times so far that she lacked little of quarrelling with Osnovski.

Osnovski, casting from his soul that feeling of disappointment which he had not been able to ward off at first, tried now with all his power to decrease the significance of the catastrophe, and show that Ignas was in general an exceptional match, and even in a financial view, quite a good one.

"I do not think," said he, "that he would have stopped writing had he been old Zavilovski's heir; but the mere management of such an immense property would have taken so much time that his talent might have suffered. As the question is of Ignas, I remember, aunt, what Henry VIII. said, when some prince threatened Holbein: 'I can make ten lords out of ten peasants, if the fancy comes to me; but out of ten lords I cannot make one Holbein.' Ignas is an exceptional man. Believe me, aunt, I have always considered Lineta a charming and honest girl, and have always loved her; but she really rose in my eyes only when she appreciated Ignas. To be something in the life of a man like him, is what any woman might envy her. Is it not true, Anetka?"

"Of course," answered Pani Osnovski; "it is pleasant for a woman to belong to a man who is something."

Osnovski seized his wife's hand, and, kissing it, said, half in jest, half in earnest,—

"And dost thou not think that this often torments me, that such a being as thou art should belong to such a zero as Yozio Osnovski? But it is hard to help it! The thing has happened; and, besides, the zero loves much."

Then he turned to Pani Bronich,—

"Think, aunt," said he, "Ignas has a number of thousands of rubles of his own; and, besides, after his father's death he will have what old Zavilovski secured to him. Poor he will not be."

"Oh, naturally," answered Pani Bronich, shaking her head contemptuously; "Nitechka, in accepting Zavilovski, did not look for money, of course; if she had looked for money, it would have been enough for us to raise a hand at Pan Kanafaropulos."

"Aunt! Mercy!" exclaimed Pani Aneta, laughing.

"But nothing has happened," said Osnovski. "It is sure that Panna Helena will not marry, and the property will pass sometime, if not to Ignas, to his children,—that's the whole affair."

Seeing, however, that the face of Pani Bronich was depressed continually, he added after a while,—

"Well, aunt, more agreement with the will of God! more calmness. Ignas is not an inch less."

"Of course," answered she, with a tinge of anger; "of course all that changes nothing. Zavilovski in his way has talent; and every one must confess that in his way he forms a match beyond all expectations. Oh, yes; of this there cannot be two opinions. Of course nothing is to be said of the property, all the more since people tell various things of the ways by which old Pan Zavilovski increased it so greatly. May God be good to him, and pardon him for having deceived me, it is unknown why! This very day Nitechka and I prayed for his soul. It was difficult to do otherwise. Of course I should prefer that he had not had that inclination to untruth, for it may be a family trait. Nitechka and I would prefer, too, that Pan Ignas had given us less frequently to understand that he would be an heir of Pan Zavilovski."

"I beg pardon most earnestly," interrupted Osnovski, with vigor. "He never gave that to be understood. Aunt will permit — this is too much. He did not wish to mention it; aunt asked him in my presence."

But Pani Bronich was in her career, and nothing could stop her; so she said, with growing irritation, —

"He did not give Yozio to understand this, but he gave me to understand it. Nitechka can testify. Besides, I said to Yozio, 'Never mind this matter.' Of course nothing has changed; and if we have some grief, it is at least not from this cause. Yozio has never been a mother; and as a man he can never understand how much fear we mothers feel at the last moment before giving a child into strange hands. I have learned of late, just now, that Zavilovski, with all his qualities, has a violent temper; and he has. I have always suspected him of something similar; and that being so, it would be simply death for Nitechka. Pan Polanyetski himself did not deny that he has a violent temper. Pan Polanyetski himself, though his friend, so far as men can be friends, gave to understand that his father, too, had a violent temper, and because of it fell into insanity, which may be in the family. I know that Pan Ignas seems to love Nitechka, in as far as men can love truly; but will that love last long? That he is selfish, Yozio himself will not deny; for that matter, you are all selfish. Then let Yozio not be astonished that in these recent hours terror seizes me when I think that my darling may fall into the hands of a tyrant, a madman, and an egotist."

"No," cried Osnovski, turning to his wife; "as I love thee, one's ears simply wither; one may simply lose one's head."

But Pani Aneta seemed to amuse herself with that conversation as she would in a theatre. The quarrels of her husband with Pani Bronich always amused her; but now she was carried away more than usual, for Pani Bronich, looking at Osnovski as if with pity, continued, —

"Besides, that sphere! All those Svirskis and Polanyetskis and Bigiels! We are blinded in Zavilovski, all of us; but, to tell the truth, is that sphere fit for Nitechka? Hardly. The Lord God himself made a difference between people; and from that comes a difference in breeding. Perhaps Yozio does not give himself a clear account of this, for, in general, men are unable to give account to themselves of such matters; but I tell Yozio that there are shades and shades, which in life may become enormously important. Has Yozio forgotten who Nitechka is, and that if anything pains such a person as Nitechka, if anything wounds her, she may pay for it with her life? Let Yozio think who those people are, speaking among ourselves, — such people as the Polanyetskis, and such men as Svirski, and that whole company with which Pan Ignas associates, and with which he will force Nitechka to associate, perhaps!"

"Well, let us take things from that point of view," interrupted Osnovski. "Very well! Let it be so. First of all, then, who was old Pan Zavilovski? That aunt knows clearly enough, even out of regard to her own relations with him. If it is a question, aunt, of the sphere, I have the honor to say that we all, in relation to such people as the Polanyetskis, are parvenus, and are taking liberties with them. I never enter into genealogies; but since aunt wants them, let aunt have them. Aunt must have heard that the Svirskis are princes. That line which settled in Great Poland dropped the title, but has the right to it; that is who they are. As to us, my grandfather was a manager in the Ukraine, and I do not think of denying that. Out of what did the Broniches grow? Aunt knows better than I do. I do not touch that matter; but, since we are alone, we can speak openly. Of the Castellis, too, aunt knows."

"The Castellis are descended from Marino Falieri," exclaimed Pani Bronich, with enthusiasm.

"Beloved aunt! I remind thee that we are alone."

"But it depended on Nitechka to become the Marchioness Colimaçao."

"*La vie parisienne!*" answered Osnovski. "Aunt knows that operetta. There is a Swiss admiral in it."

Pani Aneta was amused to perfection; but it became disagreeable to Osnovski that he had raised in his own house reminiscences which were not agreeable to Pani Bronich, hence he added, —

"But why all our talk? Aunt knows how I have always loved Nitechka, and how from the core of my heart I wished her to be worthy of Ignas."

But this was pouring oil on the flames, for Pani Bronich, hearing this blasphemy, lost the last of her cool blood, and exclaimed, —

"Nitechka worthy of Ignas? Such a — "

Happily the entrance of Pani Mashko interrupted further conversation. Aunt Bronich was silent, as if indignation had stopped the words in her mouth; Pani Aneta began to inquire of Pani Mashko what the rest of the company were doing, and where she had left them.

"Pan Kopovski, Lineta, and Stefania remained in the conservatory," answered Pani Mashko; "the two ladies are painting orchids, and Pan Kopovski amused us."

"How?" asked Osnovski.

"With conversation; we laughed heartily. He told us that his acquaintance, Pan Vyj, who very likely is a great man at heraldry, told him in all seriousness that there is a family in Poland with the escutcheon, 'Table legs.'"

"If there is one," muttered Osnovski, humorously, "it is the family of the Kopovskis, beyond doubt."

"And did Steftsia remain, too, in the conservatory?" asked Pani Aneta.

"Yes; they are sketching together."

"Dost wish to go to them?"

"Let us go."

But at that moment the servant brought letters, which Pan Osnovski looked over, and delivered. "For Anetka, for Anetka!" said he; "this little literary woman has an enormous correspondence always. For you," added he, turning to Pani Mashko; "for aunt; and this is for Steftsia, — somehow a known hand, quite familiar. The ladies will permit me to carry her this letter."

"Of course; go," said Pani Aneta, with animation; "and we will read ours."

Osnovski took the letter and went in the direction of the conservatory, looking at it, and repeating, "Whence do I know this hand? — as if — I know that I have seen this hand."

In the conservatory he found three young people, sitting under a great arum at a yellow iron table, on which the orchid was standing. Both ladies were painting it in albums. Kopovski, a little behind them, dressed in a white-flannel costume and black stockings, was looking over the shoulders of the young ladies into the albums, smoking meanwhile a slender cigarette, which he had taken from an elegant cigarette-case lying near the flower-pot.

"Good-day!" said Osnovski. "What do you think of my orchids? Splendid, are n't they? What peculiar flowers they are! Steftsia, here is a letter; ask the company to excuse thee, and read it, for it seems to me that I know the handwriting, but I cannot in any way remember whose it can be."

Panna Ratkovski opened the letter, and began to read. After a while her face changed; a flame passed over her forehead, then paleness, and again a flame. Osnovski looked at her with curiosity. When she had finished reading, she showed him the signature, and said, with a voice which trembled somewhat, —

"See from whom the letter is."

"Ah!" said Osnovski, who understood everything at once.

"May I ask thee for a moment's talk?"

"At once, my child," answered he, as if with a certain tenderness; "I will serve thee."

And they went out of the conservatory.

"But they have left us alone for once even," said Kopovski, naively.

Lineta did not answer; but, taking Kopovski's white-leather cigarette-case, which was lying on the table, began to draw it across her face gently.

He looked at that beautiful face with his wonderful eyes, beneath which she simply melted. Lineta had known for a long time what to think of him; his boundless stupidity had no longer any secret from her. Still the exquisiteness and incomparable beauty of that dullard brought her plebeian blood into some uncommon movement. Every hair in his beard had a certain marvellous and irresistible charm for her.

"Have you noticed that for a long time they are watching us, like I know not whom?" continued Kopovski.

But she, feigning not to hear, continued to draw the cigarette-case across her delicate face, and, bringing it nearer and nearer to her lips, said, —

"How soft this is; how pleasant to the touch!"

Kopovski took the cigarette-case; but he put it to his lips and began to kiss lightly the part which a while before had touched Lineta's face. Then a moment of silence rose between them.

"We must go from here," said Lineta.

And, taking the pot of orchids, she wished to put it on steps in the conservatory; she was not able to do so, however, because of the slope of those steps.

"Permit me," said Kopovski.

"No, no!" answered Lineta; "it would fall, and be broken; I will put it on the other side."

Saying this, she went with the pot of orchids in her

hands around to the other side of the steps, where between them and the wall was a narrow passage. Kopovski followed her. There she stepped on to a pile of bricks, and put the orchids on the highest step; but at the moment when she turned to descend, the bricks moved under her feet, and she began to totter. Just at that moment, Kopovski, who was standing behind, caught her by the waist.

For a few seconds they remained in that posture, she leaning with her shoulder against his breast, he drawing her toward him. Lineta leaned over more, so that at last her head was on his shoulder.

"What are you doing? This is wrong!" she began to whisper, with panting breast, surrounding him with her hot breath.

But he, instead of an answer, pressed his mustaches to her lips. All at once her arms embraced his neck with a passionate movement, and she began breathlessly and madly to return his kisses.

In their ecstasy, neither observed that Osnovski, in returning through the open doors of the conservatory, passed along on the soft sand beyond the entrance, and looked at them with a face changed and pale as linen from emotion.

## CHAPTER LVI.

MEANWHILE Pan Ignas spent the time between Warsaw and Buchynek, going from one place to the other daily, remaining now here, now there, just as his work and business commanded. Since his marriage was to take place in the fall, immediately after the season in Scheveningen, Pan Stanislav told him that it was time to find a dwelling, and furnish it, even in some fashion. He and Bigiel promised every assistance in that affair. Pani Bigiel was to see to the part which pertained to housekeeping. Pan Ignas's presence in Buchynek was necessary also in view of his relations with Panna Helena. Though the will of her father, bearing date a year earlier, made her the only heiress of the whole immense property, she did not hide in the least that she knew that her father did not make another will simply because either he had not foreseen a death so sudden, or had deferred the matter from day to day, in the manner of old people. She had not the least doubt, however, that her father wished to do something for a man of the same name, and a relative; and she said openly that she held it a duty to carry out her father's wish. No one, it is true, could foresee in what measure she would decide to do that; and for her too it was difficult to answer such a question, before she had made an exact inventory of all the properties and moneys; meanwhile, however, she began to present Pan Ignas with everything which, in her opinion, male heirs should inherit. In this way, she gave him a part of the household plate, left after the deceased, as well as a considerable and valuable collection of arms, which the old man prized, and horses greatly esteemed by him, — these Polanyetski took on commission; and, finally, that collection of pipes the fate of which had concerned Kopovski so much.

Cold, and apparently indifferent to all, intimidating people by her severe and concentrated expression of face, she had for Pan Ignas alone, in her voice and look, a certain something almost motherly; just as if with the property she had inherited from her father his inclination for the young man. He was indeed the only person on earth with whom she was connected by bonds of blood, or at least by identity of name. Learning from Pan Stanislav of the steps taken by Pan Ignas toward furnishing a house, she begged him to put in the bank for her a considerable sum in the name of "Pan Ignas," for outlays toward that end, begging, however, not to mention the matter to him immediately.

Pan Ignas, who had a young and grateful heart, became attached to her quickly, as to an elder sister; and she felt perfectly that sympathy of two natures, who wish each other well, and feel mutual confidence. Time usually changes original sympathies of that sort into great, enduring friendship, which in evil periods of life may be of great support. But at that juncture, Pan Ignas could devote to her barely a tiny part of his soul; for he had applied soul, heart, and all his powers, with the entire exclusiveness of a fanatic in love, to the greater and greater adoration of "Nitechka."

Meanwhile he was as busy as a fly in a pot, between Buchynek and the city, and even made new acquaintances. One of these was Professor Vaskovski, who had returned from his pilgrimage among the "youngest of the Aryans." He had visited the shores of the Adriatic, and the entire Balkan peninsula; but the state of his health was so pitiful that Pan Stanislav took him for good to Buchynek, to save the poor man from being cheated, and to give him needful care, which in his loneliness he could not have found in another place. Pan Ignas, himself a person of lofty soul, and ready to grasp every broad idea, though it might seem absurd to common-sense fools, conceived from the first day a love for the old man, with his theory of a historical mission predestined to the youngest of the Aryans. Of this theory he had heard already more than once from Svirski and Polanyetski, and considered it a splendid dream. But it struck him and Svirski and the Polanyetskis that the professor, on returning from his journey, answered only that "No one could escape the service which Christ had preordained to him;" then he gazed forward with his mystic eyes, as if seeking something, or looking for something in infinity, and his old face took on an expression of such deep sorrow, and even of such pain, that no one had the heart to touch that particular question. The doctor called in by Polanyetski declared that the greasy kitchen of the youngest of the Aryans had given the old man a serious catarrh of the stomach, to which was added *marasmus senilis.* The professor had, in fact, a serious catarrh of the stomach; but Pan Ignas divined in him something else,—namely, a desperate struggle between doubt and that in which he believed, and to which, as a real maniac-idealist, he had devoted a lifetime. Pan Ignas alone understood the whole tragedy of such a final *ergo erravi;* and he was doubly moved,—first, as a man with a heart, second, as a poet, who at once saw a theme for a poem: the old man before the house, in the sun, sitting on the ruin of his life and beliefs, with the words, "vanity, vanity," on his lips, and waiting for death, whose steps he hears now in the distance.

But with the professor it was not so bad, perhaps, as Pan Ignas had imagined. "The youngest of the Aryans" might, indeed, have disappointed him; but there remained the faith that Christianity had not uttered its last word yet, and that the coming epoch in the life of humanity would not be anything else than a spreading of the spirit of Christ, and a transfer of it from relations between individuals to general human relations. "Christ in history" did not cease to be for him a vision of the future. He believed even always that the mission of introducing love into history was predestined to the youngest of the Aryans; but from the time of his journey a deep sadness had seized him, for he understood that, before that could be realized, not only he, but whole generations, must die of catarrh of the stomach, caused by the indigestible kitchen of principalities on the Danube.

Meanwhile he shut himself up in himself, and in silence which had more the appearance of life-sorrow than it was in reality. Of his "idea," he hardly ever spoke directly, but the idea was evident. Just as the hand of a clock, stopped at a certain hour, never indicates any hour but that, so the indicator of his thought did not desert that idea; for to various questions he answered with words which were rather connected with it than the thing touching which he was questioned. Whenever they wished to call him back to reality, it was needful to rouse him. In dress he neglected himself utterly, and seemed every day to forget more and more that buttons on a vest, for example, are there to be buttoned. With his eternal absence of mind; with his eyes both short-sighted and child-like, reflecting in some mechanical way external impressions; with a face of concern, on which pimples had become still more evident because of defective digestion; finally, with a neglect of dress, and his wonderful trousers, which, it is unknown for what reason, were twice as wide as the trousers of other men, — he roused mirth in strangers, and became frequently the object of jokes more or less malicious. It seems that he roused such feelings first of all in the "youngest of the Aryans." In general, they considered him as a man in whose head the staves lacked a hoop; but some showed him compassion. The word "harmless" struck his ears frequently, but he feigned not to hear it. He felt, however, that at Pan Stanislav's he was comfortable; that no one laughed at him, no one showed him the compassion shown idiots.

Finally, neither the too greasy kitchen of the "youngest of the Aryans," nor the catarrh of the stomach, had taken away his boundless forbearance, and his kindness to people. He was always that dear old professor who fell into revery, but who recovered his senses when it was a question of others. He loved, as of old, Marynia, Pan Stanislav, Pani Emilia, Svirski, the Bigiels, even Mashko, — in a word, all those with whom life had brought him in contact. In general, he had a certain strange understanding of people; namely, that all, whether willing or unwilling, were serving some purpose, and were like pawns which the hand of God is moving for reasons which He Himself knows. Artists, like Svirski, he esteemed as envoys who "reconcile."

He looked in the same way on Pan Ignas, whose poetry he had read before. On becoming acquainted with the author, he looked at him as curiously as at some peculiar object; but in the morning, when the poet had gone to the city, and they began to talk about him during tea, the old man raised his finger, and, turning to Marynia, said, with a look of mystery, —

"Oh, he is God's bird! He does not know what God wrote on his head nor to what He designed him."

Marynia told him of Pan Ignas's approaching marriage, of his feeling for Panna Lineta, and of her, praising her goodness and beauty.

"Yes," said the professor, when he had heard all, "you see she too has her mission, and she too is 'chosen.' God commanded her to watch over that flame; and since she is chosen, she should be honored for having been chosen. Do you see? Favor is upon her." Then he grew thoughtful and added, "All this is precious for humanity in the future."

Pan Stanislav looked at his wife, as if wishing to say that the professor was dreaming disconnectedly; but the latter blinked somewhat, and, looking before him, continued, —

"There is in the sky a Milky Way; and when God wishes, He takes dust from it and makes new worlds. And you see, I think there is likewise a spiritual Milky Way, made up of all that people have ever thought and felt. Everything is in it, — what genius has accomplished, what talent has wrought; in it are the efforts of men's minds, the honesty of women's hearts, human goodness, and people's pains. Nothing perishes, though everything turns to dust, for out of that dust, by the will of God, new spiritual worlds are created for people."

Then he began to blink, weighing what he had said; after that, as if coming to himself, he looked for the buttons of his vest, and added, —

"But that young woman must have a soul pure as a tear, since God pointed her out and designated her to be the guardian of that fire."

Svirski's arrival interrupted further conversation. For Marynia it was not a surprise, as the artist had promised her that either he would come himself or write to inform her what turn his affair had taken. Marynia, seeing him now through the window, was nearly certain that all had ended auspiciously; but when he had entered the room and greeted every one, he looked at her with such a strange face that she did not know what to divine from it. Evidently he wished to speak of the affair, and that immediately; but he did not like to do so before the old professor and Pan Stanislav. So the latter, to whom Marynia had told everything, came to his aid, and, pointing to his wife, said, —

"She needs a walk greatly; take her to the garden, for I know that she and you have some words to say."

After a while they found themselves in the alley among the white poplars. They walked a time in silence, he swaying on his broad hips of an athlete, and seeking for something from which to begin, she bent somewhat forward, with her kindly face full of curiosity. Both were in a hurry to speak, but Svirski began at another point.

"Have you told all to your husband?" asked he, on a sudden.

Marynia blushed as if caught in a fault, and answered, —

"Yes; for Stas is such a friend of yours, and I do not like to have secrets from him."

"Of course not," said Svirski, kissing her hand. "You did well. I am not ashamed of that, just as I am not ashamed of this, that I got a refusal."

"Impossible! You are joking," said Marynia, halting.

"I give you my word that I am not." And, seeing the pain which the news caused her, he began to speak as if with concern. "But don't take it more to heart than I do. That happened which had to happen. See, I have come; I am standing before you; I have not fired into my forehead, and have no thought of doing so; but that I got a basket[1] is undoubted."

"But why? what did she answer you?"

"Why? what did she answer me?" repeated Svirski. "You see, just in that is hidden something from which there is a bitter taste in my mouth. I confess to you sincerely that I did not love Panna Ratkovski deeply. She pleased me; they all please me. I thought that she would be an honest and grateful heart, and I made a declaration here; but more through calculation, and because it was time for me. Afterward I had even a little burning at the heart. There was even a moment when I said to myself, 'Thy declaration in Buchynek was not precise enough; better put it forward another corner.' I grew shamefaced. 'What the deuce!' thought I; 'thou hast crossed the threshold with one foot; go over with the other.' And I wrote her a letter, this time with perfect precision; and see what she has written as an answer."

Then he drew a letter from his coat-pocket, and said, before he began to read it, —

"At first there are the usual commonplaces, which you know. She esteems me greatly; she would be proud and happy (but she prefers not to be); she nourishes for me sincere sympathy. (If she will nourish her husband as she does that sympathy, he will not be fat.) But at the end she says as follows: —

"'I have not the power to give you my heart with such delight as you deserve. I have chosen otherwise; and if I never shall be happy, I do not wish at least to reproach myself hereafter with not having been sincere. In view of what has happened here I cannot write more; but believe me that I shall be grateful to you all my life for your confidence, and henceforth I shall pray daily that God permit you to find a heart worthy of you, and to bless you all your life.'

"That is all."

[1] Was rejected.

A moment of silence followed; then Svirski said, —

"So far as I am concerned, these are empty words; but they mean, I love another."

"That is the case, I suppose," replied Marynia, sadly. "Poor girl! for that is an honest letter."

"An honest letter, an honest letter!" cried Svirski. "They are all honest, too. That is why it is a little bitter for me. She does n't want me. All right; that is permitted to every one. She is in love; that, too, is permitted. But with whom is she in love? Not with Osnovski or Pan Ignas, of course. With whom, then? With that head of a walking-stick, that casket, that pretty man, that tailor's model, — with that ideal of a waiting-maid. You have seen such beautiful gentlemen depicted on pieces of muslin? That is he, perfectly. If he should stand in a barber's window, young women would burst in the glass. When he wishes, he puts on a dress-coat; when not, he goes so, and all right! You remember what I said of him, — that he was a male houri? And this is bitter, and this is ill-tasting" (he spoke with growing irritation, accenting with special emphasis the word *is*), "and this speaks badly of women; for be thou, O man, a Newton, a Raphael, a Napoleon, and wish thou as thy whole reward one heart, one woman's head, she will prefer some lacquered Bibisi. That 's how they are."

"Not all women, not all. Besides, as an artist, you should know what feeling is. Something falls on a person, and that is the end of all reasoning."

"True," said Svirski, calmly; "I know that not all women are so. And as to love, you say that something falls, and there is an end. Perhaps so. That is like a disease. But there are diseases by which the more noble kinds of creatures are not affected. There is, for instance, a disease of the hoofs. You will permit me to say that it is needful to have hoofs in order to get this disease. But there has never been a case that a dove fell in love with a hoopoo, though a hoopoo is a very nice bird. You see that does n't happen to the dove. Hoopoos fall in love with hoopoos. And let them fall in love for themselves, if only they will not pretend to be doves. That is all I care. Remember how I spoke once against Panna Castelli at Bigiel's. And still she chose Pan Ignas at last. For me, it is a question of those false aspirations, that insincerity, and those phrases. If thou art a hoopoo's daughter, have the courage to own it. Do not pretend; do not lie; do not deceive. I, a man of experience, would have wagered my neck on this, that Panna Ratkovski is simply incapable of falling in love with Kopovski; and still she has. I am glad that here it is not a question of me, but of comedy, of that conventional lying, — and not of Panna Ratkovski, but of this, that such a type as Kopovski conquers."

"True," said Marynia; "but we ought to find out why all this has become entangled somehow."

But Svirski waved his hand. "Speaking properly," said he, "it is rather unravelled. If she had married me! surely I should have carried her at last in my arms. I give you my word. In me immensely much tenderness is accumulated. I should have been kind to her, and it would have been pleasant for both of us. I am also a little sorry for it. Still, she is not the only one on earth. You will find some honest soul who will want me; and soon, my dear lady, for in truth at times I cannot endure as I am. Will you not?"

Marynia began to be amused, seeing that Svirski himself did not take the loss of Panna Ratkovski to heart so very greatly. But, thinking over the letter a little more calmly, she remembered one phrase, to which she had not turned attention at first, being occupied entirely with the refusal, and she was disquieted by the phrase.

"Have you noticed," asked she, "that in one place, she says, 'After what has happened here I cannot write more'? Can you think what that may be?"

"Perhaps Kopovski has made a declaration."

"No; in such a case she would have written more explicitly. If she has become attached to him, she is a poor girl indeed, for likely she has no property, and neither is Pan Kopovski rich, they say; therefore he would hardly decide —"

"True," said Svirski; "you know that that came to my mind, too. She is in love with him, — that is undoubted; but he will not marry her." Then he stopped, and said, "In such a case, why is he staying there?"

"They amuse themselves with him, and he amuses himself," answered Marynia, hurriedly, while turning away her face somewhat, so that Svirski might not notice her confusion.

And she answered untruly. Since Pan Stanislav had shared his views with her touching Kopovski's relations with Pani Osnovski, she had thought of them frequently;

the stay of the young man in Prytulov seemed to her suspicious more than once, and explaining it by the presence of Panna Ratkovski dishonest. This dishonesty was increased, if Panna Ratkovski had fallen in love really with Kopovski. But all those intrigues might come to the surface any moment; and Marynia thought with alarm then whether the words of Panna Ratkovski — "after what has happened here" — had not that meaning precisely. In such a case it would be a real catastrophe for that honest Pan Osnovski and for Panna Steftsia.

Really everything might be involved in a tragic manner.

"I will go to-morrow to Prytulov," said Svirski; "I wish to visit the Osnovskis, just to show that I cherish no ill-feelings. If anything has happened there really, or if any one has fallen ill, I shall discover it and let you know. Pan Ignas is not there at this moment."

"No. Pan Ignas is in the city. To-morrow, or after to-morrow surely, he will come here, or go to Yasmen. Stas, too, is preparing for the city to-day. Sister Aniela is ill, and we wish to bring her here. Since I cannot go, Stas is going."

"Sister Aniela? That one whom your husband calls Pani Emilia, — a Fra Angelico face, a perfectly sainted face, a beautiful face! I saw her perhaps twice at your house. Oh, if she were not a religious!"

"She is sick, the poor thing. She can barely walk. She has disease of the spine, from overwork."

"Oh, that is bad," said Svirski. "You will have the professor, and that poor woman — But what kind people you are!"

"That is Stas," replied Marynia.

At that moment Pan Stanislav appeared at the end of the walk, and approached them with a hurried step.

"I hear that you are going to the city to-day," said Svirski; "let us go together."

"Agreed!"

And, turning to his wife, he said, —

"Marynia, hast thou not walked enough? Wilt thou lean on me?"

Marynia took his arm, and they walked to the veranda together; after that she went in to give command to bring the afternoon tea.

"I have received a wonderful despatch," said Pan Stanislav; "I did not wish to show it before my wife. Osnovski asks me where Ignas is, and asks that I go to the city on his affair. What can that be?"

"It is a wonderful thing," answered Svirski. "Panna Ratkovski writes me that something has happened there."

"Has any one fallen ill?"

"They would have sent for Pan Ignas directly. If it were Panna Castelli or Pani Bronich, they would summon him at once."

"But if Osnovski did n't wish to frighten him, he would telegraph to me."

And both looked each other in the eyes with alarm.

## CHAPTER LVII.

Next day, half an hour after Pan Stanislav's arrival, Osnovski rang at his house. At the sound of the bell, Pan Stanislav, who had been in great alarm since the day before, went himself to the door. He had admitted for some time that a bomb might burst in Prytulov any day; but he struggled in vain with his thoughts, to discover what connection the explosion might have with Pan Ignas.

Osnovski pressed his hand at greeting with special force, as is done in exceptional circumstances; and when Pan Stanislav invited him to his study, he asked on the way, —

"Are you living in Buchynek?"

"I am; we are perfectly alone."

In the study, Osnovski, when he had sat in the armchair pointed out to him, bent his head and was silent for a while, breathing hurriedly meantime; for in consequence of excessive exercise he was affected somewhat with distention of the lungs. At present emotion, and the steps, obstructed his breath still more. Pan Stanislav waited patiently for some time; at last his inborn curiosity conquered, and he asked, —

"What has happened?"

"A misfortune has happened," said Osnovski, in deep sorrow. "Ignas's marriage is broken off."

"Why?"

"Those are things so disagreeable that it would be better for Ignas perhaps not to know the reasons. For a time, I even hesitated to mention them. But he ought to know all; for this is a question of more importance than his self-love. Indignation and disgust may help him to bear the misfortune. The marriage is broken, for Panna Castelli is not worthy of such a man as Pan Ignas; and if to-day there could be a talk of renewing the relation, I would be the first to veto it decisively."

Here Osnovski began to catch breath again; but Pan Stanislav, who had been listening as if fixed to the floor, burst out suddenly, —

"By the dear God, what has happened?"

"This has happened, that those ladies went abroad three days ago, with Kopovski as the betrothed of Panna Castelli."

Pan Stanislav, who a moment before had sprung up from the chair, sat down again. On his face, with all its emotion and alarm, was reflected unspeakable astonishment. He looked for some time at Osnovski, and then, as if unable to collect his thoughts, said, —

"Kopovski? — and has Panna Castelli gone too?"

But Osnovski was too much occupied with the affair itself to turn attention to the particular form of Pan Stanislav's inquiry.

"It is unfortunate," said he; "you know that I am related to those ladies: my mother was a sister of Pani Bronich, and also of Lineta's mother; and for a time we were reared together. You will understand that I would rather spare them. But let that go. Our relations are broken; and, besides, if Lineta were my own sister, I would say what I say now. As to Pan Ignas, since my wife and I are going, and that to-day I may not find him, I will even say openly that I lack courage to talk with him; but I will tell you what I saw. You, as his near friend, may be able to soften the blow; he should know everything, for in a misfortune of this kind, there is no better cure than disgust."

Here he began to tell Pan Stanislav what he had seen in the conservatory. Excited himself, he lost breath at moments, but was unable to resist a certain astonishment at sight of the feverishness with which Pan Stanislav listened. He had hoped for cool blood in the man; he could not, of course, divine that Pan Stanislav had personal reasons, in virtue of which a narrative of that sort acted more powerfully on his nerves than would news even of the death of Pan Ignas or Panna Castelli.

"At the first moment I lost my head," continued Osnovski; "I am not hasty, but how I avoided breaking his bones, I know not. Perhaps I remembered that he was my guest; perhaps, since it is a question here of something more important than he, I thought of Ignas; perhaps I thought of nothing. I lost my head, and went out. After a time I returned, and told him to follow me. I saw that he was pale, but decided. In my own room I told him that he had acted unworthily; that he had abused the hospitality of an honorable house; and that Lineta was a wretch, for whom I had not sufficient words of contempt; that, by this same act, her marriage with Pan Ignas was broken, — but that I would force him to marry her, though I had to go to extremities. Here it turned out that they must have taken counsel during the interval in which I left them alone; for he told me that he had been in love with Lineta a long time, and that he was ready to marry her at any moment. As to Pan Ignas, I felt that Kopovski was repeating words which Lineta had dictated, for he told me that which he could not have come at himself. He said that he was ready to give every satisfaction, but that he was not bound to count with Pan Ignas, for he had no obligations touching him: 'Panna Lineta has chosen me finally; that,' said he, 'is all the worse for him, but it is her affair.' What was going on meanwhile between aunt and Lineta, I cannot tell; it is enough that before I had finished with Kopovski, Aunt Bronich rushed in like a fury, with reproaches, saying that I and my wife had not permitted Lineta to follow the natural impulse of her heart; that we had thrust her on Pan Ignas, whom she had never loved; that Lineta had cried whole nights, and that she would have paid for that marriage with her life; that what happened now was by the express will of God, — and so for a whole hour. We are to blame; Pan Ignas is to blame, — they alone are faultless."

Here Osnovski rubbed his forehead with his hand, and said, —

"I am thirty-six years of age; but before this affair I could not even imagine what woman's perversity may be. I cannot understand yet such an inconceivable power of perverting things, of placing them bottom upward. I understand what the situation was; I understand that they thought everything finished with Pan Ignas, even for this alone, that I hindered, and that there was no one left for them save Kopovski. But the ease with which white was made black, and black white; that lack of moral sense, that absence of truth and justice, — that egotism without bound or bottom. The deuce might take them were it not for Ignas. He would have been most unhappy with them; but what a blow for a man of such nature, and so much in love; what a deception! But Lineta! Who could have supposed? Kopovski, such a fool, such a fool! And that young woman thought to be so full of impulses; she who a few weeks before exchanged rings, and gave her word! And she the betrothed of Pan Ignas! As God lives, a man might lose his senses."

"A man might lose his senses," repeated Pan Stanislav, as an echo.

A moment of silence followed.

"But is it long since this happened?" asked Pan Stanislav, at last.

"Three days ago they went to Scheveningen together. They started that very day; Kopovski had a passport. See how a supreme ass may still have some cunning. He had a passport ready, for he pretended to pay court to Panna Ratkovski, my cousin, and to be ready to go abroad with us; he pretended to be courting this one, so as to have the chance of turning the other one's head. Ai, poor Pan Ignas, poor man! I give you my word, that if he had been my brother, I should not have had more sympathy for him. Better, better, that he had not bound himself to such a Lineta; but what a crash!"

Here Osnovski took out a handkerchief and rubbed his glasses, blinking meanwhile with a suffering and helpless expression of face.

"Why did you not inform us earlier?" inquired Pan Stanislav.

"Why did I not inform you earlier? Because my wife fell ill. Nervous attacks — God knows what! You will not believe how she took it to heart. And no wonder! Such a woman as she is — and in our house! With her sensitiveness, that was a blow, for it was a deception on the part of Lineta, whom she loved so much; and her sorrow for Ignas, and that contact with evil, and her disgust! On such a pure and sensitive nature as hers is, that was more than was needed. At the first moments I thought that she would be dangerously ill, and even now I say, God grant that it have no fatal effect on her nerves! We simply cannot give an account to ourselves of what takes place in a soul like hers at the very sight of evil."

Pan Stanislav looked carefully at Osnovski, bit his mustache, and was silent.

"I sent for the doctor," continued Osnovski, after a while, "and lost my head a second time. Happily, Stefania Ratkovski was there, and that worthy Pani Mashko. Both occupied themselves with Anetka so earnestly that I shall be grateful to them for a lifetime. Pani Mashko seems cold, but she is such a cordial person — "

"I judge simply," said Pan Stanislav, wishing to turn the conversation from Pani Mashko, "that if old Zavilovski had left his property to Ignas, all this would not have happened."

"Perhaps not; but for me again it is not subject to doubt that if Lineta had married Ignas, and even if he owned all Pan Zavilovski's property, her instinct would attract her toward as many Kopovskis as she might chance to meet in her lifetime; she is that kind of soul. But I understand some points; I have said that it is possible to lose one's mind at the thought that things are as they are, but I give a partial account to myself of what has happened. Hers is too common a nature to love really such a man as Pan Ignas; she needs Kopovskis. But they talked into her various lofty impulses, and finally she talked into herself that which did not exist. They seized on Ignas through vanity, through self-love, because of public opinion, and because they had no true knowledge of themselves; but what is insincere cannot last. From the moment when their vanity was satisfied, Ignas ceased to interest those ladies. Then they were afraid that with him, perhaps, they would not have such a life as alone is of worth to them; perhaps he, with his too lofty style, began to weary them. Add to this the story of the will, which, without being certainly the main cause of the catastrophe, diminished Pan Ignas in their eyes; add, before all, the instincts of Lineta's nature; add Kopovski, and you have an answer to all. There are women like Pani Polanyetski or my Anetka; there are women, also, like Lineta and her aunt."

Here Osnovski was silent again for a time; then he said,—

"I see the regret and indignation of your wife, and I am sorry that you have not seen how this affected mine—or even Pani Mashko. Yes, there are women and women; but I tell you that we ought to thank God every day on our knees for having given us such wives as we have." And his voice trembled with emotion.

Pan Stanislav, though for him it was a question mainly of Pan Ignas, was simply astounded that a man who, some minutes before, understood things so profoundly and well, could be so naive. A bitter smile came on him, too, at mention of Pani Mashko's indignation. In general, he was seized by a feeling of a certain crushing irony of life, the whole immensity of which he had never seen before so distinctly.

"Will you not see Ignas?" asked he, after a while.

"I tell you plainly that I do not feel sufficient courage; to-day I return to Prytulov, and to-day we will go from our station. I must take my wife abroad, — first, because she herself begged me tearfully to do so, and second, perhaps her health will be restored by change of air. We will go somewhere to the seaside, only not to Scheveningen, where they went with Kopovski. But I have a great request to make of you. You know how I love and value Ignas? Let me know by letter how the poor man receives the news, and what happens to him. I would ask the favor of Svirski, but I may not see him."

Then Osnovski covered his face and said, —

"Ai! how sad all this is, how sad!"

"Very well," said Pan Stanislav; "send me your address, and I will report to you how matters turn. But since the grievous mission falls to me of telling Ignas what has happened, lighten it for me. It is necessary that he receive information not from a third person, or a fourth, but from some one who saw everything. If he hears of the event from me, he may think that I represent the affair inaccurately. In such cases a man grasps at every shadow of a hope. Sit down and write to him. I will give him your letter in support of what I tell him; otherwise he may be ready to fly after them to Scheveningen. I consider such a letter indispensable."

"Will he not come here soon?"

"No; his father is sick, and he is with him. He thinks that I shall be here only in the afternoon. Write to him surely."

"You are right, perfectly right," said Osnovski. And he sat down at the writing-desk.

"Irony of life, irony of life!" thought Pan Stanislav; "bloody irony is this which has met Pan Ignas. What is such a person as Panna Castelli, with her bearing of a swan, and her instincts of a chambermaid, — that 'chosen of God,' as Vaskovski said only yesterday? What is Pani Bronich, and Osnovski, with faith in his wife, and the nervous attacks of that wife, caused by the mere contact with evil, of *such a pure* soul, and the indignation of Pani Mashko? Nothing but a ridiculous human comedy, in which some are deceiving others, and others deceiving themselves; nothing but deceived and deceivers; nothing but mistakes, blindness, and errors, and lies of life, and victims of error, victims of deceit, victims of illusions:

a complication without issue; a ridiculous, farcical, and desperate irony, covering the feelings, the passions, and hopes of people, just as snow covers fields in winter—and that is life."

These thoughts were for Pan Stanislav more grievous because, rising on a basis purely personal, they became at once a kind of reckoning with his conscience. He was enough of an egoist to refer everything to himself; and he was not fool enough not to see that in that most ironical human comedy he was playing a rôle immensely abject. His position was of that sort that he wished with all the power of his breath to hiss that Panna Castelli; and still he understood that if there was any one who was not free to judge her, it was he. In what was he better? In what was he less vile? She had betrayed a man for a fool; he had betrayed his wife for a brainless puppet. She had followed her instincts of a milliner; he had followed his instincts of an ape. But she had trampled on artificial phrases merely, with which she deceived herself and others; he had trampled on principles. She had betrayed confidence, and broken her word; he had betrayed confidence also, and broken more than a word,—he had broken an oath. And in view of this what can he say? Has he the right to condemn her? If there is no way to justify her, if he is ready to acknowledge that it would be unjust and deserving of indignation for a person like her to become the wife of Pan Ignas, with what right is he the husband of Marynia? If he can find even one word of condemnation for Panna Castelli,—and it is impossible not to find it,—and he wishes to be consistent, he should separate from Marynia, which he will never have either the will or the power to do. There is a vicious circle for you. Pan Stanislav had passed many bitter moments because of his *success*; but this moment was so grievous that it even filled him with amazement. By degrees it became simply a torture. At last, through the simple instinct of self-preservation, he began to seek for something to give him even momentary relief. But in vain did he say to himself that such people as Kopovski would not have taken his position to heart so. That was the same consolation to him as if he had thought that a cat or a horse would not have taken it to heart so either. In vain he remembered the words of Balzac: "Infidelity, when undiscovered, is nothing; when discovered, it is a trifle." "That 's a lie," repeated he, gritting his teeth, "a pleasant *nothing*, which burns so!" He understood, it is true, that behind the fact itself there may be something which heightens or lessens its criminality; and he understood also that in his case all the circumstances are of a kind to make the fault immense and unpardonable. "Here," thought he, "it takes from me the right of judging, the right of serving with my conscience. Those women sacrificed a man of the loftier kind for an idiot; they trampled him; they pushed him into misfortune, into tragedy, which may break him; they did this in a mean and abject manner, and I cannot, even in my soul, brand such a woman as Panna Castelli." And never before had the truth become to him so nearly tangible that as a man for certain crimes is deprived of a share in public life, so he now had become deprived of a share in moral life. He had had remorse enough already, but now he saw still new desolations, which he had not noted at first. The more he thought over the tragedy of Pan Ignas, and took in its extent with growing clearness, the more he was seized by a dull alarm, and a kind of prescience that in virtue of a higher and mysterious logic, something terrible must happen in his fate as well. For the man who bears in his system the germs of mortal disease, death is a question of time simply.

At last, however, he found this relief, that his thoughts turned exclusively to the present, and to Pan Ignas. How will Pan Ignas receive the news? How will he bear it? In view of the man's exaltation, in view of his deep, blind faith in Lineta, and the love which he feels for her, these questions were simply terrible. "Everything in him will be broken; all will slide away from under his feet in a moment," thought Pan Stanislav. It seemed to him that there was something repulsive and monstrous in this, that even those relations of life which do not bear in them germs of tragedy, and which ought to end well, end badly without any reason; and that life is, as it were, a forest in which misfortunes hunt a man more venomously than dogs hunt a wild beast, for they hunt in silence. Pan Stanislav felt suddenly that besides faith in himself, which he had lost already, there might fail in him various other things too, which are more important, because they are more fundamental.

In this moment, however, he thought more of Pan Ignas than of anything else. He had a good heart, and Pan

Ignas was near him; hence he was touched sincerely by his misfortune. "But that man is simply writing his sentence," thought he, as he heard the squeak of Osnovski's pen in the next room. "Poor fellow! And this is so undeserved."

Osnovski finished the letter at last, and, opening the door, said, —

"I have written guardedly, but written the whole truth. May God give him strength now! Could I think that I should have to send him such news!"

But under the sincere sorrow was evident, as it were, a certain satisfaction with his own work. Clearly he judged that he had succeeded in writing better than he had expected.

"And now I repeat once again an earnest prayer: send me even a couple of words about Ignas. Oh, if this were not so irreparable!" said he, extending his hand to Pan Stanislav. "Till we meet again! till we meet again! I will write to Ignas, too, but now I must go, for my wife is waiting. God grant us to see each other in happier times! Till we meet! A most cordial greeting to the lady," and he went out.

"What is to be done?" thought Pan Stanislav. "Limit myself to sending the letter to Pan Ignas in his lodgings, or look for him, or wait for him here? It would be well not to leave him alone at such a time; but I must return in the evening to Marynia, so that he will be alone in any case. Besides, who can hinder him from hiding? In his place, I should hide too, — I must go to Pani Emilia's."

He felt so tired from that sudden tragedy, from thoughts about himself, and thoughts about the difficult rôle which he had to play with Pan Ignas, that he remembered with some satisfaction that he must go to Pani Emilia's and take her to Buchynek. For a moment he was tempted to defer the interview with Pan Ignas, and the delivery of the letter, till the following day; but it occurred to him that if Pan Ignas did not find him at home, he might go to Buchynek.

"Better let him know everything here," thought he; "in view of Marynia's condition, I must keep everything perfectly secret from her, — both what has happened, and what may happen hereafter. I must warn every one to be silent. Pan Ignas would do better to go abroad; I could tell Marynia that he is in Scheveningen, and later, that they disagreed and separated there."

Now again he began to walk with long strides through the room, and repeat, —

"The irony of life! the irony of life!"

Then bitterness and reproaches flamed in on his soul with a new current. He was seized by a wonderful feeling, as it were, of some kind of responsibility for what had happened. "Deuce take it!" repeated he; "but I am not to blame at least in this matter." After a while, however, it came to his head that if he were not to blame personally, he, in every case, was a stick from the same forest as Panna Castelli, and that such as he had infected that social-moral atmosphere in which such flowers might spring up and blossom. At this thought he was carried away by savage anger.

The bell in the entrance was heard now. Pan Stanislav was a man of courage, but at the sound of that bell he felt his heart beat in alarm. He had forgotten his promise to lunch with Svirski, and at the first moment he was sure that Pan Ignas was coming. He recovered only when he heard the voice of the artist, but he was so wearied that Svirski's coming was disagreeable.

"Now he will let out his tongue; he will talk," thought he, with displeasure.

But he decided to tell Svirski all, for the affair could not be kept secret in any case. The point for him was that Svirski, if he visited Buchynek, should know how to bear himself before Marynia. He was mistaken in supposing that Svirski would annoy him with theories about ungrateful hearts. The artist took the matter, not from the side of general conclusions, but that of Pan Ignas. To conclusions he was to come later; at present, while listening to the narrative, he only repeated, "A misfortune! May God protect!" But at times, too: "May the thunderbolts crush!" when his fists of a Hercules were balled in anger.

Pan Stanislav was carried away somewhat, and attacked Panna Castelli without mercy, forgetting that he was uttering thereby a sentence on himself. But, in general, the conversation gave him relief. He regained at last his usual power of management; he concluded that in no case could he leave Pan Ignas at such a moment, so he begged Svirski to take his place, conduct Pani Emilia to Buchynek, and excuse to Marynia his absence with counting-house duties. Svirski, who had no reason now to visit

Prytulov, agreed very willingly, and since the carriage engaged by Pan Stanislav had arrived, both drove to Pani Emilia's.

Labor beyond her strength — labor which, as a Sister of Charity, she had to fulfil — brought on a disease of the spine. They found her emaciated and changed, with a transparent face and eyelids half closed. She walked yet, but by leaning on two sticks and not having full use of her lower limbs. As labor had brought her near life, so sickness had begun to remove her from it. She was living in the circle of her own thoughts and reminiscences, looking at the affairs of people somewhat as though a dream, somewhat as from the other shore. She suffered very little, which the doctors considered a bad sign; but, as a Sister of Charity, she had learned something of various diseases, and knew that there was no help for her, or, at least, that help was not in human power, and she was calm. To Pan Stanislav's inquiries she answered, raising her eyelids with effort, —

"I walk poorly; but it is well for me that way."

And it was well for her. One moral scruple alone gave her trouble. In her soul she believed most profoundly that were she to visit Lourdes she would regain her health surely. She did not wish to go because of the remoteness of Lourdes from Litka's grave, and because of her own wish for death. But she did not know whether she had a right to neglect anything to preserve the life given her, and especially whether she had a right to put a hindrance in the way of grace and miracles, and she was disturbed.

At present, however, the thought of seeing Marynia smiled on her, and she was ready for the road; Svirski was to take her at five. The two men went now to the lunch agreed on, for Svirski, in spite of his amazement at the affair of Pan Ignas, felt as hungry as a wolf. After they had sat down at table, they remained a while in silence.

"I wanted to make one other request of you," said Pan Stanislav at last, "to inform Panna Helena of everything that has happened, and also to tell her not to mention the matter to my wife."

"I will do so," said Svirski. "I will go this very day to Yasmen, as if to walk, and try to see her. Should she not receive me, I will send her a note, stating that it is a question of Pan Ignas. If she wishes to come to Warsaw, I will bring her, for I shall return to-day in every case. Did

Osnovski say whether Panna Ratkovski had gone with them," inquired the artist, after a pause, "or will she stay in Prytulov?"

"He said nothing. Usually Panna Ratkovski lives with her old relative, Pani Melnitski. If she goes, it will be as company for Pani Osnovski, whose angelic nature got a palpitation of the heart at sight of what has happened."

"Ah!" said Svirski.

"Yes. There is no other cause for it. Panna Ratkovski was stopping with the Osnovskis, so that Kopovski might seem to court her; but since he was courting another, there is no further reason for her stay there."

"As God lives, this is something fabulous!" said Svirski; "so that all, with the exception of Pani Osnovski, fell in love with that hoopoo."

Pan Stanislav smiled ironically and nodded his head; on his lips were sticking the words, "without exception, without exception!"

But now Svirski began his conclusions about women, from which he had refrained so far.

"Do you see; do you see? I know German and French and especially Italian women. The Italians in general have fewer impulses, and less education, but they are honester and simpler. May I not finish this macaroni, if I have seen anywhere so many false aspirations and such discord between natures which are vulgar and phrases which are lofty! If you knew what Panna Ratkovski told me of Kopovski! Or take that 'Poplar,' that 'Column,' that 'Nitechka,' that Panna Castelli, that Lily, is it not? You would swear that she was a mimosa, an artist, a sibyl, a golden-haired tall ideal. And here she is for you! She has shown herself! She has chosen, not a living person, but a lay-figure; not a man, but a puppet. When it came to the test, the sibyl turned into a waiting-maid. But I tell you that they are all palpitating for fashionable lay-figures. May thunderbolts singe them!"

Here Svirski extended his giant fist, and wanted to strike the table with it; but Pan Stanislav stopped the hand in mid-air, and said,—

"But you will admit that something exceptional has happened."

Svirski began to dispute, and to maintain that "they are all that way," and that all prefer the measure of a tailor to that of Phidias. Gradually, however, he began to regain his balance, and acknowledge that Panna Ratkovski might be an exception.

"Do you remember when you inquired touching the Broniches, I said the ladies are *canaille, canaille!* neither principles nor character, parvenu souls, nothing more? He was a fool, and you know her. God guarded me; for if they had known then that I have some stupid old genealogical papers, would n't they have made sweet faces at me, and I might have fixed myself nicely! May the woods cover me! I will go, as you see me, with Pan Ignas abroad, for I have enough of this."

They paid, and went out on to the street.

"What will you do now?" inquired Svirski.

"I shall go to look for Pan Ignas."

"Where will you find him?"

"I think among the insane, with his father; if not, I will wait for him at my own house."

But Pan Ignas was approaching the restaurant just at that moment. Svirski was the first to see him at a distance.

"Ah, there he goes!"

"Where?"

"On the other side of the street. I should know him a verst away by his jaw. Will you tell him everything? If so, I will go. You have no need of spectators."

"Very well."

Pan Ignas, on seeing them, hurried his steps and stood before them, dressed elegantly, almost to a fit, and with a glad face.

"My father is better," said he, with a voice panting a little; "I have time and will drop in at Prytulov to-day."

But Svirski, pressing his hand firmly, went off in silence. The young man looked after him with surprise.

"Was Pan Svirski offended at anything?" asked he, looking at Pan Stanislav; and he noticed then that his face too had a serious, almost stern, expression.

"What does this mean?" asked he, "or what has happened?"

Pan Stanislav took him by the hand, and said, with a voice full of emotion and cordiality, —

"My dear Pan Ignas, I have esteemed you always, not only for exceptional gifts, but for exceptional character; I have to announce very bad news to you, but I am sure that you will find in yourself strength enough, and will not give way to the misfortune."

"What has happened?" asked Pan Ignas, whose face changed in one moment.

Pan Stanislav beckoned to a droshky, and said, —

"Take a seat. To the bridge!" cried he, turning to the driver. Then, taking out Osnovski's letter, he gave it to Pan Ignas.

The young man tore open the envelope hurriedly, and began to read.

Pan Stanislav put his arm with great tenderness around his friend's body, not taking his eyes from his face, on which as the man read were reflected amazement, incredulity, stupefaction, and, above all, terror without limit. His cheeks became as white as linen; but it was evident that, feeling the misfortune, he did not grasp its extent yet, and did not understand it thoroughly, for he looked at Pan Stanislav as if without sense, and inquired with a low voice, full of fear, —

"How — how could she?"

Then, removing his hat, he passed his hand through his hair.

"I do not know what Osnovski has written," said Pan Stanislav, "but it is true. There is no reason to diminish the affair. Have courage; say to yourself that this has happened, and happened beyond recall. You were lost on her, for you are worth more than all that. There are people who know your worth, and who love you. I am aware that this is a mighty misfortune; your own brother would not be pained on your behalf more than I am. But it has happened! My dear Pan Ignas, they have gone, God knows whither. The Osnovskis too. There is no one in Prytulov. I understand what must take place in you; but you have a better future by yourself than with Panna Castelli. God destined you to higher purposes, and surely gave greater power to you than to others. You are the salt of the earth. You have exceptional duties to yourself and the world. I know that it is difficult to wave your hand at once on that which has been loved, and I do not ask you to do so; but you are not permitted to yield to despair like the first comer. My dear, poor Pan Ignas!"

Pan Stanislav spoke long, and spoke with power, for he was moved. In the further course of his speech he said things which were not only heartfelt, but wise: that misfortune has this in itself, that it stands still; while a man, whether he wishes or wishes not, must move on into the future; therefore he goes away from it ever farther and farther. A man drags, it is true, a thread of pain and remembrance behind him; but the thread grows ever more slender, for the force of things is such that he lives in the morrow. All this was true, but it was something by itself; far nearer, more real, more tangible was that which Osnovski's letter mentioned. Beyond the fact described in that letter there existed only empty sounds, striking on his ears externally, but without meaning, and for Pan Ignas as devoid of sense as the rattle of the iron lattice-work on the bridge, past which he was driving with Pan Stanislav. Pan Ignas could feel and think only in an immensely dull way; he had, however, the feeling first that what had happened was simply impossible, but still it had happened; second, that in no measure could he be reconciled to it, and never would he be reconciled, — a fact, however, which had not the least significance. There was no place in his head for another idea. He was not conscious of having lost anything except Lineta. He was not conscious of pain or sorrow or ruin or desolation, or the loss of every basis of life; he knew only that Lineta had gone, that she had not loved him, that she had left him, that she had gone with Kopovski, that the marriage was broken, that he was alone, that all this had happened, and that he did not want it, — as a thing incredible, impossible, and dreadful. Still, it had happened.

The droshky moved slowly beyond the bridge, for they were passing through a herd of oxen driven toward the city; and in the midst of the heavy tramping of these beasts, Pan Stanislav continued. Pan Ignas's ears were struck by the words, "Svirski, abroad, Italy, art;" but he did not understand that Svirski meant an acquaintance, abroad a journey, Italy a country. Now, he was talking to Lineta: "That is all well," said he; "but what will become of me? How couldst thou forget that I love thee so immensely?" And for a time it seemed to him that if he could see her, if he could tell her that one must think of the suffering of people, she would fall to weeping and throw herself on his neck. "And so many things unite us," said he to her; "besides, I am the same, thine." And suddenly his jaw protruded; it began to tremble; the veins swelled in his forehead, and his eyes were filled with a mist of tears. Pan Stanislav, who had an uncommonly kind heart, and who thought, besides, that he might touch his feelings, put his arm around his neck suddenly, and, being affected himself, began to kiss him on the cheek. But Pan Ignas's emotion did not continue; he returned to the feeling of reality. "I will not tell her that," thought he, "for I shall not see her, since she has gone with her betrothed, — with Kopovski." And at that thought his face became rigid again. He began then to take in effectively the whole extent of the misfortune. The thought struck him for the first time that if Lineta had died, his loss would have been less. The gulf caused by death leaves to believers the hope of a common life on the other shore; to unbelievers, a common nothingness; hence, to some the hope of a union, to others a common fate. Death is powerless against love which passes beyond the grave; death may wrest a dear soul from us, but cannot prevent us from loving it, and cannot degrade it. On the contrary, death makes that soul sacred; makes it not only beloved, but holy. Lineta, in taking from Pan Ignas herself,—that is, his most precious soul,—took from him at once the right of loving and grieving and yearning and honoring; by going herself, she left a memory behind her which was ruined in full measure. Now Pan Ignas felt clearly that if he should not be able to cease loving her, he would thereby become abject; and he felt that he would not be able to cease loving. Only in that moment did he see the whole greatness of his wreck, ruin, and suffering. In that moment he understood that it was more than he could bear.

"Go with Svirski to Italy," said Pan Stanislav. "Suffer out the pain, my dear friend; endure till it is over. You cannot do otherwise. The world is wide! There is so much to see, so much to love. Everything is open before thee; and before no one as before thee. Much is due to the world from thee; but much also to thee from the world. Go, my dear. Life is around thee; life is everywhere. New impressions will come; thou wilt not resist them; they will occupy thy thought, soften thy pain. Thou wilt not be circling around one existence. Svirski will show thee Italy. Thou wilt see what a comrade he is, and what horizons he will open. Besides, I tell thee that a man such as thou art, should have that power which the pearl oyster has, of turning everything into pearl simply. Listen to what thy true friend says. Go, and go at once. Promise me that thou wilt go. God grant my wife to pass her illness safely; then we may journey there also in spring. Thou wilt see how beautiful it will be for us. Well, Ignas, promise me. Dost thou say yes?"

"Yes," answered Pan Ignas, hearing the last word, but not knowing in general what the question was.

"Well, now, praise God," replied Pan Stanislav. "Let us return to the city, and spend the evening together. I have something to do in the counting-house, and I have left home for two days."

Then he gave command to turn back, for the sun was toward setting. It was a beautiful day, of those which come at the end of summer. Over the city a golden, delicate dust was borne; the roofs, and especially the church towers, gleamed at the edges, as it were with the reflection of amber, and, outlined clearly in the transparent air, seemed to delight in it. The two men rode for some time in silence.

"Wilt thou go to my house, or to thy own lodgings?" asked Pan Stanislav, when they entered the city.

The city movement seemed to calm Pan Ignas, for he looked at Pan Stanislav with perfect presence of mind, and said, —

"I have not been at home since yesterday, for I spent the night with my father. Perhaps there are letters for me; let us drive to my lodgings."

And he foresaw correctly, for at his lodgings a letter from Pani Bronich in Berlin was awaiting him. He tore open the envelope feverishly, and began to read; Pan Stanislav, looking at his changing face, thought, —

"It is evident that some hope is hidden yet in him."

Here he remembered all at once that young doctor, who in his time said of Panna Kraslavski, "I know what she is, but I cannot tear my soul from her."

Pan Ignas finished reading, and, resting his head on his hand, looked without thought on the table and the papers lying on it. At last he recovered, and gave the letter to Pan Stanislav.

"Read," said he.

Pan Stanislav took the letter and read as follows: —

"I know that you believed really in your feeling for Nitechka, and that at the first moment what has happened will seem to you a misfortune; believe me, too, that to me and to her it was not easy to resolve on the decisive step. Perhaps you will not be able to estimate Nitechka well, — there are so many things which men cannot estimate; but you ought to know her at least enough to know how much it costs her when she is forced to cause the slightest pain, even to a stranger. But what can we do! such is the will of God, which it would be a sin not to obey. We both act as our consciences dictate; and Nitechka is too just to give her hand to you without a real attachment. What has taken place, has taken place not only in conformity with the will of God, but in conformity with your good and hers; for if, without loving you sufficiently, she had become your wife, how would she be able to resist the temptations to which such a being would with certainty be exposed in view of the corruption of society? Besides, you have your talent; therefore you have something Nitechka has only her heart, which violence would break in one moment; and if it seems to you that she has disappointed you, think conscientiously whose fault is the greater? You have done much harm to Nitechka, for you fettered her will, and you did not let her follow the natural impulse of her heart; and by thus doing you sacrificed, or were ready to sacrifice, through your selfishness, her happiness, and even her life, for I am convinced that under such conditions she would not have survived a single year. Nevertheless may God forgive you as we forgive; and be it known to you that this very day we prayed for you at a Mass ordered purposely for your intention, in the church of Saint Yadviga.

"You will be pleased to send the ring to Pan Osnovski's villa; your ring, since the Osnovskis had to go abroad too, will reach you through the hands of Panna Ratkovski. Once more, may God forgive you everything, and keep you in His protection!"

"This is something unparalleled!" said Pan Stanislav.

"It is evident that truth may be treated as love is," said Pan Ignas, with a heart-rending sorrow; "but I had not supposed that."

"Listen to me, Ignas," said Pan Stanislav, who under the impulse of sympathy had begun to say *thou* to Zavilovski; "this is not merely a question of thy happiness, but of thy dignity. Suffer as much as may please thee; but it is thy duty to find strength to show that thou art indifferent to all this."

A long silence followed. But Pan Stanislav, remembering the letter, repeated from time to time,—

"This passes human understanding." Finally he turned to Pan Ignas,—

"Svirski is returning to-day from Buchynek, and late in the evening he will come to my house. Come thou too. We will pass the evening together, and he and thou will talk of the journey."

"No," said Pan Ignas; "on my return from Prytulov, I was to spend the night with my father, so I must go to him. To-morrow morning I will be with you and see Svirski."

But he merely said that, for he wanted to be alone. Pan Stanislav did not oppose his intention of spending the night at the institution, for he judged that occupation near the sick man, and care for him, would occupy his mind, then weariness and need of sleep would come. He determined, however, to drive with him to the institution.

In fact, they took farewell only at the gate. Pan Ignas, however, after he had remained a few minutes in the institution and inquired of the overseer touching his father, went out and returned home by stealth.

He lighted a candle, read Pani Bronich's letter once more, and, covering his face with his hands, began to meditate. In spite of Osnovski's letter and in spite of everything which Pan Stanislav had told him, a certain doubt and a certain hope had lingered in his soul, yet he knew that *all was over;* but at moments he had the feeling that that was not reality, but an evil dream. It was only Pani Bronich's letter that had penetrated to that little corner of his soul which was unwilling to believe, and burned out in it the remnant of illusion. So there was no Lineta any longer; there was no future, no happiness. Kopovski had all that; for him were left only loneliness, humiliation, and a ghastly vacuum. There was left to him also the impression that if "Nitechka" could have snatched from him that talent too, of which Pani Bronich made mention, she would have snatched it and given it to Kopovski. What was he for her in comparison with Kopovski? "I shall never really understand this," thought he; "but it is so." And he began to meditate over this, what was there in him so abject that she should sacrifice him thus without mercy, without the least consideration, to take less note of him than the meanest worm. "Why does she love Kopovski and not me, the man to whom she confessed love?" And he recalled how once she had quivered in his arms, when after the betrothal he gave her good-night. But now she is quivering in Kopovski's arms in precisely the same way. And at this thought he seized his handkerchief and squeezed it between his teeth, so as not to scream from pain and madness. "What is this? Why has it happened?" But there was a time when he, Ignas, did not love her; why did she not marry Kopovski at that time? What motive could she have to trample him without need?

And again he caught after the letter of Pani Bronich, as if hoping to find in it an answer to these terrible questions. He read once more the passage about the will of God, and about this, — that he was guilty, that he had done much harm to "Nitechka," and that she forgave him, and about the Mass, which was celebrated for his intention in Saint Yadviga's; and when he had ended he began to gaze at the light, blinking and saying, —

"How is that possible? How have I offended?" And suddenly he felt that the understanding of what truth is and what falsehood, of what evil is, and what good, and what is proper and improper, began to desert him. Lineta had gone from him, taken herself from him, taken his future, and now one after another all the bases of life were gliding away — and reason and thought and life itself. He saw yet that he had always loved this "Nitechka" of his beyond life, and in no way was he able to wish any harm to her; but besides that impression, everything which composes a thinking being was crushed into dust in him, and flew apart like dust in that mighty wind of misfortune.

Still he loved. Lineta became divided for him now into the Lineta of to-day and the Lineta of the past. He began to call to mind her voice, her face, her bright golden hair, her eyes and mouth, her tall form, her hands, and that warmth which so many times he had felt from her lips. His powerful imagination recreated her almost tangibly; and he saw that not only had he loved his own distant one, but he loved her yet, — that is, he yearned for her beyond measure, and was suffering beyond measure for the loss of her.

And, recognizing this, he began again to speak to her:

"How couldst thou think me able to bear this?"

At that moment he had not the least doubt of this either, that God knew the position very well. He sat a long time more in silence, and the light had burned out half its length almost when he came to himself.

But something uncommon took place in him then. He had an impression as if he were going from land in a ship, and that seemed to him which seems always on such an occasion, that it was not he who was moving away, but the shore on which he had dwelt hitherto. Everything — that was he, and in general his life; all thoughts, hopes, ambitions, objects, plans, even love, even Lineta, even his loss; and those vicious circles, and those tortures through which he had passed — seemed not merely removed from him, but foreign, and belonging exclusively to that land off there. And gradually they sank, gradually they melted, becoming ever smaller, ever more visionary, ever more dreamlike; and he went on, he became more distant, feeling that to that foreignness he does not wish to return, that he cannot return, and that all which is left of him belongs to the space which has taken him to itself, and opened its bosom before him, immense and mysterious.

## CHAPTER LVIII.

FOUR days later, on the Assumption of the Most Blessed Lady, which was also Marynia's name's[1] day, the Bigiels and Svirski went to Buchynek. They did not find Marynia at home, for she was at vespers in the church of Yasmen with Pani Emilia. When Pani Bigiel learned this, she followed them with the whole crowd of little Bigiels. The men, left alone, began to talk of the event of which for a number of days the whole city had been talking, — that was of the attempted suicide of the poet Zavilovski.

"I went to see him to-day three times," said Bigiel; "but Panna Helena's servants have the order to admit no one except the doctors."

"As for me," said Pan Stanislav, "this is the first day on which I have not been able to visit him; but during the previous days I spent a number of hours with him regularly. I tell my wife that I am at the counting-house on business."

"Tell me how it happened," said Bigiel, who wanted to know all the details, so as to consider them exactly afterward in his fashion.

"It happened this way," said Pan Stanislav. "Ignas told me that he was going to the institution, to his father. I was glad, for I judged that that would keep him away from his thoughts. I took him, however, to the gate, and he promised to visit me next day. Meanwhile it turned out that he wanted to be rid of me, so as to shoot himself undisturbed."

"Then you were not the first to find him?"

"No; I suspected nothing of that kind, and I should have looked for him next day. Luckily Panna Helena came at the mere news that the marriage was broken."

"I informed her," said Svirski, "and she took the matter to heart so much that I was astonished. She had a forewarning, as it were, of what would follow."

"She is a wonderful person," said Pan Stanislav. "I have not been able to learn how it happened; but she found him; she saved him; she called in a whole circle of doctors, and finally gave command to take him to her house."

[1] Name's day, day of that saint whose name a given person bears.

"But the doctors insist that he will live?"

"They know nothing yet definitely. In shooting, he must have turned the pistol so that the ball, after passing through his forehead, went up and lodged under the skull. They found the ball, and extracted it easily enough; but whether he will live — and if he lives, whether his mind will survive — is unknown. One doctor fears a disturbance in his speech; but his life is in question yet."

The event, though known generally, and described every day in the papers, had made so great an impression that silence continued awhile. Svirski, who, with his muscles of an athlete, had the sensitiveness of a woman, burst forth, —

"Through such women!"

But Vaskovski, sitting near, said in a low voice, —

"Leave them to the mercy of God."

"Is it possible?" said Bigiel, turning to Pan Stanislav; "and thou hadst no suspicion?"

"It did not come to my head even that he would shoot himself. I saw clearly that he was struggling with his feelings. For a while, when we were riding, his chin trembled, as if he wished to burst into weeping; but he is a brave soul. He restrained himself at once, and to appearance was calm. He deceived me mainly by his promise to come next day."

"Do you know what seems to me?" continued he, after a while; "the last drop which overflowed the cup was Pani Bronich's letter. Ignas gave it to me to read. She wrote that what had happened was the will of God; that the fault was on his side; that he was an egotist; but that they were obeying the voice of conscience and justice; that they forgave him, and begged God to forgive him too, — in a word, unheard of things! I saw that that made a desperate impression on him, and I imagine what must have taken place in a man so injured and of such spirit, when he saw that in addition to everything else injustice was attributed to him; when he understood that it is possible for people to set everything at naught and distort it, to trample on reason, truth, and the simplest principles of justice, and then shield themselves behind the Lord God. For that matter I was not concerned; but when I saw the cynicism, the want of moral understanding, as God lives, I asked myself this question: Am I mad, and are truth and honesty mere illusions on earth?"

Here Pan Stanislav was so indignant at Pani Bronich's letter that he tugged at his beard feverishly, and Svirski said, —

"I understand that even a believer may spit upon life in such moments."

Here Vaskovski rubbed his forehead with his hand, and then said to himself, —

"Yes; I have seen that kind, too. For there are people who believe, not through love, but as it were because atheism is bankrupt, as it were from despair, who imagine to themselves that somewhere, off behind phenomena, there is not a merciful Father, who places his hand on every unfortunate head, but some kind of He, unapproachable, inscrutable, indifferent; it is all one, in such case, whether that He is called the Absolute, or Nirvana. He is only a concept, not love. It is impossible to love this He; and when misfortune comes, people spit on life."

"That is well," answered Svirski, testily; "but meanwhile Pan Ignas is lying with a broken skull, and they have gone to the seashore, and it is pleasant for them."

"Whence do you know that it is pleasant for them?" answered Vaskovski.

"The deuce fire them!" said Svirski.

"But I say to you that they are unhappy. No one may trample on truth and go unpunished. They will talk various things into each other, but one thing they will not be able to talk into each other, — that is, self-respect; they will begin to despise themselves in secret, and at last even that attachment which they had for each other will be turned into secret dislike. That is inevitable."

"The deuce fire them!" repeated Svirski.

"The mercy of God is for them, not for the good," concluded Vaskovski.

Meanwhile Bigiel talked with Pan Stanislav, admiring the kindness and courage of Panna Helena.

"For there will be a fabulous amount of gossip from this," said he.

"She does not care for that," answered Pan Stanislav. "She does not count with society, for she wants nothing of it. She, too, is a resolute soul. She showed Pan Ignas always exceptional attachment, and his act must have shocked her tremendously. Do you know the history of Ploshovski?"

"I knew him personally," said Svirski. "His father

was the first man in Rome to predict success to me. Of Panna Helena they say, I think, that she was betrothed to Ploshovski."

"No, she was not; but in her secret heart perhaps she loved him greatly. Such was his fortune. It is certain that since his death she has become different altogether. For a woman so religious as she is, his suicide must in truth have been dreadful, for just think, not to be able even to pray for a man whom one has loved. And now again Pan Ignas! If any one, it is she who is doing everything to save him. Yesterday I was there; she came out to me barely alive, pale, weary, without having slept. And there is some one else to watch with her. Panna Ratkovski told me of her, that for four days she had n't slept one hour, perhaps."

"Panna Ratkovski?" inquired Svirski, quickly; and he began mechanically to seek with his hand in the coat pocket where he had her letter.

He remembered then her words: *"I have chosen otherwise, and if I shall never be happy, I do not wish at least to reproach myself afterwards with insincerity."* "Now for the first time I understand the meaning and real tragedy of those words. Now, in spite of all social appearances, without regard to the tongues of people, this young girl has gone to watch over that suicide. What could this mean? The case is clear as the sun. It is true that Kopovski went abroad with another; but she had expressed always openly what she thought of Kopovski, and if she had cared nothing for Pan Ignas, she would not have gone this time to watch at his bedside. It seems to me that I am an ass," muttered Svirski.

But that was not the only conclusion to which he came after mature consideration. All at once a yearning for Panna Ratkovski took hold of him, and sorrow that that had not happened which might have happened, as well as immense pity for her. "Thou hast become a poodle again, old fellow," said he to himself, "and it serves thee right! A good man would have felt sorrow, but thou didst begin to be angry and condemn her for loving a fool and pretending to aspiration, and for having a low nature; thou didst talk ill of her before Pani Polanyetski and before him; didst do injustice to a kind and unfortunate person, not because her refusal pained thee too greatly, but through thy own self-love. Served thee right, right! thou art an ass; thou art not worthy of her; and thou wilt be knocking around alone till death, like a mandrill, behind a menagerie grating."

In these reproaches there was a portion of truth. Svirski had not fallen in love decidedly with Panna Ratkovski; but her refusal pained him more deeply than he acknowledged, and, not being able to master his vexation, he gave way to general conclusions about women, citing Panna Ratkovski as an example, and to her disadvantage.

Now he saw the whole vanity of such conclusions. "These stupid syntheses have ruined me always," thought he. "Women are individuals like all people; and the general concept woman explains nothing whatever. There is a Panna Castelli, there is a Pani Osnovski, in whom I admit various rascalities, without, however, having proof of them; but on the other hand there is a Pani Polanyetski, a Pani Bigiel, a Sister Aniela, a Panna Helena, and a Panna Stefania. Poor child! and so it serves me right. She was there suffering in silence, and I was gnashing my teeth. If that girl is n't worth ten times more than I, then that sun is n't worth my pipe. She had a sacred reason in giving a refusal to such a buffalo. I will go to the Orient, and that is the end of the matter. Such light as there is in Egypt, there is nowhere else on earth. And what an honest woman! Moreover, she has done me good, even with her refusal, for through her I have convinced myself that my theory about women should be broken on the back of a dog. But if Panna Helena puts a whole regiment of dragoons before her door, I must see that poor girl and say what I think to her."

In fact, he went on the following morning to Panna Helena's. They did not wish to admit him, but he insisted so much that at last he was admitted. Panna Helena, judging that friendship and anxiety alone had brought him, conducted him even to the chamber in which the wounded man was lying. There, in the gloom of fastened blinds, he saw Pan Ignas, from whom came the odor of iodine, his head bound, his jaw protruding; and with him those two wearied out women, the fever of sleeplessness on their faces, and really like two shadows. The wounded man lay with open lips; he was changed, and resembled himself in nothing. He was as if incomparably older; his eyelids were swollen, and protruding from under the bandage. Svirski had liked him greatly, and with his sensitiveness had not less sympathy for him than had Pan Stanislav and Osnovski; he was struck, however, this time by his deformity. "He has fixed himself," thought he; then, turning to Panna Helena, he asked in an undertone, —

"Has he not regained consciousness?"

"No," answered she, in a whisper.

"What does the doctor say?"

Panna Helena moved her thin hand in sign that all was uncertain yet.

"This is the fifth day," whispered she again.

"And the fever decreases," said Panna Ratkovski.

Svirski wished to offer his services in watching the sick man; but Panna Helena indicated with her eyes a young doctor, whom he was not able to distinguish at once in the darkness, but who, sitting in an armchair near the table, with a basin and pile of iodine wadding, was dozing from weariness, waiting till another should relieve him.

"We have two," said Panna Ratkovski, "and besides people from the hospital, who know how to nurse the sick."

"But you ladies are wonderfully wearied."

"It is a question here of the sick man," answered she, looking toward the bed.

Svirski followed her glance. His eyes were better accustomed now to the gloom, and saw distinctly the face, motionless, with lips almost black. The long body was motionless also, only the fingers of his emaciated hand, lying on the coverlet, stirred with a monotonous movement, as if scratching.

"They will take him out in a couple of days, as God is in Heaven!" thought he, remembering his colleague, that "Slav" with whom Bukatski had disputed in his time, and who, when he had shot himself in the head, died only after two weeks of torture.

Wishing, however, to give comfort to the women, he said, in spite of that of which he was certain, —

"Wounds of this kind are either mortal at once, or are cured."

Panna Helena made no answer, but her face contracted nervously, and her lips grew pale. Evidently there was a terrible thought in her soul, that he *also* might die, and she did not wish to admit that she had had enough with that other suicide, and at the same time it was for her a question of something more than saving his life for Pan Ignas.

Svirski began to take farewell. He entered with a

speech prepared for Panna Ratkovski, to whom he had resolved to acknowledge that he had judged her unjustly, and to express all the homage which he felt for her, and to beg for her friendship; but in presence of the real tragedy of those two women, and of the danger of death, and of that half corpse, he saw at once that everything which he intended to say would be poor and petty, and that it was not the time for such empty and personal matters.

He merely pressed to his lips in silence the hand of Panna Helena, and then that of Panna Ratkovski; and, going out of that room filled with misfortune and permeated with iodine, he drew a deep breath. In his artistic imagination was represented distinctly the changed Pan Ignas, ten years older, with bound head and black lips. And in spite of all the sympathy which he had for the man, indignation seized him all at once.

"He made a hole in his skull," muttered he; "he made a hole in his talent, — and does n't care! and those souls there are dragging themselves to death and trembling like leaves."

Then a feeling, as it were of jealousy, took hold of him, as if he were sorry for himself, and he began to speak in a monologue, —

"Well, old man! but if thou, for example, were to pack a bit of lead into thy talent, no one would walk at thy bedside on tiptoe."

Further meditation was interrupted by Pan Plavitski, who, meeting him at the cross-street, stopped him, and began conversation, —

"I am just from Karlsbad," said he. "O Lord, how many elegant women! I am going to Buchynek to-day. I have just seen Stanislav, and know that my daughter is well; but he has grown thin somehow."

"Yes for he has had trouble. Have you heard of Pan Ignas?"

"I have, I have! But what will you say of that?"

"A misfortune."

"A misfortune; but this too, that there are no principles at present. All those new ideas, those atheisms of yours, and hypnotisms, and socialisms. The young generation have no principles, — that is where the trouble lies."

# CHAPTER LIX.

Pan Stanislav, under the impression of the catastrophe, forgot utterly his promise to inform Osnovski by letter how Pan Ignas had borne the rupture of the marriage and the departure of Lineta. But Osnovski, having learned from the newspapers what had happened, inquired every day by telegraph about the condition of the patient, and was greatly alarmed. In the press and in public the most contradictory accounts were current. Some journals declared that his condition was hopeless; others predicted a speedy recovery. For a long time Pan Stanislav could report nothing certain; and only after two weeks did he send a despatch that the sick man had ceased to waver between death and life, and that the doctors guaranteed his recovery.

Osnovski answered with a long letter, in which he gave various news from Ostend,—

"God reward you for good news! All danger has passed then decisively? I cannot tell you what a weight fell from the hearts of both of us Tell Pan Ignas that not only I, but my wife received the news of his recovery with tears She does not speak of any one else now, and thinks only of him. Oh, what women are! volumes might be written on this subject; but Anetka is an exception, and will you believe, that in spite of all her terror and sorrow and sympathy, Ignas has increased in her eyes through this unhappy event? They seek romantic sides always; so far does this reach that even in Kopovski, as the originator of the misfortune, Anetka, who knows all his stupidity, sees now something demonic. But beyond all she praises God for the recovery of Ignas. May he live to the glory of our society, and may he find a being worthy of him! From your despatch, I infer that he is under the care of Panna Helena. May God grant her too every blessing for such an honest heart! Really she has no one in the world nearer to her than Ignas, and I imagine that he is still dearer to her through remembrance of Ploshovski

"Now, since you have quieted me as to Ignas's recovery, I can send you some news about Aunt Bronich and Lineta. Perhaps you have heard that they are here with Kopovski. They went first to Scheveningen; but, hearing that the small-pox was there, they escaped to Ostend, not supposing that we were here. We met a number of times in the Cursaal, but pretended not to know them. Kopovski even left cards with us; but we did not return his visit, though, as my wife says justly, he is far less to blame in all this than the two women. When I received your despatch, stating that Ignas is saved surely, I thought that humanity itself commanded me to send the news to them, and I did so. As matters stand, life is unpleasant for them here, since their acquaintances withdraw; so I wished them to know at least that they have no human life on their consciences, all the more since Lineta, as it would seem, felt the deed of Ignas. In fact, they called the same day on us, and my wife received them. She says truly that evil is moral sickness, and that we should not desert relatives in sickness. In general, this first meeting was awkward and painful for both sides. Of Ignas we said not a word. Kopovski appears here as Lineta's betrothed; but they do not seem very happy, though, to tell the truth, she is better fitted for him than for Ignas, and in that view at least what has happened may be considered God's work. I know also from persons aside that Aunt Bronich mentions it as such. I need not tell you how that abuse of the name of God angers me. I know that she tried to talk into some acquaintances stopping here that she and her niece broke with Ignas because of his want of religious feelings; to others she told tales of his despotism and of his disagreement in temper with Lineta. In all this she deceives not only the world, but herself. Aunt, through persuading herself and others of it unceasingly, believes at last in the lofty character of Lineta, and in this too she is immensely disappointed. She feels bound really to defend her; she invents God knows what in her behalf, and struggles like a mad woman; but a feeling of disappointment sticks in her, and I think that she grieves over it, for she has grown very thin. Evidently they value relations with us, which, as they hope, may bring them back to society; but though my wife received them, our relations cannot return to their former condition, of course. I, first of all, could not permit this, from regard to my duty of choosing a proper society for my wife. Lineta's marriage with Kopovski is to be in Paris two months from now. Of course we shall not be present. Moreover, my wife looks on the marriage very skeptically. I have written thus at length hoping to oblige you to write as much, with all details about Ignas. If his health permits, press his hand for me, and tell him that he has and will have in me a most cordial friend, who is devoted heart and soul to him."

Marynia, notwithstanding the lateness of the season, was living yet in Buchynek; so that Pan Stanislav, when he received this letter in the counting-house, showed it first of all to the Bigiels, with whom he dined.

"I am glad of one thing," said Pani Bigiel, when she had finished the letter; "she will marry that Kopovski right away. Otherwise I should be afraid that something might spring up again in Ignas, and that after he had recovered he might be ready to return to her."

"No; Pan Ignas has much character, and I think that

he would not return in any case," said Bigiel. "What is thy thought, Stas?"

Bigiel was so accustomed to ask the opinion of his partner in every question, that he could not get on without it in this one.

"I think that they, when they look around on what they have done, will be rather ready to return. As to Ignas, I have lived so many years, and seen so many improbable things, that I will not answer for any one."

At that moment these words occurred again to Pan Stanislav: "I know what she is, but I cannot tear my soul from her."

"But wouldst thou return in his place?" inquired Bigiel.

"I think not; but I will not answer for myself even. First of all, I should n't have shot myself in the forehead; but still, I don't know even that."

And he said this with great discouragement, for he thought that if there was any man who had no right to answer for himself it was he.

But Pani Bigiel began, —

"I would give I do not know what to see Ignas; but really it is easier to take a fortress than to go to him. And I cannot understand why Panna Helena keeps him from people so, even from such friends as we are."

"She keeps him from people because the doctor has ordered absolute quiet. Besides, since he has regained consciousness, the sight of his nearest friends, even, is terribly painful to him; and this we can understand. He cannot talk with them about his deed; and he sees that every one who approaches him is thinking of nothing else."

"But you are there every day."

"They admit me because I was connected with the affair from the beginning; I was the first to report the rupture of the marriage, and I watched him."

"Does he mention that girl yet?"

"I asked Panna Helena and Panna Ratkovski about this; they answered, 'Never.' I have sat for hours with him alone, and have heard nothing. It is wonderful: he is conscious; he knows that he is wounded, knows that he is sick; but he seems at the same time to remember nothing of past events, just as if the past had no existence whatever. The doctors say that wounds in the head cause various and very peculiar phenomena of this kind. For the rest, he recognizes every one who approaches him, exhibits immense gratitude to Panna Helena and Panna Ratkovski. He loves Panna Ratkovski especially, and evidently yearns for her when she goes for a while from him. But they are both, as God lives! — there are no words to tell how good they are."

"Panna Ratkovski moves me especially," said Pani Bigiel.

Bigiel put in, "Meditating over everything carefully, I have come to the conclusion that she must have fallen in love with him."

"Thou hast spent time for nothing in meditating," answered Pan Stanislav, "for that is as clear as the sun. The poor thing hid this feeling in herself till misfortune came. Why did she reject such an offer as Svirski's? I make no secret of this, for Svirski himself tells it on every side. It seems to him that he owes her satisfaction because he suspected her of being in love with Kopovski. When Pan Ignas shot himself, she was living with her relative, Pani Melnitski, after the Osnovskis had gone; but when she learned that Panna Helena had taken Ignas, she went and begged permission to remain with her. All know perfectly how to understand this; but she does not mind such considerations, just as Panna Helena herself does not mind them."

Here Pan Stanislav turned to Pani Bigiel, —

"Panna Ratkovski moves you deeply; but think, as God lives, what a tragic figure Panna Helena is. Pan Ignas is alive, at least, but Ploshovski aimed better; and, according to her ideas, there is no mercy for him, even in that world But she loves him. There is a position! Finally, after such a suicide, comes another; it tears open all wounds, freshens every memory. Panna Ratkovski may be a touching figure; but the other has her life broken forever, and no hope, nothing left but despair."

"True, true! But she must be attached to Ignas, since she cares for him so."

"I understand why she does it; she wants to beg of the Lord God mercy for the other man, because she has saved Pan Ignas."

"That may be," said Bigiel. "And who knows that Pan Ignas may not marry Panna Ratkovski, when he recovers?"

"If he forgets that other, if he is not broken, and if he recovers."

"How, if he recovers? Just now thou hast said that his recovery is undoubted."

"It is undoubted that he will live; but the question is, will he be the former Ignas? Even though he had not fired into his head, it would be difficult to say whether such an experience would not break a man who is so sensitive. But add a broken head; that must be paid for. Who knows what will happen further? but now, for example, though he is conscious, though he talks with sense, at times he breaks off, and cannot recollect the simplest expression. Before, he never hesitated. This, too, is strange,—he remembers the names of things well, but when it is a question of any act, he stops most generally, and either remembers with effort, or forgets altogether."

"What does the doctor say?"

"In God is his hope that it will pass; the doctor does not lose hope. But even yesterday, while I was going in, Ignas said, 'Pani—' and stopped. Evidently he was thinking of Marynia, whom he recalled on a sudden, but he could not ask about her. Every day he talks more, it is true; but before he recovers, much time may pass, and certain traces may remain forever."

"But does Marynia know of everything?"

"While there was no certainty that he would live, I kept everything in secret; but after that I thought it better to tell her. Of course I was very cautious. It was hard to keep the whole matter from her longer. People were talking too much about it, and I feared that she might hear from people on one side. I told her, moreover, that the wound was slight, and that nothing threatened him, but that the doctors forbade him visitors. Even thus she was greatly affected."

"When will you bring her to the city?"

"While the weather is good, I prefer to keep her in the country."

Further conversation was interrupted by a letter, which the servant gave Pan Stanislav. The letter was from Mashko, and contained the following words:—

"I wish to see thee in thy own interest. I will wait for thee at my house till five."

"I am curious to know what he wants," said Pan Stanislav.

"Who is it?"

"Mashko; he wants to see me."

"Business and business," said Bigiel; "he has business above his ears. Sometimes I wonder really whence he gets endurance and wit for all this. Dost thou know that Pani Kraslavski has come home, and that she has lost her sight altogether? She sees nothing now, or what is called nothing. We visited those ladies before they left their country house. Wherever one turns there is misery, so that at last pity seizes one while looking."

"But in misfortune each man or woman shows his or her real nature," said Pani Bigiel. "You remember that we considered Pani Mashko as somewhat dry in character, but you will not believe how kind she is now to her mother. She does not let a servant come near her; she attends her herself everywhere, waits on her, reads to her. Really she has given me a pleasant surprise, or rather both of them, for Pani Kraslavski has lost her former pretentiousness thoroughly. It is pleasant to see how those women love each other. It seems that there was something in Pani Mashko which we could not discover."

"Both, too, were terribly indignant at the behavior of Panna Castelli," added Bigiel. "Pani Kraslavski said to us, 'If my Terka had acted in that way, I should have denied her, though I am blind, and need care.' But Pani Mashko is as she is, and she would not have acted in that way, for she is another kind of woman."

Pan Stanislav drank his cup of black coffee, and began to take farewell. For some time past every conversation about Pani Mashko had become for the man unendurable; it seemed to him, moreover, that he was listening again to an extract from that strange human comedy which people were playing around him, and in which he, too, was playing his empty part. It did not occur to him that human nature is so composed that even in the very worst person some good element may be found, and that Pani Mashko might be, after all, a loving daughter. In general, he preferred not to think of that, but began to halt over the question, what could Mashko want of him? Forgetting that Mashko had written in the letter that he wanted to see him, not in his own, but in his (Pan Stanislav's) interest, he supposed, with a certain alarm, that he wanted money a second time.

"But I," thought he, "will not refuse now."

And it occurred to him that life is like the machinery of a watch. When something is out of order in one wheel, all begin to act irregularly. What connection could there be between his adventure with Pani Mashko and his business, his money, his mercantile work? And still he felt that even as a merchant he had not, at least with reference to Mashko, the freedom that he once had.

But his suppositions proved faulty. Mashko had not come to ask money.

"I looked for thee in the counting-house, and at thy residence," said he; "at last I divined that thou must be at the Bigiels', and I sent my letter there. I wished to speak with thee on thy own business."

"How can I serve thee?" asked Pan Stanislav.

"First of all, I beg that what I say may remain between us."

"It will; I am listening."

Mashko looked for a time in silence at Pan Stanislav, as if to prepare him by that silence for some important announcement; at last he said, with a wonderful calmness, weighing out every expression, —

"I wished to tell thee that I am lost beyond redemption."

"Hast lost the will case?"

"No; the case will come up only two weeks from now but I know that I shall lose it."

"Whence hast thou that certainty?"

"Dost remember what I told thee once, that cases against wills are won almost always because the attack is more energetic than the defence; because usually the overthrow of the will concerns some one personally, while maintaining it does not? Everything in the world may be attacked; for though a thing be in accordance with the spirit of the law, almost always, in a greater degree or less, it fails to satisfy the letter, and the courts must hold to the letter."

"True. Thou hast said all that."

"Well, so it is, too, in this case which I took up. It was not so adventurous as may seem. The whole question was to break the will; and I should, perhaps, succeed in proving certain disagreements in it with the letter of the law, were it not that there is a man striving with equal energy to prove that there are none such. I will not talk long about this; it is enough for thee to know that I have to contend not merely with an opponent who is a lawyer and a finished trickster, but a personal enemy, for whom it is a question, not only to win the case, but to ruin me. Once I slighted him, and now he is taking revenge."

"In general, I do not understand why you have to do with any one except the State Attorney."

"Because there were legacies to private people in defence of which the opposite side employed Sledz, that advocate. But let this rest. I must lose the case, for it is in conditions for being lost; and if I were Sledz, I would win just as he wins. I know this in advance, and I do not deceive myself. Enough now of this whole matter."

"But go on; appeal."

"No, my dear friend, I cannot go on."

"Why?"

"Because I have more debts than there are hairs on my head; because, after my first defeat, creditors will rush at me; and because"—here Mashko lowered his voice—"I must flee."

Silence followed.

Mashko rested his elbow on his knee, his head on his palm, and sat some time with his head inclined; but after a while he began to speak, as if to himself, without raising his head,—

"It is broken. I tied knots desperately, till my hands were wearied; strength would have failed any man, still I kept knotting. But I cannot knot any longer! God sees that I have no more strength left. Everything must have its end; and let this finish sometime."

Here he drew breath, like a man who is terribly tired; then he raised his head, and said,—

"This, however, is my affair merely, and I have come to talk of thy affairs. Listen to me! According to contract concluded at the sale of Kremen, I was to make payments to thy wife after the parcelling of Magyerovka; thou hast a few thousand rubles of thy own money with me. I was to pay thy father-in-law a life ánnuity. Now I come to tell thee that if not in a week, then in two, I shall go abroad as a bankrupt, and thou and they will not see a copper."

Mashko, while telling all this with the complete boldness and insolence of a man who no longer has anything to lose, looked Pan Stanislav in the eyes, as if seeking for a storm.

But he was deceived most thoroughly. Pan Stanislav's face grew dark for one twinkle of an eye, it is true, as if from suppressed anger; but he calmed himself quickly, and said,—

"I have always expected that this would end so."

Mashko, who, knowing with whom he had to deal, supposed that Pan Stanislav would seize him by the shoulder, looked at him with amazement, as if wishing to ask what had happened.

But at that moment Pan Stanislav thought, —

"If he had wanted to borrow money for the road, I could not have refused him."

But aloud he said, "Yes; this was to be foreseen."

"No," answered Mashko, with the stubbornness of a man who will not part with the thought that only a concurrence of exceptional circumstances is to blame for everything. "Thou hast no right to say this. The moment before death, I should be ready to repeat that it might have gone otherwise."

But Pan Stanislav inquired, as if with a shade of impatience, —

"My dear, what dost thou want of me specially?"

Mashko recovered, and answered, —

"Nothing. I have come to thee only as to a man who has shown me good-will at all times, and with whom I have contracted a money debt, as well as a debt of gratitude; I have come to confess openly how things stand, and also to say to thee: save what is possible, and as much as possible."

Pan Stanislav set his teeth; he judged that even in that irony of life, whose chattering he heard round about him continually for some time past, there ought to be a certain measure. Meanwhile Mashko's words about friendship and a debt of gratitude seemed to him as simply passing that measure. "May the devils take the money and thee — if thou would only go!" thought he, in spirit. But compressing in himself the wish to utter this audibly, he said, —

"I see no way."

"There is only one way," answered Mashko. "While it is still unknown to people that I must break, while hopes are connected with the will case, while my name and signature mean something, thou hast a chance to sell thy wife's claim. Thou wilt say to the purchaser that it is thy wish to capitalize the whole property, or something of that sort. Appearances are easy. A purchaser will be found always, especially if thou decide to sell at a certain reduction. In view of profit, any Jew will buy. I prefer that any other should lose rather than thou; it is permitted thee not to hear what I have told thee of my coming bankruptcy, and it is permitted thee to hope that I shall win the case. Thou canst be sure that he who will buy the claim of thee, would sell it to thee, even though he knew that it would not be worth a broken copper on the morrow. The world is an exchange; and on the exchange most business is transacted on this basis. This is called cleverness."

"No," answered Pan Stanislav, "it has a different name. Thou hast mentioned Jews; there are certain kinds of business which they describe with one word, '*schmuzig!*' I shall save my wife's claim in another way."

"As may please thee. I, my dear friend, know the value of my system; but, seest thou, in spite of all, I said to myself that I ought to tell thee this. It is perhaps the honor of a bankrupt; but now I cannot have another. It is easy for thee to divine how hard it is for me to say this. For that matter, I knew in advance that thou wouldst refuse; hence with me it was a question only of doing my own. And now give me a cup of tea and a glass of cognac, for I am barely living."

Pan Stanislav rang for the tea and the cognac.

Mashko continued, —

"I must pluck a certain number of people, — there is no help for that; hence I prefer to pluck indifferent ones rather than those who have rendered me service. There are positions in which a man must be an opportunist with his own conscience."

Here Mashko laughed with bitterness.

"I did not know of that myself," continued he; "but now new horizons open themselves before me. One is learning till death. We bankrupts have a certain point of honor too. As to me, I care less for those who would have plucked me in a given case than those who are near me, and to whom I owe gratitude. This may be the morality of Rinaldini, but morality of its own kind."

The servant brought in tea now. Mashko, needing to strengthen himself evidently, added to his cup an overflowing glass of cognac, and, cooling the hot tea in that way, drank it at a gulp.

"My dear friend," said Pan Stanislav, "thou knowest the position better than I. All that I could say against flight, and in favor of remaining and coming to terms with creditors, thou hast said to thyself of course, therefore I prefer to ask of something else: Hast thou something to grasp with thy hand? Hast thou even money for the road?"

"I have. Whether a man fails for a hundred thousand, or a hundred and ten thousand, is all one; but I thank thee for the question."

Here Mashko added cognac to a second cup of tea, and said, —

"Do not think that I am beginning to drink from despair; I have not sat down since morning, and I am terribly tired. Ah, how much good this has done me! I will say now to thee openly that I have not thrown up the game. Thou seest that I have not fired into my forehead. That is a melodrama! that is played out. I know, indeed, that everything is ended for me here; but in this place I could not sail out anyhow. Here the interests are too small simply, and there is no field. Take the west, Paris! There men make fortunes; there they take a somersault, and rise again. What is to be said in the case if it is so? Dost thou know that Hirsh had not, perhaps, three hundred francs on leaving this country? I know, I know! from the standpoint of local mustiness and stupidity here, this will seem a dream, — the fever of a bankrupt. But still, men inferior to me have made millions there, — inferior to me! Lose or win. But if I come back at any time — "

And evidently the tea and cognac had begun to rouse him, for, clinching his fist, he added, —

"Thou wilt see!"

"If that is not dreaming," answered Pan Stanislav, with still greater impatience than before, "it is the future. But now what?"

"Now," said Mashko, after a while, "they will count me a swindler. No one will think that there are falls and falls. I will tell thee, for instance, that I have not taken from my wife a single signature, a single surety, and that she will have everything which she had before marriage. I am going now; and until I am settled she will remain here with her mother. I do not know whether you have heard that Pani Kraslavski has lost her sight. I cannot take them at present, for I am not even sure where I shall live, — in Paris perhaps, perhaps in Antwerp. But I hope that our separation will not be lasting. They know nothing yet. See in what the drama is! See what tortures me!"

And Mashko put his palm on the top of his head, blinking at the same time, as if from pain in his eyes.

"When wilt thou go?" inquired Pan Stanislav.

"I cannot tell. I will let thee know. Thou hast had the evident wish to aid me, and thou mayest, though not in money. People will avoid my wife at first; show her, then, a little attention; take her under thy protection. Is it agreed? Thou hast been really friendly to me, and I know that thou art friendly to her."

"As God lives, one might go mad," thought Pan Stanislav; but he said aloud, —

"Agreed."

"I thank thee from the soul of my heart; and I have still a prayer. Thou hast much influence over those two ladies. They will believe thy words. Defend me a little in the first moments before my wife. Explain to her that dishonesty is one thing, and misfortune another. I, as God lives, am not such a rogue as people will consider me. I might have brought my wife also to ruin, but I have not done so. I might have obtained from thee a few thousand more rubles; but I preferred not to take them. Thou wilt be able to put this before her, and she will believe thee. Is it agreed?"

"Agreed," replied Pan Stanislav.

Mashko covered his head with his hands once more, and said, with a face contracted as if from physical pain, —

"See where real ruin is! See what pains the most!"

After a while he began to take farewell, thanking Pan Stanislav, meanwhile, again for good-will toward his wife, and future care of her.

Pan Stanislav went out with him, sat in a carriage, and started for Buchynek.

On the road he thought of Mashko and his fate; but at the same time he repeated to himself, "I too am a bankrupt!"

And that was true. Besides this, for a certain time some sort of general uncomprehended alarm had tormented him; against this he could not defend himself. Round about he saw disappointment, catastrophes, ruin; and he could not resist the feeling that all these were for him, too, a kind of warning and threat of the future. He proved to himself, it is true, that such fears could not be logically justified; but none the less, the fears did not cease to stick in the bottom of his soul somewhere, and sometimes he said to himself again, "Why should I be the one exception?" Then his heart was straitened with a foreboding of misfortune. This was still worse than those pins which, without wishing it, people, even the most friendly, drove into him by any word, unconsciously. In general, his nerves had suffered recently, so that he had become almost superstitious. He returned daily to Buchynek in alarm, lest something bad might have happened in the house during his absence.

This evening, he returned later than usual because of Mashko's call, and drove in about the time when real darkness had come. Stepping out before the entrance on the sandy road, which dulled the sound of the carriage, he saw through the window Marynia, Pani Emilia, and the professor sitting near a table in the middle of the parlor. Marynia was laying out patience, and was evidently explaining the play to Pani Emilia, for her head was turned toward her, and she had one finger on the cards. At sight of her Pan Stanislav thought that which for some time he had been repeating mentally, and which filled him at once with a feeling of happiness, and with greater anger at himself: "She is the purest soul that I have met in life." And with that thought he entered the room.

"Thou art late to-day," said Marynia, when he raised her hand to his lips with greeting; "but we are waiting for thee with supper."

"Mashko detained me," answered he. "What is to be heard here?"

"The same as ever. All happy."

"And how art thou?"

"As well as a fish!" answered she, joyously, giving him her forehead for a kiss.

Then she began to inquire about Pan Ignas. Pan Stanislav, after the disagreeable talk with Mashko, breathed for the first time more freely. "She is in health, and all is right," thought he, as if in wonder. And really he felt well in that bright room, in that great peace, among those friendly souls and at the side of that person so good and reliable. He felt that everything was there which he needed for happiness; but he felt that he had spoiled that happiness of his own will; that he had brought into the clear atmosphere of his house the elements of corruption and evil, and that he was living under that roof without a right.

## CHAPTER LX.

In the middle of September such cold days came that the Polanyetskis moved from Buchynek to their house in the city. Pan Stanislav, before the arrival of his wife, had the house aired and ornamented with flowers. It seemed to him, it is true, that he had lost the right to love her, but he had lost only his former freedom with reference to her; but perhaps, just because of this, he became far more attentive and careful. The right to love no one gives, and nothing can take away. It is another case when a man has fallen, and in presence of a soul incomparably more noble than his own, feels that he is not worthy to love; he loves then with humility, and does not dare to call his feeling by its name. What Pan Stanislav had lost really was his self-confidence, his commanding ways, and his former unceremoniousness in his treatment of his wife. At present in his intercourse with her he bore himself sometimes as if she were Panna Plavitski, and he a suitor not sure of his fate yet.

Still that uncertainty of his had the aspect of coldness at times. Finally, their relation, in spite of Pan Stanislav's increased care and efforts, had become more distant than hitherto. "I have not the right!" repeated Pan Stanislav, at every more lively movement of his heart. And Marynia at last observed that they were living now somehow differently, but she interpreted this to herself variously.

First, there were guests in the house, before whom, be what may, freedom of life must be diminished; second, that misfortune had happened to Pan Ignas, — a thing to shock "Stas" and carry his mind in another direction; and finally Marynia, accustomed now to various changes in his disposition, had ceased also to attach to them as much meaning as formerly.

Having gone through long hours of meditation and sadness, she came at last to the conviction that in the first period, while certain inequalities and bends of character are not accommodated into one common line, such various shades and changes in the disposition are inevitable, though transient. The sober judgment of Pani Bigiel helped her also to the discovery of this truth; she, on a time when Marynia began to praise her perfect accord with her husband, said,—

"Ai! it did n't come to that at once. At first we loved each other as it were more passionately, but we were far less fitted for each other; sometimes one pulled in one and the other in another direction. But because we both had honesty and good-will the Lord God saw that and blessed us. After the first child all went at once in the best way; and this day I would n't give my old husband for all the treasures of earth, though he is growing heavy, and when I persuade him to Karlsbad he will not listen to me."

"After the first child," inquired Marynia, with great attention. "Ah! I would have guessed at once that it was after the first child."

Pani Bigiel began to laugh.

"And how amusing he was when our first boy was born! During the first days he said nothing at all; he would only raise his spectacles to his forehead and look at him, as at some wonder from beyond the sea, and then come to me and kiss my hands."

The hope of a child was also a reason why Marynia did not take this new change in "Stas" to heart too much. First, she promised herself to enchant him completely both with the child, which she knew in advance would be simply phenomenal, and with her own beauty after sickness; and second, she judged that it was not permitted her to think of herself now, or even exclusively of "Stas." She was occupied in preparing a place for the coming guest, as well in the house, as in her affections. She felt that she must infold such a figure not only in swaddling clothes, but in love. Hence she accumulated necessary supplies. She said to herself at once that life for two living together might be changeable; but for three living together it could not be anything but happiness and the accomplishment of that expected grace and mercy of God.

In general, she looked at the future with uncommon cheerfulness. If, finally, Pan Stanislav was for her in some way a different person, more ceremonious, as it were, and more distant, he showed such delicacy as he had never shown before. The care and anxiety which she saw on his face she referred to his feeling for Pan Ignas, for whose life there was no fear, it is true, but whose misfortune she felt with a woman's heart, understanding that it might continue as long as his life lasted. The knowledge of this gave more than one moment of sadness to her, and to the Bigiels, and to all to whom Pan Ignas had become near.

Moreover, soon after the arrival of the Polanyetskis in the city, news came all at once from Ostend which threatened new complications. A certain morning Svirski burst into the counting-house like a bomb, and, taking Bigiel and Pan Stanislav to a separate room, said, with a mien of mysteriousness, —

"Do you know what has happened? Kresovski has just been at my studio, and he returned yesterday from Ostend. Osnovski has separated from his wife, and broken Kopovski's bones for him. A fabulous scandal! All Ostend is talking of nothing else."

Both were silent under the impression of the news; at last Pan Stanislav said, —

"That had to come sooner or later. Osnovski was blind."

"But I understand nothing," said Bigiel.

"An unheard of history!" continued Svirski. "Who could have supposed anything like it?"

"What does Kresovki say?"

"He says that Osnovski made an arrangement one day to go with some Englishmen to Blanckenberg to shoot dolphins. Meanwhile he was late at the railroad, or tramway. Having an hour's time before him, he went home again and found Kopovski in his house. You can imagine what he must have seen, since a man so mild was carried away, and lost his head to that degree that, without thinking of the scandal, he pounded Kopovski, so that Kopovski is in bed."

"He was so much in love with his wife that he might have gone mad even, or killed her," said Bigiel. "What a misfortune for the man!"

"See what women are!" exclaimed Svirski.

Pan Stanislav was silent. Bigiel, who was very sorry for Osnovski, began to walk back and forth in the room. At last he stopped before Svirski, and, thrusting his hands into his pockets, said, —

"But still I don't understand anything."

Svirski, not answering directly, said, turning to Pan Stanislav, "You remember what I said of her in Rome, when I was painting your wife's portrait? Old Zavilovski called her a crested lark. I understand how just that was; for a crested lark has another name, —'the soiler.' What a woman! I knew that she was not of high worth, but I did not suppose that she could go so far — and with such a man as Kopovski! Now I see various things more clearly. Kopovski was there all the time, as if courting Panna Castelli, then as if courting Panna Ratkovski; and of course he and the lady were in agreement, inventing appearances together. What a cheery life the fellow had! Castelli for dinner, and Pani Osnovski for dessert! Pleasant for such a man! Between those two women there must have been rivalry; one vying with the other in concessions to attract him to herself. You can understand that in such a place woman's self-esteem had small value."

"You are perfectly right," said Pan Stanislav. "Pani Osnovski was always most opposed to the marriage of Kopovski to Castelli; and very likely for that reason she was so eager to have her marry Pan Ignas. When, in spite of everything, Kopovski and Castelli came to an agreement, she went to extremes to keep Kopovski for herself. Their relation is an old story."

"I begin to understand a little," said Bigiel; "but how sad this is!"

"Sad?" said Svirski; "on the contrary. It was cheerful for Kopovski. Still, it was not. 'The beginning of evil is pleasant, but the end is bitter.' There is no reason to envy him. Do you know that Osnovski is hardly any weaker than I? for, through regard for his wife, he was afraid of growing fat, and from morning till evening practised every kind of exercise? Oh, how he loved her! what a kind man he is! and how sorry I am for him! In him that woman had everything, — heart, property, a dog's attachment, — and she trampled on everything. Castelli, at least, was not a wife yet."

"And have they separated really?"

"So really that she has gone. What a position, when a man like Osnovski left her! In truth, the case is a hard one."

But Bigiel, who liked to take things on the practical side, said, "I am curious to know what she will do, for all the property is his."

"If he has not killed her on the spot, he will not let her die of hunger, that is certain; he is not a man of that kind. Kresovski told me that he remained in Ostend, and that he is going to challenge Kopovski to a duel. But Kopovski will not rise out of bed for a week. There will be a duel when he recovers. Pani Bronich and Panna Castelli have gone away, too, to Paris."

"And the marriage with Kopovski?"

"What do you wish? In view of such open infidelity, it is broken, of course. Evil does not prosper, they, too, were left in the lurch. Ha! let them hunt abroad for some Prince Crapulescu[1] — for after what they have done to Ignas, no one in this country would take Castelli, save a swindler, or an idiot. Pan Ignas will not return to her."

"I told Pan Stanislav that, too," said Bigiel; "but he answered, 'Who knows?'"

"Ai!" said Svirski, "do you suppose really?"

"I don't know! I don't know anything!" answered Pan Stanislav, with an outburst. "I guarantee nothing; I guarantee nobody; I don't guarantee myself even."

Svirski looked at him with a certain astonishment.

"Ha! maybe that is right," said he, after a while. "If any one had told me yesterday that the Osnovskis would ever separate, I should have looked on him as a madman."

And he rose to take farewell; he was in a hurry to work, but wishing to hear more about the catastrophe of the Osnovskis, had engaged to dine with Kresovski. Bigiel and Pan Stanislav remained alone.

"Evil must always pay the penalty," said Bigiel, after some thought. "But do you know what sets me thinking? that the moral level is lowering among us. Take such persons as Bronich, Castelli, Pani Osnovski, — how dishonest they are! how spoiled! and, in addition, how stupid! What a mixture, deuce knows of what! what boundless pretensions! and with those pretensions the nature of a waiting-maid. So that it brings nausea to think of them, does it not? And men, such as Ignas and Osnovski, must pay for them."

"And that logic is not understood," answered Pan Stanislav, gloomily.

Bigiel began to walk up and down in the room again, clicking his tongue and shaking his head; all at once he stopped before Pan Stanislav with a radiant face, and, slapping him on the shoulder, said, —

[1] A fanciful Roumanian name formed from the French *crapule*, a debauchee.

"Well, my old man, thou and I can say to ourselves that we drew great prizes in life's lottery. We were not saints either; but perhaps the Lord God gave us luck because we have not undermined other men's houses like bandits."

Pan Stanislav gave no answer; he merely made ready to go.

Conditions had so arranged themselves lately that everything which took place around him, and everything which he heard, became, as it were, a saw, which was tearing his nerves. In addition, he had the feeling that that was not only terribly torturing and painful, but was beginning to be ridiculous also. At moments it came to his head to take Marynia and hide with her somewhere in some tumble-down village, if only far away from that insufferable comedy of life which was growing viler and viler. But he saw that he could not do that, even for this reason, — that Marynia's condition hindered it. He stopped, however, the bargaining for Buchynek, which had been almost finished, so as to find for himself a more distant and less accessible summer place. In general, relations with people began to weigh on him greatly; but he felt that he was in the vortex, and could not get out of it. Sometimes the former man rose in him, full of energy and freshness, and he asked himself with wonder, "What the devil! why does a fault which thousands of men commit daily, swell up in my case beyond every measure?" But the sense of truth answered straightway that as in medicine there are no diseases, only patients, so in the moral world there are no offences, only offenders. What one man bears easily, another pays for with his life; and he tried in vain to defend himself. For a man of principles, for a man who, barely half a year before, had married such a woman as Marynia, for a man whom fatherhood was awaiting, his offence was beyond measure; and it was so inexcusable, so unheard of, that at times he was amazed that he could have committed it. Now, while returning home under the impression of Osnovski's misfortune, and turning it over in his head in every way, he had again the feeling as if a part of the responsibility for what had happened weighed on him. "For I," said he to himself, "am a shareholder in that factory in which are formed such relations and such women as Castelli or Pani Osnovski." Then it occurred to him that Bigiel was right in saying that the moral level was lowering, and that the general state of mind which does not exclude the possibility of such acts is simply dangerous. For he understood that all these deviations flowed neither from exceptional misfortunes, nor uncommon passions, nor over-turbulent natures, but from social wantonness, and that the name of such deviations is legion. "See," thought he, "only in the circle of my acquaintances, Pani Mashko, Pani Osnovski, Panna Castelli; and over against them whom shall I place? My Marynia alone." And at that moment it did not occur to him that, besides Marynia, there were in his circle Pani Emilia, Pani Bigiel, Panna Helena, and Panna Ratkovski. But Marynia stood out before him on that ground of corruption and frivolity so unlike them, so pure and reliable, that he was moved to the depth of his soul by the mere thought of her. "That is another world; that is another kind," thought he. For a moment he remembered that Osnovski, too, had called his own wife an exception; but he rejected this evil thought immediately. "Osnovski deceived himself, but I do not deceive myself." And he felt that the skepticism which would not yield before Marynia would be not only stupid, but pitiable. In her there was simply no place for evil. Only swamp birds can sit in a swamp. He himself had said once in a jest to her, that if she wore heels, she would have inflammation of the conscience from remorse, because she was deceiving people. And there was truth in this jest; he saw her now just there before him as clearly as one always sees the person one thinks of with concentrated feeling. He saw her changed form and changed face, in which there remained always, however, that same shapely mouth, a little too wide, and those same clear eyes; and he was more and more moved. "Indeed, I did win a great prize in life's lottery," thought he; "but I did not know how to value it. 'Evil must always pay the penalty,' said Bigiel." And Pan Stanislav, to whom a similar thought had come more than once, felt now a superstitious fear before it. "There is," thought he, "a certain logic, in virtue of which evil returns, like a wave hurled from the shore, so that evil must return to me." And all at once it seemed to him perfectly impossible that he could possess such a woman in peace, and such happiness. Just in that was lacking the logic which commands the return of the wave of evil. And then what? Marynia may die at childbirth, for instance. Pani Mashko, through revenge, may say some word about him, which will stick in Marynia's mind, and in view of her condition, will emerge afterward in the form of a fever.

Not even the whole truth is needed for that effect. On the contrary, Pani Mashko may boast even that she resisted his attempts. "And who knows," said Pan Stanislav to himself, "if Pani Mashko is not making a visit to Marynia this moment? in such an event the first conversation about men — and a few jesting words are sufficient."

Thinking thus, he felt that the cap was burning on his head; and he reached home with a feeling of alarm. At home he did not find Pani Mashko; but Marynia gave him a card from Panna Helena, asking him to come after dinner to see her.

"I fear that Ignas is worse," said Marynia.

"No; I ran in there for a moment in the morning. Panna Helena was at some conference with the attorney, Kononovich; but I saw Panna Ratkovski and Pan Ignas. He was perfectly well, and spoke to me joyously."

At dinner Pan Stanislav resolved to tell Marynia of the news which he had heard, for he knew that it could not be concealed from her anyhow, and he did not wish that it should be brought to her too suddenly and incautiously.

When she asked what was to be heard in the counting-house and the city, he said, —

"Nothing new in the counting-house; but in the city they are talking about certain misunderstandings between the Osnovskis."

"Between the Osnovskis?"

"Yes; something has happened in Ostend. Likely the cause of all is Kopovski."

Marynia flushed from curiosity, and asked, —

"What dost thou say, Stas?"

"I say what I heard. Thou wilt remember my remarks on the evening of Pan Ignas's betrothal? It seems that I was right; I will say, in brief, that there was a certain history, and, in general, that it was bad."

"But thou hast said that Kopovski is the betrothed of Panna Castelli."

"He has been, but he is not now. Everything may be broken in their case."

The news made a great impression on Marynia; she wanted to inquire further, but when Pan Stanislav told her that he knew nothing more, and that in all likelihood more detailed news would come in some days, she fell to lamenting the fate of Osnovski, whom she had always liked much, and was indignant at Pani Aneta.

"I thought," said she, "that he would change her, and attract her by his love; but she is not worthy of him, and Pan Svirski is right in what he says about women."

The conversation was interrupted by Plavitski, who, after an early dinner at the restaurant, had come to tell the "great news," which he had just heard, for all the city was talking of it. Pan Stanislav thought then that he had done well to prepare Marynia, for in Plavitski's narrative the affair took on colors which were too glaring. Plavitski mentioned, it is true, in the course of his story, "principles and matrons" of the old time; but apparently he was satisfied that something of such rousing interest had happened, and evidently he took the affair, too, from the comic side, for at the end he said, —

"But she is a mettlesome woman! she is a frolicker! Whoever was before her was an opponent! She let no man pass, no man! Poor Osnosio! but she let *no man* pass."

Here he raised his brows, and looked at Marynia and Pan Stanislav, as if wishing to see whether they understood what "no man" meant. But on Marynia's face disgust was depicted.

"Fe! Stas," said she, "how all that is not only dishonorable, but disgusting!"

## CHAPTER LXI.

After dinner Pan Stanislav went to Panna Helena's. Pan Ignas wore a black bandage on his forehead yet, with a wider plaster in the centre, covering a wound; he stuttered, and, when looking, squinted somewhat; but, in general, he was coming to himself more and more, and looked on himself as recovered already. The doctor asserted that those marks which remained from the wound yet were disappearing without a trace. When Pan Stanislav entered, the young man was sitting at a table in a deep armchair, in which old Pan Zavilovski used to sit formerly, and was listening with closed eyes to verses which Panna Ratkovski was reading. But she closed the book at sight of a visitor.

"Good-evening," said Pan Stanislav to her. "How art thou, Ignas? I see that I have interrupted a reading. In what are you so interested?"

Panna Ratkovski turned her closely-clipped head to the book,—her hair had been luxuriant before, but she cut it so as not to occupy time needed for the sick man,—and answered,—

"This is Pan Zavilovski's poetry."

"Thou art listening to thy own poetry?" said Pan Stanislav, laughing. "Well, how does it please thee?"

"I hear it as if it were not my own," replied Pan Ignas. After a while he added, speaking slowly, and stuttering a little, "But I shall write again as soon as I recover."

It was evident that this thought occupied him greatly, and that he must have mentioned it more than once; for Panna Ratkovski, as if wishing to give him pleasure, said,—

"And the same kind of beautiful verses, and not too long."

He smiled at her with gratitude, and was silent. But at that moment Panna Helena entered the room, and pressing Pan Stanislav's hand, said,—

"How well it is that you have come! I wanted to take counsel with you."

"I am at your service."

"I beg you to come to my room."

She conducted him to the adjoining room, indicated a chair to him, then, sitting down opposite, was silent, as if collecting her thoughts.

Pan Stanislav, looking at her under the lamp, noticed, for the first time, a number of silvery threads in her bright hair, and remembered that that woman was not thirty yet.

She began to speak in her cool and decisive voice, —

"I do not request counsel precisely, but assistance for my relative. I know that you are a real friend of his, and, besides, you have shown me so much kindness at the death of my father that I shall be grateful the rest of my life for it; and now I will speak more openly with you than with any one else. For personal reasons, which I will not touch, and of which I can only say that they are very painful, I have decided to create for myself other conditions of life, — conditions for me more endurable. I should have done so long since, but while my father was living I could not. Then Ignas's misfortune came. It seemed to me my duty not to desert the last relative bearing our name, for whom, besides, I have a heartfelt and real friendship. But now, thanks be to God! he is saved. The doctors answer for his life; and if God has given him exceptional capacities and predestined him to great things, nothing stands in the way of his activity."

Here she stopped, as if she had fallen to thinking suddenly of something in the future, after which, when she had roused herself, she spoke on, —

"But by his recovery my last task is finished, and I am permitted to return to my original plan. There remains only the property of which my father left a considerable amount, and which would be altogether useless to me in my coming mode of life. If I could consider this property my own personally, I might dispose of it otherwise, perhaps; but since it is family property, I consider that I have no right to devote it to foreign objects while any one of the family is alive who bears the name. I do not conceal from you that attachment to my cousin moves me; but I judge that I do above all that which conscience commands, and besides carry out the wish of my father, who did not succeed in writing his will, but who — I know with all certainty — wished to leave a part of his property to Ignas. I have provided for myself not in the degree which my father thought of doing, but still I take more than I need. Ignas inherits the rest. The act of conveyance has been written by Pan Kononovich according to all legal rules. It includes this house, Yasmen, the property in Kutno, the estates in Poznan and the moneys with the exception of that portion which I have retained for myself, and a small part which I have reserved for Panna Ratkovski. It is a question now only of delivering this document to Ignas. I have asked two doctors if it is not too early, and if the excitement might not harm him. They assure me that it is not too early, and that every agreeable news may only act on his health beneficially. This being the case, I wish to finish the matter at once, for I am in a hurry."

Here she smiled faintly. Pan Stanislav, pressing her hand, asked, with unfeigned emotion, —

"Dear lady, I do not inquire through curiosity, What do you intend?"

Not wishing evidently to give an explicit answer, she said, —

"A person has the right always to take refuge under the care of God. As to Ignas, he has an honest heart and a noble character, which will not be injured by wealth; but the property is very considerable, and he is young, inexperienced; he will begin life in conditions changed altogether, — hence I wish to ask you, as a man of honor and his friend, to have guardianship over him. Care for him, keep him from evil people, but above all remind him that his duty is to write and work further. For me it was a question, not only of saving his life, but his gifts. Let him write; let him pay society, not for himself only, but for those too whom God created for His own glory and the assistance of men, but who destroyed both themselves and their gifts."

Here her lips became pale on a sudden, her hands closed, and the voice stopped in her throat. It might seem that the despair accumulated in her soul would break all bounds immediately; but she mastered herself after a while, and only her clinched hands testified what the effort was which that action had cost her.

Pan Stanislav, seeing her suffering, judged that it would be better to turn her thought in another direction, toward practical and current affairs; hence he said, —

"Evidently this will be an unheard of change in the life of Ignas; but I too hope that it will result only in good. Knowing him, it is difficult to admit another issue. But could you not defer the act for a year, or at least half a year?"

"Why?"

"For reasons which do not lie in Ignas himself, but which might have connection with him. I do not know whether the news has reached you that the marriage of Panna Castelli to Kopovski is broken, and that the position of those ladies is tremendously awkward in consequence. Through breaking with Ignas, they have made public opinion indignant, and now their names are on people's tongues again. It would be for them a perfect escape to return to Ignas; and it is possible to suppose that when they learn of your gift, they will surely attempt this, and it is unknown whether Ignas, especially after so short an interval, and weakened as he is, might not let himself be involved by them."

Panna Helena looked at Pan Stanislav with brows contracted from attention, and, dwelling on what he said, she answered, —

"No. I judge that Ignas will choose otherwise."

"I divine your thought," said Pan Stanislav; "but think, — he was attached to that other one beyond every estimate, to such a degree that he did not wish to outlive the loss of her."

Here something happened which Pan Stanislav had not expected, for Panna Helena, who had always such control of herself and was almost stern, opened her thin arms in helplessness, and said, —

"Ah, if that were true, — if there were not for him any other happiness save in her! Oh, Pan Polanyetski, I knew that he ought not to do that; but there are things stronger than man, and they are things which he needs for life absolutely — and besides — "

Pan Stanislav looked at her with astonishment; after a while she added, —

"Besides, while one lives, one may enter on a better road any moment."

"I did not suppose that I should hear anything like this from her," thought Pan Stanislav. And he said aloud, —

"Then let us go to Ignas."

Pan Ignas received the news first with amazement, and then with delight; but that delight was as if external. It might be supposed that, by the aid of his brain, he understood that something immensely favorable had met him, and that he had told himself that he must be pleased with it, but that he did not feel it with his heart. His heart declared itself only in the care and interest with which he asked Panna Helena what she intended to do with herself, and what would become of her. She was not willing to answer him, and stated, in general terms, that she would withdraw from the world, and that her resolve was unchangeable. She implored of him this, which clearly concerned her most, not to waste his powers and disappoint people who were attached to him. She spoke as a mother, and he, repeating, "I will write again the moment I recover," kissed her hands and had tears in his eyes. It was not known, however, whether those tears meant sympathy for her, or the regret of a child abandoned by a good and kind nurse; for Panna Helena told him that from that moment she considered herself a guest in his house, and in two days would withdraw. Pan Ignas would not agree to this, and extorted the promise from her to remain a week longer. She yielded at last, through fear of exciting him and injuring his health. Then he grew calm, and was as gladsome as a little boy whose prayer has been granted. Toward the end of the evening, however, he grew thoughtful, as if remembering something, looked around with astonished eyes on those present, and said, —

"It is wonderful, but it seems to me as if all this had happened before some time."

Pan Stanislav, wishing to give a more cheerful tone to the conversation, asked, laughing, —

"Was it during previous existences on other planets? It was, was it not?"

"In that way everything might have happened some other time," said Pan Ignas.

"And you have written the very same verses already — on the moon?"

He took up a book lying on the table, looked at it, grew thoughtful, and said at last, —

"I will write again, but when I recover completely."

Pan Stanislav took farewell and went out. That evening Panna Ratkovski removed to her little chamber at Pani Melnitski's.

## CHAPTER LXII.

THE separation of the Osnovskis, who in social life occupied a position rather prominent, and the great fortune which fell on a sudden to Pan Ignas, were the items of news with which the whole city was occupied. People who supposed that Panna Helena had taken the young man to her house to marry him were stunned from amazement. New gossip and new suppositions rose. People began to whisper that Pan Ignas was a son of old Zavilovski; that he had threatened his sister with a law-suit for concealing the will; that she chose to renounce all and go abroad rather than be exposed to a scandalous law-suit. Others declared that the cause of her departure was Panna Ratkovski; that between those two young ladies scenes had taken place unparalleled, — scenes to arouse indignation. In consequence of this, self-respecting houses would not permit Panna Ratkovski to cross their thresholds. There were others, too, who, appearing in the name of public good, refused simply to Panna Helena the right of disposing of property in that fashion, giving at the same time to understand that they would have acted more in accord with public benefit.

In a word, everything was said that gossip and meddling and frivolity and low malice could invent. Soon new food for public curiosity arrived under the form of news of a duel between Osnovski and Kopovski, in which Osnovski was wounded. Kopovski returned to Warsaw soon after with the fame of a hero of uncommon adventures in love and arms, — stupider than ever, but also more beautiful, and in general so charming that at sight of him hearts young and old began to beat with quickened throb.

Osnovski, wounded rather slightly, was under treatment in Brussels. Svirski received from him a brief announcement soon after the duel, that he was well, that in the middle of winter he would go to Egypt, but, before that, would return to Prytulov. The artist came to Pan Stanislav with this news, expressing at the same time the fear that Osnovski was returning only to avenge his wrongs afresh on Kopovski.

"For I am sure," said he, "that if he is wounded, it is because he permitted it. According to me, he wished to die simply. I have shot with him more than once at Brufini's, and know how he shoots. I have seen him hit matches, and am convinced that had he wished to blow out Koposio, we should n't see him to-day."

"Perhaps not," answered Pan Stanislav; "but since he talks of going to Egypt, 't is clear that he does not intend to let himself be killed. Let him go, and let him take Pan Ignas."

"It is true that Pan Ignas ought to see the world a little. I should like to go from here to see him. How is he?"

"I will go with you, for I have not seen him to-day. He is well, but somehow strange. You remember what a proud soul he was, shut up in himself. Now he is in good health, as it were, but has become a little child; at the least trouble there are tears in his eyes."

After a while the two went out together.

"Is Panna Helena with Pan Ignas yet?" inquired Svirski.

"She is. He takes her departure to heart so much that she has pity on him. She was to go away in a week; now, as you see, the second week has passed."

"What does she wish specially to do with herself?"

"She says nothing precise on this point. Probably she will enter some religious order and pray all her life for Ploshovski."

"But Panna Ratkovski?"

"Panna Ratkovski is with Pani Melnitski."

"Did Pan Ignas feel her absence much?"

"For the first days. Afterward he seemed to forget her."

"If he does not marry her in a year, I will repeat my proposal. As I love God, I will. Such a woman, when she becomes a wife, grows attached to her husband."

"I know that in her soul Panna Helena wishes Ignas to marry Panna Ratkovski. But who knows how it will turn out?"

"I am sure that he will marry her; what I say is the imagining of a weak head. I shall not marry."

"My wife said that you told her that yesterday; but she laughed at the threat."

"It is not a threat; it is only this, that I have no happiness."

Their conversation was interrupted by the coming of a

carriage, in which were Pani Kraslavski and Pani Mashko. Those ladies were going in the direction of the Alley, wishing evidently to take the air. The day was clear, but cold; and Pani Mashko was so occupied with drawing a warm cloak on her mother that she did not see them, and did not return their salutation.

"I called on them the day before yesterday," said Svirski. "She is a kindly sort of woman."

"I hear that she is a very good daughter," answered Pan Stanislav.

"I noticed that when I was there; but, as is usual with an old sceptic, it occurred to me at once that she finds pleasure also in the rôle of a careful daughter. Do you not see women often doing good of some special sort because they think that it becomes them?"

And Svirski was not mistaken. In fact, Pani Mashko found pleasure in the rôle of a self-sacrificing daughter. But that itself was very much, since such a satisfaction flowed still from real attachment to her mother, and because at sight of her misfortune something was roused in the woman, something quivered. At the same time Svirski did not wish, or did not know how, to draw this further conclusion from his thoughts: that as in the domain of the toilet a woman in addition to a new hat needs a new cloak, a new dress, new gloves, so in the domain of good deeds once she has taken up something she wants to be fitted out anew from head to foot. In this way the rebirth of a woman is never quite impossible.

Meanwhile they arrived at Pan Ignas's, who received them with delight; because, for some time past, the sight of people gave him pleasure, as it does usually to patients returning to life. When he had learned from Svirski that the latter would go soon to Italy, he began to insist that he should take him.

"Ah, ha!" thought Svirski; "then somehow Panna Ratkovski is not in thy head?"

Pan Ignas declared that he had been thinking long of Italy; that nowhere else would he write as there, under those impressions of art, and those centuries crumbling into ruins entwined with ivy. He was carried away and pleased by that thought; hence the honest Svirski agreed without difficulty.

"But," said he, "I cannot stay long there this time, for I have a number of portraits to paint in this city; and, besides, I promised Pan Stanislav to return to the christening." Then he turned to Pan Stanislav, —

"Well, what is it finally, the christening of a son or a daughter?"

"Let it be what it likes," answered Pan Stanislav, "if only, with God's will, in good health."

And while the other two began to plan the journey, he took farewell, and went to his counting-house. He had a whole mail from the previous day to look over, so, shutting himself in, he began to read letters, and dictate to a writer in short-hand those which touched affairs needing immediate transaction. After a while, however, a newly hired servant interrupted his labor by announcing that some lady wished to see him.

Pan Stanislav was disturbed. It seemed to him, it is unknown why, that this could be no other than Pani Mashko; and, foreseeing certain explanations and scenes, his heart began to beat unquietly.

Meanwhile the laughing and glad face of Marynia appeared in the door most unexpectedly.

"Ah, well, have n't I given a surprise?" inquired she.

Pan Stanislav sprang up at sight of her, with a feeling of sudden and immense delight, and, seizing her hands, began to kiss them, one after the other.

"But, my dear, this is really a surprise!" said he. "Whence did it come to thy head to look in here?"

And thus speaking, he pushed an armchair toward her, and seated her as a dear and honored guest; from his radiant face it was evident what pleasure her presence was giving him.

"I have something curious to show thee," said Marynia; "and because I must walk a good deal, anyhow, I came in. And thou, what didst thou think? Whom didst thou look for? Own up, right away!"

Thus speaking, she began to threaten him while laughing; but he answered, —

"So much business is done here, in every case I did n't think it was thou. What hast thou to show?"

"See what a letter I have!"

Dear and Beloved Lady, — It will astonish you perhaps that I turn to you; but you, who are to become a mother soon, are the only person on earth who will understand what must take place in the heart of a mother — even if she is only an aunt — who sees her child's unhappiness. Believe me it is a question for me of nothing else than bringing even temporary relief to an unhappy child; and it interests me the more, that in all this that has happened I myself am to blame chiefly. Perhaps these words too will astonish you, but it is the case. I am to blame. If a bad and spoilt man, at the moment when Nitechka was tottering and losing her balance, dared to touch her with his unworthy lips, I should not have lost my head and sacrificed the child. Indeed, Yozio Osnovski is to blame too: he put the question of marriage on a sharp knife; he suspected something and wanted to rid his house of Kopovski. May God forgive him, for it is not proper to defend one's self at the cost of another's happiness and life. My dear lady! it seemed to me at the first moment that the only issue was marriage with the unworthy Kopovski, and that Nitechka had no longer the right to become the wife of Ignas. I wrote even purposely to Ignas that she followed the impulse of her heart, and that she would give her hand to Kopovski with attachment; and I thought that in this way Ignas would bear the loss of her more easily, and I wanted to decrease his pain. Nitechka for Kopovski! The merciful God did not permit that; and when I too saw that that union would have been death for Nitechka, we were thinking only of this, how to be free of those bonds. It is no longer a question for me of returning to former relations, for Nitechka too has lost faith in people and in life, so that probably she would never be willing to agree to a return. She does not even know that I am writing this letter. If the beloved lady had seen how Nitechka has paid for all this with her health, and how terribly she felt the act of Pan Ignas, she would have pitied her. Pan Ignas should not have done what he has done, even out of regard for Nitechka; alas! men in such cases count only with their own wishes. She is as much to blame in all this as a newly born infant; but I see how she melts before my eyes, and how from morning till evening she is grieving because she was the unconscious cause of his misfortune, and might have broken his life. Yesterday, with tears in her eyes, she begged me in case of her death to be a mother to Ignas, and to watch over him as over my own son. Every day she says that maybe he is cursing her, and my heart is breaking, for the doctor says that he answers for nothing if her condition continues. O God of mercy! but come to the aid of a despairing mother; let me know even from time to time something about Ignas, or rather write to me that he is well, that he is calm, that he has forgotten her, that he is not cursing her, so that I might show her that letter and bring her even a little relief from her torture. I feel that I am writing only in half consciousness, but you will understand what is taking place in me, when I look on that unhappy sacrifice God will reward you and I will pray every day that your daughter, if God gives you a daughter, be happier than my poor Nitechka.

"What is thy thought about that?" inquired Marynia.

"I think," said Pan Stanislav, "that news of the change

in Pan Ignas's fortune has spread rather widely; and second, I think that this letter, sent to your address, is directed really to Ignas."

"That may be. It is not an honest letter; but still they may be very unhappy."

"It is certain that their position cannot be pleasant. Osnovski was right when he wrote that there is even for Pani Bronich an immense disappointment in all this, and that she is trying vainly to deceive herself. As for Panna Castelli, you know what Svirski told me? I do not repeat to thee his words literally; but he said that now only a fool, or a man without moral value, would marry her. They understand this themselves, and certainly it is not pleasant for them. Perhaps, too, conscience is speaking; but still, see how many dodges there are in that letter. Do not show it to Ignas."

"No, I will not," answered Marynia, whose warmest wishes were on the side of Panna Ratkovski.

And Pan Stanislav, following the thought which was digging into him for some time past, repeated to her, word for word almost, what he had repeated to himself, —

"There is a certain logic which punishes, and they are harvesting what they sowed. Evil, like a wave, is thrown back from the shore and returns."

Hereupon Marynia began to draw figures on the floor with her parasol, as if meditating on something; then, raising her clear eyes to her husband, she said, —

"It is true, my Stas, that evil returns; but it may return, too, as remorse and sorrow. In that case the Lord God is satisfied with such penance, and punishes no further."

If Marynia had known what was troubling him, and wanted to soften his suffering, and console the man, she could not have found anything better than those few simple words. For some time Pan Stanislav had been oppressed by a foreboding that some misfortune must meet him, and he was in ceaseless fear of it. From her only did he learn that his sorrow and remorse might be that returning wave. Yes, he had had no little remorse, and sorrow had not been wanting in him; he felt, too, that if suffering might and could be a satisfaction, he would be ready to suffer twice as grievously. Now a desire took him to seize in his arms that woman full of simplicity and honesty, from whom so much good came to him; and if he did not do so, it was only from fear of emotions for her, and out of regard for her condition, and that indecision which fettered him in his relations with her. But he raised her hand to his lips, and said, —

"Thou art right, and art very kind."

She, pleased with the praise, smiled at him, and began to prepare for home.

When she had gone, Pan Stanislav went to the window, and followed her with his eyes. From afar he saw her curved form advancing with heavy step, her dark hair peeping from under her hat; and in that moment he felt with new force, greater than ever, that she was the dearest person in the world to him, and that he loved her only, and would love her till his death.

## CHAPTER LXIII.

Two days later Pan Stanislav received a note from Mashko, containing a few words of farewell.

"I go to-day," wrote he. "I shall try absolutely to run in once more to thee; but in every case I bid thee farewell, and thank thee for all proofs of friendship which thou hast shown me. May the Lord God prosper thee better than He has prospered me so far! I should like to see thee, even for a moment; and if I can, I shall run in about four o'clock. Meanwhile I repeat the request to remember my wife, and protect her a little when people drop her. I pray thee also to defend me before her against people's tongues. I am going to Berlin at nine in the evening, and quite openly. Till we meet again! and in every case, be well, — and once more, thanks for everything.

"MASHKO."

Pan Stanislav went to the counting-house about four, but he waited beyond an hour in vain. "He will not come," thought he, at last; "so much the better." And he went home with the feeling of satisfaction that he had succeeded in avoiding a disagreeable meeting. But in the evening a species of pity for Mashko began to move him: he thought that the man had gone by a bad and feverish road, it is true; but he had had his fill of torment and tearing, and in the end had paid dearly; that all which had happened was to be foreseen long before; and if those who foresaw it had associated with him, and received him at their houses, they ought not to show him contempt in the day of his downfall. He knew, too, that he should give Mashko pleasure by his appearance at the station; and after a moment of hesitation he went.

On the road he remembered that likely he should find Pani Mashko, too, at the station; but he knew that in any event he must meet her, and he judged that to withdraw because of her would be a kind of vain cowardice. With these thoughts he went to the station.

In the hall of the first class, which is not large, there were several persons, and on the tables whole piles of travelling-cases, but nowhere could he see Mashko; and only after he had looked around carefully did he recognize in a young veiled lady, sitting in one corner of the hall, Pani Mashko.

"Good-evening," said he, approaching her. "I have come to say good-by to your husband. Where is he?"

She bowed slightly, and answered, with the thin, cold voice usual to her, —

"My husband is buying tickets."

"How tickets? Are you going with him?"

"No; my husband is buying a ticket."

Further conversation under these conditions seemed rather difficult; but, after a while, Mashko appeared in company with a railway servant, to whom he gave the ticket and money, with the order to check the baggage. Wearing a long travelling overcoat and a soft silk cap, he looked, with his side whiskers and gold glasses, like some travelling diplomat. Pan Stanislav deceived himself, too, in thinking that Mashko would show uncommon delight at his coming. Mashko, when he saw him, said, it is true, "Oh, how thankful I am that thou hast come!" but, as it were, with a kind of indifference, and with the hurry usual to people who are going on a journey.

"Everything is checked," said he, looking around the hall. "But where are my hand packages? Ah, here they are! Good!"

Then he turned to Pan Stanislav, and said, —

"I thank thee for having come. But do me still one kindness, and conduct my wife home; or, at least, go out with her, and help her to find a carriage. Terenia, Pan Polanyetski will take thee home. My dear friend, come one moment; I have something more to say to thee."

And, taking Pan Stanislav aside, he began to speak feverishly, —

"Take her home without fail. I have given a plausible form to my journey; but do thou say to her, so, in passing, that thou art surprised that I am going such a short time before the calling of the will case, for if any event should detain me, the case must be lost. I wanted to go to thy house just to ask this of thee; but, as thou knowest, on the day of a journey — The case will come up in a week. I shall fall ill; my place will be taken by my assistant, a young advocate, a beginner, and of course he will lose. But the affair will be plausible through my illness. I have secured my wife; everything is in her name, and they will not take one glass from her. I have a plan which I shall lay before a shipbuilding company in Antwerp. If I make a contract, timber will rise in price throughout this whole country; but who knows, in that case, if I shall not return, for the whole affair of Ploshov is a trifle in comparison with this business? I cannot speak more in detail. Were it not for the grievous moments which my wife must pass, I should keep regret away; but that just throttles me."

Here he touched his throat with his hand, and then spoke still more hurriedly, —

"Misfortune fell on me; but misfortune may fall on any man. For that matter, it is too late to speak of this. What has been, has been; but I did what I could, and I shall do yet what I can. And this, too, is a relief to me, — that thou wilt get thy own even from Kremen. If I had time to tell thee what I have in mind, thou couldst see that it would not come to the head of every man. Maybe I shall have business even with thy firm. I do not give up, as thou seest — I have secured my wife perfectly. Well, it's over, it's over! Another in my place might have ended worse. Might he not? But let us return to my wife now."

Pan Stanislav listened to Mashko's words with a certain pain. He wondered, it is true, at his mental fertility; but at the same time he felt that in him there was lacking that balance which makes the difference between a man of enterprise and an enterprising adventurer. It seemed to him, too, that there was in Mashko already something of the future worn-out trickster, who will struggle for a long time yet, but who, with his plans, will be falling lower and lower till he ends, with boots worn on one side, in a second-rate coffee-house, telling, in a circle of the same kind of "broken men," of his former greatness. He thought, also, that the cause of all this was a life resting to begin with on untruth; and that Mashko, with all his intelligence, can never work himself out of the fetters of falsehood.

See, he pretends yet, and even before his wife. He had to do so; but when the hall began to fill with people, some acquaintances stepped up to greet the two men, and exchange a couple of such hurried phrases as are used at railroads. Mashko answered them with such a tinge of loftiness and favor that anger seized Pan Stanislav. "And to think," said he, "that he is fleeing from his creditors! What would happen were that man to reach fortune?"

But now the bell sounded, and beyond the window was heard the hurried breath of the engine. People began to move about and hasten.

"I am curious to know what is going on in him now?" thought Pan Stanislav.

But even at that moment Mashko could not free himself from the bonds of lying. Maybe his heart was straitened by an evil foreboding: maybe he had a gleam of second sight, that that wife whom he loved he should never see again; that he was going to want, to contempt, to fall; but it was not permitted him to show what he felt, or even to say farewell to his wife as he wished.

The second bell sounded. They went out on the platform, and Mashko stood still a while before the sleeping-car. The gleam of the lamp fell directly on his face, on which two small wrinkles appeared near the mouth. But he spoke calmly, with the tone of a man whom business constrains to a few days' absence, but who is sure that he will return.

"Well, till we meet again, Teresia! Kiss mamma's hands for me, and be well. Till we meet, till we meet!"

Thus speaking, he raised her hand, which, moreover, he kept long at his lips. Pan Stanislav, going aside a little by design, thought, —

"They see each other now for the last time. In some half year a separation in form will follow."

And the peculiar lot of those two women struck him, the same for mother and daughter. Both married with great appearances of brilliancy; and the husbands of both had to run away from their domestic hearths, leaving only shame to their wives.

But now the bell sounded the third time. Mashko entered. For a while, in the wide pane of the sleeping-car, his side whiskers were visible, and his gold-rimmed eye-glasses; then the train pushed out into darkness.

"I am at your service," said Pan Stanislav to Pani Mashko.

He was almost certain that she would thank him dryly for his society, and reject it; he was even angry, for the reason that he had determined to tell her not only something about her husband, but something from himself. But she inclined her head in agreement; she, too, had her plan. So much bitter dislike for Pan Stanislav and such a feeling of offence had been rising in her heart for a long time, that, thinking him likely to take advantage again of a moment which they were to pass together, she determined to give him a slap which he would remember for many a day.

But she was mistaken altogether. First, through her he had been crushed as ice is crushed against a cliff, and therefore for some time he had felt for her not only dislike, but even hatred. Second, if later, through a feeling of conviction that the fault was on his side exclusively, that hatred had passed, then he had changed so much that he had become almost entirely another man. His mercantile reckoning with himself had taught him that such transgressions are paid for too dearly; he was in a phase of immense desire for a life without deceit; and finally remorse and sorrow had eaten up desire in him as rust eats up iron. When assisting her into the carriage, and when he touched her shoulder, he remained calm; and when he had taken his seat, he began at once to speak of Mashko, for he judged that through a feeling of humanity alone he ought to prepare her for the coming catastrophe, and soften its significance.

"I wonder at the daring of your husband," said he. "Let one bridge fall on the road during his stay in Berlin, he will not be able to return to the will case, on which, as you know, of course, all his fate depends. He must have gone for important reasons; but it is always hazardous to act thus."

"The bridges are strong," answered Pani Mashko.

But he, unconquered by that not over-encouraging answer, spoke on, drawing aside before her gradually the curtain of the future; and he spoke so long that while he was talking they arrived before the Mashko dwelling. Then she, not understanding the meaning of his words evidently, and angry, perhaps, that she had not had the chance to give him the intended blow, said, when she had stepped out of the carriage, —

"Had you any personal object in disquieting me?"

"No," answered Pan Stanislav, who saw that the moment had come to tell her that which he had resolved to say from himself. "In relation to you, I have only one object, —to declare that, with reference to you, I have offended unworthily, and that from my whole soul I beg your pardon."

But the young woman went into her house without

answering a single word. Pan Stanislav, to the end of his life, did not know whether that was the silence of hatred or forgiveness.

Still he returned home with a certain encouragement, for it seemed to him that he ought to have acted thus. In his eyes that was a small act of penitence; it was all one to him how Pani Mashko understood him. "Maybe she judged," said he to himself, "that I begged pardon of her for my subsequent treatment; in every case I shall be able to look her more boldly in the eyes now."

And in that thought of his there was undoubtedly some selfishness; but there was also the will to escape from the toils.

## CHAPTER LXIV.

PANNA HELENA, also, before her departure, received a letter from Pani Bronich, in the style of that which Marynia had received, and, like Marynia, she did not show it to Pan Ignas. Besides, Pan Ignas went away with Svirski a week later without visiting any acquaintance except Panna Ratkovski. Svirski, in person, kept him from all visits; and Pan Stanislav, in conversations with his wife, declared that he had acted rightly. "At present," said he, "it would be disagreeable both for Ignas, and for us. Those who saw him every day are different, for they are used to him; but no one else could refrain from looking at the scar which is left on his forehead. Besides, Ignas has changed very much. During the journey he will recover perfectly; on his return we shall receive him as if nothing had happened; and strangers will see in him, above all, a wealthy young lord."

And it might have been so in reality. But meanwhile, there was loneliness around the Polanyetskis, because of that departure. Their circle of acquaintances had scattered on all sides. Osnovski remained still in Brussels; where Pani Aneta had gone no one knew. Pani Bronich and Panna Castelli were in Paris; there was no one at Yasmen. Pani Kraslavski and her daughter shut themselves in, and lived only for each other; and finally sickness had confined to her bed poor Pani Emilia, once and forever.

There remained only the Bigiels and the professor. But he was sick, too, and, moreover, he had become so peculiar that strangers considered him a lunatic. Some said with a certain irony that a man who thinks that the spirit of Christianity will penetrate into politics as it has into private life, must be indeed of sound mind. He began himself to think about death, and to make preparations for it. Frequently he repeated to Pan Stanislav his desire to die "in the ante-chamber to the other world," and in view of that was preparing for Rome. But since he loved Marynia greatly, he wished to wait till after her sickness.

In this way time passed in great seclusion for the Polanyetskis. It was for that matter necessary for Marynia, who in recent days had felt very ill, and necessary for her state of feeling. Pan Stanislav worked over business in the counting-house, and over himself; he was working out in himself a new man, and watching over his wife. She, too, was preparing herself for a new epoch in life; and she was preparing herself gladly, for it seemed to her that what she did would act upon both of them. Pan Stanislav became daily less absolute in some way, more condescending in his judgments of people, and milder, not only in relation to her, but in relation to all persons with whom life brought him into contact. He surrounded her with exceptional, with thoughtful care; and though she supposed that this care had in view not so much her person as the child, she recognized this as proper, and was grateful. She was astonished at times by a kind of timidity and, as it were, hesitation in his treatment of her; but not being able to divine that he was simply curbing his feeling for her, she ascribed such exhibitions to "Stas's" fear as to whether all would end well in her case.

Whole weeks passed in this manner. Their monotony was broken sometimes by a letter from Svirski, who, when he could seize a free moment, reported what he could of himself and Pan Ignas. In one of those letters he inquired in Pan Ignas's name if Pani Polanyetski would permit him to send a description of his impressions in the form of letters to her. "I spoke with him of this in detail," wrote Svirski. "He contends first that it might be agreeable to the lady to have echoes from a land which has left her so many pleasant memories; and second, that it would lighten his work greatly were he to write as if privately. He is well; he walks, eats, and sleeps perfectly. Every evening I see too that he sits at his desk and prepares to write. I concluded that he was trying poetry, also. Somehow it does not succeed, for he has not written anything yet, so far as I know. I suppose, however, that all will come out by degrees, and in season. Meanwhile the form of letters would lighten his work, perhaps, really. I will add in conclusion that he mentions Panna Helena with immense gratitude; and at every mention of Panna Ratkovski, his eyes become bright. I speak of her to him frequently, for what can I, poor man, do? When anything is not predestined, there is no help in the case; and when it is written down to a man that he must remain like a stake in a hedge, he will not put forth leaves in spring even."

In the middle of November a letter came from Rome, which roused much thought in the Polanyetskis. Svirski wrote as follows: —

"Imagine to yourselves that Pani Bronich is here and Panna Castelli, and that I have had an interview with them In Rome I am as if at home; hence I learned of their coming on the second day. And do you know what I did immediately? I persuaded Ignas to go to Sicily, in which, moreover, I found no great difficulty. I thought to myself, 'he will sit in Syracuse or in Taormina; and if by chance he falls into the hands of the Mafia the cost of his ransom will be less than what he paid for the privilege of wearing Panna Nitechka's ring for a short time.' I said to myself, 'if he and she are to meet on earth and be reconciled, let them meet and be reconciled; but I have no wish to take that work on my conscience, especially after what has happened.' Ignas is well to all seeming; but he has not recovered yet mentally, and in that state he might be brought easily to something which he would regret for a lifetime. As to those ladies, I divined at once why they came here, and I was delighted in soul that I had hindered their tricks; that my supposition was to the point is shown by this, that some days later a letter came to Ignas, on which I recognized the handwriting of the widow of that heaven-dwelling Teodor. I wrote on the envelope that Pan Ignas had gone away, it was unknown whither, and sent the letter retro.

"That, however, was only the beginning of the history. Next morning I received a letter with an invitation to a talk. I answered that I must refuse with regret: that my occupations do not permit me to give myself such a pleasure. In answer to this, I received a second letter with an appeal to my character, my talent, my descent, my heart, my sympathy for an unhappy woman; and with the prayer that I should either go myself, or appoint an hour in my studio There was no escape, — I went. Pani Bronich herself received me with tears, and a whole torrent of narratives which I shall not repeat, but in which 'Nitechka' appears as a Saint Agnes the martyr. 'With what can I serve,' ask I? She answers: 'It is not a question of anything, but a kind word from Pan Ignas. The child is sick, she is coughing, in all likelihood she will not live the year out; but she wants to die with a word of forgiveness.' At this I confess that I was softened a little, but I held out. Moreover, I could not give the address of Pan Ignas, for I did not know really at what hotel he had stopped. I was sweating as in a steam bath; and at last I promised something in general, that if Ignas would begin at any time to talk with me about Panna Castelli, that I would persuade him to act in accordance with the wish of Pani Bronich.

"But this was not all yet. When I was thinking of going, Panna

Lineta herself rushed in on a sudden, and turned to her aunt with the request to let her talk with me alone. I will say in parenthesis that she has grown thin, and that she seems taller than usual, really like 'a poplar,' which any wind might break. Hardly were we left alone when she turned to me and said, 'Aunt is trying to make me innocent, and is doing so through love for me. I am thankful to her; but I cannot endure it, and I declare to you that I am guilty, that I am not worthy of anything, and that if I am unhappy I have deserved it a hundred times.' When I heard this I was astonished; but I saw that she was talking sincerely, for her lips were quivering and her eyes were mist-covered. You may say to yourselves that I have a heart made of butter; but I confess that I was moved greatly, and I inquired what I could do for her. To this she answered that I could do nothing; but she begged me to believe at least that she took no part in those efforts of her aunt to renew relations, that after Pan Ignas's act her eyes were opened to what she had done, and that she would never forget it in her life At last she said once again, that she alone was the cause of everything, and begged me to repeat our conversation to Pan Ignas, not immediately, however, but only when he could not suspect that she wished to influence him.

"Well, and what do you think? Would you lend belief to anything like that? I see clearly two things, first, that Pan Ignas's attempt on his life, happen what may, must have shaken her terribly; and second, that she is fabulously unhappy, — who knows, she may be sick really. So the opinion of Panna Helena comes to my mind, who, as you repeated to me, says that we must not despair of a man while he is living. In every case it is something uncommon I believe too that even if Pan Ignas wished now to return to her, she would not consent, simply because she does not feel that she is worthy of him. As to me, I think that there are many better and nobler female natures than hers in the world; but may the deuce take me if I act against her!"

In continuation Svirski inquired about health, and sent obeisances to the Bigiels.

This letter made a great impression on all, and was the occasion of numerous discussions between the Polanyetskis and the Bigiels. It appeared at once too how far Pan Stanislav was changed. Formerly he would not have found words enough to condemn Panna Castelli, and never would he have believed that any chord of honor would make itself heard in a woman of her kind; but at present, when Pani Bigiel, who, as well as the other ladies, belonged soul and body to Panna Ratkovski's side, expressed doubts, and said, "Is not that merely a change of tactics on the part of Panna Castelli?" he said, —

"No; she is too young for that, and she seems to me sincere. It is a great thing if she acknowledges her fault so unconditionally, for it proves that untruth in life has disgusted her."

After a moment's hesitation, he added, —

"I remember, for example, that more than once Mashko acknowledged, as it were, that he was going by a wrong and false road; but right away he sought reasons to justify himself: 'With us it is necessary to do so;' 'That is the fault of our society;' 'I pay with the money that is current.' How much of this have I heard! And that was all untrue, too. Meanwhile there is a certain bravery in declaring, It is my fault absolutely. And whoso has that bravery has something left yet."

"Then do you judge that Pan Ignas would do well to return to her?"

"I do not judge at all, nor do I suppose that it could happen."

But the living interest roused by news from Rome, together with anxiety for Pan Ignas and Panna Castelli, passed away soon, under the pressure of a more important anxiety, which was hanging over the house of the Polanyetskis.

Toward the end of November Marynia's health began to fail evidently. It had been failing for some time, but she concealed this fact as long as possible. A painful palpitation of the heart came on her, and weakness so great that there were days when she could not move out of an armchair. Next came pains in her back and giddiness. In the course of a week she changed so much in the eyes, and grew thin to such a degree, that even the doctors, who up to that time had considered those symptoms as the ordinary forerunners of approaching labor, began to be alarmed at them. Her transparent face assumed at times a bluish tinge; and seemed, especially when the sick woman kept her eyes closed, like the face of a dead person. Even Pani Bigiel, the greatest optimist near Marynia, could not at last resist fears; the doctor declared to Pan Stanislav plainly that under such conditions the expected event might be dangerous, both in itself and in sequences. Marynia, though weaker every day and more exhausted, was indeed the only one who did not lose hope now.

But Pan Stanislav lost it. Such a grievous time came on him that all sufferings and misfortunes which hitherto in life he had gone through seemed to him nothing in comparison with his terrible dread, which often and often became utter despair. Formerly after his wedding, in his conceptions of marriage and his hopes of the future, a child was the main thing; now for the first time he felt that he would give not only one, but all the children that he could ever have, to save that one beloved Marynia. And his heart was cut when at times Marynia repeated with her weakened voice the question which before she had asked more than once, "Stas, but if it is a boy?" He would have been glad to fall at her feet, embrace them, and say, "Let the devil take it, boy or girl, if only thou art left;" but he had to smile at her, and assure her calmly that it was all one to him. His former terrors fell upon him again; and that hope, roused by Marynia's words, that by God's favor a wave of evil returns as remorse only, was dissipated without a trace. Now, at moments, he had again the feeling that Marynia's sickness might be just that returning wave. How it might be that wave he could not tell, for in vain did reason say to him that between the offence of Pani Osnovski or of Panna Castelli, for example, and the punishment which met them, there is an immediate connection which there is not in his case. Fear answered him, that evil may filter through life by such secret channels that the reason of man cannot follow it. And at this thought a dread seized him that was simply mysterious. A man in misfortune loses power of accurate reasoning; he lives under the weight of terror, and under such a weight was Pan Stanislav living. He saw only the precipice, and his own helplessness. More than once, while looking at the haggard face of Marynia, he said to himself, "One must be mad to suppose that she may not die;" and he sought desperately on the faces of those surrounding her for even a shade of hope, and with every drop of his blood, with every atom of his brain, with his whole soul and heart, he rose up against her death. It seemed to him an inconceivable injustice that she will have to close her eyes forever before he can show her how he loves her beyond every estimate; before he rewards her for all his carelessness, harsh treatment, egotism, and faithlessness; before he tells her that she has become the soul of his soul, something not only loved above all in his life, but revered. He repeated to himself that if God would not do this for him He ought to do it for her, so that in going from the world she might leave it with a feeling at least of that happiness which she had deserved. From these insolent suggestions to God of how He ought to act, he passed again to compunction, to humility, and to prayer. But meanwhile Marynia was daily more and more dangerously ill, and he, between two despairs, one of which shouted, "This cannot be," and the other, "It must be,"—he struggled as if in a vice.

Finally, from necessity, from the fear of taking hope from Marynia, he was forced to pretend in her presence that he paid little attention to her sickness. And the doctor and Pani Bigiel warned him daily not to alarm her; his own reason indicated the same to him. And here was a new torture, since it came to his mind that she might look on this as a lack of feeling, and die with the conviction that he had never loved her. Thus everything was changed in him utterly. Sleeplessness, torment, and alarm brought him to a kind of sickly exaltation, in which even the danger, which of itself was too evident, he saw in a still higher degree. It seemed to him that there was no hope, and at times he thought of Marynia as if already dead. For whole days he was thinking over every good point of her character,—her words, her kindness, her calmness. He remembered how all loved her, and he reproached himself desperately, saying that he had never been worthy of her, that he had not loved her sufficiently, that he had not valued her enough, and, to crown all, had broken faith with her; and therefore he must lose her, and lose her deservedly.

And in the feeling that a thing so terrible was also deserved, and that it was too late for any correction, was something simply heart-rending. Even persons who during life were always loved greatly, when they go from this world, leaving their friends in sorrow because they did not love the departed enough, leave behind, of all sorrows, that which is sorest.

At the beginning of December, Svirski and Pan Ignas returned, after two months' journey, from Italy. Pan Stanislav had grown so thin and haggard in that interval that they hardly knew him; and he, quite sunk in misery, turned scarcely any attention to them, and listened as in a dream to words of hope and consolation from both, as well as narratives, with which the honest artist tried to divert his suffering mind. What did he care now for Pan Ignas, Pani Bronich, Panna Castelli, in face of the fact that Marynia might die any day? Svirski, who had immense friendship for him, wishing to find from some point a little hope, betook himself to Pani Bigiel; but even she had not much hope to offer. The doctors themselves did not know well what the trouble was, for to her condition were added various complications, which could not be defined even. It was only known that the heart of the sick woman acted irregularly; they feared above all that, as a result of defective circulation, some coagulation in the veins might result, which would cause sudden death. Besides, even in case of a happy delivery, they feared a number of things,— exhaustion, loss of strength, and all those results which come only later. Svirski convinced himself that Pani Bigiel did not deceive herself either when, at the end of the conversation, she fell into tears, and said,—

"Poor Marynia! but he, poor man too. If even a child should be left him, he might find strength to bear the blow."

And when she had dried her tears, she added,—

"As it is, I do not understand how he endures it all."

That was true; Pan Stanislav did not eat and did not sleep. He had not shown himself at the counting-house for a long time; he went out only for flowers, which Marynia loved always, and the sight of which cheered her. But she was so sick that whenever he went for a bunch of chrysanthemums he returned with the terrible thought that perhaps he was bringing it for her coffin. Marynia's own eyes opened to this,—that perhaps her death was coming. She did not wish to speak of this to her husband; but before Pani Bigiel she fell to weeping one day in grief for her own life and for "Stas." She was tortured by the thought, how would he bear it, for she wanted that he should be awfully sorry for her, and at the same time, that he should not suffer much. Before him she pretended yet a long time to feel sure that all would end happily.

But later, when fainting spells came, she summoned courage to talk with him openly; this seemed to her a duty. Therefore one night, when Pani Bigiel, overcome by drowsiness, went to sleep, and he was watching near her as usual, she stretched her hand to him, and said,—

"Stas, I wanted to talk with thee, and beg for one thing."

"What is it, my love?" asked Pan Stanislav.

She thought for a time evidently how to express her prayer; and then she began to speak,—

"Promise me—I know that I shall recover surely—but promise me that should it be a boy, thou wilt love and be kind."

Pan Stanislav, by a superhuman effort, restrained the sobbing which seized his breast, and said calmly, —

"My dear love, I will always love thee and him, be sure."

Thereupon Marynia tried to raise his hand to her lips, but from weakness she was not able to do so; then she smiled at him from thankfulness. And again she said, "Do not think that I suppose for a moment anything terrible, not at all! but I should like to confess."

A shiver went through Pan Stanislav from head to feet.

"Well, my child," answered he, with a voice of fear, and as it were not his own voice.

And, recollecting that once her expression "service of God" pleased him, and wishing to let him know that it was not the question of anything else here but the performance of ordinary religious duties, she repeated, with an almost glad smile, —

"The service of God."

The confession took place next morning. Pan Stanislav was so sure that that was the end that he was almost astonished because Marynia was alive yet, and because she was even a little better in the evening.

He did not dare to admit hope into his soul. But she became brighter, and said that she breathed more easily. About midnight she began the usual warfare with him about his going to rest. Indeed, from trouble of mind and toil he looked not much better than she did. He refused at first, contending that he had slept in the daytime, and that he was refreshed, which was not true; but she insisted absolutely. He yielded all the more that there was a special woman and Pani Bigiel, besides the doctor, who for a week had slept in their house, and who assured him now that for the time there was no reason to expect any turn for the worse.

But when he went out, he did as he did usually; that is, he sat in an armchair at the door, and began to listen to what was happening in the room. In this way the hours of night passed. At the least noise he sprang up; but when the noise ceased he sat down again and began to think hurriedly and chaotically, as people do over whom danger is hanging. But at times his thoughts pressed one another, grew confused from weariness, forming, as it were, a dense crowd in which he was wandering without power to know anything. Sleep also tortured him. He had uncommon strength; but for ten days he knew not how he lived. Only black coffee and feverishness kept him on his feet. He did not yield even then, though his head was as heavy as lead and the crowd of his thoughts changed, as it were, into a black cloud, without a clear spot. He merely repeated to himself yet that Marynia was sick and he ought not to fall asleep; but these words had not the least meaning for him now.

At last toil, exhaustion, and sleepless nights conquered. A stony invincible sleep seized him, — a sleep in which there was no dreaming, in which reality perished, in which the whole world perished, and in which life itself was benumbed.

He was only roused toward morning by a knocking at the door.

"Pan Stanislav!" called the smothered voice of Pani Bigiel.

He sprang to his feet, and, gaining consciousness that moment, ran out of that room. With one glance he took in Marynia's bed; and at sight of the closed curtains his feet tottered under him.

"What has happened?" whispered he, with whitening lips.

But Pani Bigiel answered with a voice equally low, panting a trifle, —

"You have a son."

And she put her finger on her lips.

## CHAPTER LXV.

There were grievous days yet, and very grievous. Such weakness came on Marynia that her life began to quiver, like the flame of a taper. Would it quench, or would it flicker up again? At moments all were convinced that the flame was just, just dying. Still youth, and the relief brought by the coming of a child to the world, turned the scale on the life side. On a certain day the sick woman woke after long sleep, and seemed healthier. The old doctor in attendance, who witnessed the improvement, wished to convince himself more clearly that there was no deception, and asked to call in a physician with whom he had held counsel earlier. Pan Stanislav went to find him, and drove himself out of his mind almost while searching the city half a day for him; he did not dare hope yet that that turn in her sickness and in his misfortune was decisive. When at last he found the hunted doctor and brought him to the house, Pani Bigiel received him in the room adjoining the sick chamber, with moist eyelids, but with a glad face, and said, —

"She is better! decidedly better."

The woman could not say more, for tears flowed from her eyes. Pan Stanislav grew pale from emotion; but she controlled her delight with an effort, and said, smiling through her tears, —

"She is fighting for food now. A while since she asked to have the child brought. She asked also why you did not come. But now she is fighting for food; and how she is fighting! Ah, praise be to God! Praise be to God!"

And in her excitement she threw her arms around Pan Stanislav; then he kissed her hand and did not take it from his mouth for a long time. He trembled in every limb in the struggle to repress his delight, and also the groans which had gathered in him through many days of dread and torture, and which sought to burst forth now in spite of every effort.

Meanwhile the doctors came to Marynia, and sat rather long at her bedside. When the consultation was over, and they appeared again, satisfaction was evident on their faces. After Pan Stanislav's feverish inquiry, the doctor in regular attendance, an impetuous old man, with gold-rimmed glasses on his nose, and a golden heart in his breast, happy himself now, but greatly wearied, said, grumbling, —

"How is she? Go and thank God, — that is what!"

And Pan Stanislav went. Even had he been a man without belief, he would have gone at that moment, and thanked God with a heart swollen from tears and thankfulness, for having taken pity on him and let the wave return in the guise of pain and suffering, and not in the guise of death.

Later, when he had calmed himself, he went on tiptoe to his wife's room, where Pani Bigiel was. Marynia was gazing straight ahead with gladsome eyes, and at the first glance it was evident that she was much better really. When she saw him, she said, —

"Ah, see, Stas — I am well!"

"Well, my love," answered Pan Stanislav, quietly. It was not time yet for outbursts; therefore he sat down in silence near her bed. But after a while joy and great feeling for her overcame him so far that, bending down, he embraced with both hands her feet covered with the quilt, and, putting his face down to them, remained motionless.

And she, though very weak yet, smiled with satisfaction. She looked some time at him; then, just like a child which is happy because it is fondled, she said to Pani Bigiel, pointing with her transparent finger to that dark head nestled at her feet, —

"He loves me!"

Next day Marynia felt still stronger, and from that moment almost every hour brought improvement. At last that was not a gradual return to health, but a bloom, as it were, a sudden return of spring after winter, which astonished the doctor himself. Pan Stanislav wanted at moments to shout from the joy which was stifling him, as formerly sorrow had stifled. They kept Marynia in bed still, through excess of caution; but when her strength, her bloom, her wish for life, her humor, had returned, she began to call people to her, and say every evening that she would rise from her bed on the morrow. In one respect only the long illness and weakness had brought a change in her manner, which was to pass, however, with other traces of sickness. This was it, — she, who had been such a calm and wise woman formerly, had become for a certain time a kind of spoiled child, who insisted on various things frequently, and felt a real disappointment if they were refused. Pan Stanislav, in speaking with her, entered involuntarily into her tone, hence those "grimaces" were an occasion also of merriment.

Once she began to complain to him that Pani Bigiel would not give her red wine. Pani Bigiel explained that she gave as much as the doctor permitted, and must wait for permission to give more. Pan Stanislav set about comforting Marynia at once, speaking to her just as he used to speak formerly to Litka, —

"They will give the child wine, — they will give it! — the moment the doctor comes."

To which Marynia said, "Red!"

"But how red must it be!" answered Pan Stanislav; and then both began to laugh, and Pani Bigiel with them. As some time before, the fear of death and misfortune had hung over that room, so now it was lighted with frequent joy, as with sunlight. At times they fell into perfect humor, and grandfather Plavitski formed part of the company too on occasions. He, since the advent to the world of his grandson, had grown full of patriarchal, but kindly importance, which did not drive away merriment. It was varied, however, for at times a lofty and solemn manner gained the upper hand in him. On a certain day he brought his will, and forced all to listen to its paragraphs from beginning to end. In the touching words of the introduction he took farewell of life, of his daughter, of Pan Stanislav, and of his grandson, not sparing directions regarding the education of the latter into a good grandson, a good son, a good father, and a good citizen; then he made him heir of all he possessed. And in spite of the fact that since Mashko's bankruptcy he possessed only as much as Pan Stanislav gave him, still he was moved by his own munificence and preserved all that evening the mien of a pelican, which nourishes its young with its own proper blood.

A person who returns to the world after a grievous illness passes anew through all the periods of childhood and first youth, with this difference only, — that that which formerly was counted by years is counted now by weeks, or even days. So it was with Marynia. Pani Bigiel, who at first called her "baby," said, in laughing, that gradually "baby" had changed into a little girl, the little girl into a maiden. But the maiden began to find her feminine coquetry. Now, when they combed her hair, she insisted that they should place on her knees a small mirror, which she had received from her mother; and she looked into it carefully, to see if Pani Bigiel's promise that "afterward she would be still more beautiful," was being justified. On the first occasions the examinations did not satisfy her over-much, but afterwards more and more. At last she gave command one day to bring the mirror again, after her hair was dressed; and once more she made a thorough review of her complexion, her eyes, her mouth, her hair, her expression, — in a word, of everything which there was to look at. And the review must have turned out well, for she began to smile, and grow radiant; at last she turned toward Pan Stanislav's chamber, threatening with her thin fist, and said, with a very aggressive mien, —

"But wait now, Pan Stas!"

In truth, she had never been so comely. Her complexion, always very pure, had become still clearer, and more lily-like than it was when Pan Ignas had lost his head, and rhymed from morning till evening about it. Besides, the first rosy dawn of health was shining on her cheeks. From her eyes, from her mouth, from her face, which had grown smaller after sickness, there shone a species of light, a rebirth into life, a spring. It was a wonderful head simply, full of bright and clear colors, and at the same time of delicate outline, — really exquisite, and, as Pan Ignas had expressed himself once, belonging to the field, so wonderful that at moments, when it was lying on the pillow, and on its own dark hair, it was not possible to look at it sufficiently. That so-called "Pan Stas," who saw everything clearly, and who, according to the description of Bigiel, "could not move hand or foot from love," did not need to "wait" at all. Not only did he love her now as a woman and one dear to him, but he felt for her gratitude beyond bounds because she had not died, and he showed his gratitude by striving to divine her thoughts. Marynia had not even imagined at any time that she would become to such a degree the motive of his life, the sight of his eye, the soul of his thought and activity. Never had it been disagreeable to them with each other; but now, with Marynia's return to health, an unexampled happiness, an unexampled delight, came to their household.

And young Polanyetski, too, contributed actively. Marynia was not able to nourish him herself; and her husband, foreseeing this, got a nurse for his son. Wishing, moreover, to give the sick woman pleasure, he brought in an old acquaintance of hers in Kremen. She had served once with the Plavitskis; after their departure she happened in Yalbrykov, and there a misfortune befell her. It was never known strictly who the cause was; but if it was possible to reproach any of the greater proprietors with want of love for the people, it was not possible to reproach Pan Gantovski, for all Yalbrykov was full of proofs of how Gantovski loved the people. Even in the negotiations about peasant privileges of the co-residents of Yalbrykov, among other points raised was this, — that "the lord heir rides on a white horse, shoots from pistols, and looks into the girls' eyes;" and if on the one hand it was not easy to see what particular connection the above habits of Gantovski had with the agreements about peasant privileges, it became perfectly clear on the other that, thanks to those habits, Pan Stanislav found with ease a nurse for his son in Yalbrykov.

But as that was a youthful, vigorous, and buxom Mazovian, the young man could only succeed in her care. In general, that little Polanyetski was a personage who, from the first moment of his arrival in the world, became more and more a lord in the house, not counting with any one, nor thinking of anything, save his own wants and pleasures. According to his method, in moments free from sleep and feasting, he occupied himself with noise-making, and the development of his little lungs, by means of a cry which was as piercing as his early age could attain. At such times he was brought frequently to Marynia. On those occasions endless sessions began, at which all his physical and mental traits were investigated minutely, as well as every striking resemblance to his life-givers. It was asserted that he had the nose of his mother, the remark of his nurse, that he had a nose like a cat, being rejected with remarkable unanimity; it was settled, also, that he would have an immensely interesting smile; that he would be dark, with brown hair; that he would be tall without fail; that he was very lively, and would have an astonishing memory. Pani Bigiel, while Marynia was lying in bed, made, also, on her own account, various discoveries, which she announced to all in general. Once she rushed into Marynia's room with delight and haste worthy of every recognition, and said, —

"Imagine to thyself, he spread out his little fingers on one hand, and with the other thou wouldst swear that he was counting. He 'll be a mathematician, beyond doubt."

And Marynia answered in all seriousness, —

"Then he 'll take after his father."

Still she made a discovery earlier, even with reference to date, than all those of Pani Bigiel, — namely, that he was "a dear little love of a creature." As to Pan Stanislav, at the first moment he looked at the new acquaintance with astonishment and a certain distrust. In his time he had wished greatly to have a daughter, with this reason chiefly, that, being in make-up of heart a great child-man, he imagined that he could give all the tenderness in him only to a girl. There was sticking in him, it is unknown why, an idea that a son would be some kind of a big lump of a fellow with mustaches almost, speaking in a bass voice, snorting somewhat like a horse, whom it would not be worth while to approach with tenderness, for he would hold it in contempt. Only gradually, after looking at this little figure sleeping on pillows, did he begin to reach the conviction that not only was that no big "lump of a boy," but simply a poor little thing, deserving of tenderness, small, weak, defenceless, needing care and love as much as any little girl in the world. At last he said to himself, "So he is that kind of boy!" And thenceforth he became more and more tender toward the little thing; and after a few days he even tried to carry him to Marynia, which, however, he did with such an amount of purely superfluous caution, and also so awkwardly, that he brought to laughter, not only Marynia and Pani Bigiel, but, with a loss to his own dignity, even the nurse.

And laughter was heard now in the dwelling of the Polanyetskis from morning till evening. Both, waking in the morning, woke with that happy feeling that the day would bring them new delight. Bigiel, who, from the time that Marynia left her bed, was admitted in the evening with his violoncello, looking at their life, said once, after a moment of necessary meditation, "Misfortune may come to good people, as to every one; but when it is well for them, as God lives, it is better for no one else."

And, in truth, life was pleasant for them. Marynia, according to what she had heard in her time from Pani

Bigiel, and what she thought herself, judged that the cause of this new bloom of love in her husband was the child, which bound them by new bonds. One day she began even to speak of this to Pan Stanislav; but he answered with all simplicity, —

"No; I give thee my word! I love him in his way; but thee I loved already fabulously before he came to the world, for thyself, because thou art as thou art. Look around," said he, "think what is going on in the world; and to whom can I compare thee?"

Then, taking her hands, he began to kiss them, not only with immense love, but also with the greatest respect, and added, —

"Thou wilt never know what thou art for me, and how I love thee."

But, nestling up to him, she asked, with a face bright as the sun in heaven, —

"Indeed, Stas, shall I never know? Try to tell me."

## CHAPTER LXVI.

THE christening came. Immediately after his arrival in the world, the young man had been baptized with water by Pani Bigiel, to whom, impressed by the sickness of the mother, it seemed that the little one might die any moment. But he had not even thought of that, and had waited, in the best of health and appetite, for the time of the solemnity, in which he was to play the leading part. Pan Stanislav had invited all his acquaintances. Besides people of the house, and grandfather Plavitski, there were Pani Emilia, who, for that day, had rallied the remnant of her strength, the Bigiels, with the little Bigiels, Professor Vaskovski, Svirski, Pan Ignas, and Panna Ratkovski. Pani Polanyetski, now in health, and happy, looked so enchanting that Svirski, gazing at her, caught his hair with both hands, and said, with his usual outspokenness, —

"This just passes every understanding! As God lives! a man might lose his eyes."

"Well," said Pan Stanislav, puffing with satisfaction, and with that conceit evident in him that he had always seen that which others saw only now for the first time.

But Svirski answered, —

"Kneel down, nations! I will say nothing further."

Marynia was confused at hearing this, but flushed with pleasure, feeling that Svirski was right. She had, however, to occupy herself with the guests and the ceremony, and all the more since a certain disorder had crept in, to begin with. The first couple, Pani Emilia and Bigiel, were to hold little Stas; the second couple were Panna Ratkovski and Svirski. Meanwhile, this last man began to create unexpected difficulties, discovering hindrances, and evading, it was unknown why. "He would be very glad — he had come from Italy purposely — of course. That was an arranged affair; but he had never before held a child at a christening, therefore he did n't know if his god-child would remain in good health, and especially if he would have luck with women." At this Pan Stanislav laughed, and called him a superstitious Italian, but Marynia divined the trouble more quickly. She took advantage of the moment in which he had pushed back toward the window to escape, and whispered, —

"A gossip[1] of the second couple is no hindrance in this case."

Svirski raised his eyes to her, then laughed, showing his small sound teeth, and said on a sudden, turning to Panna Ratkovski, —

"It is true, this is only in the second couple; therefore, I will serve you."

All surrounded the little Stas, who, in the arms of the nurse, and dressed in muslin and lace, looked valiant, with his bald spot and his staring round eyes, in which the external world was reflected as mechanically as in a mirror. Bigiel took him now in his arms, and the ceremony began.

Those present listened with due attention to the solemn sacramental words, but the young pagan exhibited exceptional hardness of heart. First he began to kick, so that he half freed himself from Bigiel's arms; later, when Bigiel, in his name, renounced the devil and his works, the young man did all in his power to drown the words. It was only when he saw, all at once, in the midst of his screaming, Bigiel's spectacles, that he stopped suddenly, as if to let people know that if there are such astonishing objects in the world, it is a different thing.

However, the ceremony ended, and immediately after they gave him into the hands of the nurse, who put him into a splendid cradle, in the form of a wagon, the gift of Svirski, and wished to roll him out of the room. But Svirski, who never in his life, perhaps, had seen so nearly such a small person, and in whose breast beat a heart long yearning for fatherhood, stopped the nurse, and, bending down to the cradle, took the child in his arms.

"Carefully, carefully!" cried Pan Stanislav, pushing up quickly.

But the artist turned to him, and said, —

"Sir, I have held in my hands the works of Luca della Robbia."

And, in fact, he lifted the little creature, and began to swing him with as much dexterity as if he had had care of children all his life. Then he approached Professor Vaskovski, and asked, —

[1] With Panna Ratkovski, Svirski wished to avoid spiritual relationship, a hindrance to marriage.

"Well, what does the beloved professor think of his young Aryan?"

"What?" answered the old man, looking with tenderness at the child; "naturally, an Aryan, an Aryan of purest water."

"And a coming missionary," added Pan Stanislav.

"He will not turn from that in the future; he will not evade, just as you cannot evade," answered the professor.

It was not possible, in fact, to prejudge the future; but for the moment the young Aryan avoided all missions in a manner so unmistakable, and simply insulting, that it was necessary to give him to the nurse. The ladies, however, did not cease to smack their lips at him, and to be charmed with him, until they came to a decisive conclusion that he was a perfectly exceptional child, that his whole bearing showed this clearly, and that any one must be without eyes not to see that that would be the nicest man in the country, and, moreover, a genius.

But the "genius" fell asleep at last, as if he had been stunned by the incense, and meanwhile lunch was served. Marynia, in spite of all her friendship for the artist, seated Pan Ignas next to Panna Ratkovski. She wished, as, for that matter, all wished, not excepting even Svirski, that something should be made clear in their relations, for Pan Ignas acted strangely. Svirski held that he was not yet entirely normal. He was healthy; he slept and ate well; he had grown a little heavier; he spoke with judgment, even more deliberately than had been his habit,—but there appeared in him a certain infirmity of will, a certain lack of that initiative for which he had been so distinguished before. In Italy he grew radiant at remembrance of Panna Ratkovski; and when he spoke of her his eyes filled with tears at times. On his return, when some one reminded him that it would be well to make a visit to Panna Ratkovski, and especially when that one offered to go with him, he answered, "It is true," and he went with delight. But the visit made, it seemed as though he did not remember her existence. At times it was evident that in the depth of his soul something was troubling him, swallowing all his mental force. Svirski supposed for a while that it might be the remembrance of Panna Castelli; but he convinced himself, with a certain astonishment, that it was not, and at last he began to think that Pan Ignas never mentioned her because he had lost the feeling that she was real, or that she seemed to him now an impression so remote, a remembrance so blown apart, that it could not be brought into a real living whole. He was not melancholy. On the contrary, one might note at times in him satisfaction with life and the joy which he experienced, as it were, in this his second birth in it. Really sad, more and more confined in herself, and increasingly quiet, was Panna Ratkovski. It may be that, besides a lack of mutual feeling, other things in Pan Ignas alarmed her; but she did not mention those alarms to any one. Marynia and Pani Bigiel, judging that the only cause of her sadness was the conduct of Pan Ignas, showed the most heartfelt sympathy, and were ready to do anything to help her. Marynia saw Pan Ignas now for the first time since his return from Italy; but Pani Bigiel spoke to him daily, praising Panna Ratkovski, reminding him how much he owed her, and giving him to understand more and more clearly that it was his duty to pay something of the debt which he owed her. The honest Svirski, to the detriment of his own hopes, repeated the same to him; and Pan Ignas agreed to everything, but, as it were, unwillingly, or without being able to add the final conclusion. He spoke of his approaching second trip abroad, of plans of still greater journeys in the future, — in a word, of things which, by their nature, excluded the co-operation of Panna Ratkovski.

And now, sitting side by side, they spoke little to each other. Pan Ignas ate abundantly, and with appetite, even with attention; he followed with his eyes the new courses which were served first to the elder guests. Panna Ratkovski, noticing this, looked on him at moments, as if with painful sympathy. At last this began to vex Marynia; so, wishing to rouse a conversation between them, she said, bending over the table, —

"You have come so recently from travels, tell me and Steftsia something of Italy. Hast thou never been there, Steftsia?"

"I have not," answered Panna Ratkovski; "but not long since I read the account of a journey — but to read and to see are different."

And she blushed slightly, for she had betrayed the fact that she had been reading about Italy just when Pan Ignas was there.

"Pan Svirski persuaded me to go as far as Sicily," said he, "but it was hot there at that time; that would be the place to visit at this season."

"Ah!" said Marynia, "it is well that I think of it—but my letters? You asked through Pan Svirski if I wished you to write your impressions, but afterward I did not receive a single letter."

Pan Ignas blushed; he was confused, and then in a kind of strange and uncertain voice, answered,—

"No, for I have not been able yet; I will write very much, but later."

Having heard these words, Svirski approached Marynia after lunch, and indicating Pan Ignas with his eyes, said,—

"Do you know the impression which he makes on me sometimes?—that of a costly vessel which is cracked."

## CHAPTER LXVII.

A couple of days after the christening, Svirski visited Pan Stanislav in the counting-house, to inquire for Marynia's health, and to talk about various things which lay at his heart. Seeing, however, that he was late, and that Pan Stanislav was preparing to go, he said, —

"Do not stop for me. Let us talk on the street. The light is so sharp to-day that I cannot work; therefore I will walk to your door with you."

"In every case I should have been forced to beg your pardon," said Pan Stanislav. "My Marynia goes out to-day for the first time, and we are to dine with the Bigiels. She must be dressed by this time, but we have twenty minutes yet."

"As she goes out, she is well?"

"Praise be to God, as well as a bird!" answered Pan Stanislav, with delight.

"And the little Aryan?"

"The little Aryan bears himself stoutly."

"O happy man, if I had such a toad at home, not to mention such a wife, I should not know what to do — unless to walk upon house-tops."

"You will not believe how that boy takes my heart. Every day more, and in general, in a way that I did not expect, for you must know that I wanted a daughter."

"It is not evening yet; the daughter will come. But you are in a hurry; let us go then."

Pan Stanislav took his fur coat, and they went to the street. The day was frosty, clear. Around was heard the hurried sound of sleigh-bells. Men had their collars over their ears, their mustaches were frosty, and they threw columns of steam from their mouths.

"It is a gladsome sort of day," said Pan Stanislav. "I rejoice, for my Marynia's sake, that it is clear."

"It is gladsome for you in life; therefore everything seems clear to you," said Svirski, taking him by the arm. But all at once he dropped the arm, and stopping the way, said, with an expression as if he wished to quarrel, —

"Do you know that you have the most beautiful woman in Warsaw as wife? It is I who tell you this—I!"

And he began to strike his breast with his hand as if to increase thereby the certainty that it was he and no one else who was speaking thus.

"Of course!" answered Pan Stanislav, laughing, "and also the best and most honest on earth; but let us go on, for it is cold."

When Svirski took him again by the arm, Pan Stanislav added with some emotion,—

"But what I went through during her sickness, the Lord God alone knows— Better not mention it— She gave me a surprise simply by her return to life; but if God grants me to live till spring, I will give a surprise that will gladden her."

"There is nothing with which to compare her," answered Svirski.

Then, halting again, he said, as if in astonishment, "And, as I love God, so much simplicity at the same time."

They walked on a while in silence, then Pan Stanislav asked Svirski of his journey.

"I shall stay three weeks in Florence," answered the artist. "I have some work there. Besides, I have grown homesick for the light on San Miniato and Ginevra, with which, and with Cimabue, I was in love on a time. Do you remember in Santa Maria Novella, in the chapel of Rucellai? After a three weeks' stay I shall go to Rome. I wanted to talk with you about the journey, for this morning Pan Ignas came to me with the proposition that we should go again together."

"Ah! and did you agree?"

"I had not the heart to refuse, though, between ourselves, he is sometimes a burden. But you know how I loved him, and how I felt for him, so it is hard for me to say it, but he is burdensome occasionally. What is to be said in this case? he is changed immensely. At the christening I told Pani Polanyetski that at times he seems to me like a costly vessel which is cracked; and that is true. For I saw how he struggled over those letters, in which he wished to describe Italy for her. He walked whole hours through the room, rubbed his shot forehead, sat down, stood up; but the paper remained just as it was, untouched. God grant him to recover his former power. At present he repeats to every one that he will write; but he begins to doubt himself, and to grieve. I know that he grieves."

"The loss of his power would be a misfortune both for him and Panna Helena. If you knew how she was concerned to the verge of despair, not only for his life, but his talent."

"The loss of that would be a public misfortune; but the person for whom I am most sorry is Panna Ratkovski. She too begins to doubt whether he will be what he was, and that tortures her, perhaps, more than other griefs."

"Poor girl!" said Pan Stanislav, "and the more so since from all his plans of travelling one thing is clear, that he does not even think of her. It is fortunate that Panna Helena secured her independence."

"I will wait a year," answered Svirski, "and after a year I will propose a second time. She has taken hold of me, it is not to be denied! Have you noticed how becoming short hair is to her? She ought to wear it that way always. I will wait a year," and he was silent; "but after that I shall consider my hands free. It is not possible either that in her something will not change in a year, especially if he gives no sign of life. All this is wonderfully strange. Do you think that I do not do everything in my power to blow into life some spark for her? As God is true, a man has never done more against his own heart than I have. Pani Bigiel too does what she can. But it is difficult. Again, no one has the right to say to him expressly: marry! if he does not love her. And this is the more wonderful, since he does not seem even to think of the other. One Panna Ratkovski is worth more than a whole grove of such 'Poplars;' but that is another affair! For me the point is that she should not suppose that I am taking him away purposely. I have not dissuaded him, for I could not; but, my dear sir, should there ever be a conversation about our journey, say to her that, as God lives, I did not persuade Pan Ignas to the journey, and that I would give more than she supposes to make her happy, even were it at the cost of an old dog like me."

"Of course we shall do so."

"Thank you for that. Before going, I shall be with you again to say good-by to Pani Polanyetski."

"Surely in the evening, so that we may sit longer. I think too that you will return in summer; you and Pan Ignas will spend some time with us."

"In Buchynek?"

"In Buchynek or not, that is unknown yet."

Further conversation was interrupted by the sight of Osnovski, who at that moment was coming out of a fruit-shop, with a white package in his hand.

"See, there is Osnovski!" said Svirski.

"How changed!" said Pan Stanislav.

And indeed he was changed immensely. From under his fur cap gazed a pale face, grown yellow, and, as it were, much older. His fur coat seemed to hang on him. Seeing his two friends, he was vexed; it was evident that for a while he hesitated whether or not to go around, pretending that he did not see them. But the sidewalk was empty, and they had come so near that he changed his intention, and, coming up, began to speak with unnatural haste, as if wishing to cover with talk that of which all three were thinking exclusively.

"A good day to you, gentlemen! Oh, this is a chance that we meet, for I am shut up in Prytulov, and come rarely to the city. I have just bought some grapes, for the doctor orders me to eat grapes. But they are imported in sawdust, and have the odor of it; I thought they would be better here. There is frost to-day, indeed. In the country sleighing is perfect."

And they walked on together, all feeling awkward.

"You are going to Egypt, are you not?" inquired Pan Stanislav at last.

"That is my old plan, and perhaps I shall go. In the country there is nothing to do in winter; it is tedious to be alone there."

Here he stopped suddenly, for he saw that he was touching a delicate subject. And they went on in a silence still more oppressive, feeling that unspeakable awkwardness which is felt always when, by some tacit agreement, people talk of things of no interest, while hiding the main ones, which are painful. Osnovski would have been glad to leave his two friends; but people accustomed for long years to observe certain forms pay attention to appearances unconsciously, even in the deepest misfortune, hence he wanted to find some easy and natural means of leaving Pan Stanislav and the artist; but not being able to find it, he merely continued the awkward position. Finally, he began to take farewell of them in the unexpected and unnatural way of a man who has lost his head.

At the last moment, however, he determined otherwise. Such a comedy seemed to him unendurable. He had had enough of it. It flashed into his head that he ought not to make a secret of anything; that in avoidance of every mention of misfortune there is something abject. On his face constraint was clear, and suffering; but, halting, he began to say with a broken voice, losing breath every moment, —

"Gentlemen, I beg pardon for detaining you longer. But you know that I have separated from my wife — I do not see any reason why I should not speak of it, especially with persons so honorable and so near —I declare to you, gentlemen, that that was — that that happened so — that is, that I wished it myself, and that to my wife nothing — "

But the voice stuck in his throat, and he could not speak further. Evidently he wanted to take the fault on himself; but on a sudden he felt all the incredibility, all the extent and desperate emptiness of a lie like that, which must be a mere sound of words, so that not even the feeling of any duty, nor any social appearance could justify him. And, losing his head altogether, he went into the crowd, bearing with him his grapes and unfathomable misfortune.

Svirski and Pan Stanislav went on in silence under the impression of this misfortune.

"As God is true," said Pan Stanislav at length, "his heart is breaking."

"For such a man," answered the artist, "there is nothing except to wish death."

"And still he has not deserved such a fate."

"I give you my word," said Svirski, "whenever I think of him, I see him kissing her hands. He did it so often that I cannot imagine him otherwise. And what sets me to thinking again is this, that misfortune, like death, severs the relations of people, or if it does not sever relations completely, it estranges people. You have not known him long, but I, for example, lived on intimate terms with him, and now he is to me somehow farther away, while I am to him more a stranger; there is no help in this case, and that is so sad."

"Sad and wonderful —"

But Svirski stopped on a sudden, and exclaimed, —

"Do you know what? May a thunderbolt burn that Pani Osnovski! Panna Helena said that it was not permitted to despair of a man while he was living; but as to that one, let a thunderbolt shake her!"

"There was not in the world, perhaps, a woman more worshipped than she," said Pan Stanislav.

"There you have them," answered Svirski, passionately. "Women, taking them in general — "

But all at once he struck his glove across his mouth.

"No!" cried he. "To the devil with my old fault! I have promised myself not to make any general conclusions about women."

"I said that he worshipped her," continued Pan Stanislav, "because now I simply do not understand how he can live without her."

"But he must."

Osnovski was forced really to live without his wife, but he was not able. In Prytulov and in Warsaw, which were full of reminiscences of her, life soon became for him unendurable; hence a month later he started on a journey. But, already out of health when he left Warsaw, he caught cold in an over-heated car, and in Vienna fell so ill that he had to take to his bed. The cold, which at first was considered influenza, turned into a violent typhus. After a few days the sick man lost consciousness, and lay in a hotel at the mercy of strange doctors and strange people, far from home and his friends. But afterward in the fever which heated his brain and confused his thoughts it seemed to him that he saw near his bedside the face dearest in life to him, beloved at all times, beloved in loneliness, in sickness, and in presence of death. It seemed to him that he saw it even when he had regained consciousness, but was so weak that he could not move yet, nor speak, nor even arrange his own thoughts.

Later the vision disappeared. But he began to inquire about it from the Sisters of Charity, who were sent, it was unknown by whom, and who surrounded him with the most tender care; and he began to yearn beyond measure.

## CHAPTER LXVIII.

After the solemnity of the christening, and after the departure of Svirski and Pan Ignas, the Polanyetskis began to live again a secluded and home life, seeing scarcely any one except the Bigiels, Pani Emilia, and Vaskovski. But it was pleasant for them in that narrow circle of near friends, and pleasantest of all with themselves. Pan Stanislav was greatly occupied; he sat long in the counting-house and outside the counting-house, settling some business of which no one else knew anything. But, after finishing his work, he hurried home now with greater haste than when, as betrothed, he flew every day to the lodgings of the Plavitskis. His old liveliness returned, his old humor and confidence in life. Soon he made a discovery which seemed to him wonderful,—namely, that not only did he love his wife with all his power as his wife and the one dearest to him, but that he was in love with her as a woman, without alarm or effort, it is true, without transitions from joy to doubts and despair, but with all the emotions of sincere feeling, with a whole movement of desire, with a continually uniform fresh sensitiveness to her feminine charm, and with an untiring care, which watches, foresees, acts, anticipates, wishes, and strives continually not to injure happiness, and not to lose it. "I shall change into an Osnovski," said he, humorously; "but to me alone is it permitted to be an Osnovski, because my little one will never become a Pani Aneta." He said "my little one" to her often now, but there was in that as much respect as petting. He understood, too, that he never should have loved her so, if she had been other than she was; that all was the result of her immense, honest will, and of that sort of wonderful rectitude which issued from her as naturally as heat from a hearth. Pan Stanislav knew that his mind was the more active, his thought the more far-reaching, and his knowledge profounder than her knowledge; still he felt that through her, and through her alone, all that which was in him had become in some way more finished and more noble. Through her influence all those principles acquired by him passed from his head, where they had been a dead theory, to his heart, where they became active life. He noticed, too, that not only happiness, but he himself was her work. There was in this even a little disillusion for him, since he saw, without any doubt, that had he found some common kind of woman he might have turned out some common kind of man. At times he wondered even how she could have loved him; but he called to mind then her expression, "service of God," and that explained to him everything. For such a woman marriage, too, was "service of God," as was love also, not by some wild power lying beyond the will of people, but precisely by an act of honest will, by serving an oath, by serving God's law, by serving duty. Marynia loved him because he was her husband. Such was she, and that was the end of the question! For a long time Pan Stanislav was not able to see that all that which he worshipped in her was enjoined directly by the first catechism which one might take up, and that in her training had not killed the catechism. Perhaps she had not been reared with sufficient care; but she had been taught that she must serve God, and not use God to serve herself.

Pan Stanislav, not understanding well the reasons why she was what she was, admired her increasingly, honored and loved her. As to her, while taking things without exaggeration, she did not conceive an excessive opinion of herself; she understood, however, that life had never been so pleasant for her as it then was; that she had passed through certain trials; that during those trials she had acted honorably; that she had endured the trials with patience; that the Lord God had rewarded her. And this feeling filled her with peace. Her health came back completely; she felt, therewith, very pleasant, and very much beloved. That "Stas," whom formerly she had feared a little, inclined his dark head frequently to her knees with submissiveness almost; and she thought with delight that "that man was not at all bending by nature, and that if he did bend, it was because he loved much." And she just grew every day. Gratitude rose in her, and she paid him for his love with her whole heart.

The young "Aryan" filled his rôle of a ray in the house splendidly. Sometimes it was, indeed, a ray connected with noise; but when he was in good-humor, and when, lying in his favorite position, with his legs raised at right angles, he drew cries of delight from himself, all the male and female population of the house gathered around his cradle. Marynia covered his legs, calling him "naughty boy;" but he pulled off the cover every instant, thinking, evidently, that if a man of character has determined to kick, he should hold out in his undertaking bravely. He laughed while he kicked, showing his little toothless gums, crowing, twittering like a sparrow, cooing like a dove, or mewing like a cat. On such occasions his nurse and mother talked for whole hours with him. Professor Vaskovski, who had lost his head over the boy altogether, maintained with perfect seriousness that that was an "esoteric speech," which should be phonographed by scientists, for it might either disclose thoroughly the mystery of astral existence, or, at least, touch on its main indications.

In this way the winter months passed in the house of the Polanyetskis. In January, Pan Stanislav began to make journeys on some business, and after each return he had long consultations with Bigiel. But from the middle of January he stayed at home permanently, never going out, unless to the counting-house, or to take short excursions with Marynia and Stas in the carriage. The uniformity of their life, or rather the uniformity of its calmness and happiness, was interrupted only by news of acquaintances in the city, brought most frequently by Pani Bigiel. In this way Marynia learned that Panna Ratkovski, who, of late, had not shown herself anywhere, had established a refuge for children from the income secured her by Panna Helena, and that Osnovski had gone really to Egypt, not alone, however, but with his "Anetka," with whom, after returning to health, he reunited himself. Pan Kresovski, the former second of Mashko, had seen them in Trieste, and declared to Pan Stanislav ironically that "the lady had the look of a submissive penitent." Pan Stanislav, knowing from experience how a person is crushed in misfortune, and what sincerity there may be in penitence, replied with perfect seriousness that since her husband had received Pani Osnovski, no decent man had a right to be more exacting than he was.

But later news came from Italy which was more wonderful, and so unheard of that it became the subject of talk, not only for the Polanyetskis and the Bigiels, but the whole city, — namely, that the artist Svirski had asked in Rome for the hand of Panna Castelli, and that they would be married immediately after Easter. Marynia was so much roused by this that she persuaded her husband to write to Svirski and ask if it were true. An answer came in ten days; and when Pan Stanislav entered his wife's room at last with the letter, holding it by the corner of the envelope, and with the words, "Letter from Rome!" the serious Marynia ran up to him, with cheeks red from curiosity, and the two, standing temple to temple, read as follows: —

"Is it true? No, dear friends, it is not true! But that you should understand why that could not take place, and can never take place, I must speak to you of Pan Ignas. He came here three days since. First I persuaded him to remain in Florence, then to glance at Sienna, Parma, and especially Ravenna. Thence I send him to Athens, and to-morrow he will go by way of Brindisi. Meanwhile he sat with me from morning till evening. I saw that something was troubling the man, and wishing to turn direct conversation to things which concerned him more closely, I asked yesterday carelessly if he had not in his portfolio a half a dozen sonnets on Ravenna. And do you know what took place? At first he grew pale, and answered, 'Not yet,' but added that he would begin to write soon; then he threw his hat on the floor suddenly, and began to sob like a child. Never have I seen an outburst of similar suffering. He just wrung his hands, saying that he had murdered his talent; that there was nothing more left in him; that never would he have power to write another line; that he would prefer a hundred times that Panna Helena had not saved him. You see what is happening within him; while people will say, surely, that he does not write because he has money. And this, beyond doubt, will remain so. They have killed the poor man, murdered soul and talent in him, put out the strong fire from which light and warmth might have come to people. And that, see you, I could not forget. God be with Panna Castelli! but it was not right for her to pluck such feathers to make for herself a fan, which she threw out of the window soon after. No! I could not forget this! Never mind what I said in Warsaw, that now she must find a Prince Crapulescu, since no one else will take her; for, besides that kind, there are blind men in the world also, — plenty of them. As to me, I am neither Prince Crapulescu, nor blind. It is permitted to forgive wrongs done to one's self, but not those done to others; for that would be too easy. And this is all that I can tell you touching this matter, for you yourselves know the rest. I am waiting out the year; then I shall repeat my prayer to Panna Ratkovski. If she wants me, or rejects me, may God bless her in every case; but still that is my unchangeable decision."

"Indeed!" interrupted Marynia; "but whence did such news come?"

But in the continuation of the letter Svirski gave an exact answer.

"All this gossip" (wrote he), "may have arisen from this, that I have seen those ladies rather often. You remember that, during my former stay in Rome, Pani Bronich wrote to me first, and I was with them. Panna Castelli, instead of seeking evasions, blamed herself. I confess that that affected me. Let people say what they like, still in an open confession of fault there is a certain awakening of honesty, a certain courage, a certain turn, a groan of sorrow, which, if it does not redeem the offence, may redeem the soul. And believe me that in this which I say there is more than my heart of butter. Think, also, that in truth it is evil for them. Are the times few in which I have seen the hesitation with which they approach people, and how they are received by persons who have the courage of their principles? So much bitterness has gathered in these two women, that, as Vaskovski said with truth once, they are beginning to be embittered against themselves. That is a terrible position, in which one belongs, as it were, to the world, and carries the burden of a notable scandal. God be with them! Much might be written of this; but I remember always what Panna Helena said, — that one must not despair of a man while he lives. That unfortunate Lineta has changed from grief; she has grown thin and ugly, and I am very sorry for her. I am sorry even for Pani Bronich, who, it is true, bores holes in people's ears with her lies; but she does it out of attachment to that girl. Still, as I have said, it is permitted only to forgive wrongs done ourselves; but a man would be a kind of gorilla, and not a Christian, if he did not feel a little pity over the misfortunes of people. Whether I shall have the heart to go to them again after having seen the despair of Ignas, I know not. I am not sorry, however, that I was there. People will talk; they will stop talking; and after a year or so, if God grant me and that dear maiden to wait it out, they will see that they are talking nonsense."

The letter finished with a reference to the Osnovskis, of whose reunion Svirski knew; he had heard, even, various details which were unknown to Pan Stanislav.

"To think" (wrote he) "that God is more powerful than the perversity of man, and also is fabulously merciful, and that sometimes He permits misfortune to beat a man on the head as with a hammer, so as to knock some spark of honesty out of him. I believe now even in the rebirth of such as Pani Aneta. Maybe it is naïve in me, but at times I admit that there are no people in the world who are completely bad. See, something quivered in Pani Aneta even; she nursed him in his sickness. Oi, those women! Everything is so turned around in my head that soon I shall not have an opinion, not merely about them, but about anything."

Further on were questions about Stas, and heartfelt words for his life-givers, and finally a promise to return in the first days of spring.

## CHAPTER LXIX.

But spring was coming really, and, besides, it was as warm as it was early. Pan Stanislav, at the end of March and the beginning of April, began again to make journeys, and sometimes to spend a number of days away from home. He and Bigiel were so busied that often they remained in the counting-house till late in the evening. Pani Bigiel supposed that they must be undertaking something large; but it astonished her that her husband, who always spoke with her about his business, and almost thought aloud in her presence, and even frequently took counsel with her, was as silent now as if spell-bound. Marynia noticed also that "Stas" had his head filled with something in an unusual manner. He was more tender toward her than ever; but it seemed to her that in that tenderness of his, as well as in every conversation and every petting, there was some third thing, another thought, which occupied him so thoroughly that he could not keep away from it even a moment. And this state of distraction increased daily till the beginning of May, when it passed into something feverish. Marynia began to hesitate whether to ask or not, what the matter was. She was a little afraid to intrude; but for her it was important also that he should not think that his affairs concerned her too little. In this uncertainty, she determined to wait for a favorable moment, hoping that he himself would begin to touch on his business, even remotely.

In fact, it seemed to her, on a certain day soon after, that the opportune moment had come. Pan Stanislav returned from the counting-house earlier than usual, and with a face in some way wonderfully radiant, though serious, so that, looking him in the eyes, she asked, almost mechanically, —

"Something favorable must have happened, Stas?"

He sat near her, and instead of answering directly, began to talk with a voice which was strange in some sort, —

"See how calm and warm. The windows might be opened now. Dost thou know what I've been thinking of these last days? That for thy health and Stas's we ought to go soon from the city."

"But is not Buchynek rented?" asked Marynia.

"Buchynek is sold," answered he. Then, taking both her hands and looking into her eyes with immense affection, he said, —

"Listen, my dear, I have something to tell thee, and something which ought to please thee; but promise not to be excited too much."

"Well, what is it, Stas?"

"Seest thou, my little one? Mashko fled to foreign parts; for he had more debts than property. His creditors threw themselves on everything which was left after him, so as to recover even something. Everything went into liquidation. Magyerovka has been parcelled, and is lost; but Kremen, Skoki, and Suhotsin could be saved. Do not grow excited, my love; I have bought them for thee."

Marynia looked at him some time, blinking, and as if not believing her ears. But no! He was so moved himself that he could not jest. Her eyes were darkened with tears, and all at once she threw both arms around his neck.

"Stas!"

And at that moment she could not find other words; but in this one exclamation there were thanks and great love, and a woman's homage for the efficiency of that man who had been able to do everything. Pan Stanislav understood this; and in the feeling of that immense happiness which he had not known hitherto, he began to speak, holding her still at his breast, —

"I knew that this would comfort thee, and God knows there is no greater pleasure for me than thy delight. I remembered that thou wert sorry for Kremen, that that was an injustice to thee, and that it was possible to correct it; therefore I corrected it. But that is nothing! If I had bought ten such Kremens for thee, I should not have repaid thee for the good which thou hast done me, and still I should not be worthy of thee."

And he spoke sincerely; but Marynia removed her head from his shoulder, and, raising on him her eyes, which were at once moist and bright, said, —

"It is I, Stas, that am not worthy of thee; and I did not even hope to be so happy."

Then they began to dispute who was the more worthy; but in that dispute there were frequent intervals of silence, for Marynia, every moment embracing him, pushed up to him her mouth, beautiful, though a little too wide, and kissed him; and then he kissed in turn her eyes and her hands. For a long time yet she wanted now to cry, now to laugh from delight; for really her happiness surpassed everything which she had ever hoped for. Her mother had written once, with a weakening hand, "One should not marry to be happy, but to fulfil the duties which God imposes; happiness is only an addition and a gift of God." Meanwhile this addition was now too great to find place in her heart. There had been trials, there had been moments of grief to her, and even of doubt; but all had passed, and at last that "Stas" not only loved her as the sight of his eye, but he had done more than he had ever promised.

And at that moment, while walking with long strides through the room, still excited, but pleased with himself, and with an expression of complete boastfulness on his dark, challenging face, he said, —

"Well, Marys[1]! Now for the first time will work begin, will it not? For I have n't the least idea of country life. and that will be thy affair. But I think that I shall not be the worst of managers. We shall both work, for that Kremen is a big undertaking."

"My golden Stas," answered she, clasping her hands, "I know that thou hast done that for me; but will it not injure thee in business?"

"In business? It is thy idea, perhaps, that I let myself be stripped. Not at all! I bought cheaply, very cheaply. Bigiel, who is afraid of everything, still confesses that that is a good purchase; besides, I remain in company with him for the future. But only be not afraid of Kremen, Marys, or the old troubles. There will be something to work with; and I tell thee sincerely that if to-day all Kremen were to sink in the earth, we should have enough to support us, together with Stas."

"I," said Marynia, looking at him more or less as she would on Napoleon, or some other conqueror of similar size, "am certain that thou wilt do all that thou wishest, but I know that it was only for me that Kremen was bought."

"And I hope that I bought it, too, because thy mother is lying there, because I love thee, and because thou lovest

[1] Pronounced Márees, a diminutive of Marynia.

Kremen," answered Pan Stanislav. "But in thy way thou hast brought me back to the soil. I recall thy words in Venice when Mashko wanted to sell Kremen to Bukatski. Thou hast no idea of how I am under thy influence. Sometimes thou wilt say a thing, and I for the moment make no answer; still it remains in me, and later it is heard unexpectedly. So it was in this business. It seems strange to me now for a man to dwell on this planet, to have some wealth, as it were, and not have three square ells of this earth, concerning which he might say 'mine.' Then the question was settled. Then came the purchase. Perhaps thou hast noticed that for some months I have been buzzing about like a fly in a caldron. I did not wish to speak to thee till all was finished; I preferred a surprise. And thou hast it! This is because thou hast recovered, and art so beloved."

Here he seized her hands, and began to press them again to his mouth and his forehead. She wanted to kiss his hands, too, but he would not permit that; and at last they began to run after each other, like children, through the room, speaking to each other words which were kindly, and bright as sunbeams. Marynia wanted so much to go straight to Kremen, and to such a degree was she unable to think of aught else, that at last he threatened to grow jealous of Kremen, and to sell it.

"Oi! thou wilt not sell," said she, shaking her head.

"Why not?"

"Because," said she, taking his ear, and whispering into it, "thou lovest me."

And he began to nod in sign that that was true. But they agreed, to the great delight of Marynia, to go with their whole household to Kremen at the end of the week, —a thing perfectly possible, for Pan Stanislav had made the house ready for the coming of the "heiress." He assured her, too, that almost nothing had changed, and he had tried only that the rooms should not seem too empty; then he began to laugh suddenly, and said, "I am curious to know what papa will say to this."

The conjectural astonishment of "papa" was a new cause of delight to Marynia. For that matter, there was no need to wait long for Plavitski, since he came to dinner half an hour later. He had barely showed himself when Marynia, throwing herself on his shoulder, told with one breath the happy news; he was really astonished, and even moved.

Perhaps he felt the happiness of his daughter; perhaps there was roused in him an attachment for that corner, in which he had lived so many years; it is enough that his eyes grew moist. First he mentioned his sweat, with which that soil was soaked; then he began to say something of the "old man," and of his "refuge in the country;" at last, pressing Pan Stanislav's head between his palms, he said,—

"God grant thee luck to manage as well as I have managed, and be assured that I shall not refuse thee either my assistance or my counsels."

In the evening, at the Bigiels', Marynia, still intoxicated with her happiness, said to Pani Bigiel,—

"Well, now, tell me, how could I help loving a man like that?"

## CHAPTER LXX.

Next morning after the arrival of the Polanyetskis in Kremen, it was Sunday. Pan Stanislav himself rose late, for they had come at one o'clock the night previous. In Kremen the servants had been waiting with bread and salt for them. Marynia, laughing and weeping in turn, examined every corner in the house, and after that was unable to fall asleep, from emotion, till almost daylight. For all these reasons Pan Stanislav did not permit her to rise; but since she wanted to go to Mass at Vantory rather early, so as to pray at the church for her mother, he promised to have the carriage ready, and let her know when it was time. Immediately after breakfast he went out to look at his new inheritance. It was the second half of May, and the day was exceptionally beautiful. Rain had fallen in the night, and the sun was shining on little pools in the yard; and on the buildings it was reflected in diamond brightness in raindrops hanging on the leaves, and it made the wet roofs of the barns, cow-houses, and sheep-houses gleam. In that glitter, and in the bright May green of the trees, Kremen seemed altogether charming. Around the buildings there was hardly any movement, for it was Sunday; but at the stable were busied some men, who had to drive to church. This silence and sleepiness struck Pan Stanislav strangely. Having intended for some time to buy Kremen, he had been there repeatedly, and knew that it was a neglected property. Mashko had begun, it is true, to build a granary, which was covered with a red roof, but he had not finished it. He had never lived in the place himself, and toward the end could not expend anything on the property, hence neglect was visible at every step. But never had it seemed to Pan Stanislav neglected so absolutely as now, when he was able to say to himself, "This is mine." The buildings were somehow leaning; the walls in them not very solid; the fences were inclining and broken; under the walls were lying fragments of various broken agricultural implements. Everywhere the earth seemed desirous of drawing into itself that which was on its surface; everywhere was seen a kind of passive abandonment of things to themselves; everywhere carelessness was visible. Of agriculture Pan Stanislav knew only this, that there was need to be careful in expenses; for the rest, he had not the least conception of it, save some general information, which had struck his ears in childhood. But, looking at his kingdom, he divined that cultivation of its fields must coincide exactly with that carelessness which he saw around; he had a clear feeling that if anything was done there it was rather from custom, from routine, as it were, and because of this alone, that some such thing had been done ten, twenty, a hundred years earlier. That exertion, that untiring, watchful energy, which is the basis of commerce, of industry, and of city industry in general, — of that there was not a trace. "If I brought nothing more than that to this torpor," said Pan Stanislav, "it would be very much, for there is an absolute lack of energy. Besides, I have money, and at least this much knowledge, — that I know to begin with that I know nothing, and second, I know that I must learn and inquire." He remembered, besides, from his Belgian times, that even abroad, even there in Belgium, the spirit of man and the exertion of will meant more than the most powerful machines. And in this regard he counted on himself, and he was able to count. He felt that he was a persistent and active man. Everything taken in hand by him hitherto had to move, whether it would or not. He felt, besides, that in business he had a head that was not fantastic, but one reckoning accurately; and, thanks to this feeling, not only did he not lose confidence at sight of the neglect which he saw before him, but he found in it something like a spur. That torpor, that neglect, that inertia, that sleepiness, seemed to challenge him; and, casting his eyes around, he said to them almost with pleasure, "That 's all right; we 'll have a trial!" And he was even in a hurry for the trial.

These first reviews and thoughts did not spoil his humor, but took much time. Looking at his watch, he saw that if he wished to be in Vantory for Mass, it was time to start at once; giving the order, then, to attach the horses, he returned hastily to the house, and knocked at Marynia's door.

"Lady heiress!" called he, "the service of God!"

"Yes, yes!" answered the gladsome voice of Marynia through the door, "I am ready."

Pan Stanislav went in, and saw her in a light summer

robe, like that in which he saw her at his first visit in Kremen. She had dressed thus purposely; and he, to her great delight, understood her intention, for he exclaimed, stretching out his hands to her,—

"Panna Plavitski!"

And she, as if embarrassed, put her nose up to his face, and pointed to the cradle, in which Stas was sleeping.

Then they drove to the church with Papa Plavitski. It was a spring day, bright, full of warm breezes and gladness. In the groves the cuckoos were calling, and on the fields striding storks were visible. Along the road hoopoos and magpies flew from tree to tree before the carriage. From time to time a breeze sprang up and flew over the green fleeces, as over waves, bending the blades of grass, and forming quivering shades on the green of the fields. Around about was the odor of the soil, of grass, of spring. He and she were seized by a swarm of reminiscences. In her was called forth, though a little blunted by life in the city, that love of hers for land, and the country, the forest and green fields, the fruits in the fields, the pastures narrowing in the distance, the broad expanses of air, and that extent of the sky which is far greater than in cities. All this filled her with a half-conscious feeling which verged on the intoxication of delight. And Pan Stanislav remembered how once, in the same way, he had ridden to church with Pan Plavitski, and how, in like manner, the hoopoos and magpies flew from tree to tree before him. But now he felt at his side that rosy woman, whom he had seen then for the first time,—that former Panna Plavitski. In one word, he made present in his mind all that had taken place between them: the first acquaintance, and that charm with which she possessed him; their later disagreement; that strange part which Litka played in their lives; their marriage, later life, and the hesitations of happiness; the changes which, under the influence of that clear spirit, took place in him, and the present clearing up of life. He had also a blissful feeling that the evil had passed; that he had found more than he had dreamed of; that at present, it is true, misfortunes of every kind might come on him; but with reference to relations with her, his life had become clear once for all, and very honorable, almost equally the same as "the service of God," and as much more sunny than the past as that horizon which surrounded them was sunnier than that of the city. At this thought, happiness and affection for her overflowed his heart. Arriving at Vantory, he repeated "eternal repose" for the soul of that mother to whom he was thankful for such a wife, with no less devotion than Marynia herself. It seemed to him that he loved that dust, buried under the church, with the same filial affection as the dust of his own mother.

But now the bell sounded for Mass. In the church again old memories thronged into his mind. Everything around him was known somehow, so that at moments he felt the illusion that he had been there yesterday. The nave of the church was filled with the same gray crowd of peasants, and the odor of sweet flag; the same priest was celebrating Mass at the altar; the same birch branches, moved by the breeze, were striking the window from the outside; and Pan Stanislav thought again, as before, that everything passes, life passes, pains pass, hopes, impulses, pass, directions of thought and whole systems of philosophy pass, but Mass, as of old, is celebrated, as if in it alone were eternal indestructibility. Marynia alone was a new form in the old picture. Pan Stanislav, looking at moments on her calm face, and her eyes raised to the altar, divined that she was praying with her whole soul for their future life in the country; hence he accommodated himself to her, and prayed with her.

But after Mass, on the church square, neighbors surrounded them, old acquaintances of Pan Plavitski and Marynia. Plavitski, however, looked around in vain for Pani Yamish; she had been in the city for a number of days. Councillor Yamish was cured completely from catarrh of the stomach; and therefore well, and made young, at the sight of Marynia he fell into genuine enthusiasm.

"Here is my pupil!" cried he, kissing her hand, "the house mistress! my golden Marynia! Aha! the birds have come back to the old nest. But how beautiful she is always, as God is true, — a young lady, just a young damsel to look at, though I know that there is a son in the house."

Marynia was blushing from delight; but at that moment the Zazimskis approached, with their six children, and with them also Pan Gantovski, called commonly "Little Bear," the former unsuccessful rival for Marynia, and the incomplete slayer of Mashko. Gantovski approached awkwardly and with some confusion, as if dazzled by Marynia's beauty, and seized with sorrow for the happiness which had missed him. In fact, Marynia greeted him with comic awkwardness; but Pan Stanislav stretched his hand to him in friendliness, with the magnanimity of a conqueror, and said, —

"Oh, I find here acquaintances even from years of childhood. How are you?"

"In the old fashion," answered Gantovski.

But Pan Yamish, who was in excellent humor, said, looking teasingly at the young man, —

"He has his cares in regulating peasant privileges."

Gantovski grew still more confused, for the whole neighborhood was talking of those troubles. For some years the poor fellow had been barely able to live in that Yalbrykov of his. The regulation of peasant privileges and the selling of timber might have brought him to the open road at length, when in opposition to all the conditions, which more than once had been near settlement, there rose the eternal unchangeable reproach on the part of his Yalbrykov neighbors that "the lord heir rides on a white horse, fires from pistols, and looks into the girls' eyes."

Gantovski, though accustomed from years of youth to various country troubles, lost at times his patience and cried out in genuine despair, —

"Well, dog blood! what has one to do with the other? May the brightest thunderbolts shake every one of you!"

But after such a convincing dictum, the Yalbrykov peasant representatives assembled as usual a new mature council, and, after a careful consideration of everything, *for* and *against*, announced again, while scratching the backs of their heads, that all would be right, but that "the lord heir rides on a white horse, fires from pistols, and looks at the girls."

Meanwhile Marynia, who had as much attachment for Pan Yamish as if he had been one of the family, when she heard that he was a straw widower, invited him to dinner. But beyond expectation Plavitski, angry because he had not found Pani Yamish in Vantory, and mindful of his Sunday whist parties with "Gantos," invited Gantovski too, in consequence of which the Polanyetskis drove ahead very hurriedly, so that Marynia might have time to make needful arrangements. Behind them came Plavitski and the councillor; Gantovski dragged on in the rear in his brichka drawn by a lean Yalbrykov nag.

Along the road Plavitski said to Councillor Yamish, —

"I cannot tell you. My daughter is happy. He is a good man and an energetic piece, but — "

"But what?" asked Pan Yamish.

"But flighty. Thou hast in mind, neighbor, that he pressed me so hard for some wretched twelve thousand rubles that I was forced to sell Kremen. And what then? Then he bought back that same Kremen. If he had not squeezed me, he would not have had to buy Kremen, for he would have had it for nothing with Marynia after my death. He is a good-natured man, but here" (and while he was saying this, Plavitski tapped his forehead with his finger) "there is something lacking! What is true, is not a sin."

"Hm!" answered Yamish, who did not wish to cause bitterness to Plavitski by the remark that if Kremen had remained longer in *his* hands nothing would have been left of it.

Plavitski sighed, and said, —

"But for me in my old age new toil, for now everything must go by my head."

With difficulty did Pan Yamish restrain himself from shouting, "May God forbid!" but he knew Pan Stanislav well enough to know that there was no danger. Plavitski did not believe much in what he himself said; he was a little afraid of his son-in-law, and he knew well that now everything would go by another head.

Thus conversing, they drove up to the porch. Marynia, who had arranged everything already for the dinner, received them with Stas in her arms.

"I wanted to present my son to you before we sat down to table," said she; "a big son! a tremendous boy! a nice son!"

And in time to these words she began to sway him toward Pan Yamish. Pan Yamish touched Stas's face with his fingers, whereupon the "nice son" first made a grimace, then smiled, and all at once gave out a sound which might have a certain exceptionally important meaning for investigators of "esoteric speech;" but for an ordinary ear it recalled wonderfully the cry of a magpie or a parrot.

Meanwhile Gantovski came, and having hung up his overcoat on a peg in the entrance, he was looking in it for a handkerchief, when, by a strange chance, Rozulka, young Stas's nurse, found herself also in the entrance, and approaching Gantovski, embraced his knees, and then kissed his hands.

"Oh! how art thou, how art thou? What wilt thou say?" asked the heir of Yalbrykov.

"Nothing! I only wished to make obeisance," said Rozulka, submissively.

Gantovski bent a little to one side, and began to search for something with his fingers in his breast pocket; but evidently she had come only to bow to the heir, for, without waiting for a gift, she kissed his hand again, and walked away quietly to the nursery.

Gantovski went with a heavy face to the rest of the company, muttering to himself in bass, —

"Um-dree-dree! Um-dree-dree! Um-dramta-ta!"

Then all sat down at the table, and a conversation began about the return of the Polanyetskis to the country. Pan Yamish, who, of himself, was an intelligent man, and, as a councillor, must be wise by virtue of his office, and eloquent, turned to Pan Stanislav, and said, —

"You come to the country without a knowledge of agriculture, but with that which is lacking mainly to the bulk of our country residents, — a knowledge of administration, and capital. Hence, I trust, and I am sure, that you will not come out badly in Kremen. Your return is for me a great joy, not only with reference to you and my beloved pupil, but because it is also a proof of what I say always, and assert, that the majority of us old people must leave the land; but our sons, and if not our sons, our grandsons, will come back; and will come back stronger, better trained in the struggle of life, with calculation in their heads, and with the traditions of work. Do you remember what I told you once, — that land attracts, and that it is genuine wealth? You contradicted me, then, but to-day — see, you are the owner of Kremen."

"That was through her, and for her," answered Pan Stanislav, pointing to his wife.

"Through her, and for her," repeated the councillor; "and do you think that in my theory there is no place for women, and that I do not know their value? They divine with heart and conscience where there is real obligation, and with their hearts they urge on to it. But land is a real obligation, as well as real wealth."

Here Pan Yamish, who, in the image and likeness of many councillors, had this weakness, that he was fond of listening to himself, closed his eyes, so as to listen still better, and continued, —

"Yes, you have returned through your wife! Yes, that is her merit; and God grant us that such women be born more frequently! But in your way you have all come out of the soil, and therefore soil attracts you. We ought to have the plough on our escutcheons, all of us. And I tell you more, not only did Pan Stanislav Polanyetski return, not only did Pani Marynia Polanyetski return, but the family of the Polanyetskis returned, for in it was awakened the instinct of whole generations, who grew out of the soil, and whose dust is enriching it."

When he had said this, Pan Yamish rose, and taking a goblet, exclaimed, —

"In the hands of Pani Polanyetski, the health of the family of the Polanyetskis!"

"To the health of the family of the Polanyetskis!" cried Gantovski, who, having a feeling heart, was ready to forgive the family of the Polanyetskis all the sufferings of heart through which he had passed by reason of them.

And all went with their glasses to Pani Marynia, who thanked them with emotion; but to Pan Stanislav, who approached her, she whispered, —

"Ai, Stas, how happy I am!"

But when all in the company found themselves again at their places, Papa Plavitski added, on his part, —

"Keep the soil to the very last! that is what I have been advocating all my life."

"That is certain!" confirmed Gantovski.

But in his soul he thought, "If it were not for those dog blood troubles!"

And at that very time, in the nursery, Rozulka was singing little Stas to sleep with the sad village song, —

"Those ill-fated chambers.
Oi, thou my Yasenku!"

After dinner, the guests were making ready to separate; but Plavitski kept them for a "little party," so that they went away only when the sun was near setting. Then the Polanyetskis, having amused themselves first with little Stas, went out on the porch, and further, to the garden, for the evening was calm and clear. Everything reminded them of that first Sunday which they had spent there together; it seemed to them like some wonderful and pleasant dream, and reminiscences of that kind were there without number at every step. The sun was going down in the same way, large and shining; the trees stood motionless in the stillness of evening, reddening at the tops from the evening light; on the other side of the house the storks were chattering in the same way on their nests; there was the same mood of all things around them, cherishing and vesperal. They began to walk about, to pass through all the alleys, go to the fences, look at the fields, which lost themselves in the distance, at the narrow strips of woods barring the horizon, and to say quiet things to each other, and also as quietly as that evening was quiet. All this which surrounded them was to be their world. Both felt that that village was taking them into itself; that some relation was beginning to weave itself between them and it; that henceforth their life must flow there, not elsewhere, — laborers, devoted to the "service of God" in the field.

When the sun had gone down, they returned to the porch; but, as on that first occasion, so now they remained on it, waiting for perfect darkness. But formerly Marynia had kept at a distance from Pan Stanislav; now she nestled up to his side, and said, after some silence, —

"It will be pleasant for us here with each other, Stas, will it not?"

And he embraced her firmly, so as to feel her at his very heart, and said, —

"My beloved, my greatly beloved!"

Then from beyond the alder-trees, which were wrapped in haze, rose the ruddy moon; and the frogs in the ponds, having learned, evidently, that the lady had returned, she whom they had seen so often at the shore, called in the midst of the evening silence, in one great chorus, —

"Glad! glad!"

THE END.

www.ingramcontent.com/pod-product-compliance
Lightning Source LLC
La Vergne TN
LVHW030906080826
845145LV00010B/2788

*9781589635555*